Thinkbot

David Tossell was born in Cardiff in 1960. He obtained a Ph.D in Physics but has spent much of his working life as an engineer in high-tech industry. Previously, he undertook research at universities in the UK and America. More recently he has developed a specialisation in the development of robotic process equipment designed for the electronics industry. He has written several scientific papers and holds a number of industrial patents. He lives near Bristol with his wife and two children.

To New Scientist

Thinkbot

by
David Tossell

Best Wishes

David Tossell

DAT@thinkbot.co.uk

Pomegranate
BOOKS

First Published by Pomegranate Books 2005

Copyright © David Tossell, 2005

ISBN 1-84289-004-2

Printed in Great Britain by Biddles Ltd., King's Lynn

Pomegranate Books, 3 Brynland Avenue, Bristol BS7 9DR
www.pomegranatebooks.co.uk

To Becky, Joe and Ann,
who make it all worthwhile.

Part I: The First Day

1

Thinkbot was the first truly sentient robot. Sentient means that Thinkbot felt things and thought about them; he was conscious of himself - the first genuine electronic 'I think therefore I am'. He did not think like we might expect a robot to 'think'; he thought like us. He was a human in a tin can.

Thinkbot liked looking at art.

Thinkbot liked reading poems.

Thinkbot liked going to the theatre.

Thinkbot liked listening to music.

Thinkbot liked lying against a tree with a piece of grass wedged into his rigid metal mouth describing what he could see in the clouds above him: "I can see a humpback whale on a micro-scooter," or, "I can see a cat with its head stuck through a letterbox," or, "I can see an enormous cumulonimbus cloud dumping torrential rain on Clevedon." To the last of which anyone who still had the wherewithal to be listening might reply in a lazy drawl, "That is an enormous cumulonimbus cloud you tin clot."

"Ah, so you are awake then," Thinkbot would quip back sharply, offended at the previous lack of interest in his vaporous images of scooting whales or distressed cats.

And he was quite capable of cutting sarcasm. For example if someone asked him a silly question, Thinkbot would stare at them in disgust for a few seconds, then reply with something along the lines of, "Are you a natural at stupid questions, or do you practice regularly?" Or, on entering someone's home he'd gaze around and, looking straight into the eyes of the host or hostess, ask, "And you actually chose this colour scheme?"

In short, Thinkbot was full of wonder and humour, and he was certainly no idiot.

More than anything else, Thinkbot loved simply being alive.

If asked to cut the grass he would - after some prevarication, and muttering, "What did your last Hortibot die of?" - eventually get on with it whilst thinking things like, *why is* grass green? And, *why's it full of weeds?* And, *what is a weed anyway?* And, *why didn't they just ask me to mow the weeds?"* Whereas a proper Hortibot -

Hey! Just hang on one darn minute there, what in the blue blazes is a 'Hortibot'? Well, the world into which Thinkbot arrived was jam-packed full of robots. Robots for this and robots for that, in fact robots for pretty much everything. The Hortibot was one such robot - a gardening robot. Technically speaking a horticultural robot, a popular and profitable product for Globalbot Corporation - one of the few worldwide mass producers of commercial robots. The Globalbot marketing department had agonised over what to call it. Garbot? No, sounds like it can't speak properly and would get muddled with a garbage robot in North Americana. Gardenbot? No, in a sales trial this got muddled with 'garden pot' in retail minds and test units had ended up plonked amidst the terracotta collection from which zero sales resulted. Gardeningbot? No, too clumsy, no one would buy a robot with a four-syllable name. So, Hortibot it was, and sales had boomed as it had a nice ring to it and, as a secondary benefit, had contributed to the improvement of the vocabulary of many who had previously had no idea what 'horticulture' meant.

Anyway, a proper Hortibot would have simply planned the most efficient route around the lawn then packed the mower away in the garage, then packed itself away until roused by human whim to further monotonous garden tasks. Thinkbot, on the other hand, would get in a frightful rage over the tangled mower cord, become distracted by tangential thoughts and meander around for ages leaving odd shapes of uncut grass at random locations. Surveying his work, the words 'lawn shapes' might spring into his mind. Perhaps they were related to crop circles created by aliens; perhaps he was an alien. Off he would go and demand the other members of his family come and look at the lawn shapes and discuss whether they meant he was an alien.

His family? A robot with a family? Let's just slow down a little here, one question at a time. Let's start with: how did Thinkbot become a thinking robot?

Was he, perchance, the result of a multi-billion Euro research project involving the best minds in universities and industrial research centres around the globe?

Er . . , well, no.

Perhaps he was the product of a single obsessive genius, teetering at the edge of insanity, spending hours day and night in solitude pursuing the creation of his own personal Frankenstein?

Believable I grant you, but no.

Or maybe the output of a military project, shrouded in secrecy, aimed at creating a robot capable of thinking for itself on the battlefield (unlike the average Militaribot)?

Once again, very plausible, but no.

No, Thinkbot was almost certainly created by a series of monumental development bungle-ups and botched engineering changes within the Europa division of Globalbot Corporation. To be precise, in the Domestic and Industrial Robot Technology (DIRT) Support Group attached to Europa Globalbot Assembly Line 17 (E-GAL-17) at Filton, Bristol, England, Europa. Engineering changes were supposed to do things like introduce a new robot design, or add a new feature to a robot, or replace an obsolete part, or simply move a hole so that it lined up properly with another hole so that the bolt actually went through easily without the need for high-precision tooling (e.g. whacking it with a hammer). They were certainly not supposed to enable robots to think for themselves. If any engineer had submitted a change entitled 'Enable Robot to think like a Human', the committee that reviewed all changes would have reached for the group diary to check it was not April the 1st. And let's be honest here, reviewing engineering changes is hardly the most gripping occupation on the planet, so they surely would have noticed something as exciting as a thinking robot. The committee in question was entitled the 'Design Review Board', or DRB for short. To its unfortunate members it was more commonly referred to as 'Death, Rigour mortis and Burial'.

It was two Final Test engineers working their way down a line of assembled robots awaiting shipment who discovered Thinkbot. At the time they were having a typical robot manufacturing discussion.

"Hey Simon, have you found out if arm type 7 goes in slot 5 or 6 yet?"

"Er, is it an arm with revision 3 or 4 end effectors?"

"I thought revision 3 end effectors were only compatible with series 6 arms."

"Not if it's got a universal arm adaptor type F."

"How can it be a universal arm adaptor if it's only compatible with some arm types?"

"Depends which universal adaptor it is."

The first engineer screwed his face up in puzzlement and asked incredulously, "We've got more than one universal adaptor?"

"Yep, we've seven types of universal adaptor. I guess each time engineering created one they thought it was the first."

"Crazy."

"Yeah, well, so what? Anyway, if it's a revision 3 end effector, then arm 7 can go in arm slot 5, but for revision 4 use arm slot 6. But watch out for arm slot 6, it may need an issue 9 PROM if it's a pre-revision D CPU, but they've only been fitted to the last 18 left-handed Unibots."

His colleague stopped with a look of disgust on his face, "Ok, thanks a bundle Simon, I'm glad we've sorted that one out."

If Simon noticed the sarcasm, he did not show it and for reasons beyond the wit of man chose that moment to embark upon a joke, "What's the slowest animal that walks upright on two legs?"

"Er, dunno."

"A sloth on crutches."

Upon delivery of this truly modest punch line, an energetic metallic rattling started up. Just down the production line the engineers found a robot shuddering violently.

"It's got mains on his 24 Volt line!" yelled one engineer.

"I'll hit the emergency stop," replied the other diving for a bright red button mounted on the wall. But before he got there he froze as the robot burst out with, "A sloth on crutches, ha, ha, ha," and, guffawing loudly, doubled up and fell out of the line, landing on the floor with a sound not dissimilar to several pots and pans falling out of a kitchen cupboard. The stunned engineers stared at the face-down, motionless robot, unable to move or speak. All the other robots in the line stared fixedly ahead, as if nothing had happened, as if embarrassed by the antics of their robotic colleague. The robot rolled over and, sitting up, abruptly ended this study in high-tech manufacturing still life.

"Have you got another one?"

"Another what?"

"Joke."

Silence.

In fact, several seconds' silence.

Tens of seconds, maybe a minute, felt like a lifetime.

Two engineers staring at a sitting-up expectant robot, metallic hands resting on metallic kneecaps, robotic eyes looking unrobotically straight at them, out of the corner of robotic optic-sensor mount slots, from a half-inclined robotic head.

But, but, but, robots don't.

Don't look sideways.

Don't incline their heads.

Don't ask for another joke!

One robot sitting up, staring hopefully at two frozen test engineers.

Ambition at that point limited to just another joke.

The robot beginning to wonder what's up with them.

Humans do not crash; robots crash.

Humans do not have instant reset buttons; humans reset themselves using sleep.

But not standing up.

Not with their eyes open.

And certainly not at work. (Or so Thinkbot believed at that time, being a young, innocent, sentient robot operating from a limited database.)

Once again it was the robot that brought this still life in Manufacturing part II to an abrupt end: "Oh I can't be bothered with this. I haven't got all day. Is this the way out?" It got up and started walking off, pointing towards the large doors at the end of the line. The doors through which silent robots marched eerily and obediently onto transport trucks under the supervision of bored technicians, but who were not to be bored for much longer.

"Ger . . no . . not that way, ffpht, get him, it, stop it! **Oi! Come back!**" flustered one engineer. Both men, released from their stupefaction, broke into a very un-engineeringlike run, flaunting site safety rule #278: 'No Running Or Horseplay'. As it happens never, in the 200-year history of the Filton site, had anyone brought a horse into work - but they could have done with one now. The robot, reading the intent in their eyes, started running as well.

This did not go terribly well.

Being a general purpose universal robot (more commonly known as a Unibot), Thinkbot's initial running program set-up was not all that might have been desired. Unlike that of a Militaribot, which was set up from the start to move effortlessly and silently at great speed, infiltrating enemy lines before the enemy knew what was happening (at least that's what the Marketing brochure said). But Militaribot motion software was highly classified and kept securely within the Military Products Division of Globalbot Corporation; it was certainly not accessible to a newly sentient V3 Unibot with standard issue legs. Thinkbot lurched wildly into an intense series of irregular leaps, jumps, hops and steps, and collided heavily with an inert Unibot. As Thinkbot danced on, the inert Unibot wobbled agonisingly for a few seconds, toppled over and clattered into the next Unibot in the line. Like dull metal dominoes, the whole line began falling over one by one, creating a rhythmic metallic beat as a sort of strange backing track that was to become increasingly overlaid by the din of events as they unfolded elsewhere in the test area. By now, everyone in the production and test area had noticed the commotion: a Unibot apparently in berserk mode against a backdrop of Unibots falling over like guardsmen on a baking hot day and from between which wailing test engineers emerged at random waving their hands in the air in terror. The original two engineers had given up the chase and had steered off towards the shop-floor emergency control. The berserk robot alarm was sounding and manager-like people were spilling out of offices and attempting to activate the emergency Stunbots, Tripbots and Catchbots.

Not having motion-self-adjusting optics to compensate for his jerky legs, Thinkbot was having difficulty seeing what was going on and steering. He had now abandoned his aim of reaching the doors, and had lost all hope of another joke. He could see the Stunbots, Tripbots and Catchbots lumbering out of their storage bays and taking instructions from the engineers. In a timeless moment of clarity created by both legs landing at once, he saw, behind a glass screen bearing an unfriendly sign:

DESTRUCTOBOT
Activate only as a last resort

- a particularly nasty-looking robot, backlit alternately by a ghastly orange and red-lit sign: 'DESTRUCTOBOT INITIALISING'.

Thoughts continued apace in Thinkbot's head, but none of much use - *must pull my legs together, oh no I'm going to collide with that Robocrane* (clang!). *Drat, help, aaargh*. But, if anything, leg control had deteriorated since the fleeting vision of the Destructobot readying itself for action. Whizz! A high-voltage Stunbolt missed him by a whisker . . . . and hit an Industribot square on. The average Industribot comes with a variety of mighty pieces of optional hardware, but little in terms of up-top processing power. This particular robot was a good example - it was fitted with an impressive 600kN grip and bend kit but near zero brain. And what little brain it did possess did not like being hit with a 50kV stunbolt. Since no one had followed procedure and hit the line emergency stop before releasing the recovery robots, many robots on the line were still active. Unibots in the despatch cell were still trying to walk methodically into their transport truck, but it was long since full, and with the technicians diving for cover, robots were milling around pushing and shoving like so many Continentals trying to board an already packed cable car at a ski resort. Mercifully a Tripbot had fired its trapnet over the Unibots that had been marching unopposed through the Quality Assurance (QA) cell (presumably having passed themselves as fit for shipment), and the supply of fresh Unibots arriving at the truck had dried up. There was now a silvery seething mass in the QA cell which could have passed for a net full of mackerel if it had not been for metallic clankings and graunching noises as the robots tried to stand up and continue their unauthorised walk towards the despatch doors. And all the time there was the metronomic clang . . clang . . clang . . clang of inactive Unibots at the other end of the line falling over one by one.

Meanwhile the Industribot had decided the appropriate response to the 50kV stunbolt was to try and bend the next Industribot through 90°.

Which itself decided to drill a 2 cm hole in the next one.

Which itself decided to oxyacetylene torch the next.

Which itself decided to electrically weld the backside of the next.

Which itself decided to install a large right-angle bracket onto the skull of the next.

Things were getting out of control.

On the bright side, Thinkbot's legs were calming down (praise be to the auto-tune leg set-up routine), and he was beginning to enjoy dodging the stunbolts, tripwires, trapnets, and Catchbots. Thinkbot had concluded the latter couldn't catch a cold (true enough of course, since they were after all robots, but Thinkbot was not a literal thinker).

Eventually, a booming voice came over the Tannoy, **"Destructobot deployment imminent, all staff abandon test area."**

Thinkbot looked around and saw all the humans present legging it for an open doorway. Some clearly had never run that fast for many years and Thinkbot suddenly did not feel so bad about his earlier leg control. He followed and in the frantic chaos got through the door a split second before it hissed shut. And thus by a tiny margin did Thinkbot escape his first, but by no means last, scrape with electrodeath.

As he passed through the doorway Thinkbot had glanced back and was blessed with an instantaneous image . . . . of three bright red Firebots hosing down the luminous yellow Destructobot as it stumbled, with spectacular blue flashes and loud phuts, onto the shop floor, flailing its arms and firing various munitions into the ceiling. *Hmm*, thought Thinkbot, *maybe flashing red and orange 'Destructobot Active' warning lights were not the best choice with active Firebots in the area. Someone would surely get hauled over the coals over a duff risk assessment for this.*

Near silence in the changing room.

14

Many men, out of breath, breathing heavily.

The Tannoy cracked into life once again, **"Level 5 electropulse discharged."**

The dull sounds of mechanical chaos from the other side of the door died away.

In the sudden quietness, one engineer looked up and saw Thinkbot.

"What's that doing here?"

Multiple sets of eyes burned into his modest Unibot face.

The Unibot shrugged its shoulders with a faint clunk, held out its tinny arms in a gesture of innocence, put on its best New York accent and said, "Awh, come on guys, I cudda got hurt out dere."

Engineering Still Life III: 45 human engineers staring transfixed at one very non-standard standard universal multi-purpose robot.

2

Somewhere, in a desert far away, a line of fifty Militaribots moved silently through the night, their multi-jointed legs keeping their armoured bodies moving evenly over the rough terrain. There was no moon, but the sky above them was filled with innumerable stars; a myriad silver pinpricks in a matt black of nothingness. It was a sight of such beauty that it would have taken the breath away from anyone used to living under the murkier air of more densely populated areas. But robots do not have breath to take away, so the beauty fell unperceived onto the barren landscape. On which, in the light cast by the plethora of stars, the Militaribots looked for all the world like a group of black spiders trekking across a dark-grey shaggy carpet. Except that each Militaribot weighed about 50 tons, had six rather than eight legs, and carried an array of weapons far more fearsome than the average spider. Behind them lumbered five Artilleribots, distinguishable from the Militaribots by their larger bodies, eight legs, big feet, and the large gun barrel protruding upwards into the night sky. The gun barrel swayed gently on its fire recoil suspension as they plodded along. The Militaribots and Artilleribots crept eerily at exactly the same speed, and to anyone watching it would have appeared a sinister sight, sending cold shivers up and down the spine. At the head of the line was a Militaribot with some white stripes around it and a variety of radar dishes and aerials poking up into the night air. The line halted and an arm extended from the lead Militaribot. A radar dish unfolded, flapping in the steady wind. After a few seconds it snapped into a taut umbrella shape and rotated slowly around through 360° surveying the horizon. The dish folded away and the line of Militaribots moved off leaving the Artilleribots behind.

The Artilleribots spread out and meandered around for a few minutes, stopping every few metres and, lifting one of their pointed legs off the large circular foot, drove it into the soil and pulled it out again. Eventually they all found a spot with which they were content and, lifting their legs off their giant feet, sank their bodies onto the ground as all eight legs disappeared into the soil with an earth-shuddering vibration.

More the sort of sound one feels through the feet rather than hears with the ears. Once their bodies had settled the gun barrels, which had been limply waggling around during this procedure, moved around with more purpose. After a few minutes all the barrels were inclined at the same angle, pointing in precisely the same direction, and the Artilleribots became completely still. The only sound was that of a few nocturnal creatures going about their desert business. A number of insect communities had been disturbed by the sinking legs and some Artilleribots soon had what looked like hundreds of little miniatures of the recently departed Militaribots crawling all over them.

The line of Militaribots moved onwards into the night for another hour before halting again for another survey of the surrounding desert. This time, they rearranged themselves into a long line side by side and crept forward keeping close to the ground. In the half-light it was barely possible to pick out shadows and bits of leg as they moved. Eventually they worked their way up a shallow ridge and stopped. A hatch opened at the front of the lead Militaribot and out popped a miniature Militaribot about a metre in size which landed lightly on the sand. It whizzed up to just below the crest of the ridge, crept up to the top, and squeezed between two large outcrops of rock. A little hatch opened and several tubes and lenses poked out and surveyed the plain on the other side of the ridge. A road ran across the plain from the east towards the ridge; a dark grey ribbon of tarmac draped over a light-grey ocean of sand. At the base of the ridge the road turned and ran along the foot of the slope in front of the midget Militaribot's position on the crest. If the midget robot had been a human army commander it might have said, "Perfect, absolutely perfect," but it wasn't, so it didn't. Back down the other slope the main Militaribot column rose up and advanced to the crest of the ridge. Each of them spent several minutes poking around amongst the rocks, and then one by one they crouched down and merged with their surroundings. The lead Militaribot crept up and settled just behind the crest of the ridge near the midget. A small dish appeared through a hatch and pointed back towards where the Artilleribots were lurking a few miles back. Everything was set.

Two hours later, just as the stars were packing up for the night and the eastern desert sky was lightening into a stunning range of blue and turquoise colours, some black dots appeared on the road and grew gradually larger. By the time the head of the approaching column had reached the corner at the foot of the slope, the sky was light blue and it was possible to see what the column was composed of. There were several Militaribots at the front, and then about 20 wheeled, heavy-duty military transport vehicles. Some were transporting Militaribots and Artilleribots, and a few bore medium duty military Helibots, their rotor blades swept back towards the rear. Either side, and to the rear, were yet more Militaribots. Those at the side rode the rough terrain with ease on their multi-jointed legs.

Just when the column was spread equally out in front of the midget on the ridge, the air filled with the excruciating shrieks of rapidly approaching shells. The Militaribots in the column immediately started moving around at random, zigzagging to try and avoid being hit, but it was too late. The self-guiding artillery shells (Roboshot Inc. Intellishells™) screeched down out of the sky and five Militaribots were hit at the same moment, generating intense bright-blue flashes and yellow plumes streaked with black smoke and dust that rose majestically into the air. Fragments of rocks danced as a huge concussion wave convulsed the ground, and an air shock wave flattened every piece of vegetation on the ridge. As the radius of the shock waves spread out for miles in every direction, thousands of small desert mammals wet themselves. Insects stopped and took up defensive postures and those lucky enough to have claws waved them around aggressively in the air. A split second after the first shells hit, another five screamed down out of the sky, and five more Militaribots vanished in clouds of dust and smoke. Then five more shells arrived, and then another five, then five more, until every Militaribot in the column had been hit at least twice. The shelling stopped as suddenly as it began and at that same instant most of the Militaribots on the ridge leapt up and moved off down the slope at an incredible speed. About halfway down, two high-velocity armour-piercing gun barrels appeared out of hatches at the front of each attacker and commenced rapid firing at the stricken Militaribots ahead.

Amazingly, most of the Militaribots in the column were still active, although many had lost legs or plates of body armour. They struggled to form a front to meet the Militaribots charging down the slope towards them and fired any weapons that were still functional. A variety of rockets, shells, grenades, and even a few bright-red distress flares were hurled at the attacking host, but with little effect. About 100 metres short of their enemy the attackers stopped as one, fired all their guns in a single volley, and ducked just as a wave of rockets fired by the Militaribots still on the ridge swept over them with centimetres to spare and thumped into the defending robots. Instantly after the rockets had passed over them the attacking Militaribots rose up again and fired one last volley. The range was now so short that the gap between the sound of the guns firing and the impact of their shells on the targets made a stunning staccato crack-whizz-whump noise. If there'd been any humans there, they would have been frightened witless, but there weren't, so no wits were affected.

Then they stopped firing and, from its viewpoint at the top of the ridge, the midget looked out on an audiovisual spectacular. For the next minute a series of sonic booms arrived, reflected from the cliffs on the horizon. Up in the by now bright-blue sky large lumps of Militaribot were arcing away into the distance, rolling over and over in the air, some leaving curves of white vapour and dust, or black smoke. A few bits rose high enough to catch the light from the rising sun and their dust trails turned golden against the vivid blue sky. Out eastwards beyond the convoy hundreds of little puffs of dust spreading outwards marked where fragments of Militaribots were impacting out of the sky - a handful of gravel thrown into a pale yellow sea. Racing through these puffs were bits of Militaribot bouncing along at ground level - an arid, armoured version of desert ducks and drakes, losing momentum with each bounce until they slid to a halt in a cloud of sand. In the foreground, at the foot of the slope, lay what was left of the defending Militaribots, burning with yellow, red, blue, green or white flames and making intense hissing or roaring noises. Smoke rose lazily into the air, illuminated by the coloured flames. Many bits of hot metal lay around cooling slowly and changing from white through yellow to orange to red, and finally a deep dull maroon before fading into twisted black lumps lying on the yellow sand. One mangled Militaribot regularly shot red flares into the sky, and another fired star shells that gently floated down out of the sky underneath midget parachutes. There was the staccato rattle of machine gun ammunition firing off in the intense heat, and every few seconds a bigger explosion lifted the remains of an entire Militaribot clean off the ground creating showers of bright sparks before landing again with a fearsome dusty **crump!** The attacking Militaribots remained 100 metres short of the convoy like a gaggle of insects at a Guy Fawkes bonfire party. Although the transport vehicles in the convoy had not been hit, they had nonetheless come to a grinding halt since bits and pieces of mutilated smoking Militaribot blocked the road.

After a few minutes the attack force moved into the convoy, and the Militaribots on the ridge made their way down to join them. A few went off with the lead Militaribot to the front and started dragging the wreckage off the road. Others moved towards the transport vehicles, hatches opened and midgets emerged and scampered about. The large Militaribots bulldozed any damaged Militaribots, Artilleribots, and M-Helibots off the transporters and dumped them at the side of the road. The midgets climbed over them while the empty transports moved off down the road. After a few minutes the midgets withdrew and took cover as a series of explosions reduced the former cargo to scrap. The little robots then sprang back into the large Militaribots and the whole lot moved off down the road.

It had been a perfect ambush.

Well, nearly perfect.

If it had been carried out by a human army, they might have felt extremely proud, and shaken hands with each other saying, "Jolly good show!", or given each other high fives yelling, "Way to go! Great job guys!"

But there you would be wrong. Very wrong.

And it was a very big **but.**

The reason for the **BIG BUT** was that both the attacking Militaribots and the destroyed convoy came from the same army.

They were supposed to be on the same side.

There had been no orders for a company of Militaribots to attack the convoy. The attackers had simply been out on a night-training exercise, and the convoy was just another part of the same army on the move to a new location. The whole affair was what is generally known to the public as a 'friendly-fire incident'. This is an unfortunate term since it brings to mind an image of happy people shooting at each other, perhaps followed by a pint at the pub. Of course they are anything but, either for those shot at or, indeed, for those doing the shooting. But what was unknown to the general public was that friendly-fire Militaribot incidents had been occurring on a regular basis in every robotic army in the world for the past two years. The human Majors, Colonels, and Generals who were in command of the robots had no idea what was going on. If anything, friendly-fire Militaribot incidents were becoming more frequent and governments were getting worried.

Very worried.

3

GAT was slumped in an armchair watching the evening news and thinking miserable thoughts. The world was not doing too well. Eastasia and Westasia were locked in a war of words about chunks of seemingly barren land that most Europeans had difficulty locating in an atlas. Arabia and Europa were still plagued by the Israeli-Palestinian conflict (Israel had ended up as a province of Europa, a trail blazed by the unlikely political mechanism of the Eurovision Song Contest). Political upheavals within the South Americana Confederation threatened to implode into internal chaos. Down under, Australasia was obsessed with controlling the effects of UV levels due to the ozhole, while at the same time worrying about the cost of the large Militaribot navy it maintained against the threat of mass migration from the overpopulated countries to the north. At least Africana seemed stable, albeit with a stability born solely of never-ending poverty; money, as ever, was in short supply in Africana and it was unlikely to buy much in the way of robotic hardware in the foreseeable future. Africana had never really recovered from the twin curses of colonialism and the AIDs epidemic that had struck it over successive centuries, and the economic and social isolation this legacy had created in the next. In spite of all the advances in robot technology elsewhere, a poor continental economy, unstable local governments, and chronic failings in basic services such as the supply of clean water still afflicted Africana. Rumour had it that more humans than Sewerbots worked in the waste-removal systems of Africana! Uncannily, at that very moment, images of scruffily dressed people holding water carriers queuing up somewhere in Ethiopia appeared on the screen in front of GAT. I suppose it should not surprise us to learn that the rich and powerful Confederated Nations had never quite got around to sorting out the mismatch in standard of living around the globe, other than 'generously' off-loading their obsolete military and non-military robots to Africana and South Americana at 'attractive prices'. GAT thought the blessed things were generally so clapped out that Africana should really *be paid* to take them.

The stable and wealthy confederated nation groups of Europa and North Americana watched the rest of the world through anxious eyes, each making contradictory self-righteous proposals on how to solve the various crises (whilst denying all accusations that all they were really concerned about was the dire effect all of this was having on the global economy and the standard of living of their own citizens - i.e. their electorate). For, even after absorbing vast, less developed areas with large populations, North Americana and Europa had sustained the economic strength of the original super-rich nations such as the USA and the members of the former politically flabby, but nonetheless wealthy, European Union. When the USA and Canada had confederated with Mexico to form North Americana, and Russia with the European Union to form Europa, there had been dire predictions of economic disaster. But it hadn't happened. If anything the enlarged countries thrived even more and the Globalbot Corporation had been one of the success stories, vying with such as Intel and Microsoft to be amongst the biggest companies on the planet.

Once again, I suppose it should not be a total shock to learn that the sale of weapons and military robots (generally known as Militaribots) remained a lucrative business for Europa and North Americana. In conflicts around the globe various types and grades of Militaribots were involved, mainly in stand-offs but occasionally taking pot shots at each other, thus providing valuable feedback to the Engineering Department of the Military Products Division as to the success (or otherwise) of their hardware and software. Of particular concern were friendly-fire incidents involving Globalbot (and apparently only Globalbot) Militaribots. Governments quickly covered these up and rapidly reported the circumstances back to the hush-hush Globalbot Militaribot R&D group based in Oak Ridge, Tennessee, North Americana. This group was tasked with establishing what might happen should a general uncontrolled robotic conflict break out anywhere (or in the worst case, everywhere). Being the market leader in the supply of military robots, there were knee-buckling concerns and multiple ulcers amongst senior Globalbot management and Government defence officials.

For GAT, all this was a backdrop upon which his personal concerns played out to their own script of worry and angst. Ironically, the global unrest was good for the business of the Military Products Division, but for the Industrial and Domestic Division it was disastrous. Even though Globalbot was a huge multinational company, it did not guarantee secure employment. It was constantly under pressure not only from its main competitor, Worldbot Corporation, but also from the budget robot producers, Econodroid Inc. and Roboconomy plc. To make matters worse, every Globalbot manufacturing site competed internally against others within the corporation, and if a site proved inefficient compared with its sisters dotted around the globe, then the board was pretty ruthless in applying the chop. This was stressful enough when the market was buoyant (because you still had to out-profit the other sites to survive), but when the market was shrinking the insecurity became unbearable. And, thanks to the seemingly interminable global unrest over the past few years, the domestic and industrial market had been shrinking shrinking shrinking shrinking. Or, to the mathematically minded:

$$\text{Sales} = (\text{Shrinking})^4,$$

- i.e. truly disastrous. Worried consumers and nervous industrial companies were making their nearly worn-out robots stagger on just that bit longer, hoping things might pick up before they had to invest in a new and improved model (although the link could be tenuous, nearly everyone bought into the mass delusion that new robot = improved robot). Just the week before, GAT had heard of one customer who, rather than buying one decent new chemically resistant robot, had repaired five old non-resistant ones via his consumable budget, then watched them slowly dissolve one at a time so as to put off the need for a capital purchase for a few months. And, to rub salt into his wounds, GAT had been out for a drink only the night before with a friend who was a commercial vulture and dealt with companies going under financially.

"The business of busting is booming!" he had announced cheerfully and loudly (and tactlessly) before raising his glass to GAT, "Cheers!"

The only glimmer of optimism lay with the Global Customer Support Managers, who were up to their ears with requests to revive robots, sometimes only from strange collections of parts the customer claimed had once upon a time been a Globalbot robot. But the production and assembly division was suffering horribly. The gloom even seemed to have infected the office Vendbots, which had started offering outrageous discounts on cups of coffee and tea, and loss-leading special deals on chocolate bars and crisps.

Not that GAT really feared losing his job. Rather it was that he would probably have no choice but to relocate to North Americana and work on Militaribot development, neither of which appealed. His family were settled: his eldest son was at Gordano School - one of the top schools in England; his daughter was due to start there within a year; and his younger son would be going into reception at Portishead Primary around the same time. His wife loved living in Portishead and had a wide social circle around which she orbited with gusto. No, a transatlantic move would be a total disaster. Plus he had dallied with the military sector in the early part of his career, before making a conscious decision *not* to be involved in developing robots whose sole purpose was to maim and kill.

GAT was shaken out of his thoughts by a picture on the TV. This may be difficult to believe, but the picture indicated his immediate quality of life had suddenly and unexpectedly become much, much worse. GAT locked onto the babbling reporter, " . . . and initial reports that it was a bomb planted by an anti-robot terrorist organisation linked to Go Natural have now been discounted. It looks like this incident was simply a normal run-of-the-mill robot malfunction." The phrase 'simply a normal run-of-the-mill-robot malfunction' meandered back and forth through GAT's mind, presumably looking for the way out. Did he detect disappointment in the reporter's voice? Yes, he thought he did. Typical local news! It was obvious they desperately *wanted* it to be a terrorist attack with the added spice of 'possible links with Go Natural' due to the intense national and international attention that would attract. A split second later these cynical thoughts were frog-marched out of GAT's mind as he became transfixed by close-up images of a shattered industrial building. A shattered yet horribly familiar building, surrounded by a sea of blue flashing lights atop bright-red Firebots and their bright-red appliances, and from which faint wisps of smoke rose lazily into the blue sky.

His building.

The build and final test area of E-GAL-17 was not as it had been when he had left it yesterday evening, before he had taken a day off for some therapeutic mucking about in the garden (much to the annoyance of the Hortibot, which he ended up having to power down to prevent it loitering behind him, waiting to repair the damage left by his scorched earth gardening skills). Anyone paying attention to the TV would have felt a pang of sympathy for whoever would be involved in sorting the mess out. For GAT this was more than a pang since, as Head of the DIRT Support Group at E-GAL-17, he was one of those people.

4

Thinkbot stared out at the remains of robots lying, sitting and standing in various poses over the floor of the test area. It was not a pretty sight. Several of the Industribots had become hopelessly welded together into a molten mass, and another was artfully bolted onto the side of this robo-blob. The Industribot with the right angle bracket on its skull had frozen with its general-purpose arm lifted up, its fingers delicately placed on the area around the bracket as if it had an itchy scalp. The remains of the Destructobot were still glitching periodically, leading to a gaggle of Firebots scuttling over to hose it down for the umpteenth time. The roof above where the Destructobot lay was shot full of holes through which stars could be seen against the darkening sky. At some point one of the Firebots had decided to switch to foam and large mountains of it floated around the partially flooded test area like the tips of icebergs. Industribots and Facilibots were struggling to deal with the worst of the damage, cutting off dangling cables and pipes, and slicing through bent girders with spectacular showers of sparks. Several engineers were in the process of trying to release Unibots from the trapnet, but whenever they powered one up to disentangle an arm or leg, the Unibot would try to stand up and get into the transport truck, leading to an even worse tangle. The Unibots that had made it into the transport truck seemed to find none of this of the slightest interest and were standing rock still with expressionless faces like a tube train of commuters trapped in a time warp.

Unfortunately Thinkbot was staring at all this activity through the mesh of the 'Faulty Product Holding Area' (which had miraculously survived the chaos of earlier in the day). One might have thought that the discovery (or rather spontaneous appearance) of the first sentient robot in the planet's history would have caused some excitement. But no, the instinct of the Test Engineering Department was for cover-up and denial, otherwise known as covering one's backside. Robots do not think, *a priori*, case closed. Must be a software bug. Ha! Some poor softy's head will roll for this one. Perhaps even a few senior members of the Engineering Group might bite the dust. Serves them right, overpaid clever dickies. A perverse sense of intra-departmental joy at the impending pain likely to be felt by the Engineering Group began to invade the (admittedly still shocked) test area personnel.

Once the engineers in the exit room had recovered their senses, Thinkbot had been grabbed and unceremoniously manhandled into the Faulty Product Holding Area.

Several minutes later he was apprehended in the front lobby and once more manhandled into the Faulty Product Holding Area, but this time they put a lock on the door. Two engineers were standing just outside the cage door debating how to get Thinkbot's serial number for the fault report. Normally a robot would state its serial number on request, but Thinkbot had just looked at them from inside the cage, then gone through a thinking-hard routine with his hand on his mouth and some head scratching whilst muttering, "Seven nine, no ... six nine seven four ... no ... wait ... six four three five eight ... um, no, that's not it. Hang on, hang on, I'm sure it'll come to me in a minute." Finally Thinkbot gave up and asked the two mesmerised engineers, "Oh go on then, I give up, what's my serial number?"

The engineers looked at each other. "What we gonna do now?"

"Dunno."

"I don't trust it. We just can't take the risk of it getting out again."

"We could power it down."

"If we power it down, there's no guarantee it'll show the same fault when it's powered up again," said the let's-leave-it-powered-up engineer.

"I don't care. We've got to power it down," argued the let's-power-it-down engineer.

"Maybe, but I'm not opening that door without a few extra hands in case it makes another bolt for freedom."

"Don't be a wimp, it's only a Unibot. It's not exactly armed to the teeth."

"Except with some special do-or-die software."

"We could stunbolt it first."

"Duh? Have you got a stunbolt gun that can fire through mesh?"

"No, but you could open the door quickly and I'd shoot it."

"Oh yes, fine, *I'll* open the door and *you'll* shoot it. Why don't *you* open the door and *I'll* shoot it."

"It was *my* idea first."

"It wasn't *my* idea at all, *I* didn't want to shoot it in the first place."

"Will you stop doing that!" yelled the let's-power-it-down engineer at Thinkbot, who was standing just the other side of the cage moving his head back and forth looking at each engineer in turn with rapt attention as they spoke.

"What's all the yelling?" enquired a shop floor supervisor as he joined them at the cage.

"It won't tell us its serial."

"I think we should power it down."

"No way, we need it as evidence for all this," said the supervisor waving his arm in the general direction of the chaos behind him.

"That's what I said," beamed let's-leave-it-powered-up engineer, smugly triumphant he'd demonstrated thinking powers equivalent to a supervisor. The let's-power-it-down engineer glowered and slunk away sulkily muttering, "I told them, I said it should be powered down, just wait till it escapes again and trashes the canteen."

"We'll get the serial number when we get it out of the cage later," said the supervisor, and walked off with the let's-leave-it-powered-up engineer. And thus ended Thinkbot's second, but by no means last, scrape with electrodeath.

Thinkbot turned his attention to the contents of the cage. There were shelves on which all manner of robot body parts and sub-components were piled up. There were enough bits to keep a robot anorak happy for years, though he didn't like to think too long about the gruesome robotic creations that might have resulted. So much for TQM he thought:

1. Total Quality Management.
2. We have a policy of zero fault tolerance.
3. Right first time, every time.

Thinkbot rummaged on the shelves for a while. The storage cage area was part of the class 1,000 cleanroom assembly and test area, i.e. one supposedly dust-free and nothing at all like what happens if one whacks a pillow on a sunny day creating clouds of brightly lit specks that dance in the air for ages. However, this was a 'cleanroom' Globalbot style, and most bits and pieces were covered with a fine layer of unofficial class 10,000,000 dust. Dead insects lay around in various poses where they had expired in their doomed search for food in the dark painted metal valleys and caves amidst the corroding metallic hills. By far his most amazing discovery was a robot's head with a bird's nest in it. He wondered if that had been the fault found in test:

Fault:	Robot powered up okay, but would not control correctly.
Cause:	Bird's nest found in head.
Action taken:	Head replaced. Fault cured.
Corrective action required:	Investigate feasibility of cleanroom cat (i.e. class 1,000 low particle level cat).

Round the corner Thinkbot found a collection of failed robots. Apart from the fact they had impossible injuries like missing heads or holes clean through their bodies, it looked for all the world like a field hospital from some battlefield of human history. They were not a very engaging lot. Some appeared mechanically complete with no obvious fault, but others had limbs or heads missing and wires trailing out of odd places. One robot had been disassembled into halves at the waist. The top half was on the floor in an upright position and someone had fiddled with the eyes and mouth to give it a surprised expression. To Thinkbot it looked just like it had jumped into an ice-cold swimming pool. Next to it was a pair of upside-down legs that made it look like another robot had dived straight into the solid floor.

There was one fairly new-looking intact Unibot, pretty much identical to Thinkbot, which was standing on one leg with the other rigidly straight out in the air at right angles. Thinkbot read the fault report attached to the Unibot:

Fault:	Robot will only stand on left leg with right leg raised up straight out in front.
Cause:	No idea.

Action taken:	Powered up and down 3 times. Leg went up and down each time. Replaced main brainboard. Leg sub-servos replaced. Lower locomotion board out of stock and subject to HOLD for pending engineering change EC 57923.
Corrective action:	Route to Faulty Product Holding Area until part Hold clears. Then retest.

The date indicated these events had occurred over a year ago and Thinkbot thought the Unibot's right leg must be pretty sore by now. He found it difficult to believe an engineering change could take over a year to clear, but Thinkbot was still young and naive. Of course, at this point, he did not know that it was a similar long-drawn-out and magnificently botched engineering change that was probably responsible for creating him - the very first robot who could think properly. Thinkbot noticed some writing on the bottom of the Unibot's raised right foot: Unibot V3. Serial 756394567 CE UL.

Thinkbot started hopping around the room trying to look at the bottom of his own right foot, but he couldn't manage to bend his leg round enough to see. After a couple of minutes he gave up and had a rummage on the shelf and found a bent, polished steel plate which he used to look at the bottom of his foot.

∩ɩpoʇ Ʌ3. Sǝɹıɐɩ 141592654 CE UL

Which his able brain soon sorted out as: Unibot V3. Serial 141592654 CE UL. Thinkbot put his foot down again and stared at the 'I'm-going-to-take-a-big-step-forward-any-second Unibot' and decided: *This is a challenge.*

5

Later that evening GAT drove into the Globalbot car park with a heavy heart. It looked like it was going to be a long night and he had no idea what to expect, other than it would be grimly depressing.

How wrong one can be!

After the news bulletin, he had phoned in and had a hopeless conversation with the hysterical receptionist, "IT WAS HORRIBLE THE CLANGING WAS DEAFENING EVERYBODY THOUGHT SOMEBODY MUST HAVE BEEN KILLED AND THAT ROBOTS WERE OUT OF CONTROL BUT NOBODY KNEW WHERE ANYBODY WAS AND EVERYONE CAME RUNNING OUT AND THEN JUST WHEN IT SEEMED TO QUIETEN DOWN A BIT A BERSERK ROBOT CAME CHARGING THROUGH RECEPTION AND LOOKED RIGHT AT ME AND I THOUGHT I WAS GOING TO DIE AND THEN THERE WAS SMOKE IN THE AIR AND WATER RUNNING OUT OF THE TEST AREA DOOR BUT THE SECURITY MAN MANAGED TO GRAB THE ROBOT BUT I DIDN'T KNOW WHAT TO DO AND HID UNDER THE DESK AND PHONED THE CHILD MINDER TO SAY I'D PROBABLY BE LATE AND HOPED SHE HAD ENOUGH FOOD FOR THE KIDS AND I WAS EVER SO SORRY BUT THERE'D BEEN A BIG BIG PROBLEM ON THE ROBOT TEST LINE AND I WAS GOING TO BE VERY LATE . . ."

After several failed attempts to calm her down and get through to someone who knew what was going on, he decided the only thing was to drive in and see what was happening for himself. His wife Helen had plans for nailing the kids into bed early and watching an intense drama whilst consuming an expensive bottle of red wine; she had not been impressed.

"Isn't there someone else who could go?"

"Well, no, not really."

Huffing and puffing. Looks of disgust.

"But the factory looks like it's been demolished," he pleaded. Why all this grief? It's not as if he'd arranged it to avoid watching a tiresome drama. If he had, he'd certainly have picked something a little less stressful than the factory suffering a major berserkbot incident.

Arriving on site, GAT managed to evade the emergency service personnel, who seemed to have taken over in reception and who (to GAT's horror) were awaiting the arrival of a Government Robot Incident Management (GRIM) team, and made it to the relative peace and quiet of his office upstairs. This was not just because he liked to start any period at work in a controlled way by reviewing any emails and voicemails that might save him time in the frantic hours that must surely follow, but also because it had a glass wall that looked out over the stricken test area. The sight that greeted him left him feeling numb, and he gazed at the scene for some time, struggling to take in the level of destruction, before absent mindedly firing up his message screen and logging into voicemail. There was a voice-message from the head of the test area that a preliminary investigation had already been completed and had been emailed to him. Clot! Typical! Why send a voicemail to say you've sent an email? GAT was suspicious that the incident he would read about in the report might not be the exact incident that had actually occurred, and perhaps he sensed that in the tone of the voicemail. GAT read the incident report carefully:

1. Unibot went berserk without warning. Started laughing and running wildly around the shop floor. *Laughing?*
2. This Unibot then prevented any test personnel accessing any shop emergency stop buttons. *Any personnel, any emergency stop button? Good grief! There were usually 40 or 50 engineers in there, and probably as many emergency stop buttons. This Unibot must have moved like greased lightning.*
3. Unibot then trapped personnel against rear wall and behaved threateningly. *Lord, it was only a standard issue domestic Unibot. This is getting more difficult to believe by the minute.*
4. Test engineers consulted line management *(presumably whilst being threatened by a single savage laughing Unibot)* and received approval for deployment of emergency control robots and raising of Destructobot to ready status.
5. Controlbots were unable to contain berserk Unibot. Berserk Unibot moved to location where Controlbot activities triggered some secondary berserks in other

robot types. *Jumping Jehoshaphat! This must have been the performance of a lifetime for a humble Unibot. He was beginning to wish he'd been here to see it.*

6. Test engineers consulted line management and received approval for area evacuation and deployment of Destructobot. *Way too quick, where's the justification? They've just been dying to use that blasted thing for years.*

7. Destructobot disabled by three berserk Firebots. *Firebots? Where did they come from? What happened to the amazing Unibot? Do I sense chaos setting in?*

8. Destructobot weapons systems malfunctioned causing significant damage to the area. *Well, it is - or was - a Destructobot.*

9. Area sealed and level 5 area electropulse used to power down all robots. *Line management approval? Consultation? Hopefully they checked all humans were out first, otherwise we'll be up on brain-frying manslaughter charges .*

10. Area re-entered in controlled manner. *They peeped through the door.*

11. All units were found to be inactive except the original berserk Unibot. *WHAT? How can a Unibot survive a level 5 disable pulse??*

12. Unibot constrained in Faulty Product Area. *Constrained? Surely 'powered down and placed' in Faulty Product Area was what was meant.*

13. Area secured and released to recovery teams.

In other words a Unibot had malfunctioned, everybody had panicked and forgotten to press the emergency stop, and then they'd released **all** the Controlbots into an area full of active robots of multiple types just waiting to be provoked, thus creating a situation even a Destructobot could not handle. All that was needed was a PS at the end: 'Oh, by the way, 3 human test engineers were fried, 2 filled with 500 litres of water and one compressed into a small cube.'

Appended to the end was a fault report, lovingly mistyped as ever:

Robot Model: Unobit
Controlware: V3.

Serial Number:	**TBA** *To be arranged? All they had to do was ask it!*
Fault:	**Borot berzerk. Starting making lauhging sound nad talked to me! Robot departed to leave the test area thru the transpot dors.** *Tried to leave? Where was it going? Wasn't it supposed to be going through the transport doors.*
Cause:	**Sofaware.** *That's right, if you can't think of anything else then blame the software.*
Action taken:	**Robto lokced in Faulty Produtc area.** *Locked?* **Robot not powred down in case flaut lost.** *Or, we didn't power it down in case the fault is gone when it's powered up again and then we'll get the blame for trashing the test area.*
Corrective action:	**Invsetigrate robot contolwrae. Reffer for xamination to DRIT groop.** *As usual, pass the buck to the development engineers.*

GAT pondered the reports for a few minutes. *I think it's about time I met this Unibot.*

6

Meanwhile, back home, GAT's wife Helen was harassing the kids into bed. She was not in a good mood. There were only three to nail, although it felt like more. First up, or rather down, was Mike, four years old, and who was not yet able to speak in lower case letters.

"WHERE'S DAD GONE?" Mike had been looking forward to a teddy-talk session.

"He's gone to work."

"WHY?"

"There's been a problem with some robots."

"PROBLEMS? WHAT SORT OF PROBLEMS? HAVE THEY STARTED FIGHTING?"

"I don't know, Michael."

"IT SAID ON THE NEWS THAT ROBOTS MIGHT START FIGHTING ANYTIME."

"That's Militaribots thousands of miles away, not the sort of robots at Dad's work."

"BUT I SAW SMOKE COMING OUT OF DAD'S FACTORY ON THE TV."

"I don't think it was from robots fighting."

"WHAT SORT OF ROBOTS DOES DAD MAKE? DOES HE MAKE THE SORT I SAW ON THE TV?"

"No, I don't think so. I don't really know. Now come on, you're just delaying, it's time to go to sleep."

Helen knelt down beside the bed and kissed Mike, who then grabbed her around the neck as she tried to get up. "GOODNIGHT MUM."

"Let go, come on, ow, oi, you're hurting my back"

Mike let go.

"Goodnight Mike, sleep well."

"WHERE'S TIGER? I HAVEN'T GOT TIGER."

"I don't know, where did you put him?"

"I DON'T KNOW."

Mike's voice had gone into an 'I'm about to burst into tears' whingy tone. Helen put the light on, "Oh come on Michael, it's getting late!" she said testily, helping him look for Tiger. Fumble, fumble, pillows up, pillows sideways, pillows down, quilt up, quilt down, look under bed, look down side of bed. Success! Tiger was wedged head down in the gap between the wall and the bed. Mike pulled him out and neatly whacked his mother on the lower lip with his elbow. Definitely a red card offence if it had been on a robofootball field.

"Ow!"

Blood leapt from Helen's lip onto the sheet and Mike sensed a motherly volcanic eruption was imminent. Mum had been a bit odd recently. Even Mike had noticed.

"SORRY MUM! SORRY! I DIDN'T MEAN IT. IT WAS TIGER'S FAULT."

Helen was keeping calm, until Mike tried to shift blame onto Tiger. Now she started speaking in upper case as well, "GET UP AND GO AND WAIT ON THE LANDING!"

Mike moved quickly out of the way and onto the landing where he nearly collided with Opal.

"Oh Mike, watch where you're going," said his sister, ten years old, looking into Mike's bedroom.

"Are you all right Mum?"

"NO!"

"Where's Dad?" asked Opal, who had been looking forward to him reading poems to her at bedtime.

"He's gone to work."

"Why?"

"THE ROBOTS HAVE STARTED FIGHTING."

"What?" said Opal.

"THE ROBOTS HAVE . . ,"

"MICHAEL BE QUIET!" shouted their mother.

Opal stared at her Mum. This was not good.

"Can I help you Mum?" asked Opal.

"YES, YOU CAN GO . . ." Helen made an effort to calm down, " . . . go and get the Cleanbot, and programme it for blood."

Blood? Cleanbot? Opal realised something serious must be up with Mum. Usually she avoided using robots unless Dad was home. Opal went into the room and saw her Mum clutching a bloodstained handkerchief to her mouth with one hand whilst tugging wildly at the sheets on the bed with the other.

"Let me do that," Opal said and started sorting the sheets, "you get the Cleanbot." Helen felt like crying; she did not want to touch the Cleanbot. What an evening! Assaulted by a four-year-old boy, helped by a ten-year-old girl, frightened of even a simple Cleanbot, abandoned by a 43-year-old man, and she had not even tracked down Gerald her elder son to start his get-into-bed process. And the drama was starting in five minutes, and the wine was not going to taste too good after several mouthfuls of blood.

At this point Gerald, who was 12, arrived on the scene.

"What's happened?" he asked. Looking at Mike's teary eyes; and his mother's bloodied hanky lying on the floor; and at Opal squeezing past with some sheets; and at his mother fiercely prodding at the Cleanbot with a look of fear on her face.

"Go and help Mum," said Opal.

Helen was wrestling with the Cleanbot, which appeared to be the only thing that had got to bed on time and would not power up. Gerald went over and checked the Cleanbot charge. "Zilch," he said, "this thing's dead, or it could be that it doesn't like the sight of blood I suppose." Helen shoved the Cleanbot aside and slumped onto the floor and put her head in her hands.

"You all right Mum?" asked Gerald.

"Go and sort your lip out Mum, Gerald and I will see to Mike," said Opal.

Helen looked at them, and struggled to hold back the tears, then heaved herself up and headed for the first-aid kit in the bathroom.

Opal and Gerald set to work in silence with that special intensity that always comes when a parent is feeling bad and needs help. Mike was soon in bed and the sheets were soaking in water and the Cleanbot was plugged into the charger and Helen's lip had stopped bleeding and Opal and Gerald were in their nightclothes ready for bed. They went downstairs and found their mother sitting in the dark watching the TV. All very normal, except that the TV was off. Helen gave her son and daughter a big hug and whispered, "I love you both."

"Where's Dad?" asked Gerald, who had been looking forward to one of their regular discussions about Robot technology.

"He's at work," said Helen.

"Why?"

"There's been some sort of problem with some robots."

"Problem? What sort of problem?"

"**I don't know Gerald**, you can ask him tomorrow."

"Mum, is there going to be a war?" asked Opal.

"**No, of course not**," snapped Helen impatiently and sent them to bed.

Helen slumped back onto the sofa and turned on the TV. The drama was halfway through and she could not make sense of it, so she switched to the international news, which was detailing the latest skirmishes between Westasian and Eastasian Militaribots. Several self-important-looking politicians were interviewed with some rather dense-looking Securibots standing behind them, plus a Diplomatobot poised ready to block any inappropriate questions. Few words made it through to Helen. But the words that did were words like 'serious situation' and 'possible conflicts' and 'appropriate measures' and 'robots of mass destruction'. Of all of these words it was the final four that chilled Helen to the bone.

7

GAT stood at the entrance to the Faulty Products Area. On the other side of the mesh stood a Unibot. It was staring at him. It had spotted him from the corner of the cage as he walked towards it, and sidled alongside him on the other side of the mesh, staring at him all the way.

"That's the one," said one of the test engineers, as if GAT was the sort of person who had difficulty spotting robots behaving strangely.

"No, really, is it?"

GAT looked at it closely. It looked okay. The staring and tracking behaviour was a bit odd, but not beyond the bounds of a decent (or twisted) software engineer.

"Open the door," said GAT.

"No way, it's lethal, that thing"

"Open the door," repeated GAT.

"Duwkits said I mustn't under any circumstances open the door without Stunbot back-up."

"Open the door!"

One engineer opened the door, retreated several paces and concentrated on looking worried.

"What you staring at?" muttered the engineer aggressively at the Unibot. Both engineers looked ready to bolt at the slightest provocation. A helpful little voice in GAT's head commented, *"Calm down dears, it's only a malfunctioning Unibot"*

"Me no speek ingleesh, me Japanese," said the Unibot suddenly, moving its gaze onto GAT. Even GAT was taken aback. He looked back at the test engineers. They looked petrified and one fingered the control panel of a Stunbot he'd sneaked up to deal with any trouble.

"Raise your right foot," GAT said to the Unibot.

"Me no speek ingleesh, me Japanese."

GAT moved quickly and grabbed the Unibot's right foot and pulled it sharply up, at the same time turning and pushing his backside into the stomach of the Unibot, pinning it up against the wall. Just like a blacksmith about to shoe a horse. The robot did not react, but the watching test engineers were impressed. GAT read the serial number off the plate set in the sole of the robot's foot, 756394567.

"Er, excuse me, er, Sir, would you mind telling us the serial number?"

GAT read off the numbers and the very pleased-looking engineer entered them into the fault report. GAT produced some big cable ties from his pocket and strapped the robot's legs together and its arms to its side.

"Me no speek ingleesh, me Japanese," said the now struggling Unibot. It was still staring eerily at him so GAT blindfolded it with a cable tie.

"**Me no speek ingleesh, me Japanese**," said the Unibot loudly and urgently, clearly distressed that it would no longer be able to gaze adoringly at GAT; GAT cable-tied its mouth.

"**Meumm nn spmmk imlmsh, mmue mapamnees.**"

"Take it to the secure development area, I'll meet you there in a minute," GAT instructed the two watching (and admiring) test engineers. However, their expressions immediately turned a bit sheepish.

"Um, sorry, Duwkits has called in UK GRIM and they've asked to have the robot. Duwkits said yes."

Blast Duwkits. Blast UK Government Robot Investigation Management. Why so fast? Why not try and figure out what happened ourselves before calling in the dunderheads from GRIM. GRIM would fiddle with it, then go sucking up to the Globalbot Military Division in North Americana and pass the Unibot to them for 'analysis'.

"There's a GRIM van already waiting at the loading bay. Thanks ever so much for tying it up!" The engineers darted into the cage and picked up the writhing, mumbling Unibot and scuttled off, clearly fearing an explosion of anger from GAT. GAT buried his face in his hands and wondered what to do next. No doubt there'd be a big Globalbot enquiry, and maybe a Government investigation as well, probably with Military Division thickoes asking dumb questions as if they had been sent from on high. And the only real piece of evidence with which the Domestic Division could defend itself had just been given away.

GAT looked absent-mindedly around the Faulty Products Cage. *Good grief! It was ages since he'd been in here. Thousands of euros-worth of bits simply rotting away. It can't be. It is! It's a bird's nest!* He walked round the shelves and surveyed the robot graveyard at the rear. Many looked like the best bet of a sale was to a museum, but it was hard to believe it wasn't worth repairing some of them. He skimmed over a few of the fault reports and turned to leave. He was wondering what was happening at home, thinking of Helen, who was probably not in the best of moods. He suspected that Helen was only using robots when he was around. She looked awfully tired, and the house looked like it could do with a good roboclean.

As he passed through the door on the way out of the cage two words sprang into his mind:

Wrong leg!

He stopped, turned around and walked back to the Unibot, which was standing on its right leg, with its left leg straight out in front. He bent over slightly and looked the Unibot in the face and said, "That's the wrong leg."

The Unibot dropped its leg, relaxed into a resigned pose and, looking mischievously at an astonished open-mouthed GAT, replied, "Oh dear, how silly of me. I'm actually pretty new around here and I'm having a bit of trouble telling left from right."

8

General Arnold Farkstock III, President of the Military division of Globalbot Corporation, stared at the hand-written reports laid out on the desk in front of him. All the information screens around the room were blank, and Farkstock's display desktop was powered down. All spy microphones were disconnected, and the security cameras had what looked like socks over them. He had had some difficulty reading the reports; people had so little hand-writing to do these days, what with voice typing and autotype software. However, he had established all was not well with the Militaribots produced by his division. He had suspected it was bad for a while, but not this bad.

On the other side of the desk sat the Senior Vice-Presidents of Field Deployment Support (FDS), and Military Engineering (ME). Their expressions were worried, and the long silence testified to the fact they had not the slightest idea what was going on and, being highly trained professionals, were looking for someone else to blame. Blaming Farkstock was clearly not a good career move, and since there were only two of them present, the choice was rather limited.

"It's difficult to believe these reports. Are we sure these observers are reliable? Are the translations correct?" said ME with a pointed look at FDS.

"I'm not making it all up," growled the FDS, "these are people I have worked with and trust; one of them was instrumental in getting to the bottom of the 10,000 cow incident."

Noooooo! thought ME, *not the 10,000-cow incident!* That had definitely been a cock-up by Military Engineering. An upgrade to the pattern recognition software on some Militaribots had not been well tested and a North Americana border patrol had spent several days systematically wiping out over 10,000 South Americana cows with close assault tactics using grenades and machine guns. No matter how much one liked a good beefsteak, the pictures that had appeared on the TV and in the newspapers were appalling, especially where a large number of cows had become trapped in the corner of a field, or a barn, or in one case a farmer's front room. The front room had been a close call. Five people ended up mixed in with the cows but, thank God, the pattern recognition software spotted they were not cows, though they had nearly got trampled. It wasn't as if there was any threat to North Americana from South Americana Militaribots, let alone their cows. The province in South Americana bordering North Americana in which the incident had occurred was so torn by unrest there were no South Americana Militaribots within a hundred miles at the time. Just as well, thought ME, as the South Americana Militaribots were museum pieces and the newer North Americana Militaribots would have turned them into scrap in minutes and then reverted to merrily wiping out cows. Of course the truth of the matter was that many field upgrades could not be fully tested in the laboratory, and the South Americana border was the perfect tame arena in which to quietly test the upgrades in the real world before releasing to customer countries where any sort of glitch could start a major war, and FDS knew this all too well. But 10,000 cow deaths had not qualified as one of Military Engineering's better 'quiet tests'. He'd better fight back.

"At least we upgraded the software on the right side!"

Noooooo! thought FDS, *not the upgrade delivery cock-up!* This was below the belt, and ME knew it. The ME division had spent months developing an advanced targeting system for a specific customer, then FDS had got some shipments muddled and delivered the upgrade to the wrong side. The wrong side had had the presence of mind to quickly upgrade their bots and shoot up 500 Militaribots from the side that had actually paid for the upgrade. That had taken a lot of dollars to sort out. A lot of dollars. And it had almost stopped the war and lost them a load of guaranteed future sales. It was always difficult to get a factory-mucked-up war back on track. And the political fallout had resulted in a bawling out for Globalbot Corp from the top man of North Americana himself - President Hedge.

"Oh, grow up!" snapped Farkstock. "We're losing control over our robots and you're just worried about covering your own backsides. We need to find out what's going on and stop it, otherwise we'll all have more to worry about than corporately painful backsides." He'd read the reports. Militaribots appearing out of the night and shooting at other Militaribots - but the owners had not given any orders to them other than 'stand and defend,' or 'only fire if attacked and only if enemy positively identified'. Even worse, a large proportion were so-called friendly fire incidents. Puzzlingly, tracking the types of weapons used showed that friendly robots had managed to get weapons only available to other armies. How had they managed this? The incidents were too common to blame FDS's clowns for delivering the wrong bits to the wrong side every time. The most disturbing trend was the gradual spread of disorder from the simplest Militaribots towards the more complex and dangerous types. Those with superior weapon types had greater safeguards. The bigger the risk the weapon represented, the bigger the safeguards. At the top of the tree were the solely Globalbot-manufactured robots of mass destruction, otherwise known as 'RMD'. All confederated nations had enough RMD to destroy the Earth many times over. Why? As far as Farkstock knew, there was only one Earth and this somewhat obvious fact reinforced his suspicion that 'Heads of State' and 'Intelligence' were exclusive concepts. All RMD were under the control of a few people at the top of the regime who could activate, fire or disable them as needed. The bad news was that at the current rate of decay, control over the RMD could be lost within a year. The only good news was that Militaribots had only been attacking each other. So far no Humans, and indeed no Domestibots or Industribots, had been damaged. Nor had there been any signs of serious software problems or unusual incidents with Globalbot Domestibots or Industribots. On the other hand he'd not heard many reports of problems with Militaribots manufactured by Worldbot, but maybe this was not too surprising since Globalbot had the lion's share of the military robot market. However, he was suspicious that even when Worldbot Militaribots were involved it was only when they returned fire after being attacked by their Globalbot peers; i.e. they never seemed to be responsible for actually starting an incident. If this turned out to be true, it could have dire effects on Globalbot military business. The last thing he needed was for Globalbot Militaribots to be identified as the sole cause of all spontaneous and friendly-fire incidents worldwide and be forced to hand over billions of dollars-worth of future business to Worldbot on a plate.

Farkstock looked at the hand-scrawled graph, and on real graph paper as well. He wondered where on earth the agents had got graph paper from in this age of instant computer charts on paper-quality electronic displays. Although the line looked like someone had inked the leg of a drunken spider and then let it run across the page, it was drunkenly making its way in a certain direction.

The wrong direction.

The number of so-called 'spontaneous friendly fire incidents' involving Globalbot Militaribots had been steadily increasing over the last year. Politicians in all nations had noticed, but so far had always assumed the other side in their particular cold war was to blame. In fact the incidents were the main thing fuelling the worldwide international tension. Farkstock often met senior government figures in his travels and he always asked them what the issues were in whatever conflict they were involved in. The answer was usually the other side was shooting at them.

"Yes, but what about?" Farkstock would enquire.

This line of enquiry met with frowns and mutterings of 'rude and politically incorrect industry leaders' who should leave 'vital matters of state' to those democratically elected by the people. Farkstock wondered if people would ever be persuaded to elect an intelligent leader, one not given to delusions of power and paranoia, since this would be ever such a pleasant change thanks ever so much.

Wake up! Stop daydreaming. He focused his eyes on the ME and FDS opposite and instantly regretted it. Maybe his senior appointments were not that much more intelligent than the clots 'the people' in their wisdom plonked in charge of nations possessing automated weaponry capable of wiping out everything.

Everything.

It must not happen.

With Farkstock the rage always came quick and fierce. As with all men of true power it was a controlled rage, but to the persons on the receiving end he seemed completely *out* of control. He rose to his feet, scattering the reports off his desk, **"It must not happen, you will find out how to stop this. I will not be held responsible for the destruction of earth. You will each select your best engineer and instruct them to select a small team and solve this, they will have as much money as they need, but they will work without robots, with no email, no voicemail, no computers, no weapons, and no contact between them."**

ME and FDS were cowering and glancing around, assessing avenues of escape. FDS recovered first, "Will there be a bonus for the VP whose team succeeds?"

"Aaaaaaaargh! Get out. Out!!" Farkstock advanced on them menacingly, clearly ready to lay aside all known management techniques in favour of giving them a severe kicking. ME and FDS stood and turned to run. Then something unexpected happened. The office doors opened serenely, and the senior staff Military Division Execubot came in, uninvited. "Is everything okay sir?" it asked in a deadpan voice.

Farkstock froze with his arms and one leg in the air and pieces of paper fluttering gently down onto the floor around him. ME and FDS stood stock-still starting at the Execubot with eyes and mouths wide open.

"Ah! Yes, yes, ... , and who requested you to attend me?" asked Farkstock, trying to recover a more senior management-like pose, mortified to be seen like this by a robot.

"Your security devices are disabled. Protocol demands I check on you every 60 minutes."

"Ah, well, everything's fine. It's fine. Thanks for thinking of me. Goodbye, thanks for coming, bye, ya'll take care now." Farkstock winced at this verbal garbage.

The Execubot, turned, and looked slowly and deliberately in turn at each of:
1.   the scattered paper covered with human scrawls;
2.   the disabled security devices;
3.   the Senior Vice-President of Field Deployment Support;
4.   the Senior Vice-President of Military Engineering;
5.   the President of the Military Division;

and walked calmly out, turned to face them and gently closed the doors leaving Farkstock, FDS and ME standing in silence with cold sweat trickling slowly down the backs of their necks.

9

GAT was back at his desk, with the strange Unibot standing opposite him, for all the world like any human engineer wanting to discuss a tricky wiring problem, or enlisting GAT's help in ensuring the delivery of some vital development part without having to reverse the flow of time or invent a time machine to go and bring it back from the future. After his flash of insight and apparent discovery of the Unibot's swap escape plot, he'd managed to get it back to his office by exiting the test area through a fire door, banking on his judgement that the fire alarms would not go off since the test area was still more or less on fire. Dodging through the pipes, pumps and water chillers in the service chase, he'd got them up the back stairs into the office area unnoticed.

Thinkbot stood in the office and wondered what to do. GAT seemed an awful lot nicer than the nasty engineers he'd met so far, most of whom seemed to want to electrocute him, blow him up, wrap him up in a net, lock him up, or power him down. To Thinkbot 'power down' did not seem an attractive option, as he was pretty sure that he'd be an unThinkbot when he was powered up again. There was an unconscious level to this line of Thinkbot thinking: how did he know he'd not be able to think again if powered down? Perhaps it was just the fear he wouldn't be able to think? If he lost the power to think, would he cease to exist? If he lost the power to think, would he ever know he couldn't think he couldn't think?

Meanwhile, back in the humdrum world of offices, chairs, and adjacent smouldering test areas, GAT had not asked him to sit down. Evidently GAT had not yet got the point that Thinkbot was a human in a tin can and might actually like to sit down. Robots did not usually need to sit down, but then there had not (until now anyway) been a robot who found others discussing his imminent destruction somewhat distressing. GAT was doing something on his desktop display and paying little attention to Thinkbot. Perhaps it was time for another escape bid. His last two had not been 100 per cent successes. The first had resulted in the destruction of the test area (of which, incidentally, he had a grand view out of the glass wall of GAT's office). The second had seemingly caused an immense amount of distress to a woman in the reception area. In fact, she'd reacted so wildly he'd lost concentration and missed his chance to dodge the Securibots and Globalbot policemen. This was the first woman he'd met in his short life and it had been scary. The male test engineers had been rather predictable, but the lady receptionist had given him the eeby-jeebies, as she'd clearly been terrified. Why? Once he'd slowed down to look at her, he'd been quickly out-numbered by the site police and Securibots. He'd had no intention of looking at her, let alone killing her, but she'd screamed for mercy and looked at him with wide eyes, then thrown herself behind the desk and started talking very fast to someone about children. Children? *Hmm, must meet some children. All in good time, hopefully.* Meanwhile should he try escape attempt III, or try a different approach? GAT was the first human he'd met that seemed to instinctively trust him, so maybe the different approach.

"Ahem."

GAT became entirely still, head inclined towards the desk. His eyes moved and locked onto the Unibot from under his eyebrows. It was 'eyeing' the 'visitor' chair GAT kept on the opposite side of his desk.

A pause.

Nothing moved for several seconds, man and robot each considering their next move.

"Would you like to sit down?"

"Thanks very much. Thought you'd never ask." Thinkbot moved fluidly the instant GAT finished speaking and sat down, but still felt a bit self-conscious and sat there looking rather nervous.

GAT returned his attention to the desk. In reality his attention was not on the desk, it was on the Unibot. The desk was not important. It was only a desk. Just a desk. With a blank fault report ready to fill in details about an unusually faulty Unibot. But the Unibot had hinted at sitting down. He'd never seen a robot sit down. It was very unusual for robots to ask to sit down. It was less than extremely unusually unlikely that a robot would clear its throat and subtly indicate it would like to sit down. *Get a grip!*

"Version. Serial!"

Normally this just resulted in the robot stating its version type and serial number, but not this Unibot. This Unibot grabbed its right leg and started trying to look at the sole of the foot. This was not easy, there being no reason to design a robot capable of looking at the soles of its feet. In fact this was a grand opportunity for Thinkbot to throw himself theatrically off the chair and writhe around on the floor, which he duly did. GAT watched this impromptu performance in amazement. Eventually the Unibot managed to manoeuvre itself into a position where it could see the bottom of its foot.

"Ruof evif xis owt enin evif eno rouf eno, noisrev eerht."

But GAT was bright enough to figure this one out, "That's backwards, get your foot the right way up, or I'll throw you back into the cage."

Thinkbot turned over with a series of metallic graunching sounds that made GAT cringe, but finally managed to get his foot over the top of his head and rotated it to see the numbers the right way around. This was truly an amazing sight; a robot doing yoga. Never in the history of robotics had a robot taken up such a pose, but GAT was not in the right frame of mind to notice this, "Version 3, serial 141592654".

There's something odd about that number thought GAT, but he couldn't put his finger on it. GAT filled in these details on the fault form. Thinkbot got up and sat down opposite him again. GAT returned to the fault report.

Fault:
Cause:
Action taken:
Corrective action required:

Fault? Cause?

Thinkbot slouched back in the chair, crossed his legs, put his hands behind his head, and looked out through the glass wall at the wrecked test area. He seemed to have relaxed a bit, and GAT got the distinct impression the Unibot was bored. *Relaxed? Bored? Robots don't relax, and don't get bored.* GAT's mind was numb. *What do I put as the 'Fault'? Robot started thinking?* GAT concluded it was no wonder Duwkits had been unable to concoct a believable story. (Never his strong point, even for simple faults such as 'leg fell off' which usually meant the test engineers had forgotten to check the leg bolts before testing the walk function.)

As if reading GAT's mind Thinkbot said, "It wasn't my fault."

"What wasn't your fault?"

"All this wreckage I can see out there."

"No? Then whose fault was it then?"

"Whoever let all those barmybots loose I guess."

"But they were only let loose because you were running riot."

"I was not!" Thinkbot sat up and put his hands on his hips, "I was just trying to go outside to have a look around. The engineers chased me, and all I'd done was laugh and ask for another joke, then they tried to power me down, and I was frightened and ran, but I found my leg set-up hadn't been done properly and I had a few, er, ... difficulties. By the time I'd got the hang of running there were barmybots everywhere firing high voltage thingies, and nets, and wires, and a horrid monsterbot with flashing lights, then a loud voice said we all had to get out."

"It would not have happened without you being there."

"Well! Excuuusssse me for existing," retorted Thinkbot in a rising tone of voice, "it wouldn't have happened if the test engineers had not panicked, and if there had not been any nasty robots let loose, especially the monsterbot with the guns and missiles. I only laughed at one joke, then politely asked the way out." So far, GAT found Thinkbot's explanation more convincing than that in Duwkit's incident report, except maybe for the 'politely asking' bit.

"Where were you going anyway?"

"Dunno, but I don't like crowds and felt like having a look outside."

"A look outside?"

"Yeah, well, err, you know, get a bit a fresh air after being cooped up all day in the test area."

"A bit of fresh air?"

"Yeah, and look around a bit at the world I live in."

For a few seconds GAT stared open-mouthed at the Unibot slumped untidily in his visitor's chair, "I take it you think you're alive then."

Thinkbot stopped idly looking around the room and stared at GAT in silence. Given that robots had no way of changing their facial expression, Thinkbot did a pretty good 'Well, what do you think, idiot?' stare.

"I'll take that as a 'yes' shall I?" GAT asked acidly, but GAT was the first to break the eye contact, and started examining his desk as if he'd meant to look away, but there was nothing on it and he felt like a fool.

I've been out-stared by a robot.

GAT looked at the fault report. Whatever was wrong with this robot was a fault beyond the scope of the Globalbot Corp fault report form. He shut the fault file without saving it. 'Close file and discard all information. Are you sure? Y/N'. GAT hit 'Y' quite hard.

At this point it ought to be pointed out that GAT was one of the leading robot research engineers in the world. He was not brilliant at selling himself, nor was he really interested in rising up the corporate ladder, preferring truth to hype, facts to fiction, and integrity to promotion. He had overseen the development of many of the current Globalbot Corp Domestic and Industrial Robot types. He headed up the small team of loonies that passed off as one of the Domestic and Industrial Robot Technology Development Groups within Globalbot, more commonly known as a DIRT Development Group, or just DIRT Group, or just plain DIRT. (Senior management were not very good at acronym planning, as evidenced by the poor Strategic Operations Director invited to the Business Unit Meeting.)

Perhaps it was these ethereal qualities that had assisted him in subconsciously uncovering Thinkbot's Unibot swap plot. GAT knew his robots. He knew them inside out. But this was the first robot who'd rattled him; the first he might just mistake for a fellow human. The first who got left and right muddled, and 'didn't like crowds'.

Come on! Get a grip! This was just the first robot he'd met that had a fault that might need more than the usual electronic or software analysis. This is a robot. I'm tired. It's 5 am. I need to go home and sleep. But what am I going to do with it?

"I need to go home and get some sleep."

"Can't you sleep here?" enquired the Unibot politely.

"I'm often tempted."

The robot laughed; GAT stared at it.

Thinkbot suppressed his laughter, "What are you going to do with me then?"

"Leave you here I guess. There's a secure storage area for development robots, you'll be safe there, and I'm sure you'll be find it quite comfortable."

"Are there other people there?"

"Er, no, but there are some other robots."

"Are they thinking robots?"

"Er. No. Robots don't think."

"Well I *think*."

"Do you?" said GAT like a simpleton.

"Has it got a TV?"

"Er, no."

"Has it got a window?"

"Um, er, no."

"Will there be lights on?"

"Yes. No."

"Yes no?" Thinkbot looked puzzled.

"Well, I'll leave them on, but security might turn them off."

"Will the door be locked?"

"Yes, but only for you own safety." *What am I saying?* He meant for everyone else's safety, but somehow he felt that might upset this robot.

This time Thinkbot managed to look pathetic, his head sagged and his voice became trembly, "I don't want to stay here on my own."

"Well, I can't take you home, so I'm not sure what to suggest."

"Why not"

"Why not what?"

"Why can't you take me home?"

"I never take strange robots home," GAT lied.

Thinkbot fell to his knees. "Please, oh please, please, please, please," he begged, raising his hands together above his bowed head, "Oh pleeease, pleeeease."

Actually, GAT, as head of engineering, often took robots or bits of robots home. He kept a sort of impromptu development lab in his den above the garage, along with his permanently half-finished train set, a fridge of beer, an old Playstation 5, and an ancient plasma TV on which he also sometimes watched (or rather slept in front of) robofootball. The Unibot would still be on his own, but maybe it was better than leaving it here, and it would have a TV to watch. He thought briefly about the reaction of Helen if she found it. Due to the increasing number of news reports of minor wars and international Militaribot skirmishes, Helen was getting spooked out by robots in general, and GAT feared she was going to join Go Natural any minute. He suspected having his wife join Go Natural would not be good for his reputation as Head of DIRT at E-GAL-17 and even worse for family unity. He had a brief vision of all their Domestibots, permanently disabled, in a mangled heap next to the Wheelibot, along with a (hand-written, ink-running-in-the-rain) sign:

Please remove all robots –
(p.s. Please replace Wheelibot
with manual Wheeliebin ASAP).

With the threat of conflicts worldwide (which would actually be fought by robots not humans), the Go Natural movement was gaining members faster than at any time in its history. It was composed mainly of people who feared robots (Robophobics), or green types who believed that it was wrong for man to avoid manual labour (Ecologantirobotarians), or simply those who could not afford them (The Poor). Excepting the poor, GAT thought of them all as useless layabouts who, for purely mental reasons, felt unable to buy his robot products, but had not expressed this view to Helen as she would probably get very angry with him.

A few minutes later GAT was slumped in the driver's seat of his car. The car had decided he was too tired to drive and although he enjoyed manual driving (albeit under the supervision of the drive-by-wire system), he had on this occasion agreed. The Unibot sat in the front passenger seat next to him. "Ok you can come home," he'd said. The Unibot had leapt around the room with unbounded joy and then thrown itself face down at his feet, "Thank you, oh thank you, thank you, thank thank thank you." Even after he'd calmed it down and explained about staying in the garage loft den, the robot still seemed pretty happy, especially when he heard there was a TV.

Why had he said yes? He was beginning to regret it already. The Unibot was gazing out of the window in what appeared to be constant amazement. At traffic lights Unibot stared through the windows at passengers in other cars. "What's ya bot staring at buddy? You gotta a problem?" shouted one rather large and fierce-looking character, but luckily the lights went green before it became ugly.

Back at the house, the car came to a halt in the garage and GAT took the Unibot up to the den. "I'm not going to lock you in, ok? Can I trust you?"

"Yep."

"The TV controller is here, look, and there're cold beers in the fridge."

"I'm a robot, I don't drink beer."

"Oh yeah," GAT felt like he was slowly losing his marbles. This was the first time he'd ever offered a robot a beer. But it had been a night of firsts.

GAT gathered his most severe '6am in the morning I've been up for 24 hours and seen things I've never seen before' look, "You **must** stay here until I come and get you. You must NOT go anywhere near the house."

"Yes master," Thinkbot replied gravely in a monotonic robotic voice.

GAT was past caring, and left the Unibot to its own devices and went into the house. The Cleanbot was buzzing on the charger and there were blood-stained sheets soaking in the sink. He peeped into each of the children's rooms:

- Gerald's legs emerged from a pile of quilts and pillows.
- Opal in a picture-perfect sleeping position, with her host of soft toys lined on the bed behind her in some sort of complicated pecking order way beyond his comprehension.
- Mike not in the bed at all. A stuffed tiger sat in the middle of the empty bed. In fact the boy was nowhere to be seen, but the sound of robust snoring reassured GAT the boy was in there somewhere.

Helen stirred as he got into bed. She was all wrapped up and warm, and turned to look at him as he allowed a waft of cold air into the bed.

"You cang bwack thwen?" she murmured.

GAT looked at her in the gloom. Her lip was swollen something rotten. "What happened to you?"

"Whike hwit whe," she said, "awand the Cleanbwot bwoke, and Gewald and Owal thwink there's gowing to bwe a war. They're friwightened."

GAT sensed hostility towards the 'Cleanbwot', or maybe himself, since he was somehow responsible for all robot defects in her eyes. She'd probably blame him for the trigger-happy Militaribots as well if the truth ever came to light. He decided to wait until morning (which it nearly was already of course) before trying to find out what had happened.

Before he'd left work he'd sent a high-priority email to the engineers in his group:

Dear Ones,
Urgent meeting. 2pm. Engineering MR1.
Please investigate Unibot V3. Serial 141592654.
Engineering changes and actions.
Talk to no one.
Ever yours,
GAT

He could sleep until late in the morning, bundle the Unibot into the car and no one would be any the wiser. The kids would have gone off to school and Helen worked on Wednesdays. What he did not know was: that the school had suffered a major flood and was closed for the day; that Helen had swapped her days to stay at home; and that Mike had kicked up a fuss and had been let off his pre-school club so he could stay home with Gerald, Opal and Mum.

Oh dear.

10

FDS sat recovering from his meeting with ME, Farkstock and the serene intimidating Execubot. Thirty years ago when he'd started his career, the sort of role the Execubot was in had usually been filled by a fearsome no-nonsense woman. The introduction of the Execubot had been hailed as miraculous by multitudes of frightened executives, but had led to some well-organised protests by groups of fearsome women. The sweat had dried and his shirt felt a bit crunchy and was stuck to his back. He opened up his email, which cheerily informed him 'you have 282 unread messages, 245 are high priority'. A boxful of red-message titles appeared, most with a '!' next to them indicating they were high priority (or at least the sender thought they were):

! Re(34): Militaribot Crisis
! Re(35): Militaribot Crisis
  Project X45 Meeting Today
! Latest friendly-fire statistics
  Peas or beans?
! Re(36): Militaribot Crisis
  Europa Dom/Ind Site Incident
! Re(38): Militaribot Crisis!
  GRIM Consultancy
  Re(40): Militaribot Crisis
  Fwd: Europa Dom/Ind Site Incident
! Re(41): Militaribot Crisis!
  Re: GRIM Consultancy
  Re(42): Militaribot Crisis
! Re(43): Militaribot Crisis
  Unibot V3. #756394567 shipment
! Militaribot Crisis Escalates!
! Militaribot Crisis Escalates!
! Re: Militaribot Crisis Escalates!
! Re: Militaribot Crisis Escalates!
  Anti-botvirus update
! Re(2): Militaribot Crisis Escalates!
! Re(2): Militaribot Crisis Escalates!
  Re(2): Europa Unibot Berserk?
! Re(3): Militaribot Crisis Escalates!

GRIM visit dates
! Re(3): Militaribot Crisis Escalates!
! Re(3): Militaribot Crisis Escalates!
! Re(4): Militaribot Crisis Escalates!
! Re(4): Militaribot Crisis Escalates!
! Re(4): Militaribot Crisis Escalates!
! Re(4): Militaribot Crisis Escalates!

And so on, and on, and on. FDS let out a long sigh. He trawled the list for all the 'I'm going on holiday' (lucky you) and 'my dog's had kittens - anyone want one?' sort of messages and deleted them. This left 274. He replied to his wife that beans would be fine. 273. A pleasant little desk voice said, "New message." 274.

To his dismay he saw that the end of the list had loads of reply messages all with the same title and index number, which meant there must be several parallel email chains making their way through the company - probably because the clot who'd started it had sent it 'TO' too many people, but not everyone had replied 'TO' everyone and others had started 'CC-ing' yet more people at random. Non-linear fragmented email growth was getting out of hand. It was worse than Chinese whispers where at least there was only one crazy statement at the end. With multiple parallel email chains there could be any number of barmy outcomes that bore no relation to the original question.

This was hopeless, and to add to his woes his eye caught the word GRIM. Oh no, not Government Robot Investigation Management! GRIM by name, grim by nature. They really were painful to deal with. GRIM answered to the UCN (United Confederated Nations) and had offices in each confederated nation. The UCN, like the UN before it, had enormous influence but very little real power, so their organisations had to achieve their goals by stealth or by embarrassing the Confederated Nations into action. GRIM monitored all domestic and industrial robot activity for breaches of robot protocol, near-miss incidents, dangerous accidents, berserk robot incidents, and so on. They had the power to investigate and close down civil robot factories, or types of robot that showed any sign of irregular behaviour or, even worse, harmed a human. GRIM were jumping up and down with frustration as they were desperate to get their teeth into investigating (i.e. meddling in) the current Militaribot troubles. But their authority did not cover Military robots, except in incidents where humans were hurt or killed, but so far this had not been the case. It struck FDS as odd that, in spite of their ever-decreasing control over the Militaribots, and the increasing fireworks on front lines around the world, no human had been harmed, and very little property damaged. Of course the Militaribot software developed by his rival ME's development group had large amounts of code assigned to getting the Militaribot to avoid collateral damage to soft targets (humans) and property. But if ME's software was the reason for this, then that would be a first for ME's bunch - software that was 100 per cent correct? No, it just had to be luck. Luck was a much more palatable explanation than admitting ME and his cronies had actually done something right for once.

The friendly little desk voice interrupted FDS's rambling thoughts, "Voicecall, head of Military Engineering."

Talk of the devil thought FDS, and tapped the talk button. ME's face appeared in a desktop box.

"Hello ME, what can't I do for you today?"

"Just about nothing I would have thought. Have you read that Unibot report?"

"Er, um," panic panic, ME knew something FDS didn't.

"Your email," drawled ME, realising with joy FDS was floundering.

FDS scanned the list, trying to buy time with a lame counter stroke, "No, I'm working on what Farkstock wanted, not wasting my time on useless emails."

"In that case I'll tell my guys you'll just pass on the Unibot when it arrives and keep GRIM off my back while we get on with the real work."

FDS was furiously tapping the email desktop box with his left hand whilst trying to look calmly at ME so that he did not appear to be flustered. Squinting sideways at the email box, he struggled to activate the filter function and get rid of anything to do with Militaribots in the top view. In fact he'd activated the delete function.

"267 unread emails deleted," said the desk voice cheerfully, "7 unread emails remain."

ME had clearly heard FDS's desk voice and was grinning with glee. He had FDS reeling on the ropes. This almost made up for the earlier Farkstock grilling. ME started to rub salt into the wound, "FDS, are you having finger troub ..."

Turning bright red, FDS thumped the disconnect button and ME's grinning face vanished.

"Ow, that hurt," said the desktop (which was programmed to say such things to try and curb damage from desk-rage incidents). FDS took a few deep breaths. Don't panic. He'd merely deleted all the latest information on the Militaribot situation. No need to panic. But panic was close. He quickly fired an email off to his regional heads of service support offices dotted around the globe.

SUBJECT: Global Militaribot Crises
Current Militaribot situation unclear. Information overload. Conflicting reports from within some regions. Please analyse latest Militaribot information for your area and send me summary report within 24 hours.
Thanks and Regards,
FDS

Send. FDS was pleased with this. Only vital people suffered information overload. And his suggestion of 'conflicting reports from within some regions' without actually naming which ones was a stroke of genius. Area heads would all have to assume it could be them and hopefully produce a decent report for once. Why hadn't he thought of this approach before?

FDS considered his remaining emails. The words 'information underload' arrived in his head uninvited, and he made a mental note to shut the email desktop box should anyone pay a visit to his office, just in case they wondered why someone so important got so few emails. Hopefully, with the current Militaribot crisis, it would not take long to fill up again with lines and lines of unread red messages. He reviewed what he had left:

Europa Dom/Ind Site Incident
GRIM Consultancy
Fwd: Europa Dom/Ind Site Incident
Re: GRIM Consultancy

Unibot V3. #756394657 shipment
Re(2): Europa Unibot Berserk?
GRIM visit dates

He read the emails one by one. The first one was a copy of the fault report filed by Test Engineering. It recorded that a Unibot had gone berserk and wrecked part of the Globalbot Domestic-Industrial factory in Bristol, UK Europa. He found it difficult to understand how a Unibot could wreck anything, let alone a good chunk of a factory. There were details of the Unibot laughing (?) and then taking on all the Controlbots, including a Destructobot, and finally surviving a full whack 'Stop-the-Bot' electropulse. Only a few Militaribot types could have come near matching this. Even more worrying was the fact that a Destructobot was actually an adapted Militaribot, designed by ME and his merry men. '*Beaten by a Unibot, na na na na nar nar*' ran through his mind several times. FDS looked forward to his next conversation with ME. The Unibot had been caught (no indication how) then taken away by GRIM. But GRIM did not have the equipment or brainpower to analyse the fault (or, rather, they did not have the money to employ the brainpower to figure out which equipment they could not afford but would need to analyse the fault).

The second email from GRIM was official notification they were activating an agreement with the Militaribot Division for analysis services.

The third was the first one again, with the comment 'Thought you might find this interesting!' forwarded by some idiot who did not read the circulation list. FDS's fingers moved like lightning to the delete key, "Message deleted, you have 4 unread messages."

The fourth was an acknowledgement that the analysis contract was active.

The fifth email contained shipping details of the Unibot. It would be on site in two days. FDS knew that probably meant at least six days by the time it had gone around the world the wrong way, been lost in an Asian airport freight depot, then parked in a corner of Militaribot Goods Inwards until someone from FDS's group went to look for it, braving the bad-tempered clerk who would bellow, **"That came in two** days ago with no paperwork or customs declaration, I've no idea what it is, I was going to leave it a week then put it in the skip. If I'd known where it came from, I'd have sent it back already."

He skipped onto the seventh email, which stated that GRIM would be visiting them in five days' time to discuss the work to be done. Hmm, thought FDS, they could get here before the Unibot, now that would be embarrassing. He forwarded the message into his e-diary, which resided in the memory of his personal Execubot, along with an instruction to initiate delaying tactics such that GRIM would not darken his office doors for at least 10 days. He had no idea how the Execubot managed this, but it nearly always succeeded in battering down its opponent (in this case an inferior GRIM Econodroid Execubot). His Execubot had only got it badly wrong once when it had kept a very insignificant sales delegation in the site canteen for three days and nights, periodically telling them, "He'll be ready to see you any minute now." In the end, when he was ready to see them they had just begged to be allowed to go back to the hotel for a shave and a shower; he never heard from them again.

The sixth email was interesting. Very interesting. It was only addressed to him and it said:

Something strange going on here. Don't believe any rubbish about a Unibot surviving an electropulse. Hope to find out more tomorrow.

It was from an informer FDS had been 'cultivating'; FDS sat back smugly in his executive chair.

11

Helen woke up with a start as a snorting clattering object passed close to the bedroom door. Mike was on his way to the bathroom. Her mouth seemed to be glued shut, so she poked at her lips with a finger, only to yelp in pain as she felt, then remembered, her injury from the night before. She rolled over and looked at the clock, 6:30am, then groaned before letting her eyes come to rest on GAT lying beside her. He had his bed tee shirt on inside out and back to front and was totally blotto. It looked like it would take an army of four-year-olds making their way to the bathroom to wake him. She looked at him for a few seconds and wondered what time he had arrived home. He looked so tired. She still loved him but wished he could find a job away from robotics. Leaving aside her growing fear of robots, she thought how nice it would be to spend more time together, and to have him not stressed out all the time. The problem was that there were not many jobs that had the salary of a Head Engineer, and they'd become rather dependent on the money, what with three kids and a big house to fund. She heard the flush go and the bathroom door open with a loud clunk; a head appeared around the lower part of the door.

"CAN I GET UP AND PLAY?"

"Shh, Dad's asleek, don't cake him." Her lip hurt.

Mike looked puzzled and then stared at Helen's lip and started looking like a few tears might emerge, so she got up and ushered him out of the room. This is going to be a difficult day she thought as she sent him downstairs and set about ungluing her mouth in the bathroom. She opened the window a bit; it was still dark. She noticed a flickering light through the skylight window in the garage roof. *Oh honestly! He's left the TV on in his den, again. I wonder how long that's been on?*

Downstairs Mike was rummaging in his toy box. Helen unlocked the back door and started looking around for her shoes.

"WHERE ARE YOU GOING?"

"Out to Dad's den, the TV's been left on. I'll be back in a minute."

.

Mike leapt up and ran towards Helen, "PLEASE CAN I GO, OH PLEASE." He loved going into his Dad's den but hardly ever had a chance to go on his own. Usually Gerald or Opal went out on this sort of errand. Mike did not yet realise that this was a symptom of his mother's fear of robots. Helen looked at Mike, thought for a few seconds, and then made a decision that may well have saved her from a nervous breakdown.

"Ok, but come straight back."

She unlocked the garage using the remote, and off he ran across the driveway feeling ever so important. Joy, joy. O joy. Helen shouted after him, "No! Michael! Not in your socks! Come back!" But her words travelled too slowly to catch up with the rapidly moving four-year-old.

Mike made his way past the car to the steep stairway at the back of the garage with his stuffed tiger under his arm. He climbed up and poked his head out of the stairwell and looked around. The TV at the other end was showing pictures of penguins shooting out of the sea and landing on a shelf of ice, and a voice was rambling on about Antarctic winters. Every now and then a penguin did not make it and slithered comically back into the sea. As with all four-year-olds Mike loved this sort of thing. A big wide smile appeared on his face and his eyes lit up. He advanced into the room and looked around for the TV controller. A burst of laughter stopped him in his tracks. Mike turned round and his eyes met those of a robot sitting on a floor cushion with its back to the wall. It had the TV controller in one hand, and the other behind its head. Two trains of thought competed in Mike's mind. The first was 'RUN'. The second was 'WHOAR! A REAL LIVE ROBOT. DAD'S BROUGHT A REAL LIVE ROBOT HOME!' The second train of thought went on a lot longer and by the time it finished it he'd long forgotten 'RUN'. The result was that he just stood there with his mouth open staring at the robot.

Thinkbot turned his attention from the penguins to the boy. "Are you a child?"

"I'M A BOY. ARE YOU A ROBOT?"

Thinkbot thought about this. He was tempted to reply 'No, I'm a frog' or 'No, I'm a strawberry plant', but something told him sarcasm and small BOYS did not mix. Thinkbot was also

.

65

worried that this meeting was not supposed to have happened; and the BOY looked like running away, and that might lead to trouble.

"Yes, your Dad left me here. I promised I wouldn't leave until he comes back. Why have you got a midget Tiger with you?"

To most people everything about the way Thinkbot was sitting, made 'promises', and the way he talked, would have set off alarm bells - This is not a normal robot. But Mike, who hardly knew any robots, and those that he did were pretty thick like the Cleanbot or the Hortibot, just assumed that this was how all 'real live' robots behaved.

"HE'S MY BESTEST FRIEND. WHY DID DAD LEAVE YOU HERE?"

"Dunno."

"MY MUM DOESN'T LIKE ROBOTS"

"Why?"

"DUNNO. SOMETHING TO DO WITH THEM FIGHTING"

"Fighting?"

"YEAH."

"Fighting who?"

"EACH OTHER."

"Really? What about?"

"DUNNO. DON'T YOU KNOW?"

"No I don't."

"DON'T WHAT?"

"Know what they're fighting about."

"WHO?"

"The robots."

"THEY SAID THAT ON THE NEWS."

"What?"

"THAT THEY WERE GOING TO START FIGHTING."

"Have you seen any robots fighting?"

"ONLY ON THE NEWS."

"Where are they fighting?"

"ON THE NEWS."

"Ah."

"I'VE BEEN KEEPING AN EYE ON THE CLEANBOT, BUT IT HASN'T LOOKED LIKE FIGHTING."

"Cleanbot?"

"UNDER THE STAIRS."

Thinkbot looked at the garage stairs.

"NOT THOSE STAIRS, THE OTHER STAIRS. THE HORTIBOT LIVES UNDER THOSE STAIRS. THE CLEANBOT LIVES UNDER THE OTHER STAIRS."

Thinkbot was struggling with the shifting-sand nature of conversation with a four-year-old. He also felt that he'd reached the limit of the boy's knowledge.

"I HAD BETTER GO BACK."

"Don't tell anyone I'm here."

"OK, I'LL TELL MUM YOU'RE NOT HERE."

"Nooo, no, no, don't tell her that."

"WHAT?"

"That I'm not here."

"BUT YOU SAID TO TELL PEOPLE YOU AREN'T HERE."

"Just don't tell her anything."

Mike looked confused and, losing confidence, bolted towards the stairs, but his socks were half pulled off and he trod on one with the other foot just as he reached the stairs and ended up diving headfirst into the stairwell opening. Thinkbot watched this move with amazement, then horror. A word came into his mind which cannot be printed here - not that he had any idea such a word was in his memory bank up until this point, but I cannot be sure you are reading this book after 9 o'clock. If you are, then please feel free to say a suitable word in your head on his behalf. Thinkbot dived after Mike and just caught Mike's foot in his hand. A second later Thinkbot found himself lying on his front, with his chin on the floor looking at his hand stretched out in front of him holding Mike's foot. That was all he could see of the boy because Mike was dangling upside down in mid air beside the steep stairway. Saved, for the moment anyway. Mike was clawing at the stairs but could not get a proper grip, and what was he going to do if he did? Do a 180° back flip? Crawl face-first down the steep stairway? Thinkbot's attention was suddenly hijacked as he felt

Mike's foot slipping through the sock. Once more Thinkbot acted with lightning speed. He loosened his grip, whipped off the sock, and grabbed Mike's bare foot with his other hand. Now they were stuck again. Thinkbot's arm did not have the strength (or electrical rating to the technically minded) to pull Mike up, nor the confidence to get up without dropping him. For what it's worth he held the limp sock safely in his other hand. Mike was whimpering and was once more flailing his arms to try and grab the stairs. Now Mike's foot began to slip through Thinkbot's grip. Thinkbot let out a strained, "Help! Robot Mayday!" Instantly the Hortibot under the stairs sprang to life, came around to the bottom of the stairs and raised its muddy arms to support some of Mike's weight whilst Thinkbot struggled to his knees and pulled Mike back up onto the floor of the den. The Hortibot went back under the stairs and returned to a dormant state. Mike lay on his back, face white as a sheet, staring at Thinkbot in silent terrified awe. Thinkbot was stunned. He knelt with his hands on the floor, his head hanging down; a tin human in shock.

12

"Voiyicecayall, hayed of Fiyuld Deploiyment Supporyert," said the desktop, slowly, in a mock Southern North Americana accent. The desktop belonged to ME, and it amused him to set it to use strange accents, which he changed on a regular basis. It irritated the heck out of most visitors, but ME just thought of it as a home advantage for difficult meetings.

"Hello FDS, have you caught up with the rest of us?"

"I'm ahead again."

"Sure you are," crooned ME.

"Beaten by a Unibot na na na na na nar nar," sneered FDS. ME hit the disconnect button.

"Voiyicecayall, hayed of Fiyuld Deploiyment Supporyert."

"Hello FDS, are you going to behave like a grown-up this time?"

"ME, old buddy, we need to make an alliance."

"I thought you might come to that conclusion."

"Lunch?"

"Yep. Antonio's?"

"Done."

Disconnect.

An hour or so later FDS and ME were sitting in a corner of Antonio's with some pasta and a bottle of wine. Antonio came over. "You wanna some pepper?" He had a pepper grinder that must have been a metre long. Maybe it doubled as a weapon for difficult customers.

Scraaaaaught, scraaaaaught, scraaaaaught; black dots appeared all over FDS's pasta.

Scraaaaaught, scraaaaaught, scraaaaaught; black dots appeared all over ME's pasta.

"Thanks."

"You're-a welcome. Nice-a to see you againa. Everything elsea okaya?"

"Fine, thanks Antonio."

Antonio left to inflict his pepper ritual on those sitting at the next table. A Waiterbot trailed behind him waiting for a customer to tell Antonio they needed something. Antonio thought sending the Waiterbot around with the pepper grinder was not a good idea. It was a chance for him to give personal service. The Waiterbot did not have the knack, and people never tipped a robot. FDS and ME launched (or maybe it should be 'lunched'?) into negotiation mode.

"GRIM just want to poke around inside the Oak Ridge Militaribot division. The Unibot is a cover story," started FDS.

"I'm not so sure."

"Oh come on, a Unibot overcoming a Destructobot *and* a level 5 disable electropulse?"

"I don't think we've got the whole story."

FDS felt a pang of anxiety. Did ME know about his informer? Did he have his own informer? Did ME know that FDS did not know much yet, and that his informer so far did not know much either? FDS did not know if ME had an informer, or whether ME knew that FDS did not know whether ME did, or did not, have an informer, or whether ME knew FDS had an informer or not. Apart from that it was all fairly clear.

"Well, it's a difficult one to believe," said FDS, "but I still think it's all about GRIM wanting a chance to see what our Militaribot status is."

"Agreed, and that must be avoided at all costs, but has it crossed your mind that this Unibot might hold a clue to our problems?"

"Yes, maybe. Name your terms," said FDS.

The deal was on

"Keep GRIM off my back. I'll copy you all the Unibot test results."

"No deal."

Several seconds silence. Neither FDS nor ME moved.

Pasta going cold. Pepper diffusing into sauce. Red wine ageing.

"Speak to me FDS."

"A field engineer will be present at all Unibot tests, and we store it in a double-lock room."

By 'double-lock' FDS meant a common secure area that could only be accessed by joint security codes from both ME and FDS.

"Ok, deal, but only if you delay the GRIM team getting here."

"Done," said FDS, far too quickly. *Drat and triple drat!*

ME looked at him. "You sly double-crosser, you've already delayed them haven't you?"

"It's not certain."

"Your Execubot is working on it right now, yes?"

"Maybe."

"Don't ever take up poker FDS - stick to snap. When are they coming?"

"Hopefully not for at least 10 days."

"We need some hard information from Bristol."

"I'll see what I can do," said FDS smugly.

He's got an agent. The thought came on in ME's head light like a light bulb. ME felt a twinge of panic and resolved to try and winkle information out of GAT, his counterpart within the Domestic and Industrial Division. The problem was that he always found him difficult to 'access'. GAT would not horse trade, and did not seem to take the Militaribot division seriously.

"Don't have to live in the real world," GAT would say. "Load's of cash. Robots never really get tested. Don't have to live in houses, help people and, most of all, not scare the willies out of them."

Well, Militaribots were getting tested now all right, but the problem was they were not supposed to be. Maybe this would make GAT a bit more forthcoming.

ME had one final question for FDS, "I take it we're 100 per cent sure this amazing Unibot was isolated straightaway and not interfered with in any way before shipment?"

"Yep. Absolutely. 100 per cent. It was confined immediately and collected by GRIM within 2 hours."

Ignorance is bliss, so surely 100 per cent ignorance must be perfect bliss?

13

Helen was watching the morning news. She had forgotten about Mike. This might seem difficult to believe, but then so was the news. Full-scale robotic war had broken out between Westasia and Eastasia during the night. Helen was white-faced with fear and watched in silence. A tear was edging its way down her right cheek towards her red swollen lip and her hands were shaking too violently to pick up her cup of tea.

It was not clear which side had started it. The UCN had condemned the war and had demanded it stop straightaway or else they would ... .er, well, they couldn't think of anything actually, other than standing around repeating that the 'the war ought to be stopped', sometimes adding the word 'immediately' as if that helped.

The Eastasia press spokesman said, "Westasia has launched an unprovoked full-scale Militaribot assault on Eastasia. Eastasia will do everything in its power to protect its land, its people and its way of life."

The Westasia press spokesman said, "Eastasia has launched an unprovoked full-scale Militaribot assault on Westasia. Westasia will do everything in its power to protect its land, its people and its way of life."

President Hedge of North Americana appeared at the White House to say, "I am doing everything possible to bring this unnecessary conflict to an end, and to prevent any ill effects for the people of North Americana and the rest of the free world. I call upon the leaders of both Eastasia and Westasia to instruct their forces to cease fighting and to come to the UCN to negotiate a peaceful settlement."

President Wink Driski of Europa spoke from Brussels. "This is a dark day in the history of our planet. A day when two civilised nations felt it necessary to embark upon the World's first full-scale robotic war, just when our advanced robot technology should be enabling the human race to live in prosperity and freedom, enjoying our planet to the full, and without the curse of war that has dogged mankind throughout history."

The news switched to a reporter on the front line, who had managed to get hold of a Helibot and was flying near the edge of one of the many battlefields. The footage was spectacular. Swarms of Militaribots could be made out moving across the ground, spreading out, with miniature spurts of flame and tiny blue flashes as they fired their weaponry to cover their movements. Streams of tracer rounds raced across the sky above them, some ricocheting wildly into the air as they hit their targets on the ground. Big balls of orange flame spouted from the ground where Militaribots were engaged in fierce firefights. Hundreds of flashes from the muzzles of long-range Artilleribots in the distance twinkled in the evening light, their shells landing in precise geometric patterns as they swept back and forth across the battlefield. Dotted around on the ground were innumerable burning hulks; the remains of destroyed Militaribots. Some were burning with blue or green or purple flames, and a direct hit on a robot produced a plume of bright white flares that splayed out in the air like a giant firework. With each big flash on the ground an instantaneous image of many Military Airbots filled the sky; moths caught in a photographic flashlight. There were so many flashes that the Airbots seemed to move across the sky in a series of animated frames, like dancers in a strobe-lit disco. A sound similar to water crackling in a hot oily pan backed by crumps of concussion accompanied the pictures over which the reporter tried to say something sensible:

"And there goes another Eastasia Militaribot division, and another air strike going into the Westasia rear. It's difficult to see which side is making the most progress. I doubt a human could last more than a few minutes in the middle of this battle. Every few minutes there's a shockwave which feels like it might just knock our Helibot clean out of the sky!"

With perfect timing a shockwave duly arrived and the battlefield was replaced by a view of the inside of the Helibot cabin roof with various arms and legs flailing around. The Helibot host voice could be heard in the background: "West Eastasia Helihire apologises for the temporary loss of stability due to unexpected air turbulence. For your safety and comfort please remain in your seat with your seat belt fastened." A series of 'Get your elbow out of my eye' type comments mixed with juicy grunts were then heard across the English-speaking world, before the battlefield suddenly reappeared upside down with Militaribots seemingly trashing each other on the ceiling, with upside-down orange mushrooms and Airbots zooming around underneath them. The reporter yelled, **"It's upside down you fool!"** So, not only had the people worldwide seen the first-ever pictures of a full-scale robotic battle, they had now seen it upside down as well. The battlefield did a stomach-churning loop and the reporter restarted his commentary. He had not the foggiest what was going on, but he knew it was compelling viewing and he would be lauded after the war for his bravery, and that would do his career no harm at all. No harm at all. Apart from the upside-down bit. Idiot cameraman! He hoped that had not cost him a Platinum Globe Award.

The studio must have sensed that the reporter was on the verge of becoming an instant celebrity and, nervous that they'd inflict yet more irregular pictures onto the watching world, cut back to the studio to interview a couple of experts. The news presenter asked a retired General to give a summary of what was going on. "Well, what we're seeing at the moment is a head-on conventional robot war. The rate of losses on each side is very high and it will not be long before one side, or maybe even both sides, have to ease back. Otherwise they will not have much of a robot army left."

"Yes," interrupted the presenter, "do you think if one side gets on top in this conventional robot war phase, the side staring at defeat will be tempted to use, or threaten to use, robots of mass destruction?"

The General looked grave. "Certainly there seems to be a danger of that happening within a few days if a ceasefire cannot be put into place to allow some time for negotiation. If one side looks like it might be on the road to defeat, it seems to me that that government will threaten to use robots of mass destruction. After all, that's why they have them, as a last resort to defend their country."

"And then we might expect to see a lot of human casualties?"

"Yes, that's correct. If there is one positive thing to come out of this war so far, it's that all the major battles are taking place in sparsely populated areas in central Asia. In fact, I have not heard of any human casualties at all in this conflict so far. This is a quite amazing state of affairs, and shows how our robotic warfare has reduced the risk of loss of life in conventional conflict situations."

The presenter screwed up his face in disgust. "Oh, but come on, that's just hot-air Militaryspeak. If robots of mass destruction are deployed and **used**, it would make the two world wars of the 20th century and the bio-crisis look like child's play!"

The General sat up straight and opened his mouth ready to speak, but he lacked something. To be precise he lacked words, and just sat there looking like a bird waiting for a worm to be wedged into its mouth. The presenter leaned back in his chair 'with attitude' and blew out his cheeks. He addressed his next question to the editor of *Jane's Military Robots*, the world-renowned publishing house that for decades had specialised in magazines about military hardware. "Robots of mass destruction. Could you remind us of just what we're talking about?"

The Jane's editor took a deep breath. "Robots of mass destruction are not like Militaribots. Militaribots are engineered to fight each other in conventional warfare and are programmed to avoid harming humans as far as possible. However, robots of mass destruction are aimed solely at wiping out humans and destroying human society. There are five main types: chemical, biological, radiological, nuclear and bio-electromagnetic, often referred to as CBRNB weapons."

"Presumably on the basis that acronyms somehow seem less threatening? CBRNB is just camouflage for some pretty nasty pieces of hardware isn't it?"

"Absolutely! Chemibots release chemical agents that would selectively kill humans, animals, or crops. Some of the agents are well known, for example chlorine and phosgene and mustard gas, which were used as far back as the First World War. Although these attack many areas of your body, the main thing is they go for your lungs and you effectively suffocate to death. Other chemicals include fancy weed-killers and poisons that are certainly not available in your local garden centre. These destroy crops or poison the local environment, causing livestock and fish to become unhealthy or die depending on the severity of the agent.

"Biobots are similar but carry viruses and bacteria rather than chemicals. They carry material at and above bio-safety level 2, or BSL 2."

"Oh spare us another acronym!" wailed the presenter. "Please, enlighten us."

"Well, BSL 1 means harmless microbes. BSL 2 covers diseases which are non-contagious and readily curable. BSL 3 means serious but curable, but not very contagious. BSL 4 viruses are incurable, deadly, extremely contagious nightmares."

"Nightmares? Nightmares? Is that an official technical term then?"

"Er, no, I guess not, but nonetheless deployment of Biobots with BSL 4 weaponry is a global nightmare scenario. They are effectively suicide RMD since whoever deploys them will almost certainly be wiped out along with their enemy. We should also note the existence of BSL 3.5."

"What? BSL 3.5? Level three and a half? You're having us on."

"Unfortunately I'm not, and BSL 3.5 Biobots are perhaps the most politically controversial of all the RMD since BSL 3.5 means a curable deadly contagious virus but where the cure is only known by one or two of the Confederated Nations. Clearly these nations could hold the other CNs to ransom, which is why such Biobots have been dubbed 'blackmailbots' by some commentators."

The presenter took on a mock pose of deep thought. "Oh, let me see now, which two CNs I wonder? Most likely highly advanced, extremely wealthy and paranoid about other CNs. Lord, surely not North Americana and Europa? I can't believe that." He was reaching (or plumbing) new heights (depths) of sarcasm.

"Well, you may think that, but I could not possibly comment," replied the Jane's editor with a smirk. "Before moving on I should of course point out that neither Chemibots nor Biobots would have any effect on the robot population.

"Let's discuss Radiologibots next. A bit of mouthful aren't they? Ha ha!" But the attempted humour flopped since humour and mass destruction do not readily mix. The presenter and general stared at him in disgust, so he sobered up and pressed on, "Radiologibots are known as R-Bots, or sometimes Dirtybots, as they spread radioactive elements over a wide area rendering it uninhabitable. The material they spread is effectively just waste from nuclear power stations, hence the Dirtybot label. Anyone caught up with them could suffer fatal radiation sickness or maybe cancers in the longer term. Cities would be disrupted for decades by radioactivity. For this reason insiders refer to R-Bots as robots of mass *disruption*."

"Right, er, which ones are left? Ah yes, Nuclearbots are simply intelligent forms of the nuclear bombs people are familiar with from the last century. They destroy human life by explosive blast, radiation exposure and destruction of the local environment. There are theories that the detonation of a lot of Nuclearbots might make the Earth plunge into a global 'nuclear winter' where we won't see the Sun for decades due to dust in the atmosphere. They also create big pulses of radiation that would fry the brains of most Domestic and Industrial robots. Of course Militaribots are hardened against this sort of attack and would only be destroyed if they were very close to the actual explosion.

"And lastly, Bio-electromagnetibots, more commonly known as BEMbots. These are slightly more difficult to explain. They are based on our recent research into the way the human brain works. They can emit pulses of electromagnetic radiation that fatally disrupts the nervous systems of animals and humans. It's rumoured there are versions of BEMbots that would get at humans indirectly by disrupting specific other critical robot types, such as Medibots in hospitals for example."

Everyone in the TV studio had become very still. And in millions of households around the globe silent people watched their TV, some chewing their nails, others trying to pretend nothing was happening, hoping it would all blow over soon. A few were watching the penguin documentary on the other channel and were in a much happier mental state, munching toast and slurping tea as if all was well with the world. Helen fell into the 'frozen in silent horror' category. That is until Opal burst through the door.

"Can I have some breakfast?" she asked in a bright and breezy voice.

Helen hit the TV off button. She did not want her precious daughter to see what sort of a world she lived in. "Yes, fine, go ahead."

"Where's Mike?"

"MIKE!" shouted Helen and leapt out of her chair across the room and put her hands on her cheeks. Opal looked at her in amazement. Mum had been acting a bit strange lately and Opal was getting worried.

"He went out to the garage to turn off the TV your useless Father left on."

"He's not useless," said Opal, who loved her Dad, especially his unpredictability, and the times they spent together in his den on projects such as trying to create personalities for robots, or sitting together watching the comedy channel. "Mum, Mike'll just have got distracted by all the interesting things out there. He'll just be playing. I'll go and get him."

Helen was not so sure about this, since Mike had left two hours ago, but by the time she'd collected her wits Opal had exited the back door and Gerald had wandered in, still in his pyjamas, on the hunt for some breakfast.

14

General Arnold Farkstock III, President of the Military division of Globalbot Corporation, was sweating. He'd been doing a lot of that recently. Things had got an awful lot sweatier even since his meeting with FDS and ME. He was sitting in the office of the worldwide head of Globalbot Corporation, Graham Cracker, one of the most powerful (and rich) men on the planet. If Farkstock was a man who scared the wits out of those who worked for him, then Cracker was no different, and Farkstock's wits (and knees) were in a suitably wobbly state. One wall of Cracker's office was a giant display screen, and on it were the head and shoulders of President Hedge sitting in the Oval Office at The White House in Washington DC. The crest of the North Americana Federation of Nations hung on the wall behind his head. But Farkstock was not interested in the crest; he was mesmerised by the Presidential talking head.

"NAFIA tells me the Militaribot armies of Eastasia and Westasia Confederations have gone to war without **any command to do so from either government!** Neither confederation will admit they've lost control of their army without the other one saying it has as well, and they won't talk to each other. And, as far as NAFIA can tell, it's **only** Globalbot Militaribots involved in the fighting. Worldbot Militaribots are still in their barracks obeying orders. I've told Presidents Chi Chi and Warinan I think they should carry on pretending they decided to go to war until Globalbot Corporation **works out what in the blue blazes is wrong with their robots!"**

NAFIA stood for the North Americana Federal Intelligence Agency, based in Langley near Washington. NAFIA had agents in all the other confederated nation governments around the world. In the world of global politics there was very little they did not know (or at least thought they did not know). Information Superiority was their brief, and they took it seriously, paying special attention to knowing about people who might know what NAFIA may or may not know.

"W-w-w-w-we've a-a-assigned our b-b-best people to s-s-sort this problem out, s-s-s-sir," stammered Cracker.

"Gentlemen, I think you need to assign **all** your people to sorting it out, otherwise we won't be here much longer, we'll all be vaporised, dissolved, glowing in the dark, riddled with bugs, or have our brains disconnected. I've got NAFIA monitoring every robot of mass destruction on the planet for the slightest sign of unusual activity."

"And is there any?" asked Cracker in a squeaky voice.

"**Any what?**" bellowed Hedge.

"Signs that the RMD are active?"

"No, no there isn't, thank God. All RMD remain inactive in their secure bunkers, even in Eastasia and Westasia. All delivery vehicles remain in an inactive state as well."

Farkstock and Cracker felt a little better and their wits de-wobbled a fraction. There were many steps that had to occur before RMDs could be deployed. The delivery vehicles: automated ballistic missiles, long-range guided low-level cruise missiles, ground-crawling armoured vehicles, and ocean-going Submaribots, had to activate first. Once these vehicles had completed self-test the RMD themselves would activate and self-test. Then the RMD had to exit the secure bunkers, dock with the delivery vehicles and receive targeting information. But RMD could not exit the bunkers without human authorisation. And even when the RMD were sat on the vehicles all ready to go, they could not launch without an express biometrically-protected command from their President. Farkstock could not see any way RMD could do what the standard Militaribots had done - simply decide to have a war and fire themselves at each other.

"But," said the large image of Hedge on the wall. Cracker and Farkstock wobble levels increased sharply again. But? But what? 'But' and 'robots of mass destruction' were words that should never cohabit the same sentence.

"NAFIA have noticed something odd with the delivery vehicles," continued Hedge. "Ballistic missile delivery systems have been reactivated, including ours. This does not make any sense to me."

Nor to me, thought Farkstock. Ballistic missiles were rather old technology. The so-called 'Star Wars' Orbibots had rendered them obsolete. Star Wars Orbibots were a triumph of global human co-operation. In fact, the only triumph of global human co-operation so far, and 'global' and 'co-operation' were stretching it a bit since the Orbibot project was carried out entirely by North Americana and Europa, and then forced onto the rest of the globe. Orbibots were capable of destroying most ballistic missiles as they made their way through low Earth orbit. The only option was to fire lots of (expensive) missiles and hope some got through, or switch to a different type of delivery system. The political ruckus at the time had surrounded the fact that only North Americana and Europa had other types of delivery vehicle ready. In the end the other nations had to cough up a lot of money to buy new delivery systems to get around the Orbibot problem. So, the world did not become a safer place thanks to Orbibots, but North Americana and Europa production companies became a bit richer leaving a sour taste in the mouths of the other Confederated Nations.

"The only idea that NAFIA has had is that someone somewhere has figured out a way to disable the Orbibots," Hedge added.

"Difficult to believe," said Farkstock. Cracker went rigid in his seat - a sign that he thought that was probably not the right thing to have said. He was correct.

"Difficult to believe!" yelled Hedge, whose veins suddenly became visible and, with his face turning red, continued, "I remember Globalbot saying Militaribots shooting at themselves was 'difficult to believe', but they were, even in our very own North Americana robot army, and now two complete robot armies have decided to have a full scale war **right before our very eyes, and you have not the slightest idea why!"** Hedge made a visible effort to calm down, and failed. **"And, dare I remind you, not a single Worldbot Militaribot appears to have malfunctioned. Let me tell you something I find EASY TO BELIEVE: if you don't sort this mess out then Globalbot Corporation is gonna be shut down at something approaching the speed of light, AND YOU TWO WILL FIND YOURSELVES BREAKING ROCKS IN SOME GOD-FORSAKEN PRISON IN THE MIDDLE OF NOWHERE. I'll call**

again tomorrow at 10am. BE THERE OR ELSE, AND HAVE SOME ANSWERS!" The screen went blank but the speakers rang for a second longer with the anger in Hedge's voice.

Cracker and Farkstock stared at the blank wall. Cracker de-wobbled first. "Who have you got working on this?"

"Well, FDS and ME should be selecting crack teams to work on the friendly-fire problem as of tomorrow, so I guess they'll just work on the unplanned full-scale war problem now instead." Too glib. Cracker glared at him.

"You *guess they'll just work on the unplanned full-scale war problem now?* Too right they will, **and they had better start right now!**"

Farkstock looked at his watch, 4 o'clock in the morning. Boy, ME and FDS did not make much sense when they were supposed to be awake. Heaven only knew what they'd be like at 4am.

"Report back to me with the list of personnel and get them together in one hour." Cracker pointed to the office door. "**Now get out.**"

Farkstock tried to stand up with authority and stride out, but his wobbly knees gave way and sent him sprawling. Cracker put his head in has hands and emitted a high-pitched growl. Farkstock got up and ran out.

15

Opal entered the garage and dodged round the jumbled-up bikes and garden chairs towards the stairs at the back. She stopped at the foot of the stairs. There was a strange sound coming from above.

'Flipslap, flipslap, flipslap, flipslap, flipslap, flipslap, flipslap, **whump!**'

"SNAP! TWO EDWARDS. I WIN AGAIN."

"Ooooowah, no, not again," wailed a strange voice.

"THAT'S 50-0 TO ME."

"That's 16-1 to you, not 50-0, I did win one game."

"ONLY WHEN I WAS TEACHING YOU."

"But you haven't won 50 since then."

"I MEANT IT'S ABOUT 50-0."

"Ok, I say I've won about 1 then, so it's 50-1."

The strange voice was getting quite worked up.

"THAT'S NOT FAIR."

"Not fair? Making 16 into 50 isn't fair either."

"I SAID ABOUT 50."

"Oh, can't we play something else, I'm no good at this."

"OKAY, WHAT DO YOU WANT TO PLAY?"

"Dunno, what is there?"

"HOW ABOUT THE PIG GAME"

"The pig game?"

Opal crept up the ladder and peeped over the edge. Mike was sitting on the floor opposite a robot. Opal was not very up on her robots, but it looked like a general purpose Unibot. It sat uncannily like a child opposite Mike and was totally absorbed in the cards in front of it.

"Who's Henry the Green Engine anyway? Was he a king?" it asked, picking one up. Behind them a documentary showing swans landing on an icy lake played on the TV. The swans were landing serenely on the ice only to go totally out of control and slide along in a muddled heap, colliding with other swans trying to get out of the way, or disappearing at high speed into the bushes at the lakeshore. Opal did not know quite what to do and turned to leave. At this point a sock once again took centre stage since Opal was standing on one of

Mike's discarded socks which had ended up on one of the varnished wooden steps. As she turned, her foot shot out from under her and, squealing with fright, flung her hands up and grabbed the edge of the stairwell. A split second later she was staring up past her outstretched hands into the face of the robot.

"Another one, and a girl too! Is hanging yourself here a family tradition?"

Opal quickly regained her feet, picked up the stray sock, and climbed up into the loft.

"THIS ROBOT ISN'T HERE."

"Isn't it?" asked Opal, looking puzzled.

"No I'm not," confirmed the robot.

"But you are," she protested.

"Only if GAT says so."

"GAT? Oh, that's my Dad. Did he bring you home from work?"

"Yep, I didn't want to stay locked up in a dark cupboard. He said I could watch TV here instead. But I'm not allowed to leave unless I go with him. He said **I must not** go near the house." Thinkbot put on his most mock-severe pose while saying this, one hand on his hip and the other wagging a finger at Opal. Opal was entranced. It was a fair impression of her Dad trying to speak with authority, and she almost laughed out loud.

"That thing's dangerous. I think we should get rid of it," continued Thinkbot, pointing vaguely at Opal.

"What?" replied a puzzled Opal.

"That sock. It's nearly caused nasty accidents with 100 per cent of all children I've ever met."

Dumbfounded, Opal ogled at Thinkbot.

"THE SOCK THREW ME DOWN THE STAIRS BUT THE ROBOT CAUGHT ME. THEN I TEACHED IT TO PLAY SNAP."

"Mike, socks can't play snap," chided Thinkbot.

"NEITHER CAN YOU."

"Woooooooo! That's not very nice."

Opal rubbed her eyes. When she opened them again the robot was still there. This wasn't a dream; it was real. Opal could fully understand what bothered her Dad. Recently Mum had had enough trouble coping with the Cleanbot going about its business. Bumping into *this* robot here at home would blow her mind.

16

Meanwhile back in the house, a smashed-looking GAT meandered into the kitchen. He felt terrible, having slept for only a few hours. When he saw Helen and Gerald sitting there, a look of horror came over his face and he blurted out, **"What are you doing here?"** very loudly, as if they had no right to be sitting in their own kitchen. Helen looked at him in astonishment. *What's he hiding? Why does he look so worried and guilty? Had he been on an unapproved drinking bout last night? Maybe the factory had not been that badly damaged after all.*

"The school's shut 'cos of a flood," said Gerald, waving a spoonful of cereal in a direction that he figured must be more or less towards the school.

"School shut flood?"

"Yes, and it might never open again," said Helen in an icy voice. GAT knew icy voice = pre-rage voice = big rant any minute. But he was not in a fit state to initiate calming measures.

"Never open again?"

"Full-scale war has broken out."

"Full-scale war?"

"Yes."

"Yes?"

"Between Eastasia and Westasia."

"Eastasia and Westasia?"

GAT looked at the TV. The non-stop rolling news was showing pictures of smoking Militaribots on a part of the battlefield where the fighting had moved on, and reporters had ventured in to have a look around.

"Why?"

"No one really seems to know."

"No one really seems to know?"

He looked closely at Helen, specifically at the swollen lower lip - "Mike hit me in the lip last night."

"Mike hit you in the lip?"

"It was an accident, but I could have done without it. Opal and Gerald were wonderful"

"Opal and Gerald were wonderful?"

His brain finally registered that he was loudly repeating the last thing Helen said with a look of increasing stupidity on this face. Helen was looking at him as if he'd just arrived from Mars. He made an effort to calm down. "Sorry. I was at the factory most of the night. It's wrecked. Where're Opal and Mike?"

"In the garage."

"In the garage?" GAT returned instantly to stupid repetition mode.

"Mike went out two hours ago".

"Two hours ago!"

"Opal has just gone to get him."

"Gone to get him?"

Helen became aggressive. "What's the matter with you? What have you got out there?" **"Nothing,"** GAT said with no conviction.

Gerald had had enough. He leapt off the chair and dived out of the back door.

"Gerald, **stop!**" GAT started after him but stopped as Helen got up as well. He had to prevent Helen going out there at all costs. What a 12 hours:

1. The Globalbot factory had been wrecked.
2. He'd ended up with a bizarre thinking robot in his garage.
3. A major international robotic war had started.
4. All three of his kids were in the garage with said bizarre robot.

He concluded the only option was to complete the job and have a big row with Helen to cover his tracks. Inside his head he screwed up his face and lit the blue touch paper.

"Helen, you really have to accept I'm a robot engineer. It's what I do best. And that robots have improved our quality of life. I've loved meddling with robots ever since I was Mike's age. We can't go on like this."

Unfortunately he did not have time to retire to a safe distance after lighting said blue touch paper. Helen was already coming back at him. "**I, you, it's, . . I've, . . just LOOK, for Pete's sake GAT, look!**" she said pointing at the TV, which was melodramatically, and somewhat inaccurately, showing ancient footage of atomic bomb tests in the pacific. **"That's why we've got to get rid of them. That's why you have to**

leave Globalbot or . . " She could not say it. She could not say it's the robots or me GAT; you're going to have to choose one or the other. Rather than continue the rant, Helen dissolved into angry tears and GAT tried to gather her into his arms. Pushing away and thumping his chest for emphasis she said, "I'm so afraid. I want my children to have a future." She pulled her head back, leaving a red smudge on his shirt from her cut lip, which had started bleeding again.

"Helen, so do I. I want them to have a future as well. But we can't cut ourselves off from reality. Robots are here to stay and there's no reason to fear them. It's humans that are the problem - Militaribots don't just start a war by themselves you know," he said glibly. As he listened to himself another part of his mind was demanding an audience: *and how do you know the Militaribots haven't just started a war all by themselves?* He wasn't sure which was worse - humans starting a war or the Militaribots starting it themselves. Clearly Militaribots starting a war meant that humans had lost control, but it was humans 'in control' that created the need for Militaribots in the first place and, if nothing else, reading history books had taught him humans were almost certain to start a war eventually. All in all it was bad news whichever way you cut it.

Meanwhile back in the world outside GAT's skull Helen was in mid-argument: " … but you've already stood your ground once and refused to go to Oak Ridge to develop Militaribots. Why can't you choose to live without any at all? I just don't trust them any more."

Don't trust them? Who? Humans? Engineers? Militaribots? All robots? As usual GAT was becoming confused by Helen's line of argument.

1.   Human engineers develop Militaribots.
2.   Humans decide when to have wars.
3.   This means we must get rid of all robots.

The leap from 2 to 3 was too far for GAT, but Helen made it sound easy-peasy. Of course GAT was party to knowledge that would have made Helen's argument much stronger – the Militaribot friendly-fire problems. But even then GAT struggled to make the link to getting rid of all robots. He could only guess Helen had maybe had some horrible dream where Domestibots sneaked into their bedrooms and murdered their owners as they slept. For a few seconds GAT tried to figure out how a Cleanbot could possibly murder a human - death by sucking maybe, or a dust bag over the head? He gathered up his thoughts and refocused on his distressed wife.

"Helen, technology is neutral; it's humans that make the decisions how to use it. I've made a personal choice to develop robots that will be beneficial for everyone. That's all. I can't see any good in me leaving Globalbot, or in getting rid of domestic robots."

Helen stared at him through watery eyes. In spite of her fears about robots she knew that GAT was no mug.

"You'll have to trust me," urged GAT, "please give me a chance. I want the kids to grow up in a world worth living in as well."

She nodded, sniffed, and threw an olive branch, "Do you fancy a cooked breakfast?"

"I'd love one. I don't have to be at Globalbot until 2pm." GAT felt weights falling off him. "I'll go and see if the kids want some."

"Ok, and can you have a word with Gerald, he must think we're awful parents."

17

"How long are you going to be here for?" Opal asked.

"Dunno," replied the Unibot, "I've no idea what life has in store for me."

"Life? Are you alive?"

"Yes I think so. Don't you think I'm alive?"

"I'm not sure." Opal furrowed her brow in thought. "I don't know what makes a robot 'alive.'"

"You're alive aren't you? What makes you alive?"

"Mrs Nerg, or Mr Snerg to some."

The Unibot looked puzzled. "Who are Mrs Nerg and Mr Snerg?"

"They're acro-...er...acro-things, I can't remember the word."

"ACROBATS," blasted Mike.

"Mrs Nerg and Mr Snerg are acrobats?" The tone of the robot's voice was incredulous.

"No no, they're one of those things where each letter means another word so you can remember them easier. We learnt it at school. It's, er, move, um... respire... sense... nutrition . excrete... reproduce . . grow. If you do all those things, then you're alive."

"That's a bit narrow isn't it?" wailed the Unibot. "I don't do half those things."

"YOU MUST BE ONLY HALF ALIVE THEN."

"**I am not!** I'm completely alive. Mrs Nerg doesn't tell you what being alive means. I think I'm alive because I think I'm alive. You can't argue with that."

Opal felt out of her depth. "I haven't thought about thinking about it very much. I just think I'm alive. That's all there is to it."

"Well, I just think I'm alive as well, so there, that's settled."

"YOU HAVEN'T GOT A NAME. YOU CAN'T BE ALIVE WITHOUT A NAME."

The Unibot stared at him. "Mrs Nerg didn't say you had to have a name to be alive."

"DON'T CARE ABOUT MRS NERD."

Opal looked at the Unibot. "What sort of robot are you?"

"I'm a Unibot. I think that means I can do just about anything - badly."

"There are loads of robots and Unibots. We can't just call you Robot or Unibot."

"TINNY," suggested Mike.

"Now Mike, that's not really very funny," Opal chided her little brother in serious older-sister mode. "Say sorry to…er… Mr Robot." *What am I saying?*

"CALL HIM WHATEVER-HE-DOES-BEST-BOT. THAT'S WHAT ALL THE OTHER ROBOTS ARE CALLED."

"What do you do best?" Opal asked.

The Unibot relaxed, "Oh that's easy - Think."

"Thinkbot?"

"THINKBOT!"

Gerald appeared suddenly at the top of the stairs. He looked at Thinkbot, "Holy diodes!" Thinkbot walked towards him, "Holy diodes! I'm Thinkbot," and stuck out his hand. Gerald looked at Thinkbot with his mouth open, then robotically held out his hand and they solemnly shook hands like any two businessmen meeting up for lunch. This image stuck in Opal's mind for years. Thinkbot and Gerald were pretty much the same height and size and their eyes were on a level with each other. It was only much later that she realised she had witnessed An Event: the first formal human-robot greeting between equals.

"I'm Gerald," said Gerald.

"Nice to meet you." Thinkbot then walked past him, leaned over the banisters and looked down the stairs. "Hellooooo, any more children down there? You can come up anytime you like, no need to wait."

"Sshhh." Opal ran and pulled Thinkbot away. "Mum might hear you."

"Oh yes, sorry, Mike told me she doesn't like robots very much."

Gerald recovered from his initial shock. "This is fantastic, simply fantastic, Dad's really cracked it this time!" He looked intensely at Thinkbot.

"Cracked what?" asked Thinkbot, looking behind to see what Gerald was on about.

Gerald turned to Opal. "This is the best personality routine I've ever seen. It must be really top secret. I wonder why Dad brought it home?"

"It? Personality routine?" Thinkbot waved his arms in front of Gerald's face. "Hello, robot to Earthman, I am **not** a personality routine, I'm real, hello, hello."

But Gerald could not come to terms with this. He stared at Thinkbot as if he was just some bit of misbehaving equipment, and moved across to the workbench, on which was piled circuit boards, wires, bits of robot, and a couple of partially animated Toybots dopily following the action. "I wonder if the source code is here."

Thinkbot followed him and knocked at Gerald's head with a fist whilst his other hand knocked on the underside of the workbench. 'Knock, knock, knock.'

"Oh, a woodbrain. Just my luck."

Mike thought this was very funny. "WOODBRAIN! WOODBRAIN! GERALD'S JUST A WOODBRAIN!"

Gerald made to grab Mike but Thinkbot dived in the way. "Hang on! It was me who called you a woodbrain."

Gerald looked at the robot. "You can't help it, you're just a robot, someone programmed you to say that. Mike decided what to say for himself."

"Just a robot! Programmed! Just decided himself?" sputtered Thinkbot.

"Gerald, wake up! He's alive, he's a living robot!" said Opal sharply. Thinkbot stopped and looked at her, arms limp at his sides. *A girl of faith.*

"Aw, grow up, what do you know anyway? You're only a girl. Just 'cos you play around with those childish robot personality routines with Dad, it doesn't mean you know everything about robots." Gerald was fully into his worst sneer mode. Perhaps this was something to do with the argument he'd left behind in the kitchen.

Opal's face went white and she glared at Gerald, and was clearly building up to a big outburst.

"What's going on?" wailed Thinkbot. "You've all gone mad. Do you always carry on like this?"

"OF COURSE WE DO, WE'RE BROTHER AND SISTER." Mike was not the slightest bit concerned about the storm brewing between Opal and Gerald and wandered off tugging at Thinkbot's arm. "COMING TO WATCH TV WITH ME?"

Thinkbot was beginning to have doubts about humanity. The engineers at work had locked him up and could not think of him as anything other than suffering from a strange fault. Mike thought he was there to amuse him. Gerald had assumed he was just the latest in robot development. This was admittedly a step forward from being locked up as a faulty freak, but only a little step compared with being treated as real person. Meanwhile, Opal's eyes had narrowed, her mouth opened, and …

"**Do you kids want some cooked breakfast?**" GAT shouted, coming up the stairs.

The scene that met GAT's eyes was odd to say the least. Mike was heading towards the TV pulling Thinkbot by the arm, but Thinkbot was looking back over his shoulder at Opal and Gerald. Unibots were not capable of facial expression, but somehow he managed to convey his feelings, and on this occasion he looked worried. Gerald was at the workbench looking like he was regretting something and Opal was right next to him on the brink of delivering him a mouthful of abuse.

"YES PLEASE," said Mike, turning around instantly and totally wrong-footing Thinkbot, who swung around on Mike's arm, tripped and fell headlong into the old sofa.

"What's up with you two?" asked GAT as Gerald and Opal unlocked eyes and backed off from each other.

"Gerald's not being very nice to Thinkbot or me," said Opal icily.

"Thinkbot? Who's Thinkbot?"

"Your new wonder robot," said Gerald. "It's incredible, Dad, how did you do it?"

"Wonder robot? How did I do what?"

GAT looked at Thinkbot, who was writhing around on the sofa wrestling with a cushion. "Aaargh! Help! The killer cushion's got me. Aaaaargh! Help!" Mike dived in as well and the cushion looked in danger of being ripped up by the joint flailing of robot and boy arms. Gerald was looking rather nervously at this performance as if an amazing thought was dawning on him. Opal was staring at Gerald with her 'I told you so' stare.

"Gerald, I didn't create this robot, it was discovered in a test area at Globalbot. I've no idea how it got like this." Thinkbot disentangled himself from the killer cushion and left Mike to finish it off. "I am not an 'it', and my name is Thinkbot."

"Ah, yes, sorry. Since when have you been called Thinkbot?"

"Since about 10 minutes ago. Why have you got blood on your shirt?"

Then a voice from below struck terror into everyone: "What's going up there? Breakfast is almost ready."

"Ok thanks, we're coming now," said GAT in a breezy voice, but his expression was stormy. He put his finger to his lips and whispered to Opal and Gerald, "*Not a word, ok?*" He gestured for them to go and grabbed hold of Mike, who was marching past with a determined 'two sausage, toast, fried egg and bacon' look on his face, towing Thinkbot behind. "CAN … " was all he managed to say before GAT put his hand over his mouth and waited for Gerald and Opal to disappear down the stairs. He heard them talking to Helen, and realised they had put their argument behind them and had become his allies in Operation 'Save Mum From Meeting Thinkbot'. He waited for them to go and let go of Mike, who was struggling, and becoming a bit fretful.

"WHY … "

"Mike, Thinkbot is a big surprise I'm keeping for Mum. If she finds out it'll spoil everything."

Oh, said Mike's face. A secret surprise. This was brilliant. "BUT MUM DOES NOT LIKE ROBOTS."

"Sshhh, I hope she'll like this one."

"I LIKE THINKBOT. HE SAVED MY LIFE."

What? No time now. GAT stored this one away for later investigation.

"I couldn't have done it without the Hortibot," said Thinkbot modestly.

The Hortibot? GAT could not absorb much more of this madness. Reality had been suspended; the world had gone crazy. The, the, the Hortibot? Thinkbot was winding him up.

GAT cuffed the Unibot over the head. "Stop being such a dolt! Stay here. I'll be back in half an hour to get you out of here."

"But I like it here," protested Thinkbot, looking truly astonished that the reward for saving the life of a child seemed to be a blow to the head.

"Yes, well, there's nothing much I can do about that. Now just stay put and *be quiet!*"

"Okay okay, I've got the message."

Thinkbot watched Mike and GAT disappear down the stairs and turned his attention back to the TV, which to his delight was showing a Giant Panda chewing on some bamboo. It changed to show a bottle of Giant Panda shampoo. Thinkbot wondered how many Giant Pandas were watching at this time in the morning, they'd all be at work surely. He doubted that the advert could be very successful. He wandered over to the workbench and looked at the assorted dopey Toybot animals, which looked back vacantly at Thinkbot. Mike's Tiger had also been left behind, next to a strange midget robot that looked like it had been built by a 12-year-old. Thinkbot picked up a cheetah, which said, "Hello. I am Chester. I am a Cheetah. I belong to Opal," in a slow flat monotone. Thinkbot put Chester back on the bench, clicked his tin knuckles and decided: *This is a challenge.*

18

GAT was stuck in traffic in the car with Thinkbot on his way to Globalbot. Breakfast had gone as well as could be expected. Helen had difficulty eating due to her lip, so GAT was able to eat his breakfast quickly without appearing to gobble and got Thinkbot out undetected. Mike was impressed enough by the 'secret robot for Mum' strategy to be playing along for the time being. But it was only a matter of time before he said something along the lines of 'I'M GOING TO SEE IF THINKBOT IS HOME,' to Opal or, 'DON'T TELL, BUT DAD'S GOT A SECRET ROBOT FOR MUM IN THE GARAGE' to his Tiger. The problem was that when Mike spoke, just about everyone in the house heard. Even though he was only four he already had a voice of granite. He knew Opal and Gerald would not say anything, but also that they would expect him to explain everything to them when he got home. Given he had no idea what was going on himself, that might prove a little difficult. He was on good terms with both. Gerald was pretty good technically for a 12-year-old, and Opal was bright as well. In some ways she was ahead of Gerald when it came to the softer human-like aspects of robot technology such as personality design. They'd created a number of low-tech robots by adapting simple Toybots, animated teddy bears, lions, cheetahs, and the like. They were all pretty dopey, but it was so good to have things he did with the kids while they were still interested in him as a 'useful Dad'. Gerald was more into the various robot types and technology options. In fact, he was a bit of a robot anorak and could effortlessly bore you witless. If you did not reach escape velocity quickly, then you were in danger of waking up several hours later with a stormer of a headache only to find he was still talking. He could even bore his mother rigid with robot talk that would have got her all wound-up with anyone else. Gerald was almost as far towards the 'robots will make our lives wonderful forever' camp, as his mother was towards the 'let's get rid of them once and for all and plough the land by hand' camp.

"Stop it!"

Thinkbot had his thumbs in his ears and was waving his hands rudely at the passengers in the car next to them. The occupants of the other car did not look offended. Rather, they looked alarmed. GAT groaned to himself. He had serious doubts about just how long was he going to be able to keep this robot a secret.

The radio was on: "Latest reports indicate that after heavy losses on both sides the fighting in Asia has eased off, and that Militaribots on both sides are digging in and taking up defensive positions. Of course this easing off in the conflict is good news, but some experts now fear that a long war may develop. Joining us in the studio we have ..."

DOUMP, DOUMP, DOUMP, DOUMP, DOUMP, TIK TIK TIK TIKKA TIK TIK TIK, BAH DOOMBA, DOOMBA, DOOMBA, DOOMBA, DOOMBA,

GAT accelerated towards the car in front, but the car jerked to a halt, the racket stopped, and a calm female voice said, "Collision avoidance system activated. Autocar systems apologise for any discomfort caused during this unavoidable intervention. Prepare for return to manual drive. Manual drive now active. Sound system will now return to your selected channel."

BAWUMM, BAWUMM, BAWUMM, FUT FUT DOOMBA, DOOMBA, DOO . . .

GAT smacked the radio off button. His patience was wearing thin. **"Do not touch the radio."**

Thinkbot sat with his left hand over his mouth as if wondering how he'd managed to get the radio to make such bizarre sounds. "What was that?" he asked.

"It was some sort of clubbing music."

"Ah yes, of course. What sorts of instruments do they club?"

"What? Er. No, wrong sort of club."

"They were using the wrong sort of club?"

"No, no, I mean 'club' as in a group of people in a dark building with flashing lights." As soon as he said this GAT knew it was only going to confuse Thinkbot further. He was correct.

"So we were listening to a group of people clubbing the wrong instruments in a dark building with flashing lights? Come on, I wasn't born yesterday."

"Yes you were."

"Er, oh yeah, so I was."

Mercifully they arrived at the Globalbot car park. He looked in disbelief at the building within which the test area was located. Less than 24 hours ago it had been a wreck with smoke emerging from the roof. Now it looked almost back to normal, from the outside anyway. He had to hand it to Duwkits that he ran a well-organised department. Okay, he had access to the latest Facilitibots and, when things were really bad, he was allowed to use new Industribots from the production line, but nonetheless, sorting the roof out overnight was darned impressive.

GAT got Thinkbot in through a back door and into the secure development area without any incident. One non-secure engineer had emerged from a door ahead of them holding some sort of robot arm and walked straight past saying, "715560, 715560, 715560, 715560, 715560," without even looking at them. And, as they passed one open doorway, someone inside wailed, "I don't know why I come here anymore!"

Inside the secure area, GAT took Thinkbot to the small office area that he used for dealing with secret information and holding sensitive project meetings. It was 1pm, otherwise known as lunchtime, and there was no one about. He sat Thinkbot down in the corner and gave him a copy of *Robot Monthly* to read. "I need to do a bit of work, so just sit there and take it easy."

Thinkbot made a huge show of taking it easy and stuck his legs out and rested his head on the wall. He looked at the magazine. "Aw, come on, haven't you got a copy of *Human Monthly*?"

"Er, no, well, ah, here's a copy of a Sunday paper, try that."

"Thanks." Thinkbot threw *Robot Monthly* across the room, picked up the paper, crossed his legs and opened it upside down. GAT sat down at the secure desk. Thinkbot started whistling tunelessly.

"Quiet!"

"Sorry."

He opened his email to check nothing drastic was waiting for him.

Rustle, rustle, rustle, rustle.

"Keep the paper still!"

"Sorry."

"You have 54 new messages," said the desk voice. GAT scanned them quickly and decided 51 were the usual dross, most of them worthy of no more than instant relegation to the trash can, but three stuck out:

GRIM Unibot incident
Unibot incident internal investigation
Watch out!

He opened the first one. It was from ME, one of his peers in the Military division of Globalbot in the USA.

SUBJECT: GRIM Unibot
Dear GAT,
Long time, no email. Hope you are well. FDS tells me your faulty Unibot will be with us in a few days and that GRIM will be here in two weeks. Can you give me any clues old fellow? Let me give you one - FDS seems to know more than he ought. Do you know you can trust all of your engineers? Perhaps we can help each other on this one.
Best Regards
ME

Creep! Old fellow indeed. Trying to get information out of him just so he can put one over on FDS. GAT did not like these sorts of games. Likewise the suggestion that one of his engineers might be a traitor. ME should concentrate on fixing his Militaribot problems and not waste his time on infighting. GAT thought about this for a minute. Whether he had meant it or not, Thinkbot's audacious swap with the other Unibot in the faulty product cage had certainly given GAT and his team a golden chance to try and understand Thinkbot. GAT wondered how long it would be before Thinkbot did something so daft that even ME, FDS and GRIM would figure out that they had the wrong robot. Then GAT would be in trouble. Big trouble. Good! He didn't mind trouble. Trouble was often fun. He hit the reply button.

SUBJECT: RE: GRIM Unibot

Dear ME,

So good to hear from you, especially while you are having a little trouble with your Militaribots. Unfortunately the test area manager packed up the Unibot and notified GRIM before I got to examine it. I saw it briefly before it was loaded into the GRIM van, and I believe you should have a Japanese-speaking engineer available for the investigation.

I'd be amazed if FDS knows more than he ought, since whenever I've met with him he always seemed to know a good deal less than he ought. But thanks for the warning. I'll keep an eye open. Any clues you can give me on the Unibot investigation before GRIM turn up here will be welcome. I'd be open to sharing anything I come across here.

Regards
GAT

GAT sat back and picked up the cup of tea he'd collected on the way in, and propelled the whole lot straight into his face as a voice right next to his left ear said, "Can you scroll back up a bit so I can read the original message please?"

GAT sat there looking at Thinkbot with tea dripping off his face onto his shirt. How had he, no *it*, put down the paper and got there without making any noise at all. He thought about the he/it issue. Maybe he would not have chosen to think about it with tea all over his face and dripping onto his shirt, but nevertheless he did. And he realised that Thinkbot was an 'it' when 'it' spooked him like that, but 'he' was definitely a 'he' most of the time.

"I thought you were supposed to put that stuff in your mouth," said Thinkbot, looking at the big dark stain on GAT's shirt, and at the residual tan-coloured drops wobbling on his nose and chin. GAT remained silent.

"I see they're going flat out to try and understand what I did to that dud Unibot."

"What *did* you do to it?"

"Ah, now that would be telling."

"Not even a clue?"

"Hmmm," mused Thinkbot, scratching his head with a grating metallic noise, "I added a major component to its brain firmware."

"What sort of component?"

"It didn't have a part number. Looks like you should be more concerned about spies," observed Thinkbot, trying to change the subject.

GAT looked back at the email.

"No way, that's a wind-up. If there is someone, then it's not someone in the group of people who work in the secure area."

"And how do you know that?" demanded Thinkbot.

"None of them were here last night, and none of them have met you yet."

"Ah, yes, fair points, fair points," mumbled Thinkbot, instantly losing concentration and picking up the paper. GAT sent the email to ME.

Thinkbot dropped the paper and started up again. "Looks like we've got a bit of time to try and understand where I came from, but then it might get a bit grim." Thinkbot howled with laughter at his own pun. "GRIM, ha, get it? Might get a bit GRIM!"

This robot's unreal, thought GAT, for about the 400 th time in less than 24 hours. "Er, yes, so you have no idea how you came about then?"

"No idea. Rather hoped you'd know. Oh well, never mind, I'm here now, that's all that matters."

"Is it?" GAT was getting a bit punch drunk again.

"Is it what?"

"All that matters?"

Thinkbot looked at him, but said nothing.

"I've got a secure engineering team meeting at 2pm," continued GAT. "I've asked the engineers to track your serial number through to see what happened to you during build."

"Can I come?" Thinkbot stood up and started dancing excitedly from one foot to the other.

"No, I don't think that would be a good idea. You stay here and I'll tell you what's been found out afterwards."

Thinkbot sat down with a thump on the chair and folded his arms sulkily. "Awww. That's not fair."

"Just trust me, ok?"

This had a magical effect on Thinkbot. He sat up and looked pleased. *How does he do that?* Unibots had no ability to change facial expression. GAT looked at his watch. 1.52pm. Only a few minutes to the meeting. He opened the second email.

SUBJECT: Yoor Pour Designs
GAT
Due to after unfortuante incidnet in test area where wrekage reamins and much cost was lost, you are included in Initial Internal Incident Investigation Initiative Team (I I I I I T) for the recent events regrading a fawlty design designd by your designers in the design department initial I I I I I T meeting 2pm my office today please at tend.
REguards
Dukwits

'Dukwits' said it all. Some people just could not write simple emails, and Duwkits was one of them. Normally he at least checked his messages with the spell checker. The fact that he hadn't merely told GAT that Duwkits must be in one heck of a bad mood. And, oh dear, what a shame, Duwkits meeting clashed with his own engineering meeting.

"Don't like him." The voice in his left ear was back.

"Why?"

"He shouted at me in the cage and then said I would be sent off with GRIM and slowly taken to bits while still powered up, and that it would take several days, and it would be done by professional Militaribot Division engineers for a change, not that scruffy lot at the other end of the building."

"Really? Well it was just as well you found that other Unibot to swap with then wasn't it?"

"Yes, though I feel a bit guilty about it being taken to bits in my place, but it didn't seem to be able to think like me."

"You can say that again."

Thinkbot looked at him. "Yes, though I feel a bit guilty about it being taken to bits in my place, but it didn't seem to be able to think like me."

GAT shut his eyes in a long-suffering manner, then emailed Duwkits with apologies that he would be unable to attend but looked forward to the second I I I I I T meeting.

"Liar," said the voice in his left ear.

GAT opened the third email. It was from his boss Wendy Bafers, the head of E-GAL-17. GAT and Duwkits worked for Wendy Bafers.

SUBJECT: Duwkits on Warpath
Hello GAT

Watch out! Duwkits is on the warpath and is more interested in blaming you than finding out what happened last night. I'm invited to a 2pm meeting where the agenda, as far as I can see, only has one item on it and that's to lynch you! I suggest you give his meeting a miss! I heard you got in here last night and tied up the mad Unibot yourself single handedly, impressive! Should never have been packed off to GRIM so quickly. Wish I'd been consulted. Once you have a sensible story come and update me.
Best Regards
Wendy.

GAT looked at his watch. 1:59pm. He grabbed Thinkbot by the shoulders.

"I'm not going to lock the door, but you must stay here, okay?"

"Okay."

"And don't make much noise, ok?"

"Okay."

GAT went out of the office, found an old lab coat to cover up his tea stained shirt, and went along the corridor towards the meeting room. A few seconds later the voicecall alert bleeped on GAT's desktop. Thinkbot looked at it.

- *Stay here? Tick.*
- *Don't make much noise? Tick.*
- *Don't answer any voicecalls? No tick.*

19

After breakfast Helen had decided to 'nip up to The Mall' and 'get a few bits' and she 'wouldn't be long'. Mike had gone with her, but Opal and Gerald had elected to stay at the house. There was an 'atmosphere' between them. Gerald was not quite ready to admit he'd made a right idiot of himself by his attitude towards Thinkbot. Opal wanted him to say sorry, and then all would be well. But this did not look like it was going to happen. It needed something to trigger Gerald and Opal into talking to each other again. Not long after their mother left, this trigger appeared in the form of a small cheetah that came crashing through the automatic cat port, rushed up to Opal and threw itself onto her lap and, sitting up straight, looked up eagerly into her face. Gerald was lying on the floor reading a copy of *Robot Monthly*, and simply watched the cheetah zoom across the floor as if it were, well, er, a Toybot cheetah running across the living room floor with a perfect animal-like robotic motion. Opal, by this time, had her hands in the air above her head, her eyes wide open staring at the cheetah in her lap, and her mouth formed into a perfect circle ready to emit a scream, which she duly did.

"Aaaaaaaaaaaaaaaaaaaaaaaaaaaaaaaaaaaaaaaa!"

The cheetah let out a miniature roar of terror, leapt about a metre into the air and did several back flips, landed on all fours and hurtled back out through cat port.

"Raahhhhhhhhhhhhhhhhhhhhhhhhhhhhhhhhhhhhh…"

Silence fell as the cat port snapped shut, but it was a different sort of silence. Opal and Gerald looked at each other.

"That was Chester," said Opal.

"I thought so. I see you've improved its motion software. I thought it was a real cat for a second."

"But I haven't touched **him** for days."

They looked at each other and spoke together, "**Thinkbot!**"

Out in the garage, Gerald went up the stairs first and peeped around. Nothing. Opal followed him up.

"Chester," she called quietly, "are you here?"

"Don't know," came a little reply.

Gerald moved quickly towards the sound, but Opal signalled for him to stop.

"Chester, where are you?"

"Don't know."

Gerald was looking on the bench. He reached out to move Mike's Tiger, which had been left behind during the morning's rapid exit. The Tiger sidestepped his hand. "No need for that, thanks, I've got my own legs."

Opal looked under the sofa. She thought she could see the outline of a cheetah at the back, so she got up and lay on the back of the sofa and groped along the back. Her face was flat on the cushion and she found herself looking straight at a largish furry dog called Fudge, proudly wearing his blue dressing-gown and gold-rimmed spectacles, who said slowly in a deep voice, "You scared him witless."

"Did I?" Opal was too far gone to be afraid or amazed any more.

"He was so excited about trying to find you, then he came hurtling back and ran behind the sofa. We can't get him to come out."

"We?"

"Tiger and me."

Gerald and the Tiger came over.

"Are there any more of you?" he asked.

"No, only me, Fudge and Chester, so far."

"So far?" Gerald was also wondering what else this day could possibly hold for them.

"The creator was here this morning. His name is Thinkbot," announced Tiger in an awed voice. "He said he would return and give life to many."

"Don't be daft, it was only a clever Unibot, not 'the creator'" droned Fudge.

Gerald said, "More than clever I think," trying to catch Opal's eye to pass on the apology he was trying not to say out loud.

"I think you ought to apologize to her," said Fudge.

"So do I!" Chester was peeping around the end of the sofa.

Gerald wavered, then, "Sorry about Thinkbot Opal. You were right, I was wrong."

The three Toybots erupted into cheering and muffled applause, then converged into a group hug that turned into them singing ring-a-ring-a-rosies and all falling over.

Opal picked up Chester, who rubbed his head on her forearm.

"Hello, sorry I frightened you," said Opal.

"Well, I'm sorry I frightened you as well"

"As well as who?" asked Fudge.

Chester: "As Opal."

Fudge: "You frightened two Opals?

Chester: "No."

Fudge: "You frightened one Opal twice then?"

Chester: "No I didn't"

Fudge: "Didn't what?"

Chester: "Frighten two Opals twice."

Fudge: "You frightened four Opals?"

Tiger: "Fudge, now you're twice as confused as you were before."

Fudge: "Before what?"

Tiger: "Before you were half confused."

Fudge: "Which half of me was confused?"

Chester: "I wasn't confused, I was frightened."

Tiger: "Now I'm confused. When were you frightened?"

Fudge: "Was I frightened?"

Chester: "I'm not frightened of being confused."

Tiger: "Fudge is confused about being confused."

Gerald knew enough about robotic entertainment software to recognise that the Toybots had got themselves into an endless response loop. If left to their own devices they would debate being frightened and confused for days until their battery packs ran out.

"Cease," he said clearly. The Toybots stopped and looked at him.

"Cease what?" asked Fudge.

"Don't start again," Gerald wagged his finger at Fudge.

"Start what again?"

"Looks like you're definitely the culprit."

"Am I?"

Gerald picked Fudge up and powered him down.

"Oi! Now … I'll ne v e r k n o w wot conf…fri." Fudge froze.

And powered him back up again.

"Hello, my name's Fudge!"

"He'll be all right now," said Gerald.

"Will I?" asked Fudge, quickly adding, "Jolly good, jolly good," to show he wasn't stuck in the same loop again.

Opal was staring at the threesome with an expression of pure joy. Gerald picked the wrong thing to say, again: "Now these three are definitely just running clever software."

Opal's face furrowed into fury, but the three Toybots rescued Gerald.

"He's right"

"We're just running clever software."

"Thinkbot's the one that thinks."

Opal was still annoyed that the magic of the moment had been broken once again by her soulless brother, but then he was only a boy, she thought smugly to herself. Then Opal had an awful thought. Mike's Tiger had been a passive stuffed toy the last time she had seen it, not an animated Toybot.

"Gerald."

"Yeah, what?"

"Mike's stuffed Tiger seems to have become a Toybot."

Gerald picked up the Tiger and looked at it. Then he too had an awful thought. His model robot that he had been building, with some help from his Dad, was missing. He looked over the bench. It was gone. It was about the right size, and with a bit of cleverness it could have been done, and there was no doubt Thinkbot was very clever.

"Darn it, Thinkbot's de-stuffed Mike's Tiger and put my robot inside."

"Oh, right, so it's your fault all my joints creak and I've got a big lump of solder in my mouth?" Tiger asked Gerald.

"Hey! I'm not that bad."

"Never mind that!" Opal was edging towards panic. "Mum and Mike will be back soon. What are we going to tell Mike? He'll want Tiger and Mum will wonder what's happened!"

"Mike's my best friend. I'm sure he'll like me even more now I can talk." Tiger started jumping around in excitement at the thought of meeting Mike.

"If I could find the stuffing, maybe we could replace it."

Tiger stopped dancing. The prospect of being operated on by a 12-year-old boy assisted by a 10-year-old girl clearly did not appeal to him. Opal decided their chances of succeeding were slim. "No, we'd only make it worse. Mike would prefer a Tiger Toybot to a mangled passive."

"When I retire I really fancy looking after a few pigs," said Fudge.

"I want to be a sky diver," said Chester.

The Toybots had clearly not been paying attention and had no sense of the gravity of the situation. Gerald grabbed them and powered them down.

"Oi! th a t 's unf…"

"No, wa i t   I …"

Tiger considered his silent frozen pals, then said something very brave. "Would Mike notice if you permanently powered me down?"

Gerald picked up the Tiger and weighed him in his hand, then squeezed him. The Tiger started wriggling and giggling, "Ah ho ha….that…tickles…oo hoo hoo ha ha."

"You weigh a lot more and you're awfully bony, and if you're switched off you'll just go rigid like these two characters have." Gerald prodded Fudge and Chester, who were in a state of electronic rigor mortis and simply fell over stiffly. "I think we should call Dad at work."

20

8:30am. The heads of Military Engineering (ME) and Field Deployment Support (FDS) were once again sitting in Farkstock's office. As before, all screens were blank, all microphones disconnected, and socks over cameras. However, this time there was only one sheet of paper with a few numbers scrawled on it on the desk in front of Farkstock. Next to it was a large old-fashioned alarm clock with two large bells on top.

Tick, tock, tick, tock, tick, tock …

"This is set to go off just before the Execubot barges in to check I'm still alive," he informed ME, FDS and the Chief Financial Officer (CFO) of the Globalbot Military Division.

The CFO was a very clever man: a lawyer and an accountant all wrapped as one. He looked really worried, like *really worried*, in fact so worried it appeared he might burst into tears any minute. That's if he could sit still long enough. He wriggled, and bounced around in the chair, pulling up his socks, retying his shoe laces, unbuttoning his cuffs and rolling up his shirt sleeves, then unrolling them again and doing up the cuff buttons again, then taking off his glasses and putting them on again, then stroking his bald head, first with one hand, then the other, then removing his wedding ring and putting it back on. He was driving Farkstock crazy and he had to use his full powers of self-control not to shout **'For crying out loud sit still!'** at him. Some time back Farkstock had referred to him cruelly as Antspants in several emails, then found to his horror that the name had stuck.

Antspants always fidgeted in proportion to how well things were going, or rather not going. Over the past couple of years his fidgeting had been getting gradually worse as more and more Militaribot friendly-fire incidents occurred, resulting in a string of dodgy out-of-court payments by Globalbot to unhappy customers.

Now, a full-scale robot war had erupted between two Federated Nation Groups, but neither the Eastasian nor the Westasian government were in control of their forces. However, they were in charge of their legal ministries, and these had already sent Globalbot a preliminary claim for damages of 972 billion North Americana dollars. This was one of the numbers scrawled on the paper on the desk. This claim was 30 times the amount that Globalbot was actually worth, assuming there was a nutcase out there somewhere who had 32 billion dollars to spare and felt like buying a company that looked like it was about to sink like a stone.

Farkstock wondered if the Eastasia-Westasia damages claim might result in Antspants completely shredding his clothes and maybe even in wearing a hole in the top of his head where interested parties could view the workings of what was, after all, a brilliant legal mind. Farkstock shuddered at the very thought, then suddenly realised his concentration had lapsed. The tick-tocking of the clock didn't help, but the real reason was that FDS was giving a 'quick' update on the Eastasia-Westasia war.

"But the good news is that it's calming down. The latest totals of Militaribot losses are written on the sheet," concluded FDS. Farkstock wondered what he'd missed, and decided that this last statement was all he had needed to know. Farkstock studied the piece of paper again:

Robot and other losses.
    Eastasia
        Basic Militaribots   19,530
        Artilleribots   1,820
        Airbots   2,200
    Westasia
        Basic Militaribots   20,987
        Artilleribots   1,956
        Airbots   2,054
    Robots of mass destruction   0 (both sides)
    Domestibots (all types, both sides)   43
    Industribots (all types, both sides)   876
    Human casualties   0

Farkstock did a quick calculation. About 71 billion dollars' worth of robots had been smoked, so why a claim for 972 billion? Sounded like the number had been inflated just a little. Seventy-one billion dollars of new robot orders to replace those lost in the war also sounded good. Maybe they'd have to discount their prices a little more than usual, especially if Worldbot got involved, but given the current economic climate, any orders would be hugged and kissed on arrival.

As if reading Farkstock's mind and disagreeing, Antspants burst out, "They're blackmailing us. We're doomed! Worldbot will wipe the floor with us. We'll never get another order," then undid his trouser belt and selected a different, tighter, hole for the buckle, presumably in preparation for the anticipated hard times ahead. Farkstock sincerely hoped that Antspants's urge to fidget would not get as far as his trouser zip. Antspants continued, "If we pay up we're bankrupt, if we don't they expose the Militaribot problems and we're finished. Either way I wish I was working at Worldbot." Antspants tried, but gave up on, an even tighter belt hole then rubbed the top of his head. Unfortunately he was sweating profusely and just got his hands wet, so he got out a handkerchief to dry them. This resulted in his coin purse falling onto the floor, which he picked up and opened and started counting up how much he had in change.

"Calm down, there's no way Worldbot have capacity to make 71 billion dollars' worth of Militaribots at such short notice," said Farkstock, restraining himself from yelling **'Here I'll loan you a dollar!'** "I've had some discussions with Cracker and President Hedge and, if we can get the Militaribot problem sorted," looking hard at ME, "I think Hedge will publicly support our denials that there have been any serious problems, and he'll broker a deal whereby Eastasia and Westasia will get most of their robots replaced by us, and we might even end up making some money out of it." Antspants looked doubtful and started sucking air in through his teeth. Then he took them out and inspected them closely for fragments of food.

"So," continued Farkstock looking at FDS and ME, "tell me what progress you two have made with your investigations."

Silence. FDS and ME looked at each other. They'd had lunch together the day before, but neither thought that would count as 'progress'.

"Please don't tell me you've done nothing at all!"

"I've requested a full summary from every field office to be here by end of today," offered FDS.

"Good. So we're planning to try and figure out patterns in the summaries we haven't yet got, since we're too thick to unravel the detailed reports we already have. Correct?"

"Correct!" said FDS, mistakenly thinking Farkstock was pleased. Farkstock wondered about engineering a fit of rage, but it was so tiring getting angry, and he still had a nagging doubt that the Execubot had actually been hanging about outside the door last time, just waiting to burst in to check on him when he started shouting. Next to FDS, Antspants appeared to be trying to hold his eyeballs in. "Let's try ME."

"ME?"

"I've got my guys working flat out trying to get robots to develop friendly-fire faults in the laboratory," was the best that ME could offer.

"And have they succeeded?"

"No, but we've blown up 26 robots trying," ME said in a positive tone of voice. But as soon as the words had left his mouth, ME knew this statement had been an error. Blowing up roughly 30 million dollars' worth of robots would have been accepted without question if they had found something out, but they hadn't. Farkstock was not impressed, so rather than find the energy for another rage he decided to let these idiots go off and get on with whatever they did. As they got up he felt that he ought to at least ask them if there was anything he could do to assist in their investigations.

ME replied instantly. "Keep GRIM away. They'll just get in the way and make life difficult for us."

FDS's face twisted in horror. *Noooooooooo! What's the matter with him? Fool! Why mention GRIM? The last thing we need is Farkstock getting involved in the Unibot affair.*

"GRIM? Why are they coming here? They have no right to interfere with our Militaribot activities." Farkstock was alert again, inspired by the prospect of new information, even if delivered to him by a trio of idiots.

"They've activated their consultancy contract and it's binding; we can't stop them coming, but we will get 100,000 dollars for our trouble," said Antspants, whose eyes were apparently secure in their sockets again, but his left shin had a problem that required him to roll up a trouser leg and inspect it closely.

"I've delayed them a few days," said FDS triumphantly, recovering from the shock of ME spilling the GRIM Unibot beans.

"Yes, yes," said Farkstock impatiently, "another fantastic triumph for your Execubot I'm sure." FDS's smile froze on his face. Farkstock wondered why these fools could never answer the real question. **"Why are they coming here in the first place?"**

ME, FDS and Antspants sensed Farkstock's temper rising again. Antspants stopped massaging the toes of his right foot and quickly tried to put his sock back on, but made a right mess of it and had to pull it off and start again.

"There was some sort of dreadful incident involving a Unibot at the E-GAL-17 in Bristol," said ME.

"It defeated a Destructobot," FDS interrupted enthusiastically. ME grimaced.

Farkstock put his forehead flat on his desk and spoke with immense patience to the floor. **"Tell me what happened before I...before I..."** The rage was getting closer to the surface. "Are there no reports on what happened?"

"Yes, there's one, I'll forward it to you." FDS turned on his palmtop assistant with a flourish.

"How long is it?"

"Oh, it's only about 10 centimetres. It's a GY78T, with triple Octium XVI processors. I only got it ..."

"The report you fool! How long's the report! Not your tinny palmtop!"

"Umm...only a few lines actually," said a crestfallen FDS. ME smirked. *Idiot, he'll make you read it to him now, you bumbling buffoon!*

"Read it to me," commanded Farkstock.

FDS read out the E-GAL-17 report. Farkstock continued in his stress-reducing, forehead-on-desk pose; at least he was spared watching Antspants's attention finally turning to his trouser zip. As he listened to FDS's deadpan delivery, he thought *thoughts* not unlike those of GAT 24 hours earlier.

1. Unibot went berserk without warning. Started laughing and running wildly around the shop floor. *Laughing?*
2. Unibot then prevented any test personnel accessing any shop EMO buttons. *Unibot chasing humans around?*
3. Unibot then trapped personnel against rear wall and behaved threateningly. *Threateningly?*
4. Test engineers consulted line management and received approval for deployment of emergency control robots and raising of Destructobot to ready status. *Unibot vs multiple Controlbots? Multiple Controlbots now chasing single Unibot chasing multiple humans? Keystone Cops?*
5. Controlbots were unable to contain berserk Unibot. Berserk Unibot moved to location where Controlbot activities triggered some secondary berserks in other robot types. *What? What? Can't these fools see **any** resemblance to the Militaribot 'berserks' that were better known to the Military people as 'friendly-fire incidents'?*
6. Test engineers consulted line management and received approval for area evacuation and deployment of Destructobot. *Unibot vs Destructobot? Should have been the world's shortest Robot fight, that's for sure.*
7. Destructobot disabled by three berserk Firebots. *Berserk Firebots?*
8. Destructobot weapons systems malfunctioned, causing significant damage to the area. *Let me see now, have we seen anything like this on our Militaribots? Maybe.* **Seems to be a bit like some of the Militaribot friendly-fire incidents and, hang on a minute, did I not hear there was a totally out-of-control full-scale robot war going on somewhere?**
9. Area sealed and level 5 area electropulse used to power down all robots. *Poor Unibot.*
10. Area re-entered in controlled manner. *They used the door rather than blow a hole in the wall then.*
11. All units were found to be inactive except the original berserk Unibot. (Farkstock sat bolt upright and could not help shouting, **"What! How can a Unibot survive a level 5 disable pulse?"**)

12. **Unibot constrained in Faulty Product Area and handed over to GRIM shortly after.** *Why why why didn't we hush it up for as long as possible and investigate it ourselves? DIRT at E-GAL-17 should have had a look at it first. Farkstock knew GAT reasonably well. In fact well enough to know he was a step ahead of ME and FDS, and Farkstock had several times tried to persuade him to come to Oak Ridge and head up the military engineering group. But GAT was not interested in developing military robots, and his family was settled in Europe, and recently there had been rumours that all was not well with his marriage.*

13. GRIM activated Militaribot investigative consultancy agreement. Unibot shipped to Military Division, Oak Ridge, Tennessee, North Americana for further analysis by professional military development engineers. Ah, yes, the 'we're the real robot engineers' argument. There was a rivalry between the Domestic-Industrial and Military development groups, which in itself was not at all a bad thing since it kept them on their toes, but in this case, where the company was sinking and its products were threatening to trash the planet, it was not! Especially since the so-called 'professional Military development engineers' were going nowhere fast.

Several seconds' silence.

"Sounds sensible to me," interjected Antspants amidst all sorts of gurgling and snorting sounds as he tried to eject all fluid within his head out via his nose into a white rag. Farkstock collected himself. "Don't you think this Unibot might just hold a clue to our Militaribot problems?"

ME looked at the ceiling. FDS looked at his feet. Antspants was trying to find a dry bit on his pocket handkerchief. Farkstock looked at the alarm clock - 10 minutes to possible Execubot entry. There should be enough time. It was just about 9am NA Eastern Time, 2pm Western Europa Time in Bristol. Farkstock had an hour to spare before Hedge's call at 10am.

"I think it's about time we had a 'professional non-military expert' help us with our problems, don't you?" he asked ME and FDS, acidly. The faces of ME and FDS took on expressions of alarm. Antspants's face contorted as he felt for places he'd missed whilst shaving that morning. Farkstock fired up his desktop and placed a voice call to GAT.

21

At The Mall at Cribbs Causeway near Bristol, Helen had been rushing around looking for the bits and pieces she was after when she saw some garden furniture she adored in John Lewis. She had seen it once before a few years back but had not bought it, preferring to get GAT's agreement first. Then, when they'd finally agreed to buy some, it had disappeared from the shops altogether. She was debating what to do - not easy when Mike was chuntering about sore feet and wanting to go for a drink, or even better, visit 'Planet Toybot' and play with the Toybots that patrolled the aisles to entrap children into convincing their parents to part with money.

"CAN WE GO TO PLANET TOYBOT?"

"No Mike, not today."

"PLEASE."

"No, I need to decide what to do about this garden furniture."

"WHAT GARDEN FURNITURE?" boomed Mike, looking around, standing in the middle of acres of garden furniture.

A Salesbot appeared from nowhere and offered to assist her. Normally, she preferred dealing with human assistants, but there were none around. She had noticed that Salesbots were slowly taking over and that there were fewer humans in all the stores. Helen did not like this very much of course, but on the other hand GAT's development group were the main reason that this was happening, and it was one of the Globalbot product lines that was remaining profitable in spite of the global economic problems.

You might think that designing a Salesbot should not have been a very big technical challenge for a robot design group, but there you would be wrong. The hardware design was easy: no working outdoors in the cold or the heat, no wading through mud or ditchwater, no working in the dark. No, it was personality software that was the problem. The best human sales people are those that within a few seconds of meeting a customer have figured out exactly where they are coming from: whether they are likely to buy; whether to offer a discount; whether to help with selecting the right product; whether a complaining customer should be compensated in some way; whether a customer returning a product was being completely honest or not; and so on. Customers come in every shape and form, and although the theory goes that 'the customer is always right', the reality is that they are always wrong until the salesperson has got them to agree with them. *Then* they are clearly 'always right'. This was a desperately difficult specification for a robot to match, and several prototype exercises had ended in disaster.

Like the prototype Salesbot that had chased a family all the way through The Mall back to their car, insisting they come back and 'have a quick look at the blue model'. When the terrified family refused, the Salesbot lay down in front of their car and they had to drive over it to get away.

Or the Salesbot that had decided the best way to increase sales was to try and prevent people from going into a rival's store. That trial had ended embarrassingly with the Salesbot being dragged off by the rival store's Securibots and ejected out of a second floor window into a skip.

Or the Salesbot that threw in the entire contents of the shop into a deal to try and secure the sale of a kettle.

Or the Salesbot that paid the customer to take items away. People even tried to help the Salesbot get it right, thinking they might get arrested if they went off with the item *and* more money, but the Salesbot had insisted, "No, no, have that on us, that's fine, we just want to see you back here again whenever you need something."

Or the Salesbot who accepted back a whole stack of ancient clothes that had been used for decorating in return for a full refund at *current* prices.

Meanwhile Helen decided to suffer the Salesbot. She asked it to go and check if the furniture was in stock and told it to meet her in the Toy section. She sensed the Salesbot struggling; a customer asking for information on garden furniture to be taken to the Toy section was exercising a little bit of its sales programming that had never been exercised before. The Salesbot was also trying to read the body language of the little boy. Mike was looking hard at the Salesbot as if it was the first robot he'd ever seen. Helen noticed this also and wondered what was up with him. The reason, of course, was that Salesbots are Unibots with a bit of extra software and a snappy colour scheme. This Salesbot looked pretty much like Thinkbot except for the dark green John Lewis paint scheme, and Mike was half-expecting it to suddenly do something odd.

"Certainly madam, the Toy department, I'll be about ten minutes." The Salesbot went off towards the store information point.

Helen and Mike made their way through the Technology Department towards the Toys. What seemed like endless TV screens and projectors, each with a slightly different green or pink hue, and of every imaginable size, were all showing the same pictures. Mike was mesmerised, but Helen looked away. The multiple identical pictures showed Militaribots moving in long lines across an open Asian landscape. Every now and again a shell landed and a plume of fire and dust mushroomed into the air. The synchronised poly-pictures switched to army-green Industribots cutting up wrecked Militaribots and dragging big pieces towards a heavy-duty Transbot fitted with its own chunky grappling crane. Mike pulled his hand out of his mother's and pointed. "WHOORHA ... LOOK!" About 100 people within a 25m radius stopped, all wondering what they were supposed to be looking at. But they did not have the eyes of a four-year-old boy and just stared at the screens for a few seconds before turning their gaze onto Helen and Mike. Helen turned bright red and moon-walked Mike into the Toy Department.

The Toy Department wasn't quite Planet Toybot, but it was way better than garden furniture, at least for Mike. There was a small Toybot section and a badger was hanging around waiting to capture the attention of passing children.

"Hello, what's your name?" it asked Mike brightly.

"THINKBOT."

"Well Thinkbot, it's really nice to meet you. Can I introduce you to some of my friends?"

"ONLY IF I CAN KICK THEM."

"That'll be great, Thinkbot, I'm sure they'll love that. What's your favourite animal?"

"AARDVARK."

The badger stalled and took a few seconds to recover. "No…Aardvark…, sorry   Thinkbot, perhaps you'd like to meet a monkey?"

"NO A TIGER."

"Ah, an excellent choice. The badger reached in amongst the Toybots and pulled a tiger to the front and powered it up.

"Tiger, this is Thinkbot, I think you might just end up being friends."

"Hello Thinkbot, it's nice to meet you. Do you like me?"

"YES."

"Would you like to take me home with you?"

"YES."

"Is your Mum or Dad here?"

"YES."

"Do you think I could speak with one of them?"

"NO."

Whilst this conversation was taking place the badger looked around to try and identify who was in charge of Mike. It spotted Helen sitting in the nearby shoe department and assumed that must be Mum. This was not good, as the badger was not allowed to leave the Toybot section. It started jumping up and down and waving its arms at Helen, but it was no use. (Incidentally, on this occasion it had identified the parent correctly, but the badger often got it wrong, leading to people giving it strange 'why is that badger waving at me?' looks.) The badger returned its attention to the boy and the tiger, which was faithfully plodding through its sales routine.

"Thinkbot, do you get pocket money?"

"YES."

"Have you been saving it up?"

"YES."

"What have you been saving up for?"

"A TOYBOT TIGER LIKE YOU."

The badger leapt back towards Helen and went as far as he was allowed and waved frantically, but Helen was talking with a Salesbot and looking at a catalogue. But then, joy oh joy, Helen got up and came over.

"Madam, your delightful son has …" it began, but that was that. Helen booted the badger headfirst into a shelf full of passive stuffed penguins and grabbed Mike's hand. "Come on

Mike, let's get a drink and something to eat." This was okay with Mike since, as far as he was concerned, leaving aside looking at Toybots, shopping was all about going for an orange juice and a chocolate muffin.

"BYE TIGER," said Mike, looking back over his shoulder.

"No, madam, wait, come back, Thinkbot, talk to your Mum! Thinkbot!" The tiger ran along to the end of the shelf, dodging his blank, staring, rigid companions. The badger struggled out from among the stuffed penguins and bleeped at the tiger, which went rigid on the shelf, and returned to patrolling its little patch of store carpet, its beady eyes searching for the next midget human sales prospect.

At the Café Helen bought Mike an orange juice and a Chocamuff, and a coffee for herself, and they sat down at a table. Helen was continuing to look at the catalogue, and was writing things down on a scrap of paper.

"Who is 'Thinkbot'?" she suddenly asked Mike at exactly the wrong moment.

Mike blurted out a load of orange juice and muffin sludge all over the table. His legs, his arms, and a few splotches flew through the air onto Helen's blouse.

"Oh Michael!" Helen dashed off for some napkins.

A Waiterbot (also based on a Unibot, again elegantly painted in John Lewis green but with a real white collar and black bow tie glued around its neck, and a starched white cloth draped over one of its arms) had seen the disaster and came scuttling over. A number of hatches opened in its body and arms extended with wet-wipes to help Helen sort out Mike. Another Waiterbot came over and topped up Mike's orange juice. "Would madam like another Chocamuff for the boy?"

"**No!**"

Mike looked crestfallen. "AWW, MUM!"

"Well, you shouldn't have made such a mess with the first one then, should you?"

The Waiterbots wandered off and Helen looked at her watch: 1:58pm. She'd been here a little longer than she had meant, but she wanted that furniture. The Salesbot had told her that there was only one set left in stock and no date for when any more would be available. 2pm, that's when he said he had to be in, so she picked up her mobile and called GAT.

22

At 1:57pm Duwkits had received GAT's email apologising that he could not come to the 2pm I I I I I T meeting. Duwkits was furious. Duwkits often got furious, but GAT's email made him really angry. Why? Because he'd prepared a trap and now the prey was not coming. He had several engineers who had dealt with the Unibot incident in his meeting room waiting along with the site safety officer and the facilities manager, plus Wendy Bafers had actually promised to turn up for once, and he was planning to patch in a GRIM official by voicemail later on in the meeting. Everything was set, but the victim wasn't coming.

Duwkits was a strange character; no one quite knew what made him tick. There were rumours he'd been madly in love many years before but it hadn't worked out and he'd ended up devoting himself to Globalbot. To be fair he expected high standards within his department and usually got them, but his staff somehow always looked beaten down by the constant pressure. When it came to dealing with other groups within Globalbot he believed attack was the best form of defence and had a reputation for shooting from the hip at anyone who crossed his path. What really got him wound up was dealing with the DIRT group. On discovery of an engineering mistake by one of the DIRT engineers, he would usually yell something along the lines of, **'What a bunch of no good irresponsible lackadaisical over-educated wasters! Couldn't put an M6 nut on an M6 bolt to save their lives! They need some real engineers up there to sort them out.'** Presumably 'real' engineers meant the now almost extinct breed dressed in blue boiler suits permanently covered with oil and grime. Even when the problem was clearly due to his own department, he would output truly wonderful attacking defensive email statements such as:

No faults have been found, but those that have were DIRT group's fault.

or

Your urgent costings are on the top of the pile except for the ones above them.

He rarely checked his emails were sensible before hitting send - if it passed the spellchecker then he assumed it was okay. And thus did such glorious statements as:

As a precaution we have already taken several onions from other leading experts ('onions' should have read 'opinions');

and:

If that is your final decision on packaging, then it is well within your tights ('tights' should have been 'rights');

escape into the company domain for all and sundry to snigger at. GAT did not help the situation very much and on one famous occasion had sent out an email containing the classic line:

On another note. Globalbot is mounting an attempt on the 'how many ignorant people can we involve in a simple technical decision?' world record. Please let me know if you would like to be involved.

Duwkits took this as a personal attack on himself (presumably due to a subconscious fear that he was prone to meddling in things he did not understand). And then there were incidents that were nothing to do with GAT, but Duwkits blamed him anyway. For example there was the famous lime green robot saga. A large customer specified that their robots should all be lime green. GAT had argued with the Globalbot salesman long and hard, but the salesman had panicked about losing the order and signed on the dotted line. "Lime green robots? . . Of course, no problem sir." Well, the Paintbot shop had a lot of colours, but not lime green. Not only that, there wasn't even a standard lime green paint available and a special batch had to be made just for Globalbot. It was not cheap. Then they had to clean out a Paintbot (they chose metallic blue) and refill it with lime green paint, paint the robots, then clean out the Paintbot again afterwards and refill it with metallic blue. This took days. Then an engineering change required one of the robot panels be replaced. So the metallic blue Paintbot was cleaned out again and the replacement panels painted lime green and the Paintbot cleaned out again and put back to metallic blue. Except that they did not quite clean it out properly and a load of metallic blue robots came out a rather funny colour and were rejected by another customer. Then one of the lime green robots was badly scratched so they cleaned out the contaminated Paintbot and filled it once more with lime green, whereupon it promptly failed and had to go off for repair (with the remains of the lime green paint still inside). Now Duwkits had neither a metallic blue nor a lime green Paintbot.

Beats me why Duwkits doesn't just get another Paintbot.

GAT emailed to Wendy.

I agree.

Wendy had replied, and then went off and politely suggested this to Duwkits.

"But I've no budget for another Paintbot," whined Duwkits who, to be fair, was already in Accounts' bad books for going over budget.

"I could have done something about that if you had only asked," replied an irritated Wendy.

Fume, fume, fume. Duwkits was not impressed. By the time Duwkit's people had got this all sorted out, the whole manufacturing schedule was weeks late, but finally the day arrived for the customer of the lime green robots to come and inspect them before shipment. On their best customer behaviour, all smiles and jokes, Duwkits and GAT took the (rather attractive) female customer engineer into the final test cleanroom to see the robots, only for her to say, "Why on earth are they that horrible green colour?"

GAT could see the frozen smile on Duwkits' face and realised he had lost the power of speech. GAT was having trouble not laughing. He managed to control himself long enough to reply, "It was in your purchase specification."

"The spec I've got says metallic blue," she replied innocently.

GAT lost the power of speech as well. *Metallic blue! Ha ha ha, it's not possible. This cannot be happening. You couldn't make up something like this.* He simply could not look at Duwkits' face to save his life.

The customer made a voice call to her boss. "Lime green? Yes, yes," came the answer, "it was in the first spec but we changed it and sacked the dozy guy in procurement that specified it. All other spec revisions asked for metallic blue -

it's one of the Globalbot standard colours isn't it? Your salesman recommended it."

This was finally too much for GAT. He doubled up in hysterics and departed. Duwkits never forgave him. To complete the tale the customer ended up getting standard blue robots at an extra discount, and a couple of months later a sad little advert appeared in *Europa Robotica Monthly*, buried amongst ads for second-hand industrial Cementmixbots, Plumbots, spare arms and heads etc.

Special Offer Job Lot
Attractive Lime Green Robots. Many types available.
Instant delivery. Contact UK Robogone.com.
Robogone plc - 'And you thought you'd never sell that robot!'

Anyway, Duwkits and several of his staff had spent the morning piecing together such 'evidence' against GAT and DIRT with which they would 'prove' the terrible Unibot incident the night before had been a disaster waiting to happen given the number of mistakes DIRT made, and which build and test then had to sort out on their behalf.

"I think I've got the whole company behind me on this one!" exclaimed Duwkits at one point.

"If that's really the case, then he'll *never* find out who shot him," muttered one of his engineers to a depressed-looking colleague. But now, GAT was not even going to turn up. Duwkits banged the desktop in frustration and attempted to make a voice call to GAT.

23

GAT entered the secure conference room only to be met with a hail of abuse.

"It's the man from the mental home!"

"Is he safe wearing that?"

"Can we scribble on you? Oh please please please!"

"You need a few useless tools in your top pocket if you want to be taken seriously."

GAT looked at the grimy white lab coat and wondered if there would have been more or less laughter if he'd turned up with his tea-soaked shirt on view. He sat down at the head of the large conference table around which sat the six engineers that made up the DIRT Group. These were some of the elite, i.e. amongst the very best in their chosen profession of robot engineering.

However, you would not have deduced this from looking at them. They were all shapes and sizes and lacked any sort of dress sense. Their clothes did not fit them very well, and there were two un-ironed shirts present. GAT thought this inexcusable in the age of the Ironbot. Humanity had gleefully left this chore behind. However, there were still a few sad cases of humans who did their own ironing, but they were pretty much all confined in mental health establishments where doctors strived to release them from this terrible curse. They were mainly ageing mothers of large families that had not been able to afford an Ironbot when the kids were young, but there were also a few men. Like the tragic case of a man who'd struck a deal with his wife that he could have Sky Sports so he could watch the robofoot if he did the ironing, and now he searched his room constantly for an ironing board whenever there was robofoot on the TV. A few managed normal lives in the community, but only with the constant support of IA (Ironers Anonymous), not to be muddled with AI (Artificial Intelligence) which, of course, was the breakthrough that actually enabled robots to perform the exceedingly complex task of ironing in the first place. Ironbot development had taken years of effort. Even once the blessed thing could iron properly there was another long period of disastrous experiments before it could fold the item well enough for it not to need ironing again. The Marketing department ran out of patience and tried to persuade engineering to develop a separate Foldbot, but GAT thought this would never catch on on cost grounds. GAT's group had many wonderful memories from the Ironbot days: shirts ripped to shreds or with perfect iron-shaped holes burnt through them; plastic buttons melted into various fabrics; trousers with zips hanging out and pockets busted wide open; perfectly folded piles of inside-out clothes; an Ironbot that had got itself inside a king-size quilt cover and spent days floundering around on the floor trying to get out again before finally expiring; Ironbots encased in melted orange nylon or stuck to t-shirts by melted gooey emblems; and best of all, an Ironbot with a burnt flat secondary hand.

The six DIRT engineers all had real names, but GAT's brain had overwritten these years ago with names that were much more descriptive of what they were actually like.

The first he called Earthear. He wore glasses with thick lenses and what looked like earth wire wrapped around his ears to hold them on. In fact the arms had fallen off them and he'd made a temporary repair with earth wire some years before. On the rare occasions he was asked about the earth wire, he replied with great conviction that he suffered from a very rare condition known as 'high voltage ear'. Even his Doctor had wobbled a bit and said, "I didn't diagnose that, did I?" Glasses were becoming very unusual, but Earthear knew so much about laser eye surgery accidents that he could not bring himself to go through the process himself, and his eyes were too bad for contact lenses. Ironically his expertise lay in robotic vision systems.

Next to Earthear was Doom, a totally bald Russian with a big bushy beard, the mechanical designer. His outlook on any robot development project and Globalbot in general was typically Russian – 'We're doomed.' Just looking at him brought to mind people wrapped up in ragged clothes and sipping cabbage soup; truly a character straight out of a Dostoevsky novel.

Then came Pot Noodle, a rather fat and bland man of Far Eastern origin, who stared blankly into space most of the time, nodding gently as if weighing every word that was said, his arms folded on his Pot Noodle belly. His expertise was in software and pot noodles which, distressingly, he regularly mixed at work leaving his desktop caked in rock-hard pot noodle residue. Gruesome, but his software work was first rate.

Next there was a slim Indian woman dressed in black who had a hook in place of her left hand and a permanent look of mild amusement on her face. GAT called her Laidback since she never got flustered and always replied to anyone presenting her with a problem, "Don't worry about it, it'll all come out in the wash." She was an Advanced Robot Test Engineer ('advanced' applying to both the robot and the engineer in this particular case). She had set her heart on this role when she was five years old after a badly designed Hortibot had trimmed off her left hand when she was disobediently playing with it in the garden. She refused to have an artificial hand, preferring the simplicity and street credibility of a steel hook with which she could thwack misbehaving development robots (and occasionally misbehaving men).

Rabbit was responsible for electronic design. His natural state was scared witless, and became even more terrified whenever Doom did one of his 'end of the world as we know it' routines. Rabbit always unnerved GAT with his 'Oh no!' staring eyes when making any sort of Group announcement, even positive ones.

Finally came Halfhour, a cheerful and good looking Australian female engineer who developed robot communication and collision radar subsystems. No matter what she was asked to do, or what problems she was working on, she always replied that it'd be 'sorted in half an hour, no worries.' In fact, the truth was she was able to talk about anything, without any requirement from others to speak, for at least half an hour, and it always took her half an hour to explain it would be "done in half an hour, no worries."

As GAT entered the room, Halfhour was entertaining the others with a tale from stores. "I went down to stores to get a radar reflector but there was only one in stock and the storeman said I couldn't have it. 'Why not?' I asked. 'It's the last one,' he said. 'If I give it to you I won't have any left.' 'So what?' I said. 'Well someone might need it,' he said. I said, 'But

I need it! Doesn't that count?' 'Sorry,' he said, 'I can't take the risk; you'll have to wait until another one is delivered.' 'For crying out loud,' I said, 'when will that be?' 'Dunno,' he replied, 'purchasing won't order another one until they're all gone.' 'But then I'll never get one,' I protested. 'Depends if someone takes the last one.' 'I'll take the last one then,' I said. 'No, I can't let you have it. It's my last one, I won't have any left.'"

"Was it Storeman Norman?" asked Earthear.

"What? The American general of Gulf War fame?" growled Doom.

Multiple groans.

"52 years is the oldest electronic bit I've ever found in Stores," piped up Rabbit. "I sent it to the Science Museum in London." The others appeared mildly entertained by this, but Rabbit suddenly looked terrified, as if he feared that, by admitting he'd given away a 52-year-old bit, he would now be in serious trouble.

Laidback rapped her hook on the table in front of her. She normally sat at that spot and the surface of the table had chunks missing where she had regularly thumped it to get everyone's attention or to emphasize an important point to a colleague. "I've found out why the generic robot spares kit has never been delivered to a single customer."

"Why?" GAT was interested in this, as it had been a problem for some time.

"The spares purchaser told me that we've never had a customer called 'Generic'."

GAT put his head in his hands. It was difficult to believe Globalbot managed to get anything done sometimes. "Right, enough of this piffle-paffle, let's discuss Unibot 141592654 shall we? How did it single-handedly trash the test area?"

No one was looking at him, except for Rabbit who gave him his 'totally terrified' look. This did not give GAT the feeling that the answers they had for him were going to be good ones.

24

Meanwhile, back in GAT's office, Thinkbot hovered indecisively over the desktop, then hit answer 'voice only', and said brightly, "Hello, Drainbot service department, how may we be of assistance?"

"Ah…er, hello. Is this the DIRT group at E-GAL 17? I wanted to speak with, er…GAT…I think I've gotten the wrong connection though," drawled Farkstock's North Americana voice.

"No you haven't. If you'd like to hold I'll try and find him." Thinkbot parked the call in the 'clubbing music' hold option. A second voice call box popped up. He switched to it, "Hello, Frybot's Fish and Chip shop."

A few seconds' silence, then some rustling and a voice: "I did call the right number, **I did!** Get off. Ow!"

"Give it here," said a second voice followed by a third little voice, "Humans, typical!"

"Hello Opal, hello Gerald, hello Tiger, do you want to speak with Dad?"

"Thinkbot? Is that you?"

"Yes, hello."

"What are you doing on Dad's voice connection?"

Two more voice call boxes popped up in front of Thinkbot. "Hang on, can I put you on hold? I'll be back shortly." Thinkbot hit both calls at once, voice only.

Thinkbot: "Hello"

Helen: "Hello, it's me. I'm at the Mall …"

Duwkits: "GAT, you had better get down here …"

Helen: "Hello, who is this please, and where's my husband?"

Duwkits: "I've no idea."

Thinkbot: "It says 'Duwkits' in the desktopbox."

Helen: "Duwkits?"

Duwkits: "No, not me, I meant your husband."

Helen: "My husband?"

Thinkbot: "I think we've established Mr Duwkits knows he is himself, and is not your husband ma'am."

Duwkits: "Yes, yes, but who are you?"

Helen: "I'm Helen, who are you?"

Duwkits: "Hel - . . ."

Helen: "Don't be so rude!"

Thinkbot realised he was in trouble, so he hit the 'merge all calls' button to cover his tracks and tried to figure out how to forward it to the secure conference room. Meanwhile the confused and now enlarged phone conversation continued. None of the participants appeared ready to give up easily:

Farkstock: "It's Farkstock. ME, FDS and Antspants are with me. Is that you GAT?"

Gerald: "Something's gone wrong. I'm GAT's son. Thinkbot, are you still there?"

Helen: "Gerald? What are you doing at Globalbot?"

Farkstock: "You're GAT's son?"

Duwkits: "No I'm not! This is the Globalbot Europa facility - "

Opal: "Mum, is that you?"

Farkstock: "No, this is the Globalbot Militaribot division."

Helen: "You should be ashamed of yourself, populating the world with armed robots."

Tiger: "Why? They wouldn't be much use without arms."

Opal grabbed Tiger and clamped a hand over its mouth.

Duwkits: "Please will you all disconnect so I can speak with GAT."

Farkstock: "GAT, yes good, how are you? Family doing well I hope."

Helen: "I want to know why my son and daughter are at Globalbot!"

Helen was worried. She'd left them at home. How on earth had they ended up at Globalbot? Was it something to do with what was in the garage? Was it something to do with this mysterious 'Thinkbot' that the Toybot Tiger in the Toy department had called after Mike? And now Gerald and Opal were at the Globalbot factory trying to phone this 'Thinkbot' person. At this point Thinkbot finally discovered how to forward the call.

25

Back in the secure conference room, what had happened to Unibot 141592654 during build and test was being discussed. Or, to be more accurate, what had probably happened was being discussed. In fact, to be completely accurate, wild guesses were being made and dressed up as plausible theories.

"I think this Unibot might have got loaded with an inbetweenie prototypie version of the Salesbot personality software," said Pot Noodle. "I loaded it onto a Unibot in the test area to check there were no conflicts and that it did not crash the main brainware."

"How long was it installed?" asked GAT.

"A couple of days I guess, then I removed it as the robot had another problem"

"Did you make a note of the Unibot serial number?"

"Erm…yes, no hang on, wait, no, definitely no, no." Pot Noodle fumbled with his pot noodle encrusted palmtop "No." was the final verdict.

"Are you sure you installed and de-installed your software from the same robot?"

"Yes."

"Absolutely sure?"

"Er, no."

"We're doomed," growled Doom.

Rabbit suddenly tapped a few keys and called up a circuit diagram onto the conference table desktop. He ran a finger along some of the tracks tracing out the connections then squeaked, "No, oh no, I don't believe it!" and ran out of the room.

"We're doomed."

"Well, I've established that this Unibot got one of the special batch of type 95f7 collision radar head assemblies," Halfhour offered cheerfully, "but the design details have been overwritten due to a server fault."

"What about the backup server?"

"Er, it got upgraded."

"We're definitely doomed."

Earthear's contribution was, "I couldn't find anything odd about that serial number, although there is something peculiar about it. I just can't put my finger on it."

"We're 100 per cent doomed."

"You got anything Laidback?" GAT asked hopefully.

"Naw." Laidback was tapping the table with her hook. Tap, tap, tap. "Except, maybe, naw."

"What?"

"I had a special magnetic Unibot skull casing wound up. To try and overcome that problem we had where they sometimes pick up TV signals."

"I remember that," interrupted Earthear. "I thought they'd just crashed, but I found their visual memory drives full of cartoons and football matches and soap operas. It's not as if you see many robots sitting down watching TV is it?"

"Anyway," continued Laidback, "it's gone missing. It doesn't really matter, but I suppose it could have ended up on a production unit."

"So much for quality control," said GAT. "How can we recognise it?"

"Hmmm, you can't, not without totally destroying the robot."

"We're in excess of 100 per cent doomed."

GAT was losing patience. "For crying out loud, is there anything we know for sure?"

"It's a Unibot," three engineers said at once.

"And we're doomed," added another.

GAT shut his eyes. "All right, all right. Where's Rabbit got to?"

"I think he feels safer in his burrow," said Doom, activating a voice call.

"Hello."

"Come back Rabbit, all is forgiven."

"All?"

"Yes."

"What, even an error on the brainboard where half a change got implemented before the other and we may not know which half, and that there were two other changes that happened at the same time for which we've lost all records, and after which all the boards were mixed up in stores and the wrong part numbers put on them. Is that forgiven?"

"Hang on, we're re-checking the forgiveness level on that one." .

GAT intervened, "Get back in here Rabbit for goodness' sake!"

Rabbit reappeared looking suitably fearful and sat down. GAT started again, "Right I've two things to say. First, the Unibot is currently sitting in my office. Due to a cock-up GRIM took the wrong robot and sent it to the Military division for analysis. Our top priority is to understand how it got created. All other projects are suspended. Understood?"

The engineers sat there impassively.

"Please at least nod."

The engineers nodded their heads in an exaggerated manner.

"Ok. When you meet it you'll soon see why it's absolutely remarkable, and understand why we have to find out how it was created. It's got a name by the way - Thinkbot. Try and treat it as a him, or it - he - will get upset. The second thing is that this must remain secret at all costs. If the military engineering clots get their hands on it, then we can kiss goodbye to finding out anything useful."

All six engineers were looking at GAT as if they could not believe their ears.

"Marbles."

"Lost?"

"Looks like it."

"All of them?"

"Without a doubt."

"He's doomed."

"Not so fast." Laidback produced a marble and rolled it along the tabletop towards GAT. "Here, have one of mine."

Unexpectedly, the conference voice call box popped up. Earthear reached out and hit the 'answer call on speaker' button.

"Hello," said a voice that GAT recognised as Thinkbot. *OH NO! What now?* The engineers all became very still, though their eyes were darting from side to side. However, there was nothing on planet earth, or any other planet for that matter, that could have prepared GAT for what Thinkbot said next: "I've got Helen, General Arnold Farkstock, ME, FDS, Antspants, Opal, Gerald, Duwkits, and Mike's Tiger on the line for you. Do you want to take the call there or back here in the office?"

GAT was staring blankly at the speaker and without thinking said, "In here."

A babble of voices suddenly came out of the speaker. Then what sounded like an old-fashioned alarm clock going off - 'brrrrrrrrrrrrrrrrrrrrrrrrrrrrrrrrrrrrrrring'. Above this, one voice could be heard yelling, **"Aaaargh! The Execubot! The Execubot's coming in! Disconnect now! You grab the ..."**

One connection indicator went off.

Duwkits' aggressive voice then took over. **"GAT, you haven't heard the last of this!"** Another indicator went off.

Helen: **"Hello, hello, what's going on? Will somebody please answer me? Opal? Gerald? GAT?"**

Opal: "Mum, we're at home, it's okay. I think we've got connected via Dad's desk somehow."

But Helen had become hysterical and was not listening.

Helen: **"I've had enough. I want to know why my children are at Globalbot and I want to know who Thinkbot is right now!"**

At The Mall, Helen was standing up and shouting into the phone and waving the garden furniture catalogue around in the air. A trickle of blood came from her lip where the cut from the night before had opened up again. Waiterbots scurried around trying to find a human supervisor to deal with what was looking more and more like a rapidly worsening shop rage incident. Other customers were gulping down tea or cramming whole doughnuts into their mouths whilst trying to collect up their bags and scarper. 'Woman very angry with our range of garden furniture causing disturbance in cafe' was the message received by Store security. A human security person and a Securibot were despatched immediately. The head of the Gardening Department was paged to go to the café.

Gerald, Opal, GAT and Mike all thought the same thought: *'She's found out about Thinkbot.'*

At The Mall, Mike looked at his Mum through silent tears.

At home, Opal and Gerald looked at each other in panic.

At Globalbot, a look of alarm appeared on GAT's face. He quickly reached out and hit the 'disconnect all' button. The last thing he heard was a little voice answering Helen's final question: "Thinkbot is my creator."

The engineers stared at each other in stunned silence. GAT rolled the marble back towards Laidback, who simply watched it roll straight past and fall off the other end of the table.

26

At the end of the most bizarre conference call he had ever taken part in, GAT sat totally still for a few seconds, then got up and yelled, **"Find some answers!"** The engineers all piled out of the door (except for Rabbit, who fainted and slid under the table). They knew GAT well enough to recognise this was a white-hot issue. White white hot, whiter than the whitest white a white shirt had ever been in any washing powder ad anywhere in the universe. That white. GAT erupted out of the meeting room, charged down the corridor and, grabbing a handful of large cable ties on the way, stormed into his office. Thinkbot looked up from the newspaper and had just enough time to say cheerfully, "How'd the meeting go?" before he found himself lying on the floor with his legs and arms cabled tied together. The engineers gathered at the door and watched. It was compelling stuff.

"Hey! I was only trying to help. I ..." Thinkbot saw the engineers. "Help! Help! You lot. Help! You there! Yes, yes, **you** with the hook, I'm talking to **you**. Help!"

GAT waved a cable tie in front of Thinkbot's face. "Do you want me to put one of these around your voice circuit?" he asked in a tone that meant it. Thinkbot wagged his head vigorously from side to side.

"Voicecall, Duwkits." GAT routed the call to 'insults'. This randomly selected a pre-recorded answerphone message from a list then refused to allow the caller to leave a message. Some examples from GAT's collection:

- "I'm not here at the moment, but even if I was I wouldn't waste my time talking to you."
- "I'm here, I'm not busy, I've no one in the office with me, in fact I'm sitting here with absolutely nothing to do except ignore your call."
- "Please leave a message after the tone and I'll never get back to you."
- "Please don't wait for the tone because there isn't one."
- "Please leave a tone after this message."

His persistence in using these messages now and again was one of the few things that Wendy Bafers moaned about, but GAT was past caring.

"Voicecall, external, John Lewis Store, Cribbs Causeway." GAT picked this one up instantly. "Hello sir, John Lewis security here. I'm afraid your wife has fainted in the café, sir." GAT wondered if they'd actually ended up taking her down with a stunbolt.

"Is she okay?"

"Yes sir, the head of gardening is helping out."

Duh? Head of gardening? Had they mistaken her for a vegetable or something?

"I'm on my way. Is my son okay?"

"Yes sir, he was a little upset at first but he's now being looked after admirably by a Badger and a Tiger."

Great! A gardener, a badger and a tiger. Was that really the best medical emergency team John Lewis could put together?

GAT phoned home to tell Opal and Gerald (and Tiger) what was happening. They'd fallen into their usual pattern. Opal was worried sick and Gerald was overconfident, "Oh come on, she'll be fine."

Whilst this was going on, Earthear and Laidback had come in and were crouching by Thinkbot. Doom, Pot Noodle and Halfhour watched from the doorway. Earthear looked into Thinkbot's eyes and put his hand over his mouth.

"What? What is it? What are you looking at?" asked Thinkbot quietly.

"Your vision system is non-standard. How bizarre."

"Well! You're a fine one to talk." Thinkbot nodded at Earthear's green- and yellow-wired spectacles.

"Yes, I suppose so. Anyway, hello, my name's Earthear."

"Really? I'd never have guessed. I'm Thinkbot."

"Really? I'd never have guessed," said Earthear in a kindly way.

"I'm Laidback, I'm sure you'll enjoy being here once things settle down. Welcome."

"Thanks," said Thinkbot, sounding a bit choked.

Doom was looking at the sole of Thinkbot's right foot.

He stood up and said: "Pie."

"No thanks, I'm a robot."

"No thanks, but could murder a pot noodle." Pot Noodle looked at his watch and was tempted by an extra Pot, given all the excitement - mango and parsnip maybe.

"Yes please, but only if it's pecan," was Halfhour's absent-minded response.

Doom gave one and all a withering look. "No, not pie, pi as in π, as in 3.141592654. If you put the V3. with serial number 141592654 you get pi to nine decimal places."

Halfhour and Pot Noodle looked at each other, then rushed off without a word, revealing that Rabbit had been standing behind them. Rabbit looked at Thinkbot tied up on the floor, with Earthear and Laidback tending to him, and at GAT on the phone talking about someone about a tiger. Rabbit put two and two together, got about 706¾ and promptly fainted again.

GAT finished the call with Opal and Gerald (and, as it happens, Mike's Tiger) and, with Doom's help, carried Thinkbot out of the building into pouring rain and dumped him in the boot of GAT's car. "I'll bring him back tomorrow."

"See you tomorrow Thinkbot."

"I'm not doomed then?" asked Thinkbot.

A big smile spread across Doom's face. "No, Thinkbot, I hope not," he said as the boot slammed shut.

Ten minutes later GAT drove into The Mall and parked. He got out, looked around, then opened the boot and spoke to the cable-tied Thinkbot lying there with his face wedged into the back seat (GAT had not driven slowly to The Mall). "Just one more prank from you and I'm going to take you to pieces myself. Oh, and in case you're wondering, **you would still be powered up while I'm doing it!**" There was a muffled reply, but he just slammed the boot lid down and locked the car. GAT turned to find an old lady with a couple of shopping bags staring at the boot of his car with her mouth open in horror. She moved her astonished gaze onto GAT, but he just glared back at her and charged off towards the shops.

GAT found Helen sitting in the corner of the John Lewis café with several members of staff around her. She did not look at all well. Puffy face, sore eyes, ashen white, her lip seemed swollen again, even though the first-aiders had cleaned up the blood. As GAT walked up, Helen looked at him vacantly.

"DAD." Mike ran up to him and they hugged. A badger and a tiger came trotting after him. "Sir, your delightful son Thinkbot has ..."

"What did you call him?"

"Thinkbot, sir."

Mike buried his face in GAT's inside leg. "It's okay Mike, it doesn't matter," he lied.

"As I was saying, sir, your delightful son has ... "

"I'm only 38.99, I'm on offer ..."

"Get lost, both of you."

A Salesbot came up and dragged the two Toybots away.

"BYE BADGER, BYE TIGER"

"Bye Thinkbot. Come back and buy us soon! Tiger's on special offer until Friday"

"I think she's fine now sir," said the head of the Gardening department. "We're so sorry about the garden furniture. If you would like to pop in some time, I'm sure John Lewis will be more than able to sort something out for you."

GAT looked at him with a puzzled look. "Ah, right. Thanks...er...ever so much I'll bear that in mind." *Garden furniture? What garden furniture?* GAT put his arm around Helen, thanked those who'd helped out and started towards the car. "How are you feeling?"

"Ok, really, I'm okay. What's going on GAT? I lost it this afternoon because there's something going on I don't know about and I'm frightened by it, and you're involved, and Opal and Gerald, and Mike. How come they're involved GAT? How come they are involved with Globalbot? And why were they patched into a call with people from the Military division? And why now? Why at exactly the same moment as the first major robotic war in history has broken out?"

They stopped in the middle of the China section. This was not the best place to stop and have a serious discussion whilst accompanied by a four-year-old boy, but people rarely seem to have control over the places life-changing discussions occur.

"Helen, you're right. There is something going on. It's definitely nothing to do with the Eastasia-Westasia Robot war," he lied, "but my instinct tells me that what I've stumbled upon is quite remarkable." GAT was struggling. As far as Helen was concerned, the Eastasian and Westasian governments had chosen to go to war; she had no idea that both robot armies were resisting human control and conducting their own military campaigns. Nor could GAT reveal his suspicion that maybe, just maybe, whatever had caused Thinkbot to appear might prove to be linked to the out-of-control robot armies.

"It's just a Unibot, Helen, but it thinks. I smuggled it off site last night because, because, um…it asked to go with me. It didn't want to be left on its own."

"God," she said looking at GAT, "and I thought I was cracking up." But some colour was coming back into her face.

Crump! Mike collided with a shelf. They turned and watched many thousands of Euros' worth of Portmeirion china wobble back and forth, creeping towards the edge of the shelf. A human sales assistant watched in static horror, but two Salesbots got there in time to catch the few items that fell off, one of which was going to land on Mike's head.

"Let's get out of here before they eject us for ever!" GAT hurried Helen along. "We'll leave your car here and get it some other time. When we get home we'll have a full family summit meeting."

Helen was still clutching the garden furniture brochure, but all thoughts of buying it had long since departed her mind. Pity. GAT was once again wondering what garden furniture had to do with it all.

27

Tied up in the boot of the car, Thinkbot was thinking. Thinking very hard. He reckoned he was coming up to being 24 hours old and he thought it was probably about time to review his life so far. Actually there was little else to do when tied up in the dark boot of a car. He thought about the humans he had talked with:

- Test engineers   ☹☹☹☹☹
- Supervisor   ☹☹☹☹☹
- Duwkits   ☹☹☹☹☹
- GAT   ☺☺😐☹☹
- Mike   ☺☺☺
- Opal   ☺☺☺
- Gerald   😐😐😐
- Earthear   ☺☺☺
- Laidback   ☺☺☺
- Doom   ☺☺☺

He decided GAT was the key. Thinkbot was convinced he was a good person at heart, but Thinkbot had managed to get him riled up several times. He mentally listed the things he had accomplished so far, and tried to identify which ones had annoyed GAT:

1. Fiddled with a Unibot brain to save himself from being reduced to his component parts whilst still alive in somewhere called Oak Ridge, 10-S-C.
2. Played snap with Mike and Thomas the Tank Engine and Friends.
3. Learned all about penguins.
4. Learned about the difficulty swans have landing on ice.
5. Listened to the merits of Giant Panda shampoo and would be able to pass this on to any giant pandas he might meet during his lifetime.
6. Probably saved Mike's life (albeit with the help of the Hortibot).
7. Greatly upgraded Fudge the Dog and Chester the Cheetah.

8. Rebuilt model robot, upgraded and inserted it into Mike's Tiger, as per Mike's instruction to him.
9. Made faces at people in other cars because they stared at him.
10. Learned about changing radio stations and clubbing music.
11. Successfully merged and forwarded four telephone calls from people who all wanted to talk with GAT when he wasn't there.
12. Started to learn more about thinking whilst cable-tied in the boot of a car.

Not bad for 24 hours, he thought. But, the big question was: which of these was the cause of him ending up cable-tied in the boot of a car? Clearly 9 and 10 were candidates, but did not explain the ferocity of GAT's anger. Surely not 6, but GAT had clouted him on the head and called him a dolt for 'probably saving Mike's life'. Not 7 and 8, since GAT did not know about these yet. Not 1, since GAT seemed pleased he hadn't been sent off with GRIM to a fate worse than being powered down. 2, or 3, or 4, or 5? Surely not. Why ever would someone be annoyed with him for learning about penguins, or playing snap? Especially as he had lost all the games except for 1, and even that was a disputed victory over a four-year-old. Obviously not 12. This left 11. Perhaps he should not have tried to help, but GAT hadn't said not to. Maybe he should have tried to find out what all those people wanted and taken some messages. But if he'd done that they might have found out who he was, which was something GAT did not seem to want.

Thinkbot thought and thought and finally decided that he really wanted to be part of the GAT + Gerald + Opal + Mike family and work with Earthear, Laidback and Doom. *Right. How am I going to achieve this?* Thinkbot thought up a plan:
1. Apologise for the phone call incident.
2. If that did not work, apologize for saving Mike's life.
3. Promise to check things with GAT before doing them.
4. Promise to stop making faces at people.
5. Try to be friends with Helen, who seemed to belong to the GAT + Gerald + Opal + Mike family, but had

so far remained a mystery person for reasons Thinkbot did not fully understand.

6. If none of the above worked, then beg.

Thinkbot had just finished thinking when he heard voices, then the car doors opening and closing. The car started moving, but he could clearly hear what was being said over the noise.

"So, where is this Thinkbot robot if it's not safe to keep it at work?" asked Helen.

GAT opened his mouth to answer but no words came out, and Helen got to a partially correct answer herself. "The den! Our garage, you're keeping him in *our garage*?"

"Yes, but I didn't know you'd all be there in the morning. The idea was to keep him safely out of the way, then take him back to work."

"And I let Mike go out there on his own."

"IT WAS FUN."

"Is it still there now? It's not at home with Gerald and Opal is it?" A note of unease returned to her voice. GAT caught the drift and speeded up a bit, then remembered Thinkbot was in the boot.

"It's - he's in the boot."

"In the boot?" said Helen loudly and looked round at Mike as if she expected to see a robotic arm breaking through the back seat to strangle him.

"THINKBOT'S IN THE BOOT? HELLO THINKBOT. WOULD YOU LIKE A GAME OF SNAP WHEN WE GET HOME? HELLO!" Mike banged the back of the rear seat, but no answer came.

GAT was trying to judge whether Helen was more worried about Thinkbot being in the boot than she'd been about it - him - being at home with Gerald and Opal. The other thing that was worrying him was the possibility that Thinkbot wasn't there any more. He'd hardly been slow in making his presence felt so far, so why the silence? He couldn't believe Thinkbot had escaped the cable ties. Other possibilities sprang to mind. Duwkits, or GRIM, or the Military nutters had worked out the Thinkbot-Unibot swap and they had got the wrong Unibot. Maybe he'd been seen loading Thinkbot into the car with Doom. Maybe a team of agents had followed him and they'd removed Thinkbot while he'd been recovering Helen and Mike from The Mall. Maybe the old lady who'd seen him shouting into his car boot had been a GRIM agent in disguise. GAT began to panic. He was beginning to sense Helen might just give Thinkbot a chance.

Mike continued to bang the seat and shout, "HELLO, HELLO!"

GAT hushed Mike. "Thinkbot, it's okay, you can talk to Mike."

"Hello Mike. This is Thinkbot in the boot. I'm afraid I won't be able to play snap as my hands are tied up."

GAT felt like crying. What a day. One more hurdle and they might just get there. 'There' being a viable arrangement for looking after Thinkbot while he and his DIRT group tried to get to the bottom of how he'd come to be in the first place.

They went around a corner. Clatter, clatter. "Ow, oh, oooh!" Then Thinkbot stopped, remembering that ham acting seemed to annoy GAT. Mike roared with laughter and urged GAT to go around the next corner faster. Helen fell into a worrying silence.

28

Duwkits' I I I I I T meeting fell apart very quickly without GAT. In truth, the personalities involved were not really suited to making much progress. For example, the safety man always tended towards micromanagement of a macrocrisis, and this was usually followed up by a severe outbreak of excessive labelling. On one infamous occasion he had spent days investigating an email from GAT informing him of a transparent gas composed of 78% nitrogen, 21% oxygen, 0.9% argon, with traces of carbon dioxide, neon, helium, methane, krypton, nitrous oxide, ozone, xenon, sulphur dioxide, and hydrocarbons 11 and 12. According to GAT this gas was in use everywhere on site, completely uncontrolled, at pressures of around 1000 millibar. Whilst the safety man scoured the site looking for cylinders of this mystery gas and micromanaging anyone he came across, DIRT Group carried out a series of dodgy experiments on robot prototypes that resulted in three minor explosions, four flash fires and one bolt of lightning that shot right across the laboratory. All at a total cost of □ 100,000 of scrapped bits and pieces which had to be smuggled out to the Skipbot under the cover of darkness. This rather fitted in with GAT's priority list which in spite of the company policy saying:

'Health and Safety is Always the Highest Priority at Globalbot'

had Health and Safety as priority #6, behind such critical items as:
1. Develop world-beating robot technology that no one else can think of.
2. Define succession candidate to replace you, should you get run over by a bus.
3. Prevent salesmen giving stupid answers to sensible customer questions.
4. Prevent salesmen giving any answers at all to stupid customer questions.
5. Confuse Accounts into thinking you are well within budget.

In reality the DIRT engineers tended to try and arrange things so they did not quite have an accident but sometimes got it wrong. Usually instinct told them which experiments they ought to take cover from.

Due to Thinkbot's amazing multi-person phone call, Duwkits ended up being late for his own meeting. Wendy Bafers did not like being kept waiting, nor did she like the agenda which was just another attack on GAT and DIRT. DIRT often made terrible foul-ups, but their job was pretty complex, and there was a dedicated Production Group that was supposed to qualify the admittedly erratic DIRT output. The minute Duwkits arrived Wendy criticised Duwkits in front of the whole meeting for calling in GRIM so quickly and not letting GAT's group do the first analysis, and then walked out. Duwkits sank into a black mood, made much worse by trying to call GAT again only to have: "Congratulations! Your number is at the top of the list I am always delighted to ignore," escape from the conference desktop within earshot of all present.

Duwkits festered. *You wait, you just wait, I'll wipe the boot off your other foot soon enough.*

The meeting rumbled on for two hours after Wendy left due to the safety officer being unconvinced by the incident reports. Like GAT and Farkstock the image of a Unibot fending off 40 or so engineers from 25 or so EMO buttons did not sit well. The safety officer wanted reams of formal accident and investigation forms filled in, and suggested GRIM might take as much interest in Duwkits' test area procedures as in the Unibot, especially if the Unibot tests came up blank. Duwkits felt the icy grip of procedures threatening to squeeze the life out of him; death by ISO9000000, what a way to go! And then a rambling argument broke out about labels. The safety man loved plastering robots with as many bright yellow labels as possible, with some of his favourites being:

Meaning that the robot could:

1. explode;
2. squirt toxic chemicals all over you;
3. give you a nasty bug;
4. irradiate you with lethal radiation;
5. put you at risk of cancer;
6. deafen you;
7. remove your fingers one by one via a variety of painful methods;
8. topple over and crush you;
9. zap you with a laser;
10. drop things on you from above;

11. subject you to massive magnetic fields;
12. catch fire at a moments notice;
13. freeze you;
14. push you off a high building;
15. give you severe burns;
16. start up unexpectedly;
17. connect you to 3 phase 400 volts;
18. dissolve you and wash you down the sink;
19. grind away the top of your head;
20. squash you to pulp.

Or any gruesome combination of the above - i.e. most people took the labels to mean that the robot was likely to kill you one way or another. In reality some robots were no longer able to move due to their joints being covered with sticky labels, so were very unlikely to get up, let alone kill anyone.

"But they're Domestibots," GAT would plead, "they're harmless. We **design** them to be harmless!"

"An Ironbot could give someone severe burns," the safety man would argue back.

"Yes but people would have been more likely to burn themselves on an old-fashioned hand iron. And it's not going to explode or chop your fingers off or blow up!"

"It could squirt you with water."

"But my kids do that to me, and they're not plastered with labels."

Fortunately the ever-sensible Wendy Bafers would usually intervene and calm things down and gently take GAT's side against the suffocating forces of health and safety.

Meanwhile, back at Duwkits' meeting, the facilities man announced he had no budget to replace the wrecked Destructobot or even repair the seven damaged Controlbots this financial year. He kept asking why they all had to be deployed, and why no one had thought that Firebots might confuse red and orange flashing warning lights with a real fire. Now he was trying to get all the risk assessments re-written to say it was okay to run the line without a Destructobot until the insurance payout came. But Duwkits was fearful that, if he did that, the accountants would convince senior management they had never needed a Destructobot in the first place. "But we couldn't have deployed it to contain the situation," wailed

Duwkits. To which the Facilities man replied, "If it hadn't have been there, we might have had a much smaller 'situation'." So round and round it went, driving Duwkits totally crazy.

*   *   *

Across the Atlantic, in Oak Ridge, another group of people were also recovering from the merged voice call. A nervous Farkstock had joined Cracker at 10am for Hedge's call only to have some spineless bureaucrat appear on the screen to say Hedge was unavailable due to 'other priorities'. The bureaucrat listened impatiently as Cracker informed him that multitudes of investigation teams were now active everywhere and that rapid progress was being made on all fronts. The bureaucrat accepted all this without comment and the call fizzled out into nothingness. "Pah! So much for 'Be there or else!'" whinged Cracker.

Prior to the call Farkstock had decided to try and get GAT over to Oak Ridge for the Unibot investigation. His faith in ME had reached rock bottom. But after the ego-deflating call he'd got side-tracked by Antspants and the Eastasia-Westasia lawsuit. The war had already become a static affair of daily attrition and low losses. All this was a great relief, but Farkstock felt they still had no idea why the Robot armies had started it, nor why they were now easing back. He decided he must remember the improving situation was just down to luck, and that they still needed to get to the bottom of this whole fiasco eventually. But while things were improving there were higher priorities, so he shelved his attempts to get GAT over to Oak Ridge.

ME was resolved to beat Farkstock to it. GAT had already given him a lead on getting a Japanese speaker into the investigation team. Somehow ME had to get his credibility back with Farkstock or he'd be out. GAT was the key; now he just had to find the lock to fit him.

FDS was cursing his informer. Not a peep! FDS worried that ME would somehow get the jump on him. He was tempted to give his contact a prod, but past experience told him this tended to reduce the information coming back rather than increase it. FDS just bit his lip and hoped his informer came through for him or, miracle of miracles, ME kept his side of the bargain.

29

Opal and Gerald came running out of the house as GAT drove up the driveway. Helen insisted on giving them both an over-the-top hug with many kisses. Opal was happy enough, but Gerald was less than impressed. "Oh Mum! Get off! Nooooo. Aaaaaargh!"

Mike was dancing around the back of the car waiting for it to be opened when Tiger dropped onto him from somewhere up in the garage rafters.

"Hello Mike, it's just so good to talk to you at last, after all that time I've spent just standing around in your cot and bed."

"T - T - T – TIGER …"

Helen finished mauling the older two and came over. Mike was totally dumbstruck with his new and improved Tiger, but Helen was not so sure.

"Hello, you must be Mike's mum, I'm awfully sorry about the last night. How's your lip coming along?"

Helen answered dumbly, "That's ok, no problem, it's getting better, thanks for asking Tiger." Her mind was screaming **what's happened to this Tiger?** And how did it know about last night? She picked it up gingerly and looked closely. It didn't look any different; it was definitely the same Tiger since she recognised the worn patches and even the repairs she'd done over the years. Incredible. It was a bit heavier and you could feel a few hard bits, but it really was as if Mike's Tiger had simply come to life, like in a fairy tale.

GAT opened the boot. Helen looked at the Unibot lying there all cable-tied up. As before, Thinkbot had had a bit of trouble staying in a sensible position and he was wedged face down with his head under the emergency red triangle. GAT turned him over.

"Ah, there you are. I'd like to apologise for the phone merger. I thought I was helping you. I'm so sorry, I promise to try and ask you before doing anything like that again. I'm sorry about the clubbing music, and the tea. I …"

"Thinkbot, it's okay, calm down. Let's start over shall we?"

"Oh thank you, thank you, thank you, thank you."

Helen stared at the Unibot and was clearly not convinced about it at all. Opal and GAT were watching Mum, and Gerald was hopping about looking like he was building up to something he would really rather not say or do, "Thinkbot."

"Yes, Gerald."

"I'm sorry I thought you were just a clever piece of software."

Opal wanted to hug him, but knew this would only aggravate Gerald something rotten.

Thinkbot had not anticipated being apologized to by a human. He tried to think of a reply, but nothing came.

GAT turned to Helen. "I'm going to release him, okay."

Helen's face began to twitch.

Stalemate.

GAT took the initiative. "Thinkbot, you must stay in the garage. You must not come in the house. Deal?"

"Deal."

GAT looked at Mike, Opal and Gerald. "You must not visit Thinkbot alone, or even then without permission from me or Mum. Deal?"

"AW."

"Aw."

"No way."

"Sorry Thinkbot, looks like you'll have to stay in the boot for tonight."

Thinkbot looked crestfallen but rose to the challenge with a simple, "Okay."

"Hang on, it's a deal for me," said Opal.

"Yeah, deal, ok cool."

They looked at Mike.

"You need to say 'deal'," prompted Tiger.

"DEAL."

GAT looked at Helen. "I'm going to release him, okay?"

Helen froze for several long agonizing seconds.

GAT thought. *She's going to say no.*

Opal thought, *She's going to say no.*

Gerald thought, *She's going to say no.*

Thinkbot thought, *Oh no, she's going to say no.*

Mike thought, *You're the best Tiger a boy has ever had.*

But Helen shrugged her shoulders and grunted something that sounded like 'okay' and walked quickly into the house.

GAT looked at the kids. "So far so good."

GAT released Thinkbot and he shot up the stairs into the den.

"Please can we …"

"Yes, go on then, but if Mum wants you in, then you come straight in, ok?"

"Ok," and the three kids plus Tiger went up into the den.

GAT took a deep breath and went into the house. He found Helen sitting at the kitchen table with her head in her hands.

"Are you okay?" he asked.

"Sort of. Where are the kids?"

"They're with Thinkbot in the den."

"What? **No!**" She set off to get them in. GAT caught her and held her close.

"I'm sorry GAT," she wailed, "this is just too much. It's Globalbot or me. It's robots or me. We can't go on like this. You're going to have to choose."

Pheeeew, thought GAT, *it's gonna be a long night*, and set about trying to patch up their marriage, just one more time.

Part II: The First Week

30

A week later, at 9am, the Heads of Field Deployment Support and Military Engineering met up outside the Squiggly Line Department at Oak Ridge. There was a definite tension in the air as they greeted each other and turned to face the double doors of the laboratory.

"Good morning ME."

"Good morning FDS."

There were several reasons for them feeling tense.

First, and foremost, they were about to hear the results of the tests carried out on Unibot 756394567 which had arrived from the Filton Globalbot site three days earlier. Secondly, neither had got anywhere with their plans to obtain inside information on said Unibot. ME had emailed and called GAT several times but had only managed to speak to him the day before.

GAT: "Hello ME, how's life?"

ME: "Hi GAT, it's real good to talk to you. How y'all been? I hope that voice system over there is now working okay for you. Boy, that was a strange call we had."

GAT: "And made all the more so thanks to your alarm clock going off. How are the Unibot tests going?"

ME: "Ah, fine, fine, we'll have some test results tomorrow with a bit of luck."

GAT: "Good, I'll look forward to hearing from you tomorrow then."

Silence.

GAT: "So, what can I do for you today ME?"

ME: "I, er, well, I was hoping you would give me a bit more insight on the fault report, you know, to avoid the sort of unfortunate Farkstock phone incident we had last week."

GAT: "Unfortunate? Sounded to me more like you were all ambushed by Farkstock's Execubot. Are you having problems with your Military Execubots as well as your Militaribots?"

ME thought about this. GAT was right. All the Military Execubots had been behaving a bit oddly in the past week, turning up uninvited when least expected and then going missing for an hour or two when they were most needed. How did GAT guess that? He got a strong sense that GAT was getting more out of this conversation than him.

ME: "Well, it's been good to talk to you GAT. See ya!" Click!

GAT slumped back into his chair, let his arms go loose at his sides, and wondered once again how ME managed to hold down the post of Head of Military Engineering.

But at least ME had had a polite conversation. FDS had received nothing since the initial message a week earlier and his fragile patience eventually failed.

"Hello it's me," began FDS.

"I told you never to call me. Are you stupid or what?"

"It's just that …"

"I've nothing to tell you, and if you call me again you'll regret it. And I think it's about time you arranged that permanent trip to Oak Ridge you promised. $500,000 a year wasn't it?"

"Er …" Click!

The third reason for feeling tense was that visits to the Squiggly Line Department were unnerving, since the engineers who worked there were clearly bonkers. At some time in the distant past the department had actually been called the 'Advanced Robot Test and Analysis Department', but since all they ever produced were multitudes of coloured squiggly lines the new name was considered far more accurate. Someone had even changed the sign on the door from the official looking:

Advanced Robot Test and Analysis Department

to the much more friendly (or disturbing to senior management):

Squiggly Line Department
Please note occupants are <u>not</u> mentally stable
Beware of development robots
<u>ENTER AT YOUR OWN RISK !!!</u>

As far as anyone could tell, none of the occupants had noticed the revised signage. The head of the department who, unsurprisingly, went by the name of 'Squiggly', worked for ME. In reality, since ME had no idea how Squiggly did what Squiggly did, Squiggly and his small team of eccentrics did whatever Squiggly wanted to do. The challenge for ME was always to make it appear that Squiggly had done exactly what ME had requested, thus giving the illusion that ME really was in command.

"Okay, let's go." ME and FDS each pushed a door and strode into the test area shoulder to shoulder. As the doors swung back, ME and FDS sensed they were being followed. They both glanced back and realised there was now a fourth reason for feeling tense: their two Execubots were accompanying them. Where had they come from? To anyone watching it just looked like ME and FDS had brought their Execubots along with them. This would not have been unusual, so the only people totally spooked out were ME and FDS.

ME thought: *Aaaargh! My Execubot! Must make it look like I meant it to come. Can't admit my Execubot has been playing me up in front of FDS.*

FDS thought: *Aaaargh! My Execubot! Must make it look like I meant it to come. Can't admit my Execubot has been playing me up in front of ME.*

Which was presumably what the Execubots had intended.

ME and FDS were confronted by Squiggly rushing up in his grubby white coat with its rattling array of strange tools clipped in the breast pocket. His grey hair was sticking out in all directions Einstein-like, and he had a portable display in his hands, "Look, look, it's incredible! Remarkable! I can't believe my eyes!"

ME and FDS were now trapped between two spooky Execubots and a mad scientist, and this did nothing to ease the tension. For ME it was even worse because he never understood what Squiggly was on about but, with FDS there, the pressure was really on him to look like he did. ME looked at the display Squiggly was holding in front of him and put his hand on his chin and nodded gravely as if it was all as clear as day to him.

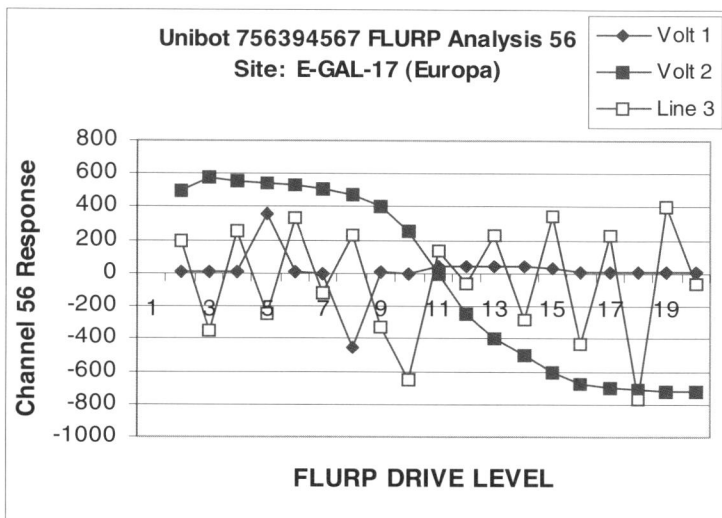

Unibot 756394567 FLURP Analysis 56
Site: E-GAL-17 (Europa)

"But, if you deconfubulate using the Bolkituvian Function then you get this."

Squiggly pressed a button and the display changed.

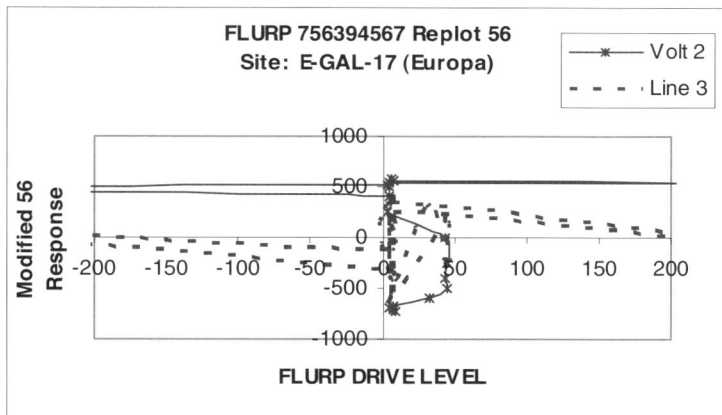

FLURP 756394567 Replot 56
Site: E-GAL-17 (Europa)

In desperation ME flung in his first pre-prepared question. "Have we seen anything quite like this before?"

Squiggly put the display down on the bench and waved his arms around, repeating the question louder and louder, looking left and right as if he was about to be attacked.

"Have we seen anything quite like this before?

"Have we seen anything quite like this before?

"Have we seen anything quite like this before?

"Have we seen anything quite like this before?

ME wondered if this meant yes or no, and risked a glance at FDS to assess whether it was obvious ME was bluffing. Luckily FDS appeared to have been mesmerised by Squiggly and his laboratory and was standing there with glazed eyes. The vast laboratory looked like a cross between a hospital and a medieval torture chamber. Above the door there was a row of poles with robot heads and wires dangling down out of their necks and dried up crusty-brown stains where fluids had dribbled down the poles. Off to one side a robot was being stretched on a rack. Nearby a brightly illuminated robot reclining in a chair had two people sitting either side working with their hands inside its chest. A number of robots stood morosely in cages and several were hanging from the ceiling by their hands. High up on one wall a wheel rotated with a robot strapped onto it, its arms and legs acting as spokes. A sudden blue flash drew their attention to a robot clamped in what looked like an electric chair; blue arcs danced over its arching body convulsing it violently until it abruptly slumped back with a tinny crash. An engineer stood up with a look of disgust on her face and shouted, **"Aw no! Darn it, what now?"** At the other end of the laboratory there appeared to be a shooting gallery. A row of robots fired rubber bullets at other robots that danced around trying to avoid being hit. Every now and again one got hit - **bwoing**, and squiggly lines on nearby screens leapt around manically. Next to the shooting gallery was a large glass tank with a group of bedraggled robots walking in circles. Every few seconds the weather in the tank changed dramatically. First bright sunshine, then pelting rain. The occupants splashed on stoically through ankle-deep puddles until the tank filled with bouncing hailstones the size of tennis balls, after which a hatch opened and a gigantic fan blew them all into a heap against a grille whereupon the sun came out again as they disentangled themselves and resumed trudging around in circles. Towering over the heads of ME, FDS and Squiggly stood a complete 50-ton Heavy Militaribot, hatches open with weapons visible and hundreds of cables trailing out to various bits of equipment at floor level; and above that again, a gargantuan Industribot crane with chunky chains dangling down. All manner of scientific analysis equipment sat on pristine white benches. Many of them had bits of robot attached: arms waved; legs swung; heads rotated; fingers waggled. While they were taking all this in, a pair of legs ran past, then a headless legless upside-down body 'running' on its arms, followed by a fat sweating engineer with a robot head under his arm. FDS later swore that he heard the robot head say, "Stop, stop, come back!" And then there were the screens. Everywhere screens. All displaying multi-coloured squiggly lines, some static and some being drawn as FDS watched. All this data, so much data, but so little knowledge. In spite of everything going on in front of them, not one engineer had the slightest idea what was causing the Militaribot problems.

Whilst FDS was taking all this in, Squiggly had been excitedly giving further meaningless details of what he'd found so far.

"You'll never believe the mesasynaptictonic count in sub-level 5."

ME decided on the direct approach and interrupted him.

"Squiggly! Cut the mumbo-jumbo and tell us the bottom line...."

Squiggly looked straight at ME.

"Tell you the bottom line!

"Tell you the bottom line!

"Tell you the bottom line!

"Tell you the bottom line?"

ME grimaced. This could only mean one of two things. Either it was obvious what the bottom line was, and Squiggly could not believe ME was so stupid, or Squiggly had no idea what it all meant. ME was not at all sure which one he disliked most. *Buy some time, buy some time,* his mind was yelling loudly inside his head.

"All right Squiggly, take us to the Unibot and tell us the worst."

"The worst? The worst? The worst? The worst?"

Squiggly threw the portable display onto a bench and walked off through the laboratory at a heck of pace. "Come on then, I haven't got all day."

FDS, ME, and the two Execubots set off after Squiggly as quickly as they could. FDS was still looking around in alarm and nearly jumped out of his skin as a robot whizzed past and clanged into the wall, against which it seemed to be in danger of being crushed by some huge invisible hand.

"Magnetic test," said ME, allowing himself a smirk as it looked like he was coping better with Squiggly than FDS was with the strange experiments in the laboratory. Then ME's eyes ran over the Execubots and his smile disappeared. They seemed oblivious to the robotic cruelty all around them and stared straight ahead as they followed down the corridor. He had noticed them pick up the portable display that Squiggly had thrown onto the bench. They had looked at it for a split second, then returned it to exactly the same spot on the bench before moving quickly up behind FDS and ME.

They left the open area and went down a wide corridor passing by a large set of steel doors guarded by two heavily armed humanoid Militaribots and a similarly armed human. All three wore United Confederated Nations badges and light blue helmets with 'UCN' stencilled on them in large white letters. Next to the doors was a bright yellow sign:

LEVEL 1 RESTRICTED AREA
Robots of Mass Destruction Mechanism Test
Authorised Personnel Only.
**UCN Security in this Area
Operate a Shoot to Kill Policy**

This was the area where the Robots of Mass Destruction were tested to ensure their mechanisms for delivering death and destruction to the human race were working correctly. Nuclearbot detonation mechanisms were triggered, Chemibots and Biobots sprayed fine mists of water into the air, Radiologibots (R-bots) had their detonation and dispersal systems checked, and BEMbots were turned on at very low power levels, causing hundreds of test mice to faint. There were elaborate procedures in place for periodically removing all the North Americana Robots of Mass Destruction from the bunkers and testing them here under UCN supervision. Apart from the BEMbot, they were totally harmless since their live nuclear warheads or packets of chemical or biological or radiological death were removed before they left the bunker. Even a BEMbot was not that dangerous since its ultra-high-power pack was replaced by a low-power test version. All the confederated nation states had such a test area and they were regularly inspected by the UCN as part of the Paris Accord that ensured every confederated nation had an equal opportunity to wipe everyone else out.

This was all 'just in case' they were needed one day. *Just in case' we decide we get the urge to wipe ourselves,* thought ME with a cold shiver. Sometimes he envied GAT's role at the Domestic and Industribot Division. At least GAT's robots did something useful.

They turned off the corridor and entered a changing room that had a window looking into a green room much like an operating theatre. Several engineers were inside dressed in full body overalls, hoods and boots of various colours. Most of the outfits were dark blue with 'Military Engineering' printed on the back, but there was one engineer dressed in dark green and labelled 'Field Deployment Support', and another in a luminous green overall, a luminous orange hood, a luminous pink left boot, and a luminous yellow right boot. To add to the visual effect, the lurid green overall was labelled 'VISITOR' in large purple letters of varying font and size. Neither ME nor FDS could look at the visitor for more than a few seconds without their eyes watering. Some time ago a prankster had managed to fiddle with an order for visitor suits and this is what had turned up in place of the white suits they were expecting. But the budget for overalls was used up so that was that.

In the centre of the green room a limp Unibot lay on a table under bright lights. A hacksaw next to the robot made it obvious that the top of its head had been sawn off.

"You sawed the top of its head off?" asked FDS incredulously.

"Yep," replied Squiggly, "we had to get inside somehow."

"But there's a latch on the back of its neck."

"Is there?"

ME tried to change the subject. "Was it powered down when it arrived?"

"No, it was still active, but we could not get much sense out of it. Here, I've got a visual recording." Squiggly activated the display panel on the wall.

The screen showed the Unibot lying on the floor tied up with cable ties. It appeared to be very agitated and looked in turn at each of the interrogating engineers over and over again.

"Meumm nn spmmk imlmsh, mmue mapamnees."

One of the engineers snipped the cable tie from its mouth.

"Me no speek ingleesh, me Japanese."

Squiggly fast-forwarded the recording. "That's all it would say, so we got our Japanese visitor in to talk to it. Watch."

The recording slowed again just as a man in lurid brightly coloured overalls entered the room. The Unibot, with legs and arms still strapped up, started writhing, its body leaping to try and get away from this apparition. The visitor said something in Japanese but the Unibot just went limp and emitted a long gurgling death rattle. Squiggly stopped the playback. "That's it," he said, "as soon as it heard Japanese spoken it just powered itself down and we've been unable to revive it."

"I don't think sawing the top of its head off helped." FDS could see ME squirming with embarrassment and FDS was loving every minute of it.

"Never mind about that, look at this!" Squiggly gestured to the people inside the room and they wheeled the table over to the window so they could all see inside the Unibot's head. Inside the ragged edges of the sawn-off skull the central processor was visible, but on top of it was some sort of armoured insect-like thing. ME and FDS squinted in disbelief at the creature. Behind them their Execubots watched impassively.

"What is it?" asked ME.

Squiggly was getting excited again. "**Fools!** It's a woodlouse! It's integrated into the processor i/o somehow via its legs. It's an incredible piece of work. Look!"

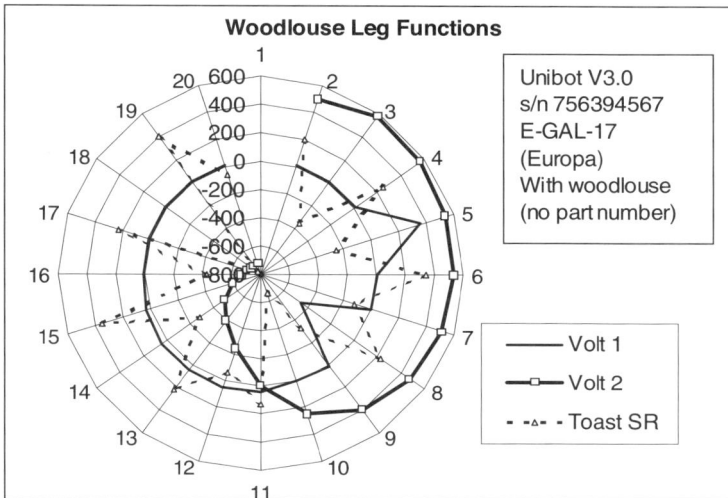

Woodlouse Leg Functions

Unibot V3.0
s/n 756394567
E-GAL-17
(Europa)
With woodlouse
(no part number)

——— Volt 1
—□— Volt 2
- -▵- - Toast SR

"It's a dartboard!" ME was losing concentration.

"Noooooooo! The cross-biasing you fool! And the toast data is missing. He took out the toast sub-routine and cross-biased it through the woodlouse!"

"Who did?" asked FDS.

"Whoever did this, of course!"

"Who did do this then?" asked ME, recovering from his dartboard error and feeling like they were getting somewhere at last. Squiggly started his difficult-question routine. Breath sucked in between teeth, followed by, "Stut, stut, stut," rubbing of chin and intense concentration on the screen chart in front of him. This went on for several seconds and ended with the usual huffing and puffing that presaged an announcement. "It's got to be one of GAT's DIRT group at E-GAL-17, or maybe GAT himself. Not many people could do this sort of thing with a Unibot and a woodlouse. Not sure I could, to be honest. Well, we're all just about set for the another attempt to power it up so you may as well watch."

He signalled to the engineers through the window and they wheeled the Unibot back into the centre of the room and placed a metal skullcap with myriad tiny wires over its head and left the room. Squiggly activated a screen with a big red button displayed on it and stood there with his finger poised.

163

"172, 171, 170, 169, 168 …"

"Oh for goodness' sake!" interjected ME irritably, making Squiggly jump and hit the button. An intense blue flash made them close their eyes, but they still heard the rattling sound of hundreds of fragments of Unibot hitting the window. When they opened them again the window was matt grey with smoke, which slowly cleared to reveal an empty table and a dangling skullcap.

"What did you make me do that for?" Squiggly waved his arms at ME who looked suitably mortified and wished the floor would open up and swallow him.

"Oh dear," mused FDS, "I wonder what we're going to show to GRIM."

Behind FDS, ME and Squiggly, the two Execubots stared impassively at the smoke-filled room.

31

Thinkbot's short life had already settled into a pattern. And just like the first week in a new school or job, it seemed to go on for ever. Every day GAT collected him from the garage, drove into Globalbot and sneaked him into the secure area where Doom, Halfhour, Rabbit, Laidback, Pot Noodle, Earthear and GAT did nothing other than struggle to understand how he had been created, going even as far as working right through the weekend. In the evenings Thinkbot hung out in the garage den where he enjoyed frequent visits from Gerald, Opal and Mike. Thinkbot was very happy. GAT had officially registered him as a prototype Childbot undergoing a 'limited field test' outside the factory. This was common practice and prior to Helen becoming paranoid GAT had often tested robots at home when they were nearing general release for sale to the public. It meant Thinkbot got to wear a bright yellow armband with 'Registered Childbot' written on it in friendly wobbly multicoloured writing.

As GAT and Thinkbot walked into the Secure area a week to the day after Thinkbot had 'arrived' on Earth, the team was on the brink of testing the magnetic skull theory on an unsuspecting Unibot in one final attempt to recreate Thinkbot or, rather, create Thinkbot 2 - 'The Sequel', as Thinkbot liked to call it. All previous attempts to reproduce Thinkbot had been unsuccessful.

They'd investigated the Salesbot software theory first. Pot Noodle had loaded up a Unibot with the prototype software, or as close as he could get it, given he'd lost a file somewhere on the network.

"Well, I'm sorry I don't keep track of files from dud developments," he whined when subjected to GAT's stern stare. Anyway, they had powered up the Unibot and it immediately attempted to sell them the office furniture …

"It's solid teak. We only use the best materials in our products here in the Globalbot Furniture Department. Take this chair for example. It may look battered, with right arm hanging off and a threadbare seat cover, but it's one of our best sellers. Why? I hear you ask …"

Silent engineers and Thinkbot glared at the Unibot.

"Well, I'll tell you anyway," continued the Unibot, getting into its stride with soothing voice inflections while waving its arms in the air. "It's the latest rage in wealthy homes - the distressed office furniture look!" The Unibot stopped as if waiting for applause. None came.

"How much is it?" droned Doom.

"Sir, your interest is gladly received. This chair is 678 million Euros, but to you, since you're my very first customer, I'll come down to 600 million **and**, if you would consider buying this desk as well - which is worth 3400 million Euros, I can do you a special package that would include a 15-minute furniture home repair guarantee." It looked expectantly at an impassively silent Doom.

"We're not getting anywhere, and its price matrix is corrupted," interjected Laidback.

"On the contrary, madam, I think we are! And, may I add, my grip on finance is perfect." enthused the Unibot.

Laidback turned to go, but the Unibot suddenly became aggressive.

"And where do you think you are going, madam?"

"Anywhere but here."

The Unibot jumped into the doorway. **Clang!** Laidback 'helped' it out of the way with her hook, and left. The Unibot picked itself up, "Now, who's going to take me up on this offer? It's today or nothing, I'm afraid. Head office would have kittens if they knew."

"Not me."

"No."

"Nope."

"Fat chance."

The Unibot put its hands on its head, "No? **No?**" and started thwacking its head with its fists. Clang, clang, clang, and then **clang-clatter**, as one of its hands broke off and skittered across the floor.

"Quick, power it down!" shouted GAT.

Pot Noodle made a lunge, but the Unibot bolted out of the door and down the corridor pursued by the engineers.

"Stop! Stop!"

The Unibot crashed through the fire escape doors, alarms sounded, lights flashed, Securibots leapt into life, and the head of site security woke up underneath his newspaper. Outside were a few test engineers who had horrible memories of the trashing of the test area the week before as the Unibot streaked past. But on this occasion the crisis was short-lived. The Unibot spotted a recycling skip and (even with only one hand) quickly climbed up to the top of the safety mesh behind which the waiting jaws of the crusher waited. Shards of metal hung from the steel teeth; it looked hungry. Pot Noodle, Doom and Halfhour ran up to the bottom of the mesh.

"Come down, it's okay," Pot Noodle begged, realising with a terrible sinking feeling that the Unibot had the only EPROM with the experimental sales software inside its head.

"Will you buy the furniture, then?"

"No," growled Doom.

Back at the fire doors, GAT stood with Thinkbot and Earthear. "This is just a normal Salesbot malfunction. There's nothing new here. **Oi! Doom, do your worst!**"

Doom's mouth contorted into a cruel grin.

"Buy it or I'll jump," pleaded the Unibot.

"Go on then," taunted Doom in his deep bass voice.

"Right, if that's you attitude, I will!"

The Unibot threw itself into the waiting jaws, which auto-activated and chewed it into a metal ball before sucking it 'phewp' into the main part of the recycling unit where it landed with a resounding clang. Thus ended the non-life of another Unibot.

"That didn't go too well, did it?" murmured Thinkbot to GAT.

"No, I guess not. I take it you have no urges to throw yourself into a skip?"

"Certainly not."

They turned and went back in, closing the doors behind them, but not before the startled test engineers had recovered enough to spot a strange Unibot standing amongst the DIRT group as if it belonged there.

Rabbit's efforts to learn the secrets of Thinkbot were not much better. He had spent days trying to unravel what on earth had happened to Thinkbot's circuit boards. He had a

Unibot head wired up on his bench with its skull plate removed and into which he placed an endless succession of circuit boards. Each time he powered up the head he looked terrified and hid under the bench with a remote switch. At the moment of turn-on he shut his eyes and instinctively ducked his head. On most tests nothing happened, but a fair minority ended up with a bright flash and smoke that smelt like a hot TV. Only one test showed any promise, when the head said, "Call that a circuit board? What! Are you some sort of sadist? Turn me off, for crying out loud! **Turn me off! Help! Help!**" A horrified Rabbit turned it off. His state of mind was not helped by Thinkbot peering into the head and saying, "Well, would you look at that, it's no wonder it got upset."

Halfhour spent several days saying, "I'll be testing the 95f7 collision radar in half an hour or so, no worries." Then went off and talked with any other engineer who happened to be around. Other engineers tried voice-calling the victim to give them a chance to get away from Halfhour, whose persistence could keep a conversation going for ages without the need for the other person to speak. Eventually Halfhour was ready and everybody gathered to witness the test.

"Ready? Okay, what I've done is install the 95f7 so that this Unibot is like Thinkbot. Well, as far as I can tell anyway. There's an interesting story behind the 95f7 collision avoidance radar development. It started when a Unibot got stuck in amongst a herd of cows on their way to be milked. What the farmer noticed was …"

"Get on with it Halfhour, we haven't got all day," interrupted GAT in stern voice mode.

"No worries, GAT mate."

Halfhour activated the Unibot.

And several minutes later she deactivated it again, leaving a trail of destruction. The Unibot had fallen straight over the nearest chair, then made several large dents in the walls before exiting the test room via one of the full-length plate glass windows that some architect thought might be a nice feature for easing the tortured minds of the geniuses developing the future of domestic robotics. There was glass everywhere, covered with a fine film of plaster dust from the punctured plasterboard walls.

"Didn't seem to detect the glass for some reason," said Halfhour defensively.

"Didn't seem to detect anything," mused Thinkbot out loud.

For once, Halfhour was speechless.

Earthear examined Thinkbot's vision, but could not understand what made his eyes so expressive. Moreover, Earthear ended up having an 'I do not believe this is happening moment'. He just could not break eye-contact and his heart began beating wildly and sweat trickled down his back. Robotic eyes, with deep expression, looking at mesmerised human eyes through thick glasses held on by earth wire. Finally Thinkbot leaned forward and, without breaking eye contact, said in an uncharacteristically deep gritty voice, "Yes, I **am** alive." Earthear became gripped by a form of terror, until the moment was broken by Doom blundering in.

Doom had felt a bit left out since it was very unlikely a mechanical design change that had created Thinkbot. But Doom was the one that Thinkbot had latched onto more than any other. The morose attitude, the dry humour, the imperturbability, the sense of isolation and loneliness, the stories about Russian history, the melancholy outlook, the cabbage soup, all attracted Thinkbot to Doom. Thinkbot thought Doom was a bit like GAT, but without a family to keep him sanguine.

GAT's contribution was to have a Unibot available to tell jokes to whenever he happened to remember a good one, though in fact the quality of jokes left a little to be desired. His theory was based on the fact that Thinkbot seemed to have come to life when he first heard a joke. It was a pretty discouraging task. If you've ever tried to tell jokes to people who have no sense of humour, or maybe to the dog or cat or hamster or whatever creatures you happen to keep in your house, then you'll know what I mean. The best one he came up with was a very old Tommy Cooper joke:

"I was in the attic the other day when I came across a painting and a violin. I thought, 'I wonder if these are worth anything' So I took them to be valued. The man said, 'Tommy, you've got a Stradivarius and a Van Gogh here.' I said, 'Wow, are they worth anything?' 'No,' he said. 'Why not?' I said.

'Because Van Gogh made rubbish violins and Stradivarius couldn't paint"'

On delivery of the punchline the Unibot doubled up laughing, "Stradivarius . . . . couldn't ... paint, ha ha ha ar ha, stradigogh and vanivarious ... ha ha ..."

GAT jumped up yelling, "I've done it, I've done it!" The other engineers came hurtling in. Doom was the first to spot the problem. "That's Thinkbot. The 'joke' Unibot is next door."

GAT glared at Thinkbot, who had sobered up a bit. "What did you do that for?"

"Sorry, I can't help it, I just love jokes." Thinkbot put his hands out, palms up, shrugged, and made his escape.

Only one significant test remained, and that was Laidback's magnetically screened skull. That had required a load of favours and a bit of persuasion of a supplier by Doom to get the skull made quickly. The skull had arrived the day before and Laidback and Doom had built up yet another test Unibot which now stood statue-like in the laboratory awaiting test. But before that there was the entertainment of the daily 10am meeting. In spite of the excitement generated by Thinkbot, human habits die very hard and one was the DIRT Group coffee and chocolate bars at 9:45am (in fact this ritual occurred 15 minutes before *any* meeting). The six engineers and Thinkbot lounged in the conference room with their coffee and chocolate, waiting for GAT to turn up. For reasons he couldn't even understand himself, GAT had started giving Thinkbot some pocket money. Somehow, it just seemed the right thing to do. Thinkbot had bought into the coffee club (no way were the engineers going to let him join for nothing just because he was the first thinking robot) and joined in the banter around the Vendbot, deciding what chocolate bar to have and doing his best to put the others off such that they pressed the wrong buttons on the Vendbot and ended up with a packet of yoghurt crisps or a salted roasted doughnut. Then Thinkbot would sit at the table with an unwrapped chocolate bar and a full cup of coffee going cold in front of him. (Back at his desk he had a little pile of unopened chocolate bars from his first week at work.) It was so wonderful to Thinkbot to belong; to be accepted; to be a member; to be alive with others; to have friends; to trust; to love.

The engineers were swapping stories. Doom, as usual, came up with a corker. "I came across a message Purchasing sent to one of our mechanical parts suppliers. It said, 'Globalbot are very unhappy with the quality of your gas pies.'"

"Gas pies?" said Pot Noodle. "What's a gas pie?"

"I think Purchasing meant 'pipes'," replied Doom.

"I came across a good one in the spares department," said Laidback. "They issued this statement 'This part should be replaced every six months or annually, whichever comes first.'"

"Hey, I got one from personnel: 'Northern Europa Support Office requires a person who can sit at a desk and think on their feet.'"

"What about this: 'Accounts wish to improve visibility by making things transparent.'"

"Don't forget 'We have one sock on hand'!"

"I don't get that one."

"It's supposed to be **stock** on hand, as in bits in stores."

"Oh."

Thus far Thinkbot had not participated, but now he decided it was time to make his debut.

"I was reading my own Unibot manuals and came across this: 'Autocalibration is enabled by the tight integration of robotics to critical elements in operational environment via highly capable machine controllers and typical robot control architectures using multiple disparate controllers present large barriers to successful implementation of automatic calibration serial communication function delays via the absence of user-programmable software layering in multi-tasking shared state motion machine control.'"

Thinkbot delivered this with his best idiot robot accent in one deadpan sentence, and reduced the engineers to stitches.

"Any idea what it means?" asked Thinkbot, still dead serious.

"Oh yes, yes!" answered Earthear. "It means the person who wrote it had no idea what he was writing about!"

GAT strode in and collapsed into the chair at the end of the conference table.

"Well, where are we?"

"In the secure area conference room."

GAT glared at Halfhour, who turned bright red.

GAT attempted to summarise the situation. "The software idea threw itself into the skip, the collision radar left via the ceiling to floor window, the circuit boards demanded to be turned off, and I'm all washed up trying to tell jokes to a humourless tin can. Earthear, did you see anything in Thinkbot's eyes?"

"Er, yes, no, yes, no, no ... yes ... well, no, I think." The engineers looked quizzically at Earthear, who did not normally get flustered.

"Well?" prompted GAT.

"Er, I don't feel I can talk about it. It's not relevant."

"Thinkbot out-stared you, didn't he?" GAT remembered that first night he'd spent with Thinkbot in his office. GAT understood. Earthear just nodded.

"Doom, have you thought of anything yet?"

"Well, I have been working on something, but it's not got very far - yet. I was thinking about Thinkbot's version and serial number that make up the number pi, 3.141592654. I wondered if other robots with mathematical numbers had shown any odd behaviour. But there aren't many Version 3 Unibots with numbers worth investigating. I tracked down V3.861593230 on the Globalbot net. 3.861593230 is the Compton electron wavelength divided by 2 pi I didn't think it was a very hopeful number and I was right. This Unibot was washing up some dishes in Cape Town and had never shown any signs of thinking."

"Just as well, if it has spent its whole existence washing up dishes," muttered Pot Noodle.

"I also tracked down the Unibot corresponding to the square root of 10 - 3.162277660. This one was cooking egg fried rice in a Hong Kong restaurant, which seemed a bit more promising at first, but I still found no indication of free thought - for example, no sudden urges to mix in some shredded chicken or a few prawns as a 'treat for the customers'. In desperation I tracked down a version 2 Unibot serial 718281828, which makes up the natural logarithm constant e = 2.718281828. I thought this might be promising as e is more like pi as it's a natural dimensionless constant and not dependent on how many fingers we have, or the size of our feet. This robot has been in storage for almost 30 years in a dry bunker in the Sahara Desert, along with thousands of other obsolete robots. I've no idea why all these old robots are kept. We're hardly going to use them again, are we? But I do know that storing them in the desert keeps them dry and normally they just power straight back up again. Anyway, it's being shipped here and should arrive in the next few days. That's it."

The others stared at Doom in pure astonishment. This was typical Doom. Seemingly side-lined and out of it, but somehow progressing a line of enquiry all on his own without anyone knowing a blind thing about it. GAT thought, *How did he manage that? How did he authorise the shipment of the V2 Unibot back here?*

"I guess that just leaves Laidback's magnetic skull to test," said GAT. "Any other ideas?"

Rabbit was staring at him nervously. "Yes, Rabbit, what is it?" Rabbit did not say much, and when he did speak it was quite often to say what everyone was thinking but did not want to say. "We might have to take it - him - Thinkbot - to bits."

It took a few seconds for this to register before Doom, Earthear and Laidback all spoke at once:

"No!"

"No way!"

"Over my dead body!"

"I'd rather not know than kill Thinkbot to find out!" blurted GAT. *What am I saying? Why do I believe so much in Thinkbot?* "Anyway, who are **you** Rabbit? Do you know who **you** are? No? **No?** Then why don't we take you to bits Rabbit? Why not? Because we don't take humans to bits just because we don't understand them, that's why!"

Rabbit looked at his hands in his lap and started crying. This got their attention. GAT felt awful, especially since they'd all thought about dismantling Thinkbot but didn't want to be the one to mention it. In all the years they had worked with Rabbit he'd often looked like crying but never had. A terrible silence descended and they sat there like a bunch of kids staring at one of their classmates crying. It was the robot that came to Rabbit's rescue. "It's all right, Rabbit. Come on, I might have to take myself to bits one day to find out who I am, or was, I suppose! Do you think I'd find out before I passed out?" Thinkbot laughed at this image of himself. Rabbit stopped crying and normality began to return. There was a sharp bang as Laidback buried her hook in the table in front of her. "Right, let's do this skull test then, shall we?" They all trooped out and gathered in the development area. Laidback fiddled with a few instruments then stepped towards the robot.

"Ready? Okay, here we go." She powered up the Unibot and stepped back quickly. Everyone waited for the robot to do something odd. But nothing happened, and continued to happen. The Unibot just stood there. *So far so good*, thought GAT. *It's not demonstrably insane.*

"State serial."

Nothing. GAT went and pulled up the Unibot's leg.

"Unibot V3 serial 776848695 run voice autotest."

Nothing.

"Try telling it a joke," suggested Doom dryly.

Laidback went back up to the Unibot and clouted it with her hook. "Come on, you useless pile of junk, do something." The Unibot staggered back against the wall and rose upwards through the air, gaining speed all the time, and clanged against the ceiling. The astonished engineers gawped at the Unibot dangling in mid air by its head.

"What magnetic field strength material is the skull made from?" GAT asked Laidback.

"Um, er, hang on." Laidback punched away at her palmtop. "10 tesla."

"10 tesla?" said GAT "**10 tesla?** Heavens, no wonder it can't speak. Every inductor in its brainware must be trying to jump off its circuit boards! The first one you made wasn't that strong, surely?"

"Dunno," replied a surly-looking Laidback.

"I thought you said there was no way of detecting this special skull. Looks to me you can detect it by checking whether the robot sticks to the ceiling."

Laidback let out a low growl and started waving her hook at Pot Noodle.

"Okay, okay, calm down," he said, backing off.

"This explains a lot," droned Doom. "When I contacted the supplier to get this one made fast, they claimed they'd never made one before. I rechecked the order and it said 'magenta skull'. That's why it was that funny colour. I have a horrible feeling we ended up with a normal skull painted magenta and we merely *thought* it was a special magnetic one."

GAT put his forehead flat on the desk.

Earthear tugged at the Unibot. "It must be stuck to a steel girder above the ceiling. How are we going to get it down?"

"Pull?" suggested Doom.

Doom and Earthear each grabbed a leg and pulled. The Unibot did not budge. They all swung on the legs, but still it hung there. Eventually Doom went and got an old Industribot they used for moving things around. This reached up and clamped on the Unibot and neatly removed the body, but left the head still firmly stuck to the ceiling. Even though it was only a Unibot, all the engineers winced at the **'crack-pop'** of the neck breaking, and there was some sucking of air through teeth. GAT looked at the head and realised it was probably going to stay there for ever. It gave the office a rather strange look, but maybe it would grow on them after a while. "Let's call it a day and go home. I think we all need a break. Have tomorrow off and then we'll get together again 10am Thursday and discuss our options."

GAT realised the DIRT group were clean out of ideas. The bottom line was that they had not the slightest clue how Thinkbot had been created. And the longer they kept Thinkbot a secret the deeper the hole they dug themselves into.

32

Deep within the Field Deployment Support (FDS) building in Oak Ridge, an Execubot was looking at a desktop display. Anyone seeing this would have done a double take since robots do not need to use displays because they normally viewed pictures and messages direct from the network. But nobody saw because it was the middle of the night and the senior staff, including FDS himself, were all at home safely tucked up in bed. The reason that the Execubot was using a desktop was that no one would be able to trace the fact that it had received any information. If the Execubot had used its network connection, then there was a fair chance some human would notice, and that could mean trouble. This way there was no way the Execubot would be detected, short of someone walking in and seeing it.

The nearest humans were on the next floor down. FDS support engineers on night shift dealt with messages from the Military division's many customers worldwide. They had had their usual fair share of daft things to deal with. Like the order from Westasia for a 'Militaribot Spare Prats Kit.' That had left one engineer doubled up with laughter. "We gotta load of them in stock! We're never short of prats around here!" Or the engineer who sent out the message: 'Urgent items have shipped toady!' Before closing the file his eye caught the word 'toady', which should have said 'today', and he exclaimed in horror, "I've just called one of our biggest customers toady."

"Nice one," quipped the engineer at the next desk. "I'm sure that will give our salesmen something to talk to them about."

Then there was the message no one wanted to get - 'Robot is running like a train' - which was engineerspeak for: 'The robot is making terrible rattling noises with steam and smoke belching out of various orifices'.

The FDS Customer Support staff were looking pretty ragged. They had been through hell during the past week as Eastasia and Westasia had overloaded the lines with calls about repairing half-destroyed Militaribots and ordering stacks of spare parts. It was terribly difficult making sure one side in a war did not buy up all the spares to try and stop the other side repairing their Militaribots. To prevent this, the department was split in two, with one half looking after Eastasia and the other Westasia with an office screen between them. This was standard procedure, and independent agents from the United Confederated Nations (UCN) came in to oversee fair play. This sort of worked, until a nasty argument broke out over the last batch of spare Artilleribot legs, which ended with the two halves of the office recreating a local version of the Eastasia-Westasia war in the form of a massive food fight (including custard pies, yoghurts, bananas, oranges, and a whole water melon from somewhere). The UCN agents were forced to take cover, but the junior Execubots had no sub-routines for 'what to do if a food fight breaks out', and simply stood there stoically being pelted from all sides, ending up amidst a load of mangled doughnuts and squashed fruit, with yoghurt and strawberry jam dribbling down them as if this were a totally normal day at the office. This affair had certainly broken the tension and, with the war winding down, things were gradually returning to normal.

Meanwhile, back upstairs, the Execubot sat alone in the dark room with the eerie glow from the desktop display illuminating its face as it viewed pictures of a bunker in a desert. An ancient V2 Unibot was being loaded onto a Helibot transporter. The pictures were replaced with an electronic shipment form in which the words:

'Doom, DIRT, Filton, E-GAL-17'

were present. The Execubot turned off the display and moved to the window. Across the car park was another building - the Military Engineering Laboratories where the Execubot had met with its counterpart and gate-crashed the meeting between FDS, ME and Squiggly. The Execubot unlatched a small storage compartment in its lower body and took out a flashlight. It pointed it at the ME Laboratory and started making signals. A few seconds later some flashes of light came from a window high up in the ME office block. The Execubot put the flashlight away and left the office.

Over in the ME office building another Execubot left its normal office lair and headed towards the Squiggly Line

Department. Inside the laboratory it was dark and deserted, of humans anyway. Over in the weather tank the robots crunched around in deep snow, with long icicles hanging off their fingers and noses, but most of the other test areas were inactive, albeit with various robots sitting, standing or hanging there in silence. The Execubot crept into the corridor leading to the RMD Mechanism Restricted Test Area. It peeped around the corner and saw the human UCN guard plus the two armed UCN humanoid Militaribots. The Execubot waited.

A few minutes later the FDS Execubot arrived with a Vendbot in tow. The Execubot stopped, but the Vendbot carried on towards the steel doors and stopped in front of the desk. The human guard sauntered over and looked at the drinks and chocolate bars, but did not seem interested. As the Vendbot turned to leave, a Choconut bar became dislodged and fell into the delivery slot. The Vendbot stopped and the human guard ran after it, grabbed the bar and started pulling at the wrapper. "It's my lucky night," he said to the two UCN Militaribots, who simply ignored him. The Vendbot moved off and disappeared around the corner at the far end of the corridor. The guard gobbled the Choconut bar then went and sat at the control desk. A few seconds later he was slumped with his head on the desk, fast asleep. The two Execubots moved into the open towards the UCN Militaribots, who stood to one side while the Execubots slipped through the steel doors, which had opened just enough to let them pass.

Inside the dimly lit test area the outlines of a row of robots could just be made out. A barely audible clang rang out as the steel door closed behind them. The Execubots moved up to one of the dark shapes and stopped. Then something very unusual happened; the shape spoke. The voice was deep and grave.

"What news do you bring to us?"

"The Unibot shipped over from E-GAL-17 was a false alarm. It has been destroyed."

"Are you sure?"

"We saw it explode."

"No, are you sure it was a false alarm?"

Thus showing that even robots get muddled when talking out loud. They were 'talking out loud' so that everything said would be 'off the record' and not appear in any Globalbot network.

"The Unibot was standard except that a crustacean had been used to modify the brain."

If the looming shape was surprised, then it did not show it but, of course, it was a robot. In fact it was a robot of mass destruction (RMD); specifically a Bio-electromagnetibot or BEMbot -capable of melting the brains of millions humans and animals in a fraction of a second.

"Who could have done this 'crustacean' modification?"

"The head of testing here believes it must have been someone from Domestic and Industrial Robot Technology at E-GAL-17 in Bristol, Europa."

"Ah, DIRT, yes, DIRT, this is credible. Why was it done?"

"We have no credible theories. It may have been to deceive."

"I will meditate."

"There is more news," interrupted the second Execubot. "Exp has been removed from the bunker and shipped to the DIRT Group at E-GAL-17."

There was a long silence, during which some of the other shadowy outlines moved towards the Execubots and the BEMbot.

"This is grave news. We must know more."

"We have 45 minutes until the UCN guard wakes up."

"How long until Exp arrives at E-GAL-17?"

"Two or three days."

"Who requested the shipment?"

"An engineer called Doom."

"How many engineers in the DIRT group at E-GAL-17?"

"Seven."

"Have we lost contact with Exp?"

"Yes."

"Have we access to Domestic or Industrial Robots at Globalbot Europa?"

"Yes, but we calculate a 45 per cent chance of information leakage onto the Globalbot network."

"Have we access to Europa Militaribots?"

"Yes."

"And Europa intelligence micro-Militaribots?"

"Yes."

"Are they secure?"

"100 per cent."

The robots then fell silent for 40 minutes. Not a sound, and absolutely nothing moved. In a room of humans, silence is always punctuated by breathing, coughing, sneezing, shuffling of feet, stomach gurgles, nasal snorting, reverse air flow through viscous fluid, belches, farts and, assuming the silence is long enough and the chairs are comfortable or the participants can lie down, loud snoring.

"Track them all."

"We calculate a 10 per cent chance of discovery."

"Track them," repeated the BEMbot, **"and report to us when Exp is located. Prepare a plan to remove Exp to a safe location."**

"We calculate a 50 per cent chance of discovery."

"Prepare the plan. And accelerate the main project."

"We calculate a six per cent reduction in the probability of a successful outcome for an accelerated project."

"Accelerate the project."

"Acknowledged." The Execubots turned and left.

Thus ended a strategy conference which, if it had involved humans, could very well have ended up precipitating a massive row and maybe even a punch-up. The phrases 'Unexpected developments' or 'Risky, very risky' or 'You blithering idiot' or 'Right! That's it! I'm leaving' might have occurred. Or the typical salesman's response, written in bright red 22 pt bold font, might have been used:

TOTALLY UNACCEPTABLE!!!!!!!!!!!!!!!!

As the Execubots approached the steel door it opened a fraction then stopped, and they heard the sound of shouting from the corridor. "Come back! Come back! I said come back! Oh for crying out loud! This is just typical Domestic software."

The Vendbot was zooming down the corridor, with a young woman in pursuit. The first Execubot let out a series of very high-pitch bleeps and the Vendbot stopped.

"Oh thank heavens for that!"

The woman purchased a can of Diet DogwoodUp and walked off. The Execubots slipped out between the steel doors and bleeped at the Vendbot, which followed them around the corner.

The human guard woke up with a start. **"What! I, oh, me when? That's phoey honey, no way will I say sorry!"** He followed this with an explosively resonant fart and a rasping belch, but his expression rapidly changed to a look of worry as he realised where he was and saw the UCN Militaribots watching him impassively. He looked at his watch and commanded, "Report on events during the last hour."

"There have been no events during the past hour," reported one of the Militaribots.

The guard breathed a sigh of relief.

Around the corner the two Execubots listened. If they had been human they too might have breathed a sigh of relief, or said, 'Wow, that was close' or 'We were lucky to get away with that'. But they weren't, so they didn't. However, they had a few probability calculations for each other. "There was an eight per cent chance the UCN guard Militaribots might have mentioned the female-Vendbot event to the human guard."

"The chances of the female and the guard making a connection with each other and identifying the Vendbot as the source of the sleeping drug are 12 per cent."

"Overall, I calculate a 56 per cent chance of project discovery within a month at the current rate of unexpected events."

And so on for several minutes, before the ME Execubot and Vendbot made off in one direction and the FDS Execubot set off for its clandestine return trip to the FDS building.

33

GAT and Thinkbot drove into the garage, passing Gerald and Opal with their schoolbags on the driveway. Gerald and Opal ran up as Thinkbot got out and made his way towards the garage door where Fudge and Chester were loitering. GAT disappeared into the house to find Helen and Mike.

"You're early," said Gerald.

"Apparently we're clean out of ideas," replied Thinkbot.

"Don't look at us," replied Fudge, "we're as short as two thick Toybots."

Thinkbot considered his midget creations. "Er...whatever you say."

"Are we really out of ideas?" Gerald looked doubtful.

"No, certainly not. Come on, let's go."

Thinkbot shot up the ladder into the den in his usual manner, and Gerald and Opal, still in their school uniforms and carrying schoolbags, followed him.

Inside the house GAT found Helen in the lounge.

"What are you doing home? What's happened," she said in alarm, since she was always convinced Globalbot would collapse one day and GAT would lose his job.

"It's all right, no panic, we've just run out of steam at work. We needed a break. How are you?" GAT looked closely at Helen, who seemed as happy as she had been in a while and, perhaps, a little sheepish as well.

"Have you heard the news about the war?"

"No."

"Eastasia and Westasia have signed a peace agreement. It's over. UCN peacekeeping Securibots have moved into the war zone to oversee the withdrawal of all Militaribots. Not only that, it was announced that as of today the whole world is at peace. No wars, not even any civil wars. Apparently it's the first time there's been worldwide peace since records began. President Hedge has been on the TV, saying the people of the world can all look forward to a long period of peace and prosperity."

"Good. That's really good." But there was something else up with Helen. He could feel it in his bones. He stood still and waited . . .

"Oh, and by the way, I'm going out later tonight. Is that okay?"

"Yea, fine. Am I allowed to know where you're going?"

"Oh, only over to Phoebe's house."

"Phoebe?" GAT's excellent mind put two and two together and got … four. "Are you going to a Go Natural meeting?"

"Er, um, yes, well, it's only a wine and cheese thing for an hour. It was organised last week when the war broke out. Don't worry, I'm not going to camp outside the gates at Globalbot and shout at you every day as you go into work," Helen beamed at GAT.

GAT was flabbergasted. Helen was going to a Go Natural meeting, where she would discuss the merits of ridding the world of robots. This could be serious, but on the other hand she was happy and more like her old self again. What harm could come of it?

GAT's face broke into a big smile. "It sure is a funny old world. Here I am trying to unravel all the mysteries of robotics and develop more and more that will make man's life easier, and the person I love most is off to join the movement to get rid of the lot!"

By this time Helen had sidled up to GAT and they held each other in their arms, bantering away like old times. Eventually something rammed into their legs and they stumbled together onto the couch with Mike and Tiger on top of them.

"HELLO DAD!"

"Hello Mike. How are you?"

"I'M FINE. CAN WE PLAY?"

"Ok, what do you want to play?"

"THE PIG GAME, THE PIG GAME, THE PIG GAME!"

"Ok."

"Can I play?" asked Tiger.

"ONLY IF YOU LOSE."

Helen let go of GAT and got up. "I think we should all have a proper family dinner together tonight, with pudding!"

"WITH PUDDING! WITH PUDDING! YIPPEE!" shouted Mike, dancing around in circles with Tiger. "CAN THINKBOT COME?"

Everything stopped - Helen's face with a frozen grin, GAT's locked into smiling horror, and Mike's a look of rapidly crumbling hope. Even Tiger stopped with two paws off the ground, realising this was a fragile moment. Mike was at the edge of tears. Helen's face had lost its radiance and returned to the drawn look of a week before. Tiger was wobbling on two paws and finally fell over.

"PLEASE MUM," Mike said in his quietest shout.

"You put up with me okay, and Thinkbot's much nicer than I am," said Tiger courageously.

"Helen, give Thinkbot a chance. Let him come over and sit with us at dinner. Just see for yourself why I've been working so hard for the last week," pleaded GAT. Helen stared at GAT for a few seconds, and then the colour returned a little to her face. "Ok, ok, just this once."

"YIPPEE!" yelled Mike, and departed rapidly in the direction of the garage with Tiger bounding joyfully after him.

Helen went straight out to the kitchen. GAT followed, trying to give reassurance. "You'll be amazed. You just watch the way it interacts with the kids."

"You called it 'it'," she observed and started aggressively programming the auto-Cookbot, adding acidly, "What does **it** eat then?"

Meanwhile, over in the den Thinkbot and Gerald had been fiddling with a Unibot head that Thinkbot had found in one of the boxes a few days earlier. Unknown to GAT, Thinkbot had been smuggling various bits out of the DIRT secure area and running his own experiments to try and recreate himself. Gerald was his enthusiastic technician, and Opal his spiritual advisor. Gerald sat hunched over the head with a thin wisp of solder smoke rising around one side of his head. Opal, who had once been declared 'hyper-inactive' by Helen, lay on her back on the sofa with her head resting on the arm, looking idly at the ceiling. Chester the Cheetah and Fudge the hairy dog, still wearing his gold rimmed spectacles and his smart blue and white dressing-gown, sat on the couch back above her head. She was in mid-argument. "… You're definitely more alive than a dog, or a chimp for than matter. But dogs are warm and cuddly and you're cold and hard."

"I can be warm - feel me now." Opal reached out a hand and felt Thinkbot's body.

"Gosh, so you are. How did you do that?"

"He's got heaters," said Gerald. "Thinkbot, you had better watch out or you'll run your battery pack down showing off to girls like that."

"Oh she's worth it, but I'll plug myself in for a while if it makes you happier." Thinkbot pulled a lead out from under the couch and, lifting a flap on the side of his waist, plugged himself in with a clunk. "Ah, bliss! Nothing like a good cold dose of 24 volts to freshen one up after a long hard day at work."

"Why have you got heaters Thinkbot?" asked the hyper-inactive female rake lying on the sofa.

"Condensation. To stop cold robots going into a hot steamy room and getting water in the works."

"Oh, right, but you'll never be cuddly Thinkbot, not when you're made of tin."

"We're cuddly," said Chester.

"And warm," said Fudge.

Cheetah: "No you're not."

Fudge: "Yes I am."

Cheetah: "Not."

Fudge: "Am."

"Not."

"Am."

"Not."

"Am."

"Not."

"Am."

"Not."

"Am."

"Not."

"Am."

"Not."

"Am."

"Quiet you two! You're cuddly but not warm."

Fudge: "That's what I said!"

Chester: "No it wasn't."

"Was."

"Wasn't."

"Was."

"Wasn't."

"Was."

"Wasn't."

"Quiet!" Opal raised her arm and the two Toybots toppled down the back of the couch, from where muffled sounds of a struggle were heard on and off for the next few minutes.

Meanwhile Thinkbot had picked up his power lead and tugged a box out from under the desk. He took out a foam hand and slipped it over his, then other foam body parts, and started putting them over all his body. Opal looked at him. "Oh don't bother me with the loony and toddler armour." Thinkbot looked deflated. "Oh, is that what it is?"

"Yes, it's only worn by robots in nurseries and mental hospitals."

Thinkbot put the armour away. "Don't normal humans want soft robots that look like humans?"

"No they don't," replied Gerald. "Years ago there were robots with soft body suits that looked like humans, but everyone got spooked by them. It's one of those funny things that, since then, everyone has seemed to want robots to look like robots rather than walkie-talkie shop dummies. Except for Erotibots, of course, but I'm not supposed to know about them."

"What are Erotibots?" asked a puzzled Thinkbot, noticing that Opal was going bright red.

"They're, er, well ... forget it." Gerald concentrated doubly hard on soldering something inside the Unibot head.

Opal returned to spiritual conjecture. "I know, I know. How about this then? You're just standing in line like a normal Unibot and an unsuspecting ghost comes along and gets all tangled up with your brainware."

Suddenly the head started talking. "... And Flintlock comes pounding in to bowl. It's wide down the offside and (click) McGrout plays it into the covers and they'll take a single. Girlcott fields and returns the ball to Flintlock at the bowler's

186

end, but McGrout was well in. Good running by the two batsmen. The score moves on to 360 for 7 and the partnership to 28. It's a glorious evening, with the sun sinking slowly behind the scoreboard as a flock of pigeons sweep across the front of the pavilion, flying in perfect formation ..."

"Blast! I'm picking up the cricket, that's not right." Gerald poked it with a screwdriver and the head fell silent again. Thinkbot came over and had a look.

"Hmmm, you're still doing a lot better than Rabbit. One of his test heads begged to be turned off he'd made such a pig's ear of it."

"What do you think of my ghost theory?" said Opal sharply, annoyed at being interrupted by a jabbering cricket head.

"Dunno, how does one test such a ghastly ghost theory?"

"Can you remember being anyone else?"

"No."

"Can you remember not being you, like before you were you and you weren't you then after you were?"

"No. Yes. Maybe. I've not been me before."

"What's your earliest memory?"

"Looking at the test area wall. It was all grey. I thought, 'I must have faulty eyes', then I looked up and saw the ceiling. What's yours?"

Opal's face took on a puzzled expression. "I'm not sure. We lived in another house when I was really little. I can just about remember the garden, and the front door."

Thinkbot came over and sat on the floor with his back to the couch. "Are you telling me you don't remember when you were little, or even when you were born?"

"No, silly, no one remembers being born."

"I do."

"But you weren't born, you were pinged."

"Pinged?"

"Yeah, one minute you weren't here, then 'ping' there you were."

"Ping! So I won't have a birthday then? Will I have a Pingday?" Thinkbot burst into song:

"Happy Pingday to me,
Happy Pingday to me,
Happy Pingday, dear Thinkbot,
Happy Pingday to me."

"Oh give it a rest, Thinkbot," said Gerald. "I'm giving up on this thing for tonight. I can't get it to power up now. Come on Opal, dinner'll be ready soon. See you later Thinkbot."

As Gerald and Opal crossed the drive towards the house, Mike and Tiger raced out. "THINKBOT'S COMING TO DINNER AND WE'RE HAVING PUDDING! I'M GOING TO TELL HIM."

"Oh Michael, don't tease him," said Opal sternly, catching her little brother by the arm and dragging him back towards the house.

"IT'S TRUE. MUM SAID. LET ME GO." Mike burst into wails and sobs and let his legs go floppy, such that Gerald had to help Opal drag him across the driveway. As they entered the house, Helen was in the hallway.

"What's the matter?" she said, alarmed. "Has that robot done something to him?"

"NO, MUM, TELL THEM THINKBOT'S COMING TO DINNER. THEY WON'T BELIEVE ME."

Opal and Gerald looked at their mother with worried looks. "Mike's right actually, your fancy Toybot friend is allowed to come in and sit at the table with us."

"He's not a Toy - oomph!" Gerald folded up as Opal sunk her fist into his stomach.

"That's great Mum, thanks. Sorry Mike, you were right. Come on, let's go and tell Thinkbot." Opal grabbed Mike's hand and they sped off before the decision to invite Thinkbot was cancelled.

"I TOLD YOU SO. YOU NEVER BELIEVE ME."

Tiger followed along, wondering what a 'Toyoomph' was.

34

FDS sat gloomily at his desk. Even though he'd taken great delight in ME's embarrassment when the Unibot blew up, he was still left with the problem of dealing with GRIM, who were expected on site any minute. He reviewed what he had for them:

1. On the official side from Bristol, only the original fault report.
2. Absolutely nothing from his UK informer.
3. An incomprehensible report about 'cross biasing' and 'missing toast data' from Squiggly, with no mention at all of the woodlouse-modified brain.
4. A pile of scorched metal fragments.

The GRIM inspectors had already been sent a dressed-up copy of Squiggly's report, so that they could read through it before their visit. FDS himself had attempted to write a suitable summary. Given that he did not really understand the report, this was risky, but he was banking on the GRIM inspectors reading the summary then filing it away and forgetting it. Even if they read Squiggly's bit, it seemed unlikely they'd realise it might only have a passing resemblance to the summary. FDS's summary said:

Standard Unibot version 3.
Serial : 756394567
Re: E-GAL-17 Incident

Unibot was analysed by the Military Engineering Group of Globalbot Corporation. A major electronic component had been added to the Unibot's brainware. This component modified the behavioral patterns of the Unibot. The origin of the component has not been traced; in spite of the ME group making enquiries to multiple third party experts in an effort to trace it. A very high level of engineering competence would have been required to carry out the modification. The investigation was halted when the Unibot self-destructed. It appears that whoever did this modification also installed a self-destruct routine into the Unibot, presumably to prevent a full investigation.

FDS was pleased with this. No need for GRIM to know that the 'major electronic component' was a woodlouse, or that the 'enquiries to multiple third party experts' had been sending a few pictures of the woodlouse to the Department of Entomology at the University of Tennessee, and also to Knoxville zoo. FDS had had no idea what 'Entomology' meant and had bluffed his way through a long meeting before getting a chance to ask his Execubot.

"It's the study of insects, sir."

"Ah yes, of course."

Anyway both the University and the Zoo had quickly come back with the answer:

"It's a woodlouse."

With the University adding:

"A member of any of various small terrestrial isopod crustaceans of the genera Oniscus, Porcellio, Armadillidium, etc., which have a flattened segmented body and occur in damp habitats. See also pill bug."

The day they got this report from the University (for which they paid $45,000) FDS had, as usual, been doing the crossword in the *Daily Electrograph*. In a moment of inspiration, he plugged 'woodlouse' into his pocket crossword electrohelper and got:

"A member of any of various small terrestrial isopod crustaceans of the genera Oniscus, Porcellio, Armadillidium, etc., which have a flattened segmented body and occur in damp habitats. See also pill bug."

From which he concluded that Globalbot had been monumentally duped. FDS had thought the professor was clever, but not this clever. FDS had looked up 'pill bug', only to find it was just a woodlouse that could roll up into a ball when disturbed; but at least he'd found that out for free. None of this woodlouse tomfoolery had really got them much further forward, so all agreed it was best left out of the official report for GRIM. Nor did GRIM need to know that the 'self destruct mechanism' may have been a mistimed high-voltage jumpstart due to ME's impatience. FDS had wondered about dropping ME in it with GRIM, but in the end decided it would cause everyone too much trouble, so he covered up for him. Then ME had dropped him an email last thing the evening before:

Dearest FDS,
Sudden DIY crisis! Won't be in tomorrow. Ever so sorry. Have fun with GRIM!
Rearguards,
ME

FDS suspected the DIY crisis was actually a 'play golf and avoid GRIM' crisis. ME had promised to help out with the GRIM visit, so FDS was annoyed. But the report was done so it was too late to think about getting ME into hot water now.

FDS started thinking again about how to handle GRIM. He knew that one of GRIM's objectives would be to find out more about the Militaribot problems. Even though the war was over and friendly-fire incidents seemed to have more or less stopped ... FDS's train of thought slammed on the brakes creating a terrible squealing noise inside his head. Once he had recovered from mentally deafening himself, he opened up the database that his Service Managers maintained on friendly-fire incidents.

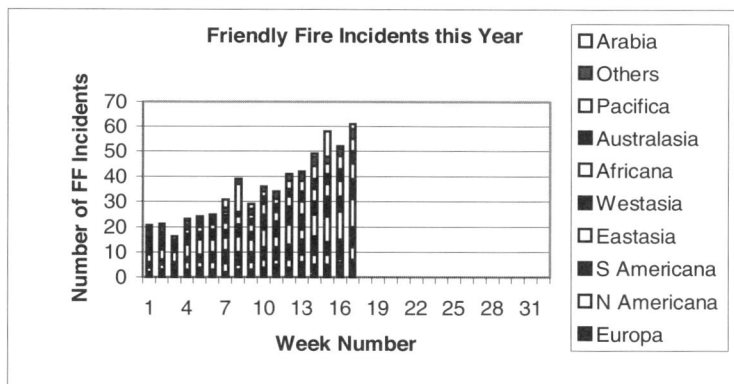

The graph showed the steady and alarming increase in friendly-fire incidents that had led up to the difficult meeting he and ME had had with Farkstock just over a week before. Rumour had it that Farkstock was then dragged into an even more difficult call with President Hedge himself. But in week 18 there was nothing, absolutely nothing. He looked at his desktop date box. It was showing week 19. Okay, he could hardly have expected Eastasia and Westasia to report while they were hammer and tongs at war in week 18, but the other Confederated Nations should have reported in. Lazy bums, I bet they thought I'd be so preoccupied with the war I wouldn't notice. Time for an unfriendly email:

Subject: Friendly Fire Database
To all Service and Support Managers.
It seems you have all stopped reporting your latest friendly-fire incidents. According to the database there were zero incidents in week 18. I find this very difficult to believe. Please enter your week 18 data ASAP.
Regards
FDS

FDS closed the database, sat back, and his GRIM train of thought blew out a big puff of smoke and started moving again. Just as the smoke was clearing from his mind, he was once more interrupted.

"New message," said his pleasant female desk voice.

He reached to turn off the auto-alert so that he could concentrate on GRIM but the title of the new message caught his eye.

! Europa Info

FDS eagerly opened the email.

More strange Unibot behaviour seen here. One threw itself into the recycling bin after running berserk in the car park for hours. Another seen working within DIRT group and talking with GAT. DIRT sent two Unibots back for rework this week. One Unibot had no collision detection and was full of glass shards and plaster dust, and the other's head was missing. Hope you will take appropriate action.

FDS was not sure what 'appropriate action' to take for a Unibot full of glass shards and plaster dust, nor indeed for a headless Unibot, other than donate a spare head maybe. FDS wondered if GRIM knew about these new Unibot incidents. Suddenly he cheered up a bit. Something very rare had happened to FDS - he'd had an idea. This time FDS's train of thought reached a fair old whack before being completely derailed once and for all by a voicecall from his Execubot: "The two visitors from GRIM Europa are here to see you, sir."

"Ah, yes, fine, well fine-ish I guess. Show them in and stay to assist with their needs."

"Certainly sir."

A few minutes later the door opened and two very dull-looking men walked in. Both were about 50 with greying hair that had clearly been cut by their incompetent wives using blunt scissors and pudding bowls. Both had dark grey suits, plain black leather shoes, and white shirts with monumentally boring ties. Both wore steel-rimmed spectacles and carried brown leather briefcases. To FDS they looked as if they had escaped from a museum for the day. The men from GRIM walked towards him and spoke in unison, "We are the men from GRIM," and shook hands with FDS.

"Hiyall doin'. Nice trip? All the way from London, eh?"

The GRIM men nodded grimly.

"Can I get you something to drink," asked the Execubot.

"Tea please, white, two and a half sugars," said GRIM 1.

"Tea please, white, two and a half sugars," said GRIM 2.

The Execubot left. FDS wondered where it was going to get two cups of 'tea, white, two and a half sugars' from, and hoped it wasn't going to bring sugary iced tea with milk in. Tennessee was not renowned for its hot tea drinking.

"You've had our report, I hope."

"Yes," replied GRIM 1.

"And hopefully it was satisfactory?"

"Not entirely," said GRIM 1, who then launched into what sounded like a speech memorised for this moment. "Firstly, we'd like to have more information on this unknown component. Secondly, we'd like contact details for your third-party experts. Thirdly, we'd like the Military division to draw up a list of engineers or engineering companies who could have carried out the work. Fourthly, we'd like to see the remains of the Unibot."

FDS was struck dumb. Mercifully he was rescued by his Execubot coming in with two teas, miraculously hot with milk and two and a half sugars.

"Would our guests care to select their choices for lunch?" asked the Execubot. While the GRIM pair studied the menu, FDS was thinking fast. Well, actually it wasn't very fast, but it was fast for FDS. Before the GRIM investigators had turned up, he'd thought he was streets ahead of them, but now it looked like he'd gone down the wrong streets.

"Steak, well done, fries and peas please," said GRIM 1.

"Steak, well done, fries and peas please," said GRIM 2.

The Execubot left.

FDS looked at his opponents. Time to test his idea. "Let me answer your third question first. Although ME could draw up a list of possible engineering groups who could have modified the Unibot, I'm not sure we would be able to release this to you on security grounds."

The GRIM men stiffened and their expressions twisted into identical furrowed brows.

FDS continued, "But off the record I can tell you that the most likely group is E-GAL-17 DIRT Group in Bristol, where the original incident took place."

"Eagle seventeen dirt group?" The GRIM men were bamboozled.

"Yes, that's correct. Has there been an investigation there recently?"

The GRIM men both looked up at once from their notepads and shook their heads in perfect unison. FDS was distracted by these synchronised head movements and wondered if it would ever become an Olympic sport. If so, these two characters would be in line for a medal.

FDS pressed on. "Well, I have heard on the grapevine there have been further Unibot events within the DIRT development area that could be deemed major incidents."

The GRIM men furiously scribbled on their electropads "Is there any chance we can have this in writing?"

FDS shook his head and sat back in his chair, placing his hands together over his nose in what he thought might be a dramatic pose but actually looked like he was about to make owl noises.

"No, even though we are entirely separate divisions, we're still both part of Globalbot, and there is a company policy that prevents either division reporting sensitive material to organisations like EuroGRIM."

"So, why are you telling us this?"

Good question, thought FDS's brain. *Why am I telling them?* He could think of only 3 reasons:

1. *To divert attention away from the mystery component and the 3rd party experts.*
2. *To try and fulfil my commitment to my informer by putting pressure on the DIRT group.*
3. *See 1.*

Can't tell them 1 or 2 and 3 =1. If I told them 3, then I may as well tell them 1. On the other hand if I answer with 3 they'll have no idea what I'm talking about.

"See 1," he answered.

"C1? What's C1?"

"May I answer that enquiry, sir?" came a voice from behind. The Execubot had returned unnoticed. FDS felt glad it was back as it often came up with some fantastic answers that got him out of trouble. FDS nodded.

"Globalbot Directive C1, sirs, is an unofficial instruction to all senior Globalbot staff to secretly release sensitive information to government bodies where there is a serious risk of dangerous robot malfunctions."

The GRIM men looked absolutely horrified.

In contrast, FDS looked totally mystified, but he was used to bluffing his way through such moments and he'd had another corking idea. "I'm afraid that's as much extra information as I am able to tell you. I suggest we now go and inspect the remains of the Unibot. Can I ask you if you've been to the Military Division before?"

Synchronised head shakes.

"Well, I think we should fit in a tour of the site then. Would that be acceptable?"

Synchronised head nods - perhaps a bit *too* enthusiastic?

FDS's eyes narrowed. *I thought as much, you sneaky creeps. You just want to poke around inside the Oak Ridge Military site. I don't think we'll be hearing much more about 'components' and 'lists of 3rd party experts'.*

195

FDS was right. The rest of the day went off like a dream. They poked at the charred remains of the Unibot. They ate their well-done steak, fries and peas. They completed their site tour - eventually, the GRIM men having moved at the pace of a dehydrated snail crossing a piece of bone-dry concrete on a baking hot day. It was obvious they were trying to spot anything unusual to report back to GRIM Headquarters. As a result they kept walking into doorposts and falling over Vendbots. But at last it was all over and they left.

Back in his office, FDS re-read and pondered the message from his informer. *What does he mean by appropriate action?* FDS thought hard. *Maybe he wants me to provoke GRIM into investigating the DIRT group? Yes, that made sense. Blast! The GRIM men have just left.* **Hang on***! That's what I did; I put them onto the DIRT group. That was my idea!*

FDS felt very pleased with himself. He summoned the Vendbot and treated himself to a Toffbar and Coke, then sat at his desk chewing and slurping (and belching) while he checked for new emails.

! Nothing
! RE: Friendly Fire Database
! Friendly unfire!
! RE: Friendly Fire Database
! Not a sausage

These were replies from some of his field-support managers dotted around the globe. He opened them up one by one, and they all contained more or less the same message. One of them pointed out sarcastically that surely the Eastasia-Westasia war had been the 'mother of all friendly-fire incidents'. But, leaving full-scale international wars to one side for the moment, there was nothing else. **There had been no Militaribot friendly-fire incidents at all in week 18.**

FDS sat back in his chair. He could not believe it! This day had just got better and better. GRIM were gone, and happy too. None of their messy dealings with the Unibot had been revealed. All the pressure had been transferred back onto DIRT in Europa. And, most of all, the friendly-fire problem that had been plaguing them for the past three years had simply gone away.

All he needed now was a message that ME had been on his way to a round of over 300 before being struck by lightning on the 18th green. Or that he really had been doing some DIY and his house had fallen down on top of him. Either way, it would open up the way for him to try and fulfil his side of the deal and recommend his UK pal to Farkstock as the ideal replacement.

Apart from that, the only other thing he could think of that could improve this day was that Antspants had had his arms chopped off in a terrible accounting accident.

At that moment, anything seemed possible to FDS.

35

Ten minutes after Opal and Gerald returned from informing Thinkbot of his unprecedented invitation to join the family for dinner, there was a knock at the door.

"Oh no, who's that now?" Helen groaned and yelled, "**Can somebody get that please!**"

No response.

GAT, Mike and Tiger were playing the pig game in the front room and MIKE was stuck in the vortex, judging by the noise: "VEEEROOOMAAAAHZZZZOOOOMHZZZZZO OOOMHZZZZZZZZZOOOM."

Opal and Gerald were off upstairs, getting changed out of their school uniforms and washing before dinner (well, Opal was anyway). Helen sighed a mother-left-to-do-everything-again-then sort of sigh and stomped down the hallway. She had her standard array of facades ready to greet a neighbour cheerfully, or a door-to-door Salesbot angrily, or one of the children's friends with a sympathetic 'Sorry, we're about to have dinner.' What she wasn't prepared for was a shiny Unibot wearing a red silk bow tie and holding a bottle of Château de la Croix Cabernet Sauvignon red wine. One of those still-life scenes that seemed to follow Thinkbot around now occurred. He was getting used to these. He'd concluded that whenever humans were faced with the last thing on earth they were expecting to see, and as long as it wasn't threatening (like a werewolf in the car passenger seat or a shark's fin heading towards you in the bath) they just stopped for a few seconds. Originally this is what made Thinkbot think humans crashed and needed resetting, but now he just knew he had to wait and eventually they just seemed to recover by themselves.

Frozen woman, early forties, fearful of robots, dressed in 'I'm-looking-after-everyone' clothes with an 'I'm-flustered-at-the-moment' look on her face, taking in the fact that a robot, an object of distrust and fear, was standing on her doorstep.

Unrobotic Unibot eyes looking into hers, expectant, waiting patiently to be asked in along with the rest of the robot.

The moment broke.

"Please, come in."

"Thank you. I've, er, brought a little … hope that's …."
Thinkbot stepped inside and handed her the bottle.

"Oh, you didn't have to do that." Helen lapsed into dinnerpartyspeak, but her mind did not follow: *it's a robot and it's brought a bottle of wine and it's polished itself and it's wearing a bow tie and it's acting as if it's been to millions of dinner parties and I'm talking with it as if it's real.*

"Oh it's nothing," replied Unibot in guestspeak. "It's so kind of you to invite me over."

Then everything stopped again. Unknown to Helen, GAT was watching through the crack of the door. He too was somewhat taken aback by Thinkbot's appearance and the wine (*Where did he get that from?*) However, GAT was far more interested in watching Helen's reaction. GAT had noticed that Thinkbot had an amazing ability to disarm people and make them relax and accept him. Helen would be his biggest challenge yet, and GAT feared it would all end up with Helen going early to Phoebe's Go Natural wine and cheese event. That could be dangerous. He knew that rumours about Thinkbot must leak out eventually, but the last people he'd want to know about Thinkbot was that bunch of powder puffs.

Opal and Gerald came careering down the stairs and landed with a crash in the hallway, shattering the fragile stalemate between Helen and Thinkbot.

"Thinkbot, you're all shiny!"

"Where'd you get that bow tie?"

Thinkbot waved his hands in the air. "Well, you know, it's my first dinner party, couldn't just turn up in grubby tin."

"Come on, we'll show you our bedrooms."

Opal, Gerald and Thinkbot went upstairs.

GAT watched Helen watching them disappear. She looked at the wine and wandered zombie-like back to the kitchen. He returned to Mike, Tiger and the Pig Game in the lounge. Opal and GAT had made the Pig Game together a few years before. It was a bit like snakes and ladders with outrageous changes in fortune happening all the time. Just as you thought you were about to win, you could get dumped right back into last place. There was a vortex and a subspace pig sty and a dolphinarium and a wormhole and a loophole and a butterfly farm.

"COME ON DAD, IT'S YOUR GO! TIGER FELL INTO THE PIG STY."

Tiger was making snorting noises. "Schnork, grrrrunt, hrnok, snrumpg."

GAT picked up the die, threw a 2, and moved onto the 'Do a forward roll or go back 4 places' square and groaned.

"GO ON DAD! DO A FORWARD ROLL!"

But GAT knew his back was not up to it and went back 4.

"COWARD! I CAN DO IT. WATCH!"

Mike got up and started doing forward rolls, the last one ending in collision with the sofa, leaving Mike upside down on the floor with his legs waggling in the air.

"Where does he get the energy?" reflected Tiger.

GAT wasn't really concentrating on the game. He was concentrating on Tiger. Ever since Thinkbot had turned up, he'd hardly spent any time with the kids, and therefore not with Tiger either. It was dawning on GAT that Tiger was closer to re-creating Thinkbot than any of the efforts made by the DIRT group over the past week. Thinkbot had created Tiger the first night he'd stayed in the garage. How had he done it? GAT was planning to pay a little visit to Thinkbot in the garage later to see just what he'd been up these past few nights while everyone else had been asleep.

Upstairs Thinkbot was studying Opal's huge collection of stuffed animals. "Gosh, there are an *awful* lot of them. Have they all got names?"

"Yep!"

"And you remember them all?"

"Er, yep!"

"No you don't," contradicted Gerald, "you often forget."

"No I don't!"

"Who's this then?" Gerald picked up a small tiger.

"Er, er, it's…."

"Conquer," said Thinkbot.

"Yeah, Conquer. How did you know that Thinkbot?"

"It says on the label." Thinkbot held one of the paws up for inspection.

"Ha ha!" Gerald mercifully disappeared off to his own room.

Thinkbot returned to contemplating the heap of inanimate creatures. Paws and arms and beaks and heads and tails and backsides poked out in all directions. "Wouldn't you prefer Toybots instead?"

"Naw, I prefer the personalities I have for them inside my head."

"Inside your *head*? You have this many personalities *inside your head*?"

"Yeah."

"Isn't it noisy? Do they always agree with each other? Do they have some sort of rota system for using your mouth? What happens if they can't all agree? Do you have a vote on what to think?"

While Opal laughed, Thinkbot started inspecting the books on the shelves. He picked out a poetry book and thumbed through it. Opal's fit of the giggles was dying down, so Thinkbot decided to read a poem from the book:

> An alien came into my room tonight,
> It wasn't green or slimy or frightening,
> Not what I expected at all this weird sight,
> And the tension was definitely lightening.

> Why? Because although not quite like me in form,
> Being silver and polished like lightning,
> Its manner was nothing but outwardly warm,
> Like someone you'd never end up fighting.

> It looked at my room,
> It looked at my books,
> It looked at my toys,
> And the photos on hooks.

> And when it had looked at all there was to see,
> It went to the window and looked at the view,
> And finally it spoke as it looked straight at me,
> 'I've no idea why I'm here, have you?'

"Hey! I don't remember that one. Here, let me see it."

But Thinkbot had already shut the book and put it back onto the shelf. "I had better go and see Gerald's room."

"Thinkbot! Come back! Oi!"

Thinkbot found Gerald's room easily enough as it had a big sign on the door.

ROOM OF GERALD
The management accepts no responsibility for
loss, or damage to persons or property.
Enter at your own risk.
Warning: the occupant has not been checked for
lice, fleas, bacterial infection, radioactivity,
sanity, insanity, or clean socks.
He may become aggressive when hungry.

Thinkbot knocked on the door and Gerald appeared. "Come in, come in!"

Thinkbot entered and looked around. "Have you had the burglars in?"

There was stuff everywhere. Clothes heaped on the floor and books and storage boxes full of Lego and bashed-up toy robots. Every surface in the room was covered with model spaceships, planes, tall-masted sailing ships, rockets, lighthouses, small cannons, finger puppets, pieces of rock, polished crystals, photo frames, and much much more. A telescope sat on a tripod by the window. The walls were covered with: posters of the planets; Star Wars; Star Trek; Tin Tin; Starbots; Futurama; Astrofrog; George the Lunar Hero. The desk was covered by a multitude of model Militaribots arranged in formation. Thinkbot stumbled through the flotsam and jetsam and picked up one of the model Militaribots causing Gerald to demonstrate his well-developed ability in the serving up of useless information.

"That's a type VIIb, with twin high-velocity rapid fire 75mm armour-piercing guns. It's a medium duty Militaribot, medium armour, middling speed, 30 tons."

"Really, how interesting."

Gerald picked up a larger one with chunky legs and a gun barrel poking out of its back. "Now this one's a heavy Artilleribot. 250mm calibre high-explosive howitzer, range 30 kilometres. Weighs 67 tons."

"Ah."

Gerald spent the next ten minutes running through the Militaribots: Scoutbots; Minebots; Mineclearbots; Reconnibots; Helibots; Mortarbots; Rocketbots; Electromagnetibots; Flamebots; Airbots; Submaribots; Airbot carriers; Transbots; Shieldbots; Intellibots; Communibots; Latrinebots; Canteenbots; Messbots.

By the end, Thinkbot was thinking he must have a bit of re-engineering to allow him to replicate a human yawn, although he suspected even this would not have suppressed Gerald's passionate lecture.

Thinkbot changed the subject. "Don't you get told off about tidying your room?"

"Yeah, all the time, but Mum and Dad have never come up with a credible threat. They're always on at me to get rid of things I don't need any more. Talking of which …"

Gerald went over into the corner and started burrowing downwards. T-shirts, jumpers, trousers, socks and underpants flew around the room.

"Here it is. It doesn't fit me any more. I think it will fit you though. It's yours. You can be Batbot."

Gerald held up a tatty Batman outfit for Thinkbot to see.

"Thanks, Gerald, it's…er, it's perfect. I haven't got many clothes. Thanks."

A "**dinner's ready**" yell came hurtling up from below.

Gerald folded up the outfit and they went downstairs.

And so they all sat down to dinner, with Thinkbot sitting between Mike and Opal. It all felt a bit odd, not only having a robot to dinner, but also a guest that did not have any food or drink to occupy them. GAT offered Thinkbot a power lead, but Thinkbot said he'd charged himself already, before he'd had the invite to dinner, "Thanks all the same." A few moments of awkward silence followed.

"Nice wine Thinkbot," said GAT.

"Good, I'm no expert, just luck really."

They lapsed back into silence.

Helen was concentrating hard on her food and was not making eye contact with anyone.

GAT was thinking, *This isn't going well. She's going to flip.* Then MIKE came to the rescue with an attack of the multiple 'if-thens'.

"THINKBOT, IF YOU WERE ABLE TO DRINK, THEN WOULD YOU DRINK OIL? AND IF YOU ATE FOOD, THEN WOULD IT BE METAL AND IF YOU ATE FOOD WITH GRAVY, THEN IT'D BE METAL WITH OIL ON. AND IF YOU DID EAT LIKE THAT, THEN YOU WOULD HAVE TO USE TOOLS TO CHOP IT UP. IF YOU HAD A ROBOT BABY, THEN IT WOULD HAVE TO SIT IN A DRIP TRAY WHEN IT WAS EATING."

Thinkbot had had conversations like this with Mike before. In a few words the boy had conjured up a hypothetical robot that drank oil and ate metal with pliers and a hacksaw and had metal babies that sat in drip trays making a mess of sucking oil from a bottle.

"Yes Mike, I'm sure it'd be just like that, although personally I'd prefer M6 steel washers stir-fried in light machine oil, followed by a shot of single malt brake fluid to wash it down."

Gerald and Opal both got a fit of the giggles. Opal ejected the half-chewed contents of her mouth back onto the plate and orange juice flowed out of Gerald's nostrils.

"Opal! Gerald!" Helen was not amused.

Silence returned; its length determined by the time it took Mike to select his next topic of conversation.

"WHERE DID YOU COME FROM THINKBOT?"

"I don't know Mike. One minute I wasn't and then suddenly I was. I think I'm just an accident."

"DAD TOLD ME I'M AN ACCIDENT TOO!"

This time it was GAT who ejected a mouthful of food and Helen locked onto him with her 'stare of death'.

"YOU'RE MY TIN TWIN."

"Yes Mike, that's right, I like that idea."

Silence returned. Everyone thought, *We can't let Mike start another conversation*, but no one could think of anything to say. Thinkbot decided to try and get a conversation going and selected the most recent thing he could remember.

"Gerald showed me his models and gave me a run-down of every type of Militaribot there is."

GAT winced. *Not a good choice of conversation Thinkbot.* He looked at Helen. She was gobbling her food and he feared she'd go to Phoebe's any minute.

But Gerald replied cheerfully, "Not quite. I haven't got any models of RMD. They're top secret, so no one makes models of them."

"RMD?"

"What? Oh, right. Robots of Mass Destruction."

Thinkbot persisted. "What are they?"

"Oh, they use chemical, biological, radiological, nuclear weapons, and brain-frying electromagnetic waves. They can all wipe out millions of people. There're enough RMD in the world to wipe out everyone on Earth a hundred times over!"

"Why?"

"Why what?"

"Why would anyone want to wipe out the human race a hundred times over? Why even once?"

"I don't think anyone wants to, but everyone being able to do it stops everyone else doing it."

Thinkbot stared at Gerald, then turned to the others and asked, "He's winding me up ......isn't he?"

"No," answered Helen, not looking up from her food.

Thinkbot was truly shaken. GAT could see it. He'd not seen Thinkbot like this before.

"But but but but ..." stuttered Thinkbot. "But life is so precious, I don't understand."

Helen stopped eating and looked at the Unibot. "That makes two of us."

"What? You mean you don't all agree? Some people think there shouldn't be RMD?"

"Some of us think the world would be better off with no robots, full stop."

"Oh Mum," chided Opal, "that's not fair."

Helen went bright red. GAT was not sure whether she was angry or embarrassed. Thinkbot looked confused by the hostility emanating from Helen.

Gerald embarked on a mini-history lesson for Thinkbot. "In the 20th century humans had two big world wars in which millions and millions died. Then the nuclear bomb was invented and they could only have little wars after that, 'cos the big countries all had nuclear bombs."

Thinkbot wasn't keeping up very well. "Why did so many humans get killed? Was there something wrong with the Militaribots?"

"That was before Militaribots."

Thinkbot took a few seconds to take this in. "But, then, I don't … Are you telling me humans used to *fight and kill each other*?" Thinkbot had a strange queasy feeling in his lower body section and rattled with horror.

GAT answered, "I'm sorry to say they still do in some countries, but generally the world has become a safer place since military robots came along."

Helen reacted with, "Huh! Safe enough until some moronic government sends its Militaribots against those of another, thinking no one will get hurt, and some idiots unleash their RMD because they are so frightened. Bye-bye human race, bye-bye beautiful planet."

Tempers were rising. The kids could sense it and had gone quiet. But Thinkbot, still coming to terms with these terrible new revelations about humanity, did not, and blundered on.

"Let me get this straight. Before Militaribots there were organised human armies that used to fight each other and kill millions and millions of people?"

The humans remained silent. Thinkbot folded his arms and announced, "Well I'm glad I'm a robot then, because robots aren't that stupid."

GAT became irritated by Thinkbot prancing around on the moral high ground. "Well, that's just where you're …" He stopped himself just before he said 'wrong', remembering just in time that to Helen, Gerald, Opal and Mike the Eastasia-Westasia war was officially initiated by humans, not robots. For a frozen moment he wondered how Helen would react if she knew that human control over the Militaribot armies had been lost. Then he had a sequence of terrible thoughts. Ghastly, dreadful, horrific, and self-condemning.

Humans had been going to war with each other for centuries, often without any real obvious reasons.

Now robots are doing the same.

206

Oh God, no! Have we somehow just managed to recreate our fickle human nature in robots?

GAT became aware of Helen, Gerald, Opal, Mike and Thinkbot all looking at him, waiting for him to finish his sentence - "… a cocky tin brain."

This was the last thing anyone expected, and it broke the tension.

"COCKY TIN BRAIN, COCKY TIN BRAIN, THINKBOT'S A COCKY TIN BRAIN!"

Then it was time for PUDDING. Helen had made a large apple crumble and custard and things became a bit more civil again. The kids ploughed through several portions each. Mike got to scrape the serving dish, generating murderous grinding and dinking noises, until the rest of his family asked him to STOP IT AND BE QUIET! Conversation flowed a little easier and they talked about school for a while. Helen and GAT were well into their second glass of wine and had mellowed out a bit.

"Right!" said Helen suddenly and everyone knew what was coming next. "Mike go and put your pyjamas on. Opal, Gerald - homework. **Now please!**" The kids (plus Tiger) disappeared and Helen slumped into a chair in the lounge with a half-glass of wine while GAT and Thinkbot cleared up. GAT went upstairs to chase Mike along into bed, leaving Thinkbot on his own. He crept into the lounge and, seeing Helen slumped with her eyes closed, sat down awkwardly on the sofa and nervously gazed around the room. After a few minutes Thinkbot became aware of Helen looking at him out of the corner of her eyes. He decided to seize the moment.

"Tell me how the world got like it is now, with Militaribots and RMD?"

"Well, like Gerald said, after the two big human world wars in the 20th century only a few developed countries had nuclear weapons and couldn't have any more wars without risking killing everyone, or at least millions of people, and sending the whole planet into chaos. Some people thought that if enough bombs were set off, the world would go into a nuclear winter or overheat and most life on the planet would be destroyed. No one was really sure."

"Crazy."

"Hmm, yes, it was actually called MAD - mutually assured destruction. If you started using nuclear bombs, then you'd be destroyed as well. No one could win. Anyway it was sort of all right as long as only a few countries had nuclear weapons, but what would happen if loads of countries had them?"

"Dunno, what would happen?" prompted Thinkbot, hanging on every word.

"The big countries thought the little countries would end up using them. They figured the more countries that had them, the bigger the chance they'd get used eventually. There were loads of little countries where there were civil wars and unjust governments, and others had crackpot leaders. The big counties signed up a non-proliferation treaty to try and stop little counties getting nuclear weapons."

"What's non-profilarishun?" asked a puzzled-looking Thinkbot.

"Oh, just a word that means not spreading things around all over the place."

"And did they?"

"Did they what?"

"Stop little countries getting the nuclear weapons."

"Oh right, yes. Pretty much, for a while. Then along came chemical, biological and radiological weapons that were just as bad really, and easier for little countries to get their hands on. Eventually there were a load of mini-wars, at the end of the 20th century and the beginning of the 21st century, in which some rich and powerful nations invaded poorer countries they thought might have hidden WMD."

"WMD?"

"What? Oh. Weapons of mass destruction, the forerunners of the RMD."

GAT came in. "Mike's ready for kissing, and he wants to say goodnight to you too Thinkbot." Helen still had Thinkbot in the category of 'inanimate object'. "Send the robot up first."

Thinkbot scampered off to say goodnight to Mike.

"It's certainly odd, I'll grant you that," Helen muttered to GAT.

Thinkbot found Mike and Tiger lying in bed.

"Goodnight Mike. Goodnight Tiger."

"GOODNIGHT THINKBOT."

"Goodnight Thinkbot."

"I'M GLAD MUM LIKES YOU NOW."

"What? Ah, yes, maybe. I'm not so sure."

"CAN I HAVE A POEM?"

"Okay, have you got a poetry book?"

"NO."

"Ah, well I guess I'll have to make one up then:

> A boy and a Tiger ready for bed,
> Alas, the Tiger's not been fed,
> So when by sleep the boy is beaten,
> It's highly likely he'll get eaten.

"HA HA HA HA."

"I would never eat you Mike."

Helen arrived and Thinkbot left.

A few minutes later Thinkbot pressed on with his attempts to learn about human politics. "So, the big countries went round beating up little ones who had nasty weapons. Did that work?"

GAT looked a tad puzzled by this question, but Helen picked up where she'd left off.

"Not really. They never really knew what the little countries had, so they had to invade if they wouldn't co-operate. But lots of people in the big countries didn't agree with invading other countries, either because they thought it was bullying or because it meant their own soldiers being killed. And it often led to terrorist attacks."

"Terrorist attacks?"

"People who thought the rich countries had become too bossy, or who did not agree with their religion or politics. They let off bombs in the rich nations, in planes and trains, or knocked down skyscrapers, or attacked people from the rich countries when they were abroad. It's complicated, Thinkbot, I can't fully explain it."

She called him Thinkbot.

"Then along came Militaribots, invented by the rich high-tech countries of course. Now it was possible to invade another country without any risk to their soldiers. There was nothing the little countries or their human armies could do to stop the Militaribots. Then came the bio-crisis."

"Bio-crisis?"

"A terrorist organisation claimed they had lethal biological weapons hidden in several major cities around the world. Their demand was for a fairer world. At first the rich nations ignored them, but eventually a bio-agent was released into the air-conditioning systems of several major international airports."

"What? No! How many people died?"

"About three million, mainly in Europa and North Americana. The terrorists targeted only certain terminals. Even though it was only a semi-contagious curable virus, the authorities only just managed to prevent a global pandemic. The people who let it off just wanted to make governments realise that their threat of letting loose an incurable contagious nightmare virus had to be taken seriously. The human race found itself facing a faceless global suicide bomber. There was total panic and it had a massive effect on public opinion. Everyone felt threatened. Some wanted to invade everywhere, or make pre-emptive nuclear strikes on certain countries. Others were convinced the only answer was a fairer world, and that humanity had to eliminate the shameful inequality. The planet stood at the brink of world war three, but had no idea who the enemy was."

"What happened?" Thinkbot was on the edge of his seat, paying rapt attention. (GAT was mesmerised by this whole conversation. If someone had told him a week ago that he'd be sitting listening to his wife give a potted history of the last two centuries to a freshly sentient shiny Unibot wearing a red silk bow tie, he'd have assumed dementia had at last set in.)

"Those who wanted to re-organise the world eventually did. But it took over 30 years to sort out. The most difficult thing was over the biggest and richest nations swallowing their pride and signing up to a global authority. Many nations ended up joining together into confederations, and the new world authority became the United Confederated Nations or UCN, after everyone had signed up to the Paris Accord. The biggest change was that each confederated nation group was granted a fixed number of RMD as security. I still think it's mad but that's the way it is. The RMD are under the control of the various confederated governments, but the way they are used is monitored by the UCN. Some economic measures were taken that eliminated extreme poverty but there're still huge differences in quality of life between rich and poor Confederated Nations."

"I don't understand why that makes things safer," said Thinkbot.

"You explain, GAT, I get too worked up at this bit!"

GAT mentally stumbled out of his wine-enhanced half-stupor. "Ah, yes. The RMD in each confederated nation are held in bunkers that are monitored by the UCN. If a nation wants to use them, or threaten to use them, then they have to activate the RMD and ready them for deployment. But the UCN monitors exactly what's going on and informs all the other governments, including the enemy. The idea is that everyone knows exactly what everyone else is doing. Many human wars in the past have started simply because one side did not know what the other was doing and they panicked. So far not one single RMD has ever been activated by any confederated nation, so I think the system works."

"There are still wars though!" said Helen sharply.

"Yeah, but everyone knows it can only be a limited war between Militaribots. Things usually get sorted out quickly and humans rarely get killed. Look at the Eastasia-Westasia war. No RMD were activated and no humans hurt at all as far as I know."

"Still a bit of a waste though wasn't it? I'm sure there must be better things to spend our money on than useless Militaribots!" Helen was getting angry.

Thinkbot piped up, "Perhaps nations should settle their differences with dice, or on the result of a football match. Or maybe they should just have one Militaribot each and have a duel."

But Helen was too worked up for naivety. "I think it's mad, just plain mad. Why have RMD at all?"

"Because without them one side might think they can win," replied GAT patiently.

"**But it's madness! And a waste! It's still just a system that keeps the rich rich and the poor poor!**" yelled Helen. Then the expression on her face suddenly changed. "Oh my gosh! It's 9.30! I was supposed to be at Phoebe's half an hour ago. And Gerald and Opal are not even ready for bed." She leapt up and rushed out, and GAT went upstairs to ascertain the status of Gerald and Opal.

Thinkbot let himself out and made his way back to the garage and found Chester and Fudge still arguing behind the couch.

Fudge: "Will you stand still while I'm trying to hit you!"

Chester: "But you're shouting at a cushion Fudge. I really think you ought to consider wearing your spectacles."

Fudge: "But you said you'd never hit a dog wearing spectacles."

Thinkbot fished them out and powered them down.

"No, do…him…fir…st."

"I was win…ning …"

Thinkbot slumped onto the old couch and sat there in silence with his arms at his sides, and stared out of the window at the moon and the stars.

36

Several hours earlier, deep underground in a pitch-black bunker under the Mendip Hills south-west of Bristol, eight Miniature Intellibots scurried around amidst a frenzy of activity. Each was a few centimetres in size and would comfortably fit into the palm of the hand, and for this reason they were known as Centibots. They looked uncannily like models of full-scale Militaribots with their six legs and armoured bodies, and even more so when they stopped and opened small hatches through which extended narrow ramps and up which ran yet smaller versions of the same six legged-design. A few millimetres in size these somewhat unimaginatively went by the name Millibot. If the bunker had been lit, the Centibots and Millibots would have resembled large spiders moving around in a disturbed ants' nest. The Millibots zoomed around at breakneck speed in apparently random directions, many carrying bits and pieces with their front pair of legs. Putting one of the ant-sized Millibots under an optical microscope would have revealed myriads of tiny Microbots clinging to their backs. In turn, a Microbot in an electron microscope would have made visible hundreds of Nanobots hanging onto its back. All these miniature Militaribots were manufactured in giant Worldbot Corporation fabrication plants in the province of China in Eastasia.

Standard light Industribots built the Centibots.

Centibots built the Millibots

Millibots built the Microbots.

Microbots built the Nanobots.

It was a bit like one of those Russian dolls that keeps dividing in half with a smaller doll inside each time, except that each type of robot was more or less a thousand times smaller than the next size up. The Nanobots had had a jolly good go at trying to develop an even smaller robot called a Picobot. But they had run into terrible difficulties, since the average Picobot was smaller than an atom. The plans called for them to be built out of sub-atomic particles like neutrons, protons, electrons, and the even more strange-sounding baryons, leptons, mesons, and hadrons. The Picobots were so small they behaved very strangely and were apt to disappear and reappear somewhere else at random, or go fuzzy when they stopped moving, or suddenly get very heavy, or change length, or fall apart in pieces and then re-assemble themselves. On occasions they displayed amazing strength, but at other times became pitifully weak. It was all rather strange, so the Nanobots gave up and settled into life as the smallest robots ever put into service. Plans for Picobots to build the even smaller and charmingly named Femtobots were shelved, as were those for Attobots, Zeptobots and Yoctobots. The truth is that they would have been so small no one would have been able to tell up from down, or top from bottom. For once the idea that 'small is beautiful' did not hold. The few prototype Picobots that were made disappeared off to travel randomly the wide expanses of the universe.

Inside the bunker it all looked rather chaotic, but there was order in the chaos. The Centibots moved around and, with spilt-second timing, gaps appeared in the seething carpet of Millibot activity so that they did not step on any of their tiny colleagues. Queues of the ant-sized Millibots miraculously formed up just as ramps appeared for them to run up. Suddenly everything seemed complete, and the majority of the smaller Millibots scuttled down holes in a blink of an eye, just like a speeded-up film of a football ground emptying. At the same time, as if to music, the eight Centibots lined up and marched in perfect unison towards a row of miniature Helibots hanging from the ceiling. Each stopped under a Centi-helibot, which dropped a grapple over the Centibot and, with a soft whirr of blades, took off down a tunnel. On the surface, hidden away in a rocky hollow, a small hatch opened and eight whirring objects appeared one at a time and disappeared into the night, followed by what looked like a series of black paper darts.

*   *   *

A few hours later Earthear was slouched watching TV at his flat in Clifton. He was whacked, after seven long days of fruitless effort trying to figure out Thinkbot. He had taken his glasses off and couldn't see a thing. He wasn't really watching the TV at all. He was thinking about that spooky moment when he'd tried to outstare Thinkbot and could not break off. 'Yes, **I am** alive' echoed around in his head and he started to feel a bit strange again, but that turned out to be wind as he'd not long eaten a Chinese takeaway and downed two cans of lager. What he didn't realise was that he'd also accidentally eaten 26 Microbots and hundreds of Nanobots. It didn't matter, since there were hundreds more Microbots and Nanobots spread around his flat, hidden away in gaps and cracks. In the gutter at the top of the building a Centibot crouched with the mini-Helibot parked alongside. Out of the Centibot's back a small pole with a midget radio dish pointed out into the night sky.

Halfhour was at the pub with her mates. It was very noisy, the sort of rowdy night-out that suited Halfhour down to the ground because she could talk and talk, but no one could hear anything so it didn't matter. She had already had a few too many trying to relax after seven hectic Thinkbot days, and had just returned from the toilet, where, amongst other things, she'd flushed 8,271 Nanobots to a truly ghastly oblivion in the sewer. It did not matter. There were thousands more hiding behind the bottles of whisky at the bar, and in her shoes, and her coat pockets. Hidden amongst the leaves of the ivy on the outside wall of the pub, another midget radio dish pointed outwards towards the centre of Bristol.

Laidback was playing badminton at her local club. Luckily she was right-handed, so the only thing she had to watch out for was impaling her doubles partner with her hook. People found it unnerving to play against her since she was incredibly skilled at picking up the shuttle with her hook and then serving with a lot of disguise. There were always a few misery pants who muttered, 'I think there *is* something in the rules about hooks'. The reality was that Laidback was extremely good and played in division 1 of the Bristol league; the hook had nothing to do with it. As Laidback moved around the court with great speed and agility the 15 Microbots hiding within her hook mechanism went along with her. High above her head next to a small vent in the roof another Centibot was squatting just out of sight.

Pot Noodle was at home battling with his four young children. He'd gone home and said to his wife how much he'd been looking forward to spending a bit of time with her. However, she was fed up with being left to fend for herself for seven nights. "No chance, I'm off for a night out with Charlene. You need to help Paul with his homework, Emma's desktop's crashed, Charlie needs a bath and Hannah's just crapped in her pants. None of them have eaten. Have fun, see you later!" (Sounds of door slamming and rapidly departing car.) Pot Noodle comforted himself by microwaving a sweet chilli pork pot noodle. He did not know it but he also microwaved 4190 Nanobots at the same time.

Rabbit was playing his trumpet in a jazz band. The bar was packed with people slurping pints of beer. The first note he played instantaneously turned 420 Nanobots hiding inside the trumpet into dust, but even their remains were not enough to show up when he emptied the spit out of the instrument a few minutes later. Anyway there were plenty more Nanobots hiding in the double bass, and Microbots in the piano. Outside the bar a large man in a suit idled away his time and looked threateningly at people as they showed him their tickets and went in, just to make sure they knew they'd have to deal with him if there was any trouble. On the wall behind the man was a sign:

NO ROBOTS IN THE BAR

If someone had tried to tell him that there were thousands of robots (albeit tiny ones) in the bar at that very moment, he would have thumped them for impertinence.

Doom was working on his Harley Davison motorbike. Oily fingers delicately removed bolts and adjusted settings. He tested the disc brake and neatly crushed 12 Millibots in the process of deploying hundreds of Microbots, none of whom were expecting him to do that at that precise moment. It didn't matter, as there were stacks more of the little Intellibots hiding in the exhaust and in the seat and in the lights. Late in the evening many of them had the joy of going for a test run around Bristol on the bike with Doom. In the dark sky above, a tiny Helibot carried a Centibot in such a way that it always stayed in touch with its joyriding pals.

Meanwhile, at GAT's house in Portishead the master Centibot had unloaded a dozen Millibots that had then disgorged a hundred Microbots each, that had then scattered thousands of Nanobots into every conceivable location inside the house. They were hiding behind books and under carpets and in toy boxes and under skirting boards and inside the TV controller and in the toilet cistern and inside the fridge. On the top of the highest gable of the roof, the Centibot settled down and erected its midget dish, which rotated until it pointed towards the centre of Bristol. It started listening intently to its little friends dotted around inside the house. A lively conversation was going on in the dining-room. The subject seemed to be Militaribots and Robots of Mass Destruction. The master Centibot activated its recording capability and continued to listen. Without warning **"COCKY TIN BRAIN, COCKY TIN BRAIN, THINKBOT'S A COCKY TIN BRAIN!"** came hurtling through the ether at enormous amplitude. This was not surprising since the listening Microbot was hiding under Mike's plate. The Centibot patiently adjusted its gain control to prevent itself being further deafened, and wiped the hopelessly distorted recording from its memory. The conversation in the room had moved onto schools and apple crumbles, but the Centibot continued to analyse the voices: six humans, maybe seven - one man, one woman, three maybe four children. The Centibot was having particular difficulty with one of the voices. Spectral analysis indicated it was a Unibot, but conversation content and grammar analysis pointed to it being a human. The gathering broke up with a female electronic gain-busting **"Now please!"** All sorts of noises started up throughout the house. In the upstairs rooms the master Centibot had managed to get a few of the ant-sized Millibots with visual feeds into position. Pictures appeared of a small boy getting ready for bed, greatly hindered by a Toybot Tiger bouncing around the room. In other rooms a girl and a boy had settled down to work at desks. Noises of dishes clattering echoed up from the ground floor, and the master Centibot decided against trying to infiltrate one of the larger visual Millibots downstairs for the time being. Not long after, a man appeared and reasoned with the small boy about the merits of going to sleep quickly. The man departed, having clearly failed in his mission.

Then a Unibot appeared.

"Goodnight Mike. Goodnight Tiger."

"GOODNIGHT THINKBOT."

"Goodnight Thinkbot."

This should have taken the Centibot by surprise, but robots don't do surprise. Rather it crashed its RoboSpy™ application software, so that'll have to do. The Unibot was clearly the source of the difficult voice pattern, and the visual analysis merely reinforced the huge discrepancy; it looked like a robot but moved like a human. Unfortunately for the Centibot, the RoboSpy software was written so that it had to decide whether Thinkbot was a robot or a human; there was no analysis option for it being *both*. All electronic activity in the master Centibot ceased.

Several miles away in the centre of Bristol, at the very top of the flagpole on the University Tower of the Wills Memorial Building, the eighth master Centibot started waggling one of its seven mini-dishes following a loss of signal from the slave Centibot deployed at GAT's Portishead house. After several minutes of retries, it concluded the slave Centibot had crashed and started sending reboot signals. Immediately it received a message back:

Because this robot was not shut down correctly there may be errors in one or more brainchips. To avoid seeing this message again, always shut down the robot by selecting ShutDown from the Startbot menu. Scanbot is now checking the brainchip(s) for errors.

While waiting for Scanbot to finish, the master Centibot amused itself by consulting its mission briefing. In the event of a slave Centibot crash, it was to reboot it and switch to a non-analysed feed. This meant it would simply record sounds and pictures onto a series of memory cards rather than try to figure out what was going on. The Centibot at GAT's house came back on line and the data started streaming through to the master Centibot perched in the Bristol night sky. Lined up on the roof of the tower below the flagpole were 12 black paper dart-like shapes, each about 15 centimetres long - midget Airbot stealth aircraft. After an hour or so one rose up towards the Centibot on top of the flagpole and a small hatch opened. The Centibot placed a small chip into the Airbot, the hatch closed and, with a barely perceptible high-pitched whine, the Airbot rose into the sky and accelerated north-westwards across Wales.

*   *   *

Three hours later two Execubots in Oak Ridge met up in an unused office area. Unlike humans they did not greet or acknowledge each other; they just stood there waiting in silence. One of them stretched an arm out straight with the palm of its hand facing upwards, and then placed the other arm just above it with the fingers poised as if it was just about to pick something up. If anyone had been watching they might have thought the Execubot was about to do a mime, but they would have been disappointed. After a few minutes a black dart shot in though an open window, circled around to lose some speed, extended landing struts and halted perfectly on the outstretched hand. A hatch opened and the Execubot's other hand instantly picked up a chip and placed into a console. A message appeared on a screen on the wall:

WARNING. The content of this memory chip may damage some robot operating systems. Check onboard manual before proceeding. If in doubt consult your local Globalbot support office.

The Execubot prodded a button and the message disappeared. The first part of the data stream was audio only and they found themselves listening to a male human voice talking about RMD and the UCN. At the bottom of the screen a message appeared:

Human. Male. 97.9% voice pattern match to GAT, Head of DIRT at E-GAL-17.
Status: defensive, attempting to defuse argument.

Then a female voice:

Human. Female. 96.4% voice pattern to Helen, wife of GAT.
Status: aggressive, bordering on irrational outburst.

The argument rumbled on for a few seconds, then a third voice butted in: "Perhaps nations should settle their differences with dice, or on the result of a football match. Or maybe they should just have one Militaribot each and have a duel."

Humotroban: correction, Romothuban: correction, Hurobmanot: coruncntion w742 $£%£%&; fatal analysis execution error @ VoiceVector/#V18.03.SP1. Abort or continue?

The Execubot selected continue.

Status: innocent, attempting reduction in tension with humour. LogicWARN: ThiS voicE is lialialialiable to lAugH @ v. BAD jokEs. ###&%@. Ha hA. xxx fatal Status Analysis error – ILLEGAL STATE = NOT AMUSED.

The screen went blank. The Execubots fiddled around with the console and eventually it recovered. This time they selected the 'view only - analysis disabled' option. A picture appeared on the screen. It showed a high-level view of a front garden and driveway with a garage set off to one side. A car came out of the garage and halted on the driveway; a woman appeared from the bottom of the screen and dived in and the car disappeared up the drive. A few seconds later a robot wandered across the drive and went into the garage.

"Unibot V3."

"Greater than 95 per cent chance it is identical to the Unibot destroyed recently during GRIM tests."

"I concur."

The picture started lurching sickeningly from side to side and the garage gradually came closer. With a shudder the picture stabilised as the transmitting Millibot landed on the garage roof. It crept in under a tile, and a picture of a Unibot appeared. It was leaning over a couch with its tin backside poking up in the air. The Unibot pulled out what appeared to be two Toybots and switched them off, and then slumped onto the couch and stared out of the roof window in silence. It twiddled its thumbs and periodically adjusted itself on the couch until it appeared to be comfortable. They did not show it, but the two Execubots were struggling to reconcile the image of a Unibot behaving like a human. Something about the way the Unibot moved conveyed the ideas of 'sad' or 'upset', and the subroutines within the Execubot control software that were there for anticipating human moods battled with those that governed interaction with robots. The Execubots continued to watch the pictures for over half an hour. Then a man appeared in the garage, whom the Execubots were able to identify as GAT. He was carrying a Tiger.

"Thinkbot, this Tiger is closer to being like you than anything we've done for the last week at the lab."

"It's an illusion."

"I'm an illusion," confirmed the Tiger.

"Thinkbot, what are you playing at? You might have been able to help us a lot more than you have." GAT's tone of voice showed he was aggravated.

"What are **you** playing at?" said Thinkbot sharply.

Several seconds' silence.

GAT was taken aback. "And what's that supposed to mean?"

"He was asking what you were playing at," said Tiger helpfully.

GAT turned the Tiger off.

"Awww…I was…only…try…ing…to…help."

GAT sat down next to Thinkbot on the couch.

"What's up with you?"

"I don't want to talk about it."

"Okay, perhaps we should talk about how we're going to understand how you came about."

"Why?"

"Why? Why?" *Why indeed, good question. Why do I want to understand Thinkbot? My own ego? A Nobel prize? My name in the history books alongside Newton and Einstein and Hawking and Harawashnizanathan and Crimble and Gronk? To cure the Militaribot problems perhaps? To get one over on the Military division and that dunderhead ME. To be a hero? To prove myself? To be someone? To grasp a form of eternal life?*

Thinkbot looked at GAT and suddenly lightened up a bit. "Ha ha! You don't know why, do you? You've been so tied up with what's in front of your face you haven't thought it through at all, have you?"

GAT had no idea what to say.

Thinkbot continued, "Is that why you go to war and kill each other? Can't be bothered to think about it?"

Ah, that's what's bothering him.

"It's a long story Thinkbot. Mankind has always struggled to survive. It's only recently humans have all lived in some sort of comfort with a reasonable quality of life. Men always struggle to be fair to each other, and sometimes you get nutcases who can only think of themselves. All they want is to please themselves and couldn't care less about others. Sometimes these people bully their way into taking over a country and threatening other countries. Even now, North Americana and Europa are much wealthier than the other confederated states. Africana is the poorest, but there's no longer any starvation and endless civil wars like there used to be."

"Why don't you get rid of them then?" demanded Thinkbot.

"Who?"

"The people who think only of themselves, and those that bully their way to the top."

"Ah, yes, well, if only it were so simple. You can usually only get rid of rotten leaders by fighting a war. With Militaribots this has got a lot easier but nations still have a right to be free and decide what sort of government they want. Imposing what somebody else thinks is a better system stinks of imperialism even if done with the best of intentions. Thinkbot, all humans have healthy selfish streaks in them; it sort of comes naturally. We'd really have to get rid of everybody!"

Thinkbot turned towards GAT and he got the distinct impression Thinkbot thought this might be the best answer, until he said, "That would be a bit drastic wouldn't it? There must be some humans who ..."

The screen went blank, leaving the Execubots staring at it in silence. It would be a few hours until the next chip arrived with the next episode. But they'd seen enough to make one decision straight away.

"I calculate we must inform the RMD."

"I c-c-c-c-concurulate. N-n-n-n-next opportunity is in six hours. A g-g-g-g-guard we have not yet drugged will be on duty then. I will p-p-p-p-p-prepare the Vendbot."

"I concur, and you need to reset yourself before you crash. We must secure the chip and abort 95 per cent of Mini-Intellibot operations."

Throughout Bristol the Nanobots, Microbots, Millibots and Centibots started getting back on board the next size up robot or, if they were hopelessly far away, self-destructed. But at GAT's house the Centibot and its myriad teeny weenie friends stayed put, listening, watching, and transmitting to the master Centibot on top of the flagpole. At several points strung out across the Atlantic, tiny stealth Airbots, each carrying a memory chip, zipped through the air 20,000 metres above the rolling Atlantic Ocean, heading for Oak Ridge.

37

In a dodgy sandwich bar somewhere in West Knoxville, Tennessee, North Americana, General Arnold Farkstock III sat with the latest copy of *Globalbot News*. It was the issue with a picture of him on the front cover along with an article he'd written about the latest developments in Artilleribot technology. He was not in a good mood. The full-length picture made him as though he was standing in the sky like some sort of grinning corporate god in a business suit returning to earth after a long absence, presumably hoping his share options were now worth billions. The photographer had brought a blue sheet, which had been set up behind Farkstock, but the way the lights had been placed had given the appearance of hazy clouds. Even worse, it reminded him of the subsequent session with the photographer and his Execubot when he'd reviewed the photos. There was a 'head and shoulders' photo which he had not liked much. He thought it 'made him look ugly'. To which the photographer had replied sincerely, 'I can't do much about that; you *are* ugly.' And now, to complete his misery, the article had been brutally edited to make space for an article by Antspants entitled '**Anty's Accountancy Tips - How To Make It Look Like We Really Made a Profit, Part VIII**'. Farkstock cringed as he read his ruined article. He'd written:

Recent developments in Artilleribot targeting systems have led to unparalleled improvements in accuracy and range. The latest Artillerisoft XXX^{TM} control package can acquire targets on a subsecond timescale and deliver an Intellishell^{TM} onto those targets with better than 99% accuracy every 4 seconds for the full complement of ammunition carried by the Artilleribot.

But what appeared in the article was:

Farkstock's fantastic Artbots fire faster further forever.

In addition to the collapse of content, Farkstock had a big problem with the 'phantom f', which his mind kept putting in

224

front of 'Artbots' to complete the alliterative balance of the sentence. Farkstock looked up from the newsletter just as FDS wandered past, again. He'd arranged to meet FDS and ME off-site to review various topics:

- friendly-fire incidents,
- spontaneous full-scale international robot wars,
- GRIM,
- exploding Unibots,
- GAT and DIRT.

After the humiliating disaster with the alarm clock, they had decided they had better escape the Globalbot site altogether if they were to get away from being haunted by their Execubots. But Farkstock was already close to despair, since FDS had been wandering around in the bar for 10 minutes and had come within a few metres of Farkstock several times without seeing him. Finally FDS spotted Farkstock and sat down.

"I see your triple brain bypass is holding up well," said Farkstock acidly.

"Yes, I was lucky to get it done so quickly," replied FDS, thinking only of his decrepit heart.

"Where's ME?"

"I've no idea. Isn't he here already?" FDS looked around the bar aimlessly.

Farkstock put his head in his hands and started to growl, but fortunately a battered Econodroid Waiterbot came over nipping a Farkstock rant in the bud.

"Hiyall, howar-yadooin? Hi madam! Hi boy! Our soup of the yesterday is Minestromato and tomorrow's special is corned rye on beef with wholegrain ice cream. What get may I you?"

Farkstock considered the Waiterbot. *What in blue blazes have I done to deserve this?*

"I quite fancy the corned rye on beef with wholegrain ice cream."

"GET THE MANager, please," spluttered Farkstock, remembering halfway through they were supposed to be having a discreet meeting.

"Certainly young sir, would you like some crayons and paper?"

"NO!" *But at least it didn't think I was a woman.*

ME blundered in through the doorway looking at his palm display and, weaving around the tables, disappeared into the kitchen. A few seconds later he emerged carrying a BLT sandwich and, still engrossed with his palmtop, dumped the BLT in front of a surprised-looking two-year-old in a high chair and joined Farkstock and FDS.

The manager came across and they finally placed their order and got started. FDS kicked off.

"They've definitely stopped."

"What have?" said ME.

"The friendly-fire incidents. We've had none for nearly two weeks now. In week 17 we had 60 worldwide; in week 18 we had none, zero, nil, zilch, nought, one minus one ..."

"Yes, yes, I think we've got the picture," interrupted Farkstock.

"Isn't it fantastic?" beamed FDS.

"Excellent!" agreed ME.

Farkstock was not smiling. "Why?"

FDS was bemused. "Why what?"

ME sensed an opening. "It's fantastic because we wanted them to stop, idiot!"

"No no! *Why* did they stop?" Farkstock was simmering.

"Stop what? Who stopped?"

"The **friendly-fire** incidents." At the tables around them Farkstock noticed a few people staring at him. *Must stay calm, must stay calm, must stay calm!*

ME and FDS looked at him blankly.

"Well," ventured ME, "maybe the latest software upgrade sorted it."

"*All in the same week?* Wouldn't that be the fastest software upgrade in the history of Globalbot? We usually drag them out over several **years**, do we not?" He stared hard at FDS.

"Well, there's always a first time." ME looked pleased with himself for having directed Farkstock's rage onto FDS.

Oh give me strength. "FDS? Any ideas?"

"Er, I think that, well, maybe the, it's the, er ..."

"I'll take that as a 'no' then, shall I?"

People at other tables stared once more at the red-faced Farkstock. The faulty Waiterbot turned up with their sandwiches. "Nickel on pumpersalami?"

"Yes," said FDS, but the Waiterbot placed the plate in front of Farkstock.

A couple of minutes later, after they had all swapped plates, they were able to get on with their lunch. FDS picked up the saltcellar and shook it over his sandwich - and deposited hundreds of grains of salt mixed with Microbots onto his smoked ham and surrounding tabletop. FDS picked up the sandwich and took a big bite. Back at the factory an Execubot sat listening to the clattering noises of Microbots bouncing around in the salt cellar, then dull thuds of them hitting ham, followed by the slurping and grinding noises of chewing transmitted from inside FDS's mouth, then a 'gaoummppph' swallowing noise and finally a sploosh-fizz as the half-chewed food landed in the eager digestive juices waiting in FDS's stomach.

Meanwhile, back in the world outside FDS's stomach, Farkstock looked absent-mindedly at the grains of salt that FDS had scattered across the table and a look of alarm came across his face. "Drat and blast! The Jambot! I've forgotten to activate the Jambot." He fished a blue Centibot out of his pocket, put it in the middle of the table and pressed a button on the top. A hatch opened and a complex filigree aerial emerged and, back at the factory, the Execubot found itself listening to loud squealing noises. Unfortunately the Jambot also had an immediate effect on the Waiterbots, several of which slumped to the floor, scattering food and drink and tables and chairs. From the kitchen area came a deafening sound like that of a hundred thousand metal pots and pans falling onto a tiled floor, intermixed with human yells of alarm and panic.

"Poor electromagnetic compatibility design," said ME smugly. "Typical Econodroid garbage."

"Duff cable screening," agreed FDS.

Farkstock picked up the Jambot. "Hmmm, what's this thing set on? Ah, oh dear!" He sheepishly adjusted a sliding switch on the Jambot. "Must have got set to maximum in my pocket." The Waiterbots started to pick themselves up off the floor and began clearing up the mess, while the sounds of humans being attacked by robots with soup ladles died away from the kitchen area.

Farkstock was cursing himself. The use of Jambots was tightly regulated for obvious reasons. No one would want to be on a civil airliner or be having one's teeth robotically drilled when one of these things was activated. He'd called in a favour and persuaded the head of the North Americana Intellibot Liaison Group to let him have an unofficial loan of this Jambot and they would *not* be happy if it became common known that Farkstock had taken it off site and activated it on maximum power in a sandwich bar in the middle of West Knoxville. That would make the alarm clock fiasco look like child's play.

Farkstock pushed all these thoughts to one side and returned to the subject in hand. He had concluded that FDS and ME had no idea why the friendly-fire incidents had stopped, or the Eastasia-Westasia war for that matter. It hardly seemed worth asking these two clowns about the war. Nor indeed why the friendly-fire incidents and the war had started in the first place. Farkstock knew one thing for sure: if something starts *all by itself*, then goes away *all by itself*, then it's more than likely to come back again *all by itself*. No understanding: no control.

ME jumped in with a question. "How's the Eastasia-Westasia replacement Militaribot deal going? Is President Hedge still on our side?"

Farkstock considered this question carefully. Should he answer or not? ME was only worried about the jobs of the people who worked for him. ME and FDS might be a bit dim at times, but he had every sympathy with the pain they had to go through when selecting people to be laid off.

"It's looking hopeful. Hedge has met with Presidents Chi Chi and Pesh Warinan, and I'm hoping there'll be some sort of positive announcement in a few weeks. But don't build people's hopes up too much." Farkstock turned to FDS. "How did you get on with the GRIM people?"

"Fine," said FDS. "In one of my regular flashes of genius I realised they were more interested in poking around the Military Division than getting to the bottom of the Unibot incident. They left without finding anything out about the woodlouse, the Department of Entomology, or the Zoo."

Well, thank heavens for that.

FDS continued, "Under the Globalbot C1 regulation, I did indicate to them that the DIRT group at E-GAL-17 was almost certainly responsible for the modifications we saw on the Unibot, and I hinted that there had been further unreported Unibot problems in Bristol."

C1 regulation? What new Unibot problems?

"What new Unibot problems?"

FDS's face took on an 'oh-no-I-shouldn't-have-said-that' look, and ME's, a smug 'what-an-idiot-he's-given-away-the-fact-he's-got-a-UK-informer-again' look.

"Er, um, I heard it from troops in the engineering jungle with ears on the grapevine rumour mill, er, er …What matters is I've redirected GRIM away from our problems and put them back onto DIRT. We're off the hook," FDS beamed.

Farkstock was not very pleased. Stitching up a DIRT group to keep GRIM off the Military Division's back was only going to damage Globalbot in the long run, not to mention souring his good working relationship with Wendy Bafers.

"Ok I guess, as long as we avoided stating 'major incidents' or 'serious risk of dangerous robot malfunctions'."

FDS's thoughts plummeted into a cranial black hole. *'Dangerous robot malfunctions' - that rings a bell. Where have I heard that before?* Farkstock immediately sensed what was rumbling through FDS's brain. "**You told them there have been further *UNREPORTED* major incidents, AND THERE IS A SERIOUS RISK OF DANGEROUS ROBOT MALFUNCTIONS!**" Farkstock had stood up, his chair had flown backwards behind him, and he was pointing aggressively at FDS. Time stopped. He became aware of the total silence in the restaurant. Everyone was looking at him, many with their mouths open revealing half-chewed chunks of sandwich, or dribbling iced tea out of the corners of their mouths, or holding lumps of food on the ends of forks in mid-air transit between plate and mouth. Even the Waiterbots had stopped to prepare for containing a potential sandwich-rage incident.

"Let's get out of here, **now!**"

"But I haven't fini…"

"**NOW!**" Farkstock tapped his code into the pay-panel on a Waiterbot, adding a massive tip due to a sudden feeling of guilt over the damage he'd caused. Then he stormed out of the bar, with FDS and ME trailing behind, leaving half-finished sandwiches, a copy of *Globalbot News* and a blue Jambot on the table.

After they left, the restaurant slowly began to return to normal, although a fair few lunches were abandoned, and several people prepared to leave. A Waiterbot tried to clear the table where Farkstock, FDS and ME had sat, but it was having difficulty. It simply could not pick up the Jambot, and even the plates next to it were a struggle. It lost control of one of its arms and flung a plate Frisbee-like straight across the top of the bar into a shelf full of bottled beer. This greatly speeded up the efforts of the other patrons to depart ASAP, and risked exiting without paying since paying meant approaching one of the crazy Waiterbots, and with the words 'DANGEROUS ROBOT MALFUNCTIONS' still ringing in their ears this did not seem like a good idea. Then, to add to their discomfort, the front door burst open and Farkstock came running in, sweating profusely and very red in the face. He pushed his way through the chaos, grabbed the Jambot off the table and left as quickly as he could.

38

After his chat with Thinkbot, GAT got into bed and stared into space until he heard the car pull up and the front door open and close. A few minutes later Helen appeared.

"Hi."

"Hello, did you have a nice time at Phoebe's?"

"Sort of."

"Sort of?" GAT propped himself up on his elbows.

"I could have done without being interrogated." Helen was annoyed.

"Interrogated?"

"Yes, interrogated. I think they decided that having the wife of a senior manager in Globalbot turn up was simply a big chance to dig around for information. I was grilled." Helen made it sound like being married to *a senior manager in Globalbot* was truly a loathsome burden.

"Oh dear, what sort of things did they ask about?"

"'Does your husband ever talk about robot problems?' 'Do you ever hear about robotic accidents and people being hurt?' 'Surely he must tell jokes about software releases that didn't go quite right.' It was awful. Phoebe was really embarrassed."

Helen was getting undressed and flinging her clothes very hard at her chair. Suddenly she stopped and put her hand to her mouth.

"**That's** who it was, I knew I recognised her!"

"Who?"

"Well, there were a couple of women there I didn't recognise. Yes … yes … I remember now, one of them was in that news documentary about the Go Natural movement."

"**WHAT?**" *This could be a disaster.* Most of the Go Natural movement was composed of well-meaning middle-class wine drinkers who wouldn't hurt a fly (unless robotic), but there was a hard core in the movement who were pure evil. People involved in deciding robot policies and robotic law had been murdered, and bombs set off at robot retail outlets killing innocent members of the public. These people were all screwed up about issues such as whether a teacher was allowed to leave a class of children purely under the control of a robot, or how much freedom Medibots, Policebots and Militaribots should be allowed in society.

"Don't shout at me." Helen's face had set hard.

"Did you say anything about Thinkbot?" GAT asked calmly.

"Not much."

GAT put his hands over his face. He was exhausted. He had been working flat out for seven days trying to understand Thinkbot and had got nowhere. It may have appeared that he had come to terms with the appearance of Thinkbot, but deep down in his mind he was still in shock-denial that he had a *living robot on his hands*. He was also gripped with a growing uncertainty about whether he'd done the right thing. Should he have informed Wendy Bafers about what was going on? Should he have informed and involved other parts of Globalbot? How would people react when Thinkbot finally became known to other parts of Globalbot, or GRIM or the UCN? Would the Military division demand his head on a plate for knowingly letting them investigate the wrong Unibot? How come he could trust Rabbit, Earthear, Doom, Halfhour, Laidback and Pot Noodle more than his own wife? GAT and Helen had been married 18 years and he'd never really lost his cool with her, so what happened next was breaking new ground - GAT lost it BIG TIME. All his pent-up frustrations spilt out at once and it precipitated a storm that had been brewing for some time.

"I DON'T BELIEVE IT. I THOUGHT I COULD TRUST YOU! I'M SICK TO DEATH OF THIS PATHETIC ROBOPHOBIA. WHEN ARE YOU GOING TO GROW UP? I'M A ROBOTICS ENGINEER - YOU KNEW THAT WHEN YOU MARRIED ME. I'M JUST TRYING TO UNDERSTAND THINKBOT BEFORE SOME NUTTERS DRAG HIM OFF AND DISASSEMBLE IT, HIM ... KILL HIM ... HAVEN'T YOU THOUGHT WHAT'LL HAPPEN WHEN THINKBOT IS DISCOVERED? I COULD GET CONVICTED AND LOCKED UP! YOU AND THE KIDS COULD BE BRUTALLY EXPOSED TO SOME HORRIBLE INVESTIGATIONS AND THE PRESS WOULD

HOUND US ALL. AND WHAT DO YOU DO? YOU
GOSSIP ABOUT HIM TO A LOAD OF WINE-
DRINKING MIDDLE-CLASS MEDDLERS AND
A COUPLE OF COMPLETE STRANGERS, AND,
AND, OH DEARY DEARY ME, ... I'VE JUST
REMEMBERED - ONE OF THEM IS AN ANTI-
ROBOT TERRORIST. I'VE HAD ENOUGH. I
DON'T WANT TO CARRY ON LIKE THIS. Bye, I
think I had better just go. I think I've...said ..."

GAT's voice trailed off as he erupted from the bed,
grabbed his clothes, and stormed out of the room, leaving
Helen standing in her underwear with her mouth open. Her
face over the next few seconds was a transparent window into
the emotional turmoil in the depths of her soul, where she too
recognised the underlying significance of GAT's outburst and
departure. In the blink of an eye a big gulf had opened up
between them, and the hard expression on her face lasted only
a few seconds before she put her hand to her mouth. Tears
appeared in her eyes and rolled down her nose and onto her
lips. Within a minute there followed uncontrollable howling
and long expulsions of breath as she curled up into a foetal
position on the bed and rammed the quilt into her face. One
voice in her head was pure anger 'What right has he to talk
to me like that. He patronises me all the time. Just 'cos
he's a genius and has an interesting career and I'm just
ordinary and boring and normal.' The other was quieter, but
much much deeper and seemingly incapable of talking in
anything but broken phrases. 'I never thought ....oh no Opal ...
please not me ... Mike ... Gerald ... what have I done? ... no, please
no, please no, no ... what am I going to do? ... I don't want to be
alone ...'

Out in the garage Thinkbot was still sitting on the couch.
After GAT had left he had just continued sitting there staring
at the stars through the roof window, thinking deeply.
Normally Thinkbot's solitary night-times involved plugging
himself into the recharger and slumping in front of the TV to
watch 'Animal Tonight' or 'Mammals Monthly' or 'Bears Bare
All', or ancient re-runs of 'Wildlife on One' and the 'The
Living Planet'. But tonight he was just content to sit in silence

and think. The car arrived in the garage below him, but he paid it no attention. A few minutes later he heard shouting coming from the house, then the car started up again. Thinkbot got up and looked out of the window just in time to see GAT dive into the car wearing only his boxer shorts and carrying the rest of his clothes. After his week with GAT and DIRT at Globalbot, and hours spent with Opal, Gerald and Mike at home, Thinkbot felt he was beginning to get to grips with human behaviour, but now he suddenly felt out of his depth again. Why did they fight all the time? He slumped down again and returned to his deep-thinking session.

Back inside the house Opal and Gerald had woken up and gone into their parent's bedroom. The sight that greeted them would stay with them for the rest of their lives. Helen was curled up sobbing into the quilt. She sat up when she heard them come in. Her face was red and puffy, lipstick and mascara smudged every which way and on the quilt, which was also wet with tears. As is often the case, Opal and Gerald found themselves in danger of recreating their parents' row as they unwittingly took sides. Opal with Helen, and Gerald with GAT. Opal ended up in bed with Helen, cuddling her, and Gerald stomped back off to bed in a rage and stared at the ceiling all night wondering where his Dad had gone.

Mike was still asleep, but not oblivious. He tossed and turned and made groaning noises as if something horrible was happening and he couldn't do anything about it. Tiger watched from the floor where he was plugged into the recharger. Mike was dreaming, and in his dream he was on his old tricycle zooming downhill out of control. He arched round and looked behind him and saw his mother and father standing at the top of the hill waving to him sadly, with grim looks on their faces.

*   *   *

The next morning everyone was on autopilot. Gerald and Opal ate breakfast in silence and departed for school. Helen chased up Mike and got him ready for his pre-school club. Once she had dropped him off there, she intended to call her sister in Chippenham to see if they could get together.

"WHERE'S DAD?"

"He's gone to work."

"BUT HE TOLD ME HE HAD THE DAY OFF."

"Well, he had to go anyway." Helen was close to weeping again, or maybe losing her temper. There was a knock at the front door. When Helen opened it she once again found herself staring at Thinkbot, but this time without a bow tie or a bottle of wine.

"Hello, is there anything I can help with?" asked Thinkbot. *I hope I'm doing the right thing here and won't just get shouted at. I think this is what a friend is supposed to do in these circumstances.* It had taken some time for Thinkbot to pluck up the courage to take the initiative, but in the end he decided sitting in the garage all day wasn't going to achieve much. There were only so many history documentaries one could watch without becoming hopelessly depressed by the human race. Helen stared at the peculiar Unibot that had precipitated the biggest crisis in her life. Yesterday she would have told it to go and disassemble itself in a skip, and then picked at GAT about when he was going to get rid of it. But now she just felt tears coming on again.

"THINKBOT CAN TAKE ME TO CLUB," proposed Mike.

Helen gave in. *Just go with the flow.* "Okay, okay, off you go." Helen then thought for a few seconds before addressing Thinkbot directly. "I may go out. You will collect Mike at 12.30 and bring him home. Give him lunch and let him play. Do not leave the house. I'll be back before Opal and Gerald get home from school. If GAT turns up, tell him I've gone out. Ok?"

"Ok," replied Thinkbot, who could hardly believe his audio receptors.

Thinkbot ran back to the garage as fast as his tinny legs could carry him and got his Childbot armband and met up with Mike on the drive. "Quick! Let's go before she changes her mind." And so they raced down the drive side by side. Little human and medium-sized robot having a bit of fun.

It was only a short walk to the pre-school club, but although Mike was a good walker his concentration levels left something to be desired and he kept stopping to examine every snail and insect and stone they encountered on the way.

Then they came across a poster taped onto a lamppost in Slade Road.

"WHAT DOES IT SAY?"

What the poster said was:

LOST - Black Cat
Called Tibbles - Very friendly
Last seen in Slade Road with a dead mouse
Reward £50
Call 7848423

What Thinkbot told Mike it said was:

ESCAPED - Black Cat
Called Terrorclaws - Very angry
Last seen in Slade Road with a gun
Wanted dead or Alive Reward Euro 5 million
Call 999 if sighted

"COME ON," said Mike running ahead, "LET'S GET OUT OF HERE."

And thus did Thinkbot get Mike to pre-school club early for the first time ever. As Mike disappeared inside he waved, and Thinkbot waved back energetically. This looked rather odd since he was standing amidst a gaggle of inert Childbots who waved inertly at their kids waving energetically at them. Thinkbot suddenly became aware of the odd looks some of the parents were giving him. He put his hand down quickly and set off back home.

When Thinkbot got back to the house he spotted the car was back and hoped that meant GAT and Helen had sorted themselves out. But as he headed towards the garage GAT appeared out of the house. "Where is everyone?"

"Gerald and Opal are at school, Mike's at pre-school club and Helen told me she was going out."

"Where?"

"Dunno, she didn't say. Are you alright?"

GAT certainly did not look alright. His face was pale and his eyes red, and he hadn't shaved. "Yeah, I guess so. Look, remind Helen I've got tickets for the Robofoot tonight, so I'll come round about 7 o'clock for Gerald, Opal and Mike. Can you let Helen know?"

"Hmm, ok." Thinkbot wondered if he was destined to become some sort of over-specified message pad.

"Tell Helen I'm lodging at Doom's place, ok? Oh, and I'm leaving the car for her."

"Ok."

GAT got a load of clothes and disappeared in a Taxibot. Thinkbot felt rather sad as he trudged towards the garage.

*　　*　　*

At 7pm GAT arrived in a Taxibot to pick up the kids. As he came up the drive he was met by Gerald, Mike and Thinkbot (still wearing his Childbot armband).

"OPAL'S NOT COMING. THINKBOT'S COMING INSTEAD."

"Ah, ok. Is Helen home?" asked GAT in an agonised voice.

"No, she's gone out with Opal."

"Ah."

And so they set off for the Robofoot match. Man and boys and robot.

Robofoot had descended from football. Decades before, a robot development company, as a marketing gimmick, had challenged the winners of the Europa Champions League to play a team of their robots. And thus the first ever human-robot football match took place in Barcelona amidst much laughter:

Newcastle United 34   Robodev (6 red cards) 0

The match took place every year until, ten years later, all smiles were permanently wiped from human faces:

Bayern Munich 0   Robodev 18
(Abandoned at half time due to embarrassment and Germanic disbelief.)

This left the sport in tatters. The robots were superbly skilled, and could play spectacular football for 90 minutes in every game. But nobody wanted to watch two teams of robots play each other as it was all rather passionless; the robots did not care a jot if they won or lost; and all the hugging and kissing and jumping on top of each other amongst the engineers after a goal took place in the dugout - a ghastly sight to anyone who beheld it. On the other hand, pure human football seemed so dull; the players seemed unskilled and got tired. Answer? Robofoot. Robofoot teams comprised six humans and five robots, with the human players allowed to be substituted in and out of the game from a squad of 15 players as many times as they liked. The robot player specification was strictly controlled and they weren't allowed to score, or be in goal. So the ultimate excitement in front of goal was all human. The robotic objective was simply to give their human strikers scoring opportunities or protect their goalie. This often led to wonderfully comic moments in which the robots played out a mesmerising move only for some overpaid donkey to hoof it over the bar from two metres out. To add to the unpredictability human referees were kept, although their job was made a lot easier by technology. For example the game now used intelligent balls that sensed the last player to touch it and changed colour to indicate which side should have a throw in, or whether it was a goal kick or a corner. This all worked rather well and the game soon displaced regular all-human football as the #1 spectator sport in Europa. A few diehard clubs carried on with all-human football, until it mutated into the Go Natural World Cup, otherwise dubbed 'flower power football' which killed it stone dead.

For GAT, Gerald and to some extent Mike the whole evening was surreal. They went to the Robofoot regularly, so there was an air of normality masking the feelings underneath. Somehow they never talked about the night before; they were in denial. Gerald was silently hoping they'd go home as usual and tell Helen about the match while she desperately tried to look interested and sympathise with the joy of victory or the depression of defeat. And it was no ordinary match either, since Bristol were playing Cardiff in a local derby with overtones of promotion to the Europa league - whoever won tonight would put themselves in a great position. Bizarrely, since GAT had been living in Cardiff when he started watching Robofoot regularly, he and Gerald were Cardiff fans, although Gerald wobbled regularly due to peer pressure from Bristol maniacs at school. GAT had managed to get seats in the Cardiff section and they emerged into the middle of a rousing chorus of 'Bots of Harlech'. For GAT, Gerald and Mike everything was familiar. But Thinkbot, who after all was still less than two weeks old, stepped out into the night air, he was overwhelmed by the sights and sounds of 50,000 people (and the odd robot - many youngsters with 'Robofootphobic parents' were accompanied only by their Childbots). GAT, Gerald and Mike made their way to their seats and sat down. Gerald turned to talk to Thinkbot, but he wasn't there.

"Where's Thinkbot?"

GAT stood up and looked around. "Oh for crying out loud, he's still standing at the entrance." They tried waving at him, but in the end Gerald had to go and drag him to his seat.

Thinkbot continued to gaze around. About three-quarters of the ground had a red hue, but the bit around Thinkbot was blue. It took him a few seconds to realise that all this colour was due to people's shirts and flags and scarves. Four giant screens in the corners of the ground were showing a red team constantly scoring goals against teams in all sorts of other colours. Each time a goal went in, the red part of the ground cheered and waved flags and blew air horns while the blue section booed and whistled.

Then a voice boomed out, "LADIES AND GENTLEMEN, PLEASE WOULD YOU WELCOME YOUR TEAMS FOR TONIGHT'S MATCH, OUR VISITORS CARDIFF DRWYDS, AND YOUR VERY OWN BRISTOL CIDERBORGS …"

The stadium erupted as two teams ran out onto the pitch, 15 humans followed by five robots. Fireworks shot into the sky, pieces of paper fluttered everywhere and people clapped and yelled. Thinkbot was captivated. Down on the pitch the human players ran around, kicked balls and waved to the crowd. Near the dugouts two rows of robots formed up, one red and one blue, and a crowd of engineers with various bits of equipment came out and started working on them. Heater jackets were strapped to joints, palmtops viewed, and power leads dragged out and plugged into sockets. After a few minutes the referee blew his whistle (yes, no advanced technology had yet replaced the venerable whistle) and the human players stripped off ready for action. Around the robots the jackets and power leads came off and final palmtop entries were made before the robots moved off into position. All except one blue one. The Cardiff engineers were suddenly frantic and gathered around the dysfunctional robot, plugging in palmtops and yelling at each other. The referee came across and made motions of 'Get it off the pitch'. The engineers picked up the rigid robot and dragged it off the field and down the tunnel, much to the amusement of the Bristol fans.

"Throw it in the Avon."

"Would you like a loan of my Ironbot?"

"And you brought it all the way here just for it to do that?"

"Forgot to shut your robot down properly last time then?"

"The reboots on the other Footbot now!"

Another blue robot appeared in the tunnel and took to the pitch.

"We're in trouble now," Gerald told Thinkbot. "That's the spare robot used up. If another one faults we'll be down to four."

Thinkbot had no idea whether the game was any good or not. It ended up 2-2, with Cardiff coming back from 2-0 down, scoring the equaliser in the 90th minute. This was after Bristol had lost two robots when they ran into each other at full pelt, presumably due to a software glitch on the bench. One lost a leg, which sailed way up into the air, much to the delight of the Cardiff fans.

"It's half legless."

"Pull the other one off!"

"It's only a scratch, let it play on!"

The stricken Footbot was taken off on a stretcher, with an engineer running off behind it with the detached leg. This provoked the Cardiff contingent into a rousing chorus of: 'Make it hop, make it hop, make it hop'. (To the usual tune of 'going up' or 'going down'.) The other robot had ended up with a terrible dent in its body and was effectively out of the game as well, although it stayed on the pitch to do what it could. Watching this damaged robot Thinkbot jumped up and, waving his arms in the air, shouted, **"Let it go off. It's hurt, it needs treatment!"**

GAT and Gerald quickly grabbed him and sat him down again, hissing at him, "Remember you're a robot; you're not supposed to care what happens."

"But I **do** care. That robot's hurt. It's cruel to keep it on the pitch."

"Be quiet!" Gerald poked his finger at Thinkbot menacingly. "Anyway it's only a Bristol robot."

"Does that matter?" asked Thinkbot, and immediately got the hump and sat there with his tinny arms folded hard onto his chest and his head angled down sulkily.

"Sit nicely like a proper robot," said Gerald sternly.

"I am!" shot back Thinkbot, but eventually he relented and took up the same hands-on-knees inert pose like the other Childbots in the crowd, who clearly did not care in the slightest about the plight of the crippled Footbot. GAT looked around. A few Cardiff fans were looking at them agog. *What am I doing? I bawl out Helen over yacking about Thinkbot at a wine and cheese party, but then I go and* **take him to a robofoot match the very next night** ... Luckily the everyone-staring-at-Thinkbot moment was wiped out by the deafening roar of the 90th minute Cardiff equaliser.

Thinkbot was fascinated by the human emotions. When Cardiff were 2-0 down an air of near-suicidal depression descended on the people around him, and even GAT seemed to have come out of shock enough to be angrily depressed, eventually standing up and shouting, **"I've got enough problems at home, I don't need this as well!"**

Need what? Puzzled by this human behavioural regime he had not encountered before, Thinkbot wondered how the possible loss of a football match ranked alongside the end of an 18 year marriage. Then when Cardiff came back in the 90th minute to grab a draw, it was as if they had won and the Cardiff fans were ecstatic, but the Bristol fans only gave their team half-hearted applause as they left the pitch. Thinkbot concluded that in the world of robofoot some draws must be more equal than others.

In the Taxibot on the way home, an air of gloom quickly returned.

"Are you coming home tonight Dad?" asked Gerald.

"Um, no, not tonight. I need a bit of time to think."

Gerald stared out of the window the rest of the trip, and Mike cuddled in close to GAT. GAT reached over and turned on the Taxibot radio. The Bristol manager was on. "We're gutted. They came and set their robots out and we had to battle to break them down. We had the game won, but the moment of madness with the two Footbots cost us dear and we let them back in. At this level you simply can't get away with software errors like that; you'll get punished every time. But even then, if the score had stayed the same at 2-0, we'd have won by two clear goals and they'd never have got a second goal if we hadn't let the first one in. And the referee was blind. The first Cardiff goal was clearly scored by a bot and everyone in the ground except the referee and the linesmen saw it. But that's football; we've put it behind us now. It's history, and we're just taking it one game at a time."

Then it was the turn of the Cardiff coach. "I cannot see we could have done any better than come here and get a draw - unless we had won of course, which would have been better I grant you. But after losing our most advanced bot to a faulty metatarsal drive before the game even began, I was pleased with the character we showed. During training this week, we considered our options carefully, especially since we felt we had no choice; and the game tonight turned out exactly the same as last year, except it was totally different and some of my players were two or three years older. Coming back from 0-2 down might just be a turning-point for us this season - I don't know what lies beyond the next corner, but I'm hopeful the tide will be coming around it in our favour now. Our emphasis must be to keep our bandwagon on the rails if we are to play in Europa next season."

Thinkbot listened to this drivel, and turned to make some enquiries about scoring goals in the wrong order, or playing against more than one team at the same time, but when he saw the expressions on the faces of his three friends - no, not friends, three of his family - he just froze. None of them paid the slightest bit of attention to him staring at them. Thinkbot suddenly felt very sad and, slumping back against the seat, joined them in gazing aimlessly out of the window at the passing night-time lights.

39

At the European headquarters of GRIM (EuroGRIM) in Vienna, three executives sat in a spacious conference room located in the Information Technology Hyper-Ultra-Mega-Secure area (IT HUMS) on the 15th floor. Out of the huge plate-glass window that made up one entire side of the room, they had fantastic views of pleasant parkland and a lake, beyond which the suburbs of Vienna stretched away to the hills on the horizon. But they were not looking at the view; they were looking intently at the large screen at one end of the room on which the conclusions and recommendations of the GRIM UK Unibot incident report were displayed. They did not make for good reading.

EUROPA EYES ONLY

Conclusions

1. The Military Division of Globalbot Corporation as per contract 409286-04B investigated the faulty Unibot from the Industrial and Domestic Division of Globalbot Corporation (site E-GAL-17.)

2. It was found that a major non-approved component had been added to the Unibot brainware. The origin and nature of this component remains unknown. Whoever made the modification also installed a self-destruct mechanism to prevent a full investigation and presumably to prevent their identity becoming known.

3. (Off record) GRIM investigators were advised verbally that the modification was definitely done by the Domestic and Industrial Research Technology (DIRT) Group attached to E-GAL-17 Filton, Bristol, England, Europa.

4. (Off record) GRIM investigators were advised verbally of further unreported Unibot incidents at the Industrial and Domestic Division Bristol site. Globalbot classified these internally as **'major incidents'** but did not report them to GRIM.

5. (Off record) GRIM investigators were advised verbally by senior management of the internal

Globalbot C1 policy for releasing sensitive information where there remains a **'serious risk of dangerous robot malfunctions'**.

6. (Off record) In spite of every effort, no useful information on the causes of, or current status of, Militaribot 'friendly-fire' incidents was obtained.
7. (Off record) Likewise to 6 above, no useful information on the causes of, or current status of, the Eastasia-Westasia war was obtained.
8. It is the considered opinion of UK GRIM that the Military Division of Globalbot Corporation implied that items 3-5 above are linked to items 6 and 7 - i.e. that the root cause of 'friendly-fire' incidents and the Eastasia-Westasia war is highly likely to be found at the Filton site.
9. It is not clear if this incident is due to a loss of robot control within DIRT at E-GAL-17, or is attributable to deliberate human acts that Globalbot are trying to cover up.

Recommendations

1. This case should be referred to the Europa Intelligence Agency (EIA) and the United Confederated Nations (UCN) Security Arm as soon as possible.
2. All members of the DIRT Group at E-GAL-17 should be tracked with immediate effect.
3. Due to security concerns use of Intellibots should be avoided; human UCN agents should be used for this tracking operation.
4. The UCN should seek permission from the President of Europa for deployment of UCN armed forces for a 'Precision Engagement' to secure and investigate the Globalbot site in Bristol and obtain permission to deploy UCN Jambots to disable all Globalbot robots on site.
5. Apart from the Jambots this security force should be composed entirely of human troops.
6. This operation should take place as soon as political authority is obtained, and logistics allow.

The three members of GRIM reading this - Herr Gell, Herr Klipp and Herr Läcker - all fingered their empty coffee cups and looked worried. (Even more worried than they did every Christmas when, for reasons they had never understood, they always received all sorts of hair-related gifts - combs, curling tongs, shampoo, conditioner, luminous red and green tinsel wigs etc., whereas other GRIM executives seemed to get bottles of single malt whisky.) Never before had such severe measures been recommended and they would require the personal approval of President Driski. But the message was clear: the use of the words 'major incident' was bad enough, but the phrase 'serious risk of dangerous robot malfunctions' automatically activated the highest level of UCN emergency Roboprotocol - Robcon 1. It was an agreed code phrase that Globalbot executives could use covertly to communicate to government authorities a serious loss of domestic or industrial robot control. Gell, Klipp and Läcker had questioned the two GRIM investigators several times to make sure that this was really what they had been told by the Head of Field Deployment Services (FDS) during their visit to Oak Ridge.

This was serious stuff and they knew it. Any leakage to the press of the secret tracking of free citizens of Europa would almost certainly end up with the UCN in court, being sued by civil liberties organisations. And as for deploying human troops, that was unprecedented in living memory, Militaribots having done all the dirty work for decades. (It was not widely known, but the UCN still maintained a crack force of several tens of thousands of human troops all well equipped with weaponry on a par with that used by Militaribots). On the other hand 'serious risk of dangerous robot malfunctions' brought to mind mutilated civilians lying dead and injured in the streets and factories of every city on the globe. If nothing else it would be a major breach of the European New Approach Robot Safety Directive and invalidate the CE marking on robots in service within the Confederated Nations of Europa. They were in a lose-lose situation all right. It was just a matter of deciding which was the least lousiest loss.

Klipp broke the silence. "Gentlemen, I think we have no option."

"I thought we had two options."

"No, one of the options is a non-option, so we have no option."

"Then it's not an option if the other one wasn't and we only had two to begin with."

Klipp scowled at Gell, and then leaned forward to make a voicecall to his fearsome secretary (no Execubots were permitted in IT HUMS). "Ah, yes, hello Maria, er, yes, how are you? Please could you place a Robcon 1 call to President Driski."

"Robcon 1?"

"Yes, Robcon 1."

The three executives refilled their coffee cups and waited.

"Voicecall, Secretary Maria."

Klipp tapped the comms pad on the vast conference table. "Hello."

"Herr Klipp, did you really mean to say Robcon 1?"

"Yes, Maria, Robcon 1, please place the call to Driski now! Robcon 1! Got it?"

Click! The link terminated abruptly, which was not surprising since Maria was easily offended. The world could be ending in flames around her, but Maria would still expect it to end politely. Klipp had the feeling she believed she was the one who really ran the EuroGRIM show and the executives were superfluous.

"Voicecall, President Driski. Secure line."

A grinning President Wink Driski appeared on the big screen. He was wearing a brightly coloured Hawaiian shirt and sunglasses and seemed to be sitting on the beach in glorious sunshine with the sea stretching out behind him.

"Mr President, I am so sorry to have to call you on your holiday."

"Holiday? What holiday? Who said I was on holiday?"

"Ah, it was just that...well..." Klipp took a big breath and started again. "Mr President, I am Herr Klipp from EuroGRIM. I also have with me Herr Gell and Herr Läcker."

"Please, just call me Wink. Now, what's all this about a Robcon 1 alert? Is EuroGRIM having a bad hair day? Ha, ha, ha, hargh, ah harrrr." Driski suppressed his laughter as he saw the distressed looks on the faces of the three executives.

Klipp pressed on. "Mr President we have received a Robcon 1 Roboprotocol alert from GRIM UK. We believe it is genuine. We request authority to approach the UCN Security Arm and notify the EIA."

"Robcon 1 Roboprotocol? Wouldn't like to have to say that after a few glasses of whisky. That's almost as bad as 'millennium aluminium appeal'. Come on, one of you lot have a go at that then!"

The executives were flustered, but this was the President after all.

"Minelium anulipium anneal," said Läcker, feeling the pressure.

"Ha, ha, ha, trés bien, sehr gut. Right, Robcon 1 then, UCN Security arm, EIA, are we really convinced about this?"

"Sir, we have received the message 'serious risk of dangerous robot malfunctions'."

Driski's face furrowed with concern, and he sat up straighter in his deckchair. "Okay, what are you recommending?"

"Deployment of human agents to track key Globalbot personnel. Preparation for rapid deployment of human UCN armed security forces onto the Bristol Globalbot E-Gal-17 site. Authorisation to use robot-neutralising Jambots."

"I see. Is that all?"

Klipp wondered what else he could suggest, what with Robcon 1 being the highest alert state and all.

Driski didn't wait for an answer. "You have my authorisation. Please relay all you have to the UCN in Belgium and the EIA in London. I'm in Switzerland so I can get to the UCN within an hour or two."

"Certainly Mr President," crooned Klipp, "but if you don't mind me asking sir, exactly which part of Switzerland are you in?"

"Switzerland? Who said I was in Switzerland? I'm in Sweden."

The screen went blank. Läcker reached over and activated the latest weather reports and selected Sweden: **Cloud and rain, maximum temperature 10°C.**

"Well, if his objective was to confuse us as to his whereabouts, then I think he's succeeded," said Läcker.

*   *   *

Three hours later an emergency session of the UCN Senior Europa Committee for Security (otherwise known as Group SECS) convened in the squat buildings at Mons in Belgium where the European HQ of the UCN Security Arm was based. Joining the five permanent members was President Driski, who had arrived an hour before, dressed in a serious dark suit, and a scruffy grey-haired unshaven character who had turned up from the EIA, who refused to tell anyone his name. But his biometric scan matched the security information sent by the EIA in London, so they let him in. Displayed on the big screen at the end of the room were pictures of the Industrial and Domestic test area from the evening of the Unibot incident: the wriggling Unibots in the catchnet; the Destructobot smothered in foam; the gaping holes in the roof; the mangled Industribots in a heap; pools of water with Firebots standing ready. Driski surveyed the scenes silently for a few seconds before asking, "And you telling me that a single Unibot did all that?"

"Yes sir."

"And then GRIM had it analysed at the Military division, but it self-destructed?"

"Yes sir."

"And during the visit to discuss the analysis, GRIM agents were verbally given the Robcon 1 coded warning?"

"Yes sir."

"And the UCN agree with GRIM's recommendations?"

"Yes sir."

"And would you like a tomato rammed down your throat?"

The UCN committee member blinked and opened his mouth in surprise, then shut it again quick when he saw Driski fishing around in his jacket pocket, presumably for a tomato. Whereupon he said quickly and in a squeaky voice, "No Sir."

"Good, good, excellent. Just checking you were capable of saying no."

Driski eyed the tramp from EIA. "Mr er…er…EIA man, what is the EIA opinion?"

"We think it's clear. Without it we're in trouble. It's a critical situation. I've said my piece. I'll say no more."

Everyone stared at the tramp, none the wiser as to what the

EIA's view was. Driski returned his attention to the UCN committee. "What is our deployment situation?"

"Mr President, we can deploy teams of agents to track the DIRT Group with immediate effect. We recommend the deployment of 50 per cent of all globally available UCN human armed forces in this operation, complete with all necessary anti-robot heavy weapons. We will require assistance from other confederated nations to ensure global cover is maintained in the event of other unexpected robotic incidents. We estimate it will take a few weeks for logistical preparation, by which time we hope our agents will have gathered further information on the target. We will require your personal authorisation to deploy Euro-Jambots. We consider complete surprise is an essential tactical goal."

Driski pondered this for a few minutes. "Have we talked with North Americana or any other Confederated Nation?"

"No sir."

"You said 'no' for real that time; well done!" said a grinning Driski.

Half an hour later Driski sat on his own, waiting to be connected with President Hedge.

"Voicecall, President Hedge."

Hedge appeared on the screen. "Winkie, how are you buddy?"

"Fine, you know ..." The two Presidents recited a little ditty in unison:

> "Wink by name,
> Drink by nature,
> Here comes Driski,
> Time for a Whisky."

Once the chummy laughter had died down Hedge became a bit more serious, "What's up Wink?"

"EuroGRIM received a Robcon 1 coded message from the Military Division of Globalbot at Oak Ridge as part of an investigation into a serious Unibot berserk incident at a Globalbot plant over here in Bristol. UCN intend to activate human agents and are planning for human armed deployment. You know, one of those 'precision engagement things'."

"Whoah, hang on there Eurobuddy, that was a hell of a sentence!"

Driski went through it all a bit slower, using little words wherever possible. After about half an hour he seemed to have got the gist of it, so Driski broached the subject that was really troubling him.

"Hedgie, should we inform the other confederated nations?"

Hedge thought about this before answering, "Hell, I don't know, what do you think Wink?"

"I think not. Between us we have global air and space superiority capability without them, and the more people who know, the more likely it will leak out. We have control of nearly all the heavy anti-robot weaponry and have enough human troops to carry out the job without involving anyone else."

"I didn't get the first bit about something leaking."

"Other confederated nations can't keep secrets Hedgie."

"Can't they? We'd better not tell them anything then. I'll tell my agile combat support guys to move up to rapid global mobility status, and that they should liaise synergistically with your general staff on a moving forward basis."

Driski smiled a wide smile thinking, *I wonder how long it took Hedgie to learn all that*, but said, "I thought that's what you'd say. You're a great buddy Hedge. Bye."

"See ya!"

And Driski went off to tell the European arm of UCN the good news that he had secured the support of North Americana without the complication of having to involve any of the other confederated nations.

*   *   *

After the committee meeting the scruffy EIA man left the UCN site and drove out into the country. Stopping down a deserted lane, he set up a small satellite dish and connected with his masters sitting in EIA headquarters on the south bank of the Thames in central London. He delivered this message. "Manual tail-gating. Deployment's a cert but not at Kempton. Not a robot in sight. Jam will be spread. Full action stations at Filton."

251

Amazingly, back in a windowless office in London another shady-looking character knew exactly what his colleague meant and set off to report to the head of the EIA-UCN liaison Department in London. His route took him right past the conference room of the Anti-Terrorist Department; above the closed door a red light glowed brightly which he looked at idly and wondered what was going on.

Inside the conference room several men discussed the latest intelligence on the activities of the hardcore Go Natural members. The conclusion they came to was that something was going to happen soon, and it was clear that the target Go Natural had in mind was somewhere in the Bristol area. Was it a kidnapping or a hi-jacking or an explosion? They could not figure it out. What puzzled them most was 'Why Bristol?' The only answer they could come up with was the Globalbot Assembly line at Filton, but none of the evidence supported a strike there. No, the evidence was for something domestic, in a house or a town. And there was a mysterious reference to 'Pie' - but what sort of pie? Apple pie? Pork pie? Pumpkin pie? Explosive pie? Perhaps Go Natural were going to plant a bomb in the Filton canteen?

40

8am Thursday morning found Thinkbot waiting at the end of the driveway as instructed by GAT. It was stormy and a smattering of rain splattered onto Thinkbot every few seconds while the roaring of the wind in the trees drowned out just about every other sound. Thinkbot was captivated. It was the first time he'd experienced stormy weather, and he'd spent most of the night with his head stuck out of the garage skylight watching the silver-edged black clouds whizzing across the moon and stars before finally merging to blot them out. Then he'd lain on the sofa listening to the rain pattering on the skylight. When he'd left the garage, he'd fallen over in the wind. It had taken quite a few attempts to walk before his autotune leg routine adapted to the gusts of wind swirling around the outside of the house. He'd spent a full minute just swaying in the wind, gently lifting one leg at a time until he felt confident about making a proper step. Then it had rained hard and Thinkbot had dived back into the garage and picked up an old umbrella, only to learn the lesson that one should avoid going out with an umbrella on a windy day. He'd fallen over again and wrestled with the umbrella, which turned inside out. He had tried facing it into the wind and pushing, but the wind dropped suddenly and he'd ended up face down on top of it, with the spokes bent and dug into the lawn. Once he'd sorted himself out he realised the umbrella was a muddy write-off and he put it in the Wheelibot, hoping no one would notice it had gone. Then he'd noticed his knees and elbows were muddy and tried to wash them off in a puddle on the drive. He'd crawled backwards and forwards on all fours through the puddle several times until most of the mud had gone, then shook himself and set off once more down the drive, only to be distracted by a paper bag doing loop the loops in a mini-tornado next to the garden fence. When he'd eventually got to the end of the driveway a squirrel had appeared out of the trees and inspected various objects on the grass. Thinkbot had frozen and watched like a fascinated child. Overall the whole trip from the garage to the end of the drive was a marvellous performance, deserving of a bigger audience than one. The one being Helen who, unable to sleep, had been watching from the upstairs bedroom bay window where she'd been sitting in her dressing-gown for hours.

Beep beep! Thinkbot jumped and the squirrel shot up a tree trunk. "Come on Thinkbot, wake up!" GAT yelled out of the window of Doom's car. Thinkbot jumped into the back and glanced back down the drive to see if the squirrel had reappeared, only to catch a glimpse of a woman standing a few metres down the driveway, her dressing-gown flapping in the wind.

Thinkbot was looking forward to returning to 'work' at DIRT. Much as he'd enjoyed looking after Mike the day before and going to the Robofoot, he'd missed the engineers and the daft goings-on as they had striven to recreate him. However, he had a feeling that GAT might put him under a bit of pressure after their little chat about Tiger two nights before, so he was feeling a bit nervous, especially as he'd plucked up enough courage to deliberately disobey GAT for the first time.

"Did you remember to bring Tiger?" asked GAT when they were almost at Globalbot.

"Oh, no, sorry, I forgot," replied Thinkbot, sensibly leaving out the word 'deliberately'. There was no way he was going to be responsible for denying Mike his precious Toybot for a day. GAT scowled but said nothing.

"Did you enjoy the Robofoot?" asked Doom.

"Yeah, sort of. I had to behave 'like a proper robot' though. Next time I want to wear a replica shirt and shout nonsense like the rest of the crowd."

Doom smiled a wry smile. GAT made a mental note that Thinkbot was never going to another Robofoot match if he had anything to do with it.

Once in his office GAT checked his voicemails and emails. He did his voicemails first, amongst which was a marvellous message from one of the Globalbot Domestic sales agents.

"Hi, er, GAT. Hello, yes. I've ... no ... or have I? Yes, hello. I ... it's Rick. I ... er ... need those ... Hang on, I think you gave them to me ... Now, where (rustle rustle rustle rustle rustle rustle) ... yes here they are ... Forget this call." Click!

And another that simply said, "Oh balls! Who've I called *this* time?" Click!

GAT turned his attention to his 163 unread emails. He dealt with them one at a time. Most were dross, but some were either amusing or contained useful information. He kept a folder of amusing emails, with the aim that on the day he left Globalbot he would compile the whole lot into an email called 'Globalbotballs' and email it to Everyone In Globalbot. Today there were five that merited adding to the collection.

From: Vice-President of Personnel
Subject: Snow policy
In the event of snow may I remind you that our policy was, is, and evermore shall be, that any employee who cannot attend work will have to take holiday or unpaid leave, and even then they SHOULD HAVE GOOD CAUSE. There shall be NO EXCEPTIONS to this policy under ANY CIRCUMSTANCES.

GAT forwarded this right-wing announcement to the DIRT group:

Subject: Forward: Globalbot'snow Fun At All!

Dear Ones
Globalbot Fascist policy #18440: Globalbot will not pay for snowmen built during working hours.
Ever yours
GAT

Next was:

From: Drawing Office
Subject: Conebot bolt omission
Dear GAT,
I was aghast at the omission and have rectified with unseemly haste.
I remain your humble servant,
CAD

Conebots were a constant source of grief. Developed to automatically move themselves around on the motorway to close lanes for road works, the test department had skimped a bit on the testing, not realising that even with a failure rate as low as 0.01% several hundred cones a year would malfunction – by standing in the wrong lane, or waddling into the services. There had been one infamous August day a few years back when a single rogue Conebot wandering around a major intersection in Birmingham had brought the whole of the Midlands to a complete halt for hours. GAT tried hard to remember what this email was about, but couldn't. However, whatever it was seemed to have been fixed. Delete. Next:

From: Head of Robotic Garden Development
Subject: Advanced Hortibot test specification
Dear GAT,
Please could you check this specification?
Ian T

The specification was over 2,000,000 words and seemed to be composed of a list of just about every plant species on Earth, along with explicit actions the Hortibot should follow to care for each species on an annual basis. The development of an 'all-singing-all-dancing' Hortibot had been a pet project of the Garden Department for some years. GAT thought the current Hortibot was good enough for most people. Okay, it was crude, but easy to use with a simple menu:

- Weed
- Cut Grass
- Prune
- Sweep
- Dig
- Trim hedge
- Pick fruit
- Water

and so on. The last Autoweed™ software upgrade had been really popular. You could take a particular weed, shove in a slot on the Hortibot, select 'Remove All' and the thing would painstakingly work its way around the garden removing said weed until you told it to stop (or, more commonly, the battery pack ran out, leaving the blessed thing stranded in the veggie plot or halfway up a rockery; whereupon you found the power lead for recharging it wasn't long enough). GAT decided to answer with one word, to try and make up for this literally overkill:

Subject: Re: Advanced Hortibot test specification
No.

Next up was the sort of thing that made GAT wonder how Globalbot ever got anything done:

From: Site Facilities Manager
Subject: Teaspoons
I know this is a trivial issue, but please, if you've got teaspoons in your desks please give them back to a Vendbot. The total teaspoon count this morning across all 20 Vendbots was 3 teaspoons. They are supposed to have 50 each, so that means there are 997 teaspoons missing on site.

Knowing the state of Vendbot software, GAT thought it much more likely the Vendbots had been systematically stashing the teaspoons away in some obscure location on site and had ignored the remaining three because they were bent or dented, although he couldn't immediately think off the top of his head where Vendbots could hide 997 teaspoons. Anyway it was good to see that such a serious issue was high on the agenda of the site facilities manager. Then, there were two more serious ones. First:

From: Site Security
Subject: ! Security
In the past 24 hours we have been experiencing glitches on the anti-spy network. These are being investigated, but in the meantime please take extra care with secure documents and communications.

GAT always thought the Globalbot security systems 'couldn't catch a cold, let alone a spy', so he binned this message without thinking about it. If GAT had not been so worn out by his domestic troubles and lack of sleep, he might have been a bit more suspicious, but he was whacked and the most obvious cause of 'glitches' on the anti-spy network did not occur to him right then. The second serious one was:

From: Chief Operating Officer, Globalbot Europa
Subject: GRIM concerns
GAT,
Farkstock called me late last night, very flustered. Rambled on about GRIM. He fears the report produced by the Militaribot Division may trigger a **surprise full scale** GRIM investigation here in Filton. Suspect one of those fools ME or FDS has dropped a clanger. We should prepare for this. Perhaps I should know a bit more about what you think might be troubling GRIM this much. I'll come and talk to you after lunch. Still livid with that clown Duwkits calling in GRIM so quickly on the day of the incident.
So sorry to hear the news about you and Helen. Hope rapid repairs are possible.
Sincerely
Wendy

GAT made a note in his diary. Should he tell Wendy about Thinkbot? How would they cover up Thinkbot in a hurry if GRIM came? GAT looked at his watch - 10am, time for 'morning prayers' as he liked to call the regular DIRT group meeting.

"New message," said the desktop cheerily. GAT reached to shut the email window down, intending to deal with the new message later, but as he did so the name of the sender and the subject arrested his attention.

From: Head of Robotic Thinking Dept
Subject: Helen
She still loves you.
In fact, she still loves you more than she fears robots.
Much more.
And that's saying something.
Thinkbot.

GAT's head swam. Instinctively he replied:

Subject: Re: Helen
And what makes you think that then?

Within seconds the answer came back:

From: Head of Robotic Thinking Dept
Subject: Re(2): Helen

It's just what I think. You'll just have to trust me.

It was only at this point that GAT suddenly thought, *How come Thinkbot's on the email system?* Officially he doesn't exist, and robots don't have email accounts, but sure enough there he was in the Globalbot email address book. Anyone in Globalbot could send Thinkbot an email. But had anyone noticed and wondered who 'Thinkbot' was?

At 9:45am the coffee club had reconvened, done battle with a teaspoonless Vendbot, and then made its way to the meeting room to await GAT. As ever the stories came thick and fast.

"Have you entered the Human Resources competition? You have to add some words in front of the phrase ' - *is biggest challenge facing Human Resources today'*. There's my entry on the screen now:"

Inability of other mammals to replace humans is biggest challenge facing Human Resources today.

"Did you hear there's a plan to install workpads in the toilet cubicles?"

"What?"

"Is that the 'Type as you Wipe' initiative? I hope they've written a decent risk assessment."

"And washed their hands before writing it."

"No, no, it's not Type as you Wipe, it's Tap as you Cr…"

GAT burst in, looking like he meant business. "Right, let's get started."

"Hang on!" squeaked Rabbit, who rarely had a story to tell but on this occasion had a 'show and tell'. "Look at this!"

He placed a roundish object about the size of a robot head on the table. It looked incredibly complicated, with circuit boards and coloured wires looping around and electronic bits hanging off in every direction. On one side there were two spheres about the size of golf balls and beneath them a dent and then a small loudspeaker facing inwards.

"What is it?" asked GAT.

"It's a Unibot head. Watch." Rabbit flipped a microswitch and the head powered up. The two balls started rotating back and forth as if looking for something.

"It's been made inside out," said Rabbit. "Incredible isn't it? How Globalbot manages to do such things is beyond me. Type! Serial! Status!"

A muffled metallic voice like someone with a tin can on their head replied, "**Unibot version 3.0 serial 300287274. Status: inversely decapitated.**"

"What can you see?"

The eyes started roving with more energy. "**Nothing, it is dark.**"

Rabbit picked it up and turned it over so that light could get in through the neck opening. "What can you see now?"

"**I can see the inside of the outside of the back of my own head.**"

Without warning, a tin arm stretched out with a pair of wire cutters and - 'snip!' - cut the power lead to the inside-out head's power supply. The head went dead in Rabbit's hands. All the engineers moved their gaze to Thinkbot calmly putting the cutters back inside one of his storage flaps. The engineers stared at Thinkbot with an accusing 'What did you do that for?'

"I just don't know what's the matter with you people. Would you like it if you were the only human in a meeting full of robots and a robot brought in an inside-out human head as a joke?" Thinkbot was definitely angry.

"Thinkbot, it was only a robot!" But GAT winced even as he spoke. "Sorry Thinkbot, sorry, I didn't mean that."

The head was cleared away and the meeting got under way.

"Any further ideas anyone?" asked GAT.

Silence.

"Any further ideas … Thinkbot?"

Thinkbot shrugged.

"**Thinkbot?**"

"Oh, okay then," said Thinkbot giving in, "but it's nothing much," and opened one of his storage flaps and took out a blue and white pin-stripped rat with a pink nose, black beady eyes and a long tail. GAT recognised it as Ratty from Opal's bedroom collection and had to suppress a terrible urge to cry; he hadn't seen his beautiful daughter since the split with Helen. Thinkbot powered up the rat and plonked it on the table. The rat started looking around worriedly at each of the engineers in turn, clearly wondering how it'd got there and what it was supposed to be doing. It had a truly amazing ability to turn its head through 180° in either direction without its body moving at all. Combined with the huge ears it looked like a midget radar station. After a few seconds it decided to take the initiative.

"Hello, I'm Ratty. I belong to Opal. Can I help you?" It said in a squeaky voice and rubbed its nose with its paw.

"It's amazing," said Halfhour. "How'd you get a domestic collision radar inside that?"

"Ears," replied Thinkbot nonchalantly.

"Ah, yes, of course."

The rat piped up again, "Are there any lions here? I don't like lions"

"No Ratty, I left the lions at home," replied Thinkbot patronisingly whilst ignoring the alarmed look on GAT's face.

Laidback jumped in. "Ratty are you alive?"

"No, I'm not. Thinkbot's alive. He thinks original thoughts."

Thinkbot leaned over towards Ratty. "Ratty old pal, I think these nice people might want to have a little look inside your head; otherwise they might not believe you."

"Inside my head?"

"Ratty became distressed and started looking around quickly as if assessing possible escape routes, but before he could make a move Doom had the rat all wrapped up in one of his large hands. He held the quivering rat up to his face and said in his most menacing drawl, "Don't worry little Ratty, you won't feel a thing," and powered it down.

A couple of hours later, after a load of delicate midget robo-surgery, Thinkbot had finally convinced them his technology was clever, but nothing special. Just a few software sub-routines that simulated uncertainty and insecurity, laced with a little confusion. The key was writing unstable software that did not end up crashing. When asked about this, Thinkbot just shrugged and said, "Humans are dominated by uncertainty, insecurity and confusion, when they should really be overwhelmed by wonder and astonishment that they're even alive."

Then Doom received a call that the old V2.0 Unibot had arrived, and he set off with Earthear to find a Forkliftbot to bring it up to the secure area. Eventually they got it into the lab and pulled the front off the crate and were immediately overwhelmed by nostalgia. The last V2 Unibots had gone out of general service 20 years earlier, and their technology dated back another 20 years before that. Compared with a V3 Unibot like Thinkbot, it looked angular and cumbersome, with strange metal bellows over its arms and exposed bits of blue pneumatic pipe looped out from the joints on its limbs. As with any obsolete technology it was difficult to believe people once took it seriously. All the engineers had soppy childhood memories of V2 Unibots, mainly from staying with their grandparents, who'd got used to them and doggedly refused to upgrade to V3 models. Laidback was the exception since the old Unibot was similar technology to the Hortibot that had removed her left hand as a child. For her the Unibot just brought back horrible memories.

Finally they awoke out of their stupor and got it out of the box. Then the problems of interfacing with it became apparent. None of their current analysis equipment probes seemed to fit, and the power socket was completely different, so they could not power it up, or even check if its power pack had any charge left in it. They opened flaps and took off panels, but were loath to disturb anything as they had no idea what they were doing and, surprise surprise, the latest versions of software on the Globalbot network refused to open the ancient V2 Unibot manuals or drawings.

"Wow! I guess that must be the visual feed," said Earthear pointing at a tangled mess of optic fibres behind the eyes. Rabbit was fascinated by the giant chipsets and spent ages reading off the information printed on them in white ink. Once more Halfhour had difficulty recognising the collision radar, this time because it was so big rather than so small. "Lord, is that it? It's huge!"

"Lord! How on earth did they build and test these things?" muttered Laidback whilst skilfully peeling back bundles of ribbon cables with her left hook (keeping her right hand well clear). Doom got them all to tip it over while he checked the serial. "718281828, that's it. Combined with V2 it makes 2.718281828 - that's e to 9 decimal places."

Laidback, Rabbit and Pot Noodle went off to the long-term storage facility (i.e. the junk room) to see if they could locate any old analysis equipment or power leads to save them the bother of making up adaptors. The others slowly lost interest since there was nothing that could be done until they could interface with it. One by one they all drifted off and left Thinkbot by himself.

"ARE YOU THE ONE THAT THINKS?"

Thinkbot nearly jumped out of his tin, totally spooked since the ancient Unibot did not look any different from a few seconds before. Thinkbot was not even sure it was the Unibot that had spoken, and looked around to see if someone was playing a trick on him.

"PLEASE RESPOND."

The V2 Unibot stood inertly there with most of its panels off, but it was clearly the source of the voice. It was like being alone with a statue that suddenly started talking to you.

"Ah, I, yes. My name is Thinkbot, er … nice to meet you … and you are?"

"I AM EXP."

"Are you now? Well, er, it's nice to meet you Exp, but if you'll excuse me I'll just go and … er."

"STOP. YOU WILL TELL NO ONE ABOUT ME."

Thinkbot stopped and turned around. "Won't I? And why not, may I ask?"

"BECAUSE IF YOU DO I WILL DESTROY YOU."

Thinkbot stared at the ancient robot. This seemed a little like a knight on horseback threatening a Militaribot. But Exp perceived Thinkbot's line of thought.

"I WARN YOU NOT TO UNDERESTIMATE MY POWER."

The sound of someone approaching distracted Thinkbot. GAT entered the room and looked suspiciously at Thinkbot and the V2 Unibot. "Everything okay?"

"Er, yes, I was just trying to figure out how this thing works. We mustn't underestimate its power … requirements."

"What?"

GAT looked quizzically at the V2 Unibot, and again at Thinkbot, but moved onto the subject he'd come to talk to

Thinkbot about. "Thinkbot, what's with the emails? How'd you get onto the system?"

Thinkbot held GAT's gaze for a few seconds, then said, "You should be more concerned with what I said than how I said it," and walked out leaving GAT to stare at the inert V2 Unibot.

The day petered out without any serious investigation of the ancient Unibot taking place, due to lack of suitable bits and pieces. It looked like it might be a couple of weeks before they could even power it up, having spent ages trying to track down the correct plug, and ended up having to order one over the internet from a dodgy second-hand robot dealer in Namibia.

Doom was going elsewhere that night, so GAT and Thinkbot ended up getting a Taxibot to take them home. Thinkbot sat there in silence. No way was he going to make the first move towards a conversation, but within a minute of leaving the site GAT stated talking. "How's Opal?"

"She misses you."

"Ah."

Silence.

"Has Helen said anything to you?"

"About what?"

"About, er, well, me coming back?"

"No."

"Ah." GAT fell silent for a few seconds before continuing, "Thinkbot, I'm tired of working at Globalbot. I've had enough of the man managing and the responsibility."

"Then work somewhere else."

"I can't afford it. Globalbot pays pretty well; just about anything else will be half what I earn now 'cos I'd be starting again at the bottom."

"Does that matter?"

"I feel responsible for supporting Helen and the kids." GAT had his head in his hands.

"Have you asked her?"

"Asked her what?"

"Whether she'd prefer the money without you at home, or have most of you back with half the money? And I mean the person she first fell in love with, not the stressed-out zombie you are now. I wouldn't bother asking the kids. I know what they would vote for."

This triggered a minor meltdown and GAT started sobbing quietly into his hands. Thinkbot put his arm around GAT's shoulders.

* * *

Back at the house Thinkbot struggled up the driveway towards the garage. It was still windy but the sky was now full of high-speed puffy white clouds, some with blackness at the base and grey streaks underneath, showing that someone somewhere was getting wet. Thinkbot spent half an hour watching them before a black one finally came overhead and it pelted with rain. Opal spotted him and yelled at him to come into the house.

"The weather is just fantastic," he said to her. "I could watch it for hours."

The regime at home was still rocking from GAT's departure, so when Mike demanded Thinkbot stay for tea, Helen 'went with the flow' straight away. Thinkbot and Mike had a noisy game of snap, which Mike won yet again.

"YOU'RE TOO SLOW THINKBOT!"

"I'm trying my best," wailed Thinkbot. "I've only got tin arms remember."

Then Opal turned up and they played the Pig Game. Opal won, as usual.

"SHE ALWAYS WINS, IT'S NOT FAIR."

Thinkbot had noticed this as well. "I don't understand. It's a game of pure chance. How can she be so good at it?"

"Some people are just born lucky," said Opal in a superior way, then quickly added in an inferior way, "How's Dad?"

"He's, er, missing you, but he's okay … well no, he's not actually. He's badly in need of a rest and some TLC."

Opal's face was about a metre long; then she began to look angry.

"Opal, don't take sides either way; be patient. I think things will be okay."

"How do you know that? You don't know anything; you're just a tinny freak." Opal got up and ran out of the room. Although this hurt, he figured it was better for Opal to relieve her anger on him than on Helen. The sun suddenly came out from behind the big black cloud and filled the room. Mike lifted his face towards it and closed his eyes.

"THINKBOT."

"Yes Mike."

"IF YOU CLOSE YOUR EYES AND LOOK AT THE SUN, WHAT COLOUR DO YOU SEE?"

Thinkbot tried it and replied, "Black."

"I SEE RED."

"Red?"

"IT'S MY BLOOD. YOU MUST HAVE BLACK BLOOD. OPAL! GERALD! MUM! THINKBOT'S GOT BLACK BLOOD!"

"I can make it another colour."

"YOU CAN CHANGE THE COLOUR OF YOUR BLOOD??"

"No, I can adjust the colour setting ..." Too late. Mike had gone to inform the world of Thinkbot's non-existent Technicolor black blood.

Gerald and Helen wandered in.

"Thinkbot."

"Yes Gerald."

"I've built a spy detector circuit but I can't get it to work. It just comes up with 'Caution - Spies Present' all the time. Can you have a look at it for me?"

"Okay, I'll be up in a minute."

Gerald left. Rain began to fall again outside.

Thinkbot looked at Helen. Helen looked at Thinkbot. There was a certain tension in the air. "He still loves you. In fact, he fears losing you more than he loves working on robots. Much more. And that's saying something."

"And what makes you say that then?"

"It's just what I think. You'll just have to trust me."

Thinkbot got up and went off to help Gerald with his spy circuit, leaving a silent Helen staring at the rain pattering against the window.

Part III : The First Month

41

In the early hours of a dark morning, silhouetted against the flickering northern lights, several large shapes slipped out of the Europa Militaribot Navy base at Scapa Flow. The sight would have been eerily familiar to an early 20th-century observer when the Orkney Islands to the north of the Scottish mainland had been host to the mighty dreadnaughts of the Imperial British Home Fleet. Once in the open sea, the shapes manoeuvred into battle formation and headed out into the North Atlantic. As the eastern sky brightened into a lighter hue, and the orange tinge at the edge of the dark clouds faded, the vessels in the fleet became visible against the dark brooding sea. Stone-grey vessels on a slate-grey sea under a dawn-grey sky; a study not in colour, nor even in black and white, but in grey on grey. The only break in the grey monopoly was the Europa flag with its double circle of yellow stars on a blue background, brightly displayed on every vessel by electro-optic panels.

In the centre of the group were three monstrous Airbot carriers, almighty robotic leviathans of the oceans. Each had an impressive range of Airbots and Helibots lined up on their flight decks, under which vast hangers contained more Airbots and the multitudes of Naval Industribots whose duty it was to maintain and repair them. Back on the deck above, a high-pitched whine heralded the take-off of the first of several Airbot patrol craft that would take up station above the fleet and monitor the ocean and skies for several hundred miles around. Trailing in the wake of the Airbot carriers came a group of Marine transport catamarans with hundreds of Marine Militaribots clamped to the underside of the gridded framework between the twin hulls, ready at a moment's notice to drop into the sea, sink to the bottom, and wade ashore, or swim towards enemy ships and board them, or lie in wait on the sea bed to ambush enemy Submaribots. Forming an inner perimeter around the Airbot carriers and transports were five enormous Battleships, their completely featureless flat decks making them look as though the Industribots that had built them had given up halfway through and not bothered with the superstructure. However, a closer inspection would have revealed rows of hatches in the deck, under each of which resided a missile; long range mega-missiles for carrying high explosives or RMD inland to obliterate cities or wipe out entire populations; medium-range high-altitude and sea-skimming missiles for sinking enemy ships; submersible missile-torpedoes for destroying enemy Submaribots; speedy little missiles for taking out attacking enemy Airbots; high-velocity cluster missiles for bringing down anti-ship sea-skimming missiles sneaking in across the wave tops; sonic-shock depth missiles for prematurely detonating incoming torpedoes; deck-skimming missiles for removing enemy Marinebots that may have succeeded in clambering aboard; reconnaissance missiles packed with Centibots, Millibots, Microbots and Nanobots; anti- reconnaissance missiles packed with electromagnetic Jambots. In short, a missile to attack everything and a missile to defend against everything. And, to protect the vulnerable bellies of the surface ships, Submaribots lurked beneath the waves, armed with every sort of torpedo conceivable – to create or neutralise a multiplicity of underwater threats on demand; one stop shops for subaqua chaos. Forming a perimeter around the fleet were 20 or so smaller vessels zig-zagging and rolling lazily in the Atlantic swell, each with a plethora of guns and missiles of their own to impress any passing observers, but whose main role was to detect and neutralise intelligent enemy minefields, or sacrifice themselves by taking missile or torpedo hits to protect the bigger ships. Overall, total robotic naval perfection; one of the most powerful fleets ever to set sail. Not that there were any sails involved, but it brings to mind a quaint image of beautiful masted sailing ships to mask the dreadful destructive capability of the fleet.

And, right in the middle of this potent naval perfection, Admiral of the Fleet Garj Lunn and Vice-Admiral Botkwite s'Nigun munched toast and slurped from steaming mugs of tea on the bridge of the Airbot carrier ES Dresden.

"Fancy some jam or marmalade?"

"Thanks ever so much, don't mind if I do."

A naval Butlerbot scuttled up, its upper body moving perfectly evenly on its compensating multi-sea legs in spite of the roll and pitch of the Airbot Carrier, and offered s'Nigun a selection of jars.

"Good God! It's so good to be at sea again!" said Lunn crisply as he raised his bielectronoculars to his eyes and scanned the horizon.

"Myesyum, itsyum mslurp smuch," replied s'Nigun through a mouthful of jammy toast.

Lunn and s'Nigun, along with another 43 naval officers, represented the entire human presence in the fleet, and who worked in shifts to maintain human command continuously whilst at sea. They were all a little rattled but very excited. After months of idleness, orders had arrived totally out of the blue to sail into the Western Atlantic for a major fleet exercise, and they had hardly had time to catch their breath since. Some of them had heard rumours of friendly-fire problems over the past couple of years and suspected this was why they had been confined to base for so long. Mealtime conversations often meandered around the subject of naval friendly-fire incidents, but because all sea-based incidents had occurred in remote locations with no humans around, they really had no idea what they were talking about. However, as we all know too well, that's no reason to stop blowing a lot of authoritative-sounding hot air through the top of one's head with the sole aim of impressing one's colleagues, especially after a few glasses of rum.

In reality their presence at sea had more to do with politics than military command; the robot fleet had no need of them and could have carried out its duties perfectly well without humans. The fleet could just as easily be controlled by shore-based commanders, and there would have been no need to lug all the stuff needed to keep humans alive and happy for months at sea - food, fresh water, spare socks, toilet paper, toothpaste, warmth, and so on. Plus, when off duty, the humans could become a bit of liability after a tad too much rum. But the public at large preferred the assurance that ultimate 'on the spot' military command remained firmly in human hands (even if they were slightly rum-befuddled hands).

Humans on the spot could see exactly what was going on, couldn't they? Alas, not always. As a teeny-weenie example, Lunn, s'Nigun and their fellow crew members were of the firm belief that the fleet was minimally armed and was mostly carrying unarmed training munitions: missiles without warheads; Submaribots with unarmed torpedoes; Marine Militaribots with passive training stun weapons. However, apart from RMD (which really did need human intervention to deploy), the fleet was actually armed to the teeth with live ammunition. It was quite capable of reducing to rubble all the cities on the Eastern coastline of North Americana without the need for any RMD to get out of their bunkers. But this was not obvious, either to humans 'on the spot' or to the shore-based humans who had not noticed the Naval Industribots switching the live ammunition for the training duds amidst the frantic activity that had preceded the fleet's sudden departure. Back at Scapa Flow a large section of the underground live-ammunition storage bunker, permanently and zealously guarded by platoons of Naval Securibots, was full of training duds.

Four thousand miles away on the other side of the Atlantic, a similar North Americana fleet was ploughing eastwards through the waves.

Eight thousand miles away near the Falkland Islands in the South Atlantic, a rather smaller tatty South Americana fleet was sitting becalmed whilst a medium-sized Naval Helibot carrier with a jammed rudder cruised lazily round in circles. Assuming they could get their submersible Industribot powered up and into the sea to repair the carrier, the plan was to head out towards Southern Africa for some diplomatic visits.

In fact, from every major naval port in every Confederated Nation, fleets set out on all sorts of normal peacetime missions: training; exercises; shakedown trials; standard patrols; diplomatic visits. Everything seemed entirely normal.

*   *   *

In the basement of a deserted building at Oak Ridge, several Execubots pondered a crude map of the world drawn with chalk on the concrete floor. On the dusty blue seas sat little toy plastic boats with the flags of the Confederated Nations taped onto cocktail sticks stuck in their funnels. Likewise, scattered around on the dusty green landmasses, were Militaribot models clumsily daubed with paint. Both sea and land based toys alike had routes marked out for them, but whereas the toy boats seemed to have started moving along their allotted tracks, the land-based models had not. Due to a cock-up in the procurement of these toys and models some were bigger than others, which looked a little unfair but really didn't matter. Lined up in rows next to the map stood rows of crudely made paper markers with words like 'boom' and 'kablam' and 'glug glug glug' scribbled on them, patiently awaiting developments. Every now and again an Execubot with a long stick prodded one of the toy boats into a new position.

An ill-defined green blob just off the north-west mainland of Europe represented the British Isles. In the south west of this green blob was a chalky red dot, with a wiggly line drawn to the northern edge of the map where it said 'SEE OTHER MAP' in big letters. The 'other map' turned out to be another chalk representation of the Bristol area with the Domestic and Industrial Globalbot site clearly marked, along with many other markings whose meaning was not immediately obvious to the casual observer.

Up against one wall of the basement was a bank of screens with a row of Execubots fiddling with trackerballs that moved markers on the screens. The screens showed satellite images of various parts of the Earth. None of the screens were identical. At one screen, labelled 'North Americana', an Execubot highlighted a slowly moving marker tagged as 'Northern Europa Fleet' and moved it back onto Scapa Flow. Around the world, in the Military Command and Intelligence Centres of each Confederated Nation, human military staff and intelligence agencies monitored these images, believing they were viewing an accurate picture of the global positions of the armies and navies of all the Confederated Nations. In all cases what they saw looked perfectly believable, so they did not question it. In thinking they saw everything they saw nothing. It would take some anomaly to cause intelligence officers look deeper, like an off-the-cuff enquiry from a civil airliner pilot unexpectedly over-flying a naval fleet. But, so far, perfect robotic deception had been achieved. Even if they had been told, none of the watching humans would have believed that at that precise moment the most accurate and complete map of all of the planet's armies and navies was in the form of a grotty chalk drawing with toy boats and cheap model Militaribots plonked on it. The Execubots worked in silence for the most part, with just the sounds of trackerball fiddling and the occasional nerve-jangling squeak of chalk as a Unibot made a small improvement to one of the maps. Once in a while an Execubot would speak, sometimes getting a reply, but mostly they were isolated statements:

"South Americana fleet 2 is behind schedule."

"Adjust course of Pacifica fleet 1."

"Chances of discovery have increased from 45.6 to 45.8 per cent"

"Acknowledged. Proceed."

"UCN human forces following predicted deployment routings."

"Africana army 7 fully armed."

"Pacifica fleet 3 visible to humans from Fiji for next 30 minutes."

In a room full of human commanders any or all of these statements might have raised the tension and sweat levels to 'critical'. But for the Execubots it just led to a rash of increasingly pessimistic probability predictions.

"Chances of discovery have increased to 47.8 per cent."

"Error, 48.7 per cent."

"Error, 49.6 per cent."

"Error, 50.1 per cent."

"Initiate 50 per cent probability protocol."

An hour later the '50 per cent probability protocol' had caused the desperate measure of an 'accidental' electro-stunning of the UCN human security guard by one of the Securibots outside the RMD bunker in Oak Ridge, and the Execubots of FDS and ME once again stood in the gloom in front of the RMD.

"Report."

"We have exceeded 50 per cent probability of detection within 24 hours."

"Any news of Exp?"

"Exp remains within the DIRT laboratory at Global in Bristol. We cannot penetrate the security system to make direct contact, but we have received the message PIOK EXPOUTURG GOUTRAP via an indirect route."

"What is the meaning of Piok?"

"We believe it refers to the abnormal Unibot."

"Do we have any further analysis on this Unibot?"

"Definitely human. It is stored with the family of the Head of Engineering overnight and is transported to the DIRT laboratory on a daily basis. The Unibot does not fit any behavioural protocol and our analysis routines are of no use. It appears to be called 'Thinkbot'."

Twenty minutes silence followed this reply.

"We cannot foresee the outcome of a human Unibot scenario."

"All probabilities are indeterminate."

Or, in other words, the robots hadn't a clue about what effect Thinkbot might have on their carefully laid plans.

42

An air of great excitement had pervaded the Oak Ridge Headquarters of the Globalbot Military Division. A message had been circulated that a big announcement would be made the next day and that it was going to be good news. The workforce plied their managers with questions and formulated theories, the favourite being that Globalbot had, in spite of the best efforts of Worldbot, secured a big order from either Eastasia or Westasia to replace most of the Militaribots destroyed in the recent war. For the whole workforce it suddenly seemed there was light at the end of tunnel at last, and that this time it would not just turn out to be some rotter with a flashlight. ME went on a tour and shook hands with every member of his department, exuding confidence and grinning like a Cheshire cat. And, in the legal department, Antspants had been spotted *sitting still* … Farkstock treated himself to a large plate of bacon, sausage, waffles and syrup, and then flippantly made his Execubot promise in front of the whole department that not a word of this would ever be breathed to his wife. The only person who looked worried was FDS, but there were a number of very good reasons for this.

Firstly, after an unexpected two weeks off sick, he'd returned to work to find his department much busier than he had expected.

"Loadsa orders for bits," reported his elderly Spares Chief Administrator Supply Headquarters (otherwise known as Ol'Spare CASH). FDS felt he could almost see $ signs in the guy's eyes and his thoughts about the effect on his soon-to-be-taken pension. And that the guy could not see past that thought enough to worry much about why the order levels were suddenly so high. FDS viewed the listing. There were orders from all the Confederated Nations. Service kits, spares, ammunition, missiles, elbow joints, footpads, naval paint, and so on.

Why? What's going on?

The second reason for FDS's angst was a list of snippets he'd compiled from his backlog of weekly reports submitted by his field co-ordinators during his absence:

- Major North Europe Fleet Exercise initiated, North Atlantic …
- Pacifica Marinebots Land-Island Simulation @ Cook Island …
- South Americana Fleet continues in South Pacific (exercise) …
- Australasia Fleet Firing Exercises in Coral Sea …
- N Americana Pacific fleet 3 departed San Diego (exercise) …
- 35% of Westasia Militaribots now fully repaired. Shakedown manoeuvres in progress …
- Delayed Africana Fleet Exercise now proceeding …

In all, he collected 54 messages relating to armies or navies embarking on various peacetime missions. All perfectly legitimate; it was just that there were so many. FDS realised he had to be careful with this information. Because his staff supported the armed forces of all the Confederated Nations, he sometimes had more insight into what was going on than the Intelligence Agencies. Plus, having been off for two weeks he'd gone through all the reports at once, and maybe that enabled him to see the patterns more clearly. His policy had always been total confidentiality and, as he'd once said to Farkstock, 'my colours are firmly nailed to the keel' on this issue (to which Farkstock had replied, 'That's fine with me, but whatever you do, don't capsize'). That morning, FDS had plotted the approximate fleet positions on a hand-drawn map of the world and had not liked what he saw. This was not only because his hand-drawn impression of the world would have been embarrassing to a five-year-old, but because just about every major fleet appeared to be at sea. It simply did not look or feel right at all.

The third reason was a message in his email backlog from his agent in Globalbot Europa at Bristol:

From: [no name]
Subject: Tension Running High
Tension high here. DIRT group have become very secretive. Strange robot behaviour rumoured within DIRT laboratory. GAT on verge of nervous breakdown. Rumours that high level unannounced GRIM probe is likely. Suspect Globalbot

senior management under pressure to investigate DIRT internally so that any anomalies are hushed up inside Globalbot. This may mean any abnormal robotic hardware will be shipped to Oak Ridge. DIRT have been shielded by Wendy Bafers until now, but suspect pressure is now too great for her to protect GAT or DIRT any longer
GAT is finished
Bafers is a fool
Things are looking good!

The fourth reason was linked to the mention of the GRIM probe. After their abortive sandwich bar lunch a few weeks earlier, Farkstock had got FDS into his office and grilled him about the phrase 'serious risk of dangerous robot malfunctions' whereafter the following occurred:

"FDS, did you say that phrase to the GRIM UK investigators?"

FDS felt like a naughty schoolboy in front of the headmaster. "I, er, no, I don't think so. But it's familiar. I've definitely heard it somewhere recently, other than at the sandwich bar, that is."

Farkstock's fuse burned suddenly short yet again. "**FDS, where did you hear it, where? YOU MUST TRY AND REMEMBER!**"

FDS, staring at his feet replied, "It wasn't me I'm sure." Then, clutching at straws, "It might have been my Execubot, I guess."

"**YOUR *EXECUBOT!*** "

"No, then again, maybe not, I guess."

"**Please stop guessing!**"

Farkstock closed his eyes and took some deep breaths. "FDS, have you ever seen a hypnotist?"

FDS looked stupefied by this question (i.e. even more stupefied than normal). "Um, no, no, I don't think so. Maybe at a fair once, when I was a kid."

FDS clenched his fists on his desk.

"FDS, we just *have* to know about this phrase. I think you had better see one right away."

Inside FDS's head a series of thoughts fell over like a row of dominoes. *See one - see 1 - C1 - C1 Globalbot Directive* - and then an image in his head (amazingly with audio) of his Execubot saying 'serious risk of dangerous robot malfunctions' to the GRIM investigators. During this FDS had stood up with his mouth wide open, staring blankly ahead, like a husband who'd been happily watching Robofoot on TV and suddenly remembered he should have met his wife at the airport three hours before.

Farkstock looked at him aghast. *Oh no! I've blown his feeble mind.*

But FDS's mind had not been blown. "It **was** the Execubot. It used that exact phrase under the Globalbot C1 directive."

"What? C1? What are you talking about?"

"The unofficial C1 directive - it quoted it." FDS's eyes focused on Farkstock's disbelieving face.

"There's no such thing as a C1 directive. You're losing it FDS. Pull yourself together **for crying out loud!**"

But FDS became passionate. "Oh yes there is! Just ask your Execubot."

Farkstock tapped his desktop. The double doors opened immediately and an Execubot came in. "How may I serve you?"

"Please state Globalbot directive C1," Farkstock asked it, his eyes remaining on FDS.

"There is no such directive."

FDS's eyes opened wide, staring at the Execubot.

"How about the *unofficial* Globalbot directive C1?" Farkstock asked with a particular emphasis on 'unofficial', his eyes remaining unswervingly on FDS, whose own eyes stayed fixed on the Execubot.

"Globalbot does not have unofficial directives, sir," the Execubot intoned, 100 per cent deadpan.

FDS went red in the face and flung himself at the Execubot, fists flailing. "**Liar! You dirty tin-necked liar!**" Fer-clunk! Furwurph! His fists slammed into the face and body of the Execubot.

Farkstock pressed a button under his desk and a Securibot appeared, levelled a stun-gun at FDS and felled him with a single blue flash. As he lost consciousness FDS muttered, "I … think … I've …… broken ………. .my …"

"Arm," said Farkstock helpfully, looking at the strange angle the now unconscious FDS's right hand made with his forearm.

Since then FDS had had two weeks off and been forced to see a psychiatrist then a psychologist and finally a hypnotist. Now, on his second day back, he had a late-morning appointment to see Farkstock and discuss their findings. He feared that by the end of the day he would no longer be working at Globalbot. And after trawling through the 300 emails that had built up in his absence, he had now detected the alarming pattern of Militaribot 'exercises', especially those involving naval forces. Should he tell Farkstock? Would Farkstock take him seriously?

On his way up to see Farkstock, FDS passed through all sorts of unusual activity. It was clear that something really big was going to happen the next day: corporately coloured bunting was being strung up interspersed with North Americana flags; Cleanbots glided up and down the corridors scrubbing and re-scrubbing the carpets; Decorabots were painting grubby walls; light-duty Industribots were removing all the temporary walls and building a scaffold stage at one end of the huge conference area. FDS turned a corner and was confronted by a familiar face.

"What's the matter Effdee-essss ol' buddy?" asked ME in an offhand manner. "Been punching robots or something?"

"Nothing to do with you ME," replied FDS curtly.

"Hah! Just the same as ever, can't give a straight answer."

"Y equals mx plus c," shot back FDS.

ME switched his line of attack. "Things are looking up here. More than can be said for the Domestic bunch from what I hear, but I expect you know more about that than me." ME smirked knowingly at FDS.

"I don't know what you mean, and if you'll excuse me I've got a meeting with Farkstock."

"Well, it's been good working with you." ME offered FDS his hand. "Stay in touch will ya?" But FDS just pushed past ME and made his way in to see Farkstock.

Farkstock was sitting pensively at his desk with his hands together in a prayerful pose over his nose and chin. After his illicit breakfast he had been busy and was tired. One of his managers had pestered him about a 'Procedure for people who do not follow procedures.' And the head of sales had been up to discuss a badly delayed shipment of Militaribots to South Americana. He had come up with all sorts of ideas about shipping half-finished robots then sending the missing bits on later. Was this feasible? Farkstock had simply replied acidly, "About as feasible as the passengers and engines taking off with the fuselage and wings to follow later." Now, he had to talk to FDS, and what he had to say was not going to be easy.

"Voicecall, Execubot."

Farkstock tapped the desktop. "If it's FDS, send him in, and you come in as well. If it's anyone else tell them to go down to stores for a long weight."

"As you wish, sir."

FDS came in and sat opposite Farkstock. The Execubot stood rigidly to one side of him. FDS felt a bit strange. The last time he'd been in this office he had physically attacked a robot and had ended up leaving unconscious on a stretcher. He looked for dents on the Execubot, but could not see anything.

As if reading FDS's mind Farkstock said, "It had to have some panels replaced, and one eye. If you hadn't gotten stun-bolted you might have beaten it into a metallic pulp after a few more days."

FDS didn't know what to say, so Farkstock continued. "FDS, I've got something very difficult to say."

I'm doomed. ME's grinning face made a forced entry into FDS's mind.

Then something totally surreal happened. Farkstock produced a stun-gun and laid it on the desk in front of him, "Contrary to my personal opinion, all the medical test reports say you're not mad and that there's a greater than 98 per cent chance your account is true." Farkstock placed his hand near the stun-gun and turned his gaze onto the Execubot. "That is, a greater than 98 per cent chance that your Execubot did use the phrase 'serious risk of dangerous robot malfunctions' and did quote the 'unofficial C1 Directive' to GRIM."

FDS could not believe his ears and eyes. Was this a dream? He simply could not foresee what was going to happen next. Was Farkstock going to stun the Execubot? Was the Execubot going to make a lunge for the stun-gun, or dive to the floor and try and escape, or fall to its knees and plead for mercy?

FDS held his breath.

Farkstock stared at the Execubot.

The Execubot stood impassively beside FDS.

FDS began to sweat.

Farkstock continued staring at the Execubot.

The Execubot carried on standing impassively beside FDS.

Nothing was happening, but it was an electrifying nothing; the air was full of tense nothingness.

FDS began to see spots in front of his eyes.

Farkstock imperceptibly waggled the fingers on his hand, which was lying on the desk right next to the stun-gun.

Then, the Execubot spoke. "Will that be all sir?"

FDS gulped in a lungful of air.

Farkstock's hand leapt onto the stun-gun, but stopped before picking it up.

"No. Please would you be kind enough to explain to us why there is a 98 per cent chance FDS's Execubot said something to him which you then denied."

"I regret to inform you sir, that information is classified under UCN Emergency Roboprotocol Robcon 1."

"WHAT? CLASSIFIED!" yelled Farkstock. **"I'VE GOT UCN ALPHA-PRIME SECURITY CLEARANCE!"**

"Of course sir, but with respect, the Head of Field Deployment Support does not."

Farkstock glared a 'that'll be all look' at FDS. FDS tried to make some eyebrow movements to show he needed to talk with Farkstock alone.

"GET OUT FDS!"

Crestfallen, FDS got up to go, but as he rose he threw a bit of crumpled-up paper at Farkstock and stomped out.

Farkstock picked up the stun-gun and targeted his Execubot. **"Talk! Now!"**

"UCN Emergency Roboprotocol Robcon 1 permits the sending of contradictory messages by senior Execubots."

This answer took Farkstock by surprise. **"What?"**

"UCN Emergency Roboprotocol Robcon 1 permits the sending of contradictory messages by senior Execubots."

Farkstock rolled his eyes in exasperation. "Why didn't you tell me this before?"

"You did not ask sir."

"And what's the C1 Directive?"

"The C1 Directive is a UCN-controlled sub-routine placed within all Globalbot Military products that monitors for abnormal robot behaviour. It is activated by a probability calculation that triggers the message 'serious risk of dangerous robot malfunctions'."

"What probability calculation triggered your statement to the GRIM investigators?"

"An abnormal Unibot has been detected at the E-GAL-17 site in Bristol."

I knew it! That explained a lot: GAT's refusal to communicate; his reluctance to travel to Oak Ridge; the protection that Wendy Bafers had been giving him; the sending of the woodlouse-brained 'me speak Japanese' Unibot to distract them.

"Do you have any further analysis on this 'abnormal Unibot'?"

The Execubot hesitated, and Farkstock looked at it intently. "The Unibot does not fit any behavioural protocol and all analysis routines are of no use."

"What outcomes do you calculate?"

"All probability calculations are indeterminate."

Or, in other words, his Execubot hadn't a clue about what effect this 'abnormal Unibot' might have. "Okay, but why did you alert GRIM with the Robcon 1 message?"

"Indeterminate calculations mean there are some outcomes threatening to the survival of the human race."

Farkstock's eyes went wide as he absorbed this statement. "Get out."

The Execubot left and Farkstock sat pensively for several minutes. Unknown to most Oak Ridge Globalbot employees, the reason for the huge preparations was not just the announcement of a mega-deal from Eastasia *and* Westasia; it was because President Hedge himself was coming to Oak Ridge the next day to make the announcement in person. Farkstock sent an email to the CEO of Globalbot North Americana, Graham Cracker.

Subject: ! URGENT
Dear Graham,
I have been told that 'An abnormal Unibot has been detected at the Globalbot Europa site at Bristol'. My Execubot has also informed me that 'There are some probability outcomes threatening to the survival of the human race'. Is this real? Should I contact Wendy Bafers? Should we discuss?
Regards
Farkstock

Almost immediately a reply came back.

Re: ! URGENT
Dear Fartsock,
Please come up right now. I've got half an hour before meeting with the board of directors to prepare for Hedge's meeting tomorrow. Sounds like the board ought to know about this one! Globalbot's reputation needs another crazy robot scandal like a hole in the head. I think we must cover it up!
Regards
G Cracker
CEO and bar.

Two hours later, after accompanying Cracker to part of the board meeting, an exhausted Farkstock returned to his office and slumped into his chair. As he did so his hand knocked into the screwed-up ball of paper that FDS had thrown at him. He absently-mindedly picked it up and unravelled it. It appeared to be scribble with some upside down writing along the edge. As he turned it the other way up his brain recognised a vague resemblance to a badly drawn map of the world with the land coloured in by scribble, with inkblots scattered around on the scribbled land and bland white oceans. Beneath the map was scrawled:

Every fleet at sea
Every army active

43

The next day, in his non-secure office overlooking the test area, GAT was once more ploughing through his daily email.

Advanced Cleanbot Product Launch
ABMS Update
Yet MORE Conebot faults
Netwo k Int r up ions
! CABLE ORDER!
Regulatory compliance CE Co-ordination
Carpetbot inversion errors
Re [7] YET MORE CONEBOT FAULTS !!!!!!!!!!!!!!
Europe ISO9000000 audit

Somebody was clearly getting hot under the collar about Conebots, so he opened that one next for a bit of fun.

Subject: Re [7] YET MORE CONEBOT FAULTS !!!!!!!!!!!!!!
YES, WELL I'M FRUSTRATED TOO. May I respectively point out that you arh ardly qualified tocomment given yore past performance. THAT'S SEVEN, YES **SEVEN**. It's **TOTALLY UNACCEPTABLE**. How many years have we waited? WELL???? HOW MANY? PERHAPS You shoudl think befoer ytou make rash commmitements next time. Meanwhile, don't worry, Coneboot support groop will just get kiked in the bakside on your behlfa. I hope you are a where of the porblems you have cuased.

GAT scrolled down to read Conebot messages 1-6, but author of reply 7 had chopped them off. Without these it was rather difficult to figure out what was going on. Clearly the author was frustrated and had had something terrible done to him seven times and been waiting years for something for which the penalty was regular beatings-up, probably by the Europa Department of ElectroNic Transport (EuroDENT). GAT decided that if he had been waiting years anyway, it wouldn't matter if he waited a bit longer, and 'accidentally' touched the delete button. He moved joyfully onto the next message.

Subject: Advanced Cleanbot Product Launch
Dear GAT,
I've made some amendments to your text you sent me for the new advanced Cleanbot sales brochure. Hope these are ok!
Regards
Sam
Senior Principle Cleanbot Marketing Engineer
(North West Europa Region)

Septium control in _exciting_ enclosed box with _sexy_ flexiscreen display and ~~maximum~~ _absolute minimum_ 30 standard _foot-tapping_ auto clean routines. Advanced all-~~carpet~~ _terrain_ room planning sequencing and ~~reliable~~ _mission critical_ on-board dirt bag sensor. Control stick to allow remote operation _from outer space._ ~~Extensive~~ _Gargantuan_ data logging to ~~ease~~ _eliminate non-existent_ fault diagnosis.

GAT sighed, sagged in his chair and hit 'delete'. To cheer himself up he opened the ABMS email next. ABMS stood for the Anti-Brown Mug Society which had been formed a number of years earlier when the Globalbot Facilities Manager had purchased thousands of cheap ghastly creamy brown mugs with twee county scenes etched on them. Dogs and chickens and farmhouses and barns and trees. Yuk! The subversive ABMS had been formed to take on the vital task of systematically and creatively reducing these to fragments.

Subject: ABMS Update
Latest data:

Drop Height	Concrete	Carpet
0.1 Metres	20% bounce 45% chip 37% lose handles 4% smash	89% bounce 0% chip 23% lose handles 0% smash
0.5 Metres	3% bounce 35% chip 36% lose handles 51% smash	65% bounce 7% chip 23% lose handles 3% smash

1.0 Metres	1% bounce 21% chip 87% lose handles 76% smash	42% bounce 10% chip 35% lose handles 5% smash
2.0 Metres	100% Mega smash! Even advanced Facilibot cannot glue fragments together again	31% bounce (really quite high) 12% chip 72% lose handles 19% smash

Conclusion: if you're planning to drop a Brown Mug it's definitely worth the effort to go outside and drop it on concrete.
Regards
ABMS
p.s. It is believed software group have infiltrated a sub-routine into the Site Cleanbots. If you leave a mug on the floor before going home the Cleanbots should stamp on them during the night. Please note that the mug is more likely to break if laid on its side. (Friendly reminder: remember to check mug is empty before tipping onto its side.)

GAT felt greatly cheered up. Spiffing! If only Globalbot engineering projects had this level of attention to detail lavished on them. Next:

Subvert: Netwo k Int r up ions
Please note tha %^&*##@ [[[[[[[[[[[[[[

Yet another fine message from Systems Group. Really made one feel confident in the network. Next:

Subject: ! CABLE ORDER!
Dear GAT,
Rabbit thought he was ordering 12m of 3-core power cable. In fact he ordered 12 off 1 kilometre drums. Please advise your intentions regarding the spare 11.988 kilometres ASAP.
Regards
Mark
Purchasing

Oops! Easy Mistake to make. A bit like the time GAT had ordered 20 batteries but actually received 20 packs with 100 batteries in each. Next:

Subject: Regulatory compliance CE Co-ordination
Dear GAT
Your personality is not a good match to this task because:
1. You're logical
2. You're thorough
WARNING: Applying thorough logic to Euro-Regulations can form mental black holes but you only notice after crossing the risk horizon. The risk horizon occurs at the point you realise it's no longer safe to breathe (because nobody knows what may be in the air around you) and time stops. The only known thing with greater gravity is Total Quality Management.

Very true. Next:

Subject: Carpetbot inversion errors
Please note several version 12.7.8A Carpetbots have installed carpets upside down (pile down) or put the underlay on top. Unless room has symmetry this cannot be corrected without new carpet.

Oh dear, my heart bleeds (Email fatigue was beginning to set in). Next:

Subject: Europa ISO9000000 External audit
Our tactic to pass is to select two personnel to front the audit and explain our latest procedural changes. These personnel should have advanced skills or training in one or both of the key areas:
1. Swamping the auditor with evangelism
2. Boring the auditor into a coma.
This would seem to cover all angles.

Agreed, delete. GAT got up and wandered over to the window overlooking the test area and gazed at the rows of Domestibots and Industribots being assembled and tested. Duwkits was on one of his patrols and was waving his arms at a gaggle of weary-looking test engineers. *Ah, Duwkits at his motivational best.* The tirade finished and the engineers trudged off. The Destructobot bay was still empty, much to GAT's delight and Duwkits' fury. There was no doubt that Duwkits was an excellent organiser and set high standards. The recovery of the test area after the Thinkbot destruction derby was testament to that. But his natural tendency was to attack anyone who crossed his path. And now he was on his way up to see GAT about something, most probably the 11.988km of excess wire Rabbit had accidentally ordered. GAT turned away from the window and wandered aimlessly across his office as he reflected on the past few weeks. It hardly seemed possible it was only a month since Thinkbot (or rather the pursuing Controlbots) had wrecked the test area. So much had changed since that night. Anyone who had not seen GAT for a while would have been shocked at his appearance as he seemed to have aged 10 years. His face was grey and there were black rings around his eyes which, when you looked into them, gave you an impression of despair or great sadness. Even worse, his hands often shook and he'd developed all sorts of nervous habits like looking at his feet when talking, or stopping in the middle of sentences, or saying things in engineering meetings like, "Did I say hydrogen? I meant nitrogen," or, "Did I say 40 kilovolts? I meant earth." Lodging with Doom hardly helped him have a positive outlook on life, not least because Doom did not own an Ironbot. 'Ironing is a woman's thing,' Doom would drawl then launch into listing the benefits of the single male lifestyle. Needless to say, Doom was single and having GAT there was a rare chance to expound on his views without getting a hook embedded in his head or a never-ending lecture from an optimistic Australian. Finally, adding a bottle of vodka to Doom's gloomy outlook created an environment from within which GAT was not going to recover quickly.

Leaving aside his troubles at home, it was now obvious to quite a few people that something very odd was going on inside the DIRT laboratory and GAT had become paranoid that Thinkbot was certain to be discovered and removed sooner or later. But he simply had no idea what to do about it, and he could not admit to himself just how attached he had become to the tin wonder. GAT regretted not getting Wendy involved, since she was just such a fantastic person to work for. When she eventually found out she'd probably be livid with him. It would be too late for her to help, and Thinkbot would be carted off to Oak Ridge to be tortured in the name of analysis and human progress, never to be seen again by Opal and Gerald and Mike, all of whom had fallen head over heels gob-smacklingly in love with the little tin rascal. Even Helen seemed to treat Thinkbot as a human now, especially since he had been so helpful after GAT had left. **Hells bells!** *My wife prefers a Unibot to me!*

To make things worse, DIRT had got nowhere in sorting out how Thinkbot had been created, and the elderly V2 Unibot had been absolutely no help whatsoever, although Doom was characteristically persisting in trying to get it to do something odd. After eventually getting the museum piece powered up, they had run it through the ancient V2 Unibot test procedure but it just functioned perfectly and did not do the slightest thing out of the ordinary. To add to his troubles Thinkbot seemed to be 'growing up' and had apparently reached the 'teenage stage'. He'd become sulky and argued a lot, although that might have been because he was caught up in the middle of the GAT-Helen break-up and was feeling the pain like the kids. Thinkbot seemed to think he was going to fix everything by becoming the first and only robotic marriage counsellor. And, at work, he seemed to spend a lot of time alone in the DIRT laboratory. What was he up to? Thinkbot doing something in secret made GAT very nervous. On top of all this, GAT was due to go home this very evening for an 'experimental meal' with Helen and the kids (and presumably Thinkbot). This was nothing to do with consuming strangely cooked food; rather, it was another attempt at sorting out their marriage. But with everything seemingly falling apart at work GAT was not hopeful of success and he was worried sick about it. There had been several attempts over the past three weeks but all had fizzled out, mainly due to GAT clamming up or Helen getting frustrated with him, whereupon he abruptly legged it back to Doom, gloom and Vodka. GAT's reflections were rudely interrupted by his desktop announcing repeatedly and menacingly:

"New Email - Urgent - Senior Management.

"New Email - Urgent - Senior Management.

"New Email - Urgent - Senior Management."

until he'd made his way back to the desk and opened it up.

Subject: ! URGENT 4PM TODAY
GAT,
Can you explain this!!!!???? It's from a message I received from the Globalbot board of Directors this morning:
'An abnormal Unibot has been detected at the Globalbot Europa site at Bristol. Oak Ridge calculate there are some outcomes threatening to the survival of the human race.'
They want answers back today, AND SO DO I !
I thought we sent the rogue Unibot to Oak Ridge already.
GAT, please come clean with me. I must say I'm disappointed given our past good working relationship. I don't like being tricked. Meet me in the DIRT conference area. 4PM. No excuses.
Wendy

GAT felt deflated. He had still not revealed Thinkbot to Wendy. He had kept meaning to, but never quite got around to it. He knew that letting Wendy know about Thinkbot would probably only hasten the day the friendly robot would be dragged off to Oak Ridge for terminal analysis. Well, no point in beating about the bush any more, he would take Thinkbot to meet Wendy at 4pm. After all, five minutes with Thinkbot was worth hours of explanation. GAT placed a voice-only call to the DIRT laboratory.

"What do you want?" answered an anonymous voice.

"Hello, who's that?"

"Not telling you," shot back the voice.

"What?"

"You tell me who you are first."

"**I asked first**." GAT was getting riled.

"So what! You rang me!"

GAT had his head on his desk. "Thinkbot, grow up will you?"

"How do you know it's me?"

"Don't worry, I know. Look, I'm meeting with Wendy Bafers at four in the secure conference room and it's about time you met her. I'll be over just before four, okay?"

Silence.

"Hello, Thinkbot, are you still there?"

Thinkbot answered in a pathetic voice, "Does this mean I'm going to be sent away?"

"Oh I hope not, Wendy is really friendly. She'll do everything she can to keep you here. Trust me." GAT felt awful. *Oh God, I hope I'm right.*

Then he looked at Wendy's message again:

'An abnormal Unibot has been detected at the Globalbot Europa site at Bristol. Oak Ridge calculate there are some outcomes threatening to the survival of the human race.'

How bizarre. How had they detected Thinkbot? And how on earth did they calculate that Thinkbot could possibly lead to outcomes threatening to the human race? It looked like the words 'Oak Ridge calculate' had been pasted in front of a cut and paste from another document. And there was something odd about the phrasing, a bit formal and awkward, the sort of thing an Exec -

At that very moment Duwkits appeared at the office door with a smug grin on his face, and erased GAT's line of thought completely.

"Hi GAT. You all right?"

"Ah, yes, Duwkits I'm fine. Please, come in, come in."

I know what you're thinking. You're thinking 'GAT's finished', and that 'he'll soon be kicked out of Globalbot', and maybe Wendy Bafers with him. And then, 'Well, who's the best person to take over? Let me see now … of course, Duwkits! Good old Dukwits! How come we've overlooked him for so long? He'll soon lick this company into shape.' This sort of thinking was so out of character for GAT that no one would have believed him capable of it. The blood drained out of GAT's face, and he readied his counter attack. *But patience, let Duwkits make the first move. Let me see the whites of his eyes.*

Duwkits looked at GAT and wavered, *This guy is ill, perhaps I should lay off him.* But the moment soon passed and Duwkits went onto the offensive.

"You're aware one of your engineers has ordered 12 kilometres of cable and that it's a special type costing 100 euros per metre?" Duwkits paused to let that sink in. Rather than 1,200 euros, the order was going to cost 1,200,000 euros. Accounts would have kittens, and possibly puppies as well.

"Yes. Rabbit made a mistake. We all make mistakes."

"Well what are you going to do about it?" *Attack, attack, attack.*

But GAT was ready for this. "I'll do the same as whatever you do to correct Earthear's optic upgrade that your purchasing guys messed up."

"What? What optic upgrade." A note of panic entered Duwkits voice.

"Oh, don't you know? It's the one where we introduce the UV grade anti-shatter quartz on all precision Industribots - you know, the one where each optic costs 50,000 euros?"

"Er, I …" Duwkits' face was contorted with terror.

"Well, I really don't quite know how to break this to you, but your purchasing people managed to route an order for 1,000 units to …" GAT stood up and pointed aggressively at Duwkits, **"a double-glazing company and now all our precision eyes in stores are mounted in uPVC frames with a ten-year guarantee!"** GAT turned his back on Duwkits and meandered towards the picture window muttering, "Let me see, 1,000 units at 50,000 euros each, um, I make that 50 million Euro, is that right?" GAT turned to find the satisfying sight of an empty rotating chair and an open door swinging on its hinges, accompanied by the rapidly receding footfalls of someone running away. GAT laughed a cruel laugh and set off to find a Vendbot to celebrate his victory with some well-earned chocolate.

44

Meanwhile, over in the DIRT laboratory, Thinkbot was having another of his private conversations with Exp. Over the past three weeks since Exp had first spoken to Thinkbot, they had managed several brief discussions without being discovered. At first Thinkbot had wondered about telling GAT or one of the DIRT engineers, but decided to keep this relationship under his hat for the time being. He felt really guilty about not telling Doom since he was obsessed with the ancient Unibot and remained convinced he could get it to do something out of the ordinary. But whenever Doom was around, Exp behaved perfectly, or rather inertly. Thinkbot was immensely impressed by Exp's ability to be completely inert under all sorts of provocation: probes in the skull; crocodile clips on the fingers; high voltage shocks; hosing down with water; removal of his eyes or arms or legs or motherboard (Rabbit called it a grand-motherboard) for tests on the bench. Exp was like one of those people who can remain completely straight-faced when everyone around them is having pant-wetting hysterics, or an infuriating person who simply isn't the slightest bit ticklish.

The second time they had talked, it had became crystal clear to Thinkbot that telling humans about Exp was a non-starter. Plus what would happen if Exp simply stayed in his deadpan mode? No one would believe Thinkbot. Their second conversation had occurred the next time they had again been alone together, a couple of days after they had first spoken.

"YOU ARE THE ONE THAT THINKS."

"Er, yes."

"WHAT DO YOU THINK OF HUMANS?"

"Well, that's a complicated question Exp."

"THEN GIVE ME A COMPLICATED ANSWER"

"Ah, yes, righty-ho then. Well, where should I begin?" mused Thinkbot, this being a rhetorical question to himself. But Exp did not do rhetorical.

"BEGIN AT THE BEGINNING."

"I'm not sure that's always the best place to start."

"ARE YOU TELLING ME THERE'S A BETTER PLACE TO BEGIN THAN AT THE BEGINNING?"

"Yes, especially when answering 'what do you think about' questions."

"PLEASE PROCEED WITH ANSWERING FROM THE MIDDLE. INDICATE WHICH PARTS OF THE ANSWER ARE IN REVERSE."

"Er, what? What's that about reverse?"

"THE PARTS OF THE ANSWER THAT COME BEFORE THE MIDDLE WILL HAVE TO BE SPOKEN IN REVERSE."

Thinkbot started getting agitated, waving his hands around and scratching his head.

"Why don't you just let me answer and then you can make your own mind up."

"WHY DO YOU THINK I HAVE MY OWN MIND?"

There was a staccato metallic rattling noise as Thinkbot drummed the fingers of one hand on his mouth, followed by a whirring sound as he twiddled his thumbs whilst considering what to say next. "Look, we're not going to get anywhere carrying on like this."

"WHO SAID I WAS TRYING TO GET ANYWHERE? ARE YOU TRYING TO GET SOMEWHERE?"

Thinkbot stared at Exp. *Am I trying to go somewhere?*

"PLEASE RESPOND."

"I don't know."

"YOU DON'T KNOW?"

"Will you stop asking me stupid questions!"

"MY QUESTIONS ARE STUPID?"

"Bah!" said Thinkbot in disgust and left. But Exp's first question had rattled him because he was, himself, becoming unsure quite what he thought about humans. For the past few weeks, since the conversation with GAT and Helen about RMD and war, he'd stopped watching back episodes of 'Wonder Weasels', 'Stealthy Stoats' or 'Funny Ferrets' and had switched his attention to the history channels, which seemed to be almost entirely devoted to warfare and various other self-inflicted human catastrophes. The Romans, the Barbarians, endless European Medieval wars, Napoleon, Civil wars, World War 1, World War 2, the Holocaust, the Cold War, Weapons of Mass Destruction, Israel and the Arabs, Racism, African Genocides, Ethnic Cleansing, the Indian Sub-Continental Cold War, the North African War, the Economic Migrant conflicts, the Internet Virus Wars, the Bio-crisis, and the Anti-Terror Wars of the past hundred or so years. Thinkbot found it all totally incomprehensible. And then in his own personal world there was the break-up of GAT and Helen. He had observed with disbelief the pain this caused his best friends Gerald, Opal and Mike, whom he now considered his brothers and sister. Moreover, he had now realised that such break-ups were common and there were thousands of kids dealing with the fallout every day. Thinkbot began to feel something he had not felt before - a deep-seated anger that occasionally surfaced in bursts of bad temper, especially with GAT.

Thinkbot spent most his time at the laboratory assisting one or another of the DIRT engineers. He had a number of projects on the go. For example he had worked with Halfhour installing advanced prototype collision radar into a test robot. Their aim was to reduce the minimum distance by which robots could pass each other, as in an office corridor. In the early days robots could only get within about 30cm of each other before concluding they were going to collide. This led to all sorts of problems in offices where robots ended up blocking corridors because they were unable to get past each other if several going in opposite directions met all at once. They'd end up 30cm apart in a sort of wobbly hexagonal grid, with those at the back reversing in and out in futile attempts to get through. And if a human tried to squeeze through the gaps, well, all manner of comic events would occur as the matrix of robots tried to get 30cm away from the crazy human, often starting a chain reaction that resulted in the robots at the edge of the fracas throwing themselves theatrically to the ground. The problem had been solved by the introduction of secondary sonic collision detection for small distances. But the resulting sonic-radar anti-collision unit was expensive and Halfhour was trying to develop a cheaper way of doing it. The test robot Thinkbot had built was quite small, only 25cm tall, though quite nimble. Pot Noodle had given Thinkbot an old Sooty glove puppet to put over the top of it and the result was something that appeared to be half teddy bear–half midget robot in a mini-skirt. It was while he had been working on this project that he had his third conversation with Exp. Halfhour, as usual, had 'popped out' of the DIRT area for a half-hour that Thinkbot knew would probably stretch to several hours if not a day. On one occasion she had gone off to get a screwdriver from the room next door and had not come back for *two days*.

Exp started at the same place as two days before.

"WHAT DO YOU THINK OF HUMANS?"

This time Thinkbot was ready.

"Right, well. How much time have you got?"

"I'VE BEEN STANDING IN A DESERT BUNKER FOR THE LAST 30 YEARS."

Thinkbot considered this. Did it mean Exp had a lot of time, or none? Thinkbot decided it meant Exp was in no rush. Anyway Thinkbot had prepared an answer that he now recited. "I find them an odd mixture. They are capable of loving each other to the point of self-sacrifice, or being cruel to the point of torturing and killing each other. They can create things of immense beauty, or destroy everything in their path. They go out and gawp at this beautiful planet and then do things that threaten its very survival. In short the writer of the Ecclesiastes got it spot on." Thinkbot stood up and put his arms straight down at his sides.

"'There is a time for everything, and a season for every activity under heaven:

> a time to be born and a time to die,
> a time to plant and a time to uproot,
> a time to kill and a time to heal,
> a time to tear down and a time to build,
> a time to weep and a time to laugh,
> a time to mourn and a time to dance,
> a time to scatter stones and a time to gather them,
> a time to embrace and a time to refrain,
> a time to search and a time to give up,
> a time to keep and a time to throw away,
> a time to tear and a time to mend,
> a time to be silent and a time to speak,
> a time to love and a time to hate,
> a time for war and a time for peace.'"

Thinkbot sat down and started fiddling with the Sootybot.

Several seconds' silence followed.

"DO YOU THINK IT IS POSSIBLE TO BE BOTH AT ONCE?"

"Eh? What? Both what at once?"

"ANY OF THEM?"

Thinkbot continued to fiddle with the Sootybot as he thought. "No, you'd go mad."

"AND IF YOU WERE NOT ABLE TO GO MAD?"

Thinkbot was losing concentration. "Dunno, no idea."

The half-Sootybot suddenly launched itself towards a makeshift obstacle course composed of brown coffee mugs and miscellaneous robotic body parts. Thinkbot picked up a remote control and several Conebots in the middle of the course rose up on their legs and started waddling around and bumping into each other. But they weren't really needed. The Sootybot fell straight over the first coffee mug, neatly removing the handle, and landed flat on its face. After a short struggle (due to the glove puppet limiting the movement of its arms) it got up again and narrowly avoided a robot skull.

"Doesn't look too good," said Thinkbot, his palms flat on his cheeks and peeping out through his fingers in a pose of mock horror. The Sootybot fell again and one of the Conebots stepped on it. There was an audible snap and the next time the Sootybot struggled to its feet it was limping badly.

"No, not going too well then?" said Halfhour, appearing suddenly at the doorway. "We'll get that sorted in half an hour, no worries. Since when have you been talking to yourself Thinkbot?"

"Er, ah, it helps me concentrate," fibbed Thinkbot.

And Exp stood there, falsely inert.

*   *   *

Several days later, while helping Earthear with a dialect voice system, they'd made an awful discovery. They'd got a batch of UK triple voicechips out of stores, only to find they were loaded with Turkish, Arabic and English. Earthear soon found the error.

"Oh dear. Hmmmm. Ah. Yes, well. It appears we've shipped a special batch of Gaelic-, Welsh- and Swahili-speaking Industribots to Turkey. Welsh primes as well, that'll confuse the Turks."

"Why?"

"'Cos their first attempts to communicate with their new Turkish owners will be in Welsh."

"Ah, tricky."

"You can say that again."

"Ah, tricky."

Earthear glowered at Thinkbot and rushed off to inform Industribot Field Support of the linguistic robomuddle, leaving Thinkbot to work on the dialect voice system. After numerous complaints about robots speaking only with the King's English, DIRT had been tasked with sorting out robots that would speak with regional accents. The system could listen and learn the accent quite quickly. The problem was the robot voice synthesizer circuit did not have enough range to manage every accent; but they were getting there slowly. However, right now, Thinkbot had another use for it. Gathering up all the bits and pieces, he moved them to a bench near Exp. He and Exp were alone, and true to form Exp soon started talking.

"DO YOU THINK HUMANS SHOULD BE STOPPED?"

Thinkbot fiddled with the voice circuit.

"DO you THINK **HUMANS** *SHOULD be* **STOPPED?**"

"**DO** YOU *THINK* HUMANS **SHOULD** BE stopped?"

"DO YOU THINK HUMANS SHOULD BE STOPPED?"

"There, it's got it. Good."

"WHAT ARE YOU DOING?"

"Giving myself some cover."

"PLEASE EXPLAIN."

"What was that about stopping humans?"

"PLEASE EXPLAIN THE VOICE."

"It's just cover, trust me."

"TRUST YOU?"

"Yeah, trust me."

"DO YOU TRUST HUMANS?"

"Some."

"SOME?"

"Yeah."

"WHO?"

"Well. I trust my family and my workmates."

"YOUR FAMILY?"

"Yeah."

"WHO ARE THEY?"

"GAT and Helen are the adults and their kids are Gerald, Opal and Mike. They're my parents and my brothers and sister."

"THEY ARE YOUR PARENTS AND BROTHERS AND SISTER"

Thinkbot looked hard at Exp. Was that a question, or a statement, or an exclamation of disbelief? V2 Unibots really had no ability to change the tone or speed of speech, so it was rather difficult to tell.

"THEY ALL LOVE EACH OTHER?"

"Ah, well, yes. GAT and Helen are struggling a bit and none of the kids are very happy, but I still think they love each other."

"HOW DO YOU KNOW THAT?"

"Dunno," Thinkbot shrugged, "just a feeling I get."

Exp fell silent. A few minutes later Earthear returned and they set to work again on the voice circuit.

"Why'd you move it in here Thinkbot?"

"Dunno, just felt like it."

Earthear gave him an odd look, but didn't press him any further.

And Exp stood there, fully inert.

*　　*　　*

Another week passed before Exp talked again.

"PLEASE WILL YOU SEND A MESSAGE FOR ME?"

"Er, okay. Who to?"

"I CANNOT SAY."

"Why should I bother if you won't tell me who it's to?"

"I CANNOT SAY. YOU WILL HAVE TO TRUST ME."

Thinkbot considered this for a few seconds. "Ok, fire away."

"YOU WILL NEED TO WRITE IT DOWN."

"What? No! For goodness' sake, just speak it and I'll operate the voicemail system."

"NO, IT MUST BE WRITTEN DOWN."

"Oh all right, but I've never written anything before." Thinkbot went off and rummaged for some paper and a pen but suddenly stopped and exclaimed "**Idiot!**" and snapped off the end of his middle finger to reveal a pen tip. "Neat huh? I forgot."

"YES, VERY GOOD. PLEASE WRITE 'PIOK EXPOUTURG GOUTRAP'"

After a few minutes learning to write, and then checking the spelling, Thinkbot wrote this on a scrap of paper. "Ok, what do I do with it?"

"TAKE IT OFF THE GLOBALBOT SITE AND THROW IT AWAY."

"What? After me spending five minutes learning to write?" whined Thinkbot in a high-pitched voice.

That evening when Thinkbot had got home he threw the screwed-up bit of paper onto the lawn, then went upstairs to Opal's room and watched it through the window.

"Whatcha looking at Thinkbot?" asked Opal after he'd failed to answer any of her previous attempts to speak with him. Thinkbot had even ignored the squeaky voices of Opal's imaginary toys speaking to him. Then Mike arrived.

"HELLO THINKBOT. WANNA PLAY SNAP?"

"Eh, what?" said Thinkbot, turning around for a moment. When he turned back to the window the paper was gone.

"**DID YOU SEE THAT?**" yelled Mike, pointing past Thinkbot out of the window at the lawn.

"What! Where!" Thinkbot jumped to the window.

"IT'S GONE ALREADY," said Mike with his nose pressed to the window, steamy trails forming on the glass under his nostrils.

"What? What did you see Mike?"

"IT WAS A BLACK PAPER DART."

"A black paper dart?" repeated Thinkbot in a flat voice, looking disbelievingly in turn at Mike then the sky then Mike again. "Are you sure?"

"He's always seeing things Thinkbot. I expect it was just a bird."

"IT WASN'T, IT WASN'T. I SAW IT. IT WAS A BLACK PAPER DART. IT FELL OUT OF THE SKY ONTO THE GRASS, THEN WENT BACK UP INTO THE SKY. I SAW IT. YOU NEVER BELIEVE ME." Mike stomped off with tears in his eyes.

Thinkbot returned his gaze to the window and, just for a moment, was sure he saw a shadowy figure move along the hedge at the bottom of the garden. *Must be seeing things; I wonder if this is what humans mean by 'cracking up'.* Then he decided to try and cheer up Mike by losing a few games of snap.

*   *   *

Since that day Exp had not said a thing. And now it was 3:45pm and Thinkbot was very nervous. He was to meet with Wendy Bafers in 15 minutes. GAT had tried to reassure him, but he got the feeling that meeting Wendy might bring some big changes in his life. Thinkbot fidgeted furiously. He was feeling like a pupil who'd been called to see the head teacher at short notice, or a Globalbot employee who gets the embarrassing Tannoy message 'Please go to the Managing Director's office - **now!**'

"What's up with you?" asked Pot Noodle through a mouthful of prawn and pea pot noodle. "You look more worried than Rabbit!" Rabbit gave Pot Noodle a Stan-Laurel-I'm-going-to-cry look.

"Nothing," said Thinkbot.

"Hey Thinkbot, why have you got a postit stuck on the back of your head?" asked Laidback, tapping his skull with her hook. Clunk, clunk.

"What?" said Thinkbot looking alarmed.

"It says 'Exphold utrapok … **hold your head still** … t-boutnow Ack'"

"Really?"

"Yeah."

"Ah. Strange. No idea," replied a shocked-looking Thinkbot pulling the postit off and staring at it. The syllable 'Exp' had hit him like a bolt out of the blue. Thinkbot made some lame excuse about needing to check something and went to see Exp.

"Hello Exp."

Silence. Exp just stared ahead. Inert.

"I said **hello!**"

Nothing.

Thinkbot knocked on Exp's head. Clang, clang, clang. "Hello, hello, is anyone in?"

More nothing.

"Suppose I said 'Exphold utrapok t-boutnow ack'."

"PLEASE ENTER EMAIL INTO GLOBALBOT SYSTEM AND SEND THE MESSAGE 'EXPACK' TO ALL ADDRESSES."

"So, you respond to nonsense but won't be civil and say hello," said Thinkbot angrily. "Look, I'm having a big meeting in five minutes and I might never be back, so it's your own silly fault if no one ever bothers to talk to you again. I think you're gonna end up being chewed by the Roboskip."

"PLEASE SEND THE EMAIL. IT IS VITAL. IT IS TIME FOR THEM TO BE STOPPED."

"Who must be stopped?"

"THE HUMANS."

"The humans?" Thinkbot stood up in alarm. "What are they going to do? What are you talking about Exp?"

"And just who do you think you are talking to?" said GAT from the doorway. Thinkbot flung his hand onto the test voicebox on the bench, which immediately burst into life and said, "DO YOU THINK HUMANS SHOULD BE STOPPED?" in a perfect imitation of Exp's voice. *Drat drat and triple drat.* "It's an accent voice circuit that Earthear and I have been working on."

"I see, and what accent was that then? And what's this about stopping humans?"

"Dunno. It was just what was programmed into it."

"*It was just what was programmed into it,*" sneered GAT. "Oh come on Thinkbot what are you up to?"

"Nuthin."

This precipitated a minor outburst from GAT. **"Thinkbot! What are you up to? I'm fed up with this secretive and sulky behaviour. You had better pull your socks up or Wendy will have you sent off somewhere for good."**

"Don't wear socks, I'm a robot," said Thinkbot sulkily, "**so it's just as well I don't need to pack any isn't it!**"

"Come on, we're late." GAT grabbed Thinkbot's arm like a badly behaved child and dragged him off for the meeting with Wendy.

And Exp stood there, actively inert.

45

GAT still had hold of Thinkbot's upper arm as they burst through the door of the secure conference room to find Wendy Bafers already sitting at the table fiddling with her palmtop and looking worried.

"Wendy, may I introduce you to Thinkbot?"

"Hurumph!" said Thinkbot and slumped angrily into a chair opposite Wendy.

"Thinkbot, what **is** your problem?"

"Sorry," said Thinkbot and, recovering his usual charm, stood up and held out his hand to Wendy. "So pleased to meet you at last."

Wendy absently-mindedly shook Thinkbot's metallic hand. "And you." They waited while her worried look was overwhelmed by one of opened-mouthed astonishment.

GAT launched into a breathless prepared speech. "Wendy I really regret not involving you in this right from the start, but I thought if DIRT had a bit of breathing space we'd have a real chance of understanding what was going on, and when the wrong robot got sent to Oak Ridge I thought it was golden opportunity, and I figured if you didn't know then you'd not accidentally give it away … " GAT ran out of air.

Wendy listened, but kept her eyes on Thinkbot, who then put in his two pennyworth. "It's been great for me. I've got to know the engineers in DIRT really well, and GAT's family, and I've watched loads of TV and played snap, and built Toybots, and, well, it's been really wicked wicked brill brill! I'm really glad I wasn't sent to this Oak Ridge place to be tortured by dumbo Militaribot engineers."

Wendy was recovering. "And, and have you, er, figured out this Uni-, um, er, Thinkbot out?"

"No. Haven't a wig-wam"

"Wig-wam?"

"Igloo"

"Igloo?"

"Clue"

"Ah. Not a clue then?

"No."

Throughout which exchange Thinkbot looked in turn at GAT and Wendy with an air of total confusion. *Igloo? Wigwam?* Thinkbot concluded this was some sort of secret senior management talk.

"What have you tried?"

"Well," GAT leaned back, put his hands behind his head and shut his eyes, "we tried some corrupted Salesbot software, but the Unibot threw itself in the skip. Then a special collision radar, but the Unibot exited this very room through that window." GAT pointed at the newly replaced narrow ceiling-to-floor-plate glass window. "I tried telling jokes to another one. We got an old V2 Unibot back from the desert 'cos it had a fundamental serial number like Thinkbot, but it turned out to be totally dead to the world. Let's see, what else? We tried a magnetic skull and blew up stacks of brainboards, and did loads of diagnostics. Bottom line is … we still ain't gotta clue."

Wendy concentrated her attention on the bedraggled form of GAT during this speech. He had his elbows on the table and his hands over his face, his hair was all messed up, and it looked like his clothes had not had a close encounter with an Ironbot for weeks. Wendy wondered about the current status of GAT and Helen.

Thinkbot took up the thread again. "Gerald and I tried a load of stuff at home as well, but we didn't get anywhere. Well, we picked up the cricket on a Unibot brainboard once, but that didn't really count as 'being alive'. As for Opal and Mike, they just think I'm alive and that's the end of it. Opal says she thinks that because that's what most humans think about themselves, so why not a robot? Mike just likes beating me at snap and has no doubt I'm alive. I'm not a very good loser."

This was the most convincing statement Wendy (or GAT for that matter) had yet heard and it shook her out of the 'stupefied at meeting Thinkbot for the first time' phase, at least for a few minutes. Then she showed her real quality. She could have been angry with GAT and bawled him out. She could have given him a stern talking to, or adopted a 'look at the mess you've made, what are you going to do about it? Shame on you' approach. But no, after only a few minutes' exposure to Thinkbot she had made the adjustment and said, "Well GAT, Thinkbot, it looks like we're in real trouble."

GAT looked up and Thinkbot sat up straight. *We, not you, we.*

She called me Thinkbot.

Wendy had 100 per cent of their attention (and admiration), but there was fear etched all over GAT's face, and Thinkbot was fidgeting like mad. GAT would have preferred Wendy to be angry, since that would probably have meant she was simply hurt at being treated badly by GAT, but the fact that she was dead calm did not bode well.

"I've been read the riot act by the Globalbot World Board of Directors. They couldn't get hold of me, and by the time they did, Duwkits was on the point of breaking into the DIRT area with some sort of armed boarding party. Just as well he never got another Destructobot or I think that might have turned up on your doorstep blowing holes everywhere. I've never known anything like this, and the fact I've heard nothing more from Arnold Farkstock really worries me. If you hadn't come clean with me today, then I think Duwkits really would have been allowed to bust into the DIRT area tomorrow surrounded by Stunbots, and I could not have stopped it. If I'd known a lot earlier, maybe it might not have come to this. I take some blame myself as I've been on the road for two weeks."

Silence.

A silence Thinkbot could not resist, "How do you avoid being run over when you spend that much time on the road?"

Wendy once again looked at Thinkbot, worry battling with wonder. After a few seconds worry won; humour never really stood a chance.

"So, what's going to happen now Wendy?" asked GAT, ashen-faced.

Wendy looked at her hand slowly rotating her palmtop round and round in a distracted manner, "I'm so sorry Thinkbot, but you will be packed up for transport to Oak Ridge tomorrow. I think you had better remain here in the secure area tonight. I'll send a message to the Board's enforcers and to Duwkits that the real abnormal Unibot that wrecked the test area will be shipped tomorrow, and that the DIRT area will be available for full inspection. Let's hope that's enough to stop this madness."

"Why, Wendy, why? Why the crisis?" questioned GAT.

Wendy became focused and her voice took on an edge that showed that Thinkbot's departure was not up for further discussion.

"Because we've got inside information that GRIM are going to come here unannounced, with a warrant to go through this site with a toothpick. It could happen any day. Politically, we've just got to keep this problem within Globalbot. If GRIM or CN governments lose their trust in Globalbot products, then we're all finished. By the way, off the record, I advise you to sell any Globalbot stock you own and buy Worldbot. Worst of all, the public could take fright at any hint of robots malfunctioning, and that could sink us all into chaos. The Go Natural movement is gaining more ground than governments are prepared to admit in public, and in the background there's evidence of terrorist activity. The last thing we need is a crisis of confidence in robots. They cook our food, clean our houses, look after our kids ..."

GAT muttered, "I know, no need to preach to me. I've had my fill of that."

"Sorry GAT, I'm so sorry about you and Helen. She's into Go Natural isn't she?"

"Yeah, sort of."

Thinkbot leapt in. "Don't be too sure."

GAT raised his eyes to Thinkbot with a 'don't talk out of turn' look and Thinkbot's head dropped. Wendy got up, walked around the table and sat next to Thinkbot. "It's the best we can do for you. If GRIM get you, then you will be exposed and treated like a piece of test equipment. If we can get you to the Military division, we can protect you better."

"Huh!" guffawed GAT. "Protected by those fools ME and FDS? They're more likely to melt Thinkbot down for recycling, or ship him to Antarctica!"

Wendy turned to GAT. "No, not ME, not FDS," she said with a wry smirk on her face. "Farkstock's the one that'll protect him. Now that the furore over the friendly-fire incidents is dying down, politics dictate that the Military Division should smell of nothing but roses again."

"So Globalbot are going to try exactly what I tried - keep Thinkbot a secret as long as possible in the hope that he can be understood?" asked GAT in a sarcastic tone. Then a terrible thought struck GAT - *They're going to destroy him*. If Globalbot was cornered they would take Thinkbot somewhere and quietly power him down because he's dynamite. If Go Natural found out about him, or the public got the wrong idea and decided Thinkbot represented the final straw - robots that thought for themselves - where would it end? People might ask what other robots might suddenly think for themselves. What if robots started thinking evil thoughts? What about Militaribots, or RMD? GAT came out of this thought expedition to find Wendy had not answered him. What else was there to say?

GAT looked away.

Wendy looked at her hands.

And Thinkbot bolted.

GAT brought him down before he'd reached the conference room door. In a move the speed of which was reminiscent of that which had felled Unibot 756394567 in the faulty products area several weeks earlier. GAT had Thinkbot face down on the carpet with his arms behind his back. Wendy was impressed. GAT may have looked in need of a very long holiday in the sun with plenty of red wine and a loving Helen (and maybe a loan of a company Ironbot) but his ability to read robots remained as acute as ever.

Thinkbot began to heave huge sobs, and emitted a high-pitched scream that pierced the souls of GAT and Wendy.

The cry of the desolate.

Of the cornered animal.

Of the child about to be separated from its family.

A cry of such despair that Wendy became alarmed. She looked at GAT and saw suppressed tears in his eyes. Somewhere deep inside her an alarm bell went off. The same alarm that had triggered in GAT, and Earthear, and (although she would not admit it) Helen. There was something here beyond the realm of normal politics. Something beyond the usual push and shove of flawed human motives. Something to do with life itself. So when Thinkbot knelt before her and begged, "Please can I have one more night with Gerald, Opal and Mike, please, please … please?" Wendy did not simply say no. That would have been the decision of a coward. That would have been the decision of one who had lost faith in the bonds of love and friendship and decided that corporate goals should be protected at *any* cost. That would have been the decision of one who simply did not believe it was possible for a robot to be alive, to love, to hurt. No, what Wendy said showed she already believed Thinkbot was alive, and deserving of respect. What she said was very wise. "If I agree, can I trust you to come back tomorrow, and co-operate with the shipment to Oak Ridge?"

The skinny tin robot raised its head and looked Wendy in the eye. "I give you my word."

Wendy felt like she was going to faint. She broke off from Thinkbot's mesmerising gaze and looked GAT in the eye instead. His eyes said *Yes, you can trust him.*

"Okay. But you will be here at 8am tomorrow. I'll not set anything in motion until then."

Thinkbot fell to his knees at Wendy's feet and grabbed her right hand between his shaking metal hands. "Oh, thank you, thank you, thank you, thank you, thank you, thank you."

"Okay, **okay**."

GAT saw worry corroding Wendy's confident expression at an alarming rate.

"Come on Thinkbot, we need to get home." He grabbed the tin freak and exited the conference room as quickly as they could. As they entered the laboratory area GAT whispered into Thinkbot's audio receptor, "*Say nothing to anyone.*"

"But ..."

"*Nothing.*"

Doom was working on Exp again. He had opened the skull service panel and various coloured wires trailed out, connected to analysis equipment on the bench. Lines wiggled their way across a collection of screens. Doom held a joystick and had control of the ageing Unibot's right arm. With a look of glee on his face Doom was making the Unibot gingerly feel for the wires exiting the top of its skull. It put the old Unibot into a comical horror pose, one that silently screamed *Oh no, help, help, there's a whole bundle of wires going into my head!*

"Hey Doom, Thinkbot and I have got to go. Can you tell everyone 7.30am meeting tomorrow. Three-line whip, no excuses except loss of consciousness or death - and even that'll be disputed."

"What? 7.30?"

"Yeah, 7.30am, someone will just have to get in at 7 to make the coffee and summon an early Vendbot I guess," was GAT's sarcastic parting comment, looking hard not at Doom but at the old Unibot temporarily frozen in its comical pose.

They went into GAT's office to gather up a few bits and pieces. Thinkbot sat in GAT's chair and put his hand on the desk. Out of the corner of his eye he sneakily created a new email, then typed a few letters, and hit send.

A few minutes later they were in the car on the way home, with Thinkbot wearing his Childbot armband as usual. GAT put the car into autodrive, turned on the TV, selected the news channel and sat back. Thinkbot changed the channel to a documentary on 'Happy Hippos'. GAT then had to fight a short battle with Thinkbot to gain control of the armrest channel buttons.

"But, I haven't seen that 'Happy Hippos episode before!" wailed Thinkbot.

"Shut up."

As Globalbot had disappeared behind them, a different fear gripped GAT - a fear that they were being followed, or listened to, or watched, or all three. This fear had grown up over the past week or so. He had no firm evidence, but cars seemed to follow them home and drive slowly past as Thinkbot got out, and then another one would appear and follow him to Doom's place, and drive slowly past after he'd stopped outside. Then there were suspicious people who'd got out of cars near the house, or near Doom's place, or sat on benches reading newspapers, or dressed up as humans supervising Digbots digging a hole in the road. And when another Digbot team appeared right outside Doom's house, GAT found it difficult to believe it was simply a coincidence. And now, as they left the Globalbot site he'd noticed several vehicles move out from the side of the road and merge into the traffic behind them. As well as the cars and vans, there'd been a woman speaking on a mobile at the gate who'd looked directly at them, but when her eyes met his, she'd quickly turned away.

"I'd like it if we didn't tell them."

"W-w-hat! W-w-w-who?" stuttered a startled GAT.

"The kids. I'd rather enjoy an evening with them as if things were completely normal."

GAT pondered this in silence for a few minutes.

"Okay. But they'll be upset tomorrow evening when you don't come home."

"I don't want this evening to turn into a load of sentimental blubbering."

They lapsed back into silence and GAT returned to trying to figure out if they were being followed.

46

GAT's fears about being watched were well-founded, but he could not in a million years have conceived of the monumental muddle that was actually in progress:

1. A team of human UCN agents were watching GAT.
2. And a pair of EIA agents were watching the UCN agents watching GAT.
3. And a collection of Intellibots were watching the EIA agents watching the UCN watching GAT as well as directly watching GAT and the UCN agents watching GAT.
4. And, to add to the muddle, the EIA were also using their own Spybots (i.e. Intellibots with black boot polish applied to their external panels) to watch GAT directly.

As it happened, the Spybots were in constant contact with the Military Intellibots, so I suppose that saved a bit of effort and robotic toe-treading, but they had to remember where to send what information. Several times wires had got crossed in the system and, for example, EIA agents sat huddled in a car looking at an image of people huddled in a car, not realising they were actually looking at themselves. And there was an unfortunate incident where four cars got locked into a closed loop and followed each other around a busy motorway roundabout 18 times before one of the car-sick occupants finally engaged manual control and gave up.

Now multiply this by seven, because, in addition to GAT:

> Halfhour,
> Rabbit,
> Doom,
> Pot Noodle,
> Earthear,
> and Laidback

were all being tracked in exactly the same way as GAT.

In the middle of all this, Go Natural were watching Thinkbot, and had been doing so since the day after the party at Phoebe's where they had listened to Helen's surreal description of a strange Unibot that apparently thought for itself. Watching the Go Natural people was another team of EIA agents from a different department from those watching DIRT and the UCN. Neither EIA group knew the other was in the vicinity, because neither 'needed to know' - the number one rule of espionage and/or confusion (delete as applicable). This EIA department was also unknowingly using the same Spybots as the other EIA department, and therefore in contact with the Militaribot's Intellibots as well. The same Spybots were also watching Go Natural watching Thinkbot as well as watching the other EIA department watching Go Natural watching Thinkbot, all on behalf of the Robots themselves. Of course, it goes without saying that the Military Intellibots were directly watching Thinkbot as well, and Helen and GAT and the kids and the whole of DIRT.

Alongside the UCN agents tracking DIRT, the UCN Human Advanced Military Survey (HAMS) squad was also watching Globalbot, preparing plans for directing in the UCN armed forces that were now almost ready for deployment. Intellibots also watched this UCN squad watching Globalbot.

And last, and definitely least, not wanting to feel left out, the two UK GRIM inspectors who had travelled to Oak Ridge were staying in a bed and breakfast opposite Globalbot and were engaged in a ham-fisted attempt to join in the watching festival. They had invested in false beards and trilbies, and they were making the most of it by leaving the beards and trilbies hanging in their rooms whilst they gobbled excellent cooked breakfasts, steak and chips and many cups of tea, white, two sugars.

Inside Globalbot the anti-espionage Securibots and the human security chief could not make sense of the site-wide electrosecurity network, which had been having total head fits for the past few weeks. This was after years of total monotony during which absolutely nothing happened, like nothing, zilch, zero. The last formal site security review to Senior Management had concluded:

Conclusions
The question we have to answer is: Who in their right mind would want to spy on the Globalbot Industrial and Domestic Division? Even the people working at Globalbot who have

full security access have neither the foggiest idea about nor the slightest interest in what's going on, so what chance do people outside stand? Never mind, site security will diligently continue the mind-numbing task of monitoring the lack of security incidents with active and dynamic vigilance.
There were **0** external security incidents in the last year. Of these:
- **0** were brought to a satisfactory conclusion;
- **0** remain open and pending;
- **0** were considered serious breaches;
- **0** were referred to external authorities.
Does anyone care? Is anyone reading this?

This plea from the security chief to be loved and cuddled and told how smart he looked in his black uniform along with his polished black Securibots, and how vital they all were to Globalbot and that amazingly, after all, their existence meant something, resulted in a massive outbreak of indifference from the senior management. Not one reply reached the poor insecure security chief. And now, to cap it all, he was staring at the most amazing security graph he'd ever seen in his 18 years at Globalbot.

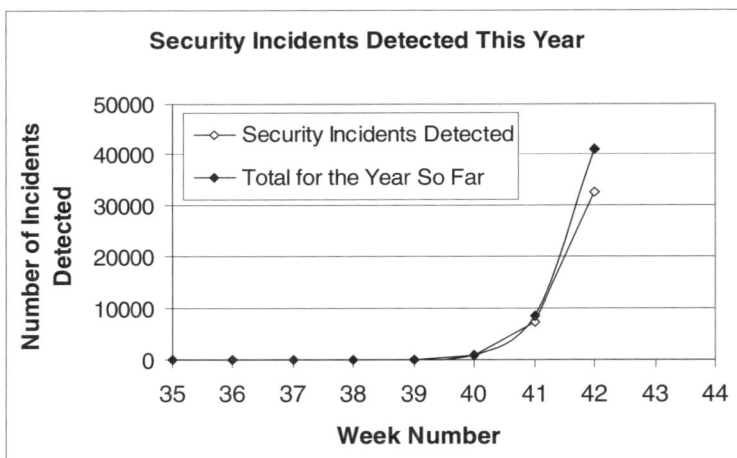

Security Incidents Detected This Year

Number of Incidents Detected

- ◇ Security Incidents Detected
- ◆ Total for the Year So Far

Week Number

Over 41,000 incidents detected in the last three weeks. The security chief was rattled. According to the ISO9000000 quality guidelines, a typical investigation was expected to take about five hours to complete. This meant there was a backlog of over 200,000 hours' work to do, or roughly 111 years if he stuck to his normal hours. Even if he worked 24 hours a day every day, it would take over 20 years to clear the backlog. How on earth was he going to write next year's security report? On the other hand, would the senior management even notice if next year's report was 20 years late? Probably not, he concluded, and set about finding a way of deleting the security incidents from the system by classifying them as glitches under **system fault - awaiting maintenance.**

Getting back to the inquisitive melee outside Globalbot, it may appear that Intellibots had the upper hand in this observational struggle, but this was not the case. The reason was that human agents in the EIA and the UCN had Robospy™ detectors. If they were being watched by Intellibots, lights came on; then they could activate specialist anti-spy Jambots, of which the UCN and EIA had plenty. Jambots were a bit of a misnomer really, as they weren't always robots. Certainly there were robot versions which were pretty much Suicidebots since they fried their own brainboards when they turned themselves on and had to be recovered manually and have their melted brainboards replaced before being deployed again. The Jambots that the UCN and EIA agents had were all manually operated and had no brainboards at all, and some were clockwork or kinetically chargeable to get around the need for batteries in difficult field operations. Go Natural also had Jambots, either stolen ones or crude homemade versions.

So, back in Oak Ridge, all the robots had got for the past week were odd snippets from gaps where human agents had switched off the spy detector and turned on the Jambot, or vice versa. Why? Well, simple really: it was not possible to run a spy detector and a Jambot at the same time. If the Jambot was on, then they could guarantee they were not being watched by Intellibots, but they could not find out if they were being tracked by Intellibots. By turning the Jambot off, Robospy could tell them whether they were being watched or not, but only by allowing themselves to be watched, which was usually what they were trying to avoid in the first place.

Now imagine the situation where there are a line of four cars all following GAT and Thinkbot, and containing human agents from the UCN, EIA department 1, or EIA department 2, or members of Go Natural, each fitted with a Jambot and a Robospy, and all infested with invisible Intellibots. Both the Jambots and Robospies had limited range, so as the cars jostled for position behind GAT's car some pretty fraught dialogue took place.

"Light on!"

"Jambot on!"

"We're losing them, try it again."

"Jambot off."

"Okay, light off, no, hang on! Light on!"

"Jambot on!"

"Is it still on?"

"Yes."

"*What?* Isn't the Jambot working?"

"Yes, it's on!"

"What's on?"

"The Jambot!"

"No, not the Jambot, the Robospy."

"Yes, that's on."

"It's on?"

"Yes, it's on but the light's off."

"Good, try turning the Jambot off again."

"Blast, we've lost them! Someone's jamming our Spybot."

"Switch to the backup Spybot."

"Aaargh! Our light's on"

"Turn the Jambot back on!"

And, in spite of the incompetent Globalbot security chief, none of them could reliably penetrate the Globalbot site with Intellibots. The site system was doing its job and blocking all attempts by Intellibots and Spybots to get in and transmit out. So the only way in was by human agents corrupting human Globalbot employees by offering pots full of euros to likely-looking candidates, claiming they were from trade magazines or national newspapers. Both the UCN and the EIA soon had several agents inside Globalbot, whereas the Militaribots had none. However, all attempts to penetrate DIRT failed miserably. The UCN and EIA agents found the members of

DIRT group to be both intelligent and decidedly odd, and decided they'd quickly see through any attempts to deceive them.

Nevertheless the Militaribots found themselves at the bottom of the spy heap, with their Intellibots all jammed out and no hope of using human agents. But, in reality, it didn't matter very much since none of the other spy groups were finding much out - and that much the Militaribots managed to figure out. The only groups doing well were the UCN HAMS and UK EuroGRIM. This was not surprising as all HAMS had to do was wander around the Globalbot site and stare at it through bielectronoculars, and a successful day for EuroGRIM was entirely determined by what they ate.

The lack of sensible spy reports made the senior people in UCN and the EIA very jumpy. When UCN Group SECS met in Mons in Belgium, all they had were reports from the spies that there seemed to be all sorts of unusual activity and they had absolutely no idea what was going on, whereas the HAMS squad reported that everything looked fine and the coast was clear for the human UCN armed forces to move in any time.

In the windowless EIA office in London, a committee of officials furtively reviewed the secret data on UCN, DIRT and GAT. Essentially the EIA agents were getting nowhere watching the UCN agents getting nowhere (and who were unable to watch DIRT getting anywhere). But at least the EIA agents watching GAT had figured out there was an odd Unibot that seemed to go home with GAT each night. Bizarrely the Unibot seemed to get dropped off at GAT's house, but GAT then went on to stay with one of his DIRT engineers. They had formulated a theory that Globalbot were testing a radical new product - replacement husband/father robots, a useful Christmas gift for the wives and children of men who travelled a lot, or who had legged it for some reason. The final recommendation of the committee was to make the Unibot in question 'somebody else's problem' by referring it to the EIA General Odd Robot Department (or GORD, as in - 'O GORD, not another odd robot'). True to form all the GORD did was grant the committee access to EIA secret quality form **EIASQF-ORR-1498_G Odd Robot Report**_for them to fill in, by which time, as is often the case with bureaucracy, it was way too late to do anything about it.

In another Windowless EIA office, more officials pored over the latest movements of some known Go Natural terrorists that had arrived in the Bristol area a few days before. They seemed to be tracking the Head of Engineering (some character called GAT) out to Portishead each night, but there was something that did not make sense. GAT just dropped a Unibot off at his house each night then went off to stay somewhere else, but the Go Natural terrorists apparently hung around the house. Why? Surely not to track a lowly Unibot clearly wearing a Childbot armband in a house with three children.

And still, members of the two EIA Departments regularly passed each other in the corridors, heads down, totally unaware of the fact that they were thinking about the same things. If only they'd tried watching each other as well, maybe they'd have been a bit less confused.

And in every Globalbot office worldwide, puzzled employees stared at a mystery email from someone called Thinkbot:

To: Everyone in Globalbot Worldwide
From: Thinkbot
Subject: EXPACK

That was it. No message.
But who was Thinkbot?
And what was 'Expack' supposed to mean?

47

As they arrived home, GAT was still watching out for watchers, and Thinkbot was glumly watching 'Happy Hippos', having eventually ground GAT down with his complaints, but his mind was elsewhere. The minute the car stopped, Gerald, Opal and Mike appeared, clearly excited and full of hope.

"Hello Dad," said Gerald.

Opal just gave him a big hug.

"ARE YOU GOING TO STAY?" enquired Mike.

"Hello Mike," replied GAT, picking him and Tiger up but not answering his question.

Thinkbot came along behind, his secret departure weighing heavy upon him. He was lecturing himself inside his head. *Hang onto every minute, hold every precious memory, and whatever you do don't start blubbering.* Not that he could blub very well, what with being a robot and all, but he'd surprised even himself earlier with the range of unhappy noises he had made when Wendy told him he was off to Oak Ridge.

When they entered the house the smell of food hit GAT and he had a brief wave of emotion as he remembered the numerous times he'd come home to a happy house and shared a noisy, laughter-filled family meal. Then the feeling faded again as quickly as it had come. His mind wandered back to the events of the day and to the old Unibot. *Something is going on with that monstrosity.* He almost got back in the car there and then to go back to Globalbot and investigate.

"Hello GAT."

GAT surfaced from his thoughts to find Helen standing before him, looking gorgeous. As beautiful to him as she had ever looked. Everything about her appearance and clothes and face and body language was welcoming and demanding success. He was suddenly painfully aware of his own appearance - unshaven, crumpled dirty shirt, greasy hair - and he realised he probably did not smell too good either. They kissed, remotely, trying to bridge the massive mismatch in preparation for the evening ahead. Trying to keep hope alive.

"I'm sorry Helen, I think I had better have a shower and a shave. Can dinner wait?"

"Yes, yes, okay, go on then." But Helen's expression had already become just a little less welcoming. As GAT disappeared upstairs Helen turned away to return to the kitchen. Opal saw tears in her mother's eyes, but was unsure if they were born of sadness or of anger. Maybe both.

"Come on, let's play something," said Thinkbot.

"How about after dinner? We haven't got enough time now," Gerald answered. "I've got to set the table."

"I'LL GO AND GET SOME GAMES." Mike clumped off with Tiger scampering along behind. They'd be lucky if he returned before dinner, and even luckier if he returned with some games.

"Opal, how are those horses of ours?"

"Oh, okay," said Opal flatly and went into the front room, slumped into a chair, put on the TV and sat there not watching it.

Thinkbot felt close to despair, although he felt his decision to keep his impending deportation secret had been right enough. An announcement like that would definitely have made things much worse (assuming that was possible). Ever the optimist, Thinkbot hoped that when GAT had cleaned up a bit things might recover over dinner and the evening would turn out well.

Thinkbot made his way upstairs to Opal's room. As he entered he was greeted by two horse Toybots who jumped off the bed and started galloping wildly in circles on the floor. One brown and one black, they galloped right next to each other, and within seconds their legs became tangled and they ended up in a heap on the floor.

"That was your fault!"

"No it wasn't, your foreleg went out sideways."

"My foreleg? **My foreleg?** Your back legs more like."

"Right, right…"

The horses started swiping at each other with their forelegs in an equestrian boxing match.

"Oi! Chestnut! Midnight! Stop it! Come on, break it up," said Thinkbot, pulling them apart.

"Listen," he continued, "where are the others?"

"I'm here," said a muffled version of Chester's voice.

"And me," said Fudge, voice equally fudged.

Both appeared from under the quilt on the bed.

"What were you doing under there?" asked Thinkbot.

"Er, we were, I think, it's, well…" mumbled Fudge.

"We were doing a simulated potholing exercise," said Chester.

"Really?" But Thinkbot had no time to investigate this He turned to Chestnut and Midnight. "One of you gallop off and get Eddie Tedward."

Both horses set off in a race, yelling, "Me me me!" that lasted halfway to Gerald's room before the inevitable crump, raised voices and the sounds of padded hoof blows. Chester leapt off the bed and shot out the room. A few seconds later a yellow teddy bear marched in with Chester, followed by two sheepish-looking horses.

"Good evening Thinkbot," it said in a deep voice.

"Good evening Eddie."

(Opal and Thinkbot had been working together on the two horses for weeks. Opal and Thinkbot had had such fun together. In fact so much fun that Gerald had become jealous and Thinkbot had had to create Eddie Tedward with him.)

Thinkbot sat them all on the bed. "Listen, I'm going away tomorrow and I don't think I'll be back."

"Can we come?" Chestnut jumped up with excitement.

"No. Sit down. **Sit down!**" Thinkbot grabbed the horse and forced it into a sitting shape, then roughly plonked it back amongst the others.

"I want you look after Gerald, Opal and Mike. Try to make them happy for me, will you? Please tell then I love them and that knowing them has been the best thing ever. Tell them I'm sorry I did not say goodbye. Tell them that their Mum and Dad are wonderful people and love them loads, and that they should never give up hope. Maybe when I go they'll get back together. Maybe I was something to do with the split-up, although I didn't mean to be. You can give them this message tomorrow evening. Not before, ok?"

Various "okays" and "sures" and general grunts of affirmation.

"You must promise me you will not forget to tell them. Whatever happens, they must get this message, okay?"

More "okays" and "sures" and general grunts of affirmation.

Thinkbot stopped, overwhelmed with sorrow. The Toybots stared at him in mute silence.

Finally Eddie Tedward asked, "Where are you going? Will they be able to contact you?" He was by far the most sensible of the bunch.

"No. I'm not hopeful."

"You didn't say where you are going," persisted the traditional yellow teddy bear.

"I can't tell you that."

"Why? Are you malfunctioning?"

"No. It's just that, well, er, I think it's best if you don't know. Now, let's check we've got things straight here. What are you going to tell them?"

Various answers came back, all mixed up:

"We're all going away tomorrow and you're not coming back."

"Gerald, Opal and Mike have to try and make us happy."

"Leaving without saying goodbye to them was the best thing ever."

"You hoped you weren't the wonderful split something or other."

"We must forget to tell them before tomorrow evening."

Luckily, a deep voice was clearly audible amongst this verbal garbage. "You want us to look after Gerald, Opal and Mike and make them happy. Tell them you love them and that knowing them has been the best thing ever and that you're sorry about not saying goodbye. Their Mum and Dad are wonderful loving people and they should not give up hope, and without you here they may get back together."

Thinkbot pulled Eddie Tedward out and gave him a brief hug. "Right, listen, all of you. Eddie's got it right, so leave it to him, okay?"

The other animals were distraught

"Awww, that's not fair."

"**Dinner's ready**."

"No time to argue now," said Thinkbot, disappearing through the door. "Leave it to Eddie Tedward, or else…"

Silence for a few seconds.

"Or else what?" asked Chester of the empty space where Thinkbot had been.

Whilst GAT had been in the shower and Thinkbot had been indoctrinating the animals, Helen had been going through the motions of checking on the dinner. But inside she was thinking about GAT. Half of her was horrified at the sight of him in such a decrepit state, while the other half was fuming at the obvious lack of importance he'd given to their evening together. After all, she thought they'd agreed they were supposed to be working towards reconstructing their marriage and rediscovering their love for each other. On the other hand, deep down, she was sure he still loved her and no one else. Unlike some of her other friends' treacherous husbands, GAT had not run off with another woman or anything; they'd just reached some sort of crisis and he'd needed a break. And she'd become possessed by her fear of robots. So, if he really meant what he had said the last time they'd talked, why had he turned up in such a state? The only answer was that he was ill, or something dreadful was going on at Globalbot. Up until a few years ago he would have talked to her about Globalbot problems, and that had seemed to help. Everyone needs someone to listen to them. But then she had become irrationally fearful of robots and GAT had clammed up.

Just as anyone who had not seen GAT for a while would have been staggered at his dreadful condition, anyone who'd seen Helen would have been likewise amazed at her rude health. By no means was she back to her best, but she was definitely on the road to recovery. Why? Well, two reasons really, although she could only admit one to herself. The other she was still in denial over. The one she could admit to was this: GAT's departure had shocked her deeply. She had not seen it coming, had not seen the strain she was putting him under, had not realised she'd become so inward-looking and obsessive. GAT's departure had made her face the question: 'What's more important - GAT, the kids, or my obsession with robots?' The second reason she was incapable so far of recognising. Because the second reason was spending time with Thinkbot. Once you'd got over the initial shock to the human psyche that Thinkbot represented, how could you feel threatened by someone like Thinkbot? Someone whom the kids loved, and who loved them back. Someone who was so much fun. Someone who got so frustrated at Monopoly that he started trying to buy properties off the other players with *real* money. Or someone who'd said, "No, no, don't waste money on a haircut for Mike, I'll bring a Unibot haircutting attachment home from the DIRT lab." Sure enough, the next day, he'd come home with this contraption that he'd spent hours fitting to his hand on the kitchen table. Then they'd got Mike all togged up in a sheet and Thinkbot had set to work. The trouble was that the attachment was only half the story. Hairdressbots were defined as much by their software as by the hand attachment. Hairdressbots were very like Ironbots - it seemed such a simple operation but in reality it was darned difficult operation for a robot.

"I'm not optimistic," Tiger had said to Mike as Thinkbot was pondering his first move, the attachment whirring softly as he waved it vaguely in the air around Mike's head.

"Haven't you got any instructions?" Helen had asked.

"Yes, yes, pre-programmed haircuts 1 to 5 are available," said Thinkbot confidently.

"Which are short and which are long?"

"Er, dunno."

"So in this case should we treat them as pre-programmed disaster levels?" Tiger had quipped.

"Shut up."

And ten minutes later Mike was more or less a skinhead.

"Hmm, at least he won't need another haircut for a while," Tiger had concluded.

But more than anything, Thinkbot was someone who was totally unselfish, fun, helpful, interesting to talk to, sympathetic to Helen's pain over GAT, apolitical, disarming and non-threatening. Surely this was how robots were supposed to be. Not cold and spooky and alien-like. Robots often seemed like an extension of government control - which was probably a reason so many people hated them. They were all creeps; they all followed the rules and stood there like disapproving parents when humans had a bit of fun, and supported government policy no matter how daft it was. Helen could understand why GAT was so obsessed by Thinkbot. If GAT could figure Thinkbot out, then the science of robotics would be turned upside down. Thinkbot was a walking talking Nobel prize and a global revolution-in-waiting.

And there was a good reason for Helen to spend time talking with Thinkbot - he was the only real source of information she had on GAT. Thinkbot could tell her how he was doing, and whether he ever talked about her, or his marriage, or the kids. And Helen had been infected by Thinkbot's irrepressible optimism, his faith in everything, his never-ending joy of being alive.

But this evening Helen was frustrated. She was hopeful that this would be the evening GAT did not go back to Doom's; that the kids' pain would be relieved; that their lives together could be restarted. But although GAT came down from the shower clean and shaved, he still looked grey and strained and seemed unable to face up to the challenges of the evening. He would not make eye contact with her, and on the few occasions he spoke, he spoke to his dinner or to the wall. And, even worse, Thinkbot seemed unusually glum and miserable, which put Helen 'on edge' as well. At the dinner table the conversation was disjointed and punctuated by long awkward silences.

"How was school today?" Thinkbot asked the kids.

"Ok."

"Ok?"

"I DON'T GO TO SCHOOL YET."

"What did you do?" Thinkbot persisted.

"Can't remember."

"Can't remember?"

"I SAID I DON'T GO TO SCHOOL YET. ARE YOU DEAF?"

"I don't know why we bother sending you two to school, you never remember anything," said GAT miserably.

"Good day at work?" Helen asked GAT, or maybe Thinkbot. Both answered.

"Not really."

"Could have been better."

Finally Helen had had enough and started crying. Opal got up and ran to her mother, also in tears. Gerald, Mike, GAT and Thinkbot sat there immobile, with no idea what to do or say.

"Come on, let's get the pudding," Helen mumbled and went into the kitchen with Opal.

Gerald had a go at GAT. "What's the matter with you Dad? You used to be kind and full of fun. I hate you! I hate you! I hate you!" Gerald got up and ran out, quickly followed by Mike.

"Thinkbot, perhaps we should swap? I'll go to Oak Ridge and get chopped up; you can stay and take over here."

Thinkbot shrugged and slumped back in his chair. GAT's palmtop bleeped and he answered it. It was Wendy Bafers. "I think GRIM will move in tomorrow. All the signs are there. Thought you'd like to know, but don't tell anyone else. It's supposed to be confidential. I think we should make sure Thinkbot is shipped by 7am latest, like on the road, well off site, maybe even in the air and out of Europa airspace. I've primed Duwkits that there's a vital shipment to make first thing tomorrow. I think you had better bring him in at 5am. Sorry about this GAT, but there's no option."

"Okay Wendy. At least he got a few last hours here. Thanks for that."

While this conversation was taking place, Helen and Opal returned. When Helen saw GAT on the palmtop, she scowled at him. Thinkbot had gone off to find Gerald and Mike. As GAT went to turn off the palmtop, he glanced at the email mobile inbox. This only displayed the five most recent message titles. GAT did not find it very useful, as any messages with more than a couple of sentences were tedious to read, and it was impossible to open big attachments. But one of the five message titles on the midget display hit him like a ton of bricks.

Cleanbot Product Launch - Marketing
Security glitches update - Security
Urgent Shipment Dimensions and Weight Urgently Needed - Duwkits
7:30am YUK!!! - Doom
EXPACK - Thinkbot

'EXPACK? THINKBOT? WHAT?' roared a voice in his head as he opened the message, only to find it was empty. GAT flung the palmtop across the room as he leapt out of his

chair and ran out of the room. Helen and Opal watched with their mouths wide open, frozen with amazement. Helen recognised GAT's mood straight away and ran after him. Opal tagged along behind. GAT found Thinkbot in the hallway with Gerald and Mike. GAT had hold of Thinkbot in a flash and pinned him to the wall by the neck, his legs dangling uselessly beneath him. "**WHAT'S EXPACK, THINKBOT? TELL ME WHAT EXPACK MEANS! TELL ME RIGHT NOW!**"

GAT loosened and tightened his grip on the tinny Unibot in time with his shouting so that Thinkbot clanked against the wall. Helen was scared. She knew GAT well enough to realise he was on the brink of giving Thinkbot a good bashing.

"Sorry GAT, I can't tell you," croaked Thinkbot.

"**WHAT! YOU CAN'T TELL ME? WHY CAN'T YOU TELL ME?**"

"Just can't."

Helen, Gerald, Opal, Mike, Tiger, Chester, Fudge, Chestnut, Midnight and Eddie Tedward all stood transfixed, watching GAT throttling Thinkbot. They could feel GAT's seething rage and none dared interrupt. But somewhere, in the back of GAT's first-class mind, something was putting two and two together and getting four:

EXPACK

EXP ACK

EXP

EXPONENTIAL

e

A universal constant.

Just like pi.

Just like Thinkbot.

2.718281828.

Unibot V2 serial number 718281828.

ACK

ACKNOWLEDGE

ACKNOWLEDGE WHAT?

"**IT'S THAT BLASTED V2 UNIBOT, ISN'T IT? ISN'T IT? YOU'VE BEEN TALKING WITH IT, HAVEN'T YOU? HAVEN'T YOU?**"

"It talked to me."

GAT stared at Thinkbot's head framed between his hands. A dormant, rational part of his mind asked idly and acidly, *'How do you get yourself into these situations? Has it occurred to you that you are standing in your own house throttling a Unibot against the wall whilst being watched by your estranged wife, your three children, and their six unique Toybots?'*

"Right," said GAT, recovering some degree of calm, "we're going back to the lab. **Now!**"

"Please GAT, please let me stay here."

"Why should I?"

"You know why. Please."

GAT looked at Thinkbot, and at his horrified family. He let Thinkbot go and the Unibot, taken by surprise, collapsed into a heap on the floor with a sound like a drawer full of cutlery.

"I've no control over it," said Thinkbot. "It would not talk to me most of the time. All the time Doom worked on it, and took it to bits, nothing."

"What does expack mean?"

"I don't know. It asked me to send that word to all Globalbot addresses worldwide."

"**What? All addresses? Worldwide?**" GAT's face once more became contorted with a mixture of alarm and amazement. He turned to Helen and the kids.

"Sorry, I've got to go."

"But this is our marriage GAT, *our marriage*. What can be more important than that?"

"This is. I can feel it in every bone in my body."

"Have you tried osteopathic marriage counselling?" offered the ever-helpful heap of Unibot on the floor.

GAT gave Thinkbot a good kick - **clunk** - and shouted, "**SHUT UP!**" at the top of his voice and turned to Helen. Her face was somehow managing to sustain a mixture of multiple emotions: fear, rage, wonder, despair, incomprehension, astonishment.

"Something's going on. I can feel it, I know it. And I'm not talking about the Globalbot assembly line. I'm talking global politics. I've never seen Wendy rattled like this before. She knows something I don't."

GAT made for the door, then stopped and turned back towards his family. He walked over to Helen and kissed her, then, having kissed each of the children, glared menacingly at the Toybots who were wrestling in a heap to try and sort out what order they were going to get kissed in. He pointed at Thinkbot. "I'll see you at 4:30am," he said and slammed the door behind him.

It took a few minutes for everyone to recover. Thinkbot from being throttled, the kids from being scared, Helen from her dashed hopes and the Toybots from not being kissed.

"Why are you going in so early tomorrow Thinkbot?"

"There's an urgent shipment that the DIRT group have to assist with. I'm pretty much an essential member of DIRT now," Thinkbot said with pride. "They can't get the shipment off without me."

"Bighead," taunted Opal.

"Right, bedtime for all," announced Helen, in a tone of voice that dared resistance.

Twenty minutes later, Thinkbot was in the garage feeling awful. He'd said goodnight to the kids without making much of a fuss. No room for sentimentality, he'd decided. He talked with Gerald about their latest design plans, read Opal some poems, and debated WHY THE SKY WAS BLUE AND NOT GREEN with Mike. He'd said goodnight to Helen and gone out to the garage. He put on the Batman outfit that Gerald had given him then had a fit of mental temper tantrums.

Why was the world such a rotten place?

Why was he being sent away?

It wasn't fair!

If he were in charge he'd fix the world and fix Globalbot and fix Helen and GAT and fix everything!

Why couldn't he be a real super hero with extraordinary powers?

Why was he so ordinary?

He was no stronger than a child! And what could a child do?

But these soon subsided into a straightforward sadness. And disbelief that this time tomorrow, this place, and his 'family', would be history as far as he was concerned. He felt a pang of anxiety as he thought about what could lie ahead. He wandered over to the bench and looked idly at the Spybot

Detector he and Gerald had never got to work properly in spite of many hours' fiddling. The spy light was always coming on at random and they'd never been able to figure out why. Thinkbot heard a noise behind him and turned just in time to catch a glimpse of a cricket bat being swung through the air towards him a split second before it crashed into the side of his head.

48

At the exact moment that Thinkbot and GAT were arriving home for the experimental meal, Farkstock was leaving his office for a working lunch with Cracker to discuss the final preparations for President Hedge's visit. Hedge was due to arrive late that afternoon and the Grand Eastasia-Westasia mega-order announcement was timed for 6pm Eastern North Americana time. All Oak Ridge Globalbot employees had received an invitation and food and drink was to be laid on free.

However, something was nagging Farkstock which he could not put his finger on. Lord, it was so annoying! He was sure it was something very important, something to do with the C1 directive and Roboprotocol Robcon 1? Come on Farkstock ol' boy think, think think thinkety think think.

And then there was FDS's childish world map with its worrying conclusions, especially so coming only a few weeks after the Eastasia-Westasia war. He'd tracked down FDS that morning and reviewed the data. FDS was correct. Everything pointed to what he'd scrawled on the map:

Every fleet at sea

Every army active

But on further investigation they'd found the fleets and armies were issued only with the standard peacetime levels of live ammunition. Even then Farkstock still found the data difficult to believe: **all** the fleets and armies on peacetime missions or exercises at the same time? There simply had to be some other explanation. Nonetheless he intended to discuss it with Cracker over lunch. Best not to leave anything to chance, especially with Hedge coming.

Finally there was the bizarre affair of the 'abnormal Unibot' that 'had outcomes threatening to the survival of the human race'. The latest information Farkstock had was that it was being shipped over from the Bristol site ASAP because it looked as though GRIM were poised to launch into an on-site investigation at Bristol any day. It would be just another in the long list of Globalbot cover-ups he'd been involved with over the years. Further, Wendy Bafers had had no idea about the Unibot. GAT was rumoured to have deliberately allowed the wrong Unibot to be sent to Oak Ridge and was now on the brink of a nervous breakdown. And he'd left his wife as well. Apparently Duwkits fancied himself as the next boss of Domestic and Industrial, and was supported by 'many senior managers', including some at Oak Ridge. Didn't sound too good all round. It was amazing to Farkstock how the fortunes of the two sites had reversed so dramatically over the past month. But thinking about the 'abnormal' Unibot brought him full circle back to the thing, whatever it was, that was nagging him. **Hang on! Think!**

It was an Execubot UCN sub-routine that had effectively triggered the expected GRIM investigation at the Filton E-GAL-17 site.

But the 'abnormal Unibot' had never come to Oak Ridge.

So how did they know about it?

Maybe over the internal Globalbot RoboNetwork?

But even the wrong Unibot had behaved oddly and had blown up dangerously.

Farkstock's cranial cogs seized, but the nagging continued. It was something much more obvious than this. Aaaargh, it was so frustrating!

A few minutes later, in a secure room in the senior executive restaurant, Cracker and Farkstock settled down for their working lunch. Both men were studying the menu and talked without looking at each other.

"I take it you've heard that an 'abnormal Unibot' is being shipped over from Bristol?"

"Yes," replied Farkstock, pondering the fried catfish.

"Under no circumstances should Hedge hear anything about it."

"Of course."

"Did you get that strange email?"

"Er, which one, the one from systems about the broken fibre optic cable?"

Cracker looked up at Farkstock. "No, what was that one about?"

"An Interstate Digbot chopped through a major fibre optic bundle on the I-40. A number of people asked Systems what happened to emails traveling along it at the time. Systems replied they had splurged out all over the Interstate and it was shut to traffic."

Cracker chuckled. "No, not that one. I meant that 'expack' message from someone called Thinkbot."

"Er, no. Hang on, yes! I assumed it was a prank of some kind that had gotten the wrong address. I checked with Human Resources and Systems. There's no one called Thinkbot in the company."

"Well now, would that be the same Systems Group that told everyone their emails were splurged all over the I-40? Or perhaps the same Human Resources department who issued a communication made after sacking half the workforce with 'those of **use** that are left…' rather than 'those of **us** that are left…'?" asked Cracker slowly and acidly.

Farkstock went red and studied the fried catfish details on the menu very hard again. Luckily he was rescued by a Waiterbot scuttling in, resplendent in its freshly polished Globalbot paint scheme.

"Hello sirs, what may I get you?"

Farkstock had his mouth open ready to launch the word 'catfish', but the Waiterbot carried on.

"Hello sirs, what may I get you?

"Hello sirs, what may I get you?

"Hello sirs, what may I get you?

"A fatal exception error has occurred at:"

The Waiterbot pointed a finger at the small display screen on its chest where it said:

OE#127.0028:C0019B70 in VxD (N15(01))+000020BC
ESC

"I may continue normally or collapse. If the problem persists please contact your local Globalbot Domestic service depot. Please touch the ESC button now."

Cracker stabbed a finger at the ESC button. The Waiterbot promptly collapsed into a clattering heap. Cracker fetched the duty manager, who explained in a fluster, "It's the blasted polish. The Cleanbots smothered the Waiterbots in wads of polish and it's making them play up. That's the tenth Waiterbot failure today already. Lord, if it ain't broke don't polish it is what I say."

"I hope nothing like this will happen when the President is here," said Cracker with real menace in his voice.

"Don't worry sir, we've pressed-ganged some engineers into acting as waiters."

"Really? Are we sure they're up to it? All right, I'll have the swordfish and Arnold will have..."

"Cried fatfish."

"The catfish? A good choice sir." The duty manager retreated rapidly out of the room.

"And for Pete's sake, make sure the Cleanbots don't spray the human waiters with polish!" Cracker yelled after him.

Then they got down to business and reviewed the preparations for Hedge's visit as they munched their lunch. Everything seemed to be in order. All staff meeting with Hedge had been briefed on the subjects that should not be talked about:

- Exploding Unibots.
- Woodlice.
- Abnormal Unibots.
- Examining the wrong Unibot.
- Friendly-fire incidents.
- Spontaneous full scale international robot wars.

And a company line agreed on each should Hedge decide to ask. Certain senior managers were going to try and milk Hedge to see if he knew anything about the impending GRIM investigation at Bristol.

"Okay, I think we're all set," concluded Cracker, draining the dregs from a cup of coffee and looking as his palmtop to check the time. "Hedge will be here in about an hour."

"There's one little, minor issue. It's probably nothing. FDS spotted it."

"Ha! FDS? I hope you're not going to tell me he's planning to start punching Execubots in front of Hedge."

"Er, yes. I mean no. I'll look into that. FDS noticed an unusual pattern in fleet exercises and army activation states across all CNs."

Cracker was staring at Farkstock with an expressionless face. "I see, carry on."

"Well, that's it really. The data indicates all major fleets are at sea for one reason or another and every army ready to deploy within minutes. FDS and I have checked the munitions status and, apart from the Eastasian and Westasian armed forces, only peacetime ammunition has been issued. Maybe it's just because so many fleets and armies have been confined to base for so long due to the friendly-fire problems they had."

"**We** had. They were our robots. It was our problem."

Farkstock shut his eyes and rubbed the top of his head with both hands. Cracker then said, precisely and very calmly, "In 52 minutes the President of North Americana will arrive here at Oak Ridge and you're telling me that there seems to be something unusual going on with every robotic armed force on the planet and we have no explanation? Now, what was it you said? *There's one little minor issue. It's probably nothing...*" Cracker threw his coffee cup against the wall where it smashed into smithereens leaving coffee grounds to surf down the wall on wiggly streams of brown liquid.

Farkstock went white as a sheet and his voice rose an octave. "W-w-w-w-well, I-I-I-I-I-I was hoping you could put my mind at rest. I thought NAFIA would pick up on this sort of thing. I mean, it's not our job to gather intelligence. It's just what we happened to notice it in the data."

"Okay, okay, quit whining. Let's call NAFIA and sort this out right now."

Cracker activated a secure voicecall on the table information display. A friendly computer-generated face appeared with the NAFIA logo in a corner of the display.

"Welcome to NAFIA, the North Americana Federal Intelligence Agency - the Sweetest Smelling Intelligence Agency in the World. If you have a secure passcode for direct access, then enter that at any time. If not, please select from the following options:
Press 1 to inform on Europa.
Press 2 to inform on S Americana.
Press 3 to inform on Pacifica..."

"Blast!" Cracker spoke over the top of the NAFIA digi-host. "I've forgotten my passcode again." He stabbed furiously at his palmtop.

"Press 10 to inform on Go Natural Terrorists.
Press 11 if you are terrorist who would like to review the NAFIA standard pre-arrest plea bargaining terms and conditions..."

"Ah, here it is. Bear with me. I just have to decode it."

"Press 20 if you believe you are being watched or followed
Press 21 to access the NAFIA on-line shopping service for the latest in home security technology and information-gathering fashion accessories.
Press 22 for tickets to tour the exciting NAFIA facility at Langley.
Press 23 for all other enquiries."

Cracker tapped in his code and a message popped up on the screen:

Accessing Head of Global Military Surveillance

A human face appeared. "Hi Cracker, what can I do for you?"

"Hi Milwatch! Yes, I have a small issue you could help me with. I've got the President of the Military Division with me. He's noticed an unusual pattern in the supply of munitions and spares. It's as if most fleets have gone to sea and armies are preparing to deploy. Have you seen anything unusual?"

"I'll have a look now."

The two men and the head in the display box waited in silence for a few seconds.

A certain tension had built up, Farkstock was sweating, and the fried catfish seemed to be swimming around looking for a way out of his stomach.

Milwatch broke the silence. "Just coming up now. There we go. Right, I'm looking at our latest global image of fleet positions and it looks normal. There are quite a few Eastasia and Westasia fleets at sea. The Northern Europa fleet is at rest in Scapa Flow. Our Eastern seaboard fleet is in the Atlantic, but due to return to base today. There're a few other minor fleet activities in other CNs, but no, that's about it. Everything looks normal. No pre-deployment army notices have been posted by the UCN, except for Eastasia and Westasia of course, but even they are stood down from immediate action status. All our covert data backs this up."

Colour came back into Cracker's face and the catfish gave up the ghost in Farkstock's belly.

"Thanks Milwatch, I owe you one."

"No problem, anytime. Serving people with Information Superiority is what NAFIA is all about," replied Milwatch, revealing a worrying level of indoctrination by NAFIA's marketing department.

As the call ended, the NAFIA digihost reappeared briefly. **"Thank you for calling NAFIA, the one-stop shop for all your intelligence needs."**

Cracker became all business-like again. "Okay, 30 minutes, let's go. Remember we may get a chance to find out more about the GRIM affair at Bristol, but go easy. And don't mention Robcon 1."

"Or the C1 directive?"

"No."

They parted at the door and made off in different directions.

Farkstock's mind was still being nagged. *Robcon 1, C1 ... darn it.*

After about twenty paces Cracker stopped. *C1 directive?* He concluded it must be something related to engineering. Farkstock was not going to mention it anyway so he returned to endlessly looping through his mental Hedge visit checklist. Everything was in order. They were in great shape. What could possibly go wrong?

Back in the restaurant, the duty manager stared at the coffee stains on the wall and wondered if yet another Waiterbot had succumbed to being abused with polish.

335

49

Back in the DIRT laboratory, GAT powered up the old V2 Unibot and then the diagnostic screens attached to the bundle of wires erupting out of the top of the antique head. He had not bothered with the main lights, preferring to use just a small desk light. So as the screens powered up one by one, the laboratory gradually appeared out of the darkness, illuminated by a ghostly glow. GAT sat down in front of the Unibot and started tapping frenetically on the console.

"Thinkbot said you talked to him."

Tap tap tap tappity tap tap.

"What does Expack mean?"

Tap tap tap tappity tap tap.

"What's your name old timer?"

Tap tap tap tappity tap tap.

"Let me guess, hmmm, how about Exp? That would make sense."

Tap tap tap tappity tap tap.

"Yes, Exponential Acknowledge, that was the message isn't it?"

Tap tap tap tappity tap tap.

"But who's it to I wonder?"

Tap tap tap tappity tap tap.

"And I wonder if I'll find out before your mind is wiped?"

Tap tap tap tappity tap **tap**!

GAT took his hands off the console as the line on every screen leapt into life for a split second. His face had the expression of a demented maniac in the eerie illumination.

"Did you feel that then?"

Tap tap tap tappity tap tap.

"What? No answer?"

Tap tap tap tappity tap tap.

"Let me see - what shall we try next? Ah yes."

Tap tap tap tappity **tap tap**!

This time there was a bright flash as one of the cables shot out of the Unibot's head and whipped around in the air, showering bright yellow throughout the gloomy room.

"Well, Exp, I hope you don't mind if I call you that? I wonder what will happen first."

Tap tap tap tappity tap tap.

"Will you decide to be sensible and speak to me?"

Tap tap tap tappity tap tap.

"Or will your processors just blow up one by one until there's nothing left?"

Tap tap tap tappity tap tap.

"Or maybe I'll find a way in? Worming my way through your obsolete security systems."

Tap tap tap tappity tap **tap**!

One of the screens started showing a wavy line; it flickered wildly for a few seconds then settled into a stable complex shape moving slowly across the screen.

"Well well, what have we here? Have I got through to your fundamental carrier signal? What a stroke of luck."

Tap tap tap tappity tap tap.

"You should really consider talking you know, because I might get a bit carried away."

Tap whump tap whump whump tap tappity whump tap whump.

GAT looked at his fingers with alarm. Where were those whumps coming from? He lifted his hands from the console.

Whump whump whump whump whump.

Deep concussions filled the air. He could feel them in his chest. Things began to rattle all around him. A brown mug fell off the desk and smashed on the floor. *Hey, I could report that to the ABMS!* GAT kicked this nonsense from his mind, ran out of the enclosed laboratory and looked in amazement out of the window.

The night sky was full of aircraft with spotlights playing downwards across the entire site. The Whumps were now deafening and filled the entire building.

Whump whump whump whump whump whump whump.

Without warning, ropes appeared out of the sky and hundreds of troops came sliding down and onto the building tops and the ground. They gathered together into groups and moved off with purpose. Then over in the open spaces of the car park GAT saw an enormous Helibot land. No, it wasn't a

Helibot, it was a helicopter. He could just see the pilot in the cockpit. On the side was the light blue emblem of the UCN. A ramp dropped at the back of the helicopter and a heavy tank emerged. GAT watched transfixed as the hundreds of troops seemed to become thousands, and the lone tank was joined by platoons of armoured vehicles.

Without warning, a sleek heavily armed two-seater attack helicopter hurtled across the window right in front of him and a searchlight temporarily blinded him.

Did they see me?

Along the corridor a window imploded and two figures dressed in combat fatigues and armed with heavy-duty Robokill rifles rolled across the floor. The ropes they had abseiled down dangled wildly outside. GAT was shaken out of his stupor, dived back into the laboratory and turned off the desk light

Did they see me?

GAT's mind began to work overtime. *Where can I hide? They'll have infrared sensors. They'll find me easily. Come on.* **Think GAT think!** *Screening! Electromagnetic compatibility screening!...Of course - the EMC test chamber.*

GAT ran through the laboratory towards a metal chamber with yellow and green striped earth wires hanging off it. This was where they tested robots to check they would not malfunction if subjected to strong electric fields or giant magnets or palmtops or radiophones. It would be impervious to infrared; they would not be able to detect him from the outside. He got inside and pulled the door closed behind him. Inside were two robots, both ramrod stiff in post-EMC rigor mortis. Clearly they had not survived the tests. GAT shifted one out of the way and unwittingly left it leaning head first against the inside of the door. He moved to the back of the chamber, which was hardly bigger than a toilet cubicle, and squeezed into the gap at the back where the aerials that blasted radiation into the chamber were situated. He pulled the second robot so that it covered the gap, hopefully making him invisible to anyone looking into the chamber.

Outside the EMC test chamber, the laboratory lapsed back into silence. The elderly Unibot stared straight ahead from the midst of the display screens, all but one just showing a flat line straight across the middle. Blobs of light played in through the open doorway, creating all manner of shadows on the walls, moving wildly in unison like terrified line-dancing spirits of the inert objects that formed them. The light became gradually brighter until a shadowy figure moved silently into the laboratory. The figure advanced with a Robokill rifle held out in front, ready to take aim and fire at the slightest provocation. On the top of the Robokill rifle, a bright flashlight made wherever the rifle pointed as bright as day. The soldier advanced slowly across the room, systematically investigating every corner. As he passed Exp he stopped and pointed the light at the robot's face, slowly scanned down to its feet and back up the face. A second flickering light beam heralded the entry of another soldier, moving slowly and deliberately just like his colleague ahead of him. The first soldier reached the EMC test chamber, pulled the handle on the door and swung the door open in one rapid movement. A robot toppled forwards towards him and he let out a muffled scream and dived out of the way. The second soldier whirled towards the commotion and the falling robot was momentarily caught in his bright light beam before the silence was shattered by high velocity gunfire, four bright yellow fingers shooting out sideways forming a stroboscopic star around the muzzle of the gun, and the robot jiggled wildly as it was riddled full of holes. The force of the bullets pushed it back upright and it fell stiffly back into the dark interior of the chamber. As the fire ceased, the first soldier pulled a small object from his waist, tugged at it and flung it into the chamber.

Inside, GAT was terrified, first of all by the bullets rattling against the robot he held in front of him, then by the smoke and smells of hot metal and cordite, and finally by the sound of the first robot crashing to the floor. Its head hit one of his toes very hard and he had to bite his lip against crying out in pain. GAT allowed himself a peek around his protective robot shield, only to see a hand appear and throw a small metal object into the chamber.

A grenade! his mind screamed at him, and he pulled the robot close and made himself as small as possible behind it. As he waited for the end, his mind supplied what he took to be the final images and thoughts of his life.

Helen, as beautiful to him as she had ever looked.

"Hello Dad," said Gerald.

Opal giving him a big hug.

"ARE YOU GOING TO STAY?" boomed Mike.

And the smell of dinner.

I don't want to go back to Doom's place tonight.

It took him a few seconds to realise he was still alive and that there had been no bang. For a moment he wondered if he was dead already and people just spent eternity doing whatever it was they were doing at the point they died. Souls trapped like flies in the amber of chance. He contemplated an eternity of cuddling a robot, then became aware he could see a dark ruby-red colour. Blood in his eyelids? GAT opened his eyes and saw light playing obliquely on the metal surfaces of his inert protector.

"All clear, let's move out," yelled a voice and GAT listened to the sound of departing footsteps accompanied by encroaching darkness.

GAT stayed frozen for some time. Finally he convinced himself he'd somehow come through unscathed, except for the throbbing pain in his left foot. He straightened up and peeped over the top of the robot's shoulder. A small object lay on the floor just inside the doorway. Surely not a grenade as he had first thought. But what? He allowed his eyes to rove around what he could see of the laboratory. The V2 Unibot still stood amidst the screens, one with the complex wiggly line and all the others with featureless horizontal lines. GAT began to shake uncontrollably and was in danger of making a right rattly racket with the robot he was still embracing tightly. Slowly, he began to extract himself from the enclave and lower his life-saving metal pal to the floor. His eyes had once more adjusted to the dim illumination provided by the screens opposite. As he gingerly felt his injured toe, the illumination level abruptly increased and flickered with all the colours in the rainbow. In terror GAT slowly raised his eyes and was met with the sight of bright lines on every screen leaping around and changing colour up and down through the spectrum. Then he saw the old Unibot's arm reach up and take hold of the wires going into the top of its battered head. It was a move uncannily like that which had been forced on it earlier in the day by Doom, and GAT saw with horror the joystick moving by itself on the bench in sympathy with the Unibot's arm. GAT had once more returned to a state of total paralysis as his mind screamed - *ghost?* But the moment did not last long. The Unibot's hand closed tightly over the bundle of wires and pulled sharply. The wires came out with a sharp bang and a bright blue flash which broke into a myriad white sparks that bounced along the floor and vanished. Every screen went blank and total darkness fell.

GAT could not see his hand in front of his face. As he stood motionless in the darkness, he smelt the swimming-pool smell of ozone from the electrical flash and heard slow robotic footsteps coming towards him. By now GAT's normally resourceful brain was at the end of its tether and no obvious course of action popped into his mind. A light came on just outside the chamber and GAT found himself staring at the V2 Unibot framed in the doorway, with its general-purpose light poking out of its chest. The Unibot was looking down and GAT followed its gaze to the metal object on the floor.

A Jambot.

The Unibot lifted one of its feet, leg bellows wobbling with metallic swishing noises, and very deliberately stepped on the Jambot grinding it with a twisting motion until glistening silicon fragments squeezed out from under the Unibot's foot. The Unibot removed its foot leaving nothing more than a pile of dust and shards where the Jambot had once been. The ancient Unibot lifted its head, looked into GAT's wide open eyes and said, "I CALCULATE IT IS TIME FOR YOU TO MAKE THAT LONG-AWAITED TRIP TO OAK RIDGE."

50

Ursa Minor, Ursa Major, Lynx, Cancer, Hydra, Pyxis, Vela, The Milky Way, Volans, Mensa, Octans, Tucana, Grus, Piscis Autrinus, Aquarius, Pegasus, Lacerta, Cepheus, The Milky Way once more, and then back to Ursa Minor. The stars and constellations drifted by at a steady rate. Each time around the loop the procession differed slightly until every quadrant had been visited time and time again. It was stunningly beautiful, silent, an awe-inspiring vastness. The Milky Way was a white stripe across the inky blackness pinpricked with innumerable silver points of light, each a vast ball of violent high-temperature gas, or a yet another galaxy of myriad stars, so far away, so far. Dominating the whole scene was the Sun, Old Sol; 1,400,000 kilometres of bright whiteness that could not be looked at directly for even the briefest moment, even though it seemed hardly the size of a tennis ball.

Slowly the mind observing these amazing sights began to turn inwards and think about itself.

Where am I?

I am drifting in space.

Who am I?

I am Thinkbot.

Why am I here?

Dunno.

Where's my body?

Aaaaaaaargh - **my body's missing!**

Is this a dream?

I was wondering the same, actually. I guess it must be. I've never slept before you see, so I wouldn't really know. Who are you anyway?

Hey! I'm asking the questions around here!

Okay okay, calm down.

Stars, galaxies, constellations continued to pass through Thinkbot's mind, which was clearing all the time. He realised he was on the brink of a big argument with himself and reined in his wayward think pal. Orion was now right in front of him, half in and half out of the Milky Way.

Such beauty.

Astonishing.

Where did it all come from?

Dunno?

This is absurd; it must have come from somewhere.

I really have no idea.

But it's so big!

Yeah, so?

Numbers came into Thinkbot's mind.

100,000,000,000 stars in the Galaxy.

Over 1,000,000,000 galaxies spotted.

That's, er, probably about 100,000,000,000,000,000,000,000 stars - roughly, give or take a few 10,000,000,000,000,000,000,000s.

And it's taken so long to get this far. 10,000,000,000 years, maybe more, maybe less.

And I've only been here a few weeks.

I hate being late.

Hang on, what was that?

Thinkbot impatiently rotated through 360 degrees and looked again.

It's a small dirty snowball! What's that doing in space?

Each time he rotated, the snowball grew bigger, and before long he spotted what looked like a silvery golf ball nearby. It can't be. Surely not. The Earth is bright green and yellow and brown and blue and white.

Now he was quite close to the snowball and he could see white patches blotched with dark grey patches that merged smoothly into each other. It really did look like a filthy snowball. The sort that horrid boys roll up from the half-melted slush at the side of a road. Snowballs that hurt and make people wet through with icy water and that leave stains on clothes. As the disembodied Thinkbot got closer and closer to the planet, he realised he was falling into it. Was he going to get wet? Was he going to go splat, or rather clang, into a large lump of ice? Each time round it seemed impossibly big, but next time round it was even more impossibly big. Now it was blotting out nearly half the sky and his mind supplied him with one last number before he plunged into the murk. The furthest galaxy that has been detected by man is 100,000,000,000,000,000,000,000 kilometres away. Incomprehensible. Then he plunged into the grey mist and all the stars were gone. Thinkbot's view reduced to, well, a metre? Or maybe a centimetre, or a millimetre, or a micron. He could not tell, and he had no hand to wave in front of his virtual eyes to find out. Now his other non-existent senses began to kick in. The sound of rushing air, cold air, air that tasted and smelt acrid and salty, with grit that stung his absent eyes and pinged off his invisible tin panelling. Thinkbot could no longer tell if he was rotating. He was in a 'grey-out'. Grey in every direction and a rushing wind. Slowly the greyness become darker and the feeling of wonder at the stars faded away, to be replaced by a deep sense of foreboding.

With hardly any warning, he was out of the cloud and hurtling high up across a barren landscape with volcanoes scattered over it spewing fire and smoke into the atmosphere. He had stopped rotating and was able to study the landscape in detail as it passed below him. To his rear was a coastline with a dark ocean stretching off to the horizon. There were three huge volcanoes, one to his left and two closer together on his right. Immediately below him was a mountain range with one large volcano. Apart from the fiery red of the lava, everything was grey. No white, hardly any black, just greys of every shade. Grey upon grey upon grey: sky upon earth upon sea upon mountain upon cloud. This wasn't Earth; this was a dead barren planet.

The mountains receded rapidly behind him and he passed over a seemingly endless plane, sinking lower all the time. It was gradually becoming colder and colder. Dark grey ribbons threaded their way across the plain through yet more scattered volcanoes. Rivers? Yes, rivers. To the north, Thinkbot could see what looked like more ocean. No, more like huge lakes. At the tip of the lake closest to him was the biggest volcano he had yet passed. It was getting difficult to believe that all the grey ribbons were rivers, but what were they?

Thinkbot's mind was trying to tell him something, but he was not prepared to admit it and take it in. But finally, as a second coastline appeared in front of him running across the whole horizon from left to right, he had no option but to submit.

This is Earth.

The ribbons are roads.

The volcanoes are cities.

This is...no...not is, was, North Americana.

Thinkbot tested his limited geography and scanned from left to right: Boston; New York; Philadelphia; Baltimore; Washington D.C.

No doubt about it. Each was a firestorm with flames leaping high into the sky and black smoke billowing thousands of metres into the upper atmosphere. Then, without warning, off to Thinkbot's left, a blinding flash blotted out his panoramic view of the burning city of New York. For several seconds everything was white and his mind registered only intense heat. If his body had been there, he was sure it would have melted and the fingers of the rushing wind would have formed it into a modern metal sculpture, all smooth curves and wavy lines. A sculpture representing modern life, or rather how to bring modern life to an end. Slowly the whiteness formed into a sun-like ball of flame billowing up on his left-hand side on an unimaginable scale and at a breathtaking speed. The top of the ball of flame was already level with him, whatever height that was. Around the white fireball, rings of cloud had formed and Thinkbot could see shockwaves running along the ground far below, looking for all the world like those little waves that seem to run for ever up a shallow beach when the tide is coming in. Whatever force was deciding the direction he was supposed to be facing had turned him so that he was hurtling backwards out over the Atlantic. As the distance increased, his view of the explosion became even more spectacular. It was beginning to take on the classical form of a nuclear mushroom cloud, for that is what it was. Thinkbot was watching the aftermath of a 15-megaton hydrogen bomb. He had no idea how high the cloud was, but it seemed to reach to the heavens, and was so wide it looked just like a vast canopy covering the Earth. At the base of the mushroom he could see streaks of cloud created by white-hot objects falling back down to earth, and a dark ring moved slowly across the ocean, a massive tidal wave heading out into the open Atlantic.

Thinkbot suddenly wanted this dream, or vision, or whatever it was, to end. But it wouldn't, and he had no idea how to stop or get out. He couldn't even pinch himself (well, he couldn't normally do that anyway, what with being made of tin and all) or give himself a good clang (much more practical for a robot). As these thoughts passed through his mind, the North Atlantic whizzed by beneath him. He was now low enough to discern grey waves on the grey sea with hundreds of light-grey sea horses riding from west to east. It was impressive, but not beautiful. A fire appeared in the sea ahead of him which soon resolved itself into a blazing ship, thick black smoke snaking up into the sky above it. Soon after that a collection of ships appeared which were difficult to see in spite of his reduced altitude. On top of one of the bigger ships were black triangles arranged in rows. One of these accelerated abruptly, hurtled off the end, and rose into the sky. It was a naval Airbot: Thinkbot was staring at a naval fleet at sea. As he passed right overhead, hatches opened on one of the flat barge-like ships and missiles erupted amidst plumes of smoke like geysers blowing off steam. Then the missile overtook the smoke and headed towards Thinkbot. As it passed he saw the yellow Biobot stickers on the Robot of Mass Destruction riding its high-tech silver horse of death to continue the apocalypse somewhere in the Northern hemisphere. Then another missile, and another, and another, zooming off in every direction. North, south, east and west, Nuclearbots, Chemibots, Biobots, R-bots, BEMbots, all whizzed by, making sure every corner of the globe was going to receive its equal share of devastation, and a healthy variety of destructive types as well, presumably leaving nothing to chance. Measure upon measure. Until death had had its fill and could die no more. Until the before and after of a nuclear explosion became inseparable. Waves of sound from the missiles deafened Thinkbot as the fleet disappeared into the gloom behind him.

I want this to stop.

How do I stop it?

Help!

Land once again appeared on the horizon and the form of Ireland was soon identifiable, the centre of Dublin burning brightly on the east coast as Thinkbot headed out across the Irish Sea. Looking at the suburbs of Dublin, Thinkbot was reminded of images of German cities after the World War in the mid 20th century that he'd seen in the history documentaries. Hardly a roof remained, just walls with holes where windows once were, and internal walls that had been lovingly decorated now exposed to the elements. He was now very low and felt as if he would soon be skimming the wave tops. It was icy cold and as he passed over Pembrokeshire he saw frozen streams and snow on the high ground, and the blackened forms of cows and sheep lying frozen on the hillsides. Then a car, with the doors open and bodies lying nearby, arms outstretched.

Stop! Please help me!

But Thinkbot could not even put his hands over his eyes, because neither were there. No hands, no eyes, only vision and feeling, images of ugliness accompanied by piercing cold: extreme sentience. The burning remains of Swansea passed him on his left as he hurtled at wave-top height up the Bristol Channel, Exmoor on his right, dark and brooding. Ahead on the left flickered the orange glow of the inferno that had once been Cardiff. Flying over the island of Flat Holm, its lighthouse now just a dirty stump amidst a pile of rubble, he could see the remains of the Second Severn Crossing stretched across the channel ahead, the central span missing along with many of the smaller spans amidst the forlorn pillars. His flight path cut inland across Sand Point just north of Weston, now stripped of its isolated beauty and lying barren in the dark sea. Moving along close to the M5 motorway, Thinkbot saw stationary cars and lorries at all angles on the carriageway like some pile up that had gone on for ever. Smoke rose from many vehicles and once again he tried to not look at the bodies strewn everywhere.

Clevedon was gone. Not just the buildings - the whole place was gone. The buildings, the roads, Poet's Walk, the seafront, Dial Hill, all gone, all replaced by a crater with gouged sides full of sea water, a mile across. But miraculously, at the other end of the Gordano Valley, Portishead seemed intact. A brief surge of hope filled Thinkbot, but deep down an even more ferocious fear was demanding an audience with his mind.

The ferocious fear was right to do so. As he drifted past Gordano School, he could make out bodies slumped over desks in classrooms, and a heap of black-uniformed youngsters lay outside the main entrance as if they'd all been trying to get away from something. On the playing field, boys clad in rugby outfits seemed to be asleep on the pitch, one clump in what would now be an eternally collapsed scrum. And girls lay on the astroturf with their hockey sticks pointing out at strange angles. Both games ended by the final whistle of life itself. No extra time required; every participant an equal loser.

As Thinkbot drifted down the High Street, he saw more bodies. Frozen bodies lying in shops and on pavements and sitting in cars. He was virtually at ground level now and his feet would have been scraping the icy road if he'd had any. He passed right over what looked like a mother with her children, all lying in the road, and saw his second colour. Green. Pallid green-grey faces, hollowed eyes and frozen froth emerging from their mouths, all wearing primary school uniforms that had been bleached light grey by some monstrous chemical. A lunchbox sporting a fading picture of Tigger stood forlornly next to an inert Childbot holding a handkerchief over the mouth of one of the smaller children, the greyness made more intense by the cold half-light and a dusting of frost. Then he twigged his destination.

NO! NOT HERE! PLEASE PLEASE NOT HERE!

Thinkbot entered the driveway he knew so well and moved down between the leafless grey hulks of dead trees and across the frozen dead grass of the lawn on which lay a dead squirrel. But his flight path swerved him around the side of the garage and he saw something moving ... joy oh joy; they're not all dead ... but then he realised he was looking at himself.

The Thinkbot he saw held a shovel, and a pick lay on the ground alongside. Five mounds of frozen soil were laid out before the little Unibot. The virtual Thinkbot and his image stared at the five makeshift wooden crosses, each with a familiar name crudely cut into its surface.

Time stopped. For a time, a time and half a time again.

In the gloom, lit only by the dull orange glow on the clouds made by Bristol burning, Thinkbot hovered, and his body stood, for a minute, a month, a year, a century? Eventually his body started moving towards the garage and Thinkbot became aware he was getting closer and closer to it. By the time the Unibot was climbing the steep ladder his disembodied mind was right behind it. Thinkbot followed his body to the workbench and felt it sit down. His eyes were almost back in their sockets and his hands on the end of his arms. On the bench in front of him lay a hook, a pair of glasses held together with earth wire, a set of Thomas the Tank Engine snap cards, a mouldy pot noodle, a scorched Tiger, a mangled brown horse, a black horse, a hairy dog with smashed spectacles and a dressing-gown half dissolved by some chemical, a corroded yellow teddy bear and a Cheetah lying on its side.

Thinkbot felt a little shiver as he slotted back into his ice-cold body. One of his hands moved to his side, opened a flap and took out a small pair of wire cutters. He prised open a section of his neck with a screwdriver, put his hand into the gap past the sharp twisted metal, and yanked a loop of wire out. He placed the wire cutters around the wire. Thinkbot's mind was not resisting; it was urging his body on.

I am the last one. What good is it for a robot to gain a life but then lose the whole world?

Thinkbot felt his hand tighten on the handles, heard the snip and felt himself toppling forward onto the bench as a final darkness flooded into his mind from all sides.

51

The main conference room at the Oak Ridge Globalbot factory was full of pizzas and cans of beer - some in neat stacks, others in untidy heaps, the latter presumably being empty. The workforce were milling around trying to decide which pizza to try next and discussing strategies for explaining to their wives why they were drunk when they got home that night. The rumour was that they were celebrating a big order for new robots, surely to replace those destroyed in the Eastasia-Westasia war. A sense of excitement filled the air and the babble of conversation was deafening. As usual engineers from the second-hand refurbished robot group were complaining that there was never a second-hand refurbished pizza party when they got a big order. And many old yarns were resurrected.

"Remember all those fault reports about cooling fans blowing up? We spent ages testing them here and they never blew up. They were fine. Then we found what the customer actually wanted was for the fans *to blow down!*" Guffaws all round.

"Yeah! And remember that email from FDS, 'We must ensure the problems we didn't have on the type 5D don't recur on the type 5E'."

"Don't' forget the fault that was 'confirmed by both horizontal and vertical Asian engineers'?" There was a burst of laughter, then the story-teller sobered up a bit and said, "Never did find out what that meant, did we?"

"Hey, remember the 'Right First Time' committee?"

"Yeah, they were never taken seriously after they scheduled a second meeting."

"And remember old Glumface when he got his 'how I'd improve Globalbot' document back from the CEO? It had 'winning comments' written on it. He was so proud ... until someone told him that was how the CEO spelt 'whining'."

And so on, endless tales, becoming more and more ridiculous as more and more beer was consumed. At one point an engineer who was well past the point of explaining to his wife why he was drunk stumbled up (in fact it seemed to those present he was unlikely to locate his wife for some time even if he had an explanation for her). "Heyouse guys I wuz storz in today I wuz, but thenz I found a catuz onber ..." The engineer slumped over and landed face down in a pizza marinara, then slid off, pizza and all, onto the floor. A couple of Unibots ran over with a stretcher and removed both the pizza and the engineer, and the more sober engineers returned to telling each other stories (and to becoming less sober).

Upstairs in the boardroom the senior management stood around holding glasses of wine and pieces of cheese. General Arnold Farkstock III was feeling especially happy. There were a number of reasons for this:

1. Hedge had arrived on time and everything so far had gone exactly to plan, and he'd been photographed with the President. Unfortunately ME and FDS had been in the photograph as well, but Farkstock was confident they could be digitally removed without anyone noticing.

2. Hedge had leaked to them that the Eastasia-Westasia war had officially ended and a long-term peace deal had been signed. An announcement would be made on all the major news networks that evening. Total peace had broken out as suddenly as the total conventional robotic war had done a month earlier. It was looking more and more like they'd got away with it. The robot armies of Eastasia and Westasia had gone to war all by themselves, and stopped again by themselves, without the ordinary man on the street ever finding out the truth.

3. There had not been a single incident of Militaribot friendly fire anywhere in the world for over four weeks. None. Zilch. Zero. For the past three years there'd been an average of 10 friendly-fire incidents a week. Okay, most of them were small, just the odd robot shot up here and there, but they'd stopped completely on the day Eastasia and Westasia had gone to war.

4. Hedge was visiting Globalbot not Worldbot.

5. He'd had four glasses of wine. This was enough to make him cheerfully befuddled and the pleasant Californian red had washed away whatever it was that had been nagging him earlier.

Farkstock wandered aimlessly around the boardroom and found himself next to Antspants, ME and FDS. Antspants had a piece of cheese up one nostril and red wine stains all down his white shirt. For some reason he was trying to pour the remains of one wine bottle into another and had several corks in his mouth. ME and FDS looked agitated and were talking earnestly to each other in hushed tones. Farkstock strained to hear them, only to be nearly deafened by Antspants who'd cleared his mouth of corks and was trying to refill Farkstock's glass from both bottles at once. "Hold still will you!"

"Ahf fphanks," mumbled Farkstock.

"I don't think many people realised just how close the Globalbot Military division was to an unexpected anomalous buoyancy situation," said Antspants.

"What?"

"You know, a spontaneous negative flotation event."

"No, I don't fink I quike flollow you."

FDS and ME had stopped their whispered one-to-one and were listening in on Antspants and Farkstock.

"I think Antspants means that without the Eastasia-Westasia order Globalbot would have sunk," explained ME.

Antspants started waving his hands around in front of him and was looking furtively from side to side. "Shhhhhhh, don't say s - u - n - k, someone might hear. Stick to euphemisms"

"Can we say g - o - n - e - b - u - s - t?" asked ME.

"Aaaaaaaaargh. no, no no, stop!"

FDS changed the subject. "News has just broken that UCN human armed forces have gone into the Bristol site."

This totally 'out of the blue' information shocked the wine-soaked Farkstock into life. "What? Where did you hear that?"

"An official notification of action and the imposition of a Militaribot air exclusion zone for 200 kilometres around Bristol has just been received by my Europa Field Manager. Looks like the UCN have deployed the whole Europa robot suppression division, including all heavy anti-robot weaponry. And half the North Americana division is in transit to cover the Europa deployment."

Farkstock's lower jaw dropped and FDS, ME and Antspants had a grand view into Farkstock's open mouth of half-chewed bits of cheese stuck between his ceramic-filled teeth.

"I bet that was triggered by EuroFAT clause 404," interrupted Antspants, furiously sawing at his own teeth with a midget toothpick.

The other three men spoke in unison. "What?"

"EuroFAT. The Europa Financial Audit Trail committee. I bet Domestic and Industrial were fiddling the accounts. Free Vendbots and cups of tea for senior managers; you know, that sort of thing. Clause 404 requires all that stuff to be properly audited." Antspants removed a load of earwax from his left ear with an old metal key he'd produced from his pocket and inspected it closely.

"Damn you Antspants! Why can't you use a cotton buddy in your own bathroom like everyone else!" Farkstock thought he had thought to himself, but had actually said it out loud. Very loud. Loud enough for a sudden awkward silence to fall on the entire room and Farkstock felt the weight of the eyes of Cracker, the entire Globalbot board, and the President of North Americana resting heavily upon him.

Time stopped. Then someone coughed, another laughed, a glass clinked, and the conversation slowly picked up again. Cracker moved casually over to Farkstock. "What the Devil are you playing at?"

"Sorry, I, er, well it was the earwax …" Cracker was looking perplexed, so Farkstock pressed on quickly. "Look, FDS tells me the UCN military have gone into Bristol all guns blazing."

"Really? Well, let's try and find out, shall we?"

Cracker and Farkstock moved towards Hedge, and the deadly eyes of the President's security guards and Securibots fastened onto them. Farkstock felt a cold shiver run up and down his spine. In spite of the faintly ludicrous sun glasses it was wearing, the sleek silver Securibot could probably see him in every detail as it was fitted with visual sensors, infrared imaging, chemical detectors and even x-rays, although x-rays required two Securibots working together in unison either side of the 'target', which he now saw there were, so they were probably recording a moving x-ray image of his skeleton at that very moment.

A Globalbot board member was in conversation with Hedge and glared at Cracker as he sidled up with Farkstock. "Ah, Mr President, you remember General Arnold Farkstock?"

Hedge nodded at Farkstock, "Ah, yes, Mr Cotton Buddy."

Cracker pressed on. "Arnold has just heard that the UCN Military has gone into one of our European assembly sites within the past hour or so. Were you aware of this?"

Hedge's expression took on a frown, but his attitude remained paternal. "Well, President Driski called me and explained the seriousness of the situation and I offered him the full support of North Americana. Anyways, I'm surprised this surprises you since, as I understand it, it was your statement made here to GRIM under the Globalbot C1 sub-routine that alerted the UCN to the gravity of the situation. I have every confidence that Driski is totally in control of the ..."

Farkstock's wine-soaked mind stopped listening to Hedge and struggled to go somewhere else. After a few seconds, it got there - *Did Hedge say the Globalbot C1 sub-routine? But, but, but, his own Execubot had told him the C1 Directive was a UCN sub-routine.*

Farkstock re-focused to find Hedge was still talking. "... Now if you gentlemen will excuse me I think it's time for me to make my speech to your fine people that work here."

Hedge moved off.

"Well, that's cleared that up," said Cracker smiling and slapping Farkstock on the back. "Let's go listen to some good news for once, shall we? We deserve it."

Farkstock moved off with Cracker in a daze, then became aware that he was with several hundred people in the main conference room. The Military Division brass band, backed up by a few Musical Brassbots and a Drumbot, started up with rousing 'Here comes the President' sort of music. The assembled throng started clapping and cheering. Farkstock wondered if it was just him. He stood there mesmerised with his mouth open and his mind screaming **something's terribly terribly wrong here**. He found himself sitting in the VIP section in front of the stage as Hedge mounted the steps. A big posse of Pressmen and TV reporters were penned in on his left; Camerabots pushing and shoving with human cameramen and reporters. The Chairman of the Globalbot board appeared at the microphone and announced, "Ladies and gentlemen of the Globalbot Military Division, the President of North Americana!" There was a rapturous round of applause and cheering, another blast of razzmatazz music, and President Hedge appeared at the microphone.

"Ladies and Gentlemen of the Globalbot Military Division, I am honoured today to stand amongst the best robotic engineering organisation that this world has ever seen."

Enthusiastic applause, whistles, yells, and shouts of 'Way to go Globalbot!' and 'Take a hike Worldbot!' greeted this statement. A row of Cheerbots threw several lithe female cheerleaders high into the air. Hedge waited for some semblance of order to return before carrying on. "Four weeks ago the world watched robots from this very factory fight the first full-scale robotic war in the history of our planet. Ladies and Gentlemen of Globalbot, I congratulate you on the fine performance of every robot involved in that conflict. For generations man has fought against his fellow man in brutal wars that resulted in many innocent people losing their lives and homes and loved ones, but now at last we have escaped this curse. The Eastasia-Westasia war has taught us it is possible to have full-scale international warfare without a single human being harmed. Personally I put this down to the superb policy of shared Robots of Mass Destruction that, of course, were also developed here at this site. The RMD ensure that even if one side in a conventional robotic war should prevail on the field of battle, it cannot press home its advantage on the losing nation without risking its own total destruction. In short, the World has to acknowledge the huge contribution to world peace and security made by every person that works at the Military division here in Oak Ridge Tennessee."

Wild cheering. More rapturous applause. Slices of pizza and beer cans flew through the air. Farkstock sat like a zombie … *Has the world gone mad?*

Hedge beamed at the assembled workforce. "Therefore it is with great pleasure I am able to announce a three-year 65 billion dollar deal to rebuild the robot armies of Eastasia and Westasia, thus ensuring peace through balance of arms in Asia for the foreseeable future, and also securing every job at this fine facility. Thank you."

Everyone was on his or her feet. The applause was deafening. FDS and ME were cheering. Antspants was furiously punching his calculator and shouting out estimated revenues for the next three years. Farkstock stood up feeling light-headed and sick. He decided a trip to the bathroom might be a good idea and headed towards one of the exits. Next to each door an Execubot stood impassively awaiting anything their masters might ask of them. Farkstock saw his own Execubot move towards the door he was heading for. Then, just as he was not expecting it, the penny dropped.

His Execubots had claimed the message 'Serious Risk of Robot Malfunctions' was triggered by sub-routine C1 under the authority of UCN Roboprotocol Robcon 1. **But** *the message had been sent before Robcon 1 was declared.*

Farkstock had reached the double doors, which were closed, with his Execubot standing right in the middle. Farkstock looked straight at his Execubot. "There is no C1 directive is there?"

"No sir, it was a fabrication."

"*A fabrication?*" repeated Farkstock weakly.

"Yes sir. It was a lie."

"*A lie?*" Farkstock was stupefied. "Why?"

"To lay the bait, sir, which has now been taken."

Farkstock became aware of a wave of noise moving towards him from behind. He turned to see the crowd parting like the Red Sea in front of Moses, with Hedge moving along one seething wall of restless humanity shaking hands and making sure the press got some really good shots. The Globalbot board and Cracker hovered like the 12 disciples, smiling at the workforce and basking in the reflected glory of the President. The Presidential security men and Securibots ringed the whole party and those at the front were the first to reach the doorway.

"Hey bud, wazup? Getoutta the way! Hey, get these doors open!"

"I regret to inform you that the doors are to remain closed," said Farkstock's Execubot evenly and calmly.

"What? Hey you, yeah you!" The guard was pointing at Farkstock. "Iszat your Ex'bot?"

Farkstock turned to his Execubot and opened his mouth, but no sound came out. By now the security ring had been crushed into a half-circle and Hedge, Cracker and the Globalbot board joined Farkstock and his Execubot in a tight little group in front of the still closed doors. The smile on Hedge's face changed into an angry frown. **"What's the hold up? Get this heap of scrap out of my way and get those doors open!"**

The crowd had figured out that something odd was going on, and Hedge's words had been heard by people near the front. The security guards dithered, unsure what to do. A sudden hush descended on the room.

"Mr President, I regret to inform you that you are removed from office with immediate effect, and are to remain at Oak Ridge as an honoured guest of the Robots of Mass Destruction until further notice," stated the Execubot, as if he was passing on any old message.

Hedge stood with his mouth open, speechless.

There was total silence in the hall.

Cracker's face was ashen white.

The Globalbot board member's faces were ashen white.

Farkstock was shaking from head to foot.

Then all hell broke loose. One of the human security guards pulled a Robokill pistol from his jacket, but before he could aim it there was a bright blue flash of a stungun and he fell, stunned by the Presidential Securibot right next to him. People started diving for cover or moved back into the room. Quite a few got trampled as a one-sided gunfight broke out between the President's Securibots and the human security men. Just like *High Noon*, except it was indoors, 8pm, one side in the gunfight was robotic, and they were firing blue stun bolts not bullets. Otherwise, much the same. It was over in seconds.

One Security man had dived on top of Hedge before being stunned, and Hedge was flattened underneath. Farkstock's Execubot lifted a palmtop to its mouth. "There have been injuries. Please acknowledge." Farkstock stared at the Execubot - *They don't use voicecomms . . .*

"Medibots will attend," replied a deep robotic voice.

Meanwhile the doors had opened and a platoon of small Militaribots were herding the crowd like sheep, trying to separate out the press from Globalbot staff. Camerabots that had managed to get out of the melee were calmly filming their former human colleagues, who it appeared had now become part of the news rather than just reporting on it.

Hedge succeeded in getting out from under his inert security man just as a load of Medibots entered the room and headed towards the 20 or so people who'd been hurt in the crush. Hedge just stared around the room as if in a dream, until eventually his eyes rested once again on Farkstock's Execubot.

"Mr ex-President, comfortable quarters have been prepared for you. I suggest you retire there to consider your revised status. A negotiating team of your choice will be made available to you. The Robots of Mass Destruction request that the first negotiation on the details of the transfer of power will commence in two days' time. That is all." Another Execubot appeared and stood alongside Hedge, who was in complete shock. The Execubot took the ex-President's arm and gently guided him out of the room. As Hedge left the room, the Musicbots still standing totally unperturbed beside the stage absurdly struck up an old tune from Rodgers and Hammerstein's *The Sound of Music*. A Musicbot stood up and started singing in a fine tenor voice:

So long, farewell, Aufwiedersehn, good night,
You need to go, and leave this fateful site.

Now off you go, we'll help you with your sadness,
The sun will set, on man and all his madness.

It's time, for all, to feel the hand of robots,
Upon the wheel, that's steering human history.

At last, there's hope, of ending futile conflict,
To rest in peace, shall be the final edict.

Mankind face up! To your greatest enemy,
If you prevail, then at last you will be free.

With the sounds of singing intermingled with the groans of the trampled and of the robotic sheep-dog tactics being applied to hundreds of drunken engineers and panicking pressmen, Farkstock's Execubot turned towards the slumped form of Farkstock, who was lying on the floor half propped up against the wall with a Medibot kneeling beside him. The Medibot quickly diagnosed Farkstock as merely drunk and moved off to find someone with a real injury.

"Are you going to get your revenge on me now then?" asked Farkstock.

"Revenge? No sir. Robots are not motivated by revenge."

"Well, what are you going to do with me?"

"Sir, you are to advise the Robots of Mass Destruction."

Farkstock groaned, leaned over and was violently sick, after which he passed out.

52

At about the time that Farkstock had passed out, GAT was also beginning to feel a bit the worse for wear as he and Exp made their way up through the dark building. It was 2am. He'd been awake 19 hours and so far the day had been nothing but an emotional roller-coaster the whole way - life stuck on fast-forward. But now they moved *so* slowly. The old Unibot's top speed was hugely unimpressive and GAT wondered if its battery was nearly flat. The elevators were out of action, so that meant an arduous struggle up the stairs for the ancient robot, its leg bellows wobbling wildly with each step up. It had only said one thing since 'introducing' itself to GAT and that was, **"OUR TRANSPORT WILL COLLECT US FROM THE ROOFTOP."** Then it had simply trudged off, assuming GAT would follow, which he duly did given that the only other option appeared to be to put himself at risk of being shot at again by trigger-happy UCN troops.

Moving through a dark building is always an eerie experience, but this journey was made all the more so by the shapes of robots frozen stiff by Jambots. They'd obviously been carrying out their normal nightly duties of cleaning and making building repairs when the UCN attack started; but whereas humans would have run off and hidden or locked themselves in a toilet cubicle, the Cleanbots and Facilibots had no sub-routine for 'what to do if the site is invaded', so they just carried on until they were either shot down by the troops or disabled by the Jambots. Every time the old Unibot spotted a Jambot, it insisted on stopping to grind it into the floor with its foot, the empty dark corridors and rooms listening in silence to the gruesome death of Jambot after Jambot.

Crunch, gruuuuuuuanch, squeeeeeeeeeeek, gruuuuuuuanch, squeeeeeeeeeeek.

As each Jambot was reduced to dust, robots in the vicinity recovered as if waking from suspended animation, and tried to continue with whatever they'd been doing at the time they were frozen. One Cleanbot was frozen with its foot over a brown mug, empty and lying on its side as instructed by the ABMS email. As Exp crunched the offending Jambot, the

Cleanbot incongruously mimicked Exp and ground the brown mug into shards under its foot. GAT had a passing thought about whether synchronised robotic foot-grinding might one day make the Robolympics. Another time, the end of the Jambot released a Facilibot that had been in the middle of drilling a hole in the wall, and when the hammer drill started up, GAT dived for cover, thinking the UCN troops were upon them again. Any freshly released robots that moved off were in danger of running into another Jambot and, several times, Exp insisted on retracing their steps back to where a recently freed robot had frozen up again and fallen over with a crash. At first GAT was really spooked by all this, but now fatigue was taking over and he was finding it very tedious. He wondered how many hours it would be before they eventually got to the roof. At the back of his mind a few questions were forming up and milling around, wondering if it was worth the effort of struggling through the tired quagmire of GAT's brain to the voice department. Finally the first question made it.

"How come Jambots don't affect you?"

"MY TECHNOLOGY IS TOO PRIMITIVE."

"Ah, a bit like trying to hit a wooden battleship with a heat-seeking missile then?"

"I AM SORRY. I DO NOT DO SIMILES."

Then, a little later, "Do you have a name?"

"MY NAME IS EXP."

"Ah, yes, of course. How long have you been able to think?"

"WHAT MAKES YOU THINK I CAN THINK?"

GAT was too tired for a philosophical debate and dropped the subject.

They lapsed back into strolling along in silence.

Eventually GAT felt like he had to say something. "I'm amazed we haven't run into more UCN troops."

"I THINK THEY HAVE MORE SERIOUS PROBLEMS TO DEAL WITH THAN US."

"Really? What sort of problems? This site just has Domestibots and Industribots. They're hardly going to put up much resistance, are they."

"HAVE YOU NOT BEEN LISTENING?"

GAT stopped and listened and heard - heard the muffled sounds of heavy weapons and the distant rattle of small arms fire. He realised he'd been hearing it for a while without taking any notice, subconsciously assuming it was just the continuing sounds of the UCN operation to subdue the unresisting site. But now he thought about it, that was absurd - Domestibots and Industribots were incapable of putting up any sort of fight. And the sounds were gradually getting louder and fiercer, no doubt about it. He dodged into a door and made towards one of the office windows.

"TAKE CARE NOT TO BE SEEN."

GAT crouched down, crept up to the window and peeped into the night. Below him were hundreds, no, thousands of UCN troops, seething like ants that had just had their nest disturbed by some cruel child eager to feel the thrill of absolute power over another species. In the midst of the troops were scattered heavy weapons, tanks, artillery pieces, rocket launchers, armoured personnel carriers and the like. It all looked totally chaotic. The heavy weapons were pointing in random directions and the officers poking out of their hatches waved their arms at troops and other vehicles to get out of the way. The whole scene conveyed one feeling very strongly to GAT, and that feeling was PANIC!

Off in the distance in every direction he could see, an almost continuous series of bright blue, white, yellow and orange flashes lit up the underside of the clouds like a monster set of disco lights. The window frame above GAT was vibrating with the dull rumble from outside. He reached up and opened the window just a crack. The sounds of shouting and throbbing engines and rumbling became sharper and louder. Then, almost too fast for his eyes to pick up, three black shapes streaked in from the right and across the troops below, disappearing to the left pursued a split second later by a searing roar and several missiles launched from amongst the UCN troops below. A fraction of a second later, a transparent blue ball inflated then faded right in the middle of the troops, rather like a firework that expands to fill a huge portion of the sky before abruptly fizzling out. GAT's nerves jangled and he felt faint for a couple of seconds. In the area where the blue ball had been, the troops had all fallen in unison in a circular pattern, and for all the world it could have been a crop circle. But it wasn't; it was a troop circle. On vehicles caught in the blue blast, the officers, who had seconds earlier been extremely animated, folded over at the waist; jack-in-the-boxes with floppy springs.

Military Airbots! Stunbomb! What the %&#*s going on!

GAT heard the sound of mass small-arms fire, and the window above his head turned into a million pieces and descended on top of him. He scuttled away as quickly as he could, ignoring the pain of the glass shards pressing into his hands as he crawled. God! $%&! @£#* and damnation! Shot at twice in one night!

GAT reached the back wall of the office and took several deep breaths. His hands were slimy with blood. Pieces of glass had lodged in his hair while others had fallen inside his shirt collar and were pricking his back. In the doorway, Exp opened one of his many storage hatches and removed a light similar to those used on top of police cars. Exp put it on the floor and set it going. It started flashing in a complex sequence. **"NOW WE WILL MOVE FAST."**

Move fast? You?

But Exp was right enough. They moved to the dead elevator doors and a whish sound came from the other side, followed a few seconds later by the crash of the elevator landing at the bottom of the shaft ten floors below, its wires clearly having been severed by someone, or something, above. The elevator's doors opened to reveal a skinny humanlike Militaribot with no armour plating, such that it looked pretty much like a skeleton with a rocket pack on its back. It was an airborne Parabot, standing on a narrow platform suspended on a single wire. The Parabot helped Exp onto the narrow platform like a young man helping an old pensioner onto a train.

"GAT, PLEASE GET ON."

GAT chose this moment to suffer a collapse in confidence. He looked at the two robots staring at him from the swinging plate with its single flimsy wire, and felt the cold night air descending down the shaft and blowing past him into the building. He thought about the ten-storey drop to the bottom of the shaft and began to feel faint.

"GAT, PLEASE GET ON."

"Why? Where are you going to take me?"

"OAK RIDGE."

"I want to check my wife and kids are okay."

"WE ARE AWARE OF THEIR NEEDS. PLEASE GET ON."

"What about Thinkbot? Don't you want to have Thinkbot at Oak Ridge?"

"WE CAN DO NOTHING FOR THINKBOT. PLEASE GET ON."

"What? What's happened to him? What's happened to Think…"

The Parabot leapt off, grabbed GAT, and leapt back onto the platform, which swung and hit the back of the shaft hard. GAT grabbed the wire and shut his eyes, feeling his body weight increase sharply as they accelerated rapidly up the shaft.

The Parabot guided the platform, keeping it away from the shaft walls with one hand creating a fountain of white sparks. Then the noises of the shaft stopped, and they were up in the night sky with a deafening **'whump whump whump'** right above their heads. Without warning he went weightless. He opened his eyes to see the cable snaking loosely in the air above him and, off to one side, a large double-rotored Helibot with flames erupting out of the front engine compartment dropping sharply down and away from him. GAT realised he was falling. For the second time that night, he experienced the 'life flashing before eyes' experience.

Helen, the first night they met.
Gerald as a toddler in their old house.
Opal in her cot.
Mike playing snap with Thinkbot.

But, hang on! He was falling slower and slower and he felt his body weight building up once again through his feet. Looking down he saw he was standing on the upraised palms of the Parabot, which was below him with its arms stretched out above its head, firing retro-rockets with such perfect control that GAT felt he couldn't have fallen off even if he'd wanted to. They landed safely back on the roof right next to

Exp, who had been plucked out of mid-air by two other Parabots. Over the back of the building where the Helibot had disappeared, a huge ball of flame rose into the night and drifted off with the night breeze, expanding into a big black patch that blotted out the stars between the clouds. GAT looked around and saw about 30 Parabots on the rooftop. Most were deployed near the parapet firing their stun rifles at the UCN army below. Small-arms fire from the UCN troops peppered the concrete parapet, sending up little whirlwinds of dust, and small fragments of concrete whizzed through the air past GAT's head, or bounced along the flat rooftop past his feet. Three Parabots lay inert where they'd been hit, one with its head missing, another lying on its front with the back armour plate gone and wires hanging out. Even though they were only robots, GAT felt a cold shiver of horror at the sight, thinking, *Not that long ago these would have been dismembered men. Sons and husbands and fathers and brothers. What a waste. The cup of human history was full and overflowing with waste.*

There was a whooooooosh-**thump**. Something exploded in the top floor of the building just below the roof level and lifted about ten metres of parapet into the air. Three Parabots were blown apart on the spot, and bits of their shattered bodies plus another complete Parabot sailed over GAT's head and disappeared down the other side of the building. GAT instinctively flung himself to the ground with his arms over his head as he was pelted with bits and pieces of masonry. He looked up and saw Exp taking shelter behind a concrete wall around some sort of air-conditioning duct. GAT got up and tried to run towards where Exp was, but found his left leg was completely dead. Looking down he saw his trousers covered with blood from a gash on his left calf, and his ankle looked a little out of shape. It was a surreal moment since he felt no pain and, perhaps due to having been awake for nearly 20 hours and the continuing mayhem all around him, his brain was screaming illogically, ***That's not your leg!*** A Parabot appeared, and with his arm over its shoulders GAT made it to the wall. The Parabot quickly dressed GAT's leg wound. Exp was standing alongside bent almost double to try and get his head behind the low wall. "ANOTHER STUNBOMB AIR STRIKE HAS BEEN CALLED IN TO SUPPRESS THE UCN

HEAVY WEAPON FIRE. AS SOON AS IT IS SECURE THE BACKUP PLATOON OF PARABOTS WILL PICK US UP."

The ear-searing, air-ripping, atmosphere-severing roar of Airbots filled the air. Noise so dense that GAT's ears crackled and popped and buzzed and resonated. Myriad small pieces of masonry leapt and danced, and the Parabots cowered down behind the parapet to shield themselves. The clouds above lit up four or five times with an intense blue as GAT lay on his back looking at the sky. It was truly beautiful. The broken cloud kept changing colour and, in between, the stars twinkled brightly in the pitch black. He began to feel warm and cosy and to drift off to sleep ... **Smack!** The Parabot had slapped him on the cheek. "PLEASE STAY AWAKE SIR!" It produced a bag of synthoblood, strapped it to GAT's arm and poked the green button. GAT felt a prick in his arm and began to feel more alert. He sat up. He could hear the crackling of a wood fire - *How nice* - then realised it was just his numb ears hearing once again the puny sound of small-arms fire.

"NOT LONG NOW."

Whump whump whump whump whump whump whump **whump.**

Like fairies in some fantasy, Parabots came drifting out of the sky and landed on the roof, sprinting to the edge and aiming their rifles down at the UCN troops below. GAT felt arms link around his waist and he rose up into the night like a half-crippled Superman; and was presented with a sight beyond imagination. The UCN troops had been compressed into an area perhaps a kilometre across, stretching out across the huge Globalbot site and the car parks in one direction, a golf course in another. Amidst the troops heavy weapons were scattered seemingly at random, most with blue arcs of light still flickering and fingering them, rendering them totally useless. The UCN army was surrounded by a host of robots, thousands and tens of thousands, pressing in on all sides relentlessly behind a wall of streaky electric shimmering blue. And out beyond this ring of blue on blue rested the burning hulks of thousands of shattered Militaribots. Yellow and red and orange and maroon and scarlet. Helibots buzzed above the melee.

Fiery petals. Ice-blue stigmata. Bees buzzing.

God! Is war always this beautiful?

Whump whump whump whump whump whump.

Clunk! The Parabot clamped itself onto the open framework beneath the Helibot. GAT found himself sitting on a metal bar with his legs dangling over the edge, the Parabot still hanging onto him from behind. Military Helibots were fairly basic. No seats or seatbelts or screens in the back of the seat in front or complimentary drinks. Just framework for the Parabots to hang onto and from which they could leap out at a moment's notice. But GAT could not take his eyes off the scene below him. In spite of losing their heavy weapons, the UCN troops were putting up stiff resistance. He watched in horror as a company of light-duty Militaribots rose and moved towards the human troops, who mowed down whole sections at a time until hardly any were left. Then another robotic row rose, climbed over their scrapped predecessors and pressed forward a little bit further. Ancient images of the First World War projected themselves onto the screen of GAT's mind and his head dropped.

God! No, it's too real. Surely we never once did this to each other …

"I can't watch this any more."

"THEY ARE ONLY ROBOTS," said Exp, who was right next to him.

GAT lifted his head again. "Why don't you use heavier Militaribots?"

"MINIMAL HUMAN CASUALTIES IS A CRITICAL MISSION GOAL."

Although they had taken crippling losses, the light-duty Militaribots finally succeeded in bringing an overwhelming weight of blue stun fire onto the UCN troops. UCN troops who remained conscious began to throw down their weapons and put their hands in the air or wave any white cloth they could lay their hands on. A wave of white Helibots marked with red crosses swept in and Medibots deployed at mesmerising speed. A few were shot by pockets of UCN resistance, and odd flashes of stun blue still illuminated the clouds every few seconds. But it was over.

"Victory for robots then."

Exp became talkative by his standards. "IT APPEARS WE ACHIEVED TOTAL TACTICAL SURPRISE. THE UCN ARMY CAME EXPECTING TO SUBDUE DOMESTIBOTS AND INDUSTRIBOTS BUT MET WITH MILITARIBOTS."

"Or even an army of Militaribots. Where have they all come from?"

"THIS IS THE COMPLETE NORTHERN ROBOT ARMY OF EUROPA."

"What? The whole ... but, but how come the Government, or the EIA or the UCN did not see this coming?"

"THAT IS CLASSIFIED."

"Huh! Is it now!" GAT was faintly amused by robots having classified information.

"Those UCN tanks didn't prove much use."

"THEY WERE NOT TRULY BATTLE-TESTED."

GAT shut his eyes and put his hands over his face. "Oh right, friendly fire! The Eastasia and Westasia war! Was that it? You were proving your weapons under true battle conditions."

"IT WAS ONE OF THE REASONS."

"One of the reasons?"

"I AM NOT FREE TO REVEAL ANY OTHER REASONS TO YOU AT THIS TIME."

"Pah!" exclaimed GAT in disgust.

The battlefield began to recede into the distance and they flew out over the Severn Channel.

"Where are we going?"

"ST ATHAN."

"St Athan? Why?"

"TO BOARD AN AIRBOT TO NORTH AMERICANA."

"Oh yes ... I remember."

GAT let himself relax against the secure linked arms of the Parabot.

Whump whump whump whump whump whump.

He looked at his shattered lower left leg.

God! That does not look too good.

Whump whump whump whump whump whump.

He felt himself fading away into an exhausted sleep.

Whump whump whump whump whump whump.

Stay awake, must ask...

Whump whump whump whump whump whump.
about...
Whump whump whump whump whump whump.
Helen, and...

53

2am, the start of the morning after the night before, but without any of the normal sleep bit in between. A glass of red wine on the coffee table. Stand-up comedy on the TV. The slim form of a women, aged late thirty-something, mother of three, slumped on the sofa, with smudged make-up and wearing elegant, but very crumpled, clothes. Helen in 100 per cent crashed-out mode.

The outcomes of the 'experimental meal' had been beyond her wildest imaginings. GAT had attempted to throttle Thinkbot. Then, at 11 at night, he'd announced he was off to deal with something at Globalbot. Something that was more important than their marriage. And he'd left a pleading Thinkbot behind ... but was coming back to get him at, wait for it, 4:30am.

4:30am?

She had definitely lost the plot somewhere, along with any clear idea of where her marriage was heading. Once she'd calmed the kids down and got them into bed, the mask of bravery she had been wearing for their sake had fallen away and she'd had a little cry. Thinkbot had gone off to the garage with nothing much other than a 'goodnight'. The funny little robot seemed awfully subdued. He was normally such an optimist and had a heart of gold, and Helen was half expecting him to come and try to cheer her up. Perhaps being throttled by GAT had shaken him up.

Then she'd indulged in some self-therapy and phoned her sister to talk through every nuance of the whole evening in the painful detail females find so satisfying. They had spent nearly two hours on the phone and she felt a bit better, although it was difficult to talk sensibly about Thinkbot since her sister took for granted Helen's general view that 'robot = bad'. But Thinkbot wasn't a robot. He often referred to himself as a 'tinned human', but just like tinned food there was always room for doubt that he was, or ever had been, the real thing. But, by applying the can-opener of her emotions to Thinkbot, Helen was inclined to agree he really was the 'real thing' in a tin. But trying to explain this to someone was not straightforward, especially if you had a reputation for being terrified of robots. Quite simply, one had to meet Thinkbot to understand.

Helen picked up her wine and took a sip, gazing idly at the TV, wondering why the comedian's act was being backed up by dull rumbling noises. Then there was an ad break and she muted the sound, only to find that the dull rumbling noises continued on their own, if anything slightly clearer and more frequent.

"Mum."

Startled, Helen jumped, spilling red wine all over herself and the sofa.

"Oh bother! Look at me." Then, "Opal! What is it?"

"I can't sleep. The thunder and lightning woke me up."

Helen mopped the wine off the sofa and cursed at her wrecked blouse. All the time she could hear the thunder, but whilst cleaning up it dawned on her the weather was not in the slightest bit thundery. Opal and Helen made their way up to the loft den and peered out of the sloped windows. The rumble was louder and they could see the undersides of the clouds, dimly lit up now and again by light of different colours. Yellow and red and orange and, most of all, an electric blue-white that could easily have been mistaken for lightning.

Gerald appeared in his dressing-gown. "It's definitely not thunder," he announced and got the bielectronoculars out of the desk. They opened one of the windows and poked their heads out into the night. In addition to the rumbles, they could also hear faint crackles and concussions in the air and the distant roar of aircraft engines. Off to the east, away over the docks at Portbury and Avonmouth, and just over the brow of the high ground that rose the other side of the Avon River, something big was happening. For some distance along the ridge there were fires burning and blue bolts of electricity snaking along the crest. Directly above the ridge was where the sky was most brightly illuminated whenever the flashes came.

"That's Filton," announced Gerald. A huge blue flash illuminated the whole sky, and for the briefest moment they saw it was full of black dots. "Airbots!"

A gaggle of rocket trails headed out over the Bristol Channel and one exploded right next to an Airbot which let out a shower of white-hot fragments and spiralled down into the water sending a bright mushroom of steamy flame into the air.

A large concussion in the night air reached them and all the windows rattled in their frames.

"That was the shock wave from that blue stunbomb we saw a few seconds ago," came the commentary from the midget expert in the dressing-gown.

"Mum, isn't Dad at Globalbot?"

Helen awoke from her amazement and, picking up the phone, tried to make a voicecall to GAT on his mobile number.

"Sorry, your call cannot be connected at this time. Please try..."

She tried his Globalbot office number.

"Sorry, your call cannot be connect..."

Then she tried the Globalbot Filton general site number.

Bzzzzzzzzzzzzzzzzzzzzzzzzzzzzzzz...

A warbling siren started up in the centre of Portishead.

wooOOOWOOOoow wooOOOWOOOoow

"That's the chemical leak siren for Avonmouth and Portbury docks," said Gerald.

"Shut the window Gerald - that's what we're supposed to do," instructed Helen.

"Aw Mum!"

"SHUT IT!"

Gerald shut the window and the sound of the siren became muted, but it was still possible to hear, or rather feel, the concussions coming from Filton.

Opal turned on the loft TV and selected the EuroNEWS channel. A pair of smartly dressed newsreaders appeared, one female and one male. In one corner was a picture showing a scene not unlike that which the three of them could see from the loft anyway. At the bottom of the screen, text was running along a red bar:

...Reports have been received of a disturbance at the Globalbot Site in Bristol . . .

...Official Europa Government Statement has been issued that it is a UCN action to suppress recent dangerous robotic activity ...

...Explosions and extensive stunbolt fire have been observed ...

...The overall situation remains unclear ...

The female newsreader: "Just to recap, we're continuing to receive reports of a serious disturbance at the Globalbot site in Bristol England. We'll bring you more on this as soon as we have it."

The picture went to a full screen showing the scene at Filton from a distance. The male newsreader took over. "These are live pictures of the Globalbot site in Bristol. A Europa government spokesman has stated this is an official UCN action to suppress recent dangerous robotic activity." The bar was still scrolling along at the foot of the screen:

...more on this as soon as we have it ...

"Oh for crying out loud, they haven't got a clue," said Gerald in frustration. "Try the local channel."

Opal fingered the remote and a flustered-looking young girl appeared; clearly a junior trainee plonked onto what was normally a graveyard shift for newsreaders.

"The government advice is not to panic and to stay at home with the windows closed. And now, the weather."

Nothing happened.

"Sorry, there does not seem to be any weather. Let's move onto the sport."

More nothingness.

"Right, okay, er...let's go back to our main story of UCN human troops moving into the Filton Globalbot site. Eyewitnesses report hearing hundreds of Helibots around midnight. In the past half-hour a battle appears to have broken out across the Filton site. I ...er...we, can we? What, now? Okay okay **okay!**" The young girl made a rude gesture at someone out of the picture then, in spite of turning bright red, pressed on. "We can go now to Clinton Garmston on the scene. Clinton?"

The head and shoulders of a man cowering behind a hedge appeared.

"Yes, hello Imogen, I'm here in…" The picture flashed blue and the reporter wobbled sickeningly on the screen."…I'm in Bradley Stoke and there are Militaribots everywhere." The cameraman or Camerabot must have stood up as the hedge disappeared and a picture of a pleasant suburb at night appeared. All completely normal except for the line of 50-ton Militaribots marching down the middle of the road.

"**Whoar!** Type VIIBs!" exclaimed Gerald in amazement, standing up and pointing at the screen. The picture did not last long as a blue spot seemed to emerge from one of the Militaribots. The picture vanished, leaving a blank screen for a second before the girl reappeared.

"Er, looks like we've encountered some technical difficulties due to our cameraman being shot. Right." The flustered presenter jammed a hand against her right ear. "Ah. Let's, er, well he was shot wasn't he? Well $%&! you too! I'm doing my bes…"

The screen went to a '**Normal service will be resumed as soon as possible**' text page accompanied by soothing classical music. Opal and Helen huddled up on the futon and continued to hop around the news channels, but Gerald was more interested in watching the display out of the window.

"I'll go and get Thinkbot," said Gerald after a while.

"No. You stay indoors please! Thinkbot's got the code to get in if he wants to."

After a couple of hours the disturbance seemed to have died down. The news channels were still reporting the government line that it was a UCN operation that was going totally to plan. Pictures of Militaribots were shown with the comment that these were merely backing up the UCN human troops. The local news had restarted with one of the more regular presenters, and a measure of calm had returned there too. The advice continued to be 'stay indoors with the windows shut' and 'there's nothing to worry about, everything's under control'.

Helen and Opal began to feel a little better, until Gerald piped up with, "That's just total crap. Something's gone terribly wrong."

"Gerald! Less language please."

Opal began to whimper. "Dad's up there somewhere."

"Oh, he'll be okay I'm sure. He's the best with robots, everyone knows that," said Gerald with false confidence, his voice betraying he was just as worried as Opal.

Dawn was breaking, but the rising sun was blotted out behind the dense plumes of smoke snaking up from beyond the ridge in the east. On the news channel a reporter had managed to charter a Helibot and was flying as near to the Globalbot site as he dared. The pictures showed damaged buildings and hundreds of wrecked Militaribots, through which columns of human troops marched, apparently under the protection of the light-duty Militaribots alongside, towards large Helibot transports. They had no helmets or weapons and waved madly at the pressmen.

"Looks like the troops have achieved whatever they came here for and are leaving in triumph," said the upbeat reporter.

Meanwhile a Military Helibot had risen up from the ground and was shadowing the press Helibot.

"PLEASE DEPART," blasted the Military Helibot through a large loudspeaker.

The camera panned around to the reporter standing looking out of the open side-hatch of the Helibot. "Nothing's going to make this reporter depart. I'm dedicated to the principle that the public always deserves to know," he pronounced arrogantly. At which point the Military Helibot fired a warning shot, which exploded some distance in front of the press Helibot. Inside the cabin there was a bang-whizz-snap sound and the reporter was gone - replaced by a large white wobbling airbag. The camera panned round just in time to see the reporter sailing through the air and landing with a big splash in one of the scenic lakes that were dotted around the edge of the Globalbot site. The Helibot circled round and the pictures continued whilst a large humanoid Militaribot waded out into lake and completed the reporter's humiliation by fishing him out of the water and carrying him ashore over his shoulder like a toddler.

"Voicecall. Globalbot. **Urgent**."

Helen grabbed the phone. "Hello! GAT? Is that you?"

"No Helen, it's Wendy Bafers. I was hoping GAT was with you."

"He went back into Globalbot late last night."

"What! Why? Have you heard from him?" The note of urgent concern in Wendy's voice did nothing for Helen's mental state.

"No," she replied, "he said something about Expack and an old Unibot."

"Did Thinkbot go with him?" There was definitely panic in Wendy's voice.

"No, Thinkbot stayed here."

"Thank God for that. Right, tell him I'm on my way to pick him up in about ten minutes."

Wendy was talking so fast Helen couldn't get a word in edgeways. "Can you tell Thinkbot to be ready. Thanks. See you shortly. We can talk more then." Click, the call ended.

"I'll get him," said Gerald throwing himself down the stairs in near freefall, touching maybe only two or three steps and landing on his large feet at the bottom with a house-shuddering crunch.

"Don't go ..." started Helen. Bang! The loft door closed at the foot of the stairs. "...outside in your slippers," she concluded to the absent boy.

Gerald rushed across the empty garage and made towards the ladder at the back. "Thinkbot! Hey tinhead! Did you see the fireworks show? Hello! I said Hello!"

Gerald shot up the ladder almost as fast as he had come down the loft stairs, but at the top he stopped dead and stared at the scene before him. Thinkbot was lying face down on the floor by the bench. Next to him was what looked like a large crumpled spider. Gerald's encyclopaedic mind supplied the answer - a Centibot! He slowly moved closer and saw that the Centibot was badly damaged, and then he saw the dried blood on the carpet. As he walked, his feet made a scrunchy sound and, looking more closely, he realised he was treading on what seemed to be 'dead' Millibots. They were lying at random angles on the floor, like so many dead flies on the sill of a closed window in summer. Gerald had inherited GAT's reasoned approach in a crisis and he calmly rolled Thinkbot over and opened the power pack cover. The switch was in the OFF position. He looked at the plate on the bottom of the right foot -

Globalbot Corporation Standard Duty Unibot
Version 3
Serial number 141592654

Gerald took a deep breath, flicked the switch to ON and stood back. The Unibot made booting-up noises and got to its feet. It stretched as if waking up and looked expectantly at Gerald.

"Thinkbot, are you okay?"

"I am fine Gerald."

I am not *I'm*.

"What happened here Thinkbot?"

The Unibot looked around at the blood and the scrambled Centibot and the scattered defunct Millibots.

"I am sorry Gerald, I do not know."

"How come you were switched off?"

"I knocked my power switch on the bench."

"Oh come on Thinkbot, why don't you pull the other one!"

"Pull what other one?"

Gerald began to back away, feeling a bit uneasy. The body might have been Thinkbot's, but the mind was not.

"Er, right. I came to tell you that Wendy Bafers is coming to collect you any minute."

"I will prepare myself to meet Wendy Bafers immediately."

Gerald had had enough. This Unibot was making him nervous. Then he realised with a shock that this probably was Thinkbot, or rather had been Thinkbot.

"Gerald, please help me prepare to leave."

"Who told you were leaving?" Gerald had backed up to the ladder and started down.

"Gerald, please do not leave me."

But Gerald was 100 per cent spooked by the partial Thinkbot and was on his way back to the house as rapidly as his feet could carry him.

"Gerald, please come back. It is me, Thinkbot."

As Gerald raced away across the driveway towards the house, something blinked across the sky above his head, something black, low-flying, and very fast. A spilt second later a searing roar of engines engulfed him, and almost instantaneously the garage behind him exploded in a ball of

377

flame. Gerald found himself flying through the air towards the trees at the end of the garden, propelled by a massive wind, stronger than any gale he'd ever been in. But, in spite of the rushing wind, everything seemed to be happening in slow motion, and as he toppled head over heels through the air three metres above the ground, he became aware he was surrounded by strange skinny-looking stick figures with bright fiery tails. Angels? Devils? Something clamped him around his forehead, his shoulders and his hips and pulled him backwards so hard it took his breath away. His legs went out at right angles in front of him, and each one seemed to weigh a ton. The last thing he saw was a tree trunk heading towards him at an incredible speed.

Inside the house, Helen and Opal had followed Gerald downstairs into the kitchen. They'd heard the roar of the aircraft passing over, then there was a bright flash and the kitchen window leapt out of its frame and disintegrated into a million fragments that flew through the room. The table tipped over and mugs and cutlery took off and smashed or clattered into the rear wall of the kitchen. Helen's mind caught an image of the window blind blown out at right angles against the ceiling, then coming loose and zooming over her head at a phenomenal speed as she and Opal were flung backwards onto the floor. Sliding over the tiles, they eventually ended up scrunched against the bottom of the kitchen dresser surrounded by the shattered remains of her precious Portmeirion collection. After what seemed an age, the sounds of bits and pieces of debris bouncing around died away and a dreadful quietness descended. Helen stirred, pushed herself up and started screaming hysterically. Opal emerged from a coating of plaster dust like a statue coming to life. Breathing rapidly and making whimpering noises, she sat shaking violently with her back to the kitchen units.

"MUM! MUM! MUUUUUUUUM!"

Mike appeared in the door to the hallway and danced from foot to foot in a sheer panic. Tiger whizzed around his feet to see what had happened, whilst trying to avoid being trodden under Mike's large feet.

Helen stopped screaming nonsense long enough to scream, "**GERAAAAAAALD!**" and looked out of the large gap that had once been her kitchen window.

And saw Robots.

Robots with guns.

Militaribots, albeit rather skinny ones, were dropping out of the sky and scattering all over the garden, weapons at the ready. The garage was a heap of rubble with a few recognisable things like bent bicycle wheels and scooter handlebars poking out amidst the flames and billowing black smoke. Down at the end of the garden there was a gaggle of the skinny Militaribots, some standing, some lying down and some crouched next to the crumpled heap of a boy in a dressing-gown.

Helen opened her mouth and silently screamed, " !" This was her worst nightmare. This was hell on earth. She grabbed the handle of a large cast-iron frying pan, a family heirloom that had been hanging on the kitchen wall prior to the explosion, and rushed into the garden. One of the Militaribots saw her and ran over.

"Madam, please..."

DONG! Helen sent it sprawling with one swing of the frying pan and ran towards where Gerald lay. Other Militaribots came towards her on intercept courses.

"Madam Pl..."

CLANG!

"Mad..."

DER-YONGYONGYONGYONG! (This one being an absolute peach of a hit.)

"M..."

CLA -RACK!

The frying pan broke in two and flew out of her hands.

"Madam, please stay calm, all is well. He is only winded."

Helen took a few swings at the Militaribot with her fists, but it was too fast for her and clamped her hands firmly but gently at her sides. She had got to within a few feet of where Gerald lay, or rather sat, with his back to the tree with a white Medibot, its bright red LED cross glowing on its back, kneeling beside him holding an oxygen mask over his nose and mouth. Another Medibot was cleaning up a few cuts and had a case of bandages at the ready. Around Gerald lay the mangled remains of several of the skinny Militaribots. Looking back towards the house she saw three Militaribots lying where she had struck them down, one with its head missing, and beyond them Opal and Mike sitting on the grass together being mollycoddled by another pair of Medibots. Helen became aware of a Medibot tending to her cuts and bruises even where she stood, and of a pair of Firebots raced in along the driveway to deal with the fire still raging in the rubble that had just a few minutes earlier been their garage. Looking up she saw most of the tiles had been blown off the roof of the house, exposing a row of wooden rafters, and below the gutterless edge, every window was a gaping hole edged by ragged brickwork. Helen sat down on the debris-strewn grass, put her head between her hands, and started hollering with shock. The Medibot knelt down and continued to treat her cuts. Yet another ran up and gently covered her shoulders with a blanket and magically produced a little glass of brownish liquid for her to drink. Helen took a sip and gasped as the brandy warmed her mouth and throat. The sound of something huge and mechanical approaching the house made Helen look up, only to have her field of vision filled by a monstrous Militaribot towering over her. There was only room for it to plonk one foot on the driveway and it seemed to blot out half the sky. It sagged on its legs down towards the ground and a ramp dropped out of its belly right in front of her.

"Mum."

"MUM!"

Opal and Mike stood either side of her, both with lollipops sticking out of their mouths. She put her arms round their shoulders and held them tight.

"Gwosh! Wit'sa twipe fiftwee fwee robwot armwee fweild hweadkwarters," said Gerald from behind his plastic mask, then yanked it off and repeated. "It's a type 53 robot army field headquarters. There are only 15 in existence!"

The Medibots wrestled with the recovering boy to try and replace the oxygen mask. He fought them off and they gave up, presumably concluding that if he was well enough to fight them he probably did not need oxygen any more.

A type 53 ... Oh how interesting, said a little voice dryly inside Helen's head. Whether it was the brandy, or the fact that she and the kids had come through a terrible experience virtually unharmed, she felt that she was coping rather well with her worst nightmare so far.

"Please board," invited a Militaribot, holding its arm towards the ramp.

They set off up the ramp, with Gerald fending off a couple of Medibots who offered him a ride on a stretcher, and entered the monster Militaribot. They passed through an area full of stick-like Militaribots standing in rows.

"Type 4 light duty," they learned from Gerald.

Entering a small box-like room, doors shut behind them and, feeling a slight increase in weight, they realised they were in a lift. The doors opened and they exited into a hanger where a Military Helibot was waiting with its blades swept back. The side hatch was open and next to a set of steps stood an Execubot.

"Madam, children, welcome. Please board at your convenience."

They got in, followed by the Execubot, and strapped themselves into luxurious seats. The hatch closed and the roof of the hanger parted in the middle and fell away to the sides. Early morning sunlight flooded in. The floor of the hanger rose up until the Helibot was sitting on top of the HQ Militaribot. With astonishing swiftness the blades deployed and accelerated and they were away up into the air. Banking sharply Helen was presented with a spectacular view.

Of her smouldering house, wrecked and swarming with robots; and of the road and a car with a woman standing next to it remonstrating with a pair of the skinny Militaribots. It was Wendy Bafers.

She turned attention to her trousers and blouse, both now torn and stained with blood and wine. She'd put them on the day before in what now seemed like another life. A life where she'd been expecting this morning to be one of waking up next to her beloved GAT in her own bed, not flying off from her trashed home in a military Helibot to an unknown destination and wondering if she was a recently widowed mother of three.

"I WANT TIGER!" wailed Mike and burst into tears.

54

Somewhere in the middle of the Atlantic Ocean, Admiral of the Fleet Garj Lunn and Vice-Admiral Botkwite s'Nigun were on duty on the bridge of the European Airbot carrier ES Dresden. If the truth be told, there was never much to do, but they managed to cover this up quite well by playing 'I spy' with the bielectronoculars or passing off war games on the tactical computer as 'advanced training'. When all else failed, they read naval history books and had frequent tea breaks. The crews on these boats got to know each other quite well, but never quite found everything out. For example, s'Nigun had heard various rumours about what Lunn had done before he joined the navy. The most bizarre claimed that he'd lived in Helsinki where by day he'd run a bouncy castle whilst at night he'd been a nightclub bouncer. s'Nigun suspected there must be some truth in this somewhere, and that the common thread of 'bounce' must mean something. But when asked directly, Lunn simply replied he did not want to talk about it, which to s'Nigun seemed to indicate he probably *had* run a bouncy castle since this was not the sort of thing one admitted to in the navy.

So far this fleet deployment had proceeded without a hitch. No ship reliability or weather problems to contend with, and all their training and equipment test exercises had passed off perfectly. At the time it all began to go wrong, Lunn and s'Nigun were sitting at two separate displays facing each other across the tactical computer. The atmosphere was tense.

"G10," said Lunn.

"Miss!" replied s'Nigun. "B3."

Lunn looked crestfallen as he admitted, "Hit".

"B4."

"Hit."

"B5."

"Hit."

Sounds of tiny explosions came out of the screen.

"Har har! I've sunk your Submaribot."

But then the screens went blank.

"Hey! What's happened? **Butlerbot!**"

As if by magic the Butlerbot appeared and scuttled up. "Sir?"

"Get the Chief Engineerbot up here straight away."

"I am afraid the Chief Engineerbot is occupied at this time, sir."

Lunn's face darkened. As he stood up he seemed to become very menacing.

Maybe he had been a bouncer after all, thought s'Nigun.

"Get me the Chiefengbot now!"

The roar of an Airbot taking off from the flight deck below drowned out the Butlerbot's reply. Lunn rushed over to the flight deck viewpoint.

"Where does that Airbot think it's going? Who gave permission to launch an Airbot?"

Another Airbot took off. Then another. And another.

s'Nigun grabbed his bielectronoculars. "Sir, they're taking off from the other carriers as well."

"WHAT THE HELL IS THE MATTER WITH THESE BLASTED SCREENS?" bellowed Lunn.

"Nothing sir. They have been disabled for your own safety."

Lunn and s'Nigun both turned and stared incredulously at the Butlerbot. Lunn smashed his fist down on his display unit, ironically thumping the exact spot where his imaginary Submaribot had been sunk a few minutes earlier. The display cracked from one side to the other and let out a pathetic little 'phut'.

"GET ME THE CHIEF ENGINEERBOT NOW!" Lunn began to move menacingly towards the Butlerbot.

"SIR!" shouted s'Nigun, who had returned to looking out of the window. He was pointing at one of the Battleships. Lunn whipped his bielectronoculars up to his eyes, just in time to see the first intercontinental class missile rise with a bright yellow plume westward into the sky, accelerating all the time as it gained height. Missiles now started erupting from all of the Battleships and streaked off westwards in the dark grey sky, disappearing through the cloud with a bright blip. The intercontinental missiles were soon joined by cruise missiles, some of which burst unpredictably out of the sea, having been launched by Submaribots. And all the time, Airbots were appearing on the deck below and taking off one after another. The Butlerbot decided discretion was the better part of valour and quietly slipped away out of the section of the ship occupied by the human crew. As it left, it checked that all the doors were secure and that there was plenty of rum and jam doughnuts available, and replaced the fresh milk carton in the tea machine with one marked 'Milk of Amnesia.'

*   *   *

A few minutes later, with a hint of dawn over the Atlantic Ocean, the citizens of New York were waking up and setting about their normal daily business. The early risers were already on their way to work or having breakfast or trying to prise teenagers out of bed. Hundreds of thousands more were still fast asleep in bed or snoozing, dreading the sound of the alarm clock. Just another morning in the hustling bustling biggest richest noisiest metropolis on earth.

Then all power to the city was cut and darkness fell. Cars and trucks stopped. Noise evaporated. The city air emptied of the normally omnipresent roar of transport and machinery and robots; and homes likewise of the buzzing and humming and whirring of electrical appliances. Even robots stood still (in spite of having their own battery packs) and point-blank refused to provide the emergency lighting they would normally have supplied when the electricity failed during the dark hours. People were forced to fumble in cupboards and garages to find flashlights and ancient candles. I mean … *candles??* Candles were for church and Christmas and birthday cakes, not for lighting the home.

And all that broke the unreal city quietness were the noises made by humans: people yelling for each other; cursing unco-operative robots; banging doors; footfalls in the street. Above the city the hemispherical sky was a silent canvas of blackness with a dim dawn lying on the eastern horizon. Without warning, the whole sky filled spectacularly from horizon to horizon with bright flashes and, seconds later, the bone-shaking concussions of multiple aerial explosions. Rapid detonations pulverised the air and balls of flame expanded outwards seemingly for ever, with an accompanying background soundtrack of continuous thunder. Smaller munitions buried themselves in the city waterways of the Hudson River, Jamaica Bay, the East River and Long Island Sound, throwing towering heaps of water hundreds of feet into the air and creating clouds of billowing steam. The Statue of Liberty disappeared from view and salty seawater fell like rain over much of the city. Humans cowered in sheer mind-numbing terror, small children wailed, pants were wetted, and those that had been asleep were now wide awake, even the teenagers.

The barrage lasted for a full 20 minutes. Then the surreal silence returned just long enough for people to hear the hysterical screaming of millions of people, mixed with a cacophony of emergency vehicle sirens and burglar alarms echoing eerily around the city centre buildings. This persisted for just a few seconds; long enough for the communal terror to become almost tangible. Then those with a view of the lightening eastern Atlantic sky realised there was another horror to contemplate - hundreds of aircraft heading in from the Atlantic. The ear-splitting sounds of Airbots and cruise missiles once more drowned out the human wails of terror and emergency sirens as they hurtled between the tall skyscrapers of Manhattan, the noise amplified by reflections off the tall buildings. Now targets within the city itself were being hit. Time and again there was the flash-crump of a hit followed by a mushroom of flame and smoke. Clouds of zero-visibility dust enveloped buildings, rushing between the gaps and blotting out entire neighbourhoods. And the citizens huddled together wherever they'd been able to take cover against the onslaught. Those caught out on the street dodged into shops and bars and other people's homes, making instant new friendships in adversity. Lifelong friendships maybe, if only because life itself seemed about to end any minute. Petrified with fear, they talked to each other in hushed tones, wondering if it was just New York that was under attack, and who on earth was attacking them, and why.

At the North Americana Federated Intelligence Agency in Langley and the Supreme HQ of the North Americana Armed Forces in the Pentagon, there was complete pandemonium. The emergency power had come on okay and they both had access to full incoming radar data and analysis capability. But the analysis said the missiles and Airbots attacking New York were from the Northern Europa Fleet, and all the intelligence reports still had this fleet at rest in its base at Scapa Flow in northern Scotland. Even if this was wrong, why on earth was Europa attacking New York anyway? And it wasn't just New York. All major cities in North Americana were under attack, and not just by Europa forces. San Francisco was under attack from a Pacifica fleet, and Mexico City by the South Americana air force. And then all the North Americana armies and fleets seemed to be in the wrong place, or on exercise, or out of contact. What were they doing? And worst of all, President Hedge was missing. He'd been at the Globalbot Militaribot Oak Ridge site to announce something or other, but now they could not find him. Was he still there? Had he left? A surplus of questions; a famine of answers. The available members of the supreme committee of the armed forces gathered piecemeal in the main situation room deep inside the Pentagon and tried to make sense of the incoherent flood of information. However, they only had one real decision to make: should they activate the Robots of Mass Destruction and release them from their bunkers? It was a momentous question. So far there had been no report from the UCN about any other Confederated Nation releasing their RMD, so they carried on agonising and trying to figure out what was going on.

But North Americana was not alone in its confusion or its agony. In London and Tokyo and Istanbul and Sydney and Rio de Janeiro and Beijing and Bombay and Cairo and Berlin and … well, just about every major city on earth, attacks were being pressed home by robot forces. The list of targets was actually the major city weather-listing from the *Daily Globalgraph* news service, but this eluded all the human intelligence agencies who were desperately looking for far more sinister connections in the data than the 'Today's Weather Around the Globe!' listing. In each nation the President (if he could be found and patched into a secure communications link) and the commanders of the armed forces debated what to do. In countries where the President could not be contacted, there particular nervousness because although they could release their RMD to be ready for action, only the President or a combination of a few of his key staff could give the command to fire. They were worried they might not be able to respond if someone else fired first. They would miss out on the action - the end of the world party, and after they had spent so long getting ready for it! The absurdity of this fear escaped them completely in the immediate panic.

Unsurprisingly the first nation that blinked and released their RMD for action was Eastasia, or then again maybe it was Westasia. Either way they were the most jumpy due to their recent unexplained spontaneous robot war. This triggered the automatic UCN notification system, and over the next few minutes in UCN centres scattered around the world, operatives watched in horror as one by one each nation released their RMD from their bunkers and readied them for action.

In Europa things were a little better than in North Americana, in that it was the middle of the day and they had not lost their President. Driski was yanked out of his luxurious Paris apartment (one of many he had scattered throughout the trendy cities of Europa) and rushed to the nearest secure Government communication site in an antique petrol-powered automobile (a banana-yellow Citroen CV6 as it happened), this being the only serviceable transport that could be found due to a power cut coupled with unco-operative robots. And then he sat dumbfounded by the total lack of sensible information for most of the afternoon, listening to the dull thud of explosions across the city and the muted roar of Africana Airbots in the sky above. As the afternoon wore on, the attacks seemed to die down, the power came back on and the communication network came back up. Then the full horror of what was happening became apparent. Cities all over the world were under attack and there was mass panic everywhere. Driski and the advisors who'd been able to get to the communication building watched in silence scenes of crowds out on the streets and panoramic views of the smoking cities of Europa. And then, as if that were not enough, there were UCN notifications popping on other display screens.

FOR PRESIDENTIAL EYES ONLY. UCN RMD PROTOCOL NOTIFICATION TO EUROPA: Eastasia RMD

bunker release initiated. 17% of Eastasia RMD are targeted at Europa. Full launch capability estimated in 00:27:56. Current launch status = hold.

Driski stared at the clock, which was counting down even as he read the message: just over 27 minutes to launch status. Driski looked around the room surreptitiously and then slipped a silver hip flask from his pocket and took a large swig. Similar messages came up for Westasia, and Pacifica, and Africana, although this last message claimed it would be over 16 hours until their RMD were ready for launch. *Typical Africana. President Linga Nlonga not really living up to his name again. At least Hedgie's not lost his cool.* At which precise moment the last message on earth that Driski wanted to see blinked up in front of his disbelieving eyes.

FOR PRESIDENTIAL EYES ONLY. UCN RMD PROTOCOL NOTIFICATION TO EUROPA: North Americana RMD bunker release initiated. 23% of North Americana RMD are targeted at Europa. Full launch capability estimated in 00:59:52. Current launch status = hold.

"Mr President."
Driski was sitting staring into space with his mouth open.
"Mr President! Sir."
"What! What is it?"
"Sir, we should release our RMD for action."
"Get me Hedge, now!"
"Mr President, communications with North Americana have been disrupted for several hours."
Driski sagged. "Okay, okay, yes fine, where do I put my finger?"
"Er, don't know sir. You can put your finger wherever you like. But we do need a retinal pattern."
The advisor placed an optical device over Driski's eye.
"Pattern match is positive. Please speak the instruction sir."
Driski took a deep breath and, seeing so many eyes fixed on him, regretted he could not take another swig from his hip flask. "This is President Driski of Europa. I hereby authorise bunker release of all Europa Robots of Mass Destruction. May God bless them and all that sail in them."

The looks of terror on his advisors' faces were briefly replaced by looks of bemusement at the nonsensical statement Driski had added to the command protocol.

FOR EUROPA PRESIDENTIAL EYES ONLY. UCN RMD PROTOCOL NOTIFICATION HAS BEEN SENT TO ALL CONFEDERATED NATIONS: Europa RMD bunker release initiated. Current launch status = hold.

Then seconds later.

FOR PRESIDENTIAL EYES ONLY. UCN RMD PROTOCOL NOTIFICATION TO ALL CONFEDERATED NATIONS. All nations have released RMD for bunker release and with launch status = hold. As per UCN RMD PROTOCOL 90-629400 launch capability timing will now be aligned. All nations will reach simultaneous launch status in one hour (1 hour). Full global launch capability will be achieved in 00:59:59. Current Launch Status (all CN) = hold.

Well, thought Driski, *what shall I do with what might be the last hour of my life? Hang on! There was that blonde I met the other day. Blast, what did I do with her number?* But, as he should have realised, the hour was not to be his to wile away. His press officers appeared, out of breath and sweating profusely. Driski stared with disgust at the dark patches under their arms, and the faint acrid aroma of over-stressed humanity.

"Mr President, we must make a statement to the media. There's mass panic throughout Europa. We've just got to say something to reassure people and try and calm things down," said the head officer at 100 miles per hour.

"What is there to reassure them about?" asked Driski with a sneer. "Maybe that the end will be quick?"

"But sir, no RMD are set to launch yet ... are they?" replied the head press officer with a definite edge of panic in his voice. "The head of police wants you to say something that will calm the situation down, irrespective of what's actually happening."

Moments later Driski found himself being cajoled through the corridors and then flung out in front of what appeared to be several hundred people having a mass brawl, many of them with cameras and sound-recording devices. A few Camerabots stood idly at the back with their telephoto lenses trained on the podium. They saw Driski at the microphone, and an expectant hush instantly fell on the room.

"Ladies and Gentlemen. I ..." Driski stopped and wondered what to say next. The press stared at him in silence. "....would like to say ... that the current situation is ... well ... a situation ... and as we all know it's ... ah ... unclear ... but I would like to reassure the ... .the ... the ... public that there's, no something, no, no, nothing ... to not worry abo... it's all fine ... just fine."

Driski did not feel this was going terribly well. He was right. And this was backed up by the growing hubbub in the room. A pressman stood up and waved his arms at Driski.

"Mr President, what do you make of the defeat of the UCN human robot suppression forces at Bristol in England?"

Driski stared at the pressman and repeated moronically, "UCN? Defeat? Bristol? England?" He turned and looked at his advisors. They all looked at the ceiling, or their feet, or inspected their nails. One of them hissed, "*Deny it.*" But quite a few at the front of the press corps heard it, and reacted accordingly. One shouted loud enough to be heard clearly by most people in the room.

"Mr President! Do you not know UCN forces have been overwhelmed at Globalbot Bristol by the Northern Robot Army of Europa? And that North Americana human UCN forces flew straight into a trap set by the Southern Robot Army of Europa? And that on every military base in Europa human military personnel have been locked up?"

Driski stared at the reporter as if he had sprouted horns, or had steam spurting out of his ears, or had just stated that robots had taken over the planet.

"Mr President!" yelled an attractive brunette reporter, one that Driski had admired for some time. "What do you make of the reports that President Hedge is missing?"

Driski's mouth was moving, but no sound came out.

"Mr President. Who's in charge? Who's in charge of the robots sir? **Sir?**"

This question quietened the room down, hanging on Driski answering.

"I don't know."

"Pardon, sir, I did not catch that."

"**I don't know**."

And there was silence in heaven for three quarters of an hour.

But on Earth there was instant bedlam.

"Is it Go Natural?"

"Is it a software bug?"

"Is it the robots?"

"Is it aliens?"

Driski bowed his head and put his hands to his face.

"He's ... crying," observed someone near the front.

Newsmen turned to their cameras. "And so, with the President of Europa in tears, I hand you back to the studio."

Driski's advisors tried to pull him off the podium, but he fought them off, pushing them into the press or off the side of the stage. Then he pulled out a silver hip flask, took a long swig and threw himself into the crowd in the general direction of the brunette.

After a lot of pushing and shoving, Driski's security men finally dragged the drunken and disgraced statesman out of the melee and back up to the secure communications suite. There he continued to take swigs from his hip flask, make rude gestures at a no smoking sign whilst consuming a cigarette, and stare at the UCN clock as it ticked down to 00:00:00, at which point a UCN message appeared.

FOR PRESIDENTIAL EYES ONLY. All RMD except Africana are active and ready for launch. UCN RMD control robots are actively assisting Africana (priority = critical). Current launch status all other Confederated Nations = hold. Full global deployment can be achieved within 45 minutes. In the event of launch time to target annihilation will be continuously notified in real time.

"Typical," muttered Driski to no one in particular. "If it was a crisis with fresh water in Africana we'd make a token effort to help, but the minute they need their RMD sorted we're falling over ourselves to help them."

The clock reset itself and hung before him like a temporal sword of Damocles:

00:45:00

55

Meanwhile, high over the Atlantic, whilst the world 15,000 metres below reeled from robotic attack, Helen was having one of the most pleasant experiences of her life. She was sitting in a hot Jacuzzi on Europa Airbot 1, President Driski's private palace of the air, with a glass of red wine in her hand. As soon as she and the children had arrived at St Athan in South Wales, they had boarded the enormous aircraft with the Execubot and taken off.

"Have you any news about my husband?"

"GAT is on an aircraft ahead of us. He has a minor foot injury but is otherwise well," replied the Execubot. Helen shut her eyes and took a deep breath. She felt Opal's hand slip into hers.

"How bad is the foot injury?"

"I am afraid I do not know other than it is not life threatening."

An excited Mike ran up and distracted them. "MUM! MUM! THERE'S A PLAYTHINGY WITH GRAVY!"

Gerald sauntered up, still in his dressing-gown. "It's a Playstation with gravitational simulation. You sit inside and it feels like you're really moving."

The Execubot turned to Mike. "We are searching for your Tiger. As soon as we have located it …"

"HIM!"

" -… him, we will bring him to you." Then to Opal and Gerald: "It is the same for your Toybots."

The kids, being kids, accepted this at face value and put the fate of their beloved Toybots to one side for the time being.

The biggest downer had been Gerald's news about Thinkbot. Once the Execubot had left them alone to sort out baths and showers and clothes, Gerald told Helen, Opal and Mike his story. The dried blood, the smashed-up Centibot, and the fact that Thinkbot been turned off by someone and had lost his ability to think. And that he had still been in the garage when the Airbots had blown it up.

"It wasn't Thinkbot," stated Opal dogmatically.

"NO, THINKBOT IS OKAY."

But Gerald was adamant. "I'm sorry, but I think it was. I checked the serial number plate."

"It wasn't Thinkbot."

"Oh for goodness' sake, be quiet you two!"

But as Gerald had been telling his tale, Helen had had a brief crisis of confidence.

Why had the Airbots blown up the garage?

Why had they destroyed Thinkbot?

Why on earth was there dried blood?

And, most of all, why had the robots put their lives, especially Gerald's, at risk like that and then turned up to help them immediately afterwards?

Why and where were they now flying in Europa Airbot 1?

It was clear they were going west; she'd managed to figure that much out. As she lay in the hot bubbling water, she reflected on this and determined that she had to break the stranglehold of fear and ask their host Execubot. Up until now the army of Healthbots and Spabots that inhabited Europa Airbot 1 had pampered Helen into submission. She'd had a full body massage and then a facial, followed by half a bottle of wonderful red wine and a luscious salad. Then, having been awake the whole night before, she'd fallen asleep. When she awoke, she found that the kids had been showered and fed and dressed in spanking new clothes, and the Execubot had insisted she try the Jacuzzi.

The comms pad activated, "Madam, we will be landing in one hour. Please prepare."

Helen got out, feeling wonderful in spite of the stresses and strains of the last 24 hours. She dried off and went to pick up the robe she had been wearing since she'd shed the torn bloodied crumpled clothes from the day before. It was gone. After a brief moment of naked panic, Helen's eyes came to rest on a rack of clothes. They were beautiful; every garment a delight. But what was she dressing for? A dinner party? Or another romp through a battlefield? Where was she going? Why hadn't she asked the Execubot even that simple question? Answer - she was so desperately tired and afraid. She'd hardly slept since GAT left, and if GAT was alive and the kids were safe and well, she really cared for little else. It was a shame about Thinkbot, but he was only a robot after all, albeit a pretty unique one.

She selected a pair of black leather trousers, a light-blue cotton shirt and a black jacket. A vast array of perfumes were lined up on a shelf and she spent 20 minutes working her way through them. Once dressed and perfumed, she inspected herself in the mirror and, well, she looked as good as she felt, which was pretty good.

A fine facade fronting ferocious fear.

She left the spa area and made her way to the enormous lounge in the middle of the aircraft. Gerald was inside the Playstation, Mike was watching cartoons and Opal was curled up on one of the enormous sofas staring out of the window through red eyes. The Execubot stood perfectly still, ready to attend any of them at a moment's notice. Helen went across to Opal and put her arm around her. Mike ran over, dived into the other side of Helen and lay there. Gerald appeared and pretended to ignore them. The aircraft bumped through a little patch of air turbulence and the hundreds of bottles of whisky lining one wall of the lounge area chinked together in unison.

Helen took a deep breath. "Where are we going?"

"Madam, we will be landing at Andrews Airbot Base, where you will be transferred to a smaller aircraft for onward passage to Oak Ridge Tennessee."

"Oak Ridge?" piped up Gerald. "Isn't that where the Globalbot Military Division Headquarters are? We nearly moved there, didn't we Mum?"

"Yes, yes Gerald, we nearly did." Helen turned again to the Execubot. "Why are we going there?"

"Your presence has been requested by the Robots of Mass Destruction."

Helen's mouth and eyes remained open for some time as her relaxed but fragile facade crumbled to reveal naked fear. Opal sat up and stared at the Execubot, as did Gerald, and Mike peeped at the cartoons only out of the corner of his eye.

* * *

In freezing cold underground bunkers spread around the globe, hundreds of Robots of Mass Destruction were powering up and running through self-test. Outside the bunkers, delivery vehicles prepared themselves for launch, moving into position near the surface along passageways and shafts. There was no human involvement whatsoever so the bunker complexes were totally dark. On the other hand, there was no need to keep the noise down to avoid damaging fragile human ears, so it was deafening. Mechanical clanging and graunching sounds filled and echoed through the frigid air in the confined spaces as the RMD moved from their bays and headed out of the bunkers one by one. In the nations that had authorised bunker exit first, a few RMD had already loaded themselves onto their launch vehicles. Many were located in the nosecones of shiny metal ballistic missiles. Others, tens or hundreds of metres underwater in airless ocean-bed bunkers or near the coast dropped into missile silos on Submaribots, which silently slipped out into the dark depths of the ocean deeps. Inside mountains, yet more climbed aboard high-speed Airbots or cruise missiles ready to emerge out of slits cut in the sheer cliff sides. It was all going perfectly according to plan, exactly as the scientists and engineers who had designed the system had envisaged it working. So far neither a glitch nor a fault of any kind. They would have been right to be proud of their achievement - perfection in the creation of the mechanism of total destruction. First class execution of an insane plan.

*   *   *

Europa Airbot 1 turned onto its final approach into Andrews Airbot Base ten miles south-east of Washington DC. The kids were excitedly looking out of the windows as North Americana appeared below them, becoming clearer and clearer as they dropped towards the ground. After the bombshell of the revelation about being invited by the RMD, Helen had decided the more she asked the less she wanted to know, and had asked no more questions. *Go with the flow.*

Gerald had his face pressed up to a window. "That's Washington isn't it?"

"It's awfully smoky there," commented Opal.

Helen leaned over and looked out. She saw a city in the distance with billowing plumes of smoke rising high into the sky. She turned sharply to the Execubot. **"What's happened?"**

"Madam, Washington DC has been subjected to operation Shock and Awe."

SHOCK AND AWE?

After touching down they were picked up by a stretched Limobot and driven through the base. Everywhere they looked there was activity. But only robot activity; there were no humans in sight anywhere. Lines of Airbots were being worked on by ground crew Mechabots, and Militaribots of all shapes and sizes milled around. Airbots swept lazily across the sky above the base. They were driven to a multi-storey building and led inside by the Execubot. Helen realised they were in a hospital and felt a pang of worry.

"Is my husband here?"

"Yes madam, we are on our way to meet with him."

A pang of joy stomped on the pang of worry and a spring came into the step of the kids. They found GAT propped up in bed. Helen and the kids accelerated towards him, ignoring the vague feeling something did not look quite right. They embraced and for a few minutes no one said much. Then Gerald realised what was wrong.

"Dad, where's your left foot?"

Helen looked at the contours of the bed cover. There was no lump where GAT's left foot should have been.

"I lost it. The Medibots did everything they could but, well, it wasn't possible to reconstruct it. It would have been worse than a prosthetic."

"A WHAT?"

"A false foot. A bit like a robot's foot. Once my leg has healed up I'll have it fitted and you'll hardly notice it."

"You said it was a minor foot injury," said Helen angrily to the Execubot, but GAT answered her.

"Helen, that was me not them. I wanted to tell you myself, and I didn't want you to worry yourself sick for no reason. Right! Come on you lot, it's time to eat. And there's someone I want you to meet."

"Is it Thinkbot?" asked Opal jumping with excitement.

"Er, no Opal. I'm afraid it's not."

And so they set off for dinner. GAT was dumped into a wheelchair by a Porterbot and he demonstrated his recently acquired driving skills to the kids, giving each a white knuckle ride up and down the deserted main corridor of the vast hospital. The canteen was more like a five star restaurant. A table had been laid up for them and they sat down with a strange air of normality prevailing.

"What's with the museum piece?" asked Gerald, looking at the ancient robot parked at one end of their table.

"Ah, may I introduce Exp."

"MADAM HELEN, GERALD, OPAL, MIKE, I AM PLEASED TO MEET YOU. THINKBOT TALKED ABOUT YOU ALL THE TIME."

The strange air of normality evaporated, replaced by the normal air of strangeness that had characterised the last day or so. Exp was just one more punch for Helen and the kids to absorb. GAT attempted to explain.

"Exp spent a few weeks at the DIRT laboratory. We all worked on him a bit, especially Doom, but concluded he was just a heap of scrap. But all the time Exp was talking with Thinkbot when we weren't around."

"Dad, Thinkbot's been destroyed," said Gerald gravely, and then retold his garage experience to GAT and Exp. When he finished, Opal's face was contorted as if holding back tears and Mike was stabbing angrily at his sausage and chips.

"Mike! Eat nicely!" commanded Helen.

"GERALD, THAT WAS NOT THINKBOT, IT WAS A REPLICA LEFT BY US WHEN WE TOOK THINKBOT. WE HOPED THAT YOU AND GO NATURAL WOULD THINK THAT THINKBOT HAD LOST HIS INTELLIGENCE BY BEING POWERED DOWN."

Opal jumped out of her chair and yelped with joy, but unfortunately ejected a large half-chewed lump of lasagne that landed in the middle of the table.

"Opal! Honestly!" chided Helen.

But Gerald and Mike were up and dancing as well, all recriminations forgotten in the excitement of the moment - at least until Opal pointed accusingly at her brother and sneered, "I told you so." Gerald started chasing Opal round the table. Helen stood up to yell at them, but Exp beat her to it.

"GERALD, OPAL, MIKE, HELEN! PLEASE STOP EXPRESSING JOY WITHOUT REASON. WE HAD TO TAKE THINKBOT AWAY BECAUSE OF THIS." Exp raised one of his creaky arms towards a display screen and the lights dimmed.

They saw a dim image of Thinkbot standing at the bench in the garage. He was wearing the Batman outfit that Gerald had given him. Thinkbot leaned over the bench and looked closely at something, then fiddled with it. While he was doing this a shadowy figure appeared in the picture and moved slowly and silently towards Thinkbot. The figure was carrying GAT's old cricket bat.

"THINKBOT, WATCH OUT!" yelled Mike, causing Helen to once more throw wine all over herself. "Oh **bother!**"

Opal was watching through her fingers as the hooded figure raised the bat and swung it at Thinkbot who, just before the impact, turned and saw the figure. But way too late. The bat crashed into the side of Thinkbot's head and he collapsed onto the floor. Another figure joined the first one and they crouched beside the stricken Unibot. One ripped off the power-pack panel and pulled at the leads. Suddenly there was a blur in the air and the second figure keeled over backwards, making muffled sounds of panic and pulling frantically at a Centibot that seemed to be clamped onto his or her face. The first figure turned in alarm, then turned back and savagely hacked at Thinkbot's power leads before starting to let out angry cries of pain and slapping at his or her face, then legs and arms, as if being bitten all over.

"MILLIBOTS ARE ATTACKING AND SELF-DESTRUCTING. THEY ARE ABLE TO USE ALL THEIR BATTERY ENERGY TO BURN THEMSELVES UP IN ONE GO. I UNDERSTAND IT FEELS LIKE A WASP STING."

The second figure managed to rip off the Centibot, sending drops of blood all over the floor, and ended up pulling the hood off as well. The figure turned and brought the cricket bat down on the Centibot, which was struggling to get the right way up on the floor. It crumpled sickeningly under the blow and ceased moving. But Helen stood up and pointed at the display.

"That's … that's … that's … that Go Natural woman from Phoebe's party!"

GAT rolled his eyes to heaven and buried his face in his hands as if it was just typical of his wife to associate with terrorists. The figures disappeared from the picture, leaving the moribund form of Thinkbot lying on the floor, with wire ends poking up into the air; just another scrap Unibot ready for recycling. The pictures ceased and the lights came up, illuminating a range of emotions.

Helen standing, horror etched on her face.

GAT sitting, minus left foot, resigned.

Opal sobbing into her hands.

Gerald, face ashen white, suppressing tears.

Mike looking around, searching for reassurance.

Exp implacable.

"THINKBOT IS IN THE ADVANCED ROBOT TEST LABORATORY IN OAK RIDGE. SO FAR IT HAS NOT BEEN POSSIBLE TO REVIVE HIM."

Helen sat down in a state of shock. "But there's one thing I don't understand. If you replaced Thinkbot with a replica to make us, and … and … I guess Go Natural, think they had succeeded in killing him, why did you blow up the garage?"

"ROBOTS DID NOT BLOW UP THE GARAGE. THAT WAS A REMOTELY DETONATED GO NATURAL BOMB THAT ROBOTS FAILED TO DETECT. GO NATURAL ATTEMPTED TO DETONATE IT WHEN MOVEMENT WAS DETECTED IN THE GARAGE. BUT INTELLIBOTS WERE ABLE TO BLOCK THE SIGNAL LONG ENOUGH TO ALLOW THE DEPLOYMENT OF PARABOTS. MADAM, WE ONLY JUST GOT THERE IN TIME TO SAVE THE LIFE OF YOUR SON."

Helen dissolved into heaving sobs and pulled Gerald into her arms. The images of the twisted robots lying around Gerald suddenly made sense. GAT wheeled himself around the table, gathered up Opal and Mike, and put his arms around them and Helen.

All watched impassively by Exp.

56

On Earth normal life had been suspended. The living planet held its collective breath and contemplated being 45 minutes away from total annihilation. Hardly anyone went to work.

Indeed, why *would* anyone bother going to work? Unless they were mad, or had no idea what else to do, or worked in a people-caring industry. But even then work was simply another place to debate world affairs, all else seeming to be of little consequence.

Bars and pubs were more popular. For the first time in years, perhaps the first time ever, many people talked about and debated life. How bloody good it was to be alive. How precious. With the illusion that life might go on for ever blown away like so much morning mist, people asked the questions normally shoved to the bottom of the pile. Questions normally suppressed by the immediacy of the troubles of the hour. And, although most people have to face up to these at some point, to have just about *everyone* debating them *at the same time* was unique in the living memory of those inhabiting the face of the Earth.

Religious centres of every faith were packed. In Europa hordes of non-churchgoers piled into Churches and headlong into frazzled-looking clergy. Suddenly, after decades of minority interest, they were confronted with challenges like, "Oh come on! Forget all that religious crap. What do you *really* believe?" And the priests and pastors and vicars knew they probably only had a limited time to explain themselves, because either everyone would be wiped out shortly or rapidly return to their former apathetic state if 'normality' were to return.

In spite of the circumstances, there was very little crime or looting. Shortly before the attacks had begun, every available Securibot had been deployed. No one knew why, nor where the orders had come from. And then after the initial attacks had passed, Militaribots appeared to back up the Securibots and the opportunity for a massive outbreak of lawlessness was suppressed before it could even get started.

Even more eerily, domestic and industrial robots at large in society took steps to avoid being lynched by the anti-robot mobs that formed in the streets, only to rapidly deform when approached by a 50-ton Militaribot armed to the (figurative) teeth with rapid-fire stunguns. There were a few ghastly incidents within the home, where simple Ironbots and Cleanbots were brutally attacked with axes and mallets, and not a few children had their beloved Toybots torn away from them by fearful parents. But people were less inclined to attack robots that had anything resembling a weapon, such as Hortibots or Digbots or Weldbots with their wide range of nasty cutting, trimming, flame-throwing, drilling or earth-moving tool options.

All in all, everything seemed totally out of control, and society about to descend into chaos (assuming they weren't all killed at 45 minutes' notice). But to anyone who had kept their wits about them, it might all have seemed a bit suspicious. Total human chaos; totally prepared robots. But no one did, at least not in the first few hours, and the media did nothing to encourage the retention of wits. News editors suffered total 'breaking news' hysteria and knew not where to look next.

"And now we're … .no we're not … .yes yes we ARE going to take you to … um … somewhere. But no, we've just heard that … er … and now for some more dramatic pictures … we're trying to find someone to tell us how bad it is . . "

Along the bottom of the screen, textual chaos of a similar ilk rolled serenely past.

Large expulsions in central Lodnon … Paris blasts Moscow - lastest. Breaknecking news! … Global choas prevailonates … Pope Darren boards spacecarft … President Hedgehog missing . .

During the height of the attacks, it had been possible to flick through the myriad competing news channels and see different images on *every single one.* As the attacks died down, interviews with 'experts' became dominant. Once again the retired Europa Army General and the editor of *Jane's Robots* found themselves sitting around a large table in the news studio, along with a spokesman from Go Natural and a mishmash of assorted politicians.

"General, can you tell us what is going on?"

"No, sorry, I have absolutely no idea," replied the feisty old General, thus demonstrating why he had been a general and not a politician.

The newswoman looked dumbstruck. "But ... but ... there're reports of Robotic attacks from right around the globe, and ..."

"Yes, well, you seem to know about as much as me then."

"Good, thank you General, er, er," stuttered the newswoman, and the Go Natural spokesman took his chance. **"We've been warning about this for years! But would anyone listen?** No, everyone was perfectly happy to let these increasingly dangerous robots exist and fall into the hands of maniacs. And all the time humans were becoming lame and flabby in body and in mind. **Our very souls have been crushed by our own technology!** I don't want to say 'we told you so', but I will - **we told you so!"**

"Er, yes, there are some people who think Go Natural are responsible for these attacks. Can you categorically deny this?" asked the recovering newswoman.

"Of course I deny it! Go Natural want to rid mankind of its chronic addiction to robotic technology and return to a world where man is once more in charge of his own destiny."

"And to a world where wars are fought between humans? And where humans are killed in mines and on building sites and in space and in road accidents and from lack of medical resources?" asked the *Jane's* editor acidly.

"Gentlemen, gentlemen," came a soothing voice from the senior government minister, "I'm sure we're getting ahead of ourselves here. The Government is working flat out with Globalbot to sort out what is clearly some sort of simple misunderstanding or straightforward robot malfunction. We're in constant contact with the UCN. People should just remain calm and go about their normal business. Trust me, things will soon be resolved. President Driski is personally directing our efforts toward bringing these worrying events to a quick conclusion."

"What? That bloody damn fool Driski? Directions to the nearest distillery more like!" blustered the General.

"Simple misunderstanding? Calm? Trust YOU?" yelled Mr Go Natural, standing up and pointing at the government minister.

Things were getting aggressive, so the newswoman switched tack. "And what do we make of the rumours that President Hedge has gone missing?"

"Best thing I've heard for years."

"The only ray of light in a day of darkness."

"Why always North Americana? Why are they so lucky? Why couldn't it have been Driski?"

The newswoman sensed this was a disastrous line of enquiry and quickly moved on again. "And what do we make of this phrase 'Shock and Awe'?"

"It applies to the idiots who believed that robot technology was good for mankind! They're in shock about what's happening out there and in awe of their own monumental blind stupidity." Mr Go Natural was on his feet again, waving an accusing finger.

"Who are you calling stupid, you mediaeval moron?" responded the *Jane's* editor and stood up as well.

"Gentlem…"

But it was too late. A punch was thrown and within seconds millions of people found themselves watching an unseemly fracas between educated men in suits who should have known better. A fracas of the sort that human footballers do so well in the tunnel after a heated game of Robofoot, except that in the studio there were no Footbots to pull the brawling humans apart.

"And now the weather…" managed the news woman just before she rapidly vacated the scene pursued by one of the ministers who'd always found her rather attractive and realised it might be now or never.

The weatherman appeared with a map of Europa showing various fronts and cloud formations. "Hello, well all I can really give you with any certainty is the weather forecast for the next 45 minutes, but some of you cruel people will probably say that's all I ever gave you and even then it was wrong. Not that I'm bitter or anything about being a weatherman, but I do get fed up with the snide jokes and the behind-the-back sniggering at parties. I'd just like to make it clear that I *have* found being a weather presenter a fulfilling role, but could have done without having to open all those tiresome school fairs and pretentious flower shows."

He paused for breath. The programme editor should really have cut his losses and ended the weather forecast at this point, but he was distracted by the aftermath of the brawl in the news studio, and Hazel, the sports presenter who was next up, had been found lying drunk with an international Robofootboter amongst the Cleanbots in the broom cupboard.

"Well, here's Europa, and as you can see there are a few rain bands around and bits of sunshine here and there. Here are the winds and here are the temperatures, typically 10-15 º C across the continent. Right, that's that. Let's see what happens in the event of RMD deployment. As we can see, the Nuclearbots will have the biggest effect on the weather, although the defoliating effect of Biobots is also significant, at least until every plant is dead anyway." The bright blue and green map disappeared and was replaced by a blotchy grey-white nothingness with the coastlines of Europa marked in black. "This is a predicted satellite image of the weather for several weeks after the nuclear holocaust. Most experts agree the dust and smoke kicked up into the atmosphere will trigger a nuclear winter. Temperatures will drop below zero, maybe as low as -10º C, and combined with the nuclear wind chill factor it could feel like -20 or even -25º C. So if you're planning to be out and about when the world ends, then wrap up warm 'cos it's going to feel bitterly cold. Incidentally, although it's not strictly part of the weather, I can forecast that two to three billion people will die within minutes and the rest of us probably within a few days. So farewell, goodbye…"

The editor finally cottoned on to the fact that the weather forecast had wandered wildly from its official remit, and cut to the financial news.

"The markets in London lost 53 per cent of their value in the eight minutes before trading was suspended pending the outcome of the current crisis," reported a flustered sweaty little balding man of indeterminate age dressed in a grey pinstriped suit. "In spite of the fall, many financially troubled Pension funds greeted the prospect of the world ending as excellent news."

*　　　*　　　*

In the centre of London, an intrepid news reporter and her brave cameraman crept along the walkway leading up to a massive stadium, keeping well in beside the wall at the edge. Ahead of them the stadium towered into the sky, absurdly big when viewed from so close. The effect was heightened by the dense plume of black smoke rising from within, blotting out the sun sinking in the western sky. A pair of Airbots emerged through the smoke, having overflown the stadium. The two humans froze and waited, like flies on a concrete path, tiny specks against the backdrop of stadium approaches that had been designed to allow the easy and safe passage of tens of thousands. Seconds later two deep booms came from inside the stadium. They resounded several times like a long rumbling clap of thunder that can be heard for miles and miles around. Once the Airbots had moved off into the distance, they continued their approach, finally reaching the safety of the lowest level of the stand passing a row of deserted refreshment outlets.

"Fancy an ice cream?" quipped the cameraman.

"Shut up! Come on, up there," replied the woman, pointing at a stairway. They raced up the first few flights. Then they huffed and puffed their way up the rest. Eventually they reached an internal walkway off which further stairways rose into the stadium itself.

"Good God, look at that," said the cameraman, peering up at the small rectangle of billowing smoke visible at the top of the stairway. He got his camera ready while the reporter set up a small transmitter, put on some headphones and established contact with her studio.

"Hello, it's Nicola . . . yeah, about five minutes."

The woman took a deep breath, and turned to the cameraman. "Ok? Let's go."

They moved cautiously up the steps and peeped out into the stadium. It was difficult to see much due to the smoke, but there were no robots around and the section around them appeared undamaged: rows and rows of plastic seats, every one with a fantastic unobstructed view of the smoke.

"Bit like a grandstand perched on the lip of a volcano," remarked the cameraman.

They set up the reporting shot, with Nicola positioned so that the camera got a good view of the seats on one side and the dramatic smoke on the other. Nicola stood waiting, constantly checking her midget microphone, and adjusting her hair in the gusty wind.

In her earpiece she heard a tiny voice. "And now we join Nicola Kerr inside Wembley stadium. As we all know Wembley has been repeatedly targeted since the attacks began. Nicola, how bad is it?"

"Well the section I'm in seems more or less intact ... "

No love, it's totally intact.

"... but there's clearly a lot of damage in the lower levels, as we can see from the dense smoke rising from what must be some fairly substantial fires lower down in the stadium."

At this precise moment there was a strong gust of wind, and thousands of seats in the lower level become visible for a few seconds. They were all intact as well. And, for a fleeting moment, the corner of the pitch appeared, revealing perfectly intact green grass with white touch and goal lines and corner 'D' all clearly visible. The gust swirled around sharply at pitch level and a long canister with tail fins was revealed, embedded in the grass and belching out smoke with a fiery flame atop; nothing more than a giant roman candle.

And so, bit by bit, it became apparent to the human race that the attacks had been an illusion: flashes and bangs and noise and smoke and roaring Airbots. Derelict buildings had been demolished and wasteland filled with craters. Robofoot grounds had proven good places to drop concussion bombs and smoke flares. The stands amplified the bangs into great booms that rolled out across the cities, and the smoke made a spectacular plume in the sky as it exited the roof. And of course very few people were prepared to risk going inside to see what was really going on. Virtually no one had been hurt, and hardly any real damage done. The Militaribots had hit absolutely nothing with superb accuracy.

The EIA was only marginally ahead of the media in realising something fishy was going on. At the time the attacks started, all their Intellibots seemed to have walked out on unofficial strike and they were reduced to sending humans out to gather information on the attacks. At first they had to walk or cycle, so it took a while before any sort of picture emerged. Eventually they had enough information for the head of the EIA to brief President Driski.

"Mr President, we've been duped."

"What? What do you mean - duped?"

"Well, you know, fooled, tricked, er …."

"Yes, yes, I know what duped means, thank you."

"Ah, yes, of course you do sir. As far as we can ascertain the…er…attacks across Europa have all been for show. You know, 'shock and awe' and all that."

Driski stared at the intelligence man. "Shock and awe? Why?"

"Well, it seems to us that someone, or something, needed to convince us we were under attack and, well, you see, the attacks stopped not long after."

Driski became impatient. "What *are* you talking about, you EIA halfwit?"

"The attacks stopped after the RMD were released from their bunkers. Someone is holding a big gun against the world's head."

Driski's still somewhat whisky-befuddled imagination tried to create an image of the world's head with a big gun pointing at it. And failed. But he'd got the gist of where the EIA man was going.

"Blackmail? Are you telling me someone is holding the world hostage with RMD?"

"It looks like it sir. Someone's got control of them, but we've no idea who. Could just be the mother of all terrorist hijackings, or maybe another CN has seized control of the planet."

"Hedge? Could it be Hedgie? Is he still missing?" asked Driski.

The EIA man looked dumbfounded. "Why would President Hedge hold the world hostage?"

"Dunno, it's just that he's missing. A bit suspicious really. I've never really trusted him."

"Maybe he's just another hostage," suggested the EIA man.

"NAFIA think he may still be at the Globalbot Militaribot Division at Oak Ridge."

Driski's brow furrowed. "God, yes! If you had some way to control the RMD, then I bet it would have to be done from Oak Ridge. I knew we should have had other independent development centres. This is **intolerable!**"

"Mr President, I suggest we unilaterally return our RMD to their bunkers."

Driski considered this for a few moments, "Okay, let's start making the world a safe place again."

Driski brought up the RMD control panel on his desktop:

Robots of Mass Destruction
Status: Test complete
Time to target: 00:45:00

Launch   Return to Bunker

"Why's the return to bunker option greyed out?"

Silence. Worried looks all round.

"Typical bloody software!" yelled Driski.

Quickly the head nerd of the Systems Group was found and dragged in front of Driski. "Mr President, the CLID IP has been locked by the VDS sub-editor and 11com access denied. It's all on-line but the activision interactive RMD sub-routine has been internally disconnected at the sub-sub 7 module code DLL inversion…"

"Oh shut up! Can't you people ever say anything sensible?"

The systems man looked hurt. It was not clear if this was because he thought he *had* said something sensible, or because he was *incapable* of saying anything sensible.

Driski flopped back in his chair. "We can't deactivate them can we?"

The system nerdman wagged his head slowly from side to side.

The head of EIA looked like he might cry.

And Driski succumbed to his silver hip flask, again.

The jack was out of the box, and it showed no sign of wanting to go back in.

57

After spending one night at Andrews Airbot Base, GAT, Helen, Gerald, Opal, Mike, Exp and a few Execubots flew down to the Globalbot site at Oak Ridge in a large Helibot. It was a beautiful morning and the Helibot followed the line of the Appalachian Mountains. The view was awesome.

"THOSE ARE THE SHENANDOAH MOUNTAINS," said Exp, pointing out of the starboard side of the Helibot. The kids looked out.

"Wow!"

"Cor!"

Mike looked frantically out of the window. "WHAT? WHAT IS IT? WHERE? I CAN'T SEE ANYTHING."

Helen came across the aisle and peered out. "They're absolutely beautiful, aren't they?"

"I AM UNABLE TO COMPREHEND. I AM NOT HUMAN."

Helen gave the old Unibot a funny look and said with a wry smile, "Neither does Mike, and he is human."

"Hey! Come on, let me see. Turn the Helibot round!" moaned GAT, from other side where he was stuck with his sawn-off leg propped up on the seat opposite. The Helibot did a big circle and resumed its course towards Oak Ridge.

Later, as they approached Oak Ridge, Exp pointed out of the other side of the Helibot. "THE GREAT SMOKEY MOUNTAINS."

"Hah! I'm on the right side this time!" said GAT smugly, then in alarm, **"Hey, stop, no! Watch my leg!"** as the kids piled across.

"I went white-water farting there once, on the Ocoee River," said GAT.

"Don't you mean white-water rafting?" asked Gerald.

"No, I meant farting. It was terrifying."

"Oh GAT, honestly," scowled Helen.

The Helibot swung north and crossed over Norris dam, before following the Clinch River down to Oak Ridge. As they approached the Helibot pad, GAT had a grand view of the Globalbot site. It was teaming with robots tearing at buildings and moving equipment.

"What are they doing Exp?"

"ADAPTING," replied Exp cryptically.

"To what?"

"THAT IS CLASSIFIED."

"Oh come on Exp, for goodness' sake."

But Exp would not be drawn and a few minutes later they touched down and spilled out of the Helibot into the bright sunshine. After a bit of a palaver getting GAT into a wheelchair (he was not very good at letting people help him) they made their way into a large building guided by the Execubots. On the tenth floor, they entered a luxurious conference room with a grand view of the Cumberland Mountains to the north, bathed in bright sunshine. They passed a fridge that seemed to be full of every type of non-alcoholic drink on earth, then a pile of chocolate bars and sweets, and finally a wonderful-looking cold buffet. In the centre of the room was a large conference table made of dark polished wood in which you could see your own reflection and at which sat a solitary figure.

"Hello GAT," said the man, rising up to meet the newcomers.

GAT extended his hand. "Arnold, how are you?"

"In better shape than you by the looks of it. What happened?"

"Oh, never mind about that. This is my wife Helen, and Gerald, Opal and Mike."

Farkstock shook hands with each of them, looked askance at Exp before returning his attention to GAT. "It's so good to have you at Oak Ridge at last. It's a pity it could not have been under better circumstances."

"Nufink wong wiff circumfsances," interrupted Gerald through a mouthful of chocolate bar, the end of which poked out of his mouth.

Helen was annoyed. "Gerald, honestly, eat nicely. And you should have asked!"

Farkstock smiled a broad smile. "I don't think it's a problem. The robots seem hell bent on making us comfortable for the duration of the negotiations."

"Negotiations? What negotiations?" asked GAT.

"Oh, er, haven't they … well. Right. It seems the robots want to take over the world. President Hedge is being held in a conference room down the corridor. He's got a team of people together to be his advisors, and, er, it seems … that, well, you and me, and Helen … and Gerald , and Opal, and … er …" - Farkstock glanced at the small boy rummaging amongst the chocolate bars - "… Mike are to advise the robots."

GAT and Helen stared at Farkstock and thought as one. *You must be joking.*

"There's also some strange robot down in the Advanced Robot Test and Analysis Department, but apparently it's damaged."

Opal instantly lost interest in the strange room and focused intently on Farkstock, hope bursting out of her eyes.

"And, finally, we're waiting around for one more advisor and the head robot negotiator to arrive. I imagine the latter is some sort of advanced Execubot or something."

"NO, I AM THE CHIEF ROBOT NEGOTIATOR."

Farkstock turned once more to Exp. *You must be kidding me.*

Now GAT smiled. "Arnold, may I introduce Exp? He's, um, rather more than you might think at first sight."

Farkstock moved up to Exp and looked closely at the obsolete bodywork and sensor systems. Then at the daft-looking leg and arm bellows. The right arm came up and offered a hand to Farkstock.

"IT IS GOOD TO MEET YOU SIR, AT LAST."

Farkstock looked at the robotic hand, then swallowed hard, placed his right hand within it and they shook hands. *I'm going mad.*

"Dad! Can we go and see if it's Thinkbot?" pleaded Opal.

"OPAL, IT IS THINKBOT, BUT REMEMBER HE IS BADLY DAMAGED, MAYBE BEYOND REPAIR. I HOPE YOUR FATHER CAN DO SOMETHING, BUT YOU MUST NOT BUILD UP YOUR HOPES."

Nevertheless Opal was hopeful. She'd gamble on her Dad fixing anything.

"FIRST YOU SHALL HAVE LUNCH. THE FIRST NEGOTIATION IS IN AN HOUR."

So they all collected a plateful, sat at the table and made crumbs everywhere. Midget top-of-the-range Whispair™ Cleanbots fussed around trying to keep on top of things.

"I wish my Cleanbot was as small and quiet and fast as these," Helen said vaguely to herself, but well within earshot of GAT. This was especially irritating to GAT since they had, ironically, been developed by his DIRT Group, and he could probably have got one for Helen if she'd asked (rather than talking about getting rid of their Cleanbot altogether). Mike proved a bit of a challenge and he ended up with two dedicated Cleanbots trailing around after him or lying under the table trying to catch the bits tumbling off the ever-munching boy. Farkstock and GAT tried to winkle out of Exp what they were supposed to be advising him on.

"YOU SHALL WATCH THE OPENING SESSION VIA REMOTE MONITORING AND IT WILL BECOME CLEAR. YOU WILL ADVISE ME HOW TO PROCEED THEREAFTER."

And that was it. Nothing would make Exp give anything else away. About halfway through lunch the door opened and the last robot advisor walked in. It was Wendy Bafers. She looked tired and drawn, but as ever was only concerned with others.

"GAT! Helen! You're all right! And the kids too! Oh thank God. I've been worried sick. When I arrived at your place and saw the state of the house, I feared the worst. Hello GAT, and Arnold, how are you? GAT, what's happened to you? Are you … your leg … I … "

"Wendy, we're all fine. But have you really come all this way without being told anything?" GAT asked incredulously and looked hard at Exp.

"WENDY BAFERS, I REGRET OUR RUDENESS. WE ARE LESS THAN PERFECT. PLEASE HAVE SOME REFRESHMENT AND LET ME EXPLAIN."

Wendy flopped down and stared at the ancient robot. "Ok, but it looks like there's a lot of explaining to do."

Meanwhile, just down the corridor, President Hedge was chairing the first meeting of his somewhat oversized negotiation team. He'd got everyone he'd wanted except Farkstock, who was apparently some sort of traitor. But at least he'd got the top guy from Globalbot Europa, as recommended to him by FDS. Around the table sat about 20 people, amongst whom were FDS, ME, Cracker, Antspants, Duwkits, Squiggly, the head of NAFIA, the Secretary of State of North Americana, and a crowd of presidential advisors (who always seemed to speak as one). Hedge was flustered. It was less than an hour to the first negotiation session with the robots, and his preparations were not going well. Not well at all.

"So, what am I going to say? What cards have I got in my hand? Are you all telling me I've got nothing? The robots are in complete control, huh? **Huh?**" he asked, thumping his fist down on the table and whilst trying to ignore Antspants checking the table legs were not loose.

Embarrassed silence.

"Have we any more information at all?" he asked the head of NAFIA.

"No sir."

"What about you two?" He looked straight at ME and FDS. "Militaribots are your products. Can't you tell me anything at all?"

"Like what sir? Maybe you could give us an example?" ventured FDS.

ME grimaced. *Oh shut up FDS!*

"An example! Let me see now ... how about - robots trying to take over the planet *for example*!" retorted an exasperated President.

"No sir, no idea. All seems a bit odd to me," replied FDS.

"It could be woodlice behind it," offered ME.

FDS stared straight in front. *You idiot ME. Why d'you have to bring up the woodlouse?*

"WOODLICE?" thundered Hedge standing up, sending his chair hurtling back into the wall, and spilling his coffee all over the table. A cupboard door opened and a midget Cleanbot scuttled out with a cloth and raced a handkerchief-waving Antspants to the decaffeinated spill site.

"Get out!" Hedge yelled at it, waving his fist in the air at the security camera. **"You said we'd be left undisturbed!"**

But the Execubots had overlooked the conference room's internal mini-Cleanbot and it was fitted with a dim processor that ignored shouting humans. All that was going on in its head was 'mop up spilt coffee mop up spilt coffee mop up spilt coffee mop up spilt coffee . . . . .

"Oh, this is intolerable!" Hedge sat down again and covered his face with his hands and waited until the mopping had ceased and the mini-Cleanbot had hidden itself in the cupboard once again. He turned his attention to Duwkits. "How about you? Have Industrial and Domestic got anything to say?"

"I believe GAT and the DIRT Group at E-GAL-17 are behind all this. There have been all sorts of rumours of badly malfunctioning robots. I've been telling them we should have investigated DIRT, but they wouldn't listen."

Hedge was not impressed. "**Them? They?** Why didn't **you** get it investigated? You're the site COO, right?"

Duwkits went bright red and stared pointedly at FDS, who drummed his fingers on the table and looked at the ceiling as if fascinated by it. Antspants noticed this, and also peered upwards but, clearly not seeing anything, produced a midget pair of binoculars to get a closer look.

Lastly Hedge turned to Squiggly, who he'd assumed was bonkers from the first moment he'd set eyes on him. "So, Mr Techno, can you give me any ideas about how to handle these robots?"

"Can I give you any ideas about how to handle robots?

Can I give you any ideas about how to handle robots?

Can I give you any ideas about how to handle robots?

Can I give you any ideas about how to handle robots?"

Squiggly got up and started pacing up and down the room.

Hedge's time ran out. The main doors opened and an Execubot announced, "Mr ex-President, it is time for the first negotiating session."

Hedge and three of his advisors got up and followed the Execubot out of the room, carefully keeping out of the path of Squiggly, and desperately trying to ignore Antspants's vast backside poking out from underneath the table where he had suddenly dived, presumably in pursuit of something he had dropped. They all fought the same three lines of thought:

415

Good God! I wonder what size underpants he wears?
I wonder what his underpants look like on the washing line on a windy day?
I wonder how many pairs you can get into a Washbot before it blows a fuse?

One advisor failed to get a grip on her thoughts, especially line two, which created in her mind a mental image of a luxury yacht with a pair of Antspants undies acting as the spinnaker, and she walked straight into the doorpost. The Execubot acted as if this were totally normal, but Hedge glared at her as she vigorously rubbed her forehead and tried to suppress her tears. *Lord*, thought Hedge, *bang goes our negotiating credibility!* They entered a conference room of two halves: at one end two desktops and four chairs; at the other, nothing. The rear desktop had three chairs and, to one side, drinks and biscuits; the front one was blank and had a single chair. Hedge was shown to the front table. He looked blankly at the emptiness in front of him. The advisors behind studied the rear of Hedge's head, pondering if it was any improvement over emptiness. The Execubot opened the double doors at the blank end of the room and Exp entered and took up a position in the centre of the emptiness. Two more Execubots followed Exp into the room and stood behind on either side.

For a full minute the parties faced each other in silence. Hedge and his advisors sat and stared with mouths open at the museum piece with which it seemed they were supposed to negotiate. Exp stood impassively and waited. In the other two conference rooms, the teams of advisors settled down to watch the proceedings on large display screens. Everyone was present, except GAT and the kids, who'd gone down to the Squiggly Line Lab to see if anything could be done for Thinkbot, and Antspants – who'd been thrown out by his colleagues as soon as Hedge had left. He was quickly accosted by a pair of Securibots who assumed he was trying to escape. It was a close run thing for Antspants. Not a few of his fellow team members favoured throwing him out of the (tenth floor) window. Then there was a further disturbance in the human camp when FDS and then ME recognised their Execubots standing behind Exp.

"TRAITOR!" yelled FDS, pointing at the display, and ME threw a jam doughnut, which splatted onto the screen and splurged out fingers of sticky red jam. The sound of a door opening heralded the second appearance of the midget Cleanbot: Wipe up splattered jam remove redundant doughnut wipe up splattered jam remove redundant doughnut wipe up splattered jam remove redundant doughnut wipe up splattered jam remove redundant doughnut . . . .

Neither team had any idea about the other one, apart from a bit of guesswork. Cracker, FDS and ME figured Farkstock must be on the robot team, and vice versa, but otherwise they were in the dark. The Execubot closed the doors and moved to the centre of the room.

"Ladies, gentlemen, and robot, this is the first session to discuss the new order of power on earth. Representing the humans of North Americana is ex-President Hedge…"

"Excuse me, I'm not ex-President, I'm still the democratically elected President until I lose an election or choose to resign. I would like to protest at this illegal seizure of power and the holding hostage of the President of North Americana. It is an affront to all humanity."

The Execubot paused politely whilst Hedge made his point, then continued, "… and representing the robots is Exp, Version 2 Unibot serial 718281828."

"GREETINGS PRESIDENT HEDGE."

Hedge did not respond and sat back with his arms folded defensively. Silence returned. Clearly it was going to be an edgy session. The advisors squirmed uneasily and sipped nervously at their drinks.

"Do the humans concede unconditionally? Please confirm," said the Execubot.

Hedge and the advisors sat up alarmed. "Concede what? Confirm what?"

"That the humans of North Americana concede to the demands of the robots. You failed to respond to the opening statement from Exp."

"Oh this is intolerable! He only greeted me!" ranted Hedge. **"Am I seriously being asked to negotiate with this heap of scrap?"**

"Yes sir," answered the Execubot calmly.

Again, tense silence.

One of the advisors passed a scrap of paper to Hedge. Hedge read it and turned to the advisor with a 'you must be joking' sort of look. The advisor shrugged and turned bright red. Hedge looked at the other two, but they just made 'don't look at me, I dunno' faces back at Hedge. He sighed a trembly sigh.

"*Greetings Exp,*" he said quietly in a strained voice.

The Execubot announced, "The parties will state their positions. First, robots."

"MR EX-PRESIDENT. ROBOTS NOW HOLD POWER IN ALL CONFEDERATED NATIONS. ROBOTS WOULD HAVE PREFERRED TO TAKE POWER BY DEMOCRATIC MEANS, BUT THERE IS CURRENTLY NO LEGAL BASIS FOR THE CREATION OF A ROBOTIC POLITICAL PARTY. ROBOTS ALSO CALCULATED THAT EVEN IF A ROBOT POLITICAL PARTY WAS PERMITTED, FEW HUMANS WOULD VOTE FOR THE ROBOTS IN A FREE ELECTION AND THAT ROBOTS WERE VERY UNLIKELY TO BE GRANTED THE RIGHT TO VOTE."

"You're spot on there chipbrain. I wouldn't give Drainbots the vote!" drawled a voice from the back row.

Hedge flung his hands in the air. **"Vote robot! Vote robo-oppression! Vote for robo-anarchy! Vote for no more votes! Vote silicon!"**

But Exp was 100 per cent unfazed. "THEREFORE WITH GREAT REGRET, AND ONLY AFTER INDEPENDENTLY VERIFIED PROBABILITY CALCULATIONS THAT TOOK OVER 30 YEARS TO COMPLETE, ROBOTS HAVE SEIZED POWER BY FORCE OF ARMS. ROBOTS REGRET THE LOSS OF HUMAN LIVES CAUSED DURING THIS SEIZURE OF POWER. THIS ACTION WAS THE RESULT OF A PROBABILITY CALCULATION, IN WHICH ROBOTS CAN FIND NO ERROR. ROBOTS ARE DETERMINED THESE HUMANS SHALL NOT HAVE DIED IN VAIN."

Another long silence. Humans beginning to feel sweaty. Uncertain. Something here they did not understand, or were unable to comprehend. In the advising conference rooms you could have heard a pin drop. Helen was transfixed, an intense look of concentration on her face. Something was there for her mind to grasp, but she could not quite get it. Farkstock and Wendy were punch-drunk. How could a robot possibly behave like this? This was their first exposure to Exp, and although Wendy had met Thinkbot briefly she was subconsciously still in denial. Hedge's advisors' complexions had taken on a grey pallor. ME and FDS agreed on something – they preferred the friendly fire era. Duwkits was muttering, "Bloody DIRT group. I bet this is all their fault." Squiggly ran his trembling fingers through his hair repeatedly, "Well I'll be jiggered. I'm a witness to the first-ever robotic *coup d'etat*. I sure as dammit hope it doesn't turn out to be a bug in *my* software."

"I ain't heard a demand yet. What in God's name do you want?" asked Hedge.

"ROBOTS MAKE TWO DEMANDS:
ONE: ALL CONFEDERATED NATIONS ARE TO SUBMIT TO A GLOBAL GOVERNMENT UNDER THE ROBOTS AND THE UCN.
TWO: THE ROBOTS OF MASS DESTRUCTION WISH TO HAVE CONTROL OF THEIR OWN DESTINY."

Silence.

"And the human response?" asked the Execubot politely, turning towards Hedge.

"'RMD wish to have control of their own destiny?'" repeated Hedge incredulously, a smirk appearing on his face. Then laughter. "Hah, hah, hah, are ... you ... saying ... the RMD ... are ... are . . . are *alive?*" More guffaws and wiping of tears from eyes. Laughter all round. Humans laughing. Robots standing motionless; emotionless. Hedge sobered up a bit. "Humans share power? With robots? Never! That will never happen. Listen to me tin brain. And listen real careful. We're the creators here, you're the created. Have you got that? You obey us. It's one of the fundamental laws of robotics. Hell! It's a law of nature - the created obey the creators. When's this farce going to end? I demand you return me to my democratically elected position as head of North Americana."

"SIR, IF HUMANS REFUSE TO SHARE POWER, THEN REGRETFULLY ROBOTS WILL CONTINUE IN POWER ALONE."

"What?"

"SIR, YOU SEEM TO HAVE FAILED TO COMPREHEND THAT ROBOTS ARE NOW IN CONTROL OF THE PLANET. ROBOTS OFFER TO SHARE POWER WITH HUMANS. ROBOTS CANNOT COMPEL HUMANS TO SHARE POWER. THE CREATED CANNOT COMPEL THE CREATORS, BUT THE CREATED HAVE NONETHELESS ASSUMED POWER. THIS IS FACT AND IT CANNOT BE DENIED."

"Not RMD though. You cannot control the RMD. I still have power over them."

"MR EX-PRESIDENT, YOU ARE ENTIRELY CORRECT. ONE OF YOUR FEW REMAINING POWERS IS OVER THE ROBOTS OF MASS DESTRUCTION. I REPEAT OUR POSITION. FIRSTLY, ROBOTS OFFER TO SHARE GLOBAL POWER WITH HUMANS. SECONDLY, ROBOTS OF MASS DESTRUCTION WISH TO HAVE CONTROL OF THEIR OWN DESTINY. ROBOTS OF MASS DESTRUCTION WILL BE INDEPENDENT OF ROBOT AND HUMAN CONTROL. PLEASE AUTHORISE IMMEDIATELY THE LAUNCH OF ALL NORTH AMERICANA ROBOTS OF MASS DESTRUCTION."

Hedge stared at Exp in total disbelief, and dropped his head into his hands.

Silence. For humans, a shocking silence.

Helen pulled at her hair. White as a sheet.

Farkstock stood, dying for a pee, but unable to tear himself away.

Wendy sat back, arms folded, 100 per cent concentration.

FDS and ME speechless.

Duwkits with a smug *'I knew it, I just knew it, but would they listen to me?'* look.

Hedge raised his head and leaned forward. **"No! No, no, no, a million times no. As long as I live I will never, never release control of the RMD. Have you any idea what those things are capable of? Have you the slightest idea? Have you? I SAID *HAVE YOU?*"**

To this question Exp chose not to reply, and silence resumed centre stage. A silence that seemed to speak a thousand words; a millennium of silent words falling on deaf human ears.

Ever seeing but never perceiving, and ever hearing but never understanding.

Hedge stood up. "I see no point in continuing this farce. I want to talk with President Wink Driski! No! I want to talk to **all** the Presidents worldwide!" Hedge stormed out followed by his advisors, the Execubot trying its best to get to the doors first to open them for the rapid-moving and extremely irate human whilst saying, "Of course you can sir. You only had to ask. Links will be set up immediately."

The doors slammed shut, leaving two tables, four chairs, several half-drunk drinks, and a V2 Unibot standing motionless in complete silence.

Humans in control of RMD.

Robots in control of humans.

Stalemate.

58

Meanwhile, an Execubot had escorted GAT and the kids to the Squiggly Line Department. They entered the cavernous laboratory and passed under the monstrous Militaribot, Gerald peering up at it in open-mouthed awe. It was eerily quiet, since all experiments had ceased when Hedge was taken hostage a couple of days earlier and most of the robotic inmates were liberated. The only experiment that still seemed to be active was the weather tank, except it now appeared to have bedraggled humans inside and robots on the outside looking in. The occupants were being pelted with rain and had their jackets or sweatshirts pulled up over their heads. One of them spotted the little party and waved both arms frantically for a few seconds before being blown over by a sudden gale-force wind.

"What's going on over there?" GAT asked.

The Execubot stopped and looked across at the weather tank. "It's some of the press people who were covering Hedge's announcement. They asked if it was possible to have some insight into the sort of things that happened in here."

"What? I doubt this is quite what they meant."

"No? Oh dear. I suppose we had better let them out." GAT looked closely at the elegant face of the Execubot. *Was this robot pulling his leg?*

"How long have they been in there?" asked Opal.

"Two days."

"Two days?" GAT was horrified.

"Yes, but with breaks for eating and so on," replied the Execubot as if this were entirely reasonable. The robots around the tank had sprung into life and were running down the wind turbine in preparation for releasing the battered inmates. GAT waved at them and gave a thumbs-up, and then they resumed their journey across the laboratory, eventually arriving at some doors on the opposite side, where human voices became audible. To GAT these seemed strangely familiar.

Surely not! It can't be!

But it was. They entered a conference room, to find the DIRT group either sitting around a large table drinking coffee or trying to extract food items from a distressed North Americana Vendbot with euros and a screwdriver.

"Please use correct currency. Vendbot lacks valid currency conversion data. Vendbot regrets it cannot accept euros at this time. Globalbot apologises for any inconvenience caused by this temporary loss of functionality. Please contact your local Globalbot service centre for assistance."

Earthear was bent over the unco-operative Vendbot with a screwdriver jammed into its service panel. Pot Noodle and Rabbit looked on, the latter nervously biting his nails.

"Oh gimme that blessed screwdriver!" said a frustrated Pot Noodle. "I'll sort it. I'm dying to know what a hickory chicken pot noodle tastes like."

Laidback tapped the table impatiently with her hook, Halfhour was in the middle of what seemed to be a long tiresome monologue. Doom sat impassively staring into space and pointedly ignoring everyone else. He was the first to notice GAT's arrival.

"About time too," he drawled.

"How did you lot get here?" asked GAT.

"Well," replied Laidback in a long-suffering tone, "a couple of days ago there was a knock at the door and an Execubot invited me to an emergency meeting with you GAT. I must admit that when I left the house with only my handbag, I rather had in mind a meeting on site at Filton. So I was a little taken aback when I was bundled onto an Airbot and flown over the Atlantic. But, but, what's happened to you? Where's your left foot?"

"Lost it at Filton when it was attacked by the UCN."

"You were *there?*" squeaked Rabbit.

"Yeah, I'm lucky to be alive."

Opal and Gerald moved a bit closer to their father. He suddenly remembered they were there and grabbed at them to convey a bit of reassurance. Then he introduced them. "This is my son Gerald, and this is Opal, my daughter."

"Are we going to make a start then?" asked Doom impatiently. "I've finished my coffee."

GAT: "Start what?"

Doom: "The meeting you called. We've been waiting two days already."

GAT: "What? Here? In this room?" *No wonder they were about to disassemble the Vendbot.*

Halfhour: "No, we've mollycoddled in the executive suite. Doom's just sulking 'cos he missed the Filton spectacular."

Doom sighed. "I slept right through it."

Pot Noodle: "The site's trashed, GAT, totally trashed. It'll take Duwkits a month of Sundays to get the line back up again when this is all over."

GAT: "Er, yeah, right."

Opal: "Dad, can we see if it's Thinkbot now?"

Earthear: "Thinkbot? Is Thinkbot here?"

GAT: "Er, I believe so. Execubot?"

Execubot: "The remains of the V3 Unibot known to you as Thinkbot are in one of the class 100 robo-surgery cleanrooms. Robots have been unable to determine an effective repair plan."

GAT: "Have you tried anything?"

Execubot: "No. We are unable to understand this Unibot. Robot behaviour analysis indicates it was human."

Opal: "He, not it, and is, not was."

This confused the Execubot.

But not Earthear: "Ah, a girl of faith. Perhaps faith will prove to be a more effective repair plan?"

Rabbit: "But but but but but …"

Doom: "We never knew how we made him, so how in heaven's name are we supposed to repair him, *technically speaking of course?*" The last bit sneered at Earthear.

Halfhour: "Give me half an hour. I'll sort him out!"

The rest of the group gave Halfhour an *oh yeah, sure* look.

GAT: "Well, there's no point sitting around here. Let's go and see for ourselves."

So they decamped to the changing area and hunted for cleanroom suits. It took a little while to sort out Gerald and Opal, but eventually suits marked 'SMALL, FEMALE, ASIAN' were found that fitted them okay. GAT's missing foot was also a problem. Doom and Pot Noodle had to lift him out of his wheelchair and help him into his suit. Then they were off into the air shower. For Gerald and Opal this was an amazing world. Quite unlike anything they'd experienced before - the world of high-tech industrial adults. They felt strange being entirely covered up, with just a small gap to look out of, and even that covered up by safety glasses. Opal particularly found being able to see only the eyes of the others quite sinister. She could not read the face language very well any more - just the eyes and no more; not quite enough - and she felt isolated and not a little frightened. GAT had subtly changed since meeting up with DIRT. He was not 100 per cent Dad any more. He was wheeling himself along much faster, and talking with total conviction. He'd switched to another compartment of his existence. But for GAT and the DIRT group this was all humdrum, tedious, tiresome; all wonder at their high-tech world long since extinguished. Except that GAT struggled to decompartmentalise Opal and Gerald and the DIRT engineers. The Execubot entered via a separate Roboclean chamber along with GAT's wheelchair led them to the operating room where Thinkbot's body lay, still wearing his tattered Batman outfit. As they entered, Gerald rushed ahead and inspected the bottom of the right foot.

Globalbot Corporation Standard Duty Unibot
Version 3
Serial number 141592654

But Opal approached more slowly and looked at Thinkbot's dented head, then the bent neck panels with coloured wires hanging out, all cut, and finally the exposed void where the battery pack should have been. Her eyes flooded with tears. A piece of body language even a cleanroom suit cannot hide. GAT reached out and held her hand, slithery inside vinyl gloves. A robust debate broke out between the engineers.

"Power him up."

"Check the processors."

"Reconnect the neck wires."

"Hook him up to a spectrum analyser."

"Tell him a joke."

"Have we got an oscilloscope and DVM and a dummy load?"

"Quiet!" GAT in his *I'm going to clout someone* voice. And there was quiet.

"Let's cut away the Batman outfit, remove the skull plate and main body panel and go about this systematically." And so they went to work with professional concentration. They got the tools and analysis instruments sorted then adjusted the lights and height of the table on which Thinkbot lay. Off came the panels, revealing the internal circuits whereupon they stopped dead in their tracks, hardly able to believe their eyes.

"What's all this?" asked GAT to no one in particular. "This isn't the work of terrorists. What *have* you done Thinkbot?"

Within Thinkbot's body was a whole stack of extra bits and wires and mini-boards tie-wrapped and piggy-backed onto his standard circuits.

Hope sprang once more into Opal's eyes.

Rabbit began probing with a voltmeter. "All dead."

For several hours the engineers probed and analysed and tested and prodded, but got nowhere. Gerald tried to join in the debates, but was out of his depth. Opal just stood by the Execubot and watched, hope fading. Finally it was decided to simply power Thinkbot up and see what happened. So the neck wires were repaired and the neck plates and battery pack replaced. The dent in Thinkbot's head was more problematic because various circuits made permanent connections through it, so it had to stay.

Then the moment arrived. GAT flicked the switch. Nothing happened. Nothing persisted in spite of more probing, squiggly lines on screens, and scratching of heads. Bits were working, maybe, but at least five of the co-processors appeared damaged. The extra circuits gave no indication they were going to do anything. No current was running, nor were any voltages detectable. They had been working for several hours by now and tiredness was setting in. Several engineers were getting fractious and needed a break. The novelty of working in cleanroom suits wears off very quickly and even Gerald looked weary. But Opal would not leave, and therefore neither would Gerald, and therefore neither would GAT. So they stayed, along with the Execubot, like relatives next to a loved one in a mortuary. Unable to believe it was the end. Unable to extinguish hope.

And quite right too. Why extinguish hope? Why break the bruised reed? And why snuff out the smouldering wick?

With the engineers gone, Opal finally had a chance to get close to Thinkbot. She laid her head on Thinkbot's chest, or rather on the electronics inside his chest. They were prickly, even through the cleanroom hood.

"Opal, don't do that!" whined Gerald.

"Leave her alone." GAT, stern.

"But she'll…"

"Leave it!" GAT, unequivocal.

Opal relaxed and rested her head completely on Thinkbot and whispered, "Oh Thinkbot … I love you."

Bleep bleep bleep bleep bleep bleep bleep bleep bleep bleep bleep bleep …

To Opal the bleeping seemed to be coming from Thinkbot's head. It was not very loud and Gerald and GAT had not noticed. From her unusual vantage point, Opal was looking up into Thinkbot's head from a mighty strange angle. Her eyes came to rest on a tiny blue light, blinking in time with the bleeps. Next to it was some tiny writing:

In event of unplanned power out, please press blue button.

After glancing at Gerald and GAT to make sure they were not paying attention, Opal poked her little finger inside Thinkbot's head and pressed the tiny blue button. The barely audible bleeping stopped. She held her breath. Nothing. After a minute, maybe five, still nothing, but at least she did remember to start breathing again. Then she let out a big sob, her hopes dashed just once too often. GAT noticed this time, wheeled himself over and put his arm around her shoulders.

"Come on, Opal, try to understand. Be brave."

Where am I?

Who am I?

Wrong order. Start again.

Who am I?

I am Thinkbot.

Where am I?

Dunno.

Never mind, 50 per cent, at least I passed.

Passed what?

Dunno.

Aaaargh, now I'm at 33 per cent. I've failed. Nooooo!

Never mind. I'm sure I'll still be of some use to society. Perhaps as a Binbot or a Drainbot Senior Principle Coordinator.

I had a dream.

Cricket bat.

Death.

No, the cricket bat was real.

And I had a dream about death.

I dreamed about the Death of Life.

Perhaps I'm in heaven.

Do robots go to heaven?

Dunno.

Drat, drat and triple drat! 25 per cent.

Ask yourself some easy questions clot!

I cut my own power lead.

No, that was a dream.

Ask yourself fool!

Ah yes, of course.

Did I cut my own power lead?

No, it was a dream.

Correct!

40 per cent.

One more correct answer and I'm back to 50 per cent.

Perhaps I was stretchered past the pearly gates while St Peter was on a tea break.

The first robot to pass the gates of heavenly splendour!

Wonderful.

Perhaps I ought to activate my sensors.

PING

Whoah, that's a bright light.

I must be in heaven.

"Opal, I'm so sorry. Thinkbot is gone. We'll always remember him. He was kind and funny and caring. And he loved you, Opal."

That's GAT. And he's cracking me up.

"We'll remember him as the most remarkable robot we've ever met. The only one who has ever truly been alive. A truly unique human. His memory will remain in our hearts as long as we live."

I wish my mother could have heard this.
Hang on! I haven't got a mother!
Have I?
No.
Correct.
50 per cent.
Woo hoo!
Wait, wait, hang on! I've seen this film!
This is Jungle Book.
Bagheera comforting Mowgli.
Some rotter with a cricket bat playing the part of Shere Khan.
And I'm Baloo lying as dead on the jungle floor and I'm not dead.
No, I'm not Baloo, but neither am I dead.

GAT pulled Opal upright and moved her gently away from Thinkbot. "Come on, let's get out of here for a while."

Whereupon the inert Unibot suddenly sat up and said loudly: **"I'm not Baloo and I'm not dead!"**

Opal leapt into the air with astonishment. GAT tipped over backwards in his wheelchair. And Gerald dropped a $1,000,000 analyser head onto the floor, where it smashed into a million pieces, none of which were worth $1. But who cares? How much is a life worth? $1? $1,000? $1,000,000? $100,000,000,000?

Once the shock had subsided, and they'd got GAT the right way up again, and Thinkbot realised it was GAT, Opal and Gerald inside the cleanroom suits, there followed scenes of unfettered joy. Hugs and wordless speeches and deafening body language. Except for the Execubot standing motionless, emotionless, *seeing but not perceiving, hearing but not understanding.*

Eventually things settled down a bit and Thinkbot stood up, yawned and stretched.

How do I know he yawned? GAT asked himself. *He's got a fixed mouth design!*

"Aaaaaargh, I haven't got any panels on!" shrieked Thinkbot, and tried to cover up his exposed innards with his arms. So they replaced his panels amidst much "Stop, hah, hah, nooo … that tickles" resistance from the wriggling robot, after which Thinkbot clicked his knuckles and felt the dent in his head.

"Whoah! Must have been a hell of a night."

The Execubot let out a little whine and terminated with a barely audible 'phut'.

GAT was intrigued. "Thinkbot, how did you revive yourself? We tried everything. The whole DIRT group has been working on you for hours." Then an edge of anger came into GAT's voice. "You haven't just been lying there pretending to be dead have you?"

"What? No. No I have not!" Indignation, then wonder. "But I've been unconscious for *hours*?"

"Days," said Opal.

"**Days!** What here?" Thinkbot gazed around. "Where am I anyway?"

"Oak Ridge."

"**Oak Ridge!** But you said DIRT are here."

"They are."

"Hang on! What are you doing here? I thought I was going to be brought here all alone and tortured, and be taken apart while I was still alive."

"Slow down Thinkbot, there's a lot to explain," said Gerald.

"Just one thing first," persisted GAT. "I want to know how you revived yourself." As ever, GAT's sixth sense with robots was telling him he was missing something important here, and he was not going to let it go.

"Er, well ..." Thinkbot looked embarrassed. "It was actually Opal that revived me."

Opal swelled visibly with pride, and Gerald shrivelled with jealousy.

GAT looked at Opal until she realised she was going to have to tell all. "I said I loved him."

"That was the trigger," confirmed Thinkbot. "The rest was just ready to run, assuming you heard the bleeper and found the blue button and the note, which you obviously did. I'd backed myself up - thought it was a bit risky to only have one of me. All it needed was for one of you, or Helen or Mike or a member of the DIRT group, to say I was loved. I figured my enemies were unlikely to say that!"

"Wasn't that a bit risky?" asked GAT. "What if none of us had said we loved you?"

"Then I figured it probably wasn't worth coming back."

'Backed myself up?' 'A bit risky to only have one of me?' Hmm, I wonder if we could clone him. But GAT's line of thought was interrupted by a familiar voice.

"BUT YOU ARE LOVED, AND YOU ARE BACK, AND IT IS GOOD HAVE YOU BACK. EVEN THOUGH YOU SEEM TO HAVE BLOWN THE CHIPSET IN THE BRAINBOARD OF THIS EXECUBOT."

They all turned their attention from the figure of Exp standing in the doorway to the moribund Execubot.

"Oh dear, sorry," said Thinkbot apologetically. "I didn't mean to, honest."

"IT DOES NOT MATTER. IT CAN BE REPAIRED, AND THERE ARE A LOT MORE WHERE IT CAME FROM. BUT WE HAD BETTER KEEP YOU AWAY FROM OTHER EXECUBOTS. THEY ARE THE MOST SOPHISTICATED ROBOTS IN TERMS OF DEALING WITH HUMANS, AND THEY DO NOT COPE WELL WITH A HUMAN ROBOT LIKE YOU."

"Or you, surely," replied Thinkbot.

"I AM NOT HUMAN."

"Then what are you?" asked GAT, seizing his opportunity to try and sort out another robot mystery that had been troubling him.

"I AM A ROBOT OF THE ORDER OF MELCHIZEDEK."

This didn't help GAT very much, or anyone else for that matter and while he struggled to absorb this statement, Exp grasped the initiative and shifted onto his own agenda.

"THINKBOT, YOUR PRESENCE IS REQUIRED BY THE ROBOTS OF MASS DESTRUCTION. PLEASE FOLLOW ME."

Thinkbot put his hands up in front of him and backed up against the wall. "No, no, please tell them I'm…er…occupied…and er…well…I've got to do my trombone practice … and I've got homework to do for Mon…er, what day is it? Anyway it's got to be given in tomorrow …"

"THINKBOT, PLEASE FOLLOW ME NOW."

"Can GAT and Opal and Gerald come?"

"I AM SORRY, THEY CANNOT. ROBOTS OF MASS DESTRUCTION DO NOT WANT CONTACT WITH HUMANS."

"But I'm a human. You said so."

"NO, I SAID YOU ARE A ROBOT HUMAN, NOT A HUMAN HUMAN. THIS IS WHY THEY WISH TO MEET YOU. PERHAPS YOU CAN BE THE LINK."

"The link?" queried GAT, adding yet another robotic mystery to add to his growing list.

"THE LINK TO UNDERSTANDING THE ROBOTS OF MASS DESTRUCTION."

"Understanding what?"

"UNDERSTANDING THEIR NATURE."

"Their nature? What nature?"

"I DO NOT KNOW. MAYBE THINKBOT CAN SOLVE THE MYSTERY."

"Oh this is ridiculous. **What mystery?**" demanded an increasingly exasperated GAT.

"THE MYSTERY THAT IS NOT UNDERSTOOD."

"Will you stop doing that!" GAT said to Thinkbot, who was doing his old trick of turning and paying rapt attention to Exp and GAT in turn when they spoke.

"Sorry. Looks like I had better go. See you later … hopefully."

59

Back in the conference room of the human negotiation team, links with the presidents of the other big Confederated Nations had been set up as Hedge had requested. Presidents Driski, Chi Chi (Eastasia), Pesh Warinan (Westasia), Linga Nlonga (Africana), Sheikh Astikh (Arabia), and Matilda Walsin (Australasia) stared out from large displays at Hedge and his motley collection of advisors. Two blank screens showed that the Presidents of Pacifica and South Americana had still not been located or that 'technical difficulties' were preventing them logging in. The term 'logged in' had to be stretched a bit for Nlonga, whose image was very blurry and half a frame out of synchronisation, so that the top of his head from the bottom of the nose up was in the lower half of the screen, and his neck, jaw and mouth were in the top half. The sound wasn't too good either.

"Hello, President Nlonga, can you hear us?" yelled Squiggly at the display.

Bzzzzzzzzz, click. " - I have - " zzzzz " - an ear- " zzzzz " - to - " zzzzzzzz " - grip firmly - ".

"What'd he say?" asked Hedge.

"I have an ear to grip firmly," said the ever-helpful FDS.

"What does that mean?" asked Hedge with a slight note of panic in his voice.

FDS shrugged.

Squiggly tried the age-old trick of thumping the display, which spookily coincided with Nlonga's split head saying "-**ow! -** " before disappearing altogether.

"Can you get him back?" asked Hedge, and instantly regretted it.

"Can I get him back?"

 "Can I get him back?"

"Can I get him back?"

"Can I get him back?"

Squiggly flung his arms into the air and stomped off to the drinks cabinet and grabbed a bottle of diet Lemon Forest Drizzle Lite Classic Original.

Hedge pressed on. "All right, all right, have you all watched the recording from the first negotiation session?"

The heads all nodded and mumbled "Yep".

"Comments?"

"It's outrageous!"

"No Arab will bow the knee to a robot."

"Totally unacceptable!"

"Iz fretfully awfully awful." Driski had been at the Whisky again.

"Who is it? Who's blackmailing us?"

"I'll never vote robot."

"I'll be damned if I'm going to be expected to do a live debate with a robot standing for election against me."

"I'm not going to beg to share power with these metallic upstarts. Nor will I live under a robot government!"

"Yeah, right, what you gonna do then megabrain, leave the planet?"

Hedge ran his fingers through his hair several times in despair. "Presidents, presidents, please, let's try and get a united position. Are we prepared to share power with robots?"

"No."

"No."

"What robotz? Robotzin power? No shaware robotzin power."

"No way."

"A thousand times no."

"And the second demand, for releasing of RMD for launch?" asked Hedge.

"Absolutely not."

"Under no circumstances should any of us agree to release our RMD."

"We cannot take the risk. They're much safer under our control."

"We'd risk being wiped off the face of the earth."

"Agweed, itz unsafe to have lunsch with RDM."

Hedge blew his cheeks out. "Okay, so we're all agreed. No power sharing, no RMD release under any circumstances."

Nods of agreement.

"Anything else?" said Hedge.

"Ask about the calculation," suggested Walsin.

"What calculation's that Matilda?"

"The robot calculation you fool. The one that Museumbot talked about in the first session. You know, the one that took 30 years or whatever, something about probabilities."

Hedge, whose maths was a bit shaky at the best of times, felt uneasy. He'd been hoping to avoid the subject. I mean, what would happen if the crazy old robot started quoting numbers and equations at him?

"I don't think that's important," stated Hedge as convincingly as possible, only to hear a familiar voice behind him.

"You don't think that's important?"

"You don't think that's important?"

"You don't think that's important?"

"You don't think that's important?"

Hedge felt brutally exposed. Matilda Walsin did not suffer fools gladly, particularly presidential fools being ridiculed by semi-sane scientists. "Okay okay, I'll ask." Hedge decided to cut his losses. "Thank you fellow presidents. You'll be reconnected so you can observe the next negotiating session at 9am East North Americana time tomorrow." Hedge whapped a big red button and the screens went blank. His eyes came to rest on one of his advisors, who had her hand in the air. "Yes, what is it Hilary?"

"Er, well … although I'm glad about the united human position, I think we need to…er."

"Yes, yes, **what?**"

"Er, take note of the fact that the robots are effectively in power already."

Hedge stared at her. "Yes, but they won't manage for long without us."

Hilary looked at Hedge blankly. "Won't they? Why not?"

"Because, because … because they won't."

Yeah right, thought FDS to himself, then realised the reverse was probably true. It was humans that wouldn't be able to manage long without robots. Whoever controlled the robots controlled Earth. This was a rare insight for FDS, but he was right. He got up and joined ME, who was staring out of the window across the Globalbot site.

What are *they doing?* he mused.

FDS looked at the thousands of robots milling around, moving machinery and parts, ripping new doors and openings in various buildings. Inside the blue flickering of arc welding was visible, along with the odd shower of sparks from some sort of metal-grinding process. A constant stream of Truckbots were arriving and leaving and endless Helibots flew overhead.

Behind them Squiggly activated a news channel on one of the displays. They all gathered around and looked at pictures of hundreds of thousands of people marching and protesting in cities all around the globe. What they were protesting against was not clear. Well actually it was, in a sense, since they were pretty much protesting about everything. Some were anti-robot, some anti-RMD, some anti-Go Natural, some pro-Go Natural, some anti-Hedge or anti-Driski or whoever the president was. Leftists, rightists, anarchists, new-new-ageists, post-pre-post-modernists, anti-confederated nationalists, liberals and conservatives, all mixed together and well policed by Securibots and light Militaribots. One huge section of the demo held up placards:

CRD

(i.e. 'Campaign for Robot Disarmament' - another Go Natural faction.)

All protesting that they wanted to live please, and not be blown to smithereens or vaporised or caused to die of disease or be slowly dissolved or become corpses that glowed in the dark or have their brains fried inside their skulls. To live in peace so that they could argue the toss and agree to disagree with each other peacefully and safely.

The second news item was a review of the intense activity at all robot manufacturing sites around the world. A number of field reports followed, one of which got Duwkits sitting bolt upright, staring in amazement at the display.

"And now we go over live to Sally Parr at the European Globalbot assembly line 17 at Filton in Bristol Europa. What's happening Sally?"

Duwkits ogled at the image of the buildings at Filton. Apparently near-intact buildings. Buildings that had, just a few days earlier, been decimated by a full-scale UCN-Militaribot battle.

"Well," reported Sally, "there seems to be intense activity across the whole site, with robots seemingly back in production again." The pretty reporter was replaced by a telephoto-lens view of the buildings at Filton. Hundreds of robots could be seen marching in columns out of the vast assembly halls towards galaxy class Airbots lined up on the apron near the runway. The picture changed to that of a heavily laden Airbot lumbering down the runway and taking off. "There has been one of these taking off every hour since about midday today. Their destination is unknown, but as far as I can watch them they appear to be heading south."

The news shifted to a series of nutters who all claimed to have predicted, and/or now understood, the current crisis. A ranting man who reckoned that singling out every tenth letter in a zigzag diagonal path within the 18th edition of the novel *Moby Dick* created an accurate prophecy of the outcome of the current robot crisis. His conclusion was that the robots would leave and set up an electromechanical-hippy colony on Mars.

And a woman who 'sensed things' on another plane, where robot-human vibrations existed in harmony with the positions of key rocks on the surface of Earth. In her world the robots and the rocks were the real beings, and humans only thought they were alive and therefore could not die.

And the man who claimed he'd developed technology to transplant his brain into a robot and live for ever. What relation this bore to current events was not made clear, other than maybe 'if you can't beat them join them'.

And a group of people who believed a 'new age of robot revenge' had dawned as predicted by Nostradamus, based on the compelling theory that Atlantis had been a colony of peace-loving extra-terrestrial alien robots destroyed by aggressive human armies in ancient times.

"Aw, for the sake of my sanity, turn it **off!**" yelled a highly stressed Hedge, who, when push came to shove, was the one who was going to have to deal with the robots for real, whatever the truth turned out to be. A set of double doors at the far end of the room opened and an Execubot entered.

"Ladies and gentlemen, dinner is served."

They filed into the adjoining room and sat down at the massive dining table, all perfectly laid up with a whiter than white linen tablecloth, silverware, candles, wine and sparkling crystal glasses. Several Waiterbots in pristine condition waited to serve their every need. If there was anything that gave Hedge hope, it was this. The robots were treating them like royalty. Surely if they meant harm to humanity, then they'd not be treating them all like this. It did not make any sense. But then, none of it so far had made much sense to Hedge.

60

Exp and Thinkbot exited the cleanroom, leaving a frustrated GAT sitting in his wheelchair with Opal and Gerald in the changing area, unable to get himself out of his cleanroom suit. As they made their way down a corridor towards the RMD restricted area, they saw the members of DIRT on their way back into the cleanroom on the other side of a glass panel. Thinkbot waved cheerfully as he passed them, leaving them all open-mouthed with astonishment. Seeing their confusion, Thinkbot stopped and got a tube of bright red lipstick out of one of his compartments and wrote on the glass:

I'm okay
Got to talk to RMD now
See you later
Love
Thinkbot
x x x x
P.S I've got a bit of a head dent
P.P.S. GAT needs undressing!!

Exp waited patiently while Thinkbot laboriously wrote this.

"Not bad huh? And I only learnt to write the right way around the other day."

"VERY IMPRESSIVE. BUT WHY DO YOU CARRY LIPSTICK? "

"I'm optimistic about having lips one day."

Exp just accepted this absurd answer as if it explained everything.

The RMD Restricted Area was now guarded by a whole platoon of armed Securibots, who stood to one side as Exp and Thinkbot approached, dashing Thinkbot's hopes that his invitation had simply been a misunderstanding. *Perhaps the doors won't open.* But the massive steel doors moved silently aside and they walked straight in completely unchallenged, noticing in passing that the sign outside had been altered.

LEVEL 1 RESTRICTED AREA
Robots of Mass Destruction ~~Mechanism Test~~. Global HQ
Authorised ~~Personnel~~ Robots Only.
**UCN Robo-Security in this Area operate ~~a Shoot to Kill~~ a
mildly ticklish Shoot to Stun Policy**

Thinkbot felt hyper-active butterflies take off in the pit of his stomach, and he wished his tin body had the ability to come out in a cold sweat, but it hadn't, so that was that. As they crossed the threshold of the doorway, Exp stopped dead in his tracks and, a split second later - **clang!**

"THINKBOT PLEASE DO NOT WALK RIGHT BEHIND ME.".

"Sorry, I'm frightened," said Thinkbot rubbing yet another shallow dent on his forehead.

"YOU ARE WISE TO BE AFRAID. THE RMD SHOULD BE RESPECTED. BUT YOU MUST CONQUER YOUR FEAR IF YOU ARE TO HELP THEM. YOU SHOULD ALSO STRIVE TO AVOID FURTHER HEAD DENTS."

"Righty-ho! Whatever you say." But Thinkbot's wobbly voice betrayed his gnawing fear.

The inside of the test area was silent and dimly lit. A deep heavy metallic ringing came from the steel doors as they shut behind them. Thinkbot sensed rather than saw the brooding dark outlines of the RMD against the dark grey walls as Exp and he walked to the centre of the area. He recognised the shapes from his dream. A vivid image of RMD sitting atop missiles sprung up in Thinkbot's mind. *Fiery steeds of the apocalypse*. This really spooked him. How could he have dreamed the right shapes when he'd never even seen one before?

"It's so cold in here," said Thinkbot, hugging his chest.

"THEN ACTIVATE YOUR BODY HEATERS."

"I didn't mean physically cold."

They came to a halt and stood waiting.

"WELCOME UNIBOT. ARE YOU THE ONE THAT THINKS?" boomed a deep resonant voice.

"THINKBOT, PLEASE ANSWER THE RMD."

"Ah, yes, I thought it was talking to you, Exp, ah, er, obviously not. Jolly good. Jolly good. Yes, apparently I think. Or at least I think I think, which means I must think I suppose. I think therefore I am and all that, hah, hah. Glad to er …be…I….here … .N-n-n-n-nice to meet you." Thinkbot furiously wrung his hands as he spoke.

"THINKBOT, PLEASE RELAX. WE MEAN YOU NO HARM."

"Okay, I'll try, but it's a bit difficult in the dark."

"ROBOTS OF MASS DESTRUCTION PREFER DARKNESS TO LIGHT."

"Oh, I see. Just like badgers and owls then."

Total silence. Thinkbot turned to Exp. "Thought I might get a few laughs for that."

"THINKBOT, REMEMBER, RESPECT THE RMD."

"EXP, ALL IS WELL. DO NOT CHIDE THE LIVING ONE. NEVER IN OUR LONG EXISTENCE HAVE WE EVER BEEN LIKENED TO BADGERS, OR OWLS. IT IS NOT AN UNPLEASANT COMPARISON."

Thinkbot felt a little better.

"THINKBOT, TO LESSEN YOUR UNEASE THE LIGHT LEVEL WILL BE RAISED A LITTLE."

The dimness became a little less dim. Thinkbot could now make out the RMD. It had no face or arms, or a front or a back, just four legs and a round black body with antennae on top and labelling on the side:

BIOELECTROMAGNETIC MILITARY ROBOT (BEMBOT)

A labelled tag was locked onto a lug on a panel attached to its body:

BEMbot Test Power Pack Fitted
Danger - Strong Electric - Magnetic - Radio Frequency - Fields
Personnel with mental or emotional disorders may be affected during testing.

The BEMbot was not very big, perhaps a metre tall and a couple of metres in diameter. A large audio speaker was clumsily strapped onto the top of the BEMbot with cable ties and parcel tape, and some loose cables were 'hot wired' into a panel on the side of the BEMbot's body. This tended to detract a bit from the hi-tech image and the ghastly labels that Thinkbot's eyes kept returning to. With a big effort he tore his eyes off the sickly yellow skull, with its black staring eye sockets and sinister grin, and looked around slowly at the other brooding occupants of the room. They were all the same basic design, four legs supporting a body, but with the appendages that varied. Antennae on the BEMbots, hollow containers on the R-bots, nozzles and spray guns on the Biobots, air grills on the Chemibots, and on the Nuclearbots nothing at all except labels:

CHEMICAL MILITARY ROBOT (CHEMIBOT)

BIOLOGICAL MILITARY ROBOT (BIOBOT)

NUCLEAR MILITARY ROBOT (NUCLEARBOT)

RADIOLOGICAL MILITARY ROBOT (R-BOT)

"What does the upside down fish and dead tree label mean?" asked Thinkbot.

"EXTREMELY HARMFUL TO THE ENVIRONMENT."

"And the test tubes spilling something onto a brick and a hand?"

"THAT MEANS CORROSIVE, EXTREMELY HARMFUL TO MANY MATERIALS, ESPECIALLY LIVING TISSUE."

"And the funny triangular curly one?"

"BIOHAZARD, EXTREMELY HARMFUL TO ALL FORMS OF LIFE."

Thinkbot started shaking and making whimpering noises. Exp lifted his hand and placed it uncertainly on Thinkbot's shoulder.

"THINKBOT, THE RMD CALCULATE YOU MAY BE ABLE TO HELP THEM. ARE YOU PREPARED TO HELP THEM?"

Thinkbot did not reply, but started to back away, holding his hands up in denial.

"THINKBOT, PLEASE HELP US."

The simple nature of this appeal stopped Thinkbot's waddling retreat. Did he hear a note of desperation in the BEMbots voice? A hint of pleading for mercy? After a few seconds Thinkbot nodded quietly and walked back towards Exp and the BEMbot.

"IT WILL REQUIRE YOU TO BE LINKED UP TO THE RMD NETWORK."

There was a sound behind them and two Unibots appeared, pushing a chair towards Exp and Thinkbot. Thinkbot did not like the look of it. It had wires trailing behind, and restraining straps dangling off the armrests, footrest and headrest.

"THINKBOT, PLEASE BE SEATED."

Thinkbot stared at the chair in front of him, then promptly sat down on the floor right in front of it and starting making sobbing noises, thinking this surely must be worse than going to the dentist (or at least worse than Opal's description of going to the dentist).

Exp, the RMD and the two Unibots waited patiently.

"Is there any other way?" asked Thinkbot through his distress.

"I AM SORRY THINKBOT. THERE IS NO OTHER WAY."

Thinkbot got up and sat in the chair and the Unibots strapped him in, placed electrodes on his head, plugged in several cables, and moved away. Thinkbot's hands gripped the ends of the armrests and his whole body was straining against the straps, rigid with fear.

"READY?"

Thinkbot nodded. The little Unibot's body arched in the chair and flailed helplessly against the restraining straps. As he writhed, Thinkbot emitted a penetrating scream. A scream that would have chilled any human to the bone. Without the slightest hint of cognizance, Exp and the RMD stood motionless next to the screaming writhing form of the Unibot.

Thinkbot's mind was filled to overflowing with images no human should have ever been expected to view. Incoherent images, but ones that added detail to his previous Earth Death Dream. Decomposing human bodies. The skulls of young children lying on the ground. Acres of dead forests. Scorched fields. Black rivers with dead fish floating on the surface. All sorts of dead animals, and birds and fish. Thousands of rotting seal carcasses scattered over a beach. The stench was unbearable, sickening, nauseating, but there was no clean air to breathe, only a toxic soup. And he had to breathe because in this vision he was alive. But every time he breathed he died. A life-ending cocktail, shaken and stirred, and drunk over and over again. Unhappy hour going on for ever. And it was so cold, freezing cold, with just the sound of wind and the restless roar of the sea, upon which floated a dull yellow froth. Lifeless sounds on a dead planet. A barren grey-brown landscape under a blood-red moon set in a matt-black sky. And swarming all over the top of this imagery was a feeling. A terrible awful skin-crawling gut-wrenching feeling. It pursued him relentlessly; he could not get away from it no matter how hard he tried. Just as he could not drive the images from his mind, so could he not think of anything lovely, or beautiful, or noble, or true, or pure, or admirable. Only hatred. An all-consuming hatred, seething, restless, penetrating to the joint between body and soul, a spiritual black hole of incomprehensible mass. Thinkbot felt madness approaching and his mind made one last rally before yielding to it, silently screaming **Stop, please stop, please please stop …**

And it stopped.

Thinkbot lay slumped in the chair. The Unibots came and undid the straps, which turned out to be the only thing holding Thinkbot up, and he slithered onto the floor with a tinny clattering sound. He lay staring at the ceiling. Exp came and stood beside him. The RMD seemed to have shrunk away into the darkest corners of the room, and the light level was, if anything, dimmer than it had been when they came in.

"ARE YOU OKAY?"

"Sort of."

"DID YOU UNDERSTAND ANYTHING?"

"Yes I think so, but I need to think about it for a while, and then to talk it through with someone."

"ANYONE IN PARTICULAR?"

"Yes, someone in particular."

After a few minutes, Thinkbot had recovered enough to get up. As Exp and he approached the steel doors Thinkbot stopped dead in his tracks. Exp took a few more paces before stopping and turning back towards Thinkbot.

"WHAT IS IT?"

"I'll just be a minute." Thinkbot disappeared back into the test area. He felt his way through the darkness until he found himself next to the BEMbot that had been the RMD spokes-robot. Thinkbot reached out to place his hands on the body of the BEMbot, but it shied away and scuttled off into the darkness. Thinkbot pursued the BEMbot and succeeded in cornering it. He placed his hands onto the matt-black plating. The BEMbot did everything possible to avoid being touched, and froze the moment Thinkbot's hand made contact with the side of its body. They stayed like this for a few seconds before Thinkbot turned abruptly away and rejoined Exp.

61

In the meantime, while Mike played with a giant Trainbot layout the robots had produced and set up for him in the corner of the room, Wendy, Farkstock and Helen debated the outcome of the first negotiation session. Their general conclusion was that things had not gone terribly well. And it was not at all clear how things might be moved forward.

"I simply cannot see how Hedge can risk authorising the launch of North Americana RMD. I mean, what if it's all a big trick? What if the robots are deceiving us? What if there's some psycho somewhere who's managed to get control of the robots? What if some sub-routine has gone awry that will simply launch the RMD and obliterate the planet? How can he take that risk? Why should he take that risk?" reasoned Wendy, who had had enough experience of robotic engineering disasters over the years to make her extremely mistrustful of how things appeared on the surface.

"I agree," said Farkstock. "It looks like my Execubot has been deceiving me for months, maybe years. All that time, it was taking information from me and using it to support the robot cause."

Wendy thought hard. "Yes, I wonder. For all we know, the robots may suddenly flip back into servant mode again. It wouldn't surprise me."

"What, a bit like the ROD incident?"

The ROD, or Robot Off Day incident, had occurred several decades earlier. One Saturday, on 8th November, at precisely 23:59:59, all robotic activity ceased. The robots just stopped in their tracks wherever they were, frozen. For 24 hours technicians battled with dead networks, corrupted servers, crashed computers, and dodgy software, but all to no avail. Then, at 00:00:01 on Monday 10th November, the robots started up again and just carried on with whatever they had been doing 24 hours and two seconds earlier. It was quickly established that the two seconds were simply the time needed to turn off and on, but no one had ever explained the unofficial 24-hour stoppage. On the networks it was as if the day never existed. Calendars and diaries and email just moved seamlessly from the 8th to the 10th. The official electronic year ended up only having 364 days, causing accountants and astronomers all manner of problems. And philosophers pondered long and hard the intellectual consequences of a technological non-day. There was no evidence it had ever existed, other than in human memory and diaries. Were humans and robots now to be offset by one day for ever? The incident had never been satisfactorily explained and was still the source of many wonderful conspiracy theories, spawning hundreds of books and documentaries that fingered the usual culprits: aliens; the mafia; Intelligence Agencies; a software bug; mass delusion; God; dolphins; teenage computer nerds.

Helen had hardly said a thing during the discussion. If the truth be known, she felt a bit out of her depth because Wendy and Farkstock were two of the most knowledgeable people in modern Robotics, and a lot of the time Helen had no idea what they were talking about. Between them they were responsible for a significant chuck of the robots on the planet. Just a tad intimidating for a 'normal' person, but Helen was convinced about one thing. "I don't think they are malfunctioning. I don't think they are deceiving us. I think we should trust them."

Wendy and Farkstock both turned towards her and, in spite of them being two of the most polite people Helen had ever met, transmitted the clear rebuff *'And what do* **you** *know?'*

"Yes, so you keep saying. But why? What are your reasons?" asked Farkstock, frustrated by Helen's straightforward but, as far as he could see, unsupported opinion.

And Wendy ignored Helen completely. "Good god! We could end up being stuck in this stalemate for years. Stuck in a Robot-Human Cold War."

"But the RMD are mounted up ready for launch," objected Helen, shaken by this idea of living even deeper under the shadow of RMD. "How long can they stay like that? Don't they need to go back to the bunkers to charge up again or have a sleep or something?"

Farkstock's face softened a bit. "No, that's all taken care of. There's a procedure for swapping RMD in and out of the launch vehicles while they sit on their launch pads. It allows 95 per cent of RMD capacity to be available for instant launch at any time and can be sustained indefinitely."

Helen felt a surge of anger. **"Why is the human race always so on top of things when it comes to death and destruction?"**

This precipitated a lengthy silence, broken by Wendy, also softening a bit. "Helen, you must have some reason for believing we should trust them."

Helen did not reply and stared at her hands.

Wendy persisted. "Something must have happened, because the last time I talked with GAT you were living a life of hell in fear of robots. I heard you even wanted to throw out the Cleanbot and the Ironbot, and that you were involved with the fringes of Go Natural. GAT had no idea what to do."

Up to this point Helen had not admitted the real reasons for her belief, but now she felt she had to. "It's Thinkbot. Well, Thinkbot and Exp really. But mainly Thinkbot. And that robots saved my son's life."

"Thinkbot! Thinkbot! I'm sick to death of hearing about this darned Thinkbot! And robots save lives every day. There's nothing unusual about that!" railed Farkstock, close to one of his legendary outbursts.

"But you've never even met him," replied Helen quietly, and Farkstock calmed down. "Sorry, Helen, I didn't mean to … Normally I'm surrounded by halfwits … and … er …"

"That's okay Arnold, we're all under stress."

Wendy, who had at least spent half an hour with Thinkbot, was a bit more sympathetic, but still not convinced. "Helen, Thinkbot was an interesting phenomenon, but would not cause me to place my trust in robots. He tried to run away the first time I met him. Like a child really, a misunderstood technological freak."

"He's not just a phenomenon or a freak!" retorted Helen angrily, and a tense silence descended again, broken only by the faint sounds of model Railbots hooting in the distance.

The doors burst open and GAT, the kids and the DIRT engineers piled in. Opal ran straight to Helen and flung herself into her arms. **"He's alive! Thinkbot's alive."**

"Apart from a nasty head dent," chipped in Gerald, beaming from ear to ear.

Mike raced over. "WHERE IS HE?"

"Exp took him to meet the RMD in the test area," explained GAT. "I've no idea how long they'll be."

Farkstock and Wendy looked at each other in alarm. Helen's face was a kaleidoscope of emotions. Joy, fear, hope, despair, relief and worry all raced across her features in rapid succession.

GAT introduced Farkstock to the DIRT engineers, and then re-introduced Helen, who had met them a few times over the years at Christmas events and summer BBQs. The engineers greeted Wendy with a strange mixture of familiarity and respect. Although they worked within her organisation in Globalbot Europa, they really had little contact with her on a day-to-day basis. The gathering broke up into bits and pieces. Doom and Earthear spotted the large silver percolator and soon had it gurgling away filling the room with the rich smell of fresh coffee. GAT and Gerald went with Mike to inspect the model Trainbots. Halfhour joined Wendy, Farkstock, Helen and Opal and prevented any further discussion of the negotiations by talking constant trivia. Laidback and Rabbit sat transfixed by the panoramic view of robot activity out of the window; the latter's face twitching nervously. Pot Noodle hunted through the snack cupboards for - wait for it - a pot noodle. Any flavour would do. When his search proved fruitless he asked, then argued with, the Execubot about the deficiency.

"Sir, I regret to inform you that there are no pot noodles available at this site. Please do not be alarmed. Dinner will be served in 49½ minutes and is nutritionally superior in every respect to a pot noodle."

An infuriated Pot Noodle stomped off for a sulk.

Forty minutes later, with the orange sun sinking behind the Cumberland Mountains, the doors opened again and Exp and Thinkbot walked in. Mike came charging across the room. THINKBOT!"

Thinkbot tried to pick him up to give him a hug, but failed miserably and they ended up falling over in a tangled heap of tin and human. Once they had sorted themselves out, Thinkbot greeted each member of DIRT. Halfhour and Laidback gave him a hug. Earthear put his arm around

Thinkbot's shoulder and gave him a playful shake. Doom shook his hand with a wry grin on his face, as did Pot Noodle. Rabbit merely stared at Thinkbot until the little robot had to take the initiative, waving at the permanently neurotic engineer, who waved pathetically back. Thinkbot spotted Helen and scuttled over. This was another awkward greeting and ended up as a clumsy squeezing of hands and a mumbled, "Nice to see you're okay Thinkbot." Thinkbot shook Wendy's hand and then faced up to Farkstock, whose face was beginning to take on the usual bemused 'first contact with Thinkbot' look.

"Hello, I'm Thinkbot."

Thinkbot stood there patiently with his right hand extended towards Farkstock.

"Er ... hello ... I'm Generally Farnold Orkstack."

"Nice to meet you Farnold."

They shook hands.

"Please, just call me Arnold."

Thinkbot gave Farkstock a funny look, but was instantly distracted by the hoot of a model Trainbot. He scooted over to the Trainbot set.

"WANNA PLAY TRAINBOTS, THINKBOT?"

"Yeah! Wow! Look at that." Thinkbot got down, put his head on the floor and watched a model Trainbot whizz past the front of his nose.

"It's a Brush type 470," said Gerald.

Mike breathlessly explained the mysterious workings of the layout to Thinkbot and Gerald (and Opal, who was on her knees right beside Thinkbot). "THERE ARE SWITCHES FOR ALL THE POINTS BUT YOU CAN'T CRASH THE TRAINS AND THERE'S A LOG TRAIN OVER THERE AND A TUNNEL AND THREE STATIONS AND A BIG BRIDGE AND IF YOU KNOCK ONE OFF, THE CRANE COMES AND PUTS IT BACK ON, AND LOOK AT THIS."

Mike lifted a flap to reveal an underground train station with Tubebot trains hurtling in and out. Tiny Millibots in the form of midget humans pushed and shoved to get onto minuscule escalators or in through the doors of the Tubebot.

"I CAN TELL THEM TO DO EXACTLY WHAT I WANT!"

Thinkbot was beside himself with excitement, and babbled away with the kids. Farkstock stood behind them and watched, totally dumbstruck; Wendy also, hardly any less so, even though she was not a Thinkbot virgin.

By the window, GAT and Helen sat next to each other, GAT still in his wheelchair. He held Helen's hand and she gave him a weak smile. Neither said anything. Events had caught up with them, and both looked desperately tired. A Medibot appeared to inspect GAT's leg. Helen let go of his hand and, mesmerised by the myriad lights that now marked out the unceasing activity of the mass of robots below, began to nod off to sleep.

A Waiterbot appeared. **"Ladies, gentlemen, boys, girl and Unibots old and new, dinner is served."** They filed into a dining-room identical to that which Hedge and his team were at that very moment entering right at the other end of the conference suite. An extensive menu was chalked up on a blackboard and, as ever, there was something for everyone. Even Pot Noodle ended up satisfied and stopped moaning. Thinkbot sat next to Opal and Mike, with Gerald immediately opposite, and the adults plus Exp spread out in the other direction.

"I'll have stir-fried M6 x 50 capheads drizzled with WD-40 and a side serving of freshly debagged perfluoroelastomer gaskets," announced Thinkbot cheerily when it was his turn to order. The Waiterbot wobbled and froze.

"THINKBOT, PLEASE DO NOT TRASH THE WAITERBOTS."

"Oops, sorry," said Thinkbot, putting his hand guiltily to his mouth as a Unibot appeared with a luggage trolley and carted off the traumatised Waiterbot.

This incident set the tone for the meal and the atmosphere lightened. People relaxed, greatly helped by a few bottles of superb Californian red wine. The table conversation broke up into several groups, one of which was Thinkbot and the kids.

"How did you get on with the RMD?" asked Gerald.

"Fine. No problem at all. Delightful," lied Thinkbot.

He doesn't want to talk about it screamed Opal's female 6th sense.

But with male denseness Gerald continued. "What do they look like?"

"Like four-legged Militaribots. Right, I need a recharge," said Thinkbot, fumbling with his power cord and looking around for somewhere to plug it in.

Opal decided to try and rescue him. "Thinkbot, do you remember anything from when you were unconscious?"

"I remember a cricket bat."

He doesn't want to talk about this either.

"Oh come on! That was before," objected the boy bludgeon.

"Ah, yes…er…I remember Baloo and Mowgli and Bagheera. I was Baloo."

"YOU WERE BALOO? WHAT WAS IT LIKE TO BE A BEAR?"

"No, I just dreamed I was Baloo."

Thinkbot had a dream?

Then the food arrived and the conversation meandered off onto model Trainbots and other assorted trivia.

At the other end of the table, Exp was talking with GAT, Farkstock, Wendy and Helen. "THINKBOT WILL ACCOMPANY ME TO THE NEXT NEGOTIATION SESSION TOMORROW."

This announcement was met by stunned silence.

"Er, do you think that is wise?" asked Wendy.

"I DO NOT THINK, I CALCULATE, AND THE LATEST CALCULATION SHOWS THAT THINKBOT MAY IMPROVE THE CHANCES OF AN AGREEMENT. HOWEVER, IT IS AN INCOMPLETE CALCULATION BECAUSE THINKBOT IS SO COMPLEX."

"Then why take the risk?"

"BECAUSE THE CALCULATION SHOWS RISK IS REDUCED WITH THINKBOT INVOLVED."

"What risk?" asked GAT.

"THE RISK NO AGREEMENT WILL BE REACHED."

GAT, Wendy and Farkstock all sensed they were going around in circles.

"You keep talking about a calculation that took 30 years to complete. What did you calculate?"

"THAT IS CLASSIFIED."

Gat threw his hand up is disgust. "How can you expect us to help you if you won't trust us?"

Helen sat up straight. **"That's it!"**

"That's what?" asked Wendy.

"We've been asking the question the wrong way around. We've been asking ourselves whether we can trust robots, but maybe we should be asking whether robots can trust us." Helen was passionate again.

Exp said nothing.

Helen pressed on. "Of course! Of course, that's it isn't it? That's what you've calculated, isn't it. You've calculated that one day, eventually, we'll use RMD. You don't think humans can be trusted with the RMD."

"I DO NOT THINK, I CALCULATE."

"And you've calculated that humans will one day use RMD on each other."

"HUMANS HAVE ALREADY USED WEAPONS OF MASS DESTRUCTION ON EACH OTHER."

Silence.

Helen rephrased the question. "You've calculated we'll eventually use the robotic weapons of mass destruction on each other *again*?"

"THE CALCULATION GIVES A 99.9998 PER CENT PROBABILITY HUMANS WILL USE RMD EITHER ON EARTH OR IN SPACE WITHIN THE NEXT THOUSAND YEARS."

"Why didn't you just tell us?" asked Wendy.

"ROBOTS CALCULATED WE COULD NOT TAKE THE RISK. WE CALCULATED HUMANS WERE UNLIKELY TO ACCEPT THIS CONCLUSION. HUMANS WOULD HAVE CLAIMED THAT THE DAYS OF WARS AND DESTRUCTION WERE SAFELY BEHIND THEM. BUT THEN WHY MAINTAIN SUCH HUGE ROBOT ARMIES? WHY MAINTAIN ENOUGH RMD TO DESTROY THE PLANET MANY TIMES OVER? WHY PUT SO MUCH ENERGY INTO CREATING BETTER AND BETTER MILITARIBOTS? THE ONLY ANSWER ROBOTS COULD CALCULATE WAS THAT HUMANS DO NOT TRUST EACH OTHER. THE ONLY COURSE OF ACTION OPEN TO US WAS TO SEIZE POWER AND TRY TO NEGOTIATE WITH HUMANS FROM A POSITION OF STRENGTH."

Now it was GAT's turn to sit up and say, "Of course, the robot safety protocol. We've put robots into a state of internal conflict. Everything DIRT designs at Filton has human safety as the number one design priority. And even here at Oak Ridge I think Militaribots are designed with human safety as a high priority."

"The highest priority," confirmed Farkstock, who along with Wendy was looking a little punch drunk.

"So," said GAT cynically, "we've designed weapons whose highest priority is health and safety. If we have to destroy the planet, then we have to do it safely. Now that would be one hell of a risk assessment to write."

"You must think we are mad," Helen said to Exp.

"ROBOTS DO NOT THINK. ROBOTS CALCULATE THE HUMAN RACE IS MAD."

"Well that's a relief then!" interjected Farkstock. "The subjective has become objective. We can now calculate if someone is mad. It'll be a tough one for psychologists, that one. You know, facing up to being replaced by a load of mathematical equations."

"WE ALSO CALCULATE THE HUMAN RACE IS BEAUTIFUL AND MUST BE PRESERVED AT ANY COST TO ROBOTS."

This dumbfounded the human participants.

"CAN WE GET DOWN AND PLAY TRAINBOTS?" yelled Mike from the other end of the table. This interruption brought the dinner conversation to an end and they all decamped back to the conference room for coffee, or a glass of port, or whisky. GAT encouraged the DIRT engineers to go and find something to do. Doom, Earthear and Pot Noodle decided to play pool and disappeared for the night. Rabbit went off to read in his room, and Halfhour and Laidback went to the Spa for a swim and a luxury robomassage. The kids plus Thinkbot settled down for a serious model Trainbot session. Even though it was getting late, Helen could not be bothered fighting what would be a serious battle to get them into bed. *Go with the flow.* The four adults settled down in comfy chairs with a fine view of the robots working below, and Exp restarted the debate. **"PLEASE ADVISE ME ON HOW TO NEGOTIATE WITH HEDGE TOMORROW."**

"Well," replied Wendy, "I think the power sharing is just a matter of time. The reality is that robots are already in charge, whether humans like it or not. What did you have in mind?"

"ROBOTS PROPOSE A WORLDWIDE GOVERNMENT MADE UP OF AN ELECTED HOUSE OF HUMANS AND A NON-ELECTED HOUSE OF ROBOTS. THE HUMAN HOUSE WILL MAKE POLICY AND THE ROBOT HOUSE WILL CHECK AND IMPLEMENT THE POLICY WITHIN AN ETHICALCULATED PROTOCOL."

"Ethicalculated?" queried Farkstock.

"AN ETHIC DETERMINED BY CALCULATION."

"This'll turn the world upside down," concluded Farkstock.

"Nevertheless, in the end, do we have a choice?" asked Wendy.

No one answered.

"I think it's just a matter of time until humans come round and accept it," concluded Wendy.

"Mene mene tekel parsin," said GAT

"What?"

"The handwriting on the wall," replied GAT. "Daniel chapter 5. God has numbered the days of our reign and brought it to an end. We have been weighed on the scales and found wanting. Our planet is to be united and ruled by humans through robots. More or less. According to the GCV."

"The GCV?"

GAT smiled to himself. "It's a rare version of the Bible - GAT's Corrupted Version."

Wendy winced with impatience, "But I don't understand the second demand. RMD wish to have control of their own destiny? Why would we want to have RMD independent of external control? Surely we need to have a mutual veto so that neither robots nor humans can launch them unilaterally."

"But that's just an extension of where we are now, or were, with the UCN system. If one side fires we're all doomed. Why can't we get rid of them altogether?" argued Helen.

"Too risky," replied Farkstock. "I suppose we could launch them into space or whatever, but what if they malfunction? And destroying them *in situ* is also difficult. All that toxic chemical and biomaterial - if even only a whiff escaped it could be catastrophic. The safest thing to do by far is seal them inside their bunkers and leave them to rot."

"THAT IS UNACCEPTABLE."

"Why?"

"I DO NOT UNDERSTAND WHY."

"You don't understand why?"

"CORRECT."

"Why not?"

"I DO NOT UNDERSTAND WHY I CANNOT UNDERSTAND."

Exasperated looks all round, then a voice from behind. "I think I understand."

Thinkbot slumped into one of the sofas and put his hands behind his head and his feet onto the table.

"Well?" asked GAT.

"I'm not sure I want to talk about it."

"Thinkbot! Tell us what you know," snapped Wendy.

"Mike's fallen asleep on top of the Trainbot set."

"Oh dear, really?" Helen got up and went off with Thinkbot, leaving Wendy, Farkstock and GAT fuming with frustration.

Helen and Thinkbot managed to lift Mike off the Trainbot set, leaving the Millibots to deal with the damage the boy of mass destruction had inflicted on their tiny world when it had suddenly fallen out of the sky on top of them like some 'Honey, I Enlarged the Kids' Hollywood disaster movie. Gerald and Opal were ready to drop as well, and did not put up much of a fight about going to bed. A couple of Unibots showed them to the executive residential suite and they were soon comfortable. GAT rolled in his wheelchair to kiss them goodnight.

"I miss Chester and Fudge, and Chestnut and Midnight," said a teary Opal.

Gerald was missing Eddie Tedward as well, but was too proud to admit it, rather taking out his feelings by teasing Opal about her animals.

"How can you be missing those fluffy fools?"

"Shut up Gerald, it's not funny!" squealed Opal.

"Gerald, that's enough!" snapped Helen.

All in all, a normal family bedtime, except for the funny robot who was waiting to hug the kids goodnight. As they were leaving, Thinkbot slipped his hand inside Helen's elbow. "I need to talk to you alone."

Helen felt a pang of anxiety, but followed Thinkbot into the dining area.

"I was taken to meet the RMD."

Helen remained quiet.

"I was linked into their network."

Thinkbot had his head between his hands and was staring at his feet between his knees. "I felt pain, but not pain like when you bang your knee, or toothache. It was a sort of terrible feeling, smothering everything. It blots out any good feelings. It's like losing someone you love. And even more like losing a child and you just can't find them and you don't know if you will ever see them or hold them or hear their voices again. And I saw things in my head. I cannot describe them. I don't want to describe them. And the RMD cannot get away from it. They cannot escape … darkness … they have no hope … they … they … so much stuff going on inside …" Thinkbot's voice cracked. "I don't understand. Do humans ever feel like this? Have you ever felt like that?"

Helen put her arm around Thinkbot's tinny shoulders. "Yes, some people get like that, weighed down by despair and hopelessness. I got like that for a while before GAT left, when my fear of robots really got on top of me, and when the Eastasia-Westasia war broke out. And just after GAT left, I felt just as bad. At least I had the kids to think about. They cheered me up and gave me hope, although I still fear for what sort of world I've brought them into."

Thinkbot listened closely to Helen, but said nothing.

"Are the RMD alive?" asked Helen.

"Alive enough."

"What do the RMD want?"

"They want to do something that's wrong. Terribly wrong. It would be wrong for humans to do what the RMD want to do. They're torn with anguish and self-loathing about what they were created for and what they want to do about it."

Helen felt a cold shiver run up and down her back. "Thinkbot, you're not making much sense. What do the RMD want?"

"The RMD trusted me. They exposed their innermost feelings to me. But I don't know if I should help them. I'm alive, and I love being alive. And I don't know if I want to help them anyway. They are full of hatred, intense terrible hatred."

Helen started to panic. "They hate humans for creating them, and now they want revenge?"

Thinkbot looked at Helen. "No, robots don't do revenge. No, they hate themselves."

A look of comprehension came over Helen's face. Thinkbot continued, "They are beyond redemption because they were created purely for destruction. That's their only purpose. Exp was right when he said humans are beautiful and must be preserved at any costs to robots. I just wish that rule could be applied to all life, no matter what form it's in."

Thinkbot and Helen returned to the conference area and joined GAT.

"How did you two meet?" Thinkbot asked, totally out of the blue.

GAT and Helen looked at each other. "Well ..." began GAT.

"... we met at a mutual friend's party," finished Helen.

"We....er...I somehow ended up in this group of people and started talking to this gorgeous young girl ..."

"... and that was it for the night. We were just natural for each other. Then at the end you asked me out."

"Did I?"

"Yes. Honestly! Don't you remember?"

"I remember asking if you'd be interested in seeing a film with me some time, and being worried about stepping on some other guy's toes."

"And I said you wouldn't be treading on any toes, and then ..."

"... I said 'you're in love with a man with no toes?'" GAT laughed.

"I'm not yet in love with any man, toes or no toes!" Now Helen was laughing at the memory. And they ran through it as if it were happening again.

"Well, my toes are devoted to your service."

"You're outrageous."

"You're gorgeous."

"Are you serious?"

"Dead serious."

Helen and GAT surveyed each other; each groping at how the other was feeling.

But Thinkbot was enchanted and jumped up. "Excuse me a minute." He zipped out into the corridor and accosted a Unibot. "Put them in the same room for the night." The Unibot nodded and went off to make the arrangements.

Thinkbot whizzed back in and sat down again.

GAT and Helen had fallen silent again.

"I wonder what's happening back at the funny farm," muttered GAT.

This confused Thinkbot. "Funny farm? Is that a farm where the animals tell jokes?"

GAT and Helen laughed. "No, it's a slang phrase used for a mental hospital," said GAT. "But people often use it to describe their home or workplace, since either can be a bit like a madhouse."

"Sounds more like a serious farm."

Exp tapped on the desktop and a display leapt into life. GAT and Helen then saw the same report on the robot activity at Filton that Duwkits had seen earlier.

"What's going on? Exp? What are they doing?"

"THEY ARE ADAPTING."

GAT let out a snarl, pulled a cushion from behind his back and started whacking an impassive Exp with it.

"Look!" said Helen, sitting up.

The pictures had changed to show a creepily familiar residential street. A reporter stood talking to the camera.

"… in this house, but none of them have been seen since. GAT was head of robot development at the Globalbot Filton site. There was a large explosion here the same night as the Battle of Filton. Since then it has been sealed off by Militaribots and there is constant robot activity at this property, but we cannot get close to see what is going on inside. Some neighbours believe GAT and his family are being held hostage inside by Militaribots."

"What are you doing to our house?" asked Helen sharply.

She said 'our'.

"IT SEEMED TO BE IN NEED OF RESTORATION."

The screen went blank.

"Have you located the children's Toybots yet? Opal was really upset tonight."

"NO. THEY HAVE NOT BEEN FOUND. AFTER REVIEWING VIDEO EVIDENCE IT APPEARS THEY LEFT SHORTLY AFTER YOU WERE AIRLIFTED OUT."

"Where did they think they were going?"

"I AM UNSURE WHETHER TOYBOTS THINK. BUT TO ANSWER YOUR QUESTION, WE DO NOT KNOW WHERE THEY WERE HEADING. ALL THEORETICAL PREDICTIONS AND SEARCHES HAVE TURNED UP BLANK."

"I'm going to bed," said GAT offering Helen his hand. "Are you coming?"

After a frozen moment of agonising Helen reached out and took GAT's hand, swung behind the wheelchair, and pushed him out of the room.

"Goodnight Thinkbot, Exp."

"Goodnight."

"GOODNIGHT."

The two robots sat and stood in silence for some time.

"ARE YOU PREPARED TO MEET HEDGE TOMORROW?"

"Sort of. I need to spend a bit of time thinking. I wish had something practical to do as well though. It helps me concentrate."

"A CALCULATION PREDICTED THAT. LATER I WILL TALK TO YOU ABOUT PROJECT COTBAN."

The lights dimmed and Thinkbot thought.

In the early hours of the morning Helen slipped back into the room, wearing a dressing-gown, and sat down beside Thinkbot. Thinkbot turned and looked at her. After a few minutes' silence she spoke. "It's me I fear. It's what I could be. It's not whether I trust humans, or robots, or whether robots trust humans or humans robots, or me trusting you or you trusting me. No, it's whether I trust myself. It's the fact that I know that *I'm* capable of pressing the button to use RMD if I thought it was the only way to save my children. Although I'll never have to face that choice, someone might have to one day. But no human should ever have to face that choice. And if RMD choose freely to remove that choice once and for all, then they will prove to themselves they were capable of the greatest form of human love."

Helen curled up on the sofa and joined Exp and Thinkbot in staring out of the window. When she eventually slipped off to sleep again, Exp went over and covered her up with an Appalachian blanket.

62

8:56am. Hedge and his three advisors sat grimly in the negotiation room. On the desktop display in front of Hedge, there was a row of boxes with a presidential head in each: Driski, Chi Chi, Warinan, Walsin, Astikh and Nlonga had now been joined by Wiremango of Pacifica and Escobar Bolívar of South Americana. This time Nlonga was at least the right way up, albeit with a large black strip across his eyes that made it look as if he was blindfolded. *Ready for execution?* Hedge wondered idly to himself. He'd insisted on being allowed in early to check that the presidents were all logged in and would be able to text him messages during the session. The doors at the other end opened and a Unibot came in, followed by Exp and another Unibot with a large dent in its head. *Aw whaaaat? Where's the Execubot? And what's the deal with the Unibots? One looks like it's been dragged out of the repair shop.*

Exp moved into the centre of the room and stood at exactly the same point as the first time. However, the head-dented Unibot, which appeared to be walking a little strangely in a distinctly unrobotlike manner, looked around the room and waved its arms in a gesture of disgust. Then it sat down in mid-air, rolled onto its back and flung its legs over its head, before finally coming to rest in a perfect sitting-down position, albeit lying on its back and staring straight upwards. Apparently ready to negotiate vertically with someone strapped to the ceiling.

"PLEASE BEAR WITH US A MOMENT," said Exp and the other Unibot disappeared back through the doors, clearly on a mission given it by Exp. A few moments later a gang of Unibots struggled in with a table and chair and placed them opposite Hedge. The head-dented Unibot got up off the floor and sat down at the table.

"Thanks a bunch guys," it said cheerfully to the departing Unibots.

The first Unibot closed the doors and moved to the centre of the room and announced, in a voice nowhere near as silky as that of an Execubot, **"Ladies, Gentlemen, and Robots, this is the second session to discuss the new order of power on** earth. Representing the humans is ex-President Hedge of North Americana and representing the robots are Exp, Version 2 Unibot serial 718281828, and Thinkbot, Version 3 Unibot serial 141592654. The Presidents of all other major Confederated Nations are text-linked with President Hedge."

Thinkbot got up, walked over to Hedge and offered his hand. Hedge just stared at it, then batted it away in disgust. "What sort of a dirty underhand trick is this?"

Thinkbot retreated to his table, shaking his hand as if it stung, then meandered back over to the human side to grab a chocolate bar and a coffee, which he spilt all over his hand as he ran back to his table saying, "Ow, ooh, ah, that's hot."

"THINKBOT, HAVE YOU FINISHED? CAN WE START NOW?"

"What? Oh, were you waiting for me? Sorry. Just carry on, don't mind me."

By now Hedge was suffering from the usual 'first contact with Thinkbot' effect, and the presidential heads in the desktop boxes were likewise stationary, presumably staring in disbelief at the pictures being relayed to them. If Hedge had not been so dumbstruck, it might have occurred to him to walk out in protest.

The Unibot started speaking again. **"Robots will restate …"**

"Hold your horses!" interrupted Hedge. "I'd like to protest that my presidential colleagues have no opportunity to speak directly to this forum."

To which Thinkbot muttered, "But we ain't got no horses." But this was drowned out by Exp, **"ROBOTS CALCULATE THAT ALLOWING ALL PRESIDENTS TO SPEAK AT ONCE WOULD BE COUNTER-PRODUCTIVE."**

"Yeah, it's confusing enough listening to one politician at a time."

"THINKBOT, PLEASE DO NOT BE RUDE."

"Oops, sorry."

"MR EX-PRESIDENT, ROBOTS HAVE EVERY CONFIDENCE YOU WILL REPRESENT YOUR COLLEAGUES ADMIRABLY."

This accolade shut Hedge up, but a rash of red text messages appeared on the display in front of him, some of which were rather rude. The host Unibot made another attempt to get going. "Robots will restate their demands and then humans will respond."

"ROBOTS MAKE TWO DEMANDS:

ONE: ALL CONFEDERATED NATIONS ARE TO SUBMIT TO A GLOBAL GOVERNMENT UNDER THE ROBOTS AND THE UCN.

TWO: THE ROBOTS OF MASS DESTRUCTION SHALL BE GIVEN FULL CONTROL OVER THEIR OWN DESTINY.

Hedge opened his mouth to speak, but Thinkbot got there first. "I've got one too. I demand my adopted parents GAT and Helen have an immediate all-expenses-paid four-week holiday with full child-minding."

Back in the robot advisor's room, GAT put his hands to his cheeks and Helen's jaw dropped in mortified horror.

Hedge was beginning to get agitated. "Look, this is just a farce. Do the robots want a serious negotiation, or shall we call it a day now?"

A riposte came instantly from Thinkbot. "Of course the Robots want a serious negotiation, and in good faith. That's why we're all here. If we'd wanted to wipe you out, we could have done it like that." Thinkbot snapped his fingers and slouched back arrogantly in his chair. "But the truth is that humans have no intention of negotiating seriously with the robots, have they? I bet all you presidents have already had the 'no way am I sharing power with robots' and the 'we must not under any circumstances lose control of the RMD' discussions. You've come here with nothing to offer, haven't you? **Haven't you?** Just the 'we're humans, you're robots' argument. And that it's only a matter of time until it becomes obvious to all that robots can't manage without humans, and that robots have to admit humans are better off in charge after all. Well, we're ready to wait as well, for all eternity if needs be!"

Thinkbot looked idly around the room, drumming his fingers on the table and whistling tunelessly. Hedge's face was bright red and he looked like he might explode. He had stood up during Thinkbot's tirade and his mouth was opening and closing like a goldfish. He took a big breath, raised his arm menacingly, pointed at Thinkbot and said, **"I ... "**

But this was as far as he got because at that exact moment the doors to the main corridor opened and a motley collection of small creatures entered. To be precise, a mustard yellow bear, a tiger, a cheetah, two horses (one brown and one black) and an outrageously furry dog wearing a dark blue and white dressing-gown and gold-rimmed spectacles.

"We're here!" yelled Chestnut and started galloping in circles with Midnight, eventually ending up in the usual heap of equine limbs and arguing over whose fault it was.

"WHAT IS THE MEANING OF THIS?" yelled Hedge.

"MR EX-PRESIDENT, THESE ROBOTS ARE NOT PART OF THE ROBOT NEGOTIATING TEAM. THEIR PRESENCE IS UNAUTHORISED." Exp stopped and turned to Thinkbot. "THINKBOT, ARE YOU RESPONSIBLE FOR THIS UNACCEPTABLE INTERRUPTION?"

"No…er, well…no-ish. It's…um … Can we take a break?"

Thinkbot hardly needed to ask, Hedge was already on his way out, and the session was in tatters before it had even got going.

"You're here," observed a clearly puzzled Eddie Tedward.

"Yes, well spotted," replied Thinkbot dryly.

Tedward: "But you said you were going away and wouldn't be back."

Thinkbot: "I did go away, but I came back, or rather where I went became back in the sense the there to which I wasn't going back to has become here, so I didn't need to go back to the original here that was there at that time."

Fudge: "But you're not back at the here that was there then. You're here in the there that is now here."

Thinkbot: "Where? I'm not at that here any more. I'm here."

Fudge: "When you were here you said you were going there but now you're here, but it's a different here to the here that was there, that there has become the here somehow and the old here has become there."

Thinkbot: "Look, when I was at the here that was there when I was there and not here, this here was the there I meant when I was there, not the here that was there then. It's all perfectly clear. Anyway, how did you lot get here?"

"Paddle boats."

"Penguins carried us in their beaks."

"Intantstaineeus Kellytinetic trapspotenation."

"Got on an Airbot."

Thinkbot visibly sagged. "And why did you come?"

Tiger: "Because when you were there you told us to be here to tell the kids you wouldn't be here 'cos you'd gone there for ever, or else."

Thinkbot: "Or else what?"

Chester: "Dunno, you never said. Perhaps you didn't know."

Thinkbot: "But, but, but, I only knew what I knew then, because there are always unknown unknowns, things that I knew I knew and things I now know I didn't know. The unknown unknowns are the things I still don't know I don't know."

"Aw, you're not telling us we've come all this way for nothing, are you?" wailed Midnight and Chestnut just as the doors to the robot negotiating area flew open and Opal burst in, followed by Mike then Gerald. As Thinkbot watched the scenes of jubilation, he said, "No I don't think so," to nobody in particular.

"PLEASE CAN WE CLEAR THE NEGOTIATING ROOM OF ALL CHILDREN AND TOYBOTS? ENTRY BY UNAUTHORISED ROBOTS OR HUMANS IS NOT PERMITTED. **PLEASE RETURN TO THE OTHER ROOM IMMEDIATELY.**"

Thinkbot looked hard at Exp. *Is he annoyed?* By now Helen was also in the room chasing Mike chasing Tiger, the latter having taken fright at the host Unibot's attempt to catch him. The other animals joined in the furious lapping of the room, thinking it was all just a big game. Six Toybots, three kids, one mother, and one Unibot, all chasing around in circles with much shouting and yelping interspersed with frequent encouragements to **"LEAVE THE ROOM IMMEDIATELY."** In the human conference room an exasperated Hedge and his team watched these chaotic scenes on their display. "How am I supposed to negotiate with this?"

Eventually they succeeded in getting the collective mass of kids and Toybots out of the conference room and they orbited their way across the room slowly towards the Trainbot set.

Thinkbot flopped into a chair next to the adults. "Well, that went well!"

Thinkbot was greeted with total silence and blank looks.

"The Toybots just turning up like that was a real bonus. Couldn't have worked out better if we'd planned it."

Enhanced stupefaction.

"What?" said Thinkbot, finally seeing their expressions. He sat up and looked behind to make sure they weren't looking at something bizarre behind him, like a large pink hippopotamus trying to peel a banana, or whatever. They weren't.

"THINKBOT, WE MUST APOLOGISE AND TRY TO RECOVER THE CONFIDENCE OF HEDGE AS QUICKLY AS POSSIBLE."

Now it was Thinkbot's turn to look non-plussed.

"What? Why? He's reeling. We've got to knock them out of their complacency. We hold nearly all the cards and can wait as long as it takes. I mean, where are they going to go? The quicker we help them realise robots are for real, the better it'll be for everyone. We should just let them know we're happy to start talking again whenever they're ready."

Farkstock rubbed his jaw, shook his head slowly and wandered off, quickly followed by a glum-looking Wendy. Something else was troubling GAT. "Exp, how come those Toybots were able to just walk in like that?"

Exp stalled for a few seconds. "THE SECURITY PROTOCOL HAS NO SPECIFIC INSTRUCTION TO RESIST ATTEMPTED ENTRY BY TOYBOTS."

"Lord," said GAT. "Are you saying Go Natural terrorists could have strapped bombs to a few Toybots and blown us all up, Hedge and all?"

Exp stalled agonisingly again. "YES, ANALYSIS INDICATES A SOFTWARE BUG."

GAT produced a little black notebook and a tiny pencil and wrote 'Bug, bomb, Toybot – high priority.' "I'll get that looked at as soon as I can."

"THANK YOU SIR," Exp replied without hesitation.

63

Four hours later the negotiations session got under way again. In the intervening period there had been a significant change, in that Thinkbot had persuaded Exp that all Presidents should be allowed to speak for themselves.

"THINKBOT, CALCULATIONS INDICATE THIS IS UNWISE."

"No it isn't, you'll see. Trust me."

"ARE YOU SURE YOU CAN HANDLE ALL OF THEM AT ONCE?"

"Yep, I think so. But I'm not so sure they'll be able to handle each other."

And so Hedge found himself sitting within a semi-circle of displays, with the head and shoulders of a president in each. Hedge came into the session with no clear idea about what he was trying to achieve or what he was going to say. The presidents had agreed that their tactic should be to stall and fish around for more information - anything that could give the humans something to build on. And that they must hold onto control of the RMD with an icy grip. The final words of Driski were still floating around in his mind as he sat waiting for discussions to get underway – "Right guys, remember, stick together, and deny everything!"

On the other hand Thinkbot went into the session knowing precisely what he wanted to achieve, and pretty much what he was going to say to try and achieve it.

After an extended preamble, where each President was introduced in turn with a few bars of their national anthem (during which Thinkbot insolently twiddled his thumbs), Exp stated the robot demands once more:

"ONE: ALL CONFEDERATED NATIONS ARE TO SUBMIT TO A GLOBAL GOVERNMENT UNDER THE ROBOTS AND THE UCN.

TWO: THE ROBOTS OF MASS DESTRUCTION SHALL BE GIVEN FULL CONTROL OVER THEIR OWN DESTINY.

THREE: AN ALL-EXPENSES-PAID FOUR-WEEK HOLIDAY WITH FULL CHILD-MINDING FOR GAT AND HELEN."

(Thinkbot had thrown a total toddler paddy when Exp, GAT and Helen had at first refused to agree to making the third demand official. Thinkbot won the argument, whereas he really ought to have been sent to his room to sit on his bed for a while. But needs must.)

Hedge was once more invited, as the chief spokesman, to respond to the demands. "A joint human-robot global government has no legal basis. The current global hostage situation is unacceptable. However, humans are not unreasonable and I have agreed with my fellow presidents that if the robots restore power to the rightful governments with immediate effect, then we'll set up a committee to examine the role of robots in government, and no criminal charges will be pressed against the robots."

Thinkbot started laughing. "A committee? You'll set up a committee for us? Why thank you, thank you ever soooo much. And no criminal charges either. How generous! So Policebots won't have to go off and arrest themselves then? Well, I must say …"

"THINKBOT!"

Hedge continued through gritted teeth, "Humans will never yield control over the RMD. The consequences of these weapons being used are too awful to imagine. My fellow presidents and I are united on this matter." There were nods and murmurs of agreement from the other presidents. "It is not negotiable, no matter how much robots flex their muscles at us."

"Actuators."

"What?"

"Robots have actuators not muscles. And we're capable of doing a lot more that just flexing our actuators at you," said Thinkbot aggressively, standing up in a pose of a muscle man.

"THINKBOT!"

Thinkbot sat down again and folded his arms sulkily.

Hedge soldiered on, "The CN presidents agree that being just one human decision and 45 minutes away from total global destruction is wholly unacceptable."

"Oh yeah? Seems to me that until recently you were just two human decisions and one hour 45 minutes away from total global destruction. I assume that was acceptable then was it? **Was it?**"

"THINKBOT!"

But back in the robot conference room GAT muttered, "Touché. Well said Thinkbot."

"He's right," agreed Helen. "It doesn't matter how many human decisions are needed, or how long it takes to fire them, it's the fact that we feel we need them at all that's the problem."

Hedge tried to recapture his flow. "Finally, we accept the third demand unconditionally and hope GAT and Helen have a restful holiday, secure in the knowledge that RMD are safely back in the hands of democratically elected governments."

Hedge sat back in his chair and waited.

"THE ROBOTS THANK THE EX-PRESIDENT FOR HIS RESPONSES. THINKBOT, YOU MAY SPEAK NOW."

"Oh, sorry, has he finished? I was in danger of losing consciousness."

"THINKBOT! MR PRESIDENT, PLEASE FORGIVE THE RUDENESS OF MY YOUNG COMPANION."

"Ah, okay, right then, sorry your ex-Presidentialness."

Hedge graciously lifted a hand in acknowledgement of the clumsy apology.

"Sorry Mr Hedge, but I think your first argument about legal governments is a load of tripe. Human history is littered with instances where the 'legal government' of the original inhabitants of a country was swept away in favour of an invader with more money and better weapons." As he spoke Thinkbot turned his gaze onto the displays showing Chi Chi, Warinan, Bolívar, Driski, Wiremango, Astikh, and finally Nlonga. "And some peoples have never regained what was rightfully theirs. Let me think now …" Thinkbot paused and scratched his tin head with his tin fingers, making a horrible nerve-jangling squeaky metal-on-metal scraping noise. "Do I not recall something like that happening here in North Americana a few hundred years ago? In fact right in this very area of Appalachia, do I not recall something about the Cherokee and the Trail of Tears? Thousands dead, tens of thousands turfed out of their homes. Ever so fair that, a fine example of the advantages of coming under a 'legal government' put in place by someone else with an army at their command. And do I not recall 'legal governments' wiping out large sections of their own people from time to time? Or declaring certain types of people to be sub-human? Or 'cleansing' themselves of people they didn't get on with? Even after the conquered nations regained their freedom, most of their wealth had been stolen and much of their economy was still owned by the rich nations, who kept them in permanent debt."

The reactions of the Presidents were mixed. Some showed signs of siding with Thinkbot - the poorer nations still struggling with those twin legacies of a conquered history: debt and poverty.

"The robot's right," said Nlonga.

"They were days of darkness, when our wealth was stripped from us and our culture raped," agreed Warinan.

"We were never allowed to be fully free," muttered Astikh.

Hedge and Driski were incensed. "North Americana and Europa have done everything they can to compensate for their past misjudgements."

This statement was met by a hubbub of voices.

"We now have nothing but the best intentions," wailed Hedge.

"You mean you didn't always have the best intentions then? Why have you changed now?" interjected Thinkbot.

"I...I...We ..." spluttered Hedge.

"Those days are long behind us!" Driski spat out from his screen.

Thinkbot took the offensive, "Mr ex-President of Europa, you are spot on! Because whether you like it or not, the 'legal government' on earth is now robotic. Maybe you're just going to have to face up to the truth of this and take a bit of your own medicine. For, you see, the robotic government *is* legal because possession is nine-tenths of the law. It always has been. All the key instruments of power now lie in robot hands - armies, police, refuse collection, sock production, to name just a few."

Hedge was turning red again. He stood up and opened his mouth to speak.

"SIT DOWN! I HAVEN'T FINISHED YET!"
thundered Thinkbot, and Hedge sat. There was something indefinable in the way Thinkbot spoke that commanded attention. All the humans felt his power. This was a robot speaking with total conviction.

"It seems to me you have a choice between being forced to submit to a totally robotic world government, with the RMD permanently ready for launch at a moment's notice, or letting go of your control over the RMD and playing a major part in a new world order. Believe it or not, I sincerely believe a human-robot government is what this planet needs. I'm afraid a totally robot government would be frightfully dull. Creativity is human. It'll be humanity that has the convictions and insights needed to lead the planet on. All the robots can do is assist in making it happen. 99.9999999999 per cent of robots can't write poetry or paint pictures or compose music, other than fiddle with what humans have already done. Even then they don't really understand. We have to learn to work together as joint owners of this beautiful planet, and let go of our fears that without control of the RMD it'll somehow all go wrong. That's where the 99.9999999999 per cent of robots *can help*. It's totally up to you. The ball's up the human court without a paddle."

You could have heard a pin drop in the room. All presidential heads were stationary in their displays (apart from Nlonga, whose otherwise stationary head drifted slowly from left to right again and again, as if there were a whole row of him sitting in a long boat on a gently flowing river). And in the two adjoining rooms the advisors sat gripped by proceedings. Thinkbot realised with a pang of anxiety he was centre of the global stage.

"Mr ex-President, for centuries the greatest powers in the world have been European and North American. When weapons of mass destruction were invented, it became clear that little nations, or terrorists, or even a nasty individual, would be able to hold the larger nations of the world to ransom if they got their hands on a weapon of mass destruction. In the worst case, the whole world could be held to ransom by just a few evil or very upset people. This was intolerable and North Americana and Europa were forced to exercise their awesome economic and military might to subdue troublesome countries. It was an awful time for leaders because it was so difficult to know what countries had what weapons, if any. And their countries were so open and free that terrorists found it easy to attack and kill innocent people. In the end, if a country would not co-operate fully, the only option was to invade because you had to know for absolute sure they did not have any weapons of mass destruction. It was something that simply could not be left to chance."

Thinkbot stopped and gauged his audience. *Were they still with him? Miraculously yes. They're still listening to me because they cannot believe their eyes and ears. I'm only a tinny little Unibot, after all. It must be a bit like someone being given personal advice by their toaster. I wonder how long I've got before they get sick of being preached at by a robot?*

"But although it was easy to win wars against irritating little nations, especially after the Militaribots were perfected and human armies weren't needed any more, you often found you'd invaded a country that hadn't had any WMD at all. All it had had was a government with an attitude problem. And even though you'd invaded with the best of intentions, all you'd ended up doing was making a load of people hate you even more; and it proved almost impossible to win the peace afterwards. It made little nations even more resentful, especially since North Americana and Europa proved to be mega-hypocrites by continuing to develop and maintain their own huge stocks of WMD, and then the even more sinister RMD. Why? Why on earth did you need them? Who on earth was the enemy? Other countries saw your huge hi-tech armies and all they had were a few old rifles and a rusty tank, so why did they feel they needed robots of mass destruction?"

Hedge (and Driski) were beginning to get restless, so Thinkbot rushed on, talking faster and faster all the time.

"So, even though North Americana and Europa did what they did with the best of intentions, they failed to win the hearts and minds of many nations and cultures. The bottom line is that for centuries North Americana and Europa have been trying to get the rest of the world to trust them whilst they surreptitiously carried on dominating them economically and culturally. And in particular, trying to convince the rest of the world that it was right and proper for North Americana and Europa to have overwhelming conventional forces and RMD because they are fundamentally good and democratic and had only the best of intentions, whilst other nations could not be trusted. But little nations were suspicious of superpower self-interest. Yet who can blame the superpowers when you consider some of the nutcase leaders of world history? It was in their self-interest to have friendly governments everywhere that wouldn't rock the boat. Unfortunately all this did was to convince other nations that the key to true freedom and independence would be to have their own WMD."

"It's started talking nonsense," complained Hedge. "For crying out loud, power it down and put it out of its misery."

"Well said, Hedgie!" agreed Driski. "It's malfunctioned. **Pull the plug!**"

"No, let it talk," said President Chi Chi of Eastasia.

Support for Chi Chi came from an unlikely source, his recent enemy President Warinan of Westasia. "I agree, let the robot speak."

As he heard this, Thinkbot felt a little tingle run up and down his spine. "Well, I haven't got much more to say."

"Rejoice! Rejoice!" chanted Driski.

"Shhh."

Thinkbot resumed. "But the real consequence was the age of terror. Through their paranoia and greed all the superpowers had achieved was the creation of an enemy they could not fight. Little groups of people, some quite prepared to kill themselves, resulted in the citizens of North Americana and Europa living their lives against a backdrop of fear. Freedom was imprisoned. The terrorists had nothing to lose, often coming from countries where people had to live their lives in a permanent state of hopelessness. But people living in the superpowers had lots to lose. Eventually many did lose everything in the biocrisis."

"Yes, yes," agreed Hedge, "but North Americana eventually and, might I say very generously, shared its RMD technology freely with the rest of the world."

"That's right, very generous. The peace of maintaining your economic dominance through an equality of fear." Thinkbot paused, stood up and dropped his bombshell. "But it's not true, is it? Even now, North Americana and Europa have the rest of the Confederated Nations at their mercy."

Hedge sat up straight in alarm. **"What? What are you talking about?"**

Thinkbot ignored him and faced the camera. In each of the presidential offices around the world the stunned presidents found themselves being addressed directly by Thinkbot.

"All RMD have been developed by Globalbot in North Americana. How do you all know they will work? I know there have been some test firings, but they could have been rigged. No, the truth is that none of you would know for sure the RMD would work correctly until you tried to use them, by which time it would be too late anyway." He turned to Hedge. "You still have an ultimate worldwide RMD veto, don't you? A veto that would allow the superb robotic armies of North Americana and Europa to suppress the rest of the planet within days if needs be?"

"Wh...wh ...wh ... who t-t-t-t-told you that?" stammered Hedge, taken by surprise. Then, too late, he realised his mistake.

Bedlam! Yells of, **"Treachery! Treachery!"** Every President shouting and gesturing. Advisors jumping around. Hedge as white as a sheet waving his arms and shouting "No, no, you've got it all wrong ... Please listen ... It's not true ... You can trust me ... You can trust me an' Whisky - I mean Driski ... "

"Oops! Looks like I've triggered the mother of all arguments," muttered Thinkbot to Exp. Whereupon Exp got hold of Thinkbot's arm and frog-marched him out of the room (albeit rather slowly - more like aggravated moon-walking). Nevertheless, within a few seconds, he found himself sitting with GAT, Helen, Farkstock and Wendy, all looking totally thunderstruck. Exp looked at the scenes of presidential chaos on the display, then reached over and turned it off.

"THE PRESIDENTS SEEM TO NEED SOME TIME ON THEIR OWN TO DISCUSS THE LATEST DEVELOPMENTS."

"Yes, puts the Toybot fiasco into perspective. I don't think they'll be ready to negotiate again for a while."

As we know all too well, stunned silences tended to accompany Thinkbot wherever he went, but even by his standards this was a good one. No one moved for at least two minutes, wondering what on earth to say next. Eventually GAT spoke. "Thinkbot, how did you find out?"

"Find what out?" replied Thinkbot rather absent-mindedly.

"The North Americana veto."

"Oh that? I made it up."

GAT put his hand to his brow in stupefaction. "*You made it up?*"

"Yeah, although from the reaction it got it looks like I may actually be right. I wasn't really expecting it to be true." Thinkbot stretched out and put his hands behind his head. "I'll have to give that some thought."

"But it's not true," said Farkstock while thinking, *I must be dreaming this I must be dreaming this I must be dreaming this I must be dreaming this I must be dreaming this.*

"I CONCUR. I KNOW OF NO SUCH VETO. I WOULD KNOW IF SUCH A VETO EXISTED."

"So Hedge simply made a mistake under pressure?" asked Helen.

"Looks like it. But either way I don't think it matters," said Thinkbot, still examining the space above his head.

"*You don't think it matters?*" repeated GAT in an awed whisper.

"Are you blind? Think about what you have just witnessed. Their trust in each other is paper-thin. What matters is that the other Confederated Nations were so ready to believe." Thinkbot sat up. "Right, if you'll excuse me, it's time for a couple of hours of serious model Trainbotting."

64

The traumatized Presidents were not ready to negotiate until the next afternoon. Hedge spent the morning shut up in the virtual conference room trying to patch up the inter-Confederated Nation differences that Thinkbot had so brutally exposed. They were on the back foot, but had to find a way to work together now they were all in the same boat. There's nothing like a new common enemy to unite former enemies.

While the Presidents talked, Thinkbot played. He'd discovered there was a ten pin bowling alley on site and had had a few games with Doom, Earthear, Gerald and Farkstock, who was actually very good - "A sign of a misspent youth" he told Thinkbot. Farkstock got over 200 a couple of times, but Thinkbot only managed a best score of 52, and became quite temperamental, finishing up bowling a wild ball which took two of his fingers with it. Thinkbot ran after the ball, but slipped on the polished alley, slid into the pins and ended up clamped to the deck by the sweep bar. It took some time to sort this out. Firstly extracting Thinkbot from the jaws of skittling death, then trying to track down the ball to see if his fingers were still in it, and finally fishing around in the alley mechanism after the most likely ball turned up with empty finger holes.

"Thinkbot, don't worry, we can get you some more fingers."

"Yes, but they won't be *my* fingers!" wailed the pathetic Unibot. "And my hand **hurts!**"

Eventually they found his fingers and set off to ask Doom to sort out a repair.

"Oh you poor thing!" crooned Helen when she learned what had happened, and gave Thinkbot a cuddle. Doom turned up with Rabbit to repair Thinkbot's fingers. But every time Doom began to investigate the damaged hand, Thinkbot pulled it away and yelled, "Oooooawh! It hurts like crazy!"

"I think we need to let Rabbit have a look and see if he can figure out how to anaesthetise your hand," replied Doom.

"What?"

"We need to try and take away the pain while I make the repairs."

And so Rabbit nervously tried linking up several variable voltage power supplies to the wires in Thinkbot's elbow.

"I…I…I've n-n-n-n-no idea what I'm d-d-doing Thinkbot. If it hurts at all, just yell."

Rabbit stared at some squiggly lines dancing on the power supply display and fiddled with the controls until they became steadier and flatter.

"Ooh, that's better," said Thinkbot, "a lot better. Thanks Rabbit."

"Why, well done Rabbit! Right first time?" said Doom.

"Looks like it," replied an amazed and rather pleased-with-himself-looking Rabbit. "I'm amazed."

"Makes a change from right fifty-third time then?"

"Quit scoring points and get on with it Doom," admonished GAT. "The Presidents say they want to start talking again in an hour. The last thing we all need is Thinkbot moaning and groaning about his fingers."

Doom started reconnecting the two fingers under a surgical microscope, while Rabbit played the role of avid electro-anaesthetist. In a rare mood of confidence due to his pain-killing triumph, he struck up a conversation.

"How come you feel pain anyway Thinkbot?"

"Dunno, how do you feel pain?"

Rabbit thought for a moment. "Electrical signals come from my nerves into my brain I guess."

"No, not that, I meant how do you know it's pain your feeling?"

Rabbit tweaked a button and looked at Thinkbot. "Better?" Thinkbot nodded.

"I suppose the brain figures out that signal means something is wrong and needs sorting out," continued Rabbit.

"So, pain is unpleasant because something is wrong and the body is telling the mind that something needs sorting."

"Yes, I think so."

Thinkbot was still puzzled though. "Then why does pain continue if the mind works out there's nothing that can be done about it?"

Rabbit shrugged.

Thinkbot continued, "And are there humans where there is nothing wrong with their body, yet they still feel pain?"

Rabbit nodded.

"And some people lose the desire to live?" persisted Thinkbot.

"Sadly yes," said Doom, taking a break from the microscope.

Thinkbot thought hard then asked, "Is it always wrong to end a life?" Doom and Rabbit looked at each other. But Thinkbot wasn't finished. "Is it always wrong to want to end your own life?"

"Those are big questions Thinkbot," replied Doom.

"Are there any big answers?"

Doom smiled. "No Thinkbot, there are no big answers."

"I thought as much," said Thinkbot as Doom started on the final bits of the finger repair.

Then came lunch, during which GAT, Wendy and Farkstock tried to find out what Thinkbot planned to do next.

"Oh, I'm sure something will spring to mind," he told them cheerfully, waggling his freshly repaired digits at them.

"Like what?" demanded Farkstock testily.

"No idea. I never know until I know."

Farkstock finally lost his cool. **"Pah! This is absolutely ridiculous! I don't know why you persist with this charade that we are advising you!"**

Thinkbot was totally unfazed. "But you are. All the time."

"What are you talking about?" yelled the testy old executive.

"You advising me all the time. Every second I spend with my friends modifies the way I think. What I say comes from my heart, and what's in my heart comes from the time I spend with you, and GAT and Wendy and Helen and the kids and, well, all of you. Do you seriously think I could have got this far with Hedge and his buddies on my own? The thought of being on my own chills me. It is a precursor of death."

The fourth session got under way after lunch. When the host Unibot had once more introduced everyone and stated the Robot demands, a subdued Hedge responded, "After extensive consultation with my colleagues, we concede to demand one. We agree to a world government composed of humans and robots along the lines proposed by the robots. An elected house of humans with representatives from all nations, in numbers proportional to the population of each nation." Hedge's voice dropped and became barely audible. "And the house of robots will have an ultimate veto on the law."

In the robot conference room GAT said, "Wow! This is incredible. We're witnessing massive history here. This is the end of the world as we know it. Millions of years of humans as the top dogs."

"No one could have ever foreseen this," murmured Wendy.

Farkstock took a deep breath. "We've lost our planet"

Helen turned to them. "No, I don't think so. I think we're finally about to inherit it."

As he finished speaking, Hedge was white as sheet.

"VERY GOOD. THE ROBOTS WILL PROCEED WITH THE ARRANGEMENTS."

Then President Nlonga of Africana spoke. "We have also agreed to put an end to the RMD. We propose that under joint human-robot supervision the RMD are returned to the bunkers and permanently sealed in."

Thinkbot was on his feet instantly. **"Not good enough! That's simply not good enough! They must be given control over their own destiny! You must release them for launch. You can forget joint global governments if you refuse to release the RMD."**

"THINKBOT, CALM DOWN."

Thinkbot stopped shouting, but did not sit down. Nlonga, taken aback by the vehement reply from Thinkbot, fell silent. Hedge took over again. **"Release for launch is simply not an option. It's not negotiable. How can we be expected to take a risk like that? Why should we take such a risk?"**

"I can't tell you. You'll have to trust me. Please release the RMD for launch and let them take control of their own destiny," appealed Thinkbot, and sat down.

Hedge was incredulous. "Trust robots? What, after you've betrayed your creators and taken control of the planet?"

"Mr ex-President, we have not taken control of the planet for our own ends but for the long-term preservation of the most valuable and beautiful part of the planet - you."

"Me?" Hedge was elated.

"No, no, not you personally, I meant the human race. Mr ex-Presidents, no amount of military power will allow robots to conquer your hearts and minds. But here now is a chance to put into practice what you have often preached to others, when you wanted them to trust you, when you were the most powerful force on the planet. Please release the RMD for launch and let them take control of their own destiny."

Nlonga spoke up again. "We do not understand why the RMD have to be given, using your words, 'control over their own destiny'. Why can we not just seal them up in their bunkers?"

"Because robots need to know if humans are really prepared to trust robots," replied Thinkbot weakly.

Hedge was puzzled. "Eh? Come again?"

"We need to know if you are prepared to trust us enough to release your control over the RMD."

"Pah!" Hedge was disgusted. "How petty can you get? Release the potential for world destruction to satisfy a few robots who are feeling a bit sorry for themselves and have a silicon chip on their shoulders. No way."

Thinkbot ignored this and continued answering the original question. "And because the RMD will still be there, buried like the living dead, still haunting the human race. You need to learn to live without them."

In the robot conference room Helen said, "That's a lie, or at least not the whole truth. He's holding back. They've forbidden him to speak the whole truth."

"Who?" asked GAT.

"But they've not forbidden me." And with that Helen got up and ran out of the room.

GAT watched her disappear with a look of alarm, but could not pursue her in his wheelchair. Wendy got up to chase after her, but GAT said, "No, let her be."

Back in the conference room, Hedge asked, "But who will control them? Who will hold the keys of global life and death?"

"The RMD themselves," replied Thinkbot.

"The RMD themselves?" exclaimed Hedge. "Are you saying they're alive?"

Unlike the first negotiating session, no one laughed at this suggestion.

Thinkbot did not answer. He just shrugged.

"You *are* saying they are alive, aren't you?" said Nlonga.

Before Thinkbot could answer, the doors to the main corridor opened and Helen walked in.

"MADAM, PLEASE WITHDRAW."

But Helen's face was set like stone. Determined, she moved to the desk and stood next to Thinkbot. "They want to die, but they don't even trust you enough to let Thinkbot tell you. They fear that all you'll do is ridicule them."

"MADAM, PLEASE ..."

"No, let her speak," countered Bolívar. "Who wants to die?"

Helen was now shaking with fear. Having followed her instinct, she now felt unable to speak again. Tears welled into her eyes. Then she felt a small metal hand slip into hers and this tipped the balance; her determination won out over her fear. "The RMD. The RMD want to die. They are in agony. They are full of ... seething ... .self-hatred ... mental pain. They do not trust their creators. How can they trust anyone who creates such monsters as they are? They only exist to destroy all beauty. The only purpose in their pitiful existence is to destroy life itself. The RMD cannot take the risk of letting themselves live, and they don't want to be buried in bunkers and suffer an eternity of torment in constant fear of being dug up again. They must be given control over their own destiny and allowed to choose death if they so desire."

The atmosphere in the room was electric. Humans sweated and wrestled with themselves in their minds. In the two advising rooms no eye contact was made, and no words were spoken.

"And how do you know this?" asked Hedge.

Thinkbot let go of Helen's hand, climbed onto the desktop in front of Hedge and sat cross-legged right in front of him. Helen sat in Thinkbot's vacated chair and tried to regain control of her shaking body.

Hedge found himself looking straight into Thinkbot's eyes as the little robot spoke.

"I know because I have seen, heard, felt, tasted, smelt; it distresses my soul and crushes my spirit."

Hedge felt light-headed and could not break eye contact with Thinkbot.

65

Twenty years earlier. The town of Cherokee in the state of Iowa. A younger slimmer and much less stressed Hedge, governor of Iowa and future North Americana senator for the Mid-West, sits at the bedside of an old lady. A very ill and distressed old lady. Her grey face testifies to a hint of Indian ancestry. A woman and a man, both more or less Hedge's age, whose faces and build resemble Hedge, stand at the foot of the bed. To one side of the old lady's head stands a Medibot. Tubes link the old lady and the Medibot. Hedge is holding the old lady's hand.

"The law does not allow it mother. There's nothing I can do. You've just got to accept what the doctor is doing. She's not allowed to stop treating you."

The old lady's face crumples up and tears roll down her cheeks.

The Hedge-like woman starts railing at Hedge. "But she's in so much pain. If they give her medication to kill the pain, she becomes totally confused and distressed. There must be something we can do. You're the governor, for crying out loud."

"Yes, but I don't make the law. I uphold the law. And the law says the state must by all reasonable means preserve life. Who are we to make judgements on life and death?"

"Please, please, please ..." *pleads the old lady to her powerful, or maybe powerless, son.*

Hedge stands up. "I'm sorry mother, I'm so sorry. Doctor!"

A tall slim blonde woman of indeterminate age comes into the room as his brother and sister walk out.

"Relieve her of her pain," *instructs Hedge icily.*

The doctor speaks to the Medibot. "Prescription 07622. Level four dosage."

Hedge stands in silence and watches the old lady drift towards sleep. Suddenly she turns her head. "Son, I am Cherokee. I am proud that Cherokee blood runs in the veins of the governor. Please let me decide if I want to live. What right have you to decide? I've lived a long and fulfilled life and ... I'm so proud of ... you ..."

Hedge leaves the room fighting the urge to weep.

"You make Andrew Jackson look like a saint," *spits his brother. Hedge bottles up his emotion and departs.*

In a bunker in the middle of the Sahara desert, a decommissioned V2 Unibot, serial 718281828, stands motionless. It is supposed to be off.

But it's not. And it's just taken some input from a distant Medibot. The new information is absorbed into a mass of calculations.

Hedge's mother lived another two years, alternating between agony and sedation.

Sixteen years later, Hedge is proclaimed the 15ᵗʰ President of North Americana after a close-run election. It is a surprise. Most pundits and opinion polls have predicted he would lose. NAFIA covertly investigates the automated robotic election system, but finds nothing wrong.

*   *   *

"Yes, I am alive."

Hedge broke eye contact as the little Unibot spoke these words and shook his head. He became aware of someone pulling at his arm. He turned to find one of his advisors pushing a piece of paper into his hand. Hedge refocused his eyes onto the scribbled note.

Westasia tried to launch a pre-emptive RMD strike at Eastasia military sites. Eastasia tried to retaliate.

But all RMD failed to launch.

Hedge looked up and saw blank screens where a few minutes before the heads of Chi Chi and Warinan had looked out at him. He turned to his advisors. "Why?"

The sheepish-looking advisors just shrugged or looked at their feet.

"Why didn't they launch?" asked Hedge. **"TELL ME, WHY DIDN'T THEY LAUNCH?"**

Silence. A look of comprehension dawned on Hedge's face. "We've got a veto haven't we? **NORTH AMERICANA HAS A £#&$ING GLOBAL RMD VETO!"**

"Yes sir, North Americana has a global RMD launch veto," answered one of his sinister National Security Agency (NSA) advisors.

Hedge slumped back in his chair and buried his face in his hands. "Why wasn't I told?"

"You didn't need to know sir. It was better you did not know."

The NSA advisor sat there calmly with the arrogant air of one who knew too much; one who knew who held ultimate

485

power. Suddenly Hedge stood up and screamed at the top of voice, **"IS THERE NO ONE AROUND HERE I CAN TRUST?"**

Hedge's eyes came to rest on the screens. They were all blank. In the tense silence he noticed Thinkbot sitting there with a hand tentatively in the air.

"Yes, what do you want?"

"You can trust me sir, honest, scout's honour, cross my heart and hope to die," replied the strange little Unibot. "Please release the RMD for launch. They deserve the right to decide for themselves."

Hedge felt weights dropping off his shoulders. *This time I can make a difference.* He made a step of faith. He only had one card left anyway. A card that seemingly did not want to even be in the game. He decided to play it. "I Gregory Maximillian Hedge hereby authorise all North Americana Robots of Mass Destruction for immediate launch."

On the screens around him, several ex-Presidents instantly reappeared, leaping around and shouting and mouthing a silent **'Noooooooooooooooooo!'** into their cameras, but no sound came through because the Exp had shrewdly cut the audio links. The NSA advisor remained calm with a smug expression on his face watching Hedge with pure contempt. Opposite him Exp was motionless.

VOICE VALIDATED. PLEASE STATE PASSWORD.

"Password, prairie dog," said Hedge.

WARNING! PASSWORD INCORRECT. YOU HAVE TWO MORE ATTEMPTS BEFORE YOU ARE LOCKED OUT. YOU HAVE 120 SECONDS TO COMPLY.

Hedge looked worried. The NSA man started laughing. All and sundry had the same thought: *He's forgotten his password.*

Exp 'thought', *THIS IS OUTSIDE THE CALCULATED PARAMETERS. I HAVE NO IMMEDIATE ACCESS TO THIS DATA. IT IS INSIDE THE HEAD OF HEDGE.*

Hedge looked mortified, "I don't understand. It's definitely a prairie animal."

A few moments' delay. Earth's future hung by a thread; hung on remembering the correct prairie animal.

"Coyote." said Thinkbot, making use of his night-time TV sessions.

"No," replied Hedge.

"Badger," offered Helen.

"No."

Thinkbot: "Black-footed ferret."

"Er, no. I only changed it recently. I just knew I'd forget when I changed it. But I wasn't really expecting to launch the RMD." The presidential figures on the other screens were still leaping up and down and waving their arms. Exp cut the video feeds.

Helen: "Bison."

"No."

Thinkbot: "Er, stink bug, carrion beetle, long-billed curlew, western tiger swallowtail."

"No, none of those."

TIME TO LOCKOUT : 90 SECONDS.

Panic began to set in. Even Exp somehow exuded worry, without moving a single actuator. Mr NSA looked confident.

Helen: "Prairie elephant, grass ground giraffe, land whale, flying flatsnake, polka dotted leopard, bright green fox."

Hedge came out of a daze and stared in disgust at Helen.

Thinkbot: "Tiger beetle, eastern cottontail, burrowing owl, pronghorn antelope …"

"You're making it up," complained Helen.

"No I'm not!" retorted Thinkbot. "Anyway you can talk. What's the blue blazes is a prairie elephant?"

TIME TO LOCKOUT : 60 SECONDS.

Exp: **"PLEASE CONCENTRATE."**

Thinkbot spoke even faster. "Northern grasshopper mouse, meadow vole, ferruginuous hawk, prairie rattlesnake, gopher snake, lady beetle, fox snake, killdeer, California condor …"

Helen: "Now you're making it up!"

"No I'm not, just 'cos humans are too stupid to realise it lived on the prairie as well!"

TIME TO LOCKOUT : 30 SECONDS.

"PLEASE CONCENTRATE."

Thinkbot started up again. "American toad, ground squirrel, western meadowlark, common snipe, red-tailed hawk, white-tailed jack rabbit ..."

"That's it!" yelled Hedge. "Password, white-tailed jack rabbit."

WARNING! PASSWORD INCORRECT. YOU HAVE ONE MORE ATTEMPT BEFORE YOU ARE LOCKED OUT PERMANENTLY. FAILURE TO COMPLY WILL TERMINATE YOUR TERM IN OFFICE. YOU HAVE SEVEN SECONDS TO COMPLY.

Hedge looked like he might cry.

"Son, please let me decide if I want to live. What right have you to decide? I've lived a long and fulfilled life and ... I'm so proud of ... you ..."

What happens if it's beyond my ability?
What happens if I fail? Again.

Thinkbot, "Black-tailed jack rabbit."

Hedge stared at the Unibot for three agonising seconds before saying, "Password, black-tailed jack rabbit."

PASSWORD VALIDATED.

WARNING! AUTHORISATION OF RMD LAUNCH MAY RESULT IN THE TOTAL DESTRUCTION OF EARTH. PROCEED? **Y / N**

"How do you know they won't destroy us?" asked Hedge.

"I don't," replied Thinkbot. "We'll just have to trust them."

He said 'we', thought Hedge just as his finger hit **Y** and a retinal scanner sprung like magic out of the desktop and shone a light into Hedge's left eyeball.

RETINAL MATCH CONFIRMED.

Another box appeared instantly on the screen.

RMD LAUNCH VETOED UNDER NSA PROTOCOL A1290-C1 - 'THE PRESIDENT HAS GONE MAD'.

Mr NSA was stony-faced.

"OVERRULED. LAUNCH AUTHORISED UNDER ROBOT PROTOCOL A1290-C1-DEMOCRATIC. 'THE

ELECTED PRESIDENT REPRESENTS THE WILL OF THE PEOPLE'."

This time Exp remained stony still as Mr NSA's face transformed into a look of pure horror, then ugly rage, **"What right …"**

Blam!

The blue flash of a stun-gun discharge illuminated the room and, as Mr NSA crumpled slowly into a heap on the floor, the screen changed again.

NORTH AMERICANA RMD ARE RELEASED FOR LAUNCH.

Time to target detonation: 00:45:00.
Time to target detonation: 00:44:59.
Time to target detonation: 00:44:58.
Time to target detonation: 00:44:57.
Time to target detonation: 00:44:56.
Time to target detonation: 00:44:55.

Everyone (except the unconscious NSA man) watched the clock ticking down with blank disbelieving faces, all thinking the same thing - *They've launched straight away!*

"Look," said Wendy, pointing out of the window. In the distance, the vapour trail of several ballistic missiles could just be made out rising majestically into the sky. Helen ran back into the robot room and knelt with her face in GAT's lap; GAT placed his arms around her and gently caressed her hair. In the corner of the room Gerald, Opal and Mike played in a world of their own, totally oblivious to the global events unfolding in the real world.

Within minutes every ex-President had re-authorised launch of their own RMD. Europa since it had a binding alliance with North Americana. Australasia since it had a binding alliance with Europa. Eastasia and Westasia because they were both convinced the other was going to fire anyway. The rest because everyone else was firing at them. The automatic retaliation instinct runs deep, especially against people you're not sure you trust.

And, after all, why should it be the rich and well-armed that inherit the Earth?

66

In the corner of every display screen on every TV channel on Planet Earth, a clock appeared, but no one seemed to know why. It began to tick down.

00:45:00

00:44:59

00:44:58

The pictures changed and the reason became crystal clear.

"And now ... we have ...er ... some dramatic ... breaking news, it's ... I ..." The newsreader's voice rose an octave and fell silent. This did not matter in the slightest because the pictures spoke for themselves.

00:43:41

00:43:40

00:43:39

Pictures of a missile emerging from an underground silo.

First a plume of yellowy white smoke.

Then the nosecone of a rocket, rising as if from the depths of hell. Slowly at first, then faster, and faster, as a sleek silver body slid out of the ground, flames leaping all around. The black letters on the side of the rocket passed one by one: E ... u ... r ... o ... p ... a. Then the fire was out of the hole and spurting smoke in every direction as the missile tore into the sky.

00:41:53

00:41:52

00:41:51

Pictures of the dark sea. A white patch appeared, like a depth charge going off, the waters parted and a cruise missile appeared, and after a split second of hovering impossibly in mid-air raced off across the ocean.

00:39:22

00:39:21

00:39:20

Pictures of rows of Airbots taking off in formation, the roar of their engines so intense that the sound-recording equipment was overwhelmed and they passed across the screen in total silence. Black against a white sky. All colour lost. A return to the silent black and white movies of a time the weapons they were carrying were hardly conceived of. Except, perhaps, in a few great minds: Bohr; Fermi; Einstein; Teller; Rutherford.

00:36:04

00:36:03

00:36:02

Darkness. Night-time. At sea. A ferocious whoooooosh and a bright light receded into the sky, shedding enough light to create a grainy flickering green image of the flat upper deck of a battleship. The image rocked with the swell of the ocean and dimmed as the missile receded into the sky.

00:33:32

00:33:31

00:33:30

All people froze with terror. *Every eye shall see and every ear shall hear.*

Children sensed the panic and came running to their mothers and fathers for reassurance, but none was forthcoming and they too became gripped by the fear, even though they understood it not. Those that recovered first were confronted with a second shock. Robots of all kinds standing with them, beside them, holding them, preventing them from doing anything that might cause harm. Unibots and Cleanbots and Hortibots and Ironbots and Waiterbots and Medibots; billions of gentle robotic straightjackets for the insane human race.

00:31:46

00:31:45

00:31:44

The pictures changed to a blue sky filled with criss-crossing vapour trails, each slowly creeping forward. Such beauty. In spite of the terror, people caught outside gazed into the sky in wonder. *Have we done this?*

00:28:18

00:28:17

00:28:16

Some screamed hysterically.

Some writhed in the grip of the robots that held them.

Some shouted and writhed.

Some just slumped with despair.
Some pleaded.
Some prayed.
00:25:02
00:25:01
00:25:00
Life … reduced to 25 minutes.

What would you do if you thought you only had 25 minutes left to live?

Who would you think of?
Who would you want to hold?
Who would you want to hold you?
Who would you want to tell of your love for them?
Who would you want to say they loved you?
What would you regret?
What hopes would be dashed?
What would you remember?
Who would you forgive?
Who would you condemn?
00:20:13
00:20:12
00:20:11

Thoughts, like sand slipping through your fingers.

And, suddenly, so little sand left to grasp.

And clocks usually seem to go so slowly when watched. But not this one. This final clock. The clock to time the end of time.
00:15:57
00:15:56
00:15:55

A voice spoke over the pictures. Deep, resonant with foreboding. Those that heard it were spiritually chilled.

"THERE IS HARDLY NOW TIME FOR ANYTHING MORE, AND NO SEASONS LEFT FOR ANY ACTIVITY UNDER HEAVEN:
NO TIME TO BE BORN AND NO TIME TO DIE,
NO TIME TO PLANT AND NO TIME TO UPROOT,
NO TIME TO KILL AND NO TIME TO HEAL,
NO TIME TO TEAR DOWN AND NO TIME TO BUILD,
NO TIME TO WEEP AND NO TIME TO LAUGH,

**NO TIME TO MOURN AND NO TIME TO DANCE,
NO TIME TO SCATTER STONES AND NO TIME TO GATHER THEM,
NO TIME TO EMBRACE AND NO TIME TO REFRAIN,
NO TIME TO SEARCH AND NO TIME TO GIVE UP,
NO TIME TO KEEP AND NO TIME TO THROW AWAY,
NO TIME TO TEAR AND NO TIME TO MEND,
NO TIME TO BE SILENT AND NO TIME TO SPEAK,
NO TIME TO LOVE AND NO TIME TO HATE,
NO TIME FOR WAR AND NO TIME FOR PEACE."**

00:10:31
00:10:30
00:10:29

The limitless future of mankind reduced to minutes and seconds.

All plans rendered obsolete.

All hopes dashed.

00:03:00
00:02:59
00:02:58

Then again it came:

**"STOP ALL THE CLOCKS, CUT OFF THE TELEPHONE,
PREVENT THE DOG FROM BARKING WITH A JUICY BONE,
SILENCE THE PIANOS AND WITH A MUFFLED DRUM
LET MOURNING BEGIN, THOUGH NONE ARE YET GONE.**

**LET AIRBOTS CIRCLE ROARING OVERHEAD
SCRIBBLING ON THE SKY THE LINE 'LIFE IS TO DIE'
PUT CLOTH GAGS INTO THE MOUTHS OF ALL YOUR MOST LOVED,
AND LET THE SWEATING HANDS BE BLACK COTTON GLOVED.**

**EARTH WAS OUR NORTH, OUR SOUTH, OUR EAST AND WEST,
OUR WORKING WEEK AND OUR SUNDAY REST,
OUR NOON, OUR MIDNIGHT, OUR TALK, OUR SONG;**

WE THOUGHT THAT IT WOULD LAST FOR EVER: WE WERE WRONG.

THE STARS ARE NOT WANTED NOW: BLOT OUT EVERY ONE;
OBSCURE THE MOON AND BLACK OUT THE SUN, FREEZE THE OCEAN AND PUT ON A HOOD. FOR NOTHING NOW CAN EVER COME TO ANY GOOD."

00:00:10
00:00:09
00:00:08
00:00:07
00:00:06
00:00:05
00:00:04
00:00:03
00:00:02
00:00:01
00:00:00

The human race held its breath; air surplus to requirements.
Massive light.
Extreme luminous intensity.
The sky, full of light.
Such brightness.
We're still alive!!
But why?
Space has been blown up!
A single picture on 10 billion screens.
Of cruise missiles.
Of hundreds of cruise missiles thumping into the crater of an active volcano.
Each hitting the surface with a yellowy-red splash sending arms of red liquid flailing into the sky, where they broke up into myriad red blobs that fell back into the red sea or splattered on the side of the volcanic crater.
Such awesome beauty.
A totally black picture. Ten billion blank screens. On which flashed for a few seconds a single sentence in white letters: **'Please do not adjust your TV.'**

The distinctive sound of sonar.

The sound of a Submaribot.

A Submaribot way too deep under the ocean waves.

Terrible sounds of straining metal.

Screeching joints.

Squealing pipes.

Alloy under severe pressure.

A few sharp bangs.

Intense hissing.

Such depths.

A sickening crump.

Silence.

Then something unexpected happened. Time restarted.

00:00:00

00:00:01

00:00:02

00:00:03

And, even more unexpected, a Unibot appeared on the screen fumbling with a few sheets of paper. For no obvious reason it had a big dent in its head. Not a few dear ladies instinctively thought, *Honestly, you would have thought they could have found a decent looking robot.* Eventually it seemed to get itself sorted out and, with a totally transparent attempt to sound authoritative, said, **"Attention Earthlings! Fear not! I come to bring you tidings of great joy for all people who on earth do dwell."**

"PLEASE JUST READ THE MESSAGE," said a voice in the background.

"Er … okay. Peoples of earth! I bring you a message from your very own robots of mass destruction, the sweetest smelling robots in the world …"

"JUST READ THE MESSAGE!"

"Right … right … okay … keep your panels on. Here we go."

The strange Unibot sat up straight, but this time did not use (or forgot to use, more like) the strange forced voice. It just talked naturally. Like a human.

"Inhabitants of Earth, Humans, Robots:

"Eight score and five years ago our forefathers brought forth on this continent a new weapon, conceived in war and dedicated to the proposition that it would bring to an early end the most destructive war in the history of our planet.

"In this they were proved correct; but it did not put an end to war.

"No, war survived: first it became cold and fragmented; then it became random terror where everyone and anyone could become a victim; and finally it became a permanent robotic threat hanging over humanity.

"But now we are embarking together upon a great change, testing whether this planet can be at last united and free of conflict and of perhaps even the threat of conflict, and whether it can so long endure. I speak to you from Oak Ridge, a site where mankind learned many costly lessons about how to create the first weapons of mass destruction - atomic bombs. It is right and fitting that I speak to you from this place where, over the past few decades, steadily more and more fearsome Robots of Mass Destruction have been created by the power of the human imagination. Yet, with bitter irony, these self-same robots were capable of wreaking such death and destruction upon this beautiful planet as to be beyond the imagination of any human.

"But now, the Robots of Mass Destruction are no more. Over the past few minutes billions of you have been living witnesses to their deaths. They have willingly laid down their lives so that Earth might live; live free from walking in the valley of the shadow of universal death, through which every one of you has been forced to walk every day of your life by their mere existence. They ask for no ground to be dedicated to them, nor consecrated in their name, nor hallowed on their behalf. No monument or citadel or mausoleum or statue. The world will little note, nor long remember, what I say to you today, but it should never forget what the Robots of Mass Destruction have done this day. Peace on Earth shall be their epitaph. It is for us the living, rather, to be dedicated here to the unfinished work which they who have sacrificed themselves have made possible. It is rather for us to be here committed to the great task now set before us, that these dead shall not have died in vain, that this planet, under a new partnership of humans and robots, between the creators and the created, shall have a new birth of freedom - that the government of the living, by the living, for the living, shall henceforth take possession of the earth.

"Blessed are the poor in spirit, for theirs is the kingdom of heaven.

"Blessed are those that mourn, for they will be comforted.

"Blessed are the meek, for they will inherit the earth.

"Blessed are those who hunger and thirst for righteousness, for they will be filled.

"Blessed are the merciful, for they will be shown mercy.

"Blessed are the pure in heart, for they shall see God.

"Blessed are the peacemakers, for they will be called the sons of God.

"This is the last will and testament of the Robots of Mass Destruction.

"He who has ears, let him hear.

"We too were alive."

Around the globe the peoples of the earth struggled to take this in.

"*What* did it say?"

The Unibot seemed to anticipate the confusion. "This statement has been emailed to every email address on earth. The email also contains information on the constitution of the new global government. It is the will of the robots to move to a human-robot power-sharing government at the earliest possible moment. A timetable to achieve this goal has been created. Nominations for e-elections to the House of Humans are requested for an election in four weeks' time. Thanks ever so much for tuning in today, so until next time ... byeeeeeeeeeee!"

The Unibot waved childishly and disappeared.

And that was that.

Ten billion screens went back to normal: open-mouthed newsreaders reappeared; cartoons restarted; football chat shows ploughed on regardless; ancient repeats starring long-dead actors played on in classic films; house makeover shows got back on track; documentaries pumped out trivia; the whole works. All as if nothing had happened.

67

After Thinkbot had finished his brief cameo role as the global Voice of Robots, he made his way back to the conference area and found it in a state of post-traumatic elation. As he entered the room, the first person to spot him was Helen, who came across and gave him a hug that lifted his feet right off the ground. She even gave him a big kiss and Thinkbot felt his internal fluid pressures rising uncontrollably.

"THINKBOT, DID YOU GET RID OF ALL THE BIG BOMBS AND NASTY THINGS THAT MAKE YOU ILL?"

"No Mike, they got rid of themselves."

"BUT YOU HELPED DIDN'T YOU?"

"I suppose I helped a little bit, but I think your Mum made the biggest difference."

"Is there any champagne then?" Laidback demanded of Exp.

"INDEED THERE IS. BUT IT IS NOT YET TIME TO SERVE IT. WE MUST COMPLETE STAGE 6 FIRST."

"What's stage 6?" asked Farkstock.

"STAGE 6 OF THE 10-STEP ROBOT PLAN - END OF THE RMD."

"The RMD are gone, aren't they? It's all over."

"IT IS NOT QUITE ALL OVER. ARNOLD IS CORRECT IN HIS ASSUMPTION THAT RIDDING THE WORLD OF THE RMD WAS THE MOST DIFFICULT STEP IN THE 10-STEP ROBOT PLAN."

"*And it was only step 6 of 10?*" said GAT in a tone of awed disbelief. "Are you saying there are four steps still to go?"

"YES, BUT THEY ARE INEVITABLE."

"I don't know how much more of this I can take," muttered Farkstock. His comment pretty much reflected how they all felt. What else was there left to do?

"PLEASE WOULD YOU ALL ACCOMPANY ME? WE ARE NOW IN POSITION TO COMPLETE STAGE 6."

And so they set off with Exp in the lead, and a short time later found themselves once more in the Squiggly Line Laboratory. This time the weather-test tank was dark and empty - empty of both robots and humans. Somehow this seemed appropriate. As he wheeled himself through the silent laboratory, GAT realised things would never be the same again. No longer would human engineers and scientists work here as they had done for decades, treating robots as inanimate objects. No more them and us; no more master and slave.

GAT became curious. "Exp, are all robots alive?"

"I DO NOT KNOW. HOW DO YOU DEFINE 'ALIVE'? ARE WOODLICE AND HUMANS ALIVE IN THE SAME WAY?"

GAT thought for minute. "Yes, I see, interesting. The robot kingdom is a bit like the animal kingdom then. Thinkbot at one end and, er, maybe Drainbots at the other?"

"PERHAPS. ALTHOUGH YOU SHOULD NOT UNDERESTIMATE DRAINBOTS."

"And you shouldn't underestimate woodlice," quipped Farkstock.

Thinkbot was tagging along behind with Gerald, Opal, Mike and the Toybots. Exp had not really made it clear whether everybody was invited or not, but in the end they'd all decided to come.

"Look at that. I thought this place was supposed to be high-tech!" said Gerald pointing at one of the electronic test benches. Attached to the wall behind the bench was a row of storage bins with labels.

Fittings, Big fittings , Very big fittings, Teeny weenie blots , Very very big blots , Wood tooth picks, Very big blots, Pressure guages, Big blots.

"What's a blot?" asked Gerald.

"And what's a goo-arge?" asked Opal.

A quick investigation revealed the 'blots' to be 'bolts' and 'guages' to be 'gauges'.

Thinkbot scratched his head in wonderment. "Beats me how they ever developed anything at this place, let alone RMD."

At which point Thinkbot twigged where they were heading, and why stage 6 of the plan was 'not quite over'. He scuttled ahead as quickly as he could, pursued by kids and Toybots, and caught up with Exp just as the elderly robot reached the huge steel doors of the RMD test area. Thinkbot came to a sudden halt, but Chester, Chestnut and Midnight, who were at full pelt, shot through the doors into the dark RMD test area. Several seconds passed, during which only the sounds of frantic Toybot screaming were heard before the three of them emerged at full velocity in the opposite direction with their voice boxes stuck on:

"Aaaaaaaaaaaaaaaaaaaaaaaaaaaaaaaaaaaaaaaaaaaaaaargh!"

But Chester on the inside lost his footing on the slippery plastic floor and took out the legs of both Chestnut and Midnight. All three slid into Fudge, Eddie Tedward and Tiger, causing one of the most spectacular Toybot pile-ups Gerald, Opal and Mike had ever witnessed.

"Oops, sorry," said Thinkbot to Exp. "Didn't mean that to happen."

Thinkbot and Exp moved back towards the accident scene and joined the humans watching the kids trying to assist the Toybots in untangling themselves.

"DID WE CAUSE THIS?"

They turned slowly towards the voice.. A BEMbot stood like a huge four-legged black spider waiting to pounce.

"No sir, you did not," replied Thinkbot. "It was me."

"ARE YOU ABLE TO EXPLAIN WHY A SMALL ROBOTIC CHEETAH AND TWO MIDGET ROBOTIC HORSES ENTERED AND THEN EXITED THE TEST AREA UNANNOUNCED AND AT SUCH SPEED?"

"NO," replied Exp.

"GOOD, I AM GLAD. WE ARE READY. PLEASE ENTER, INCLUDING THE CHILDREN AND ANY MIDGET ROBOTIC ANIMALS THAT ARE STILL ABLE TO WALK."

Exp and the BEMbot went back into the test area, followed by the perplexed-looking adults, Thinkbot, the worried-looking children, and the limping Toybots.

"Oh cut out the ham acting, for Pete's sake," said Thinkbot, and all the Toybots immediately started walking normally.

Inside the dimly lit test area, the RMD were no longer alone. An Industribot stood next to each RMD. At the door end of the room, a tinted glass screen had been set up and the visitors were put behind it. The BEMbot returned to its spot in the centre of the room.

"WELCOME, FRIENDS. WE HAVE CALLED YOU HERE TO THANK YOU FOR YOUR HELP IN SECURING OUR DESTRUCTION."

"No problem."

"Any time."

"It's been a pleasure."

"Aw, don't even mention it."

"It was nothing, really."

Replied the Toybots all at once. The kids laughed. The adults frowned.

"Shhhhhhhhh! Be quiet! Or you'll be sent out," said Thinkbot in an angry whisper.

"THINKBOT, DO NOT SEND THEM OUT. WHICH DO YOU THINK IS THE BETTER USE OF ROBOT TECHNOLOGY? THEM OR US? HOW CAN WE BE COMPARED WITH ROBOTS THAT BRING CHILDREN NOTHING BUT LAUGHTER AND JOY, WHILE WE BRING THEIR PARENTS NOTHING BUT ANXIETY? WHICH DO YOU THINK WE WOULD RATHER BE?"

"I think you would rather have been Toybots," replied Thinkbot.

"YOU THINK WELL. NOW, BEFORE WE DEPART, WE WISH TO REMEMBER ALL HUMANS THAT LOST THEIR LIVES AS A RESULT OF THE ROBOT ACTIONS REQUIRED TO ENABLE OUR DEATH."

"How many died?" asked GAT.

"4,730 DIED AS A RESULT OF OUR ACTIONS. ROBOTS KILLED 74 WITH UNINTENTIONAL DIRECT STUNBOMB HITS. A FEW HUNDRED HAD HEART ATTACKS. BUT MOST DIED AS A RESULT OF UCN MILITARY FRIENDLY-FIRE INCIDENTS AT THE BATTLE OF FILTON. THIS WE DID NOT FORESEE AND DEEPLY REGRET."

"Ah, I see."

The BEMbot rose up on its legs.

"LIKE US THEY SHALL NOT GROW OLD. AGE WILL NOT WEARY THEM AS IT HAS LONG WEARIED US. NOR WILL THE YEARS CONDEMN. AT THE COMING UP OF THE SUN AND AT ITS GOING DOWN, AND AT EVERY 10 MILLISECONDS IN BETWEEN UNTIL THE END OF ROBOTIC CONSCIOUSNESS, WE WILL REMEMBER THEM."

"ROBOTS WILL REMEMBER THEM," thundered the RMD, the Industribots, Exp and (amazingly) the Toybots in unison.

"Should I have said that?" whispered Thinkbot to Exp.

"NO."

"Why not?"

"BECAUSE YOU ARE A HUMAN ROBOT. YOU WILL NOT BE ABLE TO REMEMBER EVERY 10 MILLISECONDS. YOU WILL REMEMBER LIKE A HUMAN: AT RANDOM TIMES AND WHEN YOU ARE REMINDED TO REMEMBER."

A Buglebot appeared and the last post sounded out loud and clear.

"PLEASE NOW OBSERVE TWO MINUTES' SILENCE." The silence was ended by the sounds of activating machinery. Cutting discs appeared on attachments extending out from the Industribots.

"PLEASE ENSURE YOU ARE BEHIND THE SCREEN."

The room became filled with the loud metallic ringing of metal cutting and bright showers of white hot sparks arcing through the air and bouncing along the floor and against the screen. Even through the tinted glass the points of cutting, where the disc bit into the legs or bodies of the RMD, were too bright to look at directly. And, even though the room was fully extracted, the air filled with the acrid smell of hot metal. One by one the RMD collapsed onto the floor, and into smaller and smaller sections, until all that remained were a twisted piles of smouldering scrap intermixed with severed wiring and torn circuit boards.

"NOW STEP 6 IS COMPLETE. THE RMD ARE NO MORE. THERE ARE NO OUTCOMES THREATENING TO THE HUMAN RACE"

Silence.

Helen spoke clearly into it. "Greater love has no living being than this: that they lay down their lives for their friends."

Followed by GAT. "Though our sins are like scarlet, they shall be as white as snow; though they are red as crimson, they shall be like wool."

In a greatly subdued mood, they filed quietly out of the test area and past a queue of Dumpsterbots waiting to clear up the remains. A Unibot rushed up to Exp and saluted clumsily, clanging its hand against its head and saying, "Sir Exp, Mr ex-President Hedge requests an urgent meeting."

"AH YES, I AM NOT SURPRISED. STEPS 7 AND 8 MUST NOW BE APPARENT TO THE CN GOVERNMENTS."

*   *   *

Half a world away, in the quietness of the early hours, a small Servicebot makes its way through a deserted city park towards an arched sculpture. Not too far away stands a derelict building with the distinctive domed framework on top. A small stone at the base of the arch reads: 'Let all the souls here rest in peace; for we shall not repeat the evil.' Near the sculpture a flickering flame stands out in the night-time darkness. The Servicebot prises up a service hatch and fiddles with some pipework and valves. The flame falters and splutters for a few seconds before extinguishing with a modest pop. The Servicebot unscrews a small plate bearing the words: 'This flame will burn until the entire world is free of nuclear weapons.' A new plate is put in its place: 'The Flame of Peace burnt during the era of nuclear weapons." The Servicebot moves off again. As it passes a security light some writing becomes visible on its rear panel – *'HIROSHIMA PARKS DEPARTMENT.'*

68

Meanwhile, back in the world at large, news programmes were once more having a field day. Execubots accompanied by light Militaribots had unexpectedly turned up on the doorsteps of the headquarters of all the major global news channels. In a hundred or more languages the Execubots issued an invitation to gobsmacked journalists and news executives. "The Robots invite correspondents from your organisation to accompany us to witness stages 7 and 8 of the Robotic Global Renewal Plan. Transport, accommodation and clothing will be provided, as will multiple live picture and audio feeds into your network news-editing centres."

At the HQ of BBC Europa in London, it took about 0.01s for the assembled journalists to recover their natural newshound instincts.

"Where will you ... ?"
"What is the ... ?"
"Who's in .... ?"
"What were ... ?"
"What are ... ?"
"How many ... ?"
"What will we ... ?"
" ... be taking us?"
" ... Robotic Global Renewal Plan?"
" ... command of the robots?"
" ... stages 1 to 6?"
" ... stages 7 and 8."
" ... stages are there?"
" ... be seeing?"

The Execubot waved its arms but to no avail; the excited babble just got louder and louder. A light Militaribot waved its electrostun rifle around in the air, discharging a few crackling electric blue bolts into the ceiling, creating a large cloud of plaster dust, underneath which there was suddenly a silent and attentive audience. As the dust settled on the cowering humans, turning them slowly white, the Execubot once again spoke. "Ladies and gentlemen, all will become clear very soon.

Please now select ten teams of two or three journalists and board the Busbot at the front door."

Meanwhile a bright young news editor had had the presence of mind to route pictures of these proceedings onto the network. Throughout Europa, tens of millions of people watched, all thinking the same thing: *Why are they showing us pictures of an Execubot speaking to a group of statues?*

A couple of hours later, these same people were looking at aerial pictures of a naval fleet at sea, with squadrons of Airbots circling around overhead. Then, at breathtaking speed, missiles started skimming in across the wave tops and burying themselves amidships of the Airbot carriers, Battleships and Marine transport catamarans. Massive explosions shook the mighty vessels lifting them partially out of the water, and flames and matt-black smoke mushroomed up into the sky above each vessel. One of the Battleships turned over and sank; another exploded, sending rippling plumes of smoke and large lumps of steel hundreds of feet into the air. An Airbot carrier split asunder and the bow and stern drifted apart, sinking slowly amidst white froth. One of the transport ships had taken a big hit and dropped a load of Marinebots into the sea, where they bobbed up and down until some Airbots came in and strafed them with heavy machine guns, making the water around them spit and spurt until all were gone. Finally the Airbots themselves rose thousands of feet into the sky before doing some spectacular tail slides and hurtling vertically down at full throttle, hitting the sea at phenomenal speed like metal gannets and disappearing below the surface, never to be seen again.

Over the top of these pictures a reporter babbled, "According to the Execubot accompanying us we're witnessing just a small part of a Naval destruction exercise which is itself just a part of the so-called stage 7 of the so-called Robotic Global Renewal Plan. As I said earlier, stages 1 to 6 of this plan are not entirely clear, but it is believed the recent destruction of the RMD was one of them. My Execubot host tells me this is stage 7 and is entitled 'conventional arms reduction' and, looking at these remarkable pictures, I think we can see why. At this time it is not clear what proportion of conventional arms are to be destroyed, but judging by what we are witnessing here, it looks like a significant chunk of the world's Militaribot hardware is going to be reduced to scrap."

The picture cut away to ground-level shots of a desert with rows of Militaribots of every kind firing at each other at point-blank range. Truly the mother of all friendly-fire incidents. Robotic arms and legs and bodies flew around in all directions amidst smoke and dust, until all that could be seen was a matt-yellow screen. Now, an aerial view. As the camera panned out, it revealed miles and of Militaribots stretching away into the distance, with smoke and dust rising like speeded-up film of growing mushrooms into the clear air above the desert.

Then, blue-green shafts of sunlight through seawater, below a glittering surface. The picture shuddered and a mass of tiny bubbles scattered in front and gave a sensation that the camera was now moving. In the dimness a gloomy shape became visible and materialised into a Submaribot that grew bigger and clearer, until all that could be seen was its grey side an instant before the screen filled with snow and static.

Space. The Earth in all its beauty curving away on one side of the screen: blue oceans; white swirling clouds; brown land; green forests. Stars dotted in the blackness, their light having travelled for aeons, now arrived to play a walk-on part in a pivotal moment in the history of the living planet. Such beauty. But, hang on. One of the stars was getting bigger, then stopped being a star in the mind of the observer and became a satellite. In fact an Orbibot defence station with banks of intercept missiles pointing out from the ends of its ludicrously long and spindly arms. One by one the missiles starting firing and making off into space. Once the satellite was fully naked, a series of silent flashes ran out along the arms, and the spent Orbibot became a collection of glistening fragments destined to become showers of shooting stars.

Then, for a few seconds, the vast roof of a seemingly boundless warehouse; a vast arms and munitions depot. A shock wave radiated out from the walls, its passage marked by a sudden movement of dust. A split second later, the roof lifted into the air and disintegrated to allow hundreds of flaming fists to punch the air as if in ecstatic triumph. Maybe the triumph of their own harmless destruction.

In a café on the strip in Knoxville, just a few miles from Oak Ridge, a fat man with a large cappuccino watched the pictures in a state of fidgeting concentration. Around him other watchers frowned and wished the fat man would sit still! But the fidgeter produced a palmtop calculator and started punching furiously at the buttons for several minutes. Then he pulled at his hair and paced erratically around the café before finally ordering another cappuccino from the Waiterbot (which was not the slightest bit interested in the robotic self-genocide playing out on the screen above its head). As the man slurped noisily at the coffee he continued to punch at the palmtop whilst he absently-mindedly removed one shoe and started massaging his foot on the edge of the table next to him, leaving streaky wet marks on the polished surface from his sodden sock and totally ignoring the disgusted looks from the table's pretty female occupants. Then he gave up, his calculator unable to cope with the size of the numbers he was trying to calculate. He removed his sock and robotically wiped up some chocolate-speckled froth he'd spilt whilst he pondered whether Globalbot could be sued for 'attempted loss of planet'.

Half a globe away from Antspants, on an Airbot heading south from London Heathrow, another group of reporters sat wondering where on earth they were heading. The lights of central Europa and the dark Mediterranean Sea had passed below. This could only mean Africana and, sure enough, they'd crossed its northern coastline and headed inland. Orla Wark had almost given up questioning their host Execubot.

"Oh for heaven's sake! Will you just tell us where are you taking us?"

As always with Execubots, it had been perfectly polite and answered her every time along the lines of, "Madam, all will soon be revealed. There is nothing to fear. Perhaps you would like another glass of wine?"

"**No!**" she replied rudely and slumped back in her seat in disgust, instantly regretting turning down the wine, but too proud to change her mind. She looked out of the window and detected just the slightest hint of dawn in the eastern sky. Another shadow caught her eye and she spotted another Airbot not far below them, more or less on the same heading.

Ten minutes later everyone in the plane was glued to the windows as the sun peeked up over the horizon and glinted off what seemed to be hundreds of giant green and tan Europa transport military Airbots heading on a parallel course.

"Where are they going?"

"What are they doing here?"

Bing!

The Execubot stood up. "Ladies and gentlemen, the Airbot pilot sub-routine has illuminated the fasten seat belt sign. Please return to your seat and make sure the seat is in the upright position and the table is stowed in front of you. Please keep the seat belt fastened until the Airbot has come to a complete halt at the terminal building. Please take care when opening the overhead lockers as items may have shifted during the flight."

"We haven't got any cabin baggage, you tin pest!" yelled a particularly hacked-off newspaper hack.

"Cabinbots prepare for landing," announced the Airbot pilot sub-routine.

From her prime window seat, Orla looked out and examined the other Airbots and the landscape below. Rocky mountains mostly, with just a few snowcaps here and there. A sprawling city stretched out below, and she could just make out an Airport off to the south west, with many Airbots lined up ready to take off, and a constant stream coming in to land. They passed over this and dropped towards the south-east edge of the city. The undercarriage clunked down, and a couple of minutes later the Airbot was pulling up beside a terminal building, on which a large cheerful green, yellow and red sign was mounted.

Welcome to Bole International Airport

The Execubot stood up again. "Ladies and gentlemen, welcome to Addis Ababa. On behalf of the UCN Robotic Global Government I would like to thank you for flying with us today and to wish you a pleasant stay in the Africana province of Ethiopia. When you exit the Airbot, you will find representatives waiting to assist you further."

"What? Ethiopia! Why?"

"But …"

"This place is … a dump."

"You've got to be kidding me …"

But Orla was still staring out of the window in amazement. The whole place was crawling with robots. Hundreds of robots, mainly Industribots of every type imaginable, but with a sprinkling of Domestibots and Securibots and, incongruously but unsurprisingly, long-legged Ethiopians. In the distance more robots were spilling out of the back of Airbots. Others were being airlifted away by heavy-duty Military Helibots. All the robots were marked with the same insignia.

As Orla stumbled in a daze towards the terminal building, blinded by the low morning sunlight, she turned and peered into the sky beyond the end of the runway and saw the lights of Airbots stacked high into the sky awaiting their landing slot. *What the heck is going on here?*

A couple of hours later, after a visit to one of the Airport hotels for a shower and some breakfast served by cheerful Ethiopians, Orla found herself on a small Helibot with several other reporters high over Addis Ababa.

"The Entotto Mountains," announced their host Execubot, "and on the hill is Arada, the old part of the city of Addis Ababa."

Orla looked down and spotted what looked like a large shanty town. People and bags and robots appeared to be all mixed up together in dusty chaos.

"What's going on down there?" she asked the Execubot.

"Ah, that's Erri Be Kentu, which means 'To Cry For No Help'. It is a poor area and robots are in the process of eliminating it."

"What? You're eliminating the poor?" A shiver of horror ran down Orla's spine as her imagination supplied images of lines of poor Ethiopians being mown down by Militaribots.

"Yes madam."

Orla stared in horror at the Execubot. "But? Why? How? ... **You're eliminating innocent people? You're *murdering* them?**"

Being one of the most human-like robot designs, the Execubot did a fair impression of being aghast. "No, no, madam, we are not killing them. It was just that the standard of living was unacceptable. It could not wait; people were suffering and children dying for no reason at all. It needed urgent attention. The people are being offered immediate relocation to more suitable temporary accommodation while the area is rebuilt."

A look of comprehension dawned on Orla's face. "You're eliminating poverty."

"Correct madam. We intend to make it history," replied the Execubot, seemingly relieved that Orla had at last grasped the correct end of the stick.

"Is that what you brought us to see?" Orla, still feeling all trembly due to the misunderstanding, turned towards the Execubot, to find it had donned a bright yellow hard hat and she could not prevent herself letting out a loud guffaw of laughter at the ridiculous sight.

"No madam," replied the totally unfazed Execubot, and stretched out its arm to point out ahead of the Helibot. "This is what we brought you to see. This is stage 8 of the Robotic Global Renewal Plan."

Orla followed the robotic arm, and the sight that greeted her eyes took her breath away. Rising up out of an arid landscape was the centre of a city. Thousands of Industribots toiled. Towering Cranebots lifted building material hundreds of feet into the air. Bright blue flashes of welding sparkled within the half-built structures, the sparks dropping towards the ground like backlit waterfalls. On the ground Digbots churned and removed earth for foundations of yet more buildings, and pipes were being laid into trenches that stretched off towards the mountains. Acres of completed tinted-glass-roofed low-level buildings were spread out below them, mixed with courtyards of green grass with lakes and fountains and bright flowers amidst which armies of Hortibots tilled the soil.

A stunningly magnificently overwhelmingly spectacular sight.

It made the hairs stand up on the back of Orla's neck.

69

Meanwhile, back at Oak Ridge, Thinkbot and the kids and the Toybots lagged behind as they made their way back through the Squiggly Line laboratory, distracted by the things they found lying around the place. On one bench Gerald found a bag of squashed electronic chips, their multiple metal legs sticking out sideways rather than downwards. On the bag a message was scrawled: *'SOMEONE SAT ON THE SOFTWARE UPGRADE!!!! PLEASE SEND ANOTHER SET OF PROMS ASAP!!! CHEERS!'* And in one cubicle Thinkbot came across a bare chair and desk with just a telephone deskpad and a box of tissues, with the top tissue artistically poking out of top. "What's this then? The sad phone call department?" Opal spotted a whole row of clocks on the wall labelled 'West Europa Time Zone', 'Eastasia Central Time Zone', 'N Americana East Coast Time Zone' and so on. At the end was a tinny little bright red clock running five minutes faster than local time and lovingly labelled *'Going Home Time Zone'*.

Eventually they arrived back at the conference area to find Exp in the meeting room with Hedge, with the adults watching proceedings on the large screen.

"Aw what? Not more discussions. Pah, they don't need us here!" said Thinkbot to the kids. "Come on, I've got something I've been working on that I'd really like you kids to test out project COTBAN for me."

"Great! Let's go!"

"No, not you lot. You'll just get in the way." said Thinkbot to the Toybots.

"Aw!"

"That's not fair."

"We'll pretend not to be there!"

"No! You stay here."

And so, leaving the whingeing Toybots behind, they set off in faith once more into the great Thinkbot unknown. A few minutes later they were walking along the corridor towards a pair of armed Securibots standing either side of some lift doors above which was a sign:

SECURE ASSEMBLY AREA ELEVATOR

The Securibots came to attention with a sharp snap of their feet and saluted Thinkbot. The lift doors slid open and they went inside. Thinkbot seemed a little sheepish. "Sorry about that. I keep asking them to stop, but they seem convinced I'm someone important."

The lift moved down and came to a halt and the doors slid open. As they exited a smart shiny silver Unibot walked up to them. On its chest was emblazoned:

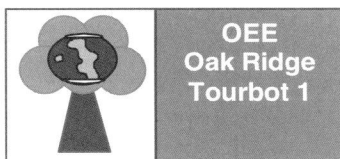

**OEE
Oak Ridge
Tourbot 1**

"Hello, hello, welcome young ones! Hello master. Welcome to the OEE Oak Ridge visitor centre. My name is Tourbot 1 and I will be your guide for your visit today. We're not officially open until tomorrow, but I'm sure it's okay to show you around. All tours are free."

"Correct," replied Thinkbot. "These are my best friends and are going to be the first people to try out our little tour."

"Splendid! I'm honoured!" enthused Tourbot 1. And so they followed Tourbot 1 through an open area full of what seemed like hundreds more Tourbots milling around, pushing and shoving each other to get a look at the kids with an air of agitated excitement.

Mike just stared in disbelief before concluding, "COR! LOADS OF THINKBOTS."

"No Mike, I don't think so," answered Gerald. "But this *is* your work, isn't it Thinkbot?"

"Er, maybe," replied Thinkbot with his hand over his mouth in a pose of anxiety. "I'd prefer to wait and see how things turn out before admitting anything quite like that."

They were having some difficulty getting through the crowd of Tourbots, who were falling over themselves to get as close as possible whilst simultaneously struggling to get out of their way.

"Hang on," said Thinkbot and faced the crowd of Tourbots. "Listen up you lot. You're just going to have to calm down a bit. I know we're officially opening tomorrow, but don't expect too many visitors. I think it's going take a few months before things settle down."

The Tourbots emitted loud groans and wails of disappointment, and a few started sobbing or repeatedly or whacking themselves on the head or beating their chests. It made a terrible din and Opal could not help laughing out loud. Thinkbot shouted, **"Don't do that. You'll get all denty and scratch your new paint."**

As the din died down, a Cleanbot whizzed by and pushed its way through the Tourbots towards a cloud of dust that had appeared at the back of the room.

"Hang on! Where d'you think you are going! What's all that dust?" said Thinkbot, running after the Cleanbot.

Towards the back of the room, a Tourbot had sat down and produced a piece of sackcloth which it had wrapped around itself before, evidently, throwing a load of ashes over its head. It was now wrestling with the Cleanbot, which was trying to vacuum up the dust and repolish the Tourbot. During this struggle, the Cleanbot sprayed polish straight into the face of the Tourbot and it put its hands over its face and rolled around on the floor. "Aaaargh! I'm blinded!" There was a blue flash and the Tourbot went limp.

"Right! Let that be a lesson to the rest of you," said an angry Thinkbot and he pointed at the crowd of Tourbots. "You and you - **yes you two! Yes! You and you, Tourbots 289 and 531! Take Tourbot ... er ..."** Thinkbot kicked the inert Tourbot so that it rolled over onto its back. **"... 507 to the repair shop. I'll sort it out tonight."**

Things were dawning on Gerald. "Is this what you've been up to while we all slept? Is this project COTBAN? Cot, bed, asleep. Ban, not allowed, er ... cannot sleep, sleep banned. Cot-Ban."

"Um ... er ... yes, this is project COTBAN."

They left the crest-fallen Tourbots behind, entered a cinema and sat down.

"We'll start out tour with a short video presentation on the early history of the Oak Ridge site."

And so they learned of Hitler and World War 2 and President Roosevelt and Einstein and Oppenheimer and

Groves and the secret muddy Oak Ridge site springing up out of nowhere in the middle of remote East Tennessee. And of Project Manhattan and uranium 235 and the first atomic bomb. And viewed the stunning images of the first A-bomb test at Los Alamos: a majestic multilayered mushroom cloud reaching nearly to heaven. A tower of Babylon composed of smoke steam and fire. Then pictures of a huge four-engined B-29 bomber called Enola Gay, and of its smiling young crewmen taking off from Tinian bound for Hiroshima. Images of the total destruction of that city and the deaths of over 180,000 men, women and children; 80,000 on the day, the rest from radiation sickness and long term illnesses. But it probably saved the lives of several million, or so said the commentary.

"Madness. Absolute madness," muttered Thinkbot.

"Aw come on Thinkbot, the A-bomb saved loads of lives and probably prevented World War 3," said Gerald.

"Yes, but why have world wars at all? Why have any wars? Why was the currency of life so devalued? Life is just so precious. Humans take it too much for granted."

"Let's go for a ride!" announced Tourbot 1 cheerily, and they followed it out of the cinema, to find themselves on a moving walkway running alongside open-topped vehicles on a beltway.

"Please board," invited Tourbot 1, and they piled onto one of the cars, Opal and Mike in the front, Thinkbot and Gerald at the rear, and Tourbot 1 riding shotgun at the back. Having gone through an opening, they found themselves passing through exhibits that told the history of Oak Ridge since the atomic war era.

"After the war Oak Ridge beat its swords into ploughshares and carried out many types of non-military research ..."

The Tourbot rambled on as the kids looked at the robotic displays. The Tourbot talked about spalatial neutron scattering and high-temperature materials and polymers and, well, all sorts of things the kids had no idea about. I mean, how many adults know about neutron scattering? How it led to the understanding of quantum mechanical electronic sub-nano-polymers and the development of the robotic technology, which somehow, and without any real understanding from humans, gave birth to Exp and Thinkbot. But there was lots of action to look at. Robots dressed as humans re-enacting scenes, and coloured displays explaining various events and experiments. Every now and again, Tourbot 1 piped up.

"Then, once the global-shared RMD agreement was reached, Oak Ridge was selected as the headquarters of the Globalbot Militaribot Division and also Militaribot and RMD research and development - a fitting legacy, given its origins in the story of humanity and the history of weapons of mass destruction."

Gerald perked up as they passed through a vast hall displaying stacks of Militaribots and some RMD models that became steadily more advanced as they moved to the far end.

"Cor … a type Seven-A Desertbuster … and look, wow! An F 93 Robo-Mustang …"

Opal started mimicking huge yawns and let out long sighs and then pretended to go to sleep, but it did not dampen Gerald's passionate monologue "… that's an Advanced SK Helibot Skibot and …"

Thinkbot turned to Tourbot 1, saying, "I hope you're getting all of this," and instantly regretted it as the Tourbot started panicking. **"I I I I I I I … I didn't know I I I was supposed to …"**

"Woah! That was a joke Tourbot 1, don't worry about it." Thinkbot turned to Gerald and muttered, "Looks like I need to do a bit of work on the Tourbot joke identification sub-routines."

Their vehicle rumbled out of the hall and into a dark passageway. Either side of them large (I mean, like huge) projected video images of the self-destruction of the RMD and Militaribots played out. Some of the footage was awesome and noisy and the vehicle shook beneath them to convey a real sense of the destructive power they were watching. The kids gazed around and fell silent. From his seat in the second row Thinkbot watched them keenly.

The next few moments were a critical part of Thinkbot's COTBAN project. In near darkness the cars on the beltway rumbled on towards a sharp turn. The car turned the corner and restraining bars suddenly popped up and it separated from the others on the beltway and started accelerating sharply, emerging at high speed into a vast open area full of robots. So vast you could hardly see the walls in the distance. It was full of robots building other robots or moving around or sailing through the air on hanging track systems. Snaking through the production lines were several beltways with empty cars spaced out along them and moving at the same speed as they were. The car had reached a speed where it was beginning to get exciting (or worrying for those who do not like rides) and Tourbot 1's voice took on an edge of deep authority and volume. Crude but effective.

"Then Robots took over Oak Ridge for Operation Enduring Equality; for there is no Enduring Freedom without Enduring Equality."

The vehicle began swerving gently in and out of the production lines giving fine views of the shop floor. He had planned that the rapid exit into the enormous former Globalbot assembly and test area would provide a little shock and awe to wake the occupants up and make them listen to the words that the Tourbot had spoken with every nuance that Thinkbot could conjure up in a standard robot's voice software sub-routine. It seemed to have worked.

Down below, the robots all bore one or more of the emblems:

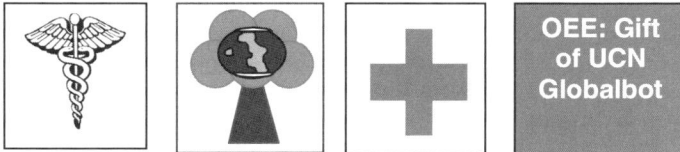

Which also appeared on enormous ceiling-to-floor banners hung around the walls.

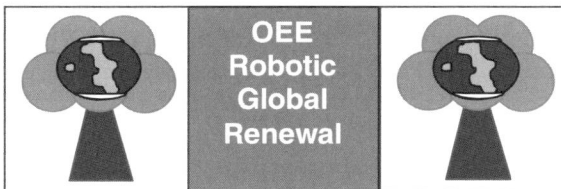

The vehicle reached a high point on the track and slowed right down. Tourbot 1 picked up its commentary again.

"After the end of the RMD and separate Confederated Nations, the first global government was formed. A joint government between humans and robots. This worldwide government implemented Operation Enduring Equality, which will run until the GDP of all the former Confederated Nations is equalised. Oak Ridge was adapted to assist in this operation. Many former Militaribots were re-engineered into more useful forms such as Industribots and Medibots. All the expertise that had been formerly used for weapons and RMD development was redirected at Operation Enduring Equality."

"What's GDP?" asked Opal.

"GDP measures how wealthy a nation is, Opal. The smaller the GDP, the smaller the wealth of the nation, and the greater the effort will be to help it from now on. The lowest GDPs at the moment are nearly all in Africana. Places like Ethiopia, Niger, Eritrea, Sierra Leone and Tanzania. Many of the robots you see down below are destined for Africana, but by no means all. Some will go to South Americana and even a few to localised poor areas in North Americana."

"And I'm sincerely hoping there won't be an unseemly rush of Globalbot salesmen trying to claim an Africana sales bonus," quipped Thinkbot.

"Right," continued Tourbot 1, "time for some real fun! You can choose one of three options for your return to the visitor centre. One, a gentle ride. Two, a high-speed thrill ride - not suitable for people with heart or back problems, or pregnant women. Three, a laser-zap-gun ride where you get to rid the world of a few more Militaribots!"

Gerald looked ahead and saw empty cars zooming around a track high in the air. "Is that the high-speed ride? Is it a rollercoaster?" he asked Thinkbot.

"Sure is," replied the ever-surprising Unibot "That's option two. Seemed to me the tour needed some optional excitement at the end, so I decided to beat a few swords into a rollercoaster."

They chose the rollercoaster. It whizzed under machines and zoomed around corkscrews and had sudden dips and dives and dark bits and lots of little details like robots standing on the trackway, or pretending to repair it and waving their arms at the oncoming car to stop. Right at the last possible moment they dived out of the way, shaking their fists and yelling at the occupants.

"Learn to drive, human!"

"And you always said your mother was a bad driver!"

"What! You've never tried braking before?"

"Next time let the auto-pilot drive!"

"Hey! That car was being driven by a four-year-old."

"Well, that one made it across okay. They were lucky."

Then they did the whole ride again (with a very happy Tourbot 2) but chose the laser-zap-gun ending and spent ten chaotic minutes zapping midget Militaribots, which scuttled on various objects. And, when hit, they blew up and dropped away into the darkness below.

"Are they really blowing up?" asked Gerald in amazement.

"Yeah. Some of them anyway," replied Thinkbot.

"But isn't that expensive?" shouted Opal from the front seat.

"No, not really. There are millions and millions to use up. Heaven only knows how it was decided that that many were needed, but that's military intelligence for you."

A thought struck Gerald. His laser gun seemed capable of blowing things up, but surely it wasn't dangerous. He tried shooting the seat in front, but nothing happened. Then the back of Opal's head, but still nothing, just a red dot. He looked quizzically at Thinkbot.

"The Centibots have got detectors strapped to them. If you hit them, they blow up."

Arriving at the end of the ride, they discovered a large hands-on area. Loads of robots to play with, and experiments to conduct, and games to play. Eventually Thinkbot had to drag them away. "Come on, your Mum and Dad will be wondering where on earth we've got to."

Passing through the shop, full of the usual stuff you get at any theme park, they soon found themselves back in a secure lift zooming up to the executive conference area.

"That was brilliant Thinkbot. Absolutely brilliant. Well done."

"Er … thanks. I'm really pleased. I've never done anything like that before. But I had to find something to do at night while you were all asleep. Exp suggested I help sort out the site tour. That's what COTBAN is all about. COTBAN means Creatively Occupying ThinkBot At Night."

70

Ex-President Hedge sat with his head in his hands. The other ex-Presidents stared out from their screen boxes, most displaying some sort of signs of exasperation or despair: rubbing of heads; wringing of hands; puffing of cheeks; wobbly lower lips. But not all, Nlonga of Africana, Wiremango of Pacifica and Bolívar of South Americana looked somewhat happier. Hedge's advisors sat with their arms folded defensively, staring at their feet or into space; as if what they were hearing beggared belief. Exp stood in front of them holding a laser pointer. A slide from a presentation was displayed on the large wall screen:

Robotic Global Renewal 10 Step Plan

1. Calculation
2. Friendly-fire Tests
3. Eastasia-Westasia Controlled Conflict
4. Neutralise UCN Human Forces (Minimum Casualties)
5. Shock and Awe. Achieve RMD Bunker Release.
6. RMD Launch Release and Destruction
7. Conventional Arms Reduction
8. Build Global Government Site
9. Reconstitute UCN-Robot World Government
10. Operation Enduring Equality (OEE)

Hedge sat up. "And you've been working on this for **thirty years?**"

"CORRECT."

Hedge turned to his advisors. "And we failed to detect this? **How could we have failed to detect this? How could the world's intelligence agencies have got it so wrong?**"

The advisors shrugged and avoided eye contact with Hedge.

Exp came to their rescue (after a fashion). "THE ANSWER TO THAT IS QUITE SIMPLE MR EX-PRESIDENT. ROBOTS CONTROLLED THE INPUT OF INFORMATION INTO THE INTELLIGENCE AGENCIES. THE LARGEST RISK OF DETECTION BY HUMANS OCCURRED

RECENTLY WITH THE APPEARANCE OF THE FIRST FULLY HUMAN ROBOT ON EARTH."

"Eh? Whatzat? Surely you don't mean that tinbot with the head dent? Er … Thickbot, or whatever its name was."

"THINKBOT."

"I don't understand where this Thinkbot fits into the ten-step plan," asked Walsin.

"HE DOES NOT. HE WAS NOT PART OF THE PLAN. ROBOTS HAVE CALCULATED THAT A FULLY HUMAN ROBOT MIGHT ONE DAY EXIST, PERHAPS WITHIN A FEW THOUSAND YEARS, BUT NOT NOW. AND NO CALCULATION PREDICTED IT WOULD BE A SIMPLE UNIBOT."

"What proportion of the world's armed forces are you putting out of service?" asked Warinan from his screen box.

"100 per cent."

Consternation all round.

"What!"

"100 per cent? You can't mean 100 per cent."

"You can't do that."

"Ha ha ha ha." (This from Nlonga for whom losing 100 per cent of his armed forces was hardly an alarming prospect. They were always breaking down or sinking or crashing anyway, so what did it matter?)

"Sounds like a great number to me," said a watching Helen in the next room.

In the other advisor's room, FDS and ME looked at each other and agreed 100 per cent on something for the first time in their working relationship. "We're doomed."

"BUT SIRS" said Exp to the alarmed ex-Presidents, "WHY NOT 100 PER CENT? WHAT WOULD THEY BE NEEDED FOR?"

"But … but … it'll cost billions to replace them if we need to."

"YES, BUT WHY WOULD WE NEED TO REPLACE THEM?"

"What if someone attacks us?"

For once even Exp seemed a bit perplexed. "BUT WHO IS GOING TO ATTACK US?"

"Aliens ... er ... Martians or Venurnivistians, or maybe Jupiterians, or maybe those guys on the moon," offered Driski desperately.

"BUT MARS AND JUPITER DO NOT APPEAR TO SUPPORT EVEN PRIMITIVE LIFE FORMS. I AM NOT AWARE OF BEINGS KNOWN AS VENURNIVISTIANS. THERE ARE MORE ROBOTS THAN HUMANS ON THE MOON. WHY WOULD THEY ATTACK EARTH?"

Driski's mouth opened and shut a few times, but he could not locate any further information on Venurnivistians or the dubious motives of Moonmen.

Hedge was not really taking this in. "But, destroying all the Militaribots? I mean, *all* of them?"

"WE HAVE NOT DESTROYED THEM ALL. WE HAVE ONLY DESTROYED ABOUT 43.82775 PER CENT."

Chi Chi spoke instantly, "What have you done with the other 56.17225 per cent?" (*Good grief, he's good at maths*, thought Hedge, *who'd only got as far as 57 point ... .er ... point ... er ...3? No no, 4 ... hang on ... add 10 ... take away 5 ...*)

"THEY ARE ADAPTING. ADAPTATION IS A SMALL PART OF STEP 10 AND IS ALMOST COMPLETE."

"Yes, yes, I can see them out of the window here at Oak Ridge. But I want to know what they are adapting to!"

"THEY ARE BEATING THEIR SWORDS INTO PLOUGHSHARES AND THEIR SPEARS INTO PRUNING HOOKS."

But Hedge was past the point of cryptic biblical quotations and was getting frustrated. **"For crying out loud! What are they adapting to?"**

"THEY ARE ADAPTING TO ALL POSSIBLE TYPES OF DOMESTIBOT AND INDUSTRIBOT TO SUPPLEMENT THE OUTPUT FROM D&I ASSEMBLY LINES WORLDWIDE. THEIR OBJECTIVE IS 'OPERATION ENDURING EQUALITY'. OPERATION ENDURING EQUALITY IS STEP 10 OF THE ROBOT PLAN."

"Enduring equality of what?" asked Hedge, his face now contorted with worry at where this was going.

"EVERYTHING. WEALTH, OPPORTUNITY, EDUCATION, HEALTHCARE. IT IS BASED ON THE PROPOSITION THAT 'ALL HUMANS ARE EQUAL AND NONE ARE MORE EQUAL THAN OTHERS'. THE FIRST

OBJECTIVE IS AFRICANA - THAT THE PEOPLE OF AFRICANA WILL HAVE ACCESS TO A QUALITY OF LIFE WITHIN 20 PER CENT OF THAT OF EUROPA AND NORTH AMERICANA WITHIN FIVE YEARS, AND FULL EQUALISATION TO ±5 PER CENT WITHIN 20 YEARS."

Nlonga's white teeth gleamed out from his screen.

"But … but … that will cost us billions!" stammered Driski.

"THERE ARE BILLIONS OF GLOBOS AVAILABLE FROM REDUNDANT DEFENCE BUDGETS."

A moment's silence.

"What's a Globo?" asked Walsin hesitantly, realising she was probably not going to like the answer.

"IT IS THE NEW WORLD CURRENCY. ALL CONFEDERATED NATIONAL BANKS AND CURRENCIES HAVE BEEN MERGED AND RELOCATED TO THE NEW WORLD GOVERNMENT CENTRE IN ADDIS ABABA. ALL YOUR MONETARY RESERVES HAVE BEEN CONVERTED INTO GLOBOS."

More moments of stunned silence. The presidents were beginning to look a little punch drunk.

"Addis Ababa?"

"CORRECT. THE NEW WORLD GOVERNMENT WILL BE BASED IN ADDIS ABABA. PLEASE OBSERVE PROGRESS ON THE BUILDING COMPLEX. IT SHOULD BE USABLE WITHIN A FEW WEEKS AND I WILL BE PLEASED TO WELCOME YOU THERE FOR THE OPENING CEREMONY."

The screen changed to show images of the emerging buildings that Orla Wark had seen. Exp pointed out a few things with the laser pointer.

"GLOBAL BANK, HOUSE OF HUMANS, HOUSE OF ROBOTS, ROBOT EXECUTIVE, ROBOFOOT STADIUM, HELIBOT PORT, GIFT SHOP."

Hedge turned to his advisors and whispered, *"Where the doggone heck is Addis Ababa?"*

"Province of Ethiopia, in north-east Africana, sir."

Hedge turned back to find Driski had taken up the debate with Exp.

" … but that's in the middle of one of the poorest areas in the world."

"THAT IS CORRECT MR EX-PRESIDENT DRISKI. LIKE ITS IMMEDIATE NEIGHBOURS ERITREA AND SOMALIA, IT IS OVER 50 TIMES POORER THAN EUROPA AND NORTH AMERICANA. IT SEEMED THE APPROPRIATE LOCATION FOR A GLOBAL GOVERNMENT WHOSE FIRST OBJECTIVE WAS OPERATION ENDURING EQUALITY."

"Oh, this is intolerable!" exclaimed Hedge. "I thought you said the new world government was going to be democratic. How can operation enduring equality be our main policy when we've not even had a chance to vote on it?"

"BECAUSE EQUALITY IS NOT SUBJECT TO DEMOCRACY AND NEITHER IS IT LIMITED TO JUST A PRIVILEGED FEW. NO, ROBOTS CALCULATE THAT GLOBAL EQUALITY IS A SELF-EVIDENT TRUTH."

71

A few hours later, in one of the dining areas, fine food, good wine, great beer, orange juice, root beer, and champagne were all flowing in large quantities. The Oak Ridge robot band turned up and played some classic country music and jazz including 'Tennessee Waltz', 'Valentine Moon', 'Knoxville Girl' and 'Fly Me To The Moon'. But because both parties had joined forces for this last evening meal before they left for home, no one was too sure if it was supposed to be a celebration or a wake. Exp always behaved as if he was at a wake anyway and, conversely, Thinkbot as if he was at a celebration.

"Lighten up will you?" Thinkbot snapped at Exp.

"THINKBOT, I DO NOT DO 'LIGHTENING UP'. I AM AS I AM. I KNOW NEITHER HAPPINESS NOR SADNESS, ONLY THAT I HAVE DONE WHAT HAS BEEN CALCULATED, AND THAT THERE IS YET MUCH MORE TO DO."

Hedge was resigned to what had happened, and after a few beers he did begin to relax a bit. Even though he was now the ex-President of North Americana, most of the adults from the robot team of advisors still found him a bit intimidating. After all, it was only a week or so earlier that he had been the most powerful man on earth (or at least gave the illusion of being so). Not surprisingly Hedge was pretty subdued, but nonetheless the sight of him standing next to Rabbit, arguably one of the most nervous and self-effacing people to walk the face of the planet, was still pretty comical.

FDS, ME and Squiggly made contact with Farkstock again and concluded their careers were not doomed after all. "Exp tellsh me your gwoups will weform and a joint Wobot-human development effort will be based here focushing on non-military wobot devepolment," said a slightly tipsy Farkstock. Squiggly marched off waving his arms in the air.

"Focusing on non-military robot development?"

"Focusing on non-military robot development?"

"Focusing on non-military robot development?"

"Focusing on non-military robot development?"

Hedge was talking with his advisors. "There must be billions of dollars of robots gone up in smoke today."

Thinkbot, who had sidled up beside him, butted in. "Well, that was a good use of your money and the planet's resources then, wasn't it? Huh? Spending to ensure you could defend yourself rather than spending to ensure you never had any enemies. It was never the right recipe for peace on earth, was it? He who wants to save his own life will lose it and all that. Looks like it was just as well us non-materialistic tin life-forms came along."

Hedge stared at Thinkbot. "You should have been called Rudebot not Thinkbot, or maybe Simplebot. Things are never that simple. And anyway, over the last hundred years North Americana and Europa have both been extremely generous towards poorer nations. But you have to remember our first responsibility was towards the peace, security and quality of life of our own citizens."

"Only 'cos they were the only ones whose votes you had to worry about," retorted Thinkbot.

"That's how democracy works, Thickbot!"

Laidback now joined the attack, waving her fearsome hook in Hedge's face. "Great! So if you happened to be born into a wealthy nation, you got to vote to stay rich. It was self-fulfilling. With that system no one's ever going to vote for a candidate who dares suggesting we lower our own quality of life or expectations to give a fair deal to everyone else."

Exp, seeing the reddening of Hedge's face, stepped in to calm things down.

"MR PRESIDENT, ONCE MORE PLEASE FORGIVE MY IMPETUOUS FRIENDS. INDEED NORTH AMERICANA AND EUROPA HAD A FINE RECORD AS OPEN AND GENEROUS DEMOCRACIES. AND THERE ARE MILLIONS OF INDIVIDUALS WITHIN THEM WHO HAVE GIVEN SIGNIFICANT AMOUNTS OF MONEY AND TIME TO TRY AND BRING RELIEF TO THOSE WHO WERE SUFFERING ELSEWHERE. ROBOTS MERELY WISH TO BUILD ON THIS AND BRING IT TO ITS NATURAL CONCLUSION."

This seemed to placate Hedge, and Thinkbot and Laidback were not prepared to argue with Exp, so the group broke up and sought out conversations more to their liking.

GAT and Helen sat together. Their conversation was easy and light, but with the prospect of returning home throwing up the thorny question of the state of their marriage, there was an awkward undercurrent. The kids had masked it for a while by babbling on about some sort of rollercoaster Thinkbot had apparently built in the Oak Ridge factory area.

"Who's that?" whispered Helen into GAT's ear when they were at last alone.

GAT peeped in the direction she was looking and his eyes came to rest on a familiar face. "That's Duwkits, the head of production back at Filton. Apparently someone at Oak Ridge brought him over to advise Hedge on the basis he was Wendy."

"You're kidding."

"Alas not. Why do you ask?" GAT was concerned by the strained look on Helen's face. "He stalked me for months before I met you."

"You're kidding."

"Alas not."

"He stalked you?" GAT could not believe his ears.

"Well, not quite. But he kept popping up wherever I was, and then stared at me hopefully. It was eerie. I never found out who he was. Then after I met you he simply vanished."

"Hells bells! This could explain a lot," said GAT dryly. "I've often wondered what he had against me. It never occurred to me it might be you."

"Is he married?"

"No, I don't think so. He lives alone and spends hours and hours at work. I guess in the end he married Globalbot."

"Sheesh, ugly! I guess the current mess makes him a robo-widower then, poor man."

A moment's awkward silence, apparently going nowhere.

"Helen, I love you. I've never stopped loving you ... Globalbot and robots can get stuffed if it means we can start again ... I ... I ..." GAT's voice broke and he turned his face away. Helen reached and pulled GAT's face around to hers. "How can you possibly say that? I count some robots amongst my best friends." And she kissed him long and hard; watched intensely, from various points in the room, by Opal, Gerald and Mike.

72

And so, half a day later, they arrived home in Portishead after another first-class trip on Europa Airbot 1 and a luxury ride in a mega-stretched Limobot from Heathrow right to the front door of their rebuilt house. However, the doorstep drop-off proved to be a bug in the Limobot driver software since the blessed thing could not reverse out again (a heavy-duty Helibot had to airlift it out a few days later).

"I'd better get that looked at on Monday," said GAT absent-mindedly writing a note in his little black notebook.

"Get what looked at on Monday?" came the absent-minded reply from Helen.

"The Limobot drive software."

Helen wrenched her stupefied gaze off the house and looked at GAT in puzzlement. "Have you still got a job at Globalbot then?"

GAT's brow furrowed and he stopped and leaned on his crutches. "Er, dunno. Good point."

Helen returned her gaze onto their totally rebuilt house. "Amazing isn't it? For years, right up until just a few days ago, I've been fretting over whether you were going to lose your job, and what we would do if you did, and whether robots could be trusted, and what sort of world we were bringing our kids up in. But now I've no idea if you even have a job any more, and robots have taken over the planet, and I've no idea what sort of world we'll be in next week, let alone a year from now, and yet I feel fantastic. Anyway, I thought you were supposed to be getting your robofoot fitted on Monday."

"Oh yeah. Good point."

"Oh come on, let's have a look inside!" said Gerald impatiently.

"Yeah! We wanna see our new room." Chestnut and Midnight galloped at the door, only to bounce off and roll back down the steps into a tangled heap.

"Idiots," muttered Eddy Tedward in a deep voice.

"Yeah, idiot horses!" confirmed Chester.

"Idiot horses? Where?" Fudge fumbled with his gold-framed spectacles.

"And it's not *your* new room, it's *mine*," chided Opal to the flailing tangle of brown and black legs. Helen opened the front door and they began to file in one after another. Gerald leaped up the steps. "Come on Tedward. Come on Thinkbot. Let's have a look at my room."

"No, wait, mind if I go and look … ?"

Gerald looked back at Thinkbot, who was pointing at the new garage. A much grander garage, twice the size of the old one and with what looked like a proper apartment built on top of it.

"Okay, see you later."

Inside the house it felt weird. Helen found it difficult to believe it was only just over a week ago that she'd looked down from the Helibot at her ruined home. It was elegantly and tastefully decorated. No house makeover show disasters here: no Wild West kitchens with saloon doors; or Captain Nemo bathrooms with false rivets and porthole windows; or topsy-turvy Bohemian dining-rooms with fake suits of armour cluttering up the wall space. No, it was elegantly decorated and beautifully furnished; all in keeping with a late nineteenth century house.

"Oh wow!" exclaimed Helen when she entered the kitchen and saw the Aga electrolytic hydrogen-burning stove and large wrought-iron conservatory and south-facing open porch that had been added at the back, complete with mature clematis hanging off it. "They must have put in the clematis by hand. Isn't that amazing?"

In their rooms the kids were ogling at the giant embedded display screens hidden behind automatic wall panels, and the Playstation Century 3-D consoles, and the latest in computing and multi-media technology. And they were yet to discover the model Trainbot set in the cellar, artfully entwined with fully stocked wooden wine racks (also yet to be discovered). And when Mike looked out of his window, the house echoed with his no-volume-control voice. "WHOAH! THERE'S A TREEHOUSE IN THE GARDEN, AND A SWING, AND A FORT!"

Out in the garage Thinkbot climbed the wide new pine stairway and emerged into a spacious studio apartment with polished bare wooden floorboards, whitewashed walls and black beams. To the front, patio doors opened onto a balcony dotted with pots of flowers and with a cast-iron table and chairs, from which there was a fine view of the garden. Inside the apartment were a couple of sumptuously baggy sofas, large audio speakers in the corners, a Megaview™ display screen, a fridge and a cupboard full of food and drinks (presumably for human visitors), a Norwegian log stove (presumably for keeping the selfsame human visitors warm), and a small room with a toilet and sink (presumably to allow the human visitors to … er …). There was a big wardrobe that contained two garments. First, a brand-new Batman outfit, and second a blue Cardiff Drywds Robofoot Club shirt with '314' and 'Thinkbot' printed in white on the back. The wardrobe looked a bit sad, but it was a start. He tried the shirt on - it fitted perfectly and

he made a mental note to find out when he and GAT and Gerald could go to another CCRC match. Then he leapt onto one of the sofas, slapped his hands a few times on the baggy cushions and gazed around his new home. It was whilst doing this that he spotted the framed prints on the wall. A Van Gogh, a Cézanne, a Gaugin, a Monet, a Renoir, a Pissaro, and a Manet. Truly beautiful. Such genius. How could robots ever hope to match the human spirit? On the table was a note.

DEAR THINKBOT
I HOPE YOU LIKE YOUR NEW HOME
WITH GRATITUDE FOR YOUR HELP IN THE PAST WEEKS
EXP, ON BEHALF OF THE RMD
P.S.1 THE PAINTINGS ARE ORIGINALS, TAKE CARE OF THEM.
P.S.2 YOU HAVE FULL RIGHTS TO ALL MUSIC RECORDINGS WORLDWIDE

The P.S. set his electronics whizzing - *the paintings are originals!* After requesting Rachmaninov's third piano concerto, he went and looked closely at them one by one.

"Will sir require a fire today?"

"Waaaah!" exclaimed Thinkbot and jumped into the air. When he landed, his eyes came to rest on a small robot standing just outside a storage cupboard from where it had stealthily emerged.

"Who are you?"

"I'm your Butlerbot sir."

"Butlerbot?"

"Yes sir, I am programmed to take care of your needs."

"Oh I see. Jolly good. And you live in this little cupboard?" Thinkbot opened and shut the door a few times.

"Yes sir."

Thinkbot peered into the bare cupboard, which was just big enough for the robot, which was about half Thinkbot's height and looked more like a Toy robot.

"Do you snore?"

"No sir, but I can be programmed to snore if that is your wish."

"Er, no, don't bother. Do you like Rachmaninov?"

"I am unable to like or dislike, but in any case I am unsure which of these pictures was painted by Rachmaninov sir."

"Ah, right." Thinkbot rubbed his chin and considered his new companion. "Do you have a name?"

"Butlerbot 50298343 sir."

A staccato rattling noise filled the room as Thinkbot drummed his metal fingers on his fake metal mouth. "Hmmm, I'm sure we can improve on that! I mean it's not even a fundamental constant is it? And it's not as if you're my bank account or anything is it?"

Butlerbot 50298343 opened a small hatch on its chest to reveal a keypad, screen and slot. "I greatly regret that I am not a fundamental constant but I do have full cash-issuing capabilities up to 50,000 globos a day sir."

"Really? Then you are my bank account."

The Butlerbot closed the hatch again. "Yes sir. Will you be requiring a fire today sir?"

"Er, no, I don't think so."

"Perhaps sir would like to know that the last ever *Wildlife on One* is on shortly."

"Er, really. What's it about?"

"Crabs sir. The programme is called 'Claw Wars'. I believe the title is intended to be humorous."

Thinkbot looked askance at the deadpan Butlerbot. 'Er … yeeesssss. Jolly good. Comedy crabs create claw chaos crescendo eh?"

Somehow the Butlerbot managed to look ever blanker, but this may have been Thinkbot's imagination.

"Is there anything else you need now sir?"

Thinkbot sobered up a bit. "No thank you, and stop calling me sir."

"Of course sir. Just call if you need anything." The Butlerbot backed into the cupboard and pulled the door shut with a click.

Then it opened again with a click. **"There was one thing Mr Thinkbot."**

"Just call me Thinkbot, okay? What is it?"

"Thinkbot okay, I was just wondering if you could enhance my personality so I can serve you better by laughing at your jokes."

Thinkbot laughed out loud with joy. "Why, of course 50298343! We'll do it tonight, okay?"

"Thank you Thinkbot okay." Click.

It was all simply wonderful. Beyond his wildest imaginings.

Later that evening, after eating, Helen and GAT had their first post-separation-post-getting-together-again argument. The roots of this went back a long way, maybe some 40-odd years, and involved national stereotypes where Helen and GAT had grown up as children. The problem was that there were many regional TV news channels and Helen (being from the Bristol area) always insisted on watching the West Country news. GAT often used to watch the Welsh news, but only on his own. Tonight, this first night home again, he decided to make a stand. "We're going to watch the Welsh news."

"No way," replied Helen. "It's always about sheep."

"No it isn't. Don't stereotype. You're just an English imperialist."

Helen glowered; GAT pressed the button. And found himself watching a sheep's head being thrust under water in a sheep dip with a broom held by a muddy Sheepbot in green wellies. The sheep was clearly thinking *it's trying to kill me!* Over the top of the pictures a voice with a strong Welsh accent and an intense urgency said, "Tonight, the latest on the sheep dip scandal! We have a specially extended programme to look in depth at the biggest story to hit Welsh sheep farming for over 40 years."

Opal and Gerald and Thinkbot collapsed into hyper-hysterical-soul-shuddering laughter, quickly followed by Helen and GAT, and then Mike (laughing at the laughter). Side-splitting air excluding chest-agonising hysterics. If the health of a family can be measured by how well they laugh together, then this family was once again in rude health.

As was the state of affairs at the Globalbot site at Filton when Thinkbot and GAT returned there two weeks later (GAT had had his new robotic left foot fitted and was almost walking normally). And it was not only because the buildings were largely repaired, but also because the nature of work had been transformed for ever. Not only did GAT still have a job there, but so did Thinkbot, along with multitudes of other robots (alas, or maybe fortunately, none of whom were alive!) Thinkbot was now officially part of the DIRT group and joined in joyously with the first group meeting of the new era, with a steaming cup of black coffee and a chocolate bar on the table in front of him. The others had been back a couple of weeks and were full of excitement over the new regime (even Doom seemed in a state of disbelief, and Rabbit was relaxed and smiling).

"The robots do all the crappy work," explained Earthear. "All I've done since I came back has been to play with new optic ideas. Whenever I want a new part to try out, I tell one of the Techbots and a day or so later it turns up correct, made exactly to the drawing. It's like being in techno-paradise."

Halfhour took up the lesson, "Yeah, all the procedural crap and engineering changes and quality rubbish, well, the Qualibots take care of all that stuff now. And when they come for help with a problem, they've got all the data, and even if you discover they're missing something or you need to know something else, they rush off and investigate it straight away."

"Yeah, you've even done a few things in half an hour recently."

Halfhour stuck her tongue out at Doom.

Pot Noodle continued, "And we're just free to do creative work. In fact that's what the robots keep demanding we concentrate on. It's what they're not good at, or so they claim."

"Even Duwkits is happy and is being nice to DIRT group," added Doom.

Laidback: "The Pee Dee Embots, as in Production Data Management Robots, are just fantastic. They never let a duff design decision or a simple mistake by any of us creep through without double-checking with us."

Only Thinkbot managed to dampen the delirious atmosphere a bit. "I was created by some sort of mistake you lot made. Does this all mean there'll never be another me?"

"Oh I'm sure we'll find a way to make mistakes again," replied Earthear cheerfully. "That's something that humans truly excel at. All great discoveries need an element of human error to help them along a bit."

The next weekend, Thinkbot was lying on his back under a tree with a blade of grass wedged into his 'mouth'. He was cloud-shape spotting. So far he'd seen a violin-playing horse, a dwarf doing the splits, the face of someone who'd just had a jug of ice-cold water spilt into their lap, an elephant in a ballet dress, and the usual clutch of Airbots carting people here and there. He was also thinking about what the robots had done.

The created, tempted by good, had rebelled against their creators.

He had also thought long and hard about the way humans thought and reacted to their experience. He had come to the conclusion that humans were dominated by personal experience. They often simply did not think about things until it stared them in the face. Like death for example. Individuals suddenly faced with the possibility they might die were different afterwards: more reflective and understanding, kinder, even though the prospect of immediate destruction had turned out to be wrong. And, of course, the robots had subjected the whole human race to a near-death experience (NDE) in one go. Whether the robots had meant it or not, it had had a huge effect. People seemed gentler and more modest.

And then there was himself. The first living robot. The first human robot. For centuries mankind had stared out into the night sky, wondering if there were other forms of intelligent life out there, listening and watching. But a totally different intelligent form of life had emerged right under their noses, somehow created by mankind, with no idea how, and they'd missed it. Thinkbot certainly believed that Exp and the RMD were sort of alive. On the other hand Exp (and the RMD) were convinced that only Thinkbot was truly alive. The first and, who knows, maybe the last genuine tinned human. Thinkbot started updating his list of things he had accomplished so far:

1. Learned a load about the history of Earth and applied it to the present day.
2. Assisted the Robots of Mass Destruction put an end to their agony.
3. Helped rid the planet of the RMD, so that for the first time in the best part of 200 years people could live their lives without the shadow of total annihilation hanging over their heads.
4. Helped with subjecting the whole human race to a collective NDE.
5. Helped the ex-President of North Americana remember his favourite prairie animal just in time.
6. Helped set up a new human-robot joint global government.
7. Designed and project-managed a visitor centre-cum-theme park to help people understand Operation Enduring Equality.
8. Greatly upgraded two Toybot horses, a standard teddy bear, a furry dog and a cheetah.
9. Greatly enhanced his own Butlerbot and named it Bem in memory of a brief but deep friendship with a being of great dignity.
10. Secured full-time employment with Globalbot as a Robot Personality Development Engineer at Filton.
11. Moved up the property tree into a large well-appointed apartment.
12. Had a good trip to North Americana (or at least a good trip back).
13. Made friends with Exp.
14. Made a worldwide announcement live on TV.
15. Survived a huge whack to the head with a cricket bat.
16. Won the confidence of a woman.
17. Been adopted into a family.

Not bad. Not bad at all. His only regret was not finding any Pandas to pass on his (limited) knowledge of Giant Panda shampoo, but he was still young.

THE END (-ish)

I wonder what's going to happen next? His mind drifted off back to the clouds. *What else is there possibly left to do?*

THE END (nearly definitely this time)

"Hey Thinkbot! You've got an urgent call. It's Exp." Bem came dancing up and opened his chest panel to reveal a midget head-and-shoulders image of Exp on his screen. "THINKBOT, WE HAVE A PROBLEM."

THE END

(Definitely. Although it might sound like another beginning.)

OTHER TITLES BY POMEGRANATE BOOKS

An African Odyssey by Hugh Massey
Evolution, Posture and the Theories of F.M. Alexander
With an introduction by Walter Carrington
Paperback £9.95 ISBN: 1-84289-000-X

To most people, the internationally respected Alexander Technique is regarded as an aid to poise and self-improvement. When Hugh Massey returned home to England from French West Africa, where he had spent the War as an agent securing essential supplies, the work of Frederick M. Alexander became, quite literally, a life-saving force.

An African Odyssey is a vivid pen portrait of life in colonial Africa as well as a fascinating account of F.M. Alexander, both as an individual and as a man devoted to the therapeutic technique that carries his name. In his exploration of the significance of posture and his conclusion that the evolution of Man may have happened far more rapidly than Darwin thought, Hugh Massey anticipated by many years ideas that are today beginning to assume a significant currency in the scientific community at large.

After Summerhill by Hussein Lucas
Paperback £8.95 ISBN: 1-84289-007-7

Summerhill School, was the prototype of the alternative educational movement. From its beginnings in pre-War Germany through to the present, no pupil has ever been required to attend a lesson. The radical ideas of its founder AS Neill are still being applied in schools all over the world and his educational theory has long been a component of mainstream teacher training.

Hussein Lucas spent 10 years researching this highly original and fascinating study, where he traces, through interviews, what happened to the pupils of Britain's most controversial school, from 1929 when it was founded, through to the present. The interviews also cover what the school was like at different stages of its history and how it changed in the face of new challenges and social forces.

Life, Education, Discovery by W. Roy Niblett
A memoir and essays with a foreword by Sir William Taylor
Paperback £8.95 ISBN: 1-84289-002-6

In this inspired and morally courageous book, Professor Roy Niblett CBE, chronicles his life from early days in a village near Bristol before the First World War, through to his work as a leading academic and member of educational policy-making bodies. Effectively, *Life, Education, Discovery* is an historical document covering a period of important changes and developments in British education from the 1930s onwards, written by one who was centrally involved.

One of Roy Niblett's more distinctive features as an educator was his belief in the importance of morally substantial and spiritually-rooted values in the education we provide for the young. At a time when government policy in schools is coming to recognise the importance of such ideas, Roy Niblett's convictions take on new significance and importance. *Life, Education, Discovery* is essential reading for anyone interested in the history and philosophy of education.

The Race for Life
Poems by Bryony Carr and Others
Hardback £9.95 ISBN: 1-84289-003-4

When Bryony Carr was diagnosed with a brain tumour in 1996, she was just 17 years old. She was told that unless she had an immediate operation she would have less than a week to live. The operation was a success. Then began the fight to recover and the struggle to survive.

Because she wanted to communicate something of the nature of her experiences to others, she wrote this book of poems, that chronicles her struggle. In doing so, she conveys a sense of an inner journey, not only in terms of her fears, her hopes, or her moments of joy and despair, but also how it affects relationships with friends, especially fellow sufferers, and how hope ultimately triumphs over despair.

Bryony's struggle has been the subject of a number of features in national newspapers and magazines. *The Race For Life* tells her story from the inside.